"I want you, Randy Hayes," Jake growled, lunging at her and seizing her wrists tightly, then pressing her against the wall. "What do you think of that?"

Miranda drew in her breath and faced him boldly, telling herself to stay calm. "I think that whatever you want to do to me, you will. After all, you're stronger than I am. Just don't take me like your father would take a woman, Jake. And don't do it just to try and scare me off, because you can't. I love you, Jake Harkner, and you damn well know it! You'd never hurt me!" Unwanted tears suddenly filled her eyes, and she felt his grip relax. He massaged her wrists for a moment.

"Damn you, woman," he said softly. "How do you know me that well?" He leaned closer, kissed her eyes, licked at her tears, then captured her mouth with his lips. Miranda responded powerfully, needfully to him, sharing a kiss that was more delicious than any she'd ever known.

Jake was wild and hard and determined, and she wanted him. . . .

OUTLAW

HEARTS

Rosanne Bittner

BANTAM BOOKS
NEW YORK · TORONTO · LONDON · SYDNEY · AUCKLAND

OUTLAW HEARTS

A Bantam Book / March 1993

ISBN 0-553-29807-0

Published simultaneously in the United States and Canada

Bantam Books are published by Bantam Books, a division of Bantam
Doubleday Dell Publishing Group, Inc. Its trademark, consisting of the
words "Bantam Books" and the portrayal of a rooster, is Registered in
U.S. Patent and Trademark Office and in other countries. Marca
Registrada. Bantam Books, 666 Fifth Avenue, New York, New York
10103.

PRINTED IN THE UNITED STATES OF AMERICA

RAD   0 9 8 7 6 5 4 3 2 1

For my sons,
Brock and Brian,
of whom I am very proud.

A Note from the Author

The locations and most of the background history of OUTLAW HEARTS are real; however, the characters and their story are entirely fictitious. Any resemblance to a person or persons who actually existed at the time of this story is purely coincidental. I would like to offer a special thank you to Dr. Michael Mayle of Coloma, Michigan, who was kind enough to answer some medical questions for me as I was writing this book.

Part

One

What we do today will become tomorrow's memory; and often the past we are now creating returns to haunt us.

CHAPTER ONE

April 1866 . . .

Miranda tried to ignore the image of her father's still-fresh grave as she flicked the reins and goaded the draft horses into a slightly faster gait. This was not a time to crumble. She had to face facts. Her father was dead, and her worthless brother was somewhere in Nevada, totally oblivious to the hardships his father and sister had faced these last months.

She was a woman alone now. If not for the war, she would still have a husband. If not for the war, there would have been no marauding outlaws to come and shoot down her father. It seemed that she had spent her entire young adult life thinking about survival, ever since her precious mother had died six years ago. She had been only fourteen then, and after that, one by one, she had lost all those she loved.

She grunted when the wagon hit a hefty rut and nearly bounced her out of her seat, but she kept a tight hold on the reins. The thirty-minute ride to Kansas City from what was left of her father's meager farm led over a rough, often muddy, dirt road. Today it was dry and hard, and the ruts and holes were more jolting; but dark clouds were moving in swiftly from the west, threatening a much-needed rain. It had been an unruly Kansas spring, warm one day, cold the next, and too dry.

Ever since the raiders had killed her father six weeks ago,

she had been in a quandary over what to do. Her friends in nearby Kansas City had been urging her to sell the farm and get herself to the safety of town, warning her that it was too dangerous for her to be staying on alone. Maybe they were right. With all the cattle and horses stolen, the chickens killed, the barn burned, what was left? It had taken her several days to get the cabin back in order, and one window, shot out by the raiders, was still boarded up. She had spent most of her and her father's hard-earned savings buying new supplies because so much had been stolen. Thank goodness most of the money was in a bank in Kansas City rather than at the cabin the day of the raid. The outlaws had torn the place apart looking for whatever they could find of value.

She was also thankful she still had the draft horses, one of the few things left that was worth something. She had finally decided to sell the farm, but she would not move to Kansas City. The first thing she should do now was try to find her brother in Nevada, and she could only pray he was actually still there. His last letter had come from Virginia City, but that had been over a year ago.

She couldn't help wondering if Wes was really worth finding, after the way he had abandoned them. Still, he was all she had left, and it seemed to her they should be together now. Besides, he should know their father was dead, and she hoped he would feel guilty about it. If he had stayed on to help with the farm, he would have been there the day of the raid to help protect things, and maybe their father would still be alive.

She felt guilty enough herself. If she had not gone to town that day to participate in a church social, maybe there would have been something she could have done herself to save her father. Then again, God only knew what the outlaws would have done to her. . . . If, if, if. She used that word a lot. If her mother had not died back in Illinois, her physician father would not have felt guilty for not being able to save her. He would not have given up his doctoring and moved to Kansas to try to farm, and consequently, he would not now be lying buried, shot down by rebel raiders.

There was no sense wondering what might have been. What was real was that she was completely alone now. She felt under the seat to make sure her father's prized Winchester rifle had not bounced too far back to reach quickly. She was determined to be ready for any would-be attackers. She had no mercy for the kind of men who had shot down her father in cold blood. Besides the rifle, she carried a derringer in her handbag. She realized the pistol was not as deadly as the rifle, but at short range, it could certainly do enough damage to stop a man in his tracks. Trouble was, for any kind of accuracy, and to do a man any real damage, that man would have to be closer to her than she would care to experience. She could only hope she would never have need of the pistol.

It seemed strange to be considering the best way to kill a man. She worried sometimes that all her losses had left her harder than she ever thought possible. Where were the gentle, loving feelings she used to have? Where was the innocent Miranda Sue Baker who had not a care in the world before her mother died? It was Hayes now, Miranda Hayes—a name taken from a man whose bed she had shared for only two weeks before he left for the war, never to return. That was three years ago. She had not shared any man's bed since.

A chilly spring wind rushed past her as the dark clouds from the west finally moved overhead. A wisp of her honey-blond hair came loose from the bun into which it was twisted, and she quickly pushed it up under her bonnet. A light spray of misty rain tickled her face, and she slapped the reins, anxious to get into town before a harder rain might begin to fall. Within minutes, increasingly bigger drops of rain began to make dark spots in the dry dirt road. She held the reins in one hand and reached behind the seat to pull out a rubber cape, managing to shake it open and fling it over her head and shoulders well enough to protect most of her person from a steady rainfall.

"Damn weather," she mumbled. Why did the rain have to wait until she made a trip to town? "Hurry it up, you two," she shouted to the horses. "Don't be so lazy!"

Jake drew his buckskin horse to a slower walk to avoid splattering mud from the street onto the horse's belly and his own knee-high leather boots and denim pants. He pulled his canvas slicker closer around him and ducked his head, and rainwater ran off his leather hat onto the black hair of the horse's mane and on down its dun-colored coat. The animal snorted and tossed its head.

"Relax, Outlaw," Jake said softly to the animal. "A few more minutes and I'll have us both out of this rain—a good livery for you and a bath and a shave for me." He looked toward a saloon, its doors closed to the fresh morning. "Later tonight maybe I'll find a good card game and end up in the bed of a woman bought with my winnings."

If Kansas City allows prostitutes to solicit openly, he thought. He wondered if he was crazy coming to such a civilized place. He was dangerously close to Missouri, where he knew posters had been tacked up showing drawings of his face and offering a reward for his capture. Thank goodness the drawings were not very good. In a large, busy town like this, a man could usually mix in better and be less noticed than in a smaller town, and Lord knew he needed to get himself some supplies and get a couple days' rest before heading west.

The still mostly unsettled land beyond the western border of Kansas seemed the only place now for a man like him. He knew other men with whom he had ridden and robbed and raided were heading in the same direction, into a lawless land where a man could live by the gun and not worry about prison. The only thing that had kept his own neck from a noose was the utter chaos the country seemed to have fallen into since the war ended. Times had been ripe the past year for hitting banks and trains and finding other ways of making easy money, and he had plenty now—enough to head west and maybe find a way to lead a normal life, if that was possible for a man who'd lived as he had. At thirty years old, he figured maybe it was time, but then life had never seemed to present the opportunity.

Maybe he could start a ranch, or some kind of business. If he could just get through Kansas, he'd be all right. He wondered if it might be best to head south first, to Indian Territory, then head west. The tangled wilds of Indian country were great protection for an outlaw, and most of the Indians themselves didn't mind putting up a stranger, for a bottle of whiskey or a little money. He'd hidden out there plenty of times in the past.

He drew Outlaw to a halt in front of a dry-goods store, noticing a little slip of a woman tying two draft horses to a hitching post. Her head was tucked under a rubber cape and she didn't see him. He watched her curiously, wondering how someone so small managed to handle two such big horses and the beat-up, awkward supply wagon they pulled. The woman rushed into the store, and Jake grinned and dismounted, his brown leather boots squishing into the mud. He tied Outlaw and patted the animal's neck. "I won't be too long, boy."

He looked around before going inside, still with the uncomfortable suspicion that he was being followed. He had considered circling back a couple of days earlier and maybe lying in wait for whoever might be on his tail, but he was sick of camping out on the cold ground and had been anxious to reach town. Now he wondered if the call of a warm bath and a soft bed had caused him to be a little too careless. If someone was following him, maybe they were waiting for him to hit a town this size, where people would see a public confrontation and it would be harder for him to get away.

He ducked his head to get more water off his hat before stepping up onto the boardwalk in front of the store. An old man was just leaving the store, and he nodded to Jake, then stepped back a little when he noticed the revolvers that hung low on Jake's hips. The old man glanced over at Outlaw, seeing the Winchester repeating rifle and the shotgun that rested in their boots on either side of the horse.

"You carry a hefty lot of firearms," the man spoke up in a grating voice.

"In these parts a traveling man has to be careful," Jake replied, keeping a friendly look on his face. "There's a lot of outlaws out there in the hills."

The old man looked him over. "That's a fact. I don't reckon if you was one of them, you'd be paradin' into a place like Kansas City now, would you?"

Jake's bearded face showed a slight grin. "No, sir, I don't think I would. A good day to you." He tipped his hat and headed into the store, hoping the old man would go on about his business and not draw attention to him. As soon as he stepped inside he glanced out the window to see the man pull a jacket over his head and shoulders and head across the street on old legs that walked uncertainly in the deepening mud.

Jake turned to realize that the store clerk and the young woman he had noticed tying the draft horses a moment ago were both now staring at him. The woman quickly turned away, embarrassed at having been caught looking. Jake nodded to the clerk. "You got tobacco? Cigars?"

"I've got just about all you need, mister, long as you've got the cash to pay for it."

"I've got the cash."

Outside the rain came down even harder. Jake began gathering needed supplies, occasionally glancing toward the woman, who seemed to be avoiding looking at him again. He supposed she thought it would be improper to meet his eyes again and be caught staring, but he wanted to see her face a second time. In that first glance she had looked pretty, and in spite of the cape she wore over her full calico dress, he had a feeling the form beneath all the clothing was slim and pleasing. It had been a long time since he had set eyes on a proper lady, one who was pretty at that. He well knew he was not the kind of man proper ladies had anything to do with, but a man could daydream. The irony was, he had fallen into a life of running against the law by *defending* a very proper lady, little more than a child. Poor young Santana. The memory of what had happened the night he found his father with the girl still haunted his sleep. He had led a lawless life ever since, had his father to thank for that. God, how he had hated that man.

Miranda refused to take a second look and risk meeting the dark eyes of the man who had just entered the store. If anyone fit the description of the kind of men who had been raiding and killing in Missouri and Kansas since the war ended, this man did. For the brief moment she had taken to look at him when he entered the store, she had noticed his eyes were shrouded in mystery. They betrayed no particular emotion, not even one of greeting. His bearded face left little else to notice but the eyes, and by the look of them, she suspected he was a dangerous man. Few men who lived and worked around Kansas City gave off such a foreboding aura. He was tall and broad-shouldered, and even when she wasn't looking at him it seemed he filled the small store with his presence. She tried to concentrate on her own list while the man's booted feet clumped back and forth as he gathered things and set them on the counter next to her own items.

She walked to where the clerk, Monty Lake, kept spools of thread, and she began choosing some, holding her handbag close. After what had happened to her father and the farm, she felt no stranger could be trusted. The man moved to stand near her then, looking at some tins of coffee. Miranda managed to keep from turning her head as she shifted her eyes enough to see a revolver hanging low on one hip. Not many men in town wore guns strapped to them as though ready for war. His dark green slicker was pushed back behind the gun, and she wondered if it was deliberate. Was this the kind of man who was always ready to grab his weapon? Maybe he intended to rob Mr. Lake instead of pay for his goods.

"Right uncomfortable weather outside, isn't it?" The man spoke up in a deep voice.

Inbred manners caused Miranda to meet his gaze then, but she refused to smile. She suspected the face behind the beard and trail dust was handsome, then chastised herself for the tiny flicker of attraction she felt to the stranger. "Yes," she answered curtly, quickly turning back to the thread.

"Don't be bothering the lady, mister," the clerk called out.

Miranda heard a sigh, and the man turned away. "Just making friendly small talk," he answered, sounding irritated. "When you travel alone a lot, it feels good to see and talk to people."

"Only when they want to talk," the clerk replied. "Mrs. Hayes there lost her father recently to no-good raiders, and she's still in mourning."

Miranda felt the stranger turn. "Sorry, ma'am," he said.

"Thank you," she answered quietly, keeping her back to him.

"Goddamn outlaws," the clerk grumbled. "Some men don't know how to let go of the war, and some got so used to fighting and killing, they don't know how to stop now; but the damned war is over. Men like that have no right attacking innocent people and stealing from them. A lot of them are angry Confederates who think they can keep the war going, think they can make up for their loss by attacking those that fought for the Union."

"Takes more than a war to make men turn to that life," the stranger answered, the words somewhat mumbled, as though he was making the comment more to himself than to Lake, Miranda thought.

"Yeah? And how would you know?" Lake retorted. Miranda stiffened at the sudden tension in the air. She wished Monty Lake would keep quiet. The stranger didn't seem like the kind of man another should rile.

"I just know, that's all," the stranger finally answered.

"What's your name, mister? I've never seen you around here before."

The stranger turned to pick up a sack of flour. "Jake. Just Jake."

"Well, mine's Monty Lake. Don't mean to be rude, but with all the raiding and such, a man can't help being cautious around strangers. You pack an awful lot of iron for a common settler. A man doesn't wear guns like that unless he's real good at using them."

"Why I wear them and how I use them are my business," Jake answered. Miranda sensed his anger rising because of Lake's nosy comments. "Your business is to start writing up these supplies and tell me what I owe you."

Miranda remained near the thread, deciding to wait there until the stranger paid for his supplies and left, then bring her things to the counter. Suddenly the front door flew open as though kicked. Miranda jumped back at the sight of the man who entered. He was nearly as big as the one called Jake but had an even more unkempt, frightening appearance about him. Her eyes widened when she noticed the sudden intruder held a rifle in his right hand, already raised and aimed at the mysterious Jake. "Jake Harkner!" the man bellowed.

Jake had already whirled when the door was kicked open, and Miranda backed farther into a corner. Jake's arms were arched to his sides as though ready to draw a gun, and a look of cunning came into his eyes. He reminded Miranda of a wild animal suddenly corralled, his dark eyes shining. His whole countenance emanated an eagerness to pounce on the one who threatened him.

"Name's Luke Putnam," the intruder sneered, a trickle of tobacco oozing out of the corner of his mouth, "and I aim to take you alive for the five thousand dollars on your head, Harkner. It's only three thousand if you're dead." He raised the rifle a little higher. "I don't really want to lose two thousand by pullin' this trigger, but if that's the way it has to be, I can't do nothin' about it. Now ease them guns from their holsters. I been followin' you for two weeks now. Figured if I got you in town, you'd never get away from me."

Miranda glanced at the counter and saw no sign of Monty Lake. The clerk had apparently ducked down when the second man barged in. Neither Jake nor Luke Putnam noticed her for the moment, and she cautiously slid her hand inside her purse, feeling for her pistol, her heart pounding wildly with fear.

"Those charges are wrong," Jake told Putnam. "I didn't do the things they say."

"That's for a jury to decide, Harkner," Putnam answered, grinning through stained teeth. "Fact remains a bank was robbed and money stolen. Innocent people were killed, a young girl abducted and raped, and it's your mug that's on the posters. Now let loose of those guns."

Miranda's stomach churned at the words—abduction and rape? And she had actually spoken to the man! She gripped the pistol as the one called Jake Harkner slowly lowered his hands to unbuckle his gunbelt. She gasped when he suddenly ducked, charging head-on into Putnam's knees. Putnam's rifle fired, the bullet shattering the glass at the front of the counter behind which Monty Lake was hiding. Lake let out a yelp, and Miranda pulled her pistol from her handbag, watching Harkner and Putnam struggle for a moment. Harkner had slammed Putnam onto his back, and now Putnam swung his rifle, cracking it across the side of Harkner's head and splitting the skin.

Everything had happened in a matter of one or two seconds. Harkner fell sideways, and in an instant he pulled a revolver as Putnam struggled to again cock his own rifle. Harkner fired, and a bloody hole exploded in Putnam's chest. He fell back without a sound against a stack of material and slid to the floor.

Harkner quickly rolled to his knees, then eyed Miranda as he stood up. His dark, angry eyes fell on the pistol she held, and with his own gun still in hand, Miranda was sure he was going to shoot her too. A survival instinct made her pull the trigger. The small pistol cracked, and Jake Harkner stumbled backward but did not fall. His eyes widened in astonishment as he looked down at his middle to see a spot of blood.

Miranda wondered which of them was the most surprised, Harkner at being shot by a woman, or she, for pulling the trigger in the first place. She waited, expecting him to shoot back, but he just shook his head. "I'll be damned," he muttered. He turned and stumbled out of the store, nearly tripping over Putnam's body. Miranda stood frozen. The rain had let up slightly, and she heard shouted voices, heard someone riding away.

"Mrs. Hayes! Dear God!" Monty Lake was coming from behind the counter, his face bleeding from where flying glass had cut him. "You shot him! I saw it! You shot that one called Jake Harkner. That bounty hunter said he was worth five thousand dollars!"

Miranda looked down at her pistol, wondering if she had just dreamed all of this.

"I'll get the sheriff," Lake told her. By then several people had gathered outside. Lake hurried out and began explaining what had happened. Miranda heard more shouts, as men quickly gathered to form a posse to try to find the wounded outlaw, who had ridden off before anyone realized what had happened.

"Mrs. Hayes! Are you all right?"

It was Sheriff McCleave. The middle-aged, big-bellied lawman had been sweet on her for a year now, but Miranda had no desire to be courted by anyone. She saw the genuine concern in his kind brown eyes.

"I'm fine, Sheriff." She looked over at the counter, wondering what the sheriff would think if he knew she was actually feeling sorry that Jake Harkner had left without being able to collect the supplies he had apparently needed. Stranger still, she felt sorry for having shot him. She couldn't understand why she should, after hearing the things he was wanted for—robbery, murder, abduction, and rape. Hadn't he denied being guilty? But then what man *wouldn't* try to deny it? It was ridiculous to feel sorry about what she had done. Maybe it was the fact that her father had been a doctor in Illinois before they had come to Kansas. She had grown up being taught it was important to save lives, not take them.

People were pressed around her now, praising her, telling her that if the posse could catch Jake Harkner, she would be a rich woman. She watched some men carry off Luke Putnam's body, heard someone say he was dead. She thought about how quickly Harkner had acted, lunging fearlessly at a man who was ready to shoot him. He had drawn his revolver with such lightning quickness that she was hardly aware he had moved his hand. Most vividly, she remembered the look in the outlaw's eyes after she shot him, such astonishment, even a hint of respect. He could so easily have shot her, or he could have threatened her, used her for a shield in order to get out of town. Instead, he had just left her there unharmed.

The sheriff rode off with a posse, and a friend from church, Bonnie Kent, was suddenly at Miranda's side. "Randy!" she exclaimed, using the more familiar shortened form of Miranda that her father had used for her practically from birth, the name by which all her friends knew her. "Oh, you poor thing! Are you hurt? Are you okay?"

"I don't know." Miranda put a hand to her eyes. "It all happened so fast!"

"Oh, this is terrible, and you still in mourning! Come to

the house for a while and rest, Randy. I'll give Mrs. Denver your list and she can see that you get everything you need here."

In a kind of daze, Randy followed Bonnie out of the store. A crowd of curious people followed, and she answered their questions as best she could while hurrying with Bonnie through a now-steady downpour. By the time they reached Bonnie's house at the west end of town, two men who reported for the Kansas City paper had also reached her. They peppered her with questions until Bonnie told everyone they must leave and let Randy rest.

Finally the door was closed, and both women removed their rain-soaked capes. Bonnie led Randy into the parlor of the small frame home she shared with her husband of one year. "I'll get you some tea," she told Miranda. "You sit right there in front of the hearth and warm yourself." She left, and Miranda remained standing, staring at the flickering flames of a small fire in the fireplace.

Suddenly everything was quiet, except for the ticking of a mantle clock. She looked up at the timepiece, shocked that it was still only ten o'clock in the morning. So much violence in one short, spring morning! And she had been a part of it! Out there somewhere rode the dangerous-looking stranger named Jake Harkner, with her bullet in his belly.

She shivered, rubbing at the backs of her arms. Would he live? He was out there suffering alone. Who would help him? Would the posse shoot him? Could she in good conscience take the reward money if they caught him? There was something barbaric about that—taking money for a man's body, dead or alive. Apparently Luke Putnam had thought nothing of it, but it gave her the chills.

Bonnie returned from her kitchen. "I'll have some water boiling soon," she told Miranda. "I wonder if my husband knows what has happened. The sawmill is on the other end of town, and those men don't always hear right away what's going on." The woman, only a year younger than Miranda, led her to a brocade love seat and made her sit down. "Randy, do you realize how rich you'll be if they catch that man?"

Miranda shuddered and immediately rose again, feeling restless. "I don't think I could take money for shooting someone, Bonnie." She turned to face her friend, and Bonnie was concerned at how pale she looked. "What frightens me is the possibility that Jake Harkner will *not* be caught! Do you think he would try to find me, to seek revenge? He's an outlaw, wanted for murder and robbery and . . . and rape!"

Bonnie rose, grasping her arms. "Randy, the man would be crazy to come back and look for you. For one thing, he's hurt. To come back here would only spell disaster for him. He'd be caught for certain. Besides, everyone would know who did it, and he'd have another crime added to the list of things he's wanted for."

Randy put a hand to her forehead and walked to a window. He was out there somewhere, bleeding, hurting. Why did she care? "He told that bounty hunter that he didn't do the things he's wanted for."

"Of course he did. Randy, a man in a pinch will say anything." Bonnie walked up behind her and patted her shoulder. "You shouldn't feel guilty about any of this, Randy. You just relax and I'll get you a sweater. You look so cold. And I think you should stay here tonight. As far as I'm concerned, you shouldn't go home at all, after what happened to your father. This just shows you, you shouldn't be living out there alone. Look what happened right here in town! I wish you'd sell that farm and get yourself a place here. I've told you before you can stay with us."

"No." Randy rubbed at her arms again, turning grateful blue-gray eyes to meet Bonnie's. "I won't intrude on young marrieds. I remember . . ." She smiled sadly. "You're lucky you met Charles toward the end of the war and that his duty was already over with. Now you can have him for a good long time."

Bonnie gave her a look of pity. "I'm sorry about your husband, Randy. You've lost so much."

Randy sighed deeply, keeping her arms folded in an unconscious protective stance. "I'll survive. I *am* going to sell the farm. That's part of the reason I came to town. I'm going to find someone who can take me to Nevada to try to find Wesley. I was at the supply store to try to decide what I might need for the trip."

Bonnie sniffed in a gesture of disgust, her taffeta dress rustling as she moved toward the doorway to go back to the kitchen. "Your brother doesn't deserve your risking your neck going to wild country like that to find him. If he cared anything at all for either you or his father, he never would have left."

Randy shrugged. "He's my brother, Bonnie. He should know what has happened. And he's all I have left."

Bonnie shook her head. "I'll go fix your tea."

The woman left, and Randy walked back to the window, which faced away from town. Somewhere out there rode Jake Harkner. What was it like to be so alone? Why did he live the way he lived? He had told Monty Lake that it took more than the war to make a man an outlaw. What had he meant? She would surely never know. He would either die from her bullet or be caught and hanged. Either way, it was her fault; and whether he was an outlaw or not, she could not help feeling she had done something terrible. She closed her eyes and whispered, "God forgive me for pulling that trigger."

Jake wasn't sure how far he had ridden in the creek. He could only hope it was far enough that anyone following him had lost his tracks. Besides that, the water washed away the blood trail he might have left if he'd stuck to land, and all the overgrowth along the creek had given him lots of protective cover.

He was almost to the point of going back and allowing himself to be caught if it meant finding someone to treat his wound. His gut felt on fire, and he was still bleeding. "Damn slip of a woman!" he grumbled. He still could not quite get over it, that young, innocent woman he had watched tying those horses had shot him! If she'd been a man, he could have blown her away before she ever found the courage to pull that trigger. But a woman! He'd done a lot of things, but he'd never killed a woman. He was just lucky she'd carried a tiny pistol in that handbag and not something like the Army .44s he used, or he would most certainly already be dead.

He headed Outlaw through a thick growth of trees and into a clearing, halting the horse and just listening for several minutes while he pressed a neckerchief to his wound. He heard no sound but the wind and birds. The morning rain had finally cleared, and it seemed as though it might warm up a little. He urged his horse to a grassy rise so he could see better. When he reached the top, he scanned the horizon in all directions, seeing no sign of anyone following. In the distance he could see what looked like a cabin and an outbuilding, as well as a larger building that had been burned. He winced and grasped at his belly, again cursing. He knew he had to get help or die. Maybe someone at the farm below could help him—if not willingly, then at gunpoint.

He urged his horse down the hill, pulling a revolver from its holster as he came closer, waiting for someone to come out and greet him—or shoot at him. Everything was quiet, and no one made an appearance. He approached the cabin. "Hello!" he called out, watching the windows carefully. One of them was broken out and boarded up. No one answered his call. He carefully surveyed the entire area, seeing no wagons, no cattle, no horses. In the distance, fencing around what appeared to be a freshly plowed field was knocked down, as was more fencing around what was once apparently a corral. He rode toward the burned-out building, which he could tell had been some kind of barn. Disaster had most certainly struck here, and from all appearances it had been a man-made disaster.

"Raiders," he muttered. He knew the signs. He had done some of this kind of work himself when he rode with Bill Kennedy and his gang; but those days were done, and Bill Kennedy and his whole bunch, or what was left of them after Jake's shootout with them, were also after Jake's hide. "I not only have the law after me, but *outlaws* too," he muttered to his horse.

He felt himself growing weaker, knew he at least had to lie down somewhere; and Outlaw also needed to rest. He managed to dismount and he led the horse to a nearby shed, opening the door cautiously at first. Inside were three empty stalls and some feed. "Here you go, boy," he said quietly to Outlaw. He led the horse inside. "I'm sorry I can't unsaddle you, but at least you can eat." He holstered his revolver and took a knife from its sheath on his belt, slitting open a sack of oats and grunting with great pain as he managed to hoist it to a feeding trough and dump it in. He stumbled against the stall then, again cursing his luck.

He removed his heavy, wet slicker and threw it over the side of the stall, then made his way back outside, closing the shed doors so his horse would not be spotted. He headed toward the cabin, then stopped for a moment at the sight of what appeared to be a fresh grave out behind the house. So, someone had died in the raid. He tried to remember when he himself had stopped killing only those who challenged him in a gunfight and had allowed himself to use his guns on innocent people. Well, he hadn't really, had he? They had all been shooting back at him at the time they died. Still, it was his own raiding and robbing that had made them raise weapons against him.

Why it bothered him lately to wonder about such things, he wasn't sure. It irked him to no end, and he thought maybe it had something to do with a man getting older and leaving the wild ways of his youth—if thirty could be considered old. Deep inside, whenever he pulled a gun on someone, he felt fourteen again, and the person staring back at him and his gun was his father. Maybe that was why he couldn't stop killing. Each man he shot was like killing his father all over again.

He mounted two low steps to the front porch of the cabin, again taking out a revolver. He knocked at the door, but there was no answer. He carefully opened the door, seeing a tidy but somewhat barren main room. Apparently the raiders had taken plenty, and whoever was left behind had straightened things up as best he or she could—most likely she, from the looks of the braided rugs on the floors and the ruffled curtains at the windows. Even the window that was boarded up still had curtains hanging on it. He figured the glass had been shot out by the raiders, or by someone shooting back at them.

He studied the room: a table and two chairs, a narrow bed in one corner, where a man's clothes hung on hooks. He spotted what looked like a doctor's bag sitting on the bed. On weakening legs he walked over to open it, seeing a doctor's instruments inside. "I'll be damned," he muttered. Maybe he had picked the right place after all. A doctor would be more likely to help him rather than try to hurt him or even turn him in; but why would a doctor be living way out here on a failing farm?

For the moment he could not afford to stand around and wonder. He could only hope whoever lived here would come back soon and would help him, either out of the goodness of their hearts, or at the point of a gun. He'd have to take the chance. To try to keep going would mean certain death.

He stumbled over to a curtained-off room to make sure no one was hiding there. The room held a homemade log bed that was neatly made and covered with a bright quilt. A single chest of drawers stood against a wall, and a washstand held a bowl and pitcher in the corner of the room. A gold-colored trunk sat against one wall. It looked old and well used. It had a deep gouge in the front of it, and the lid was painted with flowers, the colors now faded. A small table and lamp sat beside the bed.

He grunted again with pain as he walked to the bed and threw back the covers, caring little if he got blood on the blankets. He fell onto the bed, still wearing his woolen jacket and his boots. He rolled to his back, dearly wanting to stay awake and remain alert, but a blackness kept flooding over him. Finally the blackness stayed. His grip loosened on the revolver and the gun remained resting on his stomach as his hand slipped to his side.

CHAPTER
TWO

The sun was beginning to set by the time Miranda pulled her wagon to the front of her cabin. Sheriff McCleave, who had accompanied her home, rode up beside her. "Awful sorry the posse lost that man today, Mrs. Hayes," the sheriff told her. "But we aren't through searching. You sure you shouldn't have stayed in town?" The lawman dismounted and hurried over to help Miranda climb down from the wagon.

"I'll be fine, Sheriff. For one thing, Jake Harkner doesn't know anything about me or where I live, and he certainly can't go back to Kansas City and ask around now, can he?" She walked to the back of the wagon. "The man has either ridden as far from here as he can get, or he's lying dead somewhere." The words brought a sick feeling to her stomach. "Either way, I have nothing to fear from him."

"But you've got money coming to you if we can find him, dead or alive. We'll keep scouring the countryside, ma'am."

Miranda picked up a basket of supplies from the wagon and turned to face the man. "You do what you have to do, Sheriff; but if you do find him, give the money to the Methodist church. I wouldn't feel right taking it."

McCleave shook his head. "Not many folks would turn it down, and you'll need it if you still plan to go to Nevada."

"Phil Albright at the bank said he would give me what

Father had put into the farm and would take it over and resell it. It won't be much, but with what Father had left in his savings, it will be enough."

The sheriff frowned. "I don't like the idea at all, Mrs. Hayes. How is a widow woman like yourself going to get all the way to Nevada?"

"Where there is a will, there is a way, Sheriff. I just need a week or so to get things in order. Then I'll come back to town and look into perhaps going to Independence and seeing if there are some parties leaving for Nevada with whom I could travel. With all that gold and silver out there, there are new people heading to that area every spring."

The sheriff took the basket from her, shaking his head. "You're a brave lady to think about traveling all that way with strangers to find a wayward brother you don't even know will be there anymore."

Miranda turned and picked up another basket. "I don't know what else to do. The four years we've been here in Kansas have been filled with nothing but loss and heartache for me. I met my husband here and lost him to the war, Wes ran off, Father was killed, the farm has gone under." They were walking as she spoke and they both stepped up onto the porch of the cabin. "I need to get away from here, Sheriff." Miranda looked up at the man, studying the hard lines of his face. She guessed him to be perhaps forty. He was not tall, but he was brawny, his only soft spot being his hefty middle. He was neither handsome nor ugly, a rather ordinary-looking man who was always watching out for her, hoping for more than friendship. She smiled. "I think I've proven I can take care of myself."

McCleave grinned back at her. "Well, I'd agree with that." The two of them went inside and set the baskets on the table. McCleave touched Miranda's arm as she turned to go back outside for more supplies. Miranda stopped and met his gaze, seeing a mixture of concern and desire there. "I, uh, I admire you a lot, Mrs. Hayes. You're a right handsome woman, except that you could use more meat on these small bones."

Miranda blushed at the awkward compliment. "I try to put on some weight, but no matter how much I eat . . ." Her smile faded. "I know what you're saying, Sheriff, and I appreciate the compliment and the concern." She felt a tiny flash of desire, and she knew it was not because she was attracted to the sheriff, but more from the distant longings she had experienced lately of just wanting to be with a man again, to have a man love her, hold her, protect her, share her bed. "This is something I have to do, Sheriff. I'll be fine." She patted his arm. "If things don't work out, maybe I'll come back."

McCleave studied her delicate, pretty face, the eyes that sometimes looked gray and sometimes looked blue, the honey-blond hair that he liked to picture hanging loose around her bare shoulders. She had to be so lonely, he thought. He missed his own dead wife, had often thought what a pleasant wife the widow Hayes would make. The late afternoon had grown much warmer, and Miranda wasn't wearing her cape. His eyes moved over the pale blue flowered calico dress she wore, a dress that fit her nicely rounded figure temptingly, flattering her slender waist and a bosom surprisingly generous for her small frame.

The man sighed, wishing he could have sparked enough interest to make her stay around; but Miranda Hayes was a woman who had her mind set on something else, a woman who stuck to her decisions. He nodded resignedly. "Well, I hope you do come back. You just be sure to wire us at Kansas City and let all your friends know you're all right once you reach Nevada."

"I'll do that." Miranda walked back outside with him. "I can finish up here, Sheriff. You'd better get back to your duties."

"You sure?" The man looked around, his eyes resting on the burned-out barn for a moment, then to the boarded-up window of the cabin. "Mrs. Hayes, it's awful dangerous out here for you."

"Those raiders have taken what they came for. They hit most of the farms around here, and they know there's nothing left to take. Stop worrying, Sheriff. I really would like to be alone now. It's been a long day, and I just want to go inside and rest."

"You should have stayed the night at Mrs. Kent's, like she offered."

"I don't like to put people out. In fact, you didn't need to follow me out here. It really wasn't necessary."

"Well, I just thought I'd make sure there weren't any problems." The sheriff tipped his hat to her. "You take care now. Keep your door bolted once you're inside, and you get packed up and back to town as soon as you can."

"I will. I promise. And you take care of yourself."

The man smiled and walked to his horse, mounting up. "See you in a few days then."

"Yes. And keep those reporters and other nosy people away from here," she told him, shading her eyes as she looked at him against a setting sun. "I don't like being a celebrity because I shot a man. I don't want to talk anymore about it."

The man tipped his hat. "I understand, but I don't think you understand the significance of what you did, Mrs. Hayes. Jake Harkner is known for his expertise with those revolvers he wears. He's got quite a reputation—rode with Bill Kennedy and his bunch for a while. Rumor has it he started out by killing his own pa down in Texas. Don't know if that's true, but I've never heard anything good about the man. Don't you be feeling sorry for what you did. If that man is dead, you did society a favor."

He winked and rode off, and Miranda turned back to get a gunny sack full of more supplies from the wagon. She carried them inside, her stomach still in knots. She still could not quite settle her own feelings over what she had done. But— killed his own father! Was it true? What kind of man would do a thing like that? She had loved her own father so dearly, still mourned his loss. How could a man live with himself after doing such a thing? Maybe the sheriff was right. Maybe if Jake Harkner were dead from her gunshot, it was best for all. Maybe the Lord had directed her to fire that pistol.

She walked back outside and sat down on the steps for a moment, watching the sun sink behind a hill to the west. After a day of answering constant questions, telling her story again and again, she felt spent. Dangerous or not, it felt good to be here alone, to have nothing but quiet. She studied the horizon. Where was Jake Harkner? She almost hoped he was dead. She could rest easier knowing that than to think he was lying alone somewhere, bleeding, in pain, dying slowly with no help. Did a man like that deserve to die that way? Probably. He had lived by the gun and should die by the gun, the way his innocent victims had died, especially his poor father.

She sat thinking and enjoying the quiet for several minutes before deciding she had better put up the horses before it got too dark. She rose and took hold of the harness to one of the draft horses, leading the animals toward the shed and thinking how easily either horse could crush her small bones if he got the notion to be ornery. But the two gelded animals were as gentle as kittens, obedient and always willing. They had been easy to sell. Next week she would deliver them to the owner of a hardware store, and they would be used to pull delivery wagons for the business. She would miss them.

She stopped and patted the neck of each horse. "I'll have your harness off in a minute, boys." She opened the shed door, then gasped when she saw a strange horse inside the shed, nibbling away at fresh oats. The animal was still saddled, a rifle and a shotgun resting in boots on either side of the saddle.

Fear gripped Miranda in the form of real pain in her chest. Whose horse was this? She noticed a dark green slicker tossed over the side of the stall. It looked familiar. Hadn't Jake Harkner been wearing a slicker like that when she saw him in the store?

Every nerve end came alert as her gaze quickly darted around the shed, but she saw no sign of human life. She put her hand to the strange horse's flank and could feel that the animal was cool. Apparently it had been there for several hours. If so, where was the man who had ridden it?

She moved closer to study the animal, noticing dried blood on the saddle and stuck to the left side of the horse's coat. Whoever had ridden it was bleeding, which made it even more likely it was Jake Harkner! But why here? The man couldn't possibly know where she lived! And where was he? Waiting for her? Hiding somewhere, ready to shoot her down in revenge? Still, why would he put his horse up in her own shed, knowing she would surely see it?

She put a hand to her head, which suddenly ached fiercely. Her heart was pounding so hard she could feel it in her chest. She felt like a fool for not checking everything more thoroughly before Sheriff McCleave left. Now he was too far away to even hear a gunshot.

She was here alone, with a stranger, most likely a man bent on revenge, somewhere on her property, but where? She told herself not to panic. She had to think logically, be cautious. She moved past the draft horses to the wagon and reached under the seat to take out her father's own Winchester. She cocked the rifle and looked around, holding the gun in a ready position.

"Wherever you are, come out now!" she said sternly, try- ing to sound unafraid. Her only reply was the soft quiet of the early evening. She checked around the shed once more, then walked back outside, her eyes glancing in every direction, her ears alert. She decided the horses would just have to wait in harness for a while. There was no time now to tend to them.

She checked behind the shed, scanned the open land all around the cabin. Since the raid, there were really no buildings left but the shed and the cabin, and the land was so flat, except for the high hill to the west, that there really were no good hiding places outside. Even the hill itself was treeless. That left only the cabin.

The cabin! Surely whoever owned the horse wasn't inside the cabin! And to think that she and Sheriff McCleave had been inside there themselves! Was it possible someone could have been lurking in there the whole time the sheriff was with her? If so, he was either unconscious from his wound, or lying in wait for her to be alone.

She slowly approached her tiny log home, walking completely around it, seeing nothing. She approached the root cellar at the north wall of the building, swallowing back her fear as she reached down and flung open one door, then pointed her rifle into the cellar. "Come on out if you're in there!" she demanded. "Just get out and ride away and no one has to be hurt!"

Again her reply was only silence. She moved around to fling open the other heavy metal door, wishing it was brighter outside so she could see better down into the small dugout. "Did you hear me? Come out of there!" She reached down and picked up a couple of medium-sized rocks, flinging them into the dark hole, but all she heard were thuds as they hit the dirt floor. She knew from the size of the cellar and the small space in the middle of the surrounding shelves that if someone were down there, she could hardly have missed him with the rocks.

She cautiously stepped closer and kicked one door up with her foot, sending it back over and slamming closed. With her rifle aimed at what was left at the opening, she moved around to the other side and kicked that door shut. She backed away then, watching the cellar a moment longer, before turning and heading for the cabin's front door, her heart pounding even more wildly. Unless the owner of the horse had just wandered off, the cabin was the only place left where he could be. She looked down and saw a couple of spots of what could be blood on her porch. Why hadn't she or the sheriff noticed it before? How could they both have been so careless?

She cautiously pushed open the door with the barrel of her

rifle, then stepped inside. Everything still appeared to be in order. Raising the rifle to a ready position then, she headed for her curtained-off bedroom, hoping she wasn't so worked up with fright that she would pass out if confronted. She moved to the wall and pressed her back against it, then peered around just far enough to peek through a crack between the edge of the curtain and the doorframe.

At that moment Miranda Hayes thought perhaps her heart would stop beating altogether, and she found it impossible to stifle a gasp. "My God!" she whispered. There on her own bed lay Jake Harkner, apparently unconscious, one of his infamous revolvers lying on his belly. He must have been there the whole time, even when Sheriff McCleave was inside the cabin! How had he ended up here, in her own house? Did he know she lived here? Had he come to kill her but been overcome by his own wound? Was he faking now, waiting for her to get closer?

She stepped inside the room, quickly raising her rifle again when he moaned. She studied him a moment, noticing that his forehead and the skin around his eyes looked sickly pale. Blood stained the cotton blankets beneath him, and his forehead and hair were bathed in sweat as well as more blood from where Luke Putnam had slammed his rifle across Jake's head. She had worked enough with her father to know this was not a man ready to rise up and shoot her. He looked more like a dying man.

She moved a little closer, her rifle still in her right hand as she reached out with her left hand to cautiously take hold of the revolver resting on his stomach. He made no move to stop her. She turned and laid the gun on a chair, and mustering more courage, she reached across him and pulled the second revolver from its holster. When he still made no move to stop her, she set her rifle in a corner and then took the two revolvers hurriedly into the main room, placing them into a potato basket under a curtained-off counter. If he did come around, she didn't want him to be able to find his guns right away.

She hurried back to the bedroom, wondering what she should do. If she went to town for help, he could die before she got back, and she was not sure she wanted to be responsible for that. Besides that, it was getting dark, and she couldn't be traveling to town at night; nor could she let him lie there bleeding and dying while she waited for morning. There was nothing to do for the moment but try to help him.

"Mr. Harkner? Jake Harkner?" she spoke up, leaning closer.

Her only reply was a moan. She breathed deeply for courage and began removing his clothing—first his boots, then his gunbelt and his jacket. It was a burdensome project. The man was a good six feet tall and built rock-hard. On top of that, in his present state he was dead weight. With a good deal of physical maneuvering she pulled off his pants and shirt and managed to move his legs up farther onto the bed and straighten out his body. She hurriedly gathered some towels and stuffed them underneath him as best she could, then unbuttoned and pulled open the shirt of his long johns so she could see the wound, a tiny hole just below his left ribs.

She knew from working with her father and from his medical books that most vital organs were on the right side of a person's body, and she also knew that the small caliber of her pistol could mean no terribly dangerous damage had been done. The biggest problem was that the man had bled considerably, which was probably the reason he had passed out; or she supposed it could be from the vicious blow he had taken to the head. He could have a fractured skull.

She felt underneath him, pressing her hand at his back at the inside of his long johns, trying to see if perhaps the bullet had passed through him, but she already knew that for the size gun she had used, that was unlikely. She felt no wound at his back, and the sick feeling returned to her stomach. The bullet was still inside him and should come out, and there was no one but her to do it.

She knew that the first thing she had to do was to get him to drink some water to replace the body fluids he had lost from blood and perspiration. She worked quickly then, going to get a ladleful of water from the drinking bucket in the main room and bringing it back into the bedroom. She raised Jake's head and tried speaking to him again, asking him to drink the water. All she got was another groan. She managed to pour some of the water into his mouth, and she watched him swallow. More ran out of his mouth and down to the pillow. From the looks of her bed and the man in it, she knew both needed considerable cleaning up; but for the moment her biggest concern was getting out the bullet.

She went into the main room to get her father's doctor bag. "Why are you doing this, Miranda?" she muttered to herself. "Just let him die." Wouldn't society be better off?

That was what Sheriff McCleave had said. Still, her Christian upbringing had taught her that every man had value, and she reasoned there had to be a reason why this man had led the life he led. Why had he shot his father, if indeed that was true? What was the whole story? How old had he been? She could not forget the strange sadness in his voice when he had told the clerk this morning that it took more than a war to make a man lead a lawless life. Had it been only this morning? It seemed like such a long, long time ago.

She set the doctor bag on the table and quickly built a fire in the stone fireplace at the kitchen end of the cabin. She hung a kettle of water on the pothook to heat, then grabbed more towels and the doctor bag and went back into the bedroom. She watched Jake Harkner while the water heated. Had God led him here deliberately? Was she supposed to help him? How ironic that this man had invaded her life twice today. To her it seemed a kind of sign, that for some strange reason he was supposed to be a part of her life, that there was some purpose for his being here. She rolled her eyes then at the ridiculous thought.

She took a bottle of laudanum from the bag and uncorked it, again leaning over Harkner and raising his head slightly. "Try to drink some of this," she said. "It will help kill the pain. I've got to try to get out the bullet, Mr. Harkner. I doubt that it went very deep. It was a small gun I used, and the bullet had to go through your woolen jacket first."

"San . . . tana," he muttered. "I tried . . . sorry . . . Pa. Pa!"

The word "Pa" was spoken with a hint of utter despair. Miranda found herself feeling a little sorry for him, then chastised herself for such feelings. *If the man wasn't in such a state, you'd probably be dead by now,* she told herself. Again she felt like a fool for wanting to help him, yet could not bring herself to let him just lie there in pain. She shoved the slim neck of the bottle into his mouth and poured. Jake swallowed, coughed and sputtered. "No, Pa," he murmured. "Stay . . . away. Don't . . . make me drink it!" His eyes squinted up and he pressed his lips tight when Miranda took the bottle away. He let out a whimper then that sounded more like a child than a man.

Miranda stepped back in astonishment. His whole body shuddered, then he suddenly lay quiet again. He had mentioned his father twice, the first time with such utter pain, this time with an almost pitiful, childlike pleading. She reminded herself that time was important now. The laudanum would take effect quickly. She went back into the main room and rummaged through a supply cabinet until she found some rope. She went back into the bedroom and used the rope to tie Jake's wrists and ankles to the sturdy log bedposts, afraid that when she started cutting into him he would thrash around and make her hurt him more—or perhaps he would come awake and try to grab her.

"As soon as this is over and I see you don't have a fever, I'll give you a bath and a shave," she said as she fastened the ropes tightly. "You'll feel a lot better then. I don't mean you any more harm, Mr. Harkner." She had no idea if he heard her. She only knew she had to keep talking to keep up her own courage. She had seen her father remove bullets a couple of times, but she had no real experience of her own. All she knew to do was to dig with a knife, or perhaps she would have to reach inside the wound with her fingers to find the bullet. Somehow it had to come out.

She went back to the fireplace to find the water was finally hot. She poured some into a pan and brought it back into the bedroom, setting it on a small table beside the bed. She then retrieved a bottle of whiskey from her pantry, something her father always kept around for medicinal purposes only, for he had not been a drinking man himself. She thought about the time Wes had gotten into the whiskey, how there had been times when she and her father had come home from church to find her brother drunk and acting silly. It had been a source of heated arguments between her brother and their father, and one of the reasons Wes had left—so that he would be free to do as he pleased, to drink and smoke and gamble and do all the things his father hated.

She put aside those thoughts and doused Jake's wound with the whiskey. His body jerked, but his eyes did not open. She poured more whiskey over her own hands and her father's surgical knife. She drew a deep breath then and said a quick prayer. "Heavenly Father, if you meant for me to do this, then help me do it right."

Fighting to keep her hands steady, she began digging. Jake's body stiffened, and a pitiful groan exited his lips, but he did not thrash about. Miranda fought tears as she dug deeper and more sickening groans welled up from what seemed the very depths of the man. She swallowed, then reached inside the wound with her fingers, feeling around until she touched what she thought must be the bullet.

"Please let it be," she whispered. She got hold of the object between two fingers and pulled, breathing a sigh of relief when she retrieved the bullet and held it up to look at it. She smiled with great delight, an almost victorious feeling coming over her then as she dropped the bullet onto the small table beside the bed.

She wet a cloth with the hot water and began washing around the wound to get rid of as much fresh and dried blood as possible. She poured more whiskey over it, then threaded some catgut into her father's stitching needle. She soaked some gauze with whiskey and ran it over the catgut, then doused the wound again with the same whiskey before beginning to stitch up the hole.

Doctors were not sure yet of the reasons, but it seemed that if wounds were cleaned with pure alcohol, or at least whiskey, infection, which could kill a person from even a simple wound, could often be avoided. When her father left the medical profession, there had been heated debates going on at the time over how to prevent infection. She wondered how those debates had turned out. Her father had always been adamant that wounds must be washed or kept clean with alcohol.

She hoped she had done the right thing. It would be a shame now, after all her good work, if Jake Harkner should die from infection. Bad as he was, she would be very disappointed if that happened. It felt good to do what she had just done. She thought how proud her father would be, and how she had often wished women were more accepted into the medical profession. She would have liked being a doctor. There was no reason why a woman couldn't do this as well as any man.

She finished the stitches, then untied Jake's wrists and ankles and managed to get his arms out of his long johns so she could pull the top of them down under his hips. Then she wrapped the wound, reaching under his hard, heavy body over and over to bring the gauze around and then tie it. She decided then that all his clothes needed washing, and realized the man could have another kind of accident while lying there unconscious. She pulled the long johns all the way off him and tossed them to the floor, then wrapped a towel around his privates and between his legs, feeling a little embarrassed, but knowing it had to be done. Any nurse in a hospital would have done the same. When it came to medicine, there was no room for modesty.

"I'll give you a good bath when I'm sure you're all right otherwise," she told him. There came no response. She removed her prize quilt from the bed, glad to see he had gotten no blood on it. She replaced it with an older blanket and covered him, but his legs were so long that his feet hung over the end of the bed. As she drew the blanket up to his neck, she noticed another scar at his left shoulder, a sign of stitches at his right ribs, and as she drew the covers to his neck, a strange, wide scar at the right side of his neck.

She dipped some gauze into the hot water then and began washing the wound at the side of Jake's head, noting that the blow of Luke Putnam's rifle had left a deep gash from just in front of Jake's left ear across his left cheekbone. An ugly blue swelling surrounded the cut. She cleaned it as best she could and dabbed at it with more whiskey. "I'm afraid you're going to have another scar here," she said.

She jumped back then when Jake's eyes suddenly flew open. He stared at her a moment, his dark eyes looking glassy and blank. "Santana?" he muttered. His eyes closed again. Miranda put a hand to her chest and breathed deeply to stop her sudden shaking. Was she crazy to do what she had just done? She clenched her fists, forcing herself to stay calm. The man certainly couldn't do her any harm tonight, and he didn't even know where his guns were. She gathered the doctor bag and utensils and carried them out to the table, then retrieved the pan of hot water. She washed the surgeon's knife and the stitching needle and put them back into the bag. She put away the whiskey and the laudanum, and a sudden sense of utter exhaustion overcame her then. She realized that nearly every part of her body ached. It had been the longest, most trying day of her life, one that was not just a physical drain but an emotional one. She realized there was nothing more she could do for Jake Harkner tonight, and what she would do with him after this would have to be decided in the morning.

She went back into the bedroom to get her rifle. The man still lay quietly resting. She hoped it was more of a sleep now than unconsciousness. She took the rifle and set it over near her father's cot in the main room. She stoked up the fire against what she knew would be a chilly night in spite of the warm day. She straightened then, rubbing her hands at her aching lower back. She longed to just lie down now, but she remembered the poor draft horses were still in harness. She lit one lantern and set it on the table, then lit another and carried it outside.

It was dark now, which made everything seem more frightening. She hung the lantern in the shed and began the arduous task of removing the harness from the horses, a job difficult for most men and doubly difficult for her small arms, especially tonight, when her whole body screamed from a day of emotional upheaval and a tenseness that brought physical pain. The only thing that gave her the strength for this was realizing how miserable the poor, loyal horses would be if she left them in harness all night.

She finally managed to free them and herd them into their own stalls in the shed, giving each of them some oats. Feeling sorry for Jake Harkner's buckskin, she removed the gear and saddle from it also, hanging everything over the wall of the stall. She took his rifle and shotgun and hid them behind some bales of hay in the corner, deciding that at least if Harkner came to, he wouldn't be able to find his guns and use them on her.

Suddenly she realized that in her concern for the horses, she had left her own rifle inside the house. She quickly took down the lantern and closed the shed doors, then hurried back to the cabin to find everything the same. She went into the bedroom to check on Jake once more, only to find he had not moved. His breathing was deep and rhythmic, and she thought his forehead already felt a little cooler.

She picked up his clothes and carried them into the main room, where she took down a wooden laundry tub and set it near the fire. She threw his clothes into the tub, poured hot water over them and added some lye soap, figuring the clothes needed a good soaking. She would scrub them and hang them out in the morning. At least that would leave the man even more helpless for the time being—not only would he not have his guns, but he wouldn't even have any clothes to put on!

Miranda stretched and arched her back in an aching weariness. There was nothing left to do now but wait for morning. She turned down the lantern. She could think of nothing more wonderful now than to sleep, but she decided not to undress. Lord knew what Jake Harkner would do if he did come around, and she had better be ready. She turned back the covers of her father's cot and lay down, ankle-high shoes and all, then pulled the covers over her. Miranda positioned the rifle beside her in such a way that she could easily raise it and fire.

Fire? After doing what she considered a damn good job of treating a man's bullet wound, could she turn around and shoot him if he came out of that bedroom and threatened her? Had she gone through all this and saved the man just to go and get the law tomorrow so they could come and hang him? Or had she unconsciously saved the man just so she could collect five thousand dollars for him instead of three thousand?

No, she knew without a doubt that she hadn't been thinking about the money at all, and deep inside she knew it would be difficult for her to turn and hand Jake Harkner over to the law. With those two things ruled out, what else was she to do, let him ride off scot-free to rob and kill and rape again?

She couldn't say why she had done what she did, why she had shot him in the first place, or why she decided to help him. Now she had no idea what she should do about Jake Harkner tomorrow. She closed her eyes and tried to make herself sleep, realizing the much-needed rest was not going to come easily. It had been a long day. It was going to be an even longer night.

CHAPTER
THREE

Miranda saw the flash of a gun. Was it the one she was holding, or someone else's? Everyone moved slowly. A stranger turned to look at her, then reached for her. She tried to run, but her feet felt bolted to the floor. The stranger came closer. He was bleeding everywhere. He shoved a barrel out of the way to get to her, and it made a scraping sound.

It was that sound that woke her from the nightmare. She gasped and sat up, struggling to collect her thoughts as bright sunshine poured through a back window and into the main room through the bedroom doorway. The doorway! She turned to see the curtain pushed aside, and only a few feet away stood Jake Harkner, grasping the back of a chair.

Miranda grabbed up her rifle and leaped from the cot, blinking sleepy eyes in order to see better. The dream, the sound that had awakened her, the leap from her bed, had all happened in a matter of seconds. Now she knew where the sound had come from. Jake Harkner had managed to get out of bed and must have scraped the chair on the floor when he grasped it for support. Now he stood there staring at her, and she was staring back, both startled, both confused, neither saying a word. She could see Jake's body shivering and he was breathing deeply from pain. Blood stained the gauze she had wrapped around his middle, and with his free hand he held a towel in front of his privates.

"You'd best get back in that bed," she told him, trying to sound authoritative.

"You!" he said in a near growl. "You're the lady—"

"I'm the lady who shot you yesterday. And if you came here to kill me, your plan failed! My bullet nearly put an end to you before you could do the same to me."

He looked around the room, back at her. "I don't understand . . . you *live* here?"

"That's right." Miranda, most of her hair now hanging free of its once-neat bun from her tossing through a restless night's sleep, kept the gun steady. "How did you find out? You rode out of town before you could have known."

Jake blinked and shook his head, wondering if he was just having a bad dream. "I *didn't* know. I just . . . rode till I found someplace . . . where I could hole up. I was going to ask . . . whoever lived here to—" He looked down at himself, realizing he was standing naked in front of this slip of a woman, except for the towel he managed to keep in front of himself. "Where in hell are my guns?"

"You won't be needing them." Miranda swallowed as she watched an angry fire rise into his dark eyes.

"Where are my guns, damn it! Turn them over, or I'll come over there and take the one you're holding!"

"Will you?" Miranda noticed how pale he was. "My bet is you can't even walk across this room. If you want this gun, come and get it."

He let out a sigh of frustration. "Look lady . . . I didn't come here . . . to kill you. I didn't even know . . . this was . . . your place. It's just a goddamn, cruel twist of fate, but then that's my . . . kind of luck. Now give me my guns . . . and I'll get dressed . . . and get out of here. That's all I want." He looked around the room again like a caged animal. "Does the law know . . . I'm here? Is there anybody else here? A pa? A husband?"

"Have you forgotten what that clerk told you yesterday in the store? My father was shot by marauding outlaws, men like *you*!" She lowered the rifle just a little. "The law doesn't know you're here. No one does—yet. By the time I found you last night, it was too dark for me to go for help."

Jake looked down at himself again, still trying to wade through the confusion in his mind. "I don't understand. You shot me . . . but you . . . it looks like you tried to fix me up." He raised his eyes to study her again. "Why? You . . . could have just let me lie there and die and . . . collected your three thousand dollars."

"Unlike you, Mr. Harkner, I don't consider money more important than a human life, even the life of someone like you."

Jake stared at the fragile woman who looked at that moment very capable of using the rifle. She stood there with frazzled hair, wrinkled dress, tired eyes—the rifle looking almost too big for her to handle. He wondered how long she would be able to stand there holding it in a shooting position before her slender arms got too tired to keep it up. If he were not so confused and in so much pain, the sight of her would be humorous. Ordinarily, he would laugh at something like this and find a way to lunge at the puny female and get the gun away from her, but she had him at a disadvantage, and she knew it. Damn woman. How in hell did this annoying female manage to keep moving into his path and messing up his plans?

"*Nobody* values my life, lady. I know . . . why you saved me. You want . . . the extra two thousand dollars . . . I'm worth alive. Well, it won't . . . work, because . . . I'm getting dressed and getting . . . out of here." Why in hell did he feel so weak? He had to be strong, had to be firm with this woman. She was here alone. She ought to be easy to scare. "You won't . . . use that rifle on me. Not after going to . . . all this trouble of . . . fixing me up. Now you just . . . tell me where my guns are . . . my clothes. I won't . . . hurt you unless you force me to. I just want . . . to get out of here . . . and be on my way."

Miranda glanced at the gauze, and saw that the bloodstain was bigger. "I don't think you'll be going anywhere, Mr. Harkner. I suggest you get back in that bed before you pass out on the floor, in which case I would never be able to get you back in the bedroom. Then how would I hide you if someone came to visit?"

Jake frowned, watching her eyes. They were pretty eyes, kind of gray and kind of blue. If not for her frazzled appearance . . . Yet he remembered now how pretty he had thought she was when he'd seen her yesterday. Had a whole day really gone by already? "Hide me? Why would you . . . do that?"

She lowered the rifle. "I don't know myself yet. I'm as confused as you are right now, but I do believe by the look on your face that you didn't come here deliberately. If that's the case, I have to think maybe the Lord sent you here for some special reason, seeing as how I'm the one who almost ended your life. Maybe He meant for me to make amends for that by helping you, and it does seem a shame to go to all the trouble of keeping you alive only to turn you over for a hanging. But that doesn't mean I won't still do it. Now get back in that bed."

Jake wanted to argue the matter, but he knew she was right. He could feel himself growing more lightheaded by the minute. If only she'd give him his damn guns. He didn't intend to use them on her, he just wanted them. The law could come by and check on her any time, and he didn't believe she'd hide him like she said she would. He started to turn, then realized she would see his bare behind when he did. Fact was, she had apparently seen everything there was to see. It made him feel doubly vulnerable. Taking a man's clothes was as bad as putting chains on him. Where was he going to go if he couldn't get dressed? It was funny and infuriating both at the same time. "I have to take a leak," he told her, wanting to embarrass her. After all, he was embarrassed himself. He gladly watched her face redden.

"There's a covered pot in the corner of the bedroom. It's clean. Use it." Miranda wished she could keep from blushing, knew he was trying to upset her, perhaps intimidate her. Was everything she had heard about this man true? Thank goodness he was too weak to try anything, but what about when he was stronger? If she had any sense she would tie him up once she got him back into bed, and she would go for help.

"Your generosity . . . is appreciated," he answered sarcastically. He turned, and Miranda forced back a gasp at the sight of deep red scars on the man's back, which looked as though he had been whipped. She raised the rifle again and aimed it at that back, part of her telling herself to be very, very careful; another part of her strangely touched by the things he had muttered, the scars she had seen; and yet another part of her attracted to his very masculine build, the broad shoulders and solid hips.

Jake stumbled back into the bedroom, cursing his condition, even angrier that it was because of the woman who held a rifle on him now and who still had the upper hand. How in hell had he gotten into this ridiculous situation? "Do you need any help?" he heard her asking.

"Hell, no!" he growled, only hoping he was right. It took every ounce of strength and determination he had left to tend to himself. He heard her walking about in the main room, and he hated this feeling of dependency. He was entirely at the woman's mercy, when if he had his normal strength he could break her in half—her, the same woman who had shot him in the first place! God, his gut burned, and his head ached so fiercely that he kept seeing bright flashes. Was she really serious about hiding him if someone came? Why in hell would she want to do that? He was worth five thousand dollars! What was that line she fed him about a man's life being worth more than a reward? Certainly not *his* life. The woman was either stalling him or a little bit crazy. He just couldn't figure out which.

He managed to put the lid back on the pot and stand up long enough to wrap the towel completely around his waist.

"If you're able to stand a little longer, I would like to put some clean blankets on the bed, Mr. Harkner."

Jake turned to see her standing at the doorway. He twisted the towel so it would stay in place, then braced himself against the chest of drawers. "Go ahead." He watched her come into the room. She avoided his eyes as she quickly jerked some blankets off the feather mattress. "What about my horse?" he asked. "He needs his saddle—"

"I tended to him last night. Once you're settled back in this bed I'll let him and my own draft horses out to graze. There is some low ground not far from here where there is always water. They'll find it."

He swallowed against a sudden feeling of nausea, hoping she got the bed ready before he passed out. "What if somebody sees him?"

"He won't be saddled," she answered, turning to the trunk with the faded flowers on top and raising the lid. She took out clean blankets. "If anyone notices, I'll tell them I don't know where he belongs—that he strayed here from somewhere. It happens all the time—other farmers' horses get loose. You left town so fast yesterday, I don't think anyone even knew what kind of horse you were riding. I didn't know myself until I found him in the shed." There was a moment of silence as she kept working.

"Where's the rifle of yours?" he asked then.

Miranda glanced up at him. The man was all power and experience. "Hidden in the other room." She returned to tucking blankets. "I figured you were in no condition to manage to ransack a room to find it or your own guns, and I don't imagine you would even be very effective in trying to hurt me. I simply decided to take a chance on your present weakness." She quickly remade the bed, amazed at how she was able to carry on a conversation with a killer, still wondering why she was bothering to help him. She finished and stepped back. "There. You can lie back down."

She moved to the doorway, and Jake watched her a moment, seeing the fear then. She had let her guard down for a moment. A big, strong, naked man was standing in her bedroom, a man with a reputation as a killer and rapist. She must feel awfully vulnerable herself, he thought. He had never been in such an odd situation with a proper woman before. Why did he feel this sudden compassion for her? "Look, lady, you can believe me . . . or not. I didn't do . . . what that bounty hunter said. I have killed men . . . but mostly out of . . . self-defense . . . men wanting to challenge me when I'd rather be left alone. I've done a lot of wrong things . . . and I expect I deserve prison for it . . . but I've never laid a hand wrongly on a woman, never beat one, never raped one, proper . . . or not. Fact is . . . part of the trouble I'm in is . . . because I tried to help a woman . . . more than once. You don't have to be afraid of me. That's . . . the God's truth. All I want is to get well . . . and get out of here."

Their eyes held, and in spite of the honesty in his own, Miranda told herself she was crazy to believe him. "*God,* Mr. Harkner? Do you really believe in a God?"

He winced with pain as he unsteadily walked to the bed. "Oh, I believe in Him. I just . . . don't happen to believe He . . . gives a damn about me. I expect . . . He long ago gave directions to make sure . . . I go straight to Hell once I die." He grunted as he managed to lie back down, his feet again sticking out the end of the bed. "Not that most of my life . . . right here on earth hasn't been hell already."

Miranda spread another blanket over him. "You said some things last night when you were in pain that make me wonder about you, Mr. Harkner. I guess curiosity is part of the reason I'm not ready to turn you over to the law."

She opened a second blanket and spread that over the

first. "Curiosity?" Jake put a hand to his aching head. "About what?"

She folded her arms and stepped back. "Who is Santana?" Miranda almost regretted the question when she saw the pain that came into his eyes. "You said her name last night, more than once."

Jake closed his eyes. "She's just someone I knew once."

"I think maybe you loved her."

"And I think maybe it's none of your business."

"While you are here under my care, and considering your reputation and the fact that I have not turned you over to Sheriff McCleave, everything about you is my business."

"Then go ahead and get the sheriff," he grumbled, rubbing at his eyes. "My private life is my private life."

"Is she one of the women you tried to help once?"

"What the hell do you care!" Jake gave her the fiercest look he could muster. He hated personal questions.

Miranda stepped a little closer. "Because of the way you spoke her name. I didn't think you were a man capable of deep feelings, Mr. Harkner, but last night I saw a side of you I'm sure few people see. I guess that's the main reason I'm not sure I want to turn you in." Did this man really kill his father? "You also spoke the word Pa, but I couldn't determine if it was with hatred or affection."

Miranda watched his eyes. Again she saw the look of a little boy. "There are some people you can love and hate at the same time."

"Is it true you killed your own father?"

Jake just stared at her, looking surprised at first, then taking on a look of almost pitiful remorse. "Jesus, you've even heard *that* already?" He closed his eyes. "It's a long story," he said quietly, "and none of your damn business. If others say I killed him, then I killed him. Who the hell is going to believe my side of anything? And who the hell cares about what might have made me do it? Folks don't want to hear reasons. They're quick to judge without knowing the facts."

Miranda bent over and picked up the soiled blankets. "Maybe you just hang around with the wrong people, Mr. Harkner. I've never thought any man should be judged by other people's gossip. And I saw a side to you last night that tells me there are things buried inside of you that need digging up, but this isn't the time. You're hurting. Tell me what hurts the most, and I'll see if I can find something among my father's medicine to help."

Jake scowled at her. "You're a strange woman, Mrs. Hayes. I do remember your name right, don't I?"

"Yes."

"Where's your husband?"

"Killed in the war." Miranda knew she should feel uneasy when his eyes moved over her then, but instead she felt self-conscious, only then realizing how wrinkled her clothes must be and how disheveled she must look. She absently put a hand to her hair, realizing it must be in terrible disarray.

"There's nobody else?" he asked.

"A brother. He's in Virginia City, Nevada. As soon as I figure out what to do with you, I'm leaving here to go and find him. He's all I have left since my father was killed. My mother died six years ago."

"Pretty dangerous for a woman out here all alone, what with all the raiding." Jake watched the hint of a smile at the corner of her mouth.

"Yes, isn't it?" she answered sarcastically.

Jake couldn't help a slight grin of his own. "Even more dangerous to set out all alone for Nevada."

"I'll find someone reputable to take me there. I'm no fainting daisy, Mr. Harkner."

He let out a little laugh, then winced with the pain it brought. "I'll agree with that," he told her, his voice gruff with pain. "You say . . . you've got medicine? My head feels like it's coming right off my shoulders."

"My father was a doctor. I learned a lot from him. That's how I was able to take that bullet out of you last night. I'll see what I can find to help the pain."

Jake watched her slender body, heard her skirts rustle as she moved out of the room. She returned carrying a brown bottle. She handed it to Jake. "Just a couple of swallows. Too much isn't good. A man can get as dependent on this stuff as whiskey."

Jake reached out and took the bottle. Their fingers touched, and a strange warmth moved through him. He could tell by her eyes and the slight blush in her cheeks that she had felt it too. He uncorked the bottle and took a couple swallows of the bitter liquid, grimacing at the taste. Then he handed the bottle back to her.

"You should probably try to eat something," she told him.

"I'll clean up and then fix you some vegetable soup and some tea. You just rest while I get things together. I have to go let out the horses first. Maybe later this afternoon I can shave you." *You also need a bath,* she wanted to add but how could she bathe him now when he was fully conscious? That would just have to wait until he could do it himself. She turned to leave.

"Mrs. Hayes," Jake called. Miranda stopped and turned, embarrassed for feeling a sudden flash of womanly longings when his fingers had touched her own. She looked at the bed but did not meet his eyes. "Thank you," he said.

Miranda could not help looking at him then. "I'm the one who shot you, Mr. Harkner."

"You didn't really want to do that. I could tell . . . the minute you pulled the trigger. I saw the look of surprise in your eyes. And now . . . you've helped me when you could easily have . . . let me die. Not one person would have blamed you for it. They would just figure . . . society was rid of another rat."

"I have yet to decide whether I did the right thing, Mr. Harkner. And as far as my helping you last night, for all we know I botched the whole thing. I've never taken a bullet out of anyone before. You aren't out of danger of infection yet, so don't go thanking me too quickly."

Jake watched her leave, and he closed his eyes again, sinking back into the feather pillow. For the moment, he was at this woman's mercy, and there was no way around it. Fact was, he felt a kind of comfort here. This was the woman who had shot him, yet now, lying here under her care, watching her gentle eyes . . . crazy as it seemed, the woman gave him a feeling of security, something he had not felt since he was very small, in his mother's arms. He had never stopped missing his mother, never thought he would find anyone who brought out those sweet, childish feelings that he thought he had lost years ago. Mrs. Hayes was the kind of woman a man longed to know better, yet he didn't even know her first name.

For the next week Jake learned the hard way that the strange Mrs. Hayes's last words had been too true. He got worse instead of better after getting out of bed that first morning, and the next several days were spent in fits of delirium from fever and infection. He vaguely remembered gentle hands, soft words, sometimes thinking it was his mother nursing him, as she had done once when he had been attacked by yellow jackets; and again when he'd fallen and broken his arm . . . and those many times she'd tended to him after his father had beaten him.

Someone bathed him almost constantly, trying to keep him cool, and when he came around enough to think clearly again, he realized someone had shaved him. He glanced at the bedroom doorway. The curtains were drawn back, and he could see Miranda Hayes moving around in the outer room. Something smelled wonderful, and she was placing fresh-baked bread on the table.

Miranda. He remembered she had told him her name later that first day, before he got sicker than he remembered being in his entire life. After that it seemed he saw everything in a fog, or through black pain. Either his head was reeling with misery, or his gut was screaming, or he was vomiting. It occurred to him that Mrs. Hayes had put up with an awful lot of ugly things to take care of him. Why on earth had she done it?

He breathed deeply. He felt better than since he'd been shot, clearheaded, almost free of pain, and he knew he owed his life to the woman in the outer room, unless she might still choose to turn him in. She had had time while he was ill to go to town and get someone, yet she had not done so. He raised the blankets to see he still lay naked, with towels over him, but he felt clean. He sniffed his arm and smelled soap.

"When you feel up to it, I'll wash and cut your hair," came the woman's voice. Jake looked up to see her coming into the bedroom. "How are you feeling today, Mr. Harkner? Have you returned to the real world?"

He just stared at her a moment. She was actually smiling and looked relieved that he might be better. And today . . . today she was the prettiest he had ever seen her. She wore a deep blue calico dress that fit her small but nicely curved frame. Her long, honey-blond hair was hanging well past her shoulders, drawn up at the sides with combs. There was no more fear in her eyes as she came closer and touched his face with the back of her hand, and what a slender, gentle hand it was.

"The fever is finally gone. I'd say you're going to live, Mr. Harkner. And I must say, under all that trail dust and that neglected beard, you turned out to be quite a handsome man once I found your real face."

Jake's eyes moved over her, and Miranda immediately re-gretted the remark, wondering what had made her say it. She moved to the foot of the bed, draping a light blanket over his bare feet, then moved to the window and opened the curtains. "It's a beautiful day."

Jake tried to sit up, but dizziness overcame him. He groaned, and quickly Miranda was at his side, grasping his shoulders and pressing him back into the feather mattress. "Not yet. Don't be so anxious, Jake."

"How long have I been here?"

"Nearly a week now. I imagine it will be another few days before you can think about walking around, let alone riding a horse."

Again Jake tried to sit up. "I don't have another few days. I've been here too long already. Where are my guns? My clothes?"

"Jake, if you do too much too soon, everything I've done, all the hours I've sat with you through the night, will be for nothing. You'll kill yourself. Let your body heal." She straight-ened and folded her arms. "I'm not giving you any guns just yet. As far as your clothes, they've been boiled and pressed and are clean whenever you're ready to wear them again, but at the moment you are far from that."

Again he settled back into the bed, hating to admit she was right. She had called him Jake twice, using the name as easily as if he were her best friend. And was that true concern he saw in her eyes? She left the room, and he heard the sound of dishes clinking, water being poured. She returned a few min-utes later with a tray. "A cup of good, strong tea is just what you need. Good for a stomach that hasn't seen food for a long time." She set the tray on the table beside the bed. "And if you're so determined to sit up, then let's do it right. Then you can get the tea down better. If it stays down, I'll cut you a piece of bread and we'll see if that stays down."

She reached over to help him raise up a little, bracing an arm under his neck. She reached around him then to fluff the pillows and grasp an extra one to prop against the cross-poles at the head of the bed.

Jake noticed her neck was small and pretty. She was so close, smelled so good. He thought how if he were at his usual strength and felt all right, it would be very hard not to pull her to him and taste her mouth, feel her soft skin. How long had she been a widow? How often did she think about what it had been like to let a man bed her? Had it been good with her husband, or were there things he had never even taught her?

"I'll help all I can, but you're going to have to push with your hands a little." Miranda grasped him under the arms and used all her strength to help scoot him up slightly, thinking what a solid, muscular man he was, in spite of his last week of sickness. His skin was so dark, she wondered if he had Mexican or Indian blood. She struggled to ignore his closeness, tried not to think about how good it might feel to have a man hold her again in the night, treasure her, make love to her. It was certainly ridiculous to think such a thing about a man like Jake Harkner.

She got him to a sitting position and quickly moved away from him, turning to take the tray and set it across his legs. She took the cup then and raised it to his lips. "Try to drink some."

Jake took the cup into his own hands. "I can hold it."

Miranda watched him a moment, confused by her own feelings. Taking care of him, nursing him through his agony and knowing she was the cause of it, hearing the things he had said in his delirium, all made her feel closer to him, responsible for him. Her curiosity about his past had only grown stronger, as had this strange, unexplainable sympathy for him. Why on earth should she feel sorry for this man who was probably no better than those who had killed her father? Was it foolish to believe that deep inside, every man had some good in him?

"I don't know why I haven't told anyone you're here," she said. "I only know that no matter how much part of me argued for it, I simply could not turn you in for bounty money. I did go into town once." She watched his dark eyes turn distrustful again as he lowered the cup. "Don't worry. I had no intention of turning you in," she assured him. "I only went so that everything would appear normal and so my friends could see I was just fine. I wanted to avoid anyone coming here to check on me. As long as you were sick, I couldn't count on you keeping quiet if someone came around." She smiled softly. "Do you want to know the latest rumor about you?"

Jake frowned. "I'm not so sure I do."

"Oh, you'll like this one. Everyone is convinced you died alone somewhere and your body will never be found. They say you might have made it to Indian Territory, in which case you most certainly will never be found, except perhaps by wolves and buzzards who will do a fine job of consuming what is left of your body."

Jake grinned. "That so?" He took another drink of tea. "Well, as long as I'm supposed to be dead, we'll just leave things that way. It will be easier getting out of here. If I'm lucky, a certain gang of outlaws will believe the rumor and will stop looking for me."

"Bill Kennedy?"

Jake studied her eyes. "How did you know?"

"Sheriff McCleave told me you rode with him. Why is he after you?"

Jake rubbed at his eyes. "I think I told you I don't like questions."

Miranda folded her arms. "And I think that after all I've done for you, I deserve some answers."

Jake sighed, setting the cup on the tray, feeling ridiculous trying to handle the delicate little thing in his big hands. He thought how the thin china cups reminded him of Miranda Hayes. "Don't you have some good whiskey? That would do me a lot better than this tea."

Miranda walked around to the foot of the bed. "Tell me why Bill Kennedy is after you, and I'll let you have a couple of shots of whiskey."

He grinned a little. "So, now we're up to blackmail, are we?"

"Call it what you want."

He rubbed at his stomach, thinking how the tea did make him feel better. "The things that bounty hunter said, about me being wanted for rape. I wasn't with Kennedy's gang that day they robbed that bank back in Missouri, and I didn't have anything to do with them taking that woman customer off with them. But because I usually rode with them, rumor spread that I was a part of it. I didn't even know about it until I rode into Kennedy's hideaway that night and found him and the rest of them—" He glanced at her, saw her growing a little pale. "I don't think I need to go into details. Suffice it to say most women would rather have been shot, and this one wasn't even a woman. She was young, maybe only seventeen or so." A look of anger and outrage moved into his eyes. "It's like I said before, Mrs. Hayes. I've done a lot of things, but not that. And because of something that happened when I was younger, I've never been able to tolerate watching a man abuse a woman. I got her out of there, but not without a hell of a gun battle that left a lot of Kennedy's men dead. They aren't going to forget about it anytime soon, if ever. I took the girl back to town and left her off. I don't even know if she realized who helped her. Apparently she didn't, or she would have told the law I had nothing to do with abusing her."

Miranda watched his eyes. They were dark, compelling, and at the moment she believed they told the truth. The man emanated power and danger, and at the same time he had shown such vulnerability when he was sick, had again spoken the name Santana. When he had muttered about his father, it had been as though in agony, with an almost begging tone to his voice. This man carried some kind of deep hurt, and for some reason she wanted to find the good in him. She told herself to be careful, not to let his powerful personality and handsome qualities make her do something foolish. Those dark eyes had a way of making her forget all reason. She had been alone too long, that was the problem, so long that she was allowing herself to enjoy the company of an outlaw.

"What happened in your life that made you feel so defensive of women? Did it involve the one named Santana?"

He looked away. "All you need to know is that I didn't do the things I'm wanted for now. By the way, where's my gear? I need a smoke with that whiskey."

Miranda sighed. He was through talking about himself for the moment. "I'll see if I can find your tobacco, and I'll get the whiskey, but only if you promise to eat something."

"I'll try." He met her eyes again. "And I still want my guns. Anyone could come by at any time."

"That's right, Jake. And anyone who might come by would be one of my friends checking on me. Do you really think I would allow you to shoot an innocent person who might come out here just to see if I'm all right? I have betrayed my friends enough already just by saving your life and keeping you here secretly. I'm not about to let you turn around and hold a gun on them."

Jake rolled his eyes. "Mrs. Hayes—"

"Randy."

"What?"

"I told you my first name is Miranda. Friends and family just call me Randy."

"I'm not family," Jake told her. "Don't tell me you're calling me a friend! I'm no friend to anything but my guns, and I'm not eating until they're hanging over this bedpost."

Miranda stiffened. "Fine, if that's the way you want it. You can also go without your tobacco and whiskey. You just remember that you're not going to do anything but get weaker if you don't eat, and if you ever intend to ride out of here, Jake Harkner, you'd better learn to go by my rules! No guns!"

She held his eyes challengingly, then watched another hint of a smile at the corner of his mouth. "You drive a hard bargain, Randy."

"It's called survival, and I meant it about considering ourselves friends. After what we have been through together for the last week, what else can you call it?"

He put a hand to his hair, wishing it was cleaner. "I don't know. I only know that among those I run with, a man calls you friend only as long as he knows you can outdraw and outshoot him."

Miranda smiled. "Well then, I'd say it's time you learned what it's like to have a *real* friend. Besides, I *did* outshoot you, and I'm *still* calling you friend."

Jake sighed deeply. There was no outtalking this woman, and at the moment no outdoing her physically. "I give up. Just get me that whiskey, will you?"

"Are you going to eat?"

"Yes."

"Fine."

Jake watched her exit the room, his mind already whirling with how he could outsmart this woman. Friend? No woman like that one called a man like him friend, and he still couldn't quite believe she wouldn't turn him in if someone came by.

He had to find those guns! As long as he was this weak, the guns were his only protection. They were all he'd counted on most of his life, and he wasn't about to be without them now. If he could find them, Randy Hayes would have to live by his rules. He'd never lived by anyone else's, and he wasn't about to start now!

CHAPTER
FOUR

 Miranda lugged two buckets of water from the well, setting one down at the door so that she could open it, then picking the water up again and struggling inside with her heavy load. As soon as she got through the doorway she saw Jake standing near the counter under which she kept the potatoes. He had managed to pull on a pair of long johns but was still shirtless, and he held one revolver in his hand; another lay on the pantry. His gunbelts, which she had hidden in the bottom of her wardrobe, hung over one shoulder. She moved slowly to set the buckets on the floor, unsure whether or not she should be afraid. She watched Jake's eyes, saw there a mixture of victory and humor. "Potatoes?" he asked sarcastically. "I thought they'd be under a floorboard or something."

Miranda told herself to stay calm. Everything had been fine as long as he was in bed and had no weapons. She had carried her own rifle everywhere with her, leaving it on the porch just now while she got the water. "Apparently I shouldn't have left those things anywhere in the house."

Jake grinned, whirling the chamber of the revolver in his hand and holding it up to blow into it. "Potatoes have dirt on them. I'll have a time getting these things cleaned up. I usually oil them nearly every day." He glanced at her, saw the fear beginning to build in her eyes. "Don't worry, they aren't even loaded. I took the bullets out so I can clean them." He frowned then, feeling annoyed at what she must be thinking. "Look, I told you I don't go around hurting women."

Miranda leaned down and picked up the buckets. "I'm wondering why it's so important to you to have a gun in your hand. I'm certainly no threat, and I told you I have no intention of turning you in."

Jake watched her lift the buckets to the counter, seeing that it took great effort, and wondering at the fact that such slender arms could lift anything. "A man like me can't be too careful or too trusting. A whole townful of people who would love to collect the reward on me is only a half-hour from here. Not only do I have civilians and the law after me, but the men I used to ride with are after me too. I'll rest a lot better with these hanging over the bedpost."

Miranda faced him, her arms folded. "Suit yourself. You have a lot to learn about trust, Jake." She turned away and began adding more wood to the fire in the hearth. "You'd better get back in that bed. Just because you woke up this morning feeling better doesn't mean you can be up rutting around like everything was normal. You do too much too soon and you'll just land yourself in bed longer than if you'd stayed there in the first place."

Miranda heard another gun chamber whirl, and her heartbeat quickened. She had let herself believe he was telling the truth about not hurting her. She hoped her own basic instincts were right. What convinced her was the day she had shot him, the way he looked at her, the fact that he could have shot back but did not. She had seen a side to him while he was sick that she guessed few people knew anything about, and strangest of all, there was something about him she had begun to like, although she could not quite name it. Was it just a woman's reaction to such a man, or was it like feeling sorry for a wounded animal?

In her whole life she could not remember her emotions being so confused. She had always been so sure of herself, sure of what she wanted, able to clearly judge other people. But this man was an enigma, a man she had no doubt could be ruthless, but who still harbored a frightened, possibly abused child within his big, virile frame.

"Don't worry, I'm going," he answered. "But that soup you make and that shot of whiskey and a good sleep this afternoon did wonders. Give me a couple more days' rest and I can be out of your hair completely. I'm sure that will make you sleep better at night." The last words were spoken with a hint of bitterness. "If you'll bring in my gear, I can clean these guns," he added.

Miranda faced him. "So you can go on killing?"

His dark eyes turned to smoky anger, and Miranda reminded herself that this man was a drifter and a raider who probably didn't even know how many men he had killed. Now he stood here, all six feet plus of him, feeling stronger *and* ornerier. She stepped back when he cocked the revolver and pointed it directly at her, all with a lightning speed that made her gasp.

"So I can *defend* myself!" he nearly growled. He lowered the gun, an almost sad look coming into his eyes. "Hell, I told you it wasn't loaded." He shook his head. "Do you really think I'd hurt you now, after what you went through to keep me alive? You know something? My pa couldn't see any good in me either. My mother did, but then that's the way mothers are, isn't it? Trouble was, Pa didn't see the good in her either, and he had it in his head that the only way to bring out the good in anybody was to *beat* it out of them, with a board or a belt or a whip or his fists or anything else that was handy! The more whiskey he had in him, the bigger the weapon."

He walked up to her and leaned closer, his eyes on fire. "When you live your whole life defending yourself, Randy, it becomes as natural as breathing. My father taught me how *not* to trust, how *not* to let myself care about anyone. He made it very clear that I'm a worthless bastard who'll never amount to bullshit, and he was *right*! And it's because of him that I've lived a life on the run!"

He towered over her, making her want to back away, but she stubbornly refused to show any fear. He held the revolver in front of her face. "I don't expect somebody like you, a proper lady who comes from a world I've never known, to even *begin* to understand why I need these! Just know that I *do* need them, and don't *bitch* at me about it!" He stepped back, just staring at her a moment, then turned away and picked up the other revolver. He walked into the bedroom and threw the guns and belts on the bed, then came back into the main room, hating himself for the way she was still just standing there as though frozen in place. "You got a privy out back?"

She swallowed, looking a little pale. "Yes." He could see

her pretending to be unafraid. "I'll heat some water. When you're through out back, I'll help you wash your hair. I can cut it a little for you if you like."

Jake sighed deeply, thinking how at the moment she reminded him of his mother, not physically, but having that frightened look about her he had seen too many times. "Look, I'm sorry. I don't know what made me light into you like that. I guess . . . there are just things about my life you don't understand." He went to the door. "Where's your rifle? I'm not stepping outside without something to shoot with."

Miranda began dipping some water from one of the buckets into a black pot. "Do you like dumplings? I thought I would boil some for supper. I'm afraid they will have to be mixed with vegetables. I have no meat. The raiders ran off our livestock and killed all our chickens." She turned to look at him. "Well? Do you like dumplings?"

"I like them just fine." Jake thought how he would like nothing more right now than a huge steak and some fried potatoes, but then who was he to order up a meal to his liking? He was just an intruder, and besides, she had no meat. "The rifle?"

She looked away again. "Out on the porch."

Jake left, and Miranda breathed deeply to keep her composure. His bellowing voice and smoldering eyes when he had leaned close and lit into her had left her shaken, but she was not about to let him see it. His quick apology had set her more at ease again, but her mind whirled with wonder at the things he had told her. And she still wondered who Santana was. His mother? After all, it was a Mexican name, and Jake Harkner most certainly had some kind of Spanish or Indian blood in him. Still, he surely wouldn't call his mother by her first name. Was she a woman he had loved? Was Jake Harkner capable of caring for someone that much?

My father taught me how not to trust, how not to care about anyone. Were the marks on his back from beatings administered by his own father? She wondered if he realized that all the while he was yelling at her, she could see the little boy behind those blazing dark eyes. She wished he would smile more often. When he smiled, he was a changed man. He was devilishly handsome whether smiling or not, but when he did smile, there was no trace of the outlaw, or the hurt little boy or the angry man. There were only those straight, white teeth and those full lips. He looked like any decent man one might meet in town, except that few were built quite so big. Fewer still were that good-looking.

She rolled her eyes at the thought, feeling foolish and sinful. Jake Harkner had nothing to offer a woman but trouble. Besides that, he was not a man who bothered offering a woman *anything*, except maybe a little money for a roll in bed. It was not likely he had known any decent women.

She hung the kettle on the pothook and stoked up the fire. Why was that womanly side of her she had ignored since her husband's death suddenly stirred, even after he had lit into her with his harsh words? Part of her looked forward to his being well enough to leave, and another part of her didn't want him to go.

She filled a second kettle with water and hung it on another hook to heat it for washing his hair. She knew deep inside what was really happening to her. She had a man in her house again, not a father, but a man who looked at her as a woman, the way Mack had looked at her when they'd first met. It felt good to take care of a man, cook for a man, shave him. She missed those things, perhaps because she had had Mack for such a short time and had just begun to get used to being a wife when he left for the war. She had always helped her father, cooked for him, kept house and such; but doing it for a husband had been different. She and Mack had had big plans to build up the farm, build their own bigger and better house once the war was over, have children; but those dreams had died when he had.

She cut some dumplings from the dough she had rolled out on her pastry board earlier that afternoon. She began dropping them into the pot of heated water, realizing that since she was fourteen she had been taking care of men, first her father and brother, then her father and Mack, then just her father. She had missed having someone to fuss over, and she reasoned maybe that was why she hadn't really minded having Jake around.

She heard him come back inside then, and she took out a washpan and set it on a shelf her father had built onto the side of the wall for a countertop, and beneath which she stored pots and pans. She glanced at Jake, watched him set her rifle against the wall. "Bring a chair over here and lean back. I'll wash your hair," she told him.

"You don't have to if you don't want."

"I do want. It's the only part of you that still needs washing."

She turned away at the words, hoping he didn't notice the flush in her cheeks. Yes, she had bathed him when he was sick, mostly to keep him cooled down. She had noticed his flat, muscled stomach; his powerful thighs. She had tried to forget about seeing the parts of him that normally only wives and whores saw. In spite of his reputation and usually sour personality, Jake Harkner was a beautiful man physically. She wondered if he even realized it. His father had told him all his life that he was no good, a worthless bastard, in Jake's words. Did he even see himself as physically ugly too? That would take a pretty amazing imagination. Perhaps he wanted to be ugly, thought it was fitting. Maybe that was why he left himself unbathed and unshaved and let his hair grow every which way.

"Can you get the chair all right, or do you want me to do it?" she asked.

"I can do it. By the way, where are my pants? Feels kind of strange walking around in bare feet and long johns."

Her eyes widened, and without thinking she walked up to him and touched his upper arms, realizing how cold they were. "My goodness! It's so cool out this evening. I didn't even think!" She rushed past him and took his blue denim shirt, his denim pants, and a pair of socks from where they lay neatly folded on her cot. "Put these on. You should never have gone out there half dressed! You'll take sick in your condition." She handed him the clothes. "Wait a minute. I'll get the top half of your underwear. It's in the bedroom." She went into the other room and called to him. "I burned the one-piece long johns you were wearing the day I found you. They were too bloodstained to wear again. I found these in your gear."

Jake smiled to himself at her sudden concern that he might have gotten cold. She came back and handed him the underwear. He pulled it on and buttoned it, then put his arms into the sleeves of his shirt. It felt good to get dressed, made him feel less at her mercy and more in control. "I guess in our exchange of words earlier, neither one of us thought about me getting dressed." He began buttoning the shirt. "By the way, I really am sorry about exploding at you."

Miranda turned and cut more dumplings. "It's all right. I'm sorry, for judging you. In any case, I see no new blood stains on those bandages since I changed them earlier today, so you might as well get dressed. I'll wash your hair while these dumplings cook."

Jake finished dressing, except for his boots. "How's Outlaw doing?"

"Outlaw?"

"My horse."

"Oh, he's just fine. Eating me out of oats, I might add."

"I'll pay you something before I leave. And I'll see what I can do about getting you some meat—maybe shoot a couple of rabbits or something."

"That's all right. I'll be leaving myself a few days after you do. No sense stocking up on anything. I'll sell my horses and take a train to Independence, find someone there to take me to Nevada."

Jake watched her work, realized he enjoyed watching her doing womanly things, enjoyed watching the woman herself. She wore yellow today. He liked that color on her. It was a pretty dress of polished cotton, with white lace around the cuffs and around the modestly cut bodice that showed just a hint of the fullness of her breasts. Had she dressed extra nice just for him? Or was it just her beauty and quiet elegance that made the dress seem prettier than it really was? "You really still planning on going to Nevada?"

"Yes." Miranda stirred the dumplings, then picked up a hotpad and took hold of the kettle of hot water. "There's nothing left for me here but bad memories." She poured some of the water into the washpan she had set out. "My mother died from injuries from a fall when I was fourteen, and my father blamed himself for not being able to help her. For all his skills as a doctor, there was nothing he could do. That was back in Illinois." She hung the kettle back over the fire. "Father—his name was Doctor Lawrence Baker—moved here to start fresh, get away from his own bad memories. He gave up doctoring, tried to farm. I met Mack in Kansas City. Mackenzie Hayes was his full name. He was a bootmaker. We married, and two weeks later he volunteered for the war like all young men his age. He fought for the Union, of course." She glanced at Jake, saw a look of near guilt in his eyes. "I don't suppose you fought in the war?"

He folded his arms. "No. I was a gunrunner—smuggled rifles and ammunition to the Confederates for gold."

She paled slightly. "I see."

"I don't think you do. By the time the war started, I was

already well on my way to living on the wrong side of the law
and getting money however I could get it, legally or illegally.
What did I know about the reasons for that war? All I saw
were a lot of young men blowing each other's guts out for
what they thought were noble reasons. What was really happening was that the men in power were using those poor
young men as their little pawns in a political struggle. I wasn't
about to die for that, but I didn't mind making money off their
war, so I robbed Union trains and stole guns from the North,
then sold them to the South. Some of that led to robberies
after the war ended. That's when I fell in with Kennedy and
his bunch—Confederates bent on continuing their revenge.
When that's the only kind of people you've ever known,
Randy, you just end up in that kind of life."

Miranda dipped a large ladle into a bucket of cool water
and carried it over to the washpan to poor it in and cool the
hot water already there. "I would like to understand, Jake, I
really would. Sit down here and I'll wash your hair. Maybe at
supper you can tell me more about yourself."

He took the chair. "It would be pretty hard for a woman
like you to hear it."

"I'm stronger than you think."

Jake put his head back. "You were telling me about yourself."

"Nothing much more to tell." She took the ladle and
poured some of the water over his hair, letting the excess run
back into the pan. She began soaping up his hair then. "Mack
never came back. I married him in sixty-two, got the telegram
about his death in sixty-three. He didn't even die from a
wound. He died from cholera. In sixty-four my brother left
and it was nearly a year before he bothered to write and tell us
he was in Nevada. I haven't heard from him since. That's his
picture over there on the stand by the cot."

She began scrubbing his hair. "A few weeks ago Father was
killed by raiders and we lost everything of value, which left me
with this excuse of a farm and the draft horses my only collat-
eral. Since the farm isn't worth much, all I really have left is
some money Father had in the bank and what I can get for the
two draft horses of mine. I intend to load most of my furniture
into the wagon in a few days and take it and the wagon and
horses into Kansas City and sell everything. The bank is going
to take over the farm and sell it for what they can get, and I'll
be on my way to Nevada."

Jake enjoyed the gentle massage of her hands. He struggled against growing feelings for this woman whom he admired for her courage and fortitude. She was no fainting flower, in spite of her size. She had strength and determination, and she was not easily frightened. Never had he fought manly urges as much as he was right now, for besides his great admiration for her, he also could not help feeling a sexual attraction. She was bending close, her nicely rounded breasts not far from his face. He wanted to take hold of her, touch those full breasts, taste them, take pleasure in her mouth, feel her body against his own. It had been a while since he was with a woman, and he'd never bedded one like Miranda Hayes, a woman of virtue and gentleness, the kind of woman who only gave herself to a man out of love and devotion. He almost laughed out loud at the idea of her thinking of him that way.

"You're quite a woman," he told her. "Most would have gone into town a long time ago just for the protection of civilization, maybe married the first man who came along who could provide for them."

"I'll find a way to provide for myself. I married Mack because I had deep affection for him. He was a good man. It had nothing to do with wanting someone to look after me. I wanted to take care of him, give him children." She began rinsing his hair. "Have you ever thought of settling, Jake? Having sons?"

He chuckled. "Me? I've given it a thought a time or two, but a wanted man isn't one who can settle, let alone find a woman who would be willing to be on the run the rest of her life. As far as children . . ." He paused for a moment, losing his smile. "I got no teaching in how to handle children. I'd be too afraid that somehow I'd be like my own father. I'd shoot myself if I ever found myself doing that to my own kid. The way I was raised, and the way I've lived, I'd make a pretty rotten father. I'm better off leaving things just like they are."

Miranda took a towel and motioned for him to sit up straight. She began drying his hair with the towel. "Where will you go when you leave here?"

"I don't know. Indian Territory, I expect. That's the best place for wanted men to hide out. I might go on farther west from there. It's a lawless land out there. A man can make his own rules. I was on my way when that bounty hunter found me."

Miranda went to her father's washstand near the cot and

returned with a comb and a pair of scissors. Pulling the comb through Jake's tangled hair, she said, "Do you want to know something funny?"

"What's that?"

"I think I'll miss you a little when you go. I don't even fully trust you yet, and I am firmly against the way you live. But I have actually enjoyed taking care of you. It has kept me busy, kept my mind off my grief. You have brought a strangely exciting element to things lately—I've never shot a man before, never taken a bullet out of a man, never known a real outlaw. It's too bad it was your kind who killed my father. I could never fully forgive that, but I truly would like to understand it, if you would share your past with me. I feel it might be good for you to talk to someone about it. And where is the harm?"

She began snipping at his hair, thinking how full and wavy and pretty it was, so black it almost looked blue. "Once you leave here, you'll never see me again, so why not use me as a sounding board? You already did a while ago when you lit into me about how your father treated you. *Were* you a bastard, or was that all in his head?"

Jake thought about his mother, as beautiful a woman as any man could want, a dark, exotic beauty. "My father was white, an Englishman from Connecticut. He came from a very poor family. His own father abused him, kicked him out when he was twelve years old, or so he told me. I used to feel sorry for him, until he kicked or beat out any feelings I had for him." The last statement was spoken bitterly, and he paused a moment before continuing.

"At any rate," he finally spoke up again, "he wandered to Texas, worked for a while, joined Houston's army to fight for Texas's independence. He was at San Jacinto when Santa Ana surrendered. After that he wandered around northern Mexico and southern Texas, bought a young Mexican girl off her drunken father and lived with her, never married her."

"Your mother?"

Again Jake paused before answering. "Her name was Evita, and from what I can remember, she was the most beautiful woman I've ever seen. But from my earliest memories, my pa seemed to enjoy beating her. He accused her of sleeping with other men, was jealous of her beauty. I wouldn't blame her if she *did* sleep with other men, the way my pa treated her. But I don't believe in my heart she ever did. She just wasn't that type. I felt so sorry for her when I got older and realized she never had any choice in living with my father. He paid money for her, like a common whore. I'm sure she hated that. At any rate, it wasn't long before my father turned on me, believing I was the bastard son of one of my mother's lovers. I can't begin to describe what it's like, being seven, eight years old and having your giant of a father come after you with his big fists or a wide belt that leaves welts and scars."

Miranda combed through his hair again, deciding to be careful with her words. He was being unusually open, and he spoke with near trembling emotion. She was not sure how long this spell of revealing his true feelings would last. "Your back?" she asked.

"Yeah." He sighed deeply. "Scars from a three-inch-wide belt with a big buckle on the end." He stopped to swallow and clear his throat, as though the next words were too difficult to speak. "I had a younger brother once. Pa beat him one time until he was unconscious. He was only six. I tried to stop him, but Pa turned on me and wrapped a piece of thin cord around my neck, twisting it until I choked to the point of blacking out. It cut into the skin and left a scar. You probably noticed it when you were nursing me."

"Yes. I wondered about it." Miranda fought tears. She never dreamed one man could be capable of such horror against his own children, let alone that a child could survive such a thing and remain sane, if Jake Harkner could be considered sane.

"When I came around, I was still lying on the floor, blood everywhere. My little brother lay not far from me, dead. My mother was in the next room, also dead. Pa had beat her for trying to help me. I didn't see it, but I know that's what happened. Pa was outside digging graves. When he came in and found out I was still alive, he told me I'd better never tell anybody what really happened, or he'd kill me, and I damn well believed him. He told others that my mother and brother had taken sick and died from cholera. That was in a little town in northern Mexico, and most of the people there were afraid of him, so nobody questioned the explanation. Pa was a big man, like me. That's where I get my size from, but my coloring, my looks, that comes from my Mexican blood."

"I wondered. I knew you had either Spanish blood or perhaps Indian." She finished trimming his hair, then rubbed in a little of her father's hair oil to smooth it back and combed through it. She came around to stand in front of him, struck by what looked like tears in his eyes. She decided he would hate it if she acknowledged those tears, so she put on a smile. "You look wonderful. Do you want to go look in the mirror in my bedroom?"

He grinned almost bashfully. "Sure. Lord knows this is the last time I'll be clean and groomed for a while." He rose, scooting back his chair and walking into the bedroom.

Miranda wanted very much to ask him about Santana, about the circumstances of his father's death and how he had ended up living the life of an outlaw. But she had learned a woman had to tread cautiously around a man like Jake Harkner. If he wanted to tell her, he would tell her. She couldn't pressure it out of him, and she knew now that it was probably something very difficult for him to talk about. He had already told her more than she ever imagined he would.

"Looks fine," he told her from the bedroom. "I hardly recognize myself."

Miranda laughed. "Maybe that's the look you should keep. Maybe others won't recognize you either. Besides, you're an exceptionally handsome man, Jake Harkner. You shouldn't hide under all that dirt and hair."

There came no reply. She picked up the pan of water and held it against her waist with one hand as she opened the door. She walked out onto the porch and tossed the used water into the grass in front of the cabin. It was then she saw them, three riders coming. She recognized Sheriff McCleave's horse, and her heart rushed faster. The sheriff! Jake!

She hurried back inside. "Stay in the bedroom!" she called out, hurriedly shoving Jake's boots under her cot. She grabbed the comb and scissors and put them back with her father's things, pushed the chair back in place. Jake came into the main room.

"What is it?"

"Sheriff McCleave. He's coming here! I can't believe he'd come when it's nearly dark like this!"

Jake hurried into the bedroom, and Miranda ran in behind him to see him quickly loading his revolvers. "No!" she shouted, grabbing at his arm.

Jake gave her a shove, sending her stumbling backward. "I didn't go through all this to turn around and get hanged!" he growled.

Miranda grabbed his arm again. "He's a *friend*, Jake, a good man! I don't want him hurt!"

Jake whirled, grasping her wrist and pulling her hand away. He cocked the revolver. "He's the *law!*"

Desperate tears began to fill her eyes. "He's just a friend come to check on me. I can keep him outside, Jake! Even if he comes in, all your things are either in the shed or in here. I already put up the horses. He'll never know you're here if you just stay crouched down on the other side of the bed!" Her eyes teared. "Please! If you hurt him and the men with him, it will be like I did it, don't you see? If I hadn't put you up, or if I had just turned you in, none of it would have happened! Please, Jake! You *owe* me!"

Jake studied the blue-gray eyes that lately had haunted his thoughts and desires. He was becoming much too fond of this woman he could never have, beginning to feel emotions he had thought were long buried or even destroyed. "I owe you *nothing!*" he muttered. "You might have saved me, but you're also the one who shot me, so we're even."

"I also could have turned you in for five thousand dollars, so we're not even!"

"And how do I know you won't do it now?" he said bitterly. "Here's your chance, lady! Five thousand dollars can send a woman to Nevada in style. You could even hire someone to go to Nevada and find your brother, stay here and live in safety and comfort while they do it. It can buy you some damn fancy dresses and a nice little house in town!"

A tear slipped down her cheek. "I have *principles,* Jake Harkner! Now I'm trusting that *you* have principles too. Don't betray me! And you just remember that if you shoot those men out there, you'll have to shoot me, too, because I'm a *witness!* More than that, I'll get Pa's rifle and I'll kill you myself if you shoot down my friends! That will mean you'll have to defend yourself, as you keep talking about, and *kill* me!" That rifle isn't any little derringer. You won't survive if I shoot you with that! What will it be, Jake? Will you kill me too? I thought that was one thing you *did* have principles about!"

He pressed the revolver against her throat. "Don't get in my way, Randy. Don't say a word to them, and don't get in my way, or I can't guarantee anything. I've never hurt a lady on purpose, but if it comes to a shoot-out, that's a different story. You stall those men and keep them outside. Don't you betray me, woman, after all your fancy talk about not being able to take money for a man!"

Miranda swallowed, feeling the cold steel against her throat. "It's time for you to learn about friendship and trust, Jake," she said quietly, realizing the sheriff must be quite close to the cabin by now. "You just revealed some very intimate things about yourself to me, and I listened and understood. Do you really think I would turn around now and let the sheriff shoot you down or haul you away? Do you really think that?"

He took the gun away and slowly stepped back. "I don't know, but I'll damn well keep my ears open. Now get out there and make sure there is nothing around to give away my presence. And try to keep the sheriff outside!"

Miranda breathed deeply, struggling for composure. She walked back into the main room, pulling closed the curtain at the bedroom doorway, then started for the main door when she noticed the little pile of black hair on the wooden floor. Jake's hair! She quickly grabbed a broom and lifted a hand-tied rug, sweeping the hair under it and feeling Jake's dark eyes and cold gun watching her every move.

She put the broom back, glanced around the room. She smoothed her dress and ran her fingers through her hair. She opened the door then, stepping out and closing it behind her to greet Sheriff McCleave.

CHAPTER FIVE

 Miranda walked off the porch, giving Sheriff Mc-
Cleave a smile as he rode closer with two deputies. "Sheriff! What brings you out this late in the
day? It's nearly dark!"

"Evening, Mrs. Hayes. Just checking on you. Heard a rumor that someone suspected of belonging to Bill Kennedy's
bunch was snooping around town asking about the shoot-out
between that Jake Harkner and Luke Putnam. Grapevine has
it Kennedy is looking for this Harkner fellow just as hard as
the law is. Seems they had some kind of falling out, although
we don't know why; but just knowing the man might be in the
area makes me uneasy. We've been out scouting around,
checking with other farmers and such to make sure there's
been no trouble."

Tell him! Tell him! Miranda could not understand why she
could not obey the small voice that commanded her to do
what was right and logical. Did she really believe Jake could
shoot down all three of these men? Or was her reason for not
speaking up more illogical and unbelievable—that she didn't
want Jake to be hurt?

"I've been fine," she told McCleave. "Since I'm the one
who shot Jake Harkner, it's awfully farfetched to think I would
have anything to do with the man afterward, so it isn't likely
this Kennedy person would come here looking for him. People

must have told him that Mr. Harkner is probably dead or in Indian Territory by now."

"That's true, but we have to make sure. Bansen, who owns the farm east of you, said a bunch of suspicious-looking men stopped at his place and asked for food and permission to water their horses. Bansen says they looked like the kind who would just as soon shoot you as look at you, so he didn't ask for any money—gave the men what they wanted and they rode on. One of them said something about 'looking for the skunk' down in Cherokee country. My hunch is that it was Kennedy and his men, and if so, they've headed on south by now. Bansen is just damn lucky they were in an obliging mood, or him and his wife would be dead, or they might even have taken his wife with them and made her *wish* she was dead."

Jake listened from inside. So, Kennedy was on his trail, too, just like he thought. The man had gone on south, so this might be a damn good time to head north rather than into Indian Territory himself like he had planned. He was glad it wasn't Miranda's place Kennedy had stopped at. If he'd found her there alone . . .

He heard the sheriff apologizing for his reference to what Kennedy and his men might have done to Bansen's wife. "I hate to be so crude, but you've got to understand how dangerous it is for you out here, Mrs. Hayes," the man was saying. "Why don't you come back to town with us tonight? You've got friends you could stay with. Kennedy and his bunch are a bad lot, believe me. Personally I hope that Harkner fellow is dead. Anybody who would ride with men like that has to be as bad as the rest of them."

"I'm just fine right here, Sheriff. Besides, I couldn't pick up and leave at this hour. Why, I just started a pot of dumplings, and I have bread rising. You said yourself Kennedy and his men headed south, and in just a few more days I'll be leaving here myself, heading for Independence. You really must stop worrying about me." She smiled for the man. "I have a fresh-baked pie on the table. Why don't you take it back with you and share it with your men? I'll get it for you."

Jake pressed his back against the wall near the curtains as Miranda came inside. His gun was cocked and ready to fire. He heard a horse whinny, heard footsteps on the porch then, heavy ones, like those of a good-sized man.

"Sheriff," he heard Miranda say, sounding surprised. "I

was just wrapping a towel around the pie to bring it out to you. It's apple."

Jake waited, every muscle and nerve end tense and alert. McCleave was inside the house! He listened intently.

"Mrs. Hayes, I didn't really come here because of Kennedy and his bunch. I have good reason to believe they're long gone from here. I just . . . I needed an excuse to come and see you once more, since I was gone when you came into town four days ago. I feel like I have to try once more to convince you to stay in Kansas City, mostly for your own safety, but also because . . . because I'd like very much to court you."

Jake grinned a little, relaxing slightly. So, that was the reason he had followed her inside. He couldn't blame the man for being infatuated with Miranda. He expected a lot of men desired her. "Please stay, Mrs. Hayes. I beg you again, not just for my sake but for your own, don't go to Nevada. It's just too dangerous. Not only is it wild, untamed country full of unruly men, but there's a lot of Indian trouble out west."

Jake waited through a moment of silence. He couldn't see Miranda, but he could see the sheriff through a slit in the curtains. He was a big, stout man who needed to lose some weight off his middle.

"Sheriff, I have explained before why I can't stay. There are simply too many bad memories here, and I truly feel obligated to find Wesley. After that, and after I've had some time away from here, maybe I will come back."

"Well, I'll be wishing for it real hard," the sheriff told her.

Jake could see how the man looked at her, and it brought a surprising jealousy to his own heart. He had a distinct urge to shoot the man on the spot. He watched Miranda hand him a pie.

"You have to stop thinking about me and just take care of yourself, Sheriff McCleave; but I do appreciate your concern. You're very kind."

McCleave sighed deeply, bringing the pie to his face to smell it. "Well, you can't blame a man for trying." He shook his head. "What a waste. Not only are you a right handsome woman, but a good cook on top of it. It smells wonderful in here."

Miranda put a hand on his arm and walked toward the door. *That's it,* Jake thought. *Get him back outside. You're real good, Randy Hayes.*

"Well, now you can take some of that wonderful smell

home with you," she was saying. "And thank you, Sheriff, for coming out here to make sure I'm all right."

The sheriff followed her out, holding the pie, and Jake thought what an easily fooled man he was. He listened as Miranda talked sweetly to all three men. Finally he heard the horses riding off, heard the door close.

He peered through the curtains again to see Miranda leaning against the door, looking relieved. "They're gone," she said loudly.

Jake stepped out and walked past her to look out a front window. He saw the three men riding off in the distance. "Good work," he told her.

"I didn't do it for you," she answered, going back to stir the dumplings, not wanting to believe in her heart she cared anything for Jake Harkner. "I did it for them. I have no doubt you could have shot down all three of them in the blink of an eye if they tried anything. Men like that are no match for you, and I didn't want to see them die."

He turned to her. "Then if you thought they could take me, you would have told?"

"I didn't say that. I only meant that if there was trouble, if they had perhaps seen you or some sign of you, they would have foolishly tried something and they would all be dead or at least hurt. I won't have that on my conscience." She tested a dumpling. "You might have been hurt too," she added, so softly Jake barely heard her. "Sit down and I'll give you something to eat."

Jake moved to the table, still watching her, wondering at the way she had of ordering him about, wondering more at why he felt compelled to obey. It touched him that she seemed to care he might have been hurt again. He studied the lovely form that her yellow dress fit so well. The sheriff was right. It did smell wonderful in the house. She was a "right handsome" woman and a good cook. What man *wouldn't* want someone like her for a wife?

The thought so startled him that he drew in his breath and looked away from her, picking up his gun and whirling the chamber again to remove the bullets. He reasoned he had better get out of here as quickly as possible, before he lost his mind completely, if it was his mind he was losing. Maybe it was something else, though—maybe his heart. Did he still have one? He almost laughed out loud at the ridiculous thought and directed his attention to the gun then, warning himself to stop thinking about women altogether. When he was out of here and on his way north he'd find some whore who could get a few things out of his system. He reasoned that was why he thought about Miranda Hayes more fondly than made sense for a man like him. He'd just been too long without.

Miranda was setting fresh bread on the table now, and he struggled to ignore the soft look of her as she moved about the room, the way she was softly humming. The crazy woman actually seemed happy! She had just sent away a man who could have gotten a notorious outlaw out of her house. She'd just turned down an opportunity to make five thousand dollars for herself, and she was walking around humming! She poured both of them some coffee and set a bowl of dumplings and vegetables in front of him, then took a chair across the table from him.

"Well, it's nice to have someone to share a meal with," she spoke up, "and good that you can sit at the table instead of me having to carry a tray to the bed. Just go easy on that stomach of yours. Don't eat too much too fast. It will be nice to see you hold something down for once."

Jake set the gun aside and picked up a fork. He stabbed a dumpling and took a bite. "Real good," he told her. "A couple more meals like this and a little more rest and I'll be out of here. You can return to whatever kind of life is normal for you, get yourself to Nevada, whatever."

Miranda looked at him, again surprised at herself for thinking how she would miss having him around. "You still going to Indian Territory? Sheriff McCleave says that's where that Bill Kennedy probably headed."

Jake swallowed more of the dumpling stew. "I'll go north, then maybe west to Oregon or California. It's not likely anybody out west will know who Jake Harkner is. I've got a little money—might even figure out a way to live on the side of the law, kind of start over. What do you think of that?"

Miranda found herself smiling wryly. "The notorious Jake Harkner, a farmer, perhaps?"

He shrugged. "Sure. I could do that." He frowned then. "Well, maybe not a farmer—a gunsmith, maybe."

Miranda laughed lightly. "That sounds more like an occupation you could handle."

Jake watched her eyes, astounded that for a moment she looked at him almost lovingly. He looked back down at his food and took another mouthful. *Jesus, it is definitely time to get out of here,* he told himself. "What the hell am I saying?" he said aloud. "I'll never be anything but a man on the run. And why should I work for money when I can get it the easy way? There's no law farther west—perfect place for a man like me."

Miranda frowned. "You mean I nursed you back to health just so you could go back out there and rob and kill again?" She watched him stiffen at the words, watched his dark eyes quickly turn angry again as he broke off a piece of bread from the loaf she had set on the table.

"It was your choice, lady. Maybe you should have turned me in to that sheriff."

Miranda watched him dunk the bread into the juice of the stew, then bite off a piece. *You don't fool me, Jake Harkner,* she thought. *You really were thinking about changing your ways. You just don't want anyone to know that sometimes you actually have decent thoughts.* There was the little boy again. It had come out when he smiled and talked about living a normal life. It was the young boy who wanted that, but the man was telling him he couldn't hope for such things. He had gone too far down the wrong path.

Miranda picked up the bread and used a knife to cut off a piece for herself. The room hung silent except for the sound of clinking forks. Miranda thought how easily defensive he was, realized that to get him talking again she had to change the subject. He was not about to continue discussing the possibility of being a settled man and leading an ordinary life. "How old are you, Jake?"

He took a swallow of coffee. "Thirty." He finally met her eyes again. "You?"

Miranda buttered her bread. "Twenty."

He stabbed another dumpling. "That's not very old for a woman who's been through all that you have. You must have been pretty young when you married."

"I was sixteen."

Again Jake could not look at her. Sixteen. He thought how good it must have been, bedding a sixteen-year-old virgin beauty like her. Now that she had known a man, she'd probably be even better in bed. Maybe she even missed it. Damn her! He had to quit allowing those thoughts! He grabbed up his coffee cup and took another swallow, suddenly rising and scooting back his chair. "I can't eat any more. I've got to get my gear so I can oil my guns. If I can get a good night's rest, I'll be out of your way tomorrow." He headed for the bedroom to find his socks.

"Jake, that's too soon. You can't go riding off the first day you start feeling better. You're still healing."

Jake turned to meet her eyes, saw the true concern there. They just watched each other for a moment, and he knew she was feeling the same thing he was—he didn't really want to leave, and she didn't want him to go. "It's best I go," he told her. "You know I'm right, Randy."

Their eyes held in mutual understanding. *Yes,* she thought, *perhaps it is best you leave at that.* She felt her cheeks getting hot, wondered at her own stupidity at allowing herself to be concerned for the very kind of man she should despise. She turned away. "I'll go get your gear for you." She hurried out, unable to meet his dark eyes again, and unable to control the tears that were forming in her own.

She breathed deeply of the fresh air and headed for the horse shed, thinking how there was so much about Jake Harkner she still didn't know. Would he tell her what had happened with her father and the woman called Santana if she asked him? Or would he just get angry? It was so hard to tell what things he would talk about and what things might bring that fire to his eyes that frightened her a little.

She walked with hard, angry steps, chastising herself all the way to the shed, telling herself that her loneliness and loss had affected her mind. Keeping Jake Harkner in her own house, saving his life, was a traitorous act, traitorous to her father, to her friends, to Sheriff McCleave. What had possessed her to help and protect the man? He was probably right to say that he was fooling himself to think about settling. She had no doubt she had inadvertently hurt a lot of other people by helping Jake Harkner and turning him loose on society again. What an ignorant fool he must think her to be!

She went into the shed and to the place where she had hung his saddlebags and extra supply packs. She rummaged through one saddlebag to see if she could find the gun oil and cleaning brushes so that she wouldn't have to carry all his gear into the house. She pulled out one heavy leather pouch, and curiosity got the better of her. She opened it to find it was full of coins and a thick roll of paper money. "Stolen, no doubt," she muttered. "Oh, Randy, you're such a fool!"

She angrily pulled more things out of the saddlebag, looking for the gun-cleaning supplies. Out came another leather pouch, and again curiosity got the better of her. She wondered why she hadn't thought to do this when Jake was more ill and she would have had time to carefully go through all his gear, perhaps find something important, something that would have persuaded her to turn this man in.

She opened the pouch, her eyes widening when she pulled out its contents. It looked at first like just a beautiful piece of jewelry, a woman's necklace. After studying it a moment, she realized it was actually Rosary beads. She didn't know a lot about Catholics, but a Catholic girlfriend back in Illinois had shown Randy her mother's Rosary beads and had explained that they were used in prayer.

Had Jake stolen this sacred object? After all, Rosary beads were a very personal thing, as far as she knew. To steal something like this seemed just plain mean. Were they worth something? This particular necklace was beautiful, the beads a shiny black with what looked like tiny rubies spaced at intervals between the black beads. A breathtaking cross was attached to the beads, decorated with more rubies embedded in what looked as if it might be real gold. In the center of the cross was a little porcelain replica of Christ.

"What the hell are you doing?"

Miranda gasped and turned to see Jake standing at the doorway to the shed. She felt the color coming to her face as she quickly put the beads back into the pouch. "I was looking . . . for your gun-cleaning supplies," she stammered. "I didn't think it was necessary to carry all this gear into the house—"

He came closer, taking the pouch from her. "These belonged to my mother," he told her angrily. "Stay out of my personal things!" He shoved the beads and other spilled items back into the saddlebag and picked up a separate leather bag that had been attached to the saddlebags with a rawhide cord. He untied the cord and hung the saddlebags back over the hook where Randy had first put them. "This is all I need. Where are my rifle and my shotgun?"

Miranda, near tears, moved past him and dug the guns out from under the straw where she had hidden them. He grabbed them from her, looking disgusted at how dusty they were, then turned and walked out of the shed. Randy followed, closing and latching the shed door and walking to catch up with him.

"Jake, I was just—"

"You were trying to decide which things were mine legally and which were stolen," he grumbled. "Did you find my money?"

"Yes."

He stopped. "Take any?"

Her eyes widened in indignation. "Of course not!"

He turned away and kept walking. "Of course not," he repeated sarcastically. "But you're wondering if *I* stole it! Fact is, I did—some of it, anyway, from a sonofabitch who tried to attack me one night when I was camped alone. He figured he'd knock my brains out and steal my food and gear, but before he could raise a hand to clobber me with the rock that was in it, he found a pistol resting against his forehead, right between his eyes. Now there was one scared man, let me tell you! He handed over his own money right quick, money he'd stolen himself, he said, from a traveling salesman hawking everything from jewelry to pots and pans. I tied the guy to a tree so I could get some sleep, let him go the next morning before I left. He's damn lucky I didn't put a bullet in his head for sneaking up on me like he did!"

Miranda hurried to keep up with him, surprised at how briskly he was walking after being so sick. She supposed it was because he was angry. They reached the porch and he stopped and turned.

"I don't steal things like Rosary beads," he told her angrily. He turned to go inside and she touched his arm.

"Jake, I'm sorry. I really was looking for your gun oil. I just . . . I'm curious to know more about you, and I couldn't help—" She turned away, putting her hands to her flushed face. "I'm sorry," she repeated.

"You know all you need to know about me. What the hell difference does it make anyway?" He went inside.

Miranda followed him in to see him shove his bowl and cup aside and drop the leather pouch on the table beside the revolver he had left there. He laid his rifles across the table, then went into the bedroom for a moment, returning with a pair of socks, one gunbelt, and his second revolver. "Where in hell are my boots?" he asked. "I'm tired of going around barefoot."

Miranda remained silent. She walked over to the cot and pulled the boots out from under it, bringing them over and dropping them beside him. "There's no sense putting them on tonight. It's nearly dark and you have what you need. You won't be going out anymore."

Jake scowled at her and turned away to pull on his socks. For nearly two hours he remained silent. Miranda cleaned up from supper, then picked up some knitting and sat down in a rocker beside the fireplace. Occasionally she glanced over at the table where Jake had his revolvers and rifle and shotgun broken down into pieces. He carefully cleaned and oiled every part, and she thought how he probably would make a good gunsmith, just as he'd suggested he might do.

She wanted to tell him so, but the anger remained in his eyes the whole time he worked. She felt like a fool for being caught rummaging through his things like a curious child; and she was fed up trying to tread lightly with her words, never knowing what would offend him and what would not. She decided that from here on, if he wanted to talk, she would let him start the conversation. It was a good thing if he could leave tomorrow. The better he felt, the ornerier he got . . . and, most likely, the more dangerous he became.

By the time the guns were taken apart, cleaned and oiled, and put back together again, it was very late, and Miranda had finished the sleeve of the sweater she was knitting. Jake turned up the table lantern and raised one of the revolvers to its light, then began mechanically working the revolving chamber, using the gun action itself. He cocked the gun, pulled the trigger. Click. Cock and click. Cock and click, peering through each open cavity as the chamber turned. He whirled the chamber twice, then he loaded the gun. He picked up the second revolver and did the same, cocking it and pulling the trigger, checking to be sure it was working properly. He loaded the second gun.

Miranda started a second sweater sleeve, feeling nervous at the sound of the whirling and clicking. This was the first time she had been alone in the house with him when he felt good and was getting back his strength. He had his guns back, and he was angry with her. Had she been wrong to trust him? Wrong to believe him when he said he never harmed women? Now he was cocking his Winchester, checking it, loading it. "You want me to clean your rifle for you?" he suddenly spoke up.

It had been so long since he had said anything that the words startled her. She looked over at him and saw that his eyes did not show quite so much anger now. "I suppose it needs cleaning," she answered. "My father used to do it. It hasn't been cleaned since he was killed, but then it hasn't been used, either."

Jake finished polishing the barrel of his shotgun, then laid it and the Winchester carefully across the end of the table. He rose and walked to the wall against which her rifle stood. He brought it back to the table and began taking it apart. "I took the beads from my mother's jewelry box after my pa killed her," he said then, surprising Miranda with the statement. She had no idea he was still thinking about the Rosary beads. "I knew Pa would try to sell it, so I hid it. I caught him tearing through her things one day, and I knew what he was after. It was the only thing of value she owned. Her grandmother had given it to her. It was made by a goldsmith friend of her grandfather's—has real rubies in it."

Miranda continued knitting. "Your mother was a religious woman then?" she asked carefully.

"When you live with someone like my father, you do a lot of praying."

Miranda took her eyes from her knitting and watched him for a moment. *Do you ever pray, Jake Harkner?* She decided she had better not ask. It sounded like a question that might bring back his anger. "How did you come to know so much about firearms?" she asked. "It's one thing to know how to shoot a gun, but you take them apart to the last little screw and put them back together again."

"You use guns enough, depend on them to keep you alive, you learn how to take care of them. A clean, well-oiled gun won't backfire on you or fail you when you need it most. It will shoot straighter and react quicker when you pull the trigger. It even comes out of a holster faster." He opened the Winchester and began running a brush through the barrel. "I just made myself learn. Comes with the trade, like you knowing how to cook and knit—or even knowing about doctoring from helping your father." He picked up a long rod and oiled a rag, then shoved the rag through the inside of the gun barrel. "Your pa ever hit you?"

Miranda returned to her knitting. "No. He was a good man, gentle, caring. He loved helping the sick, until my mother fell and he couldn't save her. He got a little harder after that, gave up doctoring. He was never really very happy after that."

Jake snickered sarcastically. "Well, I'm sorry for all you've been through, but even at that, you've led a charmed life compared to mine. You're lucky you had a nice, normal life for as long as you did—parents who really loved each other, a father who knew how to treat his children. That brother of yours must be an ungrateful brat, taking off on your pa like that. If I had had a father like yours apparently was, I never would have left. To this day I still have nightmares about mine. He even made me drink slop water once, after he'd already washed in it and spit in it—"

"Jake, don't—"

"I just want you to understand about me, that's all. I don't know why I want you to understand. Maybe it's because I know you're wondering if you've done the right thing, putting me up like this. I can't guarantee that I won't go right back out there and kill again. You'd best understand the kind of men I rode with at times, like Kennedy and his bunch. They're as bad as they come, murder for no good reason, rape innocent women. Kennedy's right-hand man is a Mexican named Juan Hidalgo. He carries the biggest knife you ever saw and can throw it almost as fast as a man can pull a gun. He can do other things with that knife that would make you sick if I told you. I rode with them for a while, so I'm judged by what they did, and I probably deserve it. I told you I've never hurt a woman, but I'm no damn saint either. I've done some pretty bad things. I don't know why it matters to me, but I want you to understand why I've gotten into a way of life that I can't get out of. I got into it because of something that happened between me and my father."

He pulled the rag out of the barrel and then began polishing the outside of it. "Sometimes fate puts you on a road you don't want to be on, Randy. Other men come along who won't let you get off it. Once men find out you're good with a gun, it becomes a challenge. They track you down, brag that they're better, make you draw on them. Eventually you get a reputation with the gun, and no decent person wants anything to do with you. You can't get a job, nobody trusts you, but you have to survive, so you fall in with another way of life. Add to that the fact that you know you're no good in the first place, because your father has told you so all your life; and on top of that you don't have much education, you can barely read; and you've never in your whole life lived like normal people; you've had the love beaten out of you before you even understood what love is . . . and you end up a Jake Harkner."

He began carefully oiling the mechanical parts of her father's Winchester. "Don't be feeling bad about putting me up, and don't think I'm not grateful. I just want you to know that no matter what lawless things I've done, it's like I said. I wasn't with Kennedy and his men that day of the bank robbery and the abduction in Missouri, but somehow the rumor got spread that I was. You know the rest." He rubbed briskly at the metal parts of the rifle. "I'm sorry I yelled at you out there at the shed. I'll get out of your way tomorrow and you can start getting ready to go to Nevada. I hope you find your brother, although I'm betting he's not worth you going through all that danger. He might not even be where you think he is. What will you do then?"

Miranda didn't want to talk about herself. He had opened up to her again, and she wanted to know more; but she knew he had offered all he was going to offer. Her heart ached for him. She wanted to tell him it was never too late for a man to change his ways, never too late to learn to feel love. She had never known his father, but she hated him for literally destroying what might have been a decent young man. Why *shouldn't* Jake Harkner be hard and mean and angry with the world? He had seen his little brother and his mother beaten to death, had suffered great emotional and physical pain at the hands of a brutal father who had never loved him, who had convinced him he was a bastard.

"I don't know," she answered. "I might like it there, might find a job. I've heard there is all kinds of work for a woman in a busy mining town. They say women can make a fortune just cooking for all the men there looking for a hot meal."

Jake glanced at her, thinking of one occupation that could earn a woman who looked like Miranda Hayes a virtual fortune; but she was no easy woman. As though reading his mind, she suddenly returned to her knitting, looking embarrassed.

"You'd better keep this rifle handy, and that little pistol of yours. I don't think you realize how a woman like you will look to men who haven't seen a decent female in months," Jake told her. He turned his eyes back to the rifle. "After a while a man gets sick of the painted whores who'll go with any man with a coin in his pocket."

"Please don't talk that way," she said, her cheeks feeling hot again.

He sighed, picking up the rifle stock and oiling the wood. "Sorry. I just want you to think twice about what you're doing.

It's like the sheriff said. You're a beautiful woman and unattached. That's awful ripe bait for lonely men. Most will respect the lady that you are, but don't count on all of them knowing or caring about the difference between a proper lady and one that's not so proper. My mother was a proper lady, a good woman. I guess that's why in spite of the life I've led, I've always respected a good woman."

Miranda felt a rush of warmth at the words. "Well, I guess I should say thank you, if you meant that as a compliment."

"I did." He amazed her with a smile and a wink. Miranda felt herself blushing more. She set aside her knitting and added more wood to the fire, thinking about his warning about Nevada. She knew he was right about the danger of going into wild country like that alone. Even if she traveled with others, who was really going to care anything about her?

Somehow it all came together then. Jake Harkner was going west too. Why not hitch a ride with a man who could protect her better than anyone else she knew? But would he protect her? She glanced sidelong at him, watching him work. Maybe the only reason he hadn't harmed her here was because she was so close to town and someone would find her. Maybe alone with such a man, day and night out in the middle of nowhere, would be another matter. Still, when he had spoken about respecting a good woman, something rang true in his voice and his eyes.

Yes, Miranda, she thought, *you truly have lost your mind.* She stirred the coals. "You really shouldn't leave tomorrow. I'll worry about you, Jake. You can't tell me you aren't still in pain."

He began putting her rifle back together. "Sure I am. That doesn't mean I can't travel. The worst is over. I'll heal just as well on the back of a horse as in that bed, and it's too dangerous for both of us for me to be here. If someone did discover me and there was a shoot-out, you could get hurt." He looked at her. "You changed the subject. We were talking about you going to Nevada and how I think it's too damn dangerous. Take it from a man who knows how most of those worthless bastards in places like that think. That's no place for somebody like you."

Miranda had the strange sensation that she'd lost control of her speech and thoughts, that the normally sane and logical Miranda Hayes had vanished in the last few days and a stranger had occupied her body. "What if *you* took me?" she found herself asking.

The room hung uncomfortably silent for a moment as their eyes met. A look of astonishment moved through Jake's eyes, followed by cynicism. "I didn't think you were that crazy."

She folded her arms, stepping closer. *Why are you doing this, Miranda!* she argued inwardly. "I need to go to Nevada, Jake, and you said yourself how dangerous it is. I could have turned you in a long time ago, but I didn't, so you owe me something, besides the fact that you've been sleeping in my bed for over a week, eating my food. I cleaned up after you when you kept losing everything I put in your stomach. I've bathed you, cut your hair, taken a bullet out of you; and you've told me things I'll bet you've never told anyone else. I think we've gotten to be pretty good friends. I've helped you. Now you can help me. I think it's the perfect solution. I can go ahead to Independence like I said I'd do, and we could meet somewhere along the way. No one in Kansas City will know what I've done once I leave, and we wouldn't have to travel completely alone together. Maybe I'll join a wagon train, and you could join up later as just a traveler going in the same direction. Then you'd be along if I had any problems, and I'd feel safer knowing you were there."

"Safer? With a wanted man along? An outlaw?" He shook his head. "Jesus," he muttered, turning his attention back to the rifle.

Miranda waited, feeling more embarrassed and foolish with every silent moment. She watched him put the barrel back on the rifle and tighten some screws. He cocked it then and grinned sarcastically.

"I've been trying to tell you the kind of man I am. You just don't get it, do you? Men like me don't dawdle along with a wagon train full of farmers and prospectors and women and kids. We might rob them, but we don't travel with them."

"Then you could meet me at Independence and we'd go it alone." *This is insane! Totally insane!* Why did she feel this need to keep him around? Was that all it was? Was that why she had come up with such a foolish idea, just because she didn't want him to ride out of her life?

Jake held up the rifle and aimed it away from her, pulling the trigger. Another click. He rose and handed her the rifle. "You don't know what you'd be asking. I just got done telling you about lonely men and beautiful women. After a while I'd be one of those lonely men." His eyes moved over her. "I'd hate to ruin a beautiful friendship. Find somebody else to take you."

Miranda took the gun from him. "I wouldn't be afraid of you. You said yourself you respect a good woman."

"Yeah? Well, being alone on a trail for weeks can alter a man's thinking. You just give me a good breakfast in the morning and I'll be on my way. As far as all the things you've done for me, you're right. I owe you. I intend to pay you in cash before I leave. I expect you could use all the extra money you can get for your trip."

Miranda struggled against tears, feeling more embarrassed by the second. She set the gun aside. "Thank you for cleaning my rifle," she said quietly, turning away from him. "You'd better get some sleep. I'll make flapjacks in the morning, if you like."

"Sounds fine to me."

He was standing close behind her, and she could feel the brawny power he emanated, feel the danger; but the danger lay not in anything bad he might have in mind, for she trusted him. Why, she wasn't sure, but she did. The danger lay in her own attraction to him, these ridiculous feelings that were churning inside of her. "I hope you don't think me too forward," she said hesitatingly, staring at the fire. She laughed nervously. "I guess it was a pretty ridiculous suggestion, let alone how it would look to others."

She felt his big hand on her shoulder then, realized he could break her in half if he wanted, but his touch was gentle. "Trouble follows me everyplace I go, Randy, and you don't want to be along when it comes. If I wasn't a wanted man, I think I'd consider it, but you're better off without me around. Something tells me you'll make it just fine on your own. You just keep that rifle handy." He squeezed her shoulder, and then his hand was gone. He walked into the bedroom, and Miranda shivered at the realization that she would have liked to turn around and let him hold her, just for a moment, just for the comfort of a man's strong arms around her again. But Jake Harkner's arms? She wiped at a tear, outraged with herself for making the blatant suggestion that he take her to Nevada. What a fool he must think she was!

Jake closed off the curtain to the bedroom and laid back on the bed, deciding to leave his clothes on. He wanted to leave good and early, and there was no sense getting undressed. Hell, out on the trail he slept in his clothes most of the time anyway. Besides, he knew that if he got undressed and crawled under the covers tonight, he'd start fantasizing about Miranda Hayes being under there with him. Didn't she know what she did to him? Did she realize the emotions she brought forth in him, things he had never felt before?

No way was he taking her to Nevada. Come morning, he was getting the hell out of the woman's life for good. He really wasn't ready to travel yet, but he didn't dare stay near Miranda Hayes one day longer.

CHAPTER SIX

Miranda watched Jake saddle up while she held the two gunny sacks full of supplies she had prepared for him. He gave Outlaw's stomach a light punch. "Suck it in, boy," he barked. "You don't fool me, filling yourself up with air like that." The horse's belly contracted, and Jake tightened the cinch. "All I need is to be on a hard ride to get away from some marshal only to have my saddle slip on me."

Miranda saw him wince, knew he was still in pain. "Jake, can't you wait one more day?"

Jake kept his eyes on the cinch, thinking about the restless night he had had, lying awake and wondering what Mrs. Miranda Hayes would have done if he had gone out to her cot and planted his mouth on her sweet lips. "No, ma'am. Too dangerous for you having me here, what with that sheriff sweet on you and all. Hard telling when he might show up again." He let down a stirrup and turned to meet her eyes. Was that a trace of tears he saw there? No. He would not believe that. "If you had any common sense at all, you would stay here and marry the sheriff and let him take care of you."

Miranda stiffened with indignation, glad he had said something that made her momentarily forget about wanting to cry. "Why do all men think a woman needs 'taking care of'? I'll be just fine on my own. And if I did have common sense, you would be sitting in prison or hanging from a tree by now, and I would be five thousand dollars richer."

Jake grinned. "You've got me there."

Miranda thought how he looked even more handsome now in the morning light. It was the best he had looked since the first day she saw him in the supply store, bearded and mean-looking, then so sick after that. He had a fine, square jaw and dark, wide-set eyes that were perfectly outlined with dark eyelashes. Even his nose seemed perfectly matched to the rest of his face, and when he smiled, his teeth were straight and clean. She surmised that in spite of his cruelty, Jake's father must have been as handsome as his mother was beautiful, for they had produced a son that was the best of both. How sad that they had never given that son a decent home.

A faint scar on Jake's left jaw and another tiny one on his upper lip only seemed to make him even more handsome, lending a ruggedness to his looks that was accented by his tall frame and broad shoulders. She found herself wondering how his full, firm lips would feel on her mouth, how a man like Jake Harkner kissed a woman, made love to a woman. She could only guess where the scars had come from—a barroom fight, some man's knife, maybe his father.

Jake reached into a saddlebag and took out the pouchful of money. He opened it and took out fifty dollars, handing it to her. "I don't want it," she told him. "I guess helping you was the least I can do after shooting you."

Jake's gaze raked over her in a way that should have made her angry, but she only felt a rush of desire. "Well, you have your hands full there," he told her, noticing a gunny sack in each hand. Miranda gasped then when he shoved the money into the moderate neckline of her dress. She felt her cheeks going crimson at the touch of his hand between her breasts, knew she should berate him for such a daring move, but she could not take her eyes from his; nor could she ignore the tingle of fire his touch had brought to her blood.

"Keep it," he said. "I won't take no for an answer."

Miranda swallowed, handing him the sacks. "I . . . packed some food for you," she said, suddenly flustered, bewildered by her feelings. "There are some potatoes here, some fresh bread, dried apples, a little flour and sugar and salt—some crackers and carrots. There are even some muffins." He took the sacks from her, their eyes still locked on each other. Miranda felt almost faint. "You should eat the muffins and bread first," she added, her voice softer. "They'll go stale more quickly than the other things."

Jake nodded, his smile fading. Miranda wondered if he hated this as much as she did. "Thanks," he said, turning to tie the sacks onto Outlaw. He adjusted his hat then, took hold of the reins. "I guess that's about it. Far as I know, I've got everything." He met her eyes once more.

Miranda nodded. "Yes." *Everything but me,* she wanted to tell him.

Jake adjusted his hat again, suddenly looking nervous and uncomfortable. "Look, Randy, I'm sorry about not taking you to Nevada. I hope you understand." *I think I could love you, if I even know what love is.*

Miranda forced a smile. "Sure. I understand." *I think I'm falling in love with you, Jake Harkner.* "I'll make it just fine."

He smiled again. "You remember what I said about keeping that Winchester handy."

"I will." *Do you know how utterly handsome you are when you smile, Jake?* "You should smile more often, you know," she continued aloud. "I'm sure with that beard gone and a smile on your face, no one would connect you to the way you probably look on those posters."

Jake laughed lightly. "Now there's a thought. Change my appearance."

Miranda glanced at the two gunbelts worn crossed at his middle, the revolvers that hung in their holsters at either side of his hips. "It's those guns that give you away, you know."

He sighed. "I know. But I can't afford to be without them."

Miranda folded her arms and stepped back, a light morning breeze blowing her honey-blond hair in little strands across her face. She shook her head slightly to get them out of the way. "Bye, Jake."

He just stared at her a moment before stepping closer and grasping hold of her arm gently. He bent down and kissed her cheek, and Miranda wondered why she didn't stop him, why she wished he would have kissed her mouth instead. She wondered if he was thinking the same thing. He turned and mounted Outlaw.

"This whole thing has been the strangest experience of my life," he told her, wincing once again as he settled himself into his saddle. He turned Outlaw and faced her. "I don't know what to think of it, being shot by a woman, then helped by her.

You're easy to talk to, Randy, a good woman and a beautiful one. I have to say I envy the man you finally pick when you remarry. He'll be a real lucky man."

Miranda touched her cheek where he had kissed her, a kiss that had sent pricks of fire through her bloodstream. "You take care of yourself. Don't do too much riding the first day. Promise?"

"Promise."

"I'll watch the newspapers—maybe read something about you once in a while."

"It will all be bad, I can guarantee. Just don't believe most of it."

Again the tears wanted to come. "I won't. God be with you, Jake."

He gave her the familiar sarcastic grin. "I doubt He takes time for the likes of me."

Miranda suddenly couldn't find her voice.

Jake tipped his hat to her then. *"Vaya con Dios,* Randy Hayes." He turned Outlaw, heading north. Miranda wanted to call out to him to stop, beg him to take her with him, or just to hold her for a little while. She put up her hand to wave, but he did not turn around to look back. She watched man and horse move up a distant rise and disappear on the other side.

"Good-bye, Jake," she said again, this time softly. He had spoken to her in Spanish, and it had sounded beautiful. She wondered how much of his mother's language he remembered, how often he used it.

Tears blurred her sight as she walked back to the cabin. She told herself those tears were just because of her father's recent death, from all her losses, and her fear of heading into an untamed land. The tears couldn't possibly have anything to do with Jake Harkner riding out of her life.

Jake started awake when an owl hooted. In an instant his revolver was drawn and cocked, but there was only silence in the darkness around him. The owl hooted again, and a soft night wind rustled the awakening spring leaves of the trees in the hollow where he had made camp. He waited a moment, listening intently, finally deciding it was only the owl that had disturbed him. He put the gun back in its holster and sat up straighter, bracing himself against his saddle. By the dim light of his fading campfire he could see that Outlaw was still tied where he had left him.

He had made camp in a hollow somewhere on the plains of southeastern Nebraska, had been there for several days now. Miranda had been right, he thought. He was not healed enough to have left when he did. An overpowering weakness had forced him to go slowly and finally to camp for several days in this one spot so he could rest. He felt good now, much stronger again. He just wished he could sleep better. He figured sleep should come easy, now that he was healed.

He sighed with disgust, knew the reason he was so restless and so easily awakened. It had nothing to do with worrying about being followed and bushwhacked, and it had nothing to do anymore with his injury. It had to do with a woman, a little slip of a woman with honey-blond hair and gray-blue eyes who had told him all human life had value. Miranda Hayes was probably on her way to Nevada by now, and it would be a miracle if she made it alive. Even if she did, survival after she got there would be another matter. He wanted to kick himself for not taking her himself, had given himself all kinds of good reasons why he just couldn't do it; but none of his arguments had convinced him he had made the right decision. The fact remained that he would always wonder if he should have taken her, always feel guilty for not doing it.

The guilt was what really frustrated him. He hadn't felt guilty about anything in years—except for the unending guilt over his father that had stolen his desire to ever make anything of himself. That guilt made sense, but to feel guilty for not taking a woman where she wanted to go made no sense. On top of that, after being around her, he had begun to feel guilty about what had never bothered him before, his past life of raiding and robbing and killing. He thought he had long ago accepted the way he lived as just the way things were, had determined in his own mind that such things could never be changed; but that damn woman had made him think about things he had not cared about since he was in his teens. The strange thing was, she had never really preached to him, or even raised her voice. She had just dropped subtle hints, had gotten that damned disappointed look in her eyes at times that made him feel like an ass.

There had been another look in those eyes that haunted him even more, especially at night. If he wasn't so sure it couldn't possibly be true, he would bet the way she looked at him the day he left meant she had feelings for him that ran deeper than friendship. Even friendship seemed unbelievable, considering the differences between them; but to think she might have wanted more . . .

He shook his head. Damned if Mrs. Miranda Hayes didn't act as if she needed holding, and damned if he didn't want to hold her. He could not forget how soft her cheek had been when he kissed it, how good she had smelled. He had wanted to lick that cheek, taste her skin, her mouth, all the pretty places on a woman that made a man hungry. He couldn't help picturing how firm and pink her breasts must be, how hungry she might be herself to have a man share her bed again. Lord knew he would certainly like to accommodate her, but what was strange was that he didn't want it so much in a lustful sort of way he thought of most women. After all, the kind of women he had always known didn't create much of any other kind of feeling in a man. They were just there to satisfy physical needs.

But Miranda, she was different. For the first time in his life he had wanted to make love to a woman just to satisfy her and not himself, to comfort her, to be united in spirit besides in body, if that kind of thing was possible. He had found himself wanting to protect and defend the woman, which seemed pretty ridiculous when he considered the fact that she had shot him. Sometimes the way she looked at him, he had just wanted to take her in his arms and tell her she didn't have to be lonely or afraid anymore.

He sat up and reached into his supplies, taking out a cigarette paper and some tobacco. He rolled himself a cigarette and pulled a slender stick from the fire, using it to light the smoke. He took a deep drag, leaning back again and studying the stars he could still see through spaces in the treetops. They were fading, as the sky to the east began to glow red from the sunrise.

Randy. The shortened form of her name sounded like a boy, but she sure didn't look or talk like any boy. Why in hell had he been led to her house? Was there some reason for all of it? He snickered, drawing on the cigarette again. What a fool he was, contemplating what it might be like to be married to a woman like that, to bed her, protect her, provide for her. Hell, even if he seriously tried such a thing, society would never leave him alone. He would always have to worry about the law. Life could never be peaceful and happy for a man like him. Fact was, he had never known either of those pleasantries in his entire life.

"What do you think, Outlaw?" he asked the horse. "Would I have a chance with Mrs. Hayes?"

The horse snorted and shook its head, and Jake grinned, taking another drag on the cigarette. Inside he didn't want to smile. Inside he hurt. He wanted that woman, and that was the hell of it. More than that, even if he couldn't have her, he could not help thinking he should have seen her to Nevada. He could have at least done that much. He knew he would never have touched her if she didn't want him to. That wasn't why he had turned her down. He had turned her down because he was afraid of his own feelings. What if he fell in love with her, knowing such a love was impossible for her to return? He hadn't let his feelings get to him in years, and he was not about to start now. He thought he had buried all the hurt a long time ago, with his mother and his brother, with Santana and his father. That was when he stopped feeling anything. That was when he knew a man was better off letting the hardness set in, not giving a damn about anything or anyone, including himself. A few days with Miranda Hayes had opened old wounds. She had made him talk about himself, made him remember things he would rather not think about.

It had been nice, though, in that warm little cabin, always smelled good. A man could get used to coming home to a place like that, to a woman like that. He closed his eyes, smoking quietly, listening to the owl hoot again to greet the morning. The owl's call reminded him of the loneliness of traveling in the open. He had spent many a night camped out like this, knew the dangers involved. Miranda would be facing the same dangers on that trip west, only it would be worse for her because she was pretty and unattached.

"I should have done it, Outlaw," he said then, thinking what a useless life he had led. He could have done one good thing for once and taken Miranda Hayes to Nevada like she asked.

Maybe he still could. He could go back and see if she had left yet. If she had, even though he would risk being seen and identified, he could go to Independence and see if he could find out who she had ended up traveling with, which route she had taken. It was dangerous for him to go to any town in Kansas or Missouri, but since when had danger bothered him any? He only knew he could not go on like this, wondering, feeling that it would be his fault if anything happened to the woman. Maybe she was still in Independence looking for a guide. Was there still time to catch up with her?

Hell, he thought, the sun would be up soon. There was no time like the present to change his mind. He took the coffee-pot from where he had set it beside the fire and set it over the coals, opening the lid and pouring some water into it from a canteen. He added a few crushed coffee beans, then set a fry-pan on the coals, getting some bacon from his supplies and slapping some into the pan. He had sliced the bacon from a side of ham a farmer had hanging near his smokehouse, a few miles back. Jake had stopped and asked for some of the meat, paid for it, even got the man to pack it in lard for him so it wouldn't spoil. There was a time when he might have just held a gun on the man and demanded all the food he wanted, but since spending those few days with Randy, such notions didn't seem right anymore. He grinned at how she would have re-acted if he had stolen the meat.

That's not why I saved your life, Jake Harkner, so you could go back to stealing from other people. He could just hear the words, and he knew that something had changed inside him since knowing Randy, but he couldn't quite put his finger on what felt different.

"Might as well eat an early breakfast, boy," he told Out-law. "We're heading out, see if we can find that Mrs. Hayes and still help her get to Nevada. I just hope I don't get recog-nized. Maybe it's like Randy said. Maybe if I leave these guns off in town and stay cleaned up and shaved and smile like an ordinary happy man, I won't get caught. It's pretty bad when you have to shave *off* a beard to disguise yourself."

Lord, he suddenly felt good inside, better than he had felt in a long time. It didn't matter if Miranda didn't need his help anymore. He knew somewhere deep inside that he wasn't even doing this just to act as a guide or to repay her for helping him. He was doing it because he couldn't stand the thought of never seeing Miranda Hayes again. Something felt unfinished, and he knew that whatever it was, it would stay unfinished if he didn't find Randy.

Miranda followed the Reverend Wilbur Jennings to the docks on the banks of the Missouri River. The little gathering of travelers was made up of Jennings's wife and children, two brothers, his father, a nephew, a brother-in-law, and a friend, all headed for Miranda's own destination—Virginia City, Nevada.

Upon arriving in Independence, Miranda had been directed to a local Presbyterian church, where "good, Christian people" gathered who wanted to travel together to points west. The minister there, a Reverend Harold Bishop, had told Miranda about his fellow Presbyterian minister, Wilbur Jennings, from Missouri, who was headed with his family to the "wild silver town" of Virginia City to "bring Christ to its wayward, sinful citizens."

"The town is growing," Reverend Bishop had told her. "We have received letters from a former church member who went there to preach the word, and he tells us there is a great need there for missionaries and the like, people who can build a church and bring some order and civilization to what he calls 'Hell on Earth.' The Reverend Jennings has volunteered to take his entire family there and see what he can do about the sin and corruption that abound there."

What better kind of people to travel with than dedicated Christians led by a minister, Miranda thought. Reverend Bishop agreed with her before she could voice the words. "Not many heading for Nevada these days but prospectors and drifters," the reverend had warned her, "single men looking for gold or silver or the profits to be made from miners needing supplies or a night of drinking and women. And the only women heading there are the kind with whom a decent woman should never be seen, painted women who welcome single men into their dens of iniquity."

Bishop had invited Miranda to meet the Reverend Jennings and his family at a church potluck being held just two days after she'd arrived in Independence via a short train ride from Kansas City. Church members had found various ways to raise money to sponsor the trip, and Miranda was welcome to go along so that Reverend Jennings's wife would have a woman companion. They were also pleased that Miranda had a background in medicine that could be of help to them on the way, as well as in Virginia City.

The fact that Miranda had bravely shot the notorious outlaw Jake Harkner made her even more welcome. The citizens of Kansas City had made an embarrassing fuss over that fact once more before she left, throwing her a huge farewell party and saying she would be one of their most famous citizens.

"You'll go down in the history books," one man told her, "especially once Harkner's body is found." Again a feeling of traitorousness had plagued Miranda as she accepted everyone's best wishes, gifts of quilts and food for her journey, and even money that had been collected for her.

The news about the shooting had traveled to the Independence newspapers, and someone at the church where she had been directed recognized her name. Again she became a celebrity, and the Reverend Bishop had given a sermon about how sometimes God's children are forced into violence. "Perhaps it was God's hand that directed Mrs. Hayes that day, ridding Kansas and Missouri of a man who was a plague to society."

Miranda's heart only ached at the very words Jake would probably use on himself, words she felt now were so unfair. What did these people know about how or why a man turned out the way he did? A few weeks ago she would have been as quick to judge as they were, but no longer. Her only secret redemption was the fact that she had been able to help the very man whose possible death these people were celebrating.

She was glad that finally it was time to head for Nevada. There would be no more probing questions, no more praise for her bravery; she wouldn't have to talk about Jake Harkner anymore after today, bear the guilt of not telling these well-intentioned people the truth, that because of her, Jake Harkner was alive and well, or at least she hoped that he was. She had told the Jenningses that she would rather put the whole incident behind her. Once they left Independence, it was to be forgotten; and they all wisely agreed that it was best no one in Nevada heard about her exploits. Virginia City was not a town where a proper and available young lady wanted any extra attention drawn to her.

Miranda watched the steamboat that would take them upriver to Omaha, where she and the Jennings family would all depart by wagon to travel the Oregon Trail west. She remembered the trip she had taken with her father and brother across Missouri by steamboat over four years ago, when they first came to Kansas from Illinois. It was strange how people could move in and out of one's life, could be so important, like Mack and her father, and then be taken away again. She wondered if that was how it would always be for her. Maybe she would never find Wesley. Maybe she would always be alone. Strangely, she had not thought so much about loneliness until

Jake had left. Why had his departure left this unwarranted void in her soul?

The Jennings family all greeted her pleasantly, although there was an aloofness about them that left Miranda feeling like an outsider. It irritated her a little that they seemed to pity her "poor, lost brother," and were already sure his soul needed redemption after living with other "wayward men" in a "town of sin." They did seem to admire her own courage in going to find him, and Miranda felt embarrassed sometimes over the way they fussed over her because she was the woman who had bravely faced the outlaw Jake Harkner. She didn't want to be fussed over and she didn't feel brave at all. She had shot Jake out of pure defensive reflex, and she was going to find Wes because she was just plain lonely, desperate to find what was left of her family and her identity.

When she thought about the stories she had heard about Indian trouble everywhere out west, she felt even less brave; but she was determined to do this. There was no turning back now. She could only hope that the Jennings clan would be able to take care of themselves along the way. She was grateful that even though they thought him an "un-Christian, wayward man," they had hired a guide for the journey, a trader named Hap Dearing, who had been to Nevada twice and was making another trip with supplies and four other men who appeared to Miranda to know how to use the rifles they carried.

The Reverend Jennings helped his brothers carry more gear onto the steamboat, and Miranda thought how much safer she would feel if she could have made this trip with Jake. How odd that she would have been less afraid with one man than with this big family and Hap Dearing and his men.

Her thoughts whirled as she thought about the dangerous trip she was preparing to make. The day she left the farm and her father's grave had been one of the saddest she could remember. She had become a woman there, had loved and lost so much. But what hurt the most now was the memory of those last few days when Jake was there. Had it been fate, was it somehow "meant to be," that she should shoot the man and then find him lying in her own house and save his life? She couldn't help thinking there had to be a reason for all of it.

The entire Jennings family was gathered at the docks now, all eleven of them, as well as their close friend, Adam Hummer, a single man who at thirty-eight was going to Nevada to farm food he intended to supply to miners, and to grocery

stores and restaurant owners. Hummer smiled and nodded to
Miranda, and Reverend Jennings's wife, Opal, who was thirty-
two, put an arm around her waist and welcomed her. The
woman was quickly surrounded by her fourteen-year-old
daughter, Loretta; her two sons, Chester, eleven, and David,
eight; and her baby daughter, Sara, only three. Sara clung to
her mother's skirts while Reverend Jennings came back off the
boat and urged the family to form a circle for prayer before
starting their journey.

Included in the clan were the reverend's two brothers,
John, twenty-eight, and Bernard, twenty-seven, both single
men who were also going into the ministry. The reverend's
father, Clemson, who Miranda worried was too old for the
journey, was also going along, since his wife was dead and he
wanted to be with his sons. Also going with them was a
nephew, Clarence, only eighteen, and the only family member
Miranda did not care for. He seemed always to be staring at
her, always stood closer than necessary when talking to her.
Even now, Clarence was the one who pushed his way beside
her so that it was his hand she had to hold while they prayed.
James Gaylord, Clarence's father and the reverend's brother-
in-law, was also coming along. Clarence's mother, who was the
reverend's sister, had died several years earlier in childbirth.

As they prayed together on the docks, Miranda thought
how all the Jennings family looked alike: tall, lanky men, the
older ones with nearly bald heads, the younger ones with hair
so thin it was obvious they, too, would lose their hair at a
younger age than most men. What hair they all did have was
blond, and all but John Jennings had blue eyes.

The brother-in-law, James, and the friend Adam Hummer
were the only ones who looked different from the rest. James
was a short, stocky man with thick, graying hair and bags under his eyes even when he was rested; Hummer was tall but
much more rotund than the Jenningses, with dark, wavy hair.
They all dressed in plain black suits with plain black hats and
knee-length black boots, and the reverend nearly always carried a Bible.

Miranda was not completely comfortable with these people, but they seemed to her to be the best of the few choices
she had. At least they seemed trustworthy, people of moral
character and a Christian background. She decided she would
simply avoid Clarence as much as possible.

The reverend finished his prayer, and Miranda struggled

against a feeling of sudden panic and regret. She reasoned she could still change her mind, but a stubbornness had set in now, a determination that would not let her give up. She reminded herself that there was nothing left for her here but sad memories. She had taken all her personal possessions, sold most of her furniture. All she had with her now was her trunk, with its quilts and towels, a few dishes, and her clothes. Her father's Winchester was in the trunk, her trusty little derringer in her handbag. She had not forgotten Jake's warning that she keep both guns handy. Once they left Omaha by wagon, she would carry the Winchester in the wagon where it would be easy to get hold of.

Jake. It seemed her thoughts always came back to him, and she knew now that she had been hopelessly, foolishly falling in love with the man, and she had a feeling he knew it. That was why he had left before he was really ready to travel. She prayed he was all right, felt guilty for being partly responsible for his leaving too soon.

She boarded the riverboat with the Jennings clan, her thoughts on an outlaw. She actually smiled at imagining the reaction of this family if she told them what she had done the last few days before leaving Kansas City. She could not help thinking how she might actually have enjoyed this trip if she could have gone with Jake. She felt desperately alone, in spite of the company and kindness of the Jennings family. Their friendship was not the same as what she had felt with Jake, in spite of his attempts at making her think he was not worth her time.

The steamboat gave off two long whistles from its stack as it drifted away from the dock and the huge paddle wheels at either side began churning through the water. Again Miranda felt the tears wanting to come as the sight of Independence gradually disappeared when the steamboat made its way around a bend.

"Got an exciting trip ahead of us, don't we?"

Miranda felt a hand against her back in a too-familiar gesture. She turned to see Clarence Jennings standing beside her, his blue eyes sparkling with eager youth. His gaze dropped to her breasts for a moment, and he rubbed her back lightly. "Don't you be worried, Mrs. Hayes. My uncles and I will look after you."

Miranda moved away, feeling a chill at his touch. "You

look after yourself and your father, Clarence. I can take care of myself."

The young man shrugged, looking her over again. "Must be hard, being a widow, alone and all. I just wanted you to know we care." He grinned at her. "Anything you need, you just let me know."

Miranda did not miss the suggestive tone of his remark. "If there is anything I need, I will talk to your aunt or your uncle," she answered. "Right now I would like to be alone."

His smile faded, and Miranda was surprised at the hostile look that came into his eyes. He nodded to her. "Whatever you want, ma'am. Once we head out by wagon across Nebraska, you won't get much chance to be alone then, will you? We'll all be herded together like the Lord's sheep."

He gave her a wink and left, and Miranda shivered. She pulled her shawl closer, and the sickening feeling that she had made the wrong choice after all returned to plague her; but her determination to find her brother was stronger. She set her lips tight, gritting her teeth and telling herself she could do this. If Clarence Jennings tried to give her any trouble, she would quickly put him in his place. The steamer gave off another lonely sounding whistle, and she turned to go and find Opal Jennings. Thank goodness there was another woman along.

She turned away from the sight of things left behind. She must not think about Mack or her father, or the lonely little cabin at the farm, the grave behind it. And she must not think about Jake Harkner. All those things were in her past now. She had to be strong, think about the future, finding Wes. She had told everyone she could do this, that she could take care of herself. Now she had to prove she was right.

CHAPTER
SEVEN

 Jake tipped his hat and nodded politely to an elderly woman who was stepping off a boardwalk to cross the street. "Morning, ma'am," he told her, giving her his best smile. He hoped Miranda was right when she said he looked very different when he was clean and shaved and smiling.

"Good morning, sir," the woman replied, responding to his smile with one of her own. "Lovely day, isn't it?"

"Yes, ma'am." What the hell had gotten into him, risking his neck like this, sweet-talking an old lady, all to find a woman who probably would rather he didn't show up in her life again now that he was out of it. "I'm wondering if you might tell me where a man could go to find out about others traveling west. I figure most come here to Independence first. I'm looking for someone who would have needed to find decent, Christian traveling companions. Where might she have gone for that kind of help?"

The old woman squinted at the sun that was at Jake's back and eyed his horses and gear. Jake had purchased an extra horse from a farmer, loading part of his gear onto it so he could hide his rifles under blankets and keep them from being noticed. Besides that, he needed the packhorse for the extra supplies he had gathered for his journey. His revolvers were also put away, and he felt naked as a jaybird without them, but he wanted to look like a common traveler, and he knew Miranda was right about that too. He couldn't expect to go unnoticed when he wore two six-guns and packed a Winchester and a shotgun besides. Once he got out of civilized areas like this, he decided he would at least carry his revolvers again. Being without them made him too damn nervous.

"Well, sir, if a person is looking to find good, Christian folks to travel with, they would surely see the Reverend Bishop at the Presbyterian church just up the street," the old lady was telling him. "He helps good people find traveling companions. Otherwise, the person you're looking for might have just gone to the docks along the river and asked around, or north of town there's a big area where people with wagons gather. Some start right out from there by wagon, others with a little more money take the steamboats up to Omaha first."

"Thank you very much. You've been a big help." Jake nodded to her again and rode on, heading for the church. It was his last hope. He had already checked at hotels and boarding houses, had already been to the docks and to the "jumping off" area, which was what some still called the gathering place for those going west by wagon train. Rumor had it that a transcontinental railroad would someday span the West, and he knew tracks were already being built out of Omaha, but he found it hard to believe such a project would ever be completed.

The fact remained that people still had to go west by wagon, and he didn't even like to think about the danger that would be for someone like Miranda. The more he searched for her, the more anxious he became to find her, and the more guilty he felt for not going with her in the first place. He hoped that he would find his answer at the church. He had to get out of this town before he was recognized.

What if she hadn't even come to Independence first, as she said she would? He had stopped at her cabin, found a man living there alone. He had felt a terrible ache at seeing the cabin bare and unkempt, not at all as homey and warm as when Miranda lived in it. The man had said she'd been gone nearly three weeks already, that all her friends in Kansas City had thrown a farewell party for her. He imagined it must be nice to have good friends like that, and he was almost surprised Miranda hadn't stayed after all; but then she was a stubborn, independent woman who stuck to her guns once her mind was made up.

Because of the information, and the danger of being recognized, he had bypassed Kansas City and had come straight to Independence. He had hoped against hope that she would still be in town, but he had found no trace of her. His last hope was the Presbyterian church the old woman had told him about. He headed in that direction, passed a stage station on the way, then drew Outlaw to a halt when he spotted a poster on the outside wall of the station. The packhorse meandered to a halt behind him, and Jake dismounted, holding Outlaw's reins as he stepped closer to look at the poster, seeing a hand-sketched picture of himself, his dark eyes looking mean and threatening, his hair hanging long and stringy, a grizzly beard hiding most of his face. He moved to catch his reflection in a nearby window and he grinned. By God, Miranda had a point. He didn't look much like that poster at all. Still, it was eerie to see his own mug plastered up that way, with the words $5,000 REWARD printed in huge, bold letters at the top.

WANTED, he read, FOR ROBBERY, MURDER, ABDUCTION AND RAPE. JACKSON "JAKE" LLOYD HARKNER, DESCRIPTION: APPROX. 6'1", 200#, BELIEVED TO BE PART MEXICAN, DARK HAIR AND EYES, DARK SKIN. $5,000 REWARD IF CAUGHT ALIVE. $3,000 DEAD. ARMED AND DANGEROUS.

Jake stepped back and glanced around. People walked by on their busy errands, no one paying him much attention. He adjusted his hat, feeling more than uncomfortable at the sight of the poster. He decided he had better do what he came here to do and get the hell out of Missouri. He remounted Outlaw and headed for the small frame church the old lady had indicated to him. As he came closer, a short, graying man emerged from the front doors of the white building. He made his way down the steps, glancing at Jake and smiling. "Excuse me, sir!" Jake called out. "Might you be the Reverend Bishop?"

The man brightened. "Yes, I'm Reverend Bishop. Can I do something for you?"

"Possibly." Jake halted Outlaw and again dismounted, holding the reins as he removed his hat respectfully. "I'm told you often help people who are headed west find traveling companions."

"Yes, I do, but most have gone by now. You have to get an early start in the spring in order to make it all the way west before bad weather sets in."

Jake watched the man's kind, sparkling eyes, wondering at how some people were almost innocent in their trust. He wondered how the reverend would feel if he knew the truth about him. Would he still smile like that?

"I know that," he answered. "But there is someone I'm looking for, a Mrs. Miranda Hayes. Back in Illinois I was a good friend of her family," he lied, "her father, Dr. Baker, and her brother Wesley. I came here looking for them, went to Kansas City and found out the good doctor had been killed by outlaws. I was real sorry to hear that. Then they told me Wesley had gone to Nevada months ago, and that Mrs. Hayes had been married and lost her husband to the war. She just recently left to go to Nevada to find her brother." Jake shook his head, putting on a look of dire concern. "I can't imagine that poor young woman heading out alone to a place like that. I thought I'd try to find her, at least go along for extra protection. I owe that much to her father, who saved my life once."

The reverend frowned. "Oh, it is too bad you didn't show up sooner. On a trip like that, and with women and children along, you just can't have enough men to provide and protect, Mr., uh, what was your name?"

"Jake," Jake replied too quickly. He cursed himself for it, feeling he shouldn't have used any part of his real name. "Jake Turner," he finished, using the name of the farmer from whom he had purchased the packhorse. "You know Mrs. Hayes then?"

"I certainly do!"

Jake felt a rush of warmth, wondered why his heart always pounded a little faster when he thought about seeing Miranda again.

"A beautiful young woman, she is. Being widowed and all, I knew she would want good, trustworthy people with whom to travel, so I introduced her to a fellow reverend, Wilbur Jennings. Reverend Jennings is headed for Virginia City with his family. They intend to bring Christianity to the poor, lost miners there who need Christ's guidance and teaching. Reverend Jennings and his family plan to build a church there and start a school."

Jake could hardly believe how trusting this man was, so willing to give out information, apparently not doubting for a moment that he might not be telling the truth.

"Jennings?" he asked. "Is it a big family?"

"Oh, yes! The reverend and his wife have four children,

and the reverend's two younger brothers, his father, a brother-in-law and nephew, and a friend of the family are all going. In fact, they're traveling with a trader, Hap Dearing, and four extra men. Mrs. Hayes should be quite safe, I assure you. The traders know how to defend themselves. Mr. Dearing has made the trip to Nevada before. Fact is, I imagine Mrs. Hayes herself can do a good job protecting herself. Did they tell you back in Kansas City about her shooting that outlaw, Jake Harkner?"

The man's trusting ignorance made Jake almost want to laugh. "Yes, they did. I'm just glad she wasn't hurt. It must have been very unsettling for her."

"Yes, I think it was. She didn't seem to want to talk much about it. I think it still upsets her. She certainly is a brave woman." The man adjusted his hat. "Even so, I expect she'd be happy to see an old friend of her father and brother show up. I think she was pretty scared to set out for Nevada, but she's a determined lady. I expect by now they are well on their way out of Omaha—took a steamboat upriver first. I do hope they're having good weather. Spring can be mighty tricky."

"Weather out on the plains can be tricky any time of year. I traveled as far west as western Nebraska once, came back this way during the war."

"Oh, were you in the war, Mr. Turner?"

Yeah, I was a gunrunner, Jake felt like answering, just to see the look on the reverend's face. "Yes, sir," he answered. "But I would rather not talk about it."

"Oh, I see, I see." A look of true concern came into Bishop's gentle eyes, and Jake felt like an ass for having to lie to him. "Do you intend to try to find Mrs. Hayes? They are a good two or three weeks ahead of you, you know. They left May third."

Jake looked past him at the open country beyond the church. "Yes, I'll try to find her. As long as I know the party she's traveling with, that will help. I'll ride hard north to the Oregon Trail. I can probably be up there before another steamboat could make it, and I can inquire at some of the forts along the way. It won't be easy catching up to them, but a man alone can also travel a lot faster than a whole family with wagons. Those freight wagons will slow them down even more."

"Well, Mr. Turner, you're welcome to come to my home for a good home-cooked meal first to send you on your way."

Jake was dumbfounded at the offer. *You don't even know me,* he thought. *I could rob you blind!* He was not used to being around such good, trusting people. He wondered if the reverend had ever known or witnessed any form of violence in his whole life. "No, thank you," he answered. "If I'm going to catch up with Mrs. Hayes and the others, I had better get started right away. I appreciate the offer, though." He re-mounted Outlaw. "You've been a big help, Reverend. I'm very grateful."

"Well, I'm here to serve in any way I can, Mr. Turner. God be with you on your journey."

"Thank you." Jake nodded to the man and kicked Outlaw's sides lightly, heading out of town, anxious to be away from civilized places. *Thank you indeed,* he thought. He could hardly believe it had all been so easy—the old woman telling him about Reverend Bishop, the reverend so willing to give out information. Again he felt controlled by fate. Maybe he was supposed to find Randy. Maybe someone was making it easy for him.

Someone? He looked up at a puffy cloud overhead, then rolled his eyes at what he had been thinking. Men like him didn't give much thought to being helped by God. He only kept his mother's prayer beads for sentimental reasons, not to pray with. Praying was not for the likes of him. Still, if he had prayed, he couldn't have gotten a much quicker answer than what he had just gotten from Reverend Bishop. He thought finding Randy would be a lot harder than this, but then he hadn't really found her yet. He only knew where to start looking, and she had a big head start.

He pulled a thin cigar from his shirt pocket. It was getting warm already, and he wore no jacket. He slowed Outlaw to a walk while he took a match from a little pouch on his saddle and flicked it with his fingernail to light it. He held it to the cigar and took a puff, then waved out the match and threw it aside, thinking again what big country it was where he was headed. His only hope was that the Jennings family and the traders would stick to the regular Oregon Trail. It was his only chance of finding Randy.

He spurred Outlaw into a faster gait, heading north.

Miranda walked beside the wagon, swatting at a fly that kept pestering her. During the day it was flies, at night mosquitoes.

She was sure that both, along with the heat, the mud, the sudden drenching storms, the painful cramps in her calves, and the sores on her feet would be much more bearable if she could have kept Opal's friendship, as well as the friendship of the Reverend Jennings and his brothers.

Clarence had seen to it that she was left an outsider. What was most frustrating was that she could not directly accuse the young man of anything solid. She simply knew by instinct that he had been talking to his uncles about her, had been planting ideas in their heads. She realized now that she should have known by the hostile look the young man had given her the day when she turned down his advances that he would find a way to get even.

He had apparently done just that. The first three weeks of their journey out of Omaha, he had hung around her incessantly, pushing his presence on her, making her talk to him when she didn't want to, finding ways to help her, touch her. Then there were times when she would see him talking to his uncles, all of them stealing glances at her, whispering together. She had no doubt Clarence was telling the pious men that she was some kind of wanton woman who had been flirting with him, a man-hungry widow who seemed to have her eyes set on an innocent teenager.

Apparently the talk had come around to Opal, who had become colder and more distant. Losing the woman's companionship hurt more than anything. She wished she could explain. Surely Opal had seen how it was Clarence who made all the advances, had seen how hard she had tried to avoid the young man. But then Clarence was Opal's nephew. What person would believe a stranger over family?

Clarence had done a perfect job of exacting revenge and keeping her outside the family circle. Now besides Clarence's staring eyes, she had to put up with scornful looks from the rest of the Jennings clan. There were five unmarried men besides Clarence among the travelers, plus Hap Dearing and his four men, about whom she knew little. All of them seemed to take delight lately in gawking at her.

Sometimes she felt as though she was walking naked alongside the wagon, and she was utterly miserable, wondering how she was going to make it all the way to Nevada under these conditions. She was sure the Jennings family were beginning to look at her as some kind of sinful harlot who had been tempting poor, innocent Clarence. They no longer seemed to be impressed by the fact that she had shot an outlaw, but rather were beginning to use the experience as proof that she was not the pure and saintly woman they originally thought her to be. One evening at prayer, the reverend had asked God to forgive her for bringing violence against another human being, even though it had apparently been in self-defense. She thought how hypocritical they were to praise her for what she had done only until they began to think she was some kind of wayward woman herself. That made the shooting suddenly a bad thing.

They had been on the trail nearly a month now, and the past week had been miserable, both in weather and her emotions. Until today, the weather had been cold and rainy for five days, daily drenching those who had to walk. The wagons had gotten buried in mud more than once, and little Sara had taken sick. Miranda herself did not feel well. Even though today it had warmed and things were drying out, her throat hurt and her muscles ached. Walking several miles every day had at first given her terrible leg cramps and swollen feet, but now it seemed her body was getting more used to the strain and her feet did not hurt quite so much; but overall she remained in misery from emotional turmoil and loss of sleep.

At first she had shared a wagon with Opal and little Sara, while the rest of the children slept in the second wagon and all the men slept outside. The past few nights Opal had not spoken to her at all, a complete change from their long nightly conversations when they'd first started out. She claimed she was just too tired now to talk, but Miranda knew the real reason. The woman no longer wanted her friendship.

Miranda felt desperately alone, as if no one were traveling with her at all. She trudged through mud and high prairie grass, sometimes helping Loretta gather a few wildflowers, putting some into the belt of her dress just to make herself feel better. She still thought of Jake often, sure he would have been easier to talk to than these people who called themselves Christians. Jake would not be so quick to judge, certainly not the type to hold a supposed "sin" over someone's head. The worst part was being judged for something she had not done at all. She had been so sure these were the perfect people with whom to make this long journey. Now she found it ironic that she would rather be traveling with an outlaw.

Night was falling, and Dearing finally rode up to Reverend Jennings and told the man they would make camp for the night along the river. Miranda breathed a sigh of relief. It had already been decided that the women would be allowed to bathe tonight. Blankets would be hung tent-style beside the river so the women would have a place to undress. It had been ten days since any of them had done more than wash their hands and faces, and Miranda had never felt so uncomfortably grimy. She felt like cursing the brother who had brought this misery on her, but then Wesley had not asked her to come to Nevada. It had been her own decision, and now she was trapped. How could she go back? She certainly couldn't do it alone, and the wagon that carried her trunk belonged to Reverend Jennings. She had paid them a good deal of what money she had left, leaving her little to pay anyone else to take her, and how could she trust just any stranger that came along?

Somehow she had to bear up as an outcast until they reached Nevada, and she fought to hold her chin high and not let her emotional abandonment get her down. If she let herself give in to this agony, she felt she would lose her mind completely. Reverend Jennings would probably declare her mad and go on without her. The old stubbornness that had gotten her through most of her losses and grief was still there to hold her up, along with nightly prayers.

"We will each take turns bathing tonight," Opal was telling her as they both lowered the back gate of one of the wagons. "We will have to be very cautious and discreet, what with those traders along. Heaven knows if they can truly be trusted." The woman looked at her almost scathingly. "You must be extra careful, considering your widowed status, Miranda. You must understand how some men look at a thing like that."

Miranda caught the suggestion, felt the hurt. "If my being a widow so disturbs you, Opal, why did any of you agree to allow me to come along? Everything was fine in the beginning. I thought we were becoming quite good friends. I might as well say it out, because I am tired of the way all of you have been treating me lately. I have done absolutely nothing to deserve your turning on me. I don't like any of this, and I want to know why it is happening."

The woman stiffened, leaning a little closer, her usually meek demeanor suddenly, surprisingly stern and full of warning. "You seemed a very discreet, Christian young lady in the beginning; but you have been much too friendly with my nephew Clarence. Don't you understand that a young man that age is easily swayed by a beautiful, available woman he thinks is in need of a man? He looks at you as experienced and lonely, and he has confessed to my husband that the way you look at him makes him think sinful things."

Miranda's eyes widened with indignation. Fury boiled within her, but she fought to keep her voice down, realizing that to be overheard by the men would only make her look worse, not better. "I know exactly what your nephew is thinking, Opal, and it isn't because of anything I have done! I have tried to stay away from him, but he won't leave me alone! If you want the truth, I can't stand Clarence Jennings, and if he doesn't stay away from me, I'll use the same pistol on him I used on Jake Harkner! You tell him to stay away from me and stop spreading lies about me! I have no desire to tempt any man on this wagon train! I am here for one thing only, and that is to get to Nevada!"

She whirled and began angrily taking down pans and other necessities for the evening meal. Opal watched her a moment, wanting to believe her. But, after all, Clarence would never lie. He was a good, Christian young man who had never done anything but make his father proud of him. Miranda Hayes must not even realize how she was tempting the poor boy. The woman walked to the second wagon, where her husband was helping unhitch the oxen. She pulled him aside.

"I think perhaps we should consider helping Miranda find someone else to travel with when we reach the next fort, Wilbur. I am afraid this whole thing with Clarence may get out of hand. Perhaps we made a wrong decision letting her come along."

The reverend sighed, removing his hat and running a hand through his thinning red hair. "I agree. I will think about it over the next few days, discuss it with John and Berny and Father. I hate to abandon her that way, but if she's at a fort, she'll be safe until she finds other traveling companions. This is partly our fault for being so quick to take her in. I was just so anxious to have a traveling companion for you that I didn't consider that her being such an attractive widow might cause problems with all these men along. I'll pray about it."

"Thank you, Wilbur." Opal returned to her work, feeling Miranda's anger as they worked together to prepare supper. It was really too bad they would probably have to leave poor Miranda behind, but Opal could not think what else to do. After all, the family and Christian values came first.

. . .

Miranda sat down on a stump, wondering if she had ever felt more alone. Another week of putting up with stares and cold shoulders had passed since she had told Opal exactly what she thought. Thank goodness Clarence had stayed away from her lately, but several times she had seen the reverend talking privately with his brothers and father, knew they were discussing her. This hell had to end somewhere, and she had decided to come here to be alone to pray and think. She had decided that she would face the reverend and the others head-on, speak up to them before they could pompously come to her first. Her anger was taking over the hurt now. It was time to stand up to the Jenningses and get everything out in the open, even though they were the ones in charge. Enough was enough.

She put her head in her hands, listening to the soft, night breeze in the cottonwood trees. The wagon train was perhaps twenty yards away, and for the moment it felt good to be entirely alone, away from the looks and the whispers. She listened to crickets, grateful that a breeze the last two nights had kept the mosquitoes at bay.

What a fool you were to think you could go running off to Nevada, she told herself. *You should have listened to Jake, listened to Sheriff McCleave.* She had never been attracted to the sheriff, but right now being back in Kansas City and letting him court her sounded wonderful. She was sure none of her friends back there considered her as some kind of wanton woman just because she was a widow. They had known Mack, knew how hard his death had been on her. She could still be with them, but instead she had chosen this pain and discomfort and danger just to find a brother who probably didn't want to be found. It had seemed so important at the time. What was left for her if she couldn't find Wesley? Would she have lost all that was Miranda Baker Hayes?

Perhaps she already had. She was certainly a different person from the young woman who had first come to Kansas from Illinois. Sometimes she wondered who that person was. She longed for some kind of stability and she supposed that was why it was important to find Wesley. Maybe she could make a home for him, have family again. What was there for a person without family? Nothing but loneliness and a feeling of not belonging anywhere. No wonder Jake was such a lost soul. He not only had no family left, he didn't even have good memories to look back on.

Jake. How many times had her thoughts turned to him? Sometimes it was so comforting to think of him.

"A penny for your thoughts," a voice said.

Miranda jumped, startled that someone was there. Clarence! The brat had followed her here, sneaky devil that he was. How could she not have heard him, unless he had deliberately sneaked up as quietly as possible?

She immediately rose, on guard. "You have no right to be here," she said firmly. "I came here to be alone."

"Did you?"

She could see him better now in the bright moonlight. He stepped closer.

"I don't believe that, Mrs. Hayes. You were hoping me or one of the other men would see you walk off and would follow. You've been trying to find a way to be alone with one of the men this whole trip."

Miranda wished she had her handbag along. If she did, she would find it very easy to take out her pistol and shoot him here and now. "You are a stupid young man who likes to fantasize," she answered. "Now get back to the wagons."

He came even closer, close enough to touch her. "I don't take orders from anybody but Uncle Wilbur and my pa." He grasped her arms, and Miranda jerked away.

"Touch me again and I'll scream," she said in a near growl. "Your father and the holy reverend will soon learn the kind of man you really are! They'll know who's been lying and who's been telling the truth all along!"

He grabbed her again, this time his grip tight enough to hurt. Miranda realized he was a surprisingly strong young man for his slender build. "Will they?" he snarled. "Scream all you want, Mrs. Hayes. No matter how it works out, they'll see you as a *slut*! I'll make sure they know you lured me out here, that I just couldn't resist your invitation, because I'm just an innocent boy who's been manipulated by an experienced woman lonely for a man. No, lady, you won't scream, because you know that the only way out of this, the only way to save face and be allowed to stay with us, is to cooperate and give me what you know I want . . . and what I know *you* want!"

He jerked her arms behind her and pressed her close against him. Miranda could feel his hardened erection pressing at her belly. His breath smelled from the fried onions he had eaten at supper. "The best thing for you to do is just quietly let it happen, Mrs. Hayes. That way they'll never know. I sure won't tell. Will you?"

He tried to kiss her, and she turned her face away. He bit at her neck, and for one brief moment Miranda wondered if he was right. Did she really have any choice? Not one person along would believe her side of the story. Clarence pushed her to the ground, and an inner pride and fury welled up inside her. To hell with what any of them thought! Clarence Jennings was not going to get away with this, even if it meant she had to travel the rest of this trip completely alone and dragging her own trunk!

He let go of her arms to grab at her breasts, sure she would not resist. Miranda took the opportunity to jab at his eyes and face while she let out a bloodcurdling scream. She fought wildly then, scratching, biting, butting heads.

"Goddamn, you split my lip!" Clarence yelled, jumping away from her.

Miranda was immediately on her feet, gripping a rock she had grabbed as she rose. She threw it at him, and Clarence cried out when it hit him hard in the ribs.

"You bitch!" he snarled. "You slut!"

"Get out of my sight, or by God I'll find my pistol and *kill* you!" Miranda told him. She heard the sound of people crashing through the trees.

"Mrs. Hayes! What's wrong?" someone shouted. "Mrs. Hayes! Is it you out there? Are you all right?"

"Pa!" Clarence shouted back before Miranda could answer. "Pa, I think she broke my rib!"

"Clarence!" Miranda recognized James Gaylord's voice. The man came closer to his son. "What happened?"

"What is going on here?" The demand came from Reverend Jennings. The man's brothers, and his friend Adam Hummer also arrived on the scene. "Did you see Indians? What happened?"

"What's going on?"

Miranda recognized Hap Dearing's voice. She wanted to crawl in a hole, knew what they would all think. Before she could make any reply, Clarence began carrying on about how she had lured him here and made him think he could kiss her. Through tears he told how she had suddenly changed her mind and started screaming and fighting him. "She's just trying to get me in trouble, Pa," he wept. "I know I shouldn't have come out here with her. I'm sorry, Pa."

"Get back to camp!" Gaylord commanded his son. Miranda could not see his face well, but she could sense his fury.

"Your son followed me here deliberately," she told the man. "He's handing you a pack of lies to get himself out of trouble. Can't you see that? He attacked me! He tried to force himself on me!"

"Enough!" This time it was the reverend who spoke up. "We will go back to camp and talk about this." The man turned and stormed away, and the others followed, no one offering to walk with Miranda. She walked behind them, shaking from Clarence's abuse, wishing she could bathe and wash off his touch, the saliva he had left on her neck. How ironic that she had spent several days with a notorious outlaw and never once felt threatened the way she had felt around Clarence from the first day they left Independence. How she hated him! She knew already no one was going to listen to her side of the story. Their minds were made up. Clarence had given a convincing performance.

She longed for a friend, someone to turn to. She needed someone's understanding at this moment, but when she looked at the faces around the fire when they reached camp, she saw not one kind face. Hap Dearing and his men looked at her as though she were wearing rouge and a red taffeta dress. One of them looked ready to burst out laughing as his eyes boldly roved over her, as though to say he knew all along she was easy. The Jennings men, as well as the brother-in-law James Gaylord, and their missionary friend Adam Hummer, all gave her accusing stares, the Reverend Jennings glaring at her with his nose in the air like a pious judge.

"Mrs. Hayes, we have already discussed the possibility of leaving you behind at one of the forts," he told Miranda. "I am terribly sorry, but that is what we are going to have to do."

Miranda felt the panic setting in. If they left her behind, she would have to go on with strangers she didn't know anything about. And what kind of people would be at the place where they would leave her? How long would it take to find someone new to travel with? If she had to wait too long, she would never make it all the way to Nevada this summer. She would be stranded in the middle of nowhere. "I did absolutely nothing improper," she told the preacher. "Your nephew has been harrassing me ever since we left Independence. I have asked him time and again to leave me alone! He has spread lies about me and—"

"I won't listen to any more to your own lies!" Clarence's father roared.

"Why do you think I screamed and fought him!" Miranda shouted back. "Does that sound like a woman who had lured him out there for illicit purposes?"

"You just wanted to get me in trouble, to try to prove it was all me!" Clarence put in, the tears still coming. "You touched me! You said if I came out there with you, you'd show me about women!"

Miranda closed her eyes. Oh, how she wanted to kill! She felt on fire, full of rage, and she breathed deeply for control. She needed to scream and cry, but she was determined not to crumble in front of these pompous asses. She held her chin high and faced the reverend. "If you want to believe your nephew over me, there is nothing I can do about it," she told him calmly. "I am telling you that you are wrong, Reverend, and if you leave me behind, the sin will be on your head for abandoning an innocent woman. I hope it haunts you forever!"

She saw the man flinch, saw the hint of doubt in his eyes, and she hoped he'd choke on that doubt. "Go ahead and leave me behind. I really don't care anymore. I would rather walk the rest of the way with my trunk on my back than to spend the next two months with such people. And you call yourselves *Christians*!"

She turned and walked away, almost anxious now to be left behind so that she would never have to look at their faces again. *You're a survivor, Miranda Hayes,* she told herself. *You'll make it to Nevada with or without them.* Everyone had tried to tell her she couldn't do this, but by God she would!

"There's a trading post not far ahead," she heard Hap Dearing telling the reverend. "It's not very big, but at least there are supplies there in case she gets stranded for long. Lots of people stop there. I expect we could leave her off there. The sooner, the better. All this trouble is slowin' us down, and I don't intend to lose any time. If you want to stay along with me and my men for protection, I'd get rid of her at the trading post. There's men there that can look after her."

Men? What kind of men? Miranda felt sick and lonely, but she was determined not to show any fear or concern if Jennings left her at the trading post. She would get the Winchester out of her trunk and make sure every man there knew he had better leave her alone!

She blinked back tears. An owl hooted somewhere nearby, and it seemed only to accent her despair. She walked farther out into the prairie grass, found a flat rock in the moonlight, and sat down. Her feet ached from a long day's walk, and she reached down and removed her high-button shoes. She rubbed at her feet, and it was then she heard the dreaded rattling sound.

It all happened in the matter of a second. She realized what was lurking under the rock, and in that same sudden thought, before she could react to the sound of the rattler, she felt the horrid pain in her left foot and knew she had been bitten. She gasped with the pain, knew something had to be done quickly. She also knew from her father that a person bitten by a rattler should never run, but panic took away all reasoning. She clung to her shoes and ran back to the camp, collapsing when she reached the fire.

"Sssssnake!" she managed to get out before things began to go black on her.

She felt someone fussing around her foot, heard Hap Dearing tell someone to get him a knife. ". . . suck out the venom as best I can . . ." she thought she heard the man say.

"Oh, dear God, what is going to happen next?" It was Opal's voice.

"Maybe it's God's punishment on her for being bad." Clarence said with a sneer.

I'm going to die, Miranda thought, suddenly feeling very calm. *I'm going to die out here and be buried in an unmarked grave. No one will ever know what happened to me. Not Wesley . . . not even Jake.* Why did the thought of Jake not knowing hurt the most?

Good-bye Jake. She saw his face, saw his smile as he rode away from her. It was her last thought before she fell into total unconsciousness.

CHAPTER EIGHT

 Jake urged a weary Outlaw toward the trading post, wondering how much longer his two horses could keep up the pace he had forced them to endure for the past two weeks. He had been careful not to ride them so hard that they gave out on him, but he had not been nearly as easy on the animals as he would normally have been.

For two weeks he had searched among the travelers he passed heading west. None had seen or heard of the Jennings clan, so he knew that they still had to be ahead somewhere. Hope had sprung anew when he found a trader at Fort Kearny who did remember the reverend and his family, as well as the lovely young widow woman traveling with them.

"Prettiest thing I've ever seen," the man had commented, bringing a warmth to Jake's heart he was not accustomed to feeling.

"Did she seem all right?" Jake asked.

"Believe so," the trader had answered, "except that preacher and his family she was travelin' with, I don't know, they didn't seem to be too friendly to her. Maybe it was just my imagination. You know her?"

"I know her. How long ago were they here?"

"Oh, maybe five, six days."

Jake had ridden the horses even harder since then. There

was no doubt now that he had to be getting close. Again he had checked with every group of travelers he passed, but none knew anything about the party Miranda was with, which meant he was still behind them. He didn't like slowing down now, but he needed supplies. He decided he would stop at the trading post just ahead and see if they had what he needed. Maybe someone here had seen the Jenningses and could tell him how close he was.

Now that he was in dangerous, lawless country, Jake had decided to wear his revolvers again. Both were strapped on, and his rifle and shotgun rested in their boots at either side of his saddle. He knew better than most that a man couldn't be too careful, especially a wanted man. The poster back at Independence still haunted him, and he had been sure to shave every day since seeing it.

As he approached the trading post, he scanned his surroundings, a man ever alert. A bearded, dirty-looking, heavyset man stood inside a corral of horses, removing riding gear from one of them. He glanced at Jake and nodded but did not smile. Jake nodded in return, thinking what a pitiful-looking post this was. Two other men sat near an open fire to his left, watching a hunk of beef that was hung over the flames to roast. They, too, looked filthy. All kinds of trash cluttered the area, from broken-down wagons to rusted pans. Chickens clucked and fluttered about the area, and there was a general bad smell about the place.

Jake could not imagine that Jennings had stopped at a place like this, but then if they needed supplies bad enough, they might have. The post consisted of five small buildings, two log and three sod, all with sod roofs. The biggest one had a sign that read Supplies, another read Saloon, and yet another Bath House. Jake supposed the two smallest buildings were living quarters for whomever ran the meager operation. Outside the supply store were stacks of baled hay and sacks of potatoes, as well as a few buffalo skins and some blankets.

About five men, Jake thought. He had seen three outside, figured there were at least a couple more inside the buildings. There were no wagon trains or visible travelers present at the moment. In the distance a small herd of cattle grazed. He rode closer to the supply store, glad to see there were no wanted posters tacked up anywhere. He started to dismount when he spotted something familiar sitting outside the small sod house next to the supply post. It was a trunk, a gold trunk with brass trim and a faded flower design painted on the top. His heartbeat quickened and he rode a little closer, studying the trunk thoughtfully, searching his memory. He had seen that trunk before, in Randy's bedroom!

Surely this was just coincidence. What on earth would Randy's trunk be doing here? Maybe it just happened to look the same. Maybe there were a lot of trunks like this one, with the same gold background and brass trim, the same faded flower design on the lid. Still, they wouldn't all have the same gouge in the front. For some reason he had remembered that long dent in the front of Randy's trunk. No two trunks could have exactly the same damage.

What the hell was going on here? He told himself to be careful. Something smelled here, and it was more than the chickens. His dark eyes moved then to a bearded man who came out of the small house, carrying a pitcher of water. Jake was instantly wary. He had long ago learned to read a man by his eyes. That was why he was still alive and free, why he never lost when a man drew on him, why he seldom lost at poker. A man's eyes could tell a lot, and this man was hiding something. The man hastily closed the door, and Jake did not miss the quick look of worry and guilt on his face.

"Hello there! Can I help you with something?" the man asked, putting on a smile.

Jake glanced at the trunk again. If it was Miranda's, how had it gotten here? Where were the Jennings wagons? "Just need some supplies."

"Well, then come on over to my store and I'll fix you up." The man was stocky and looked dirty like the others. He scratched at a beard and then smoothed back his greasy hair as he headed toward the building next door, seeming to Jake to be much too eager to get him away from the sod house. "This whole post is my own setup," the man bragged. "I do pretty good here."

The man was grinning too much, as far as Jake was concerned. Jake led Outlaw to a hitching post and dismounted, tying the horse. The packhorse, already tied to Outlaw's saddle, halted wearily behind.

"Name's Nemus, Jack Nemus," the owner was telling him.

Jake studied the man as he came closer, wondering when he had washed last. He wore soiled cotton pants, and long johns instead of a shirt. There were sweat stains under the arms of the underwear, and some of the buttons were undone, revealing thick chest hair. He put out his hand to Jake, looking him over and appearing a little awed by Jake's height and size.

"Well, now, you're a pretty big man. Hope you ain't lookin' for clothes!" The man laughed, and Jake studied teeth stained brown from too much chewing tobacco. He shook the man's hand, forcing himself to be friendly. He put on a smile.

"Just food and such, tobacco."

"Well, we have plenty of that. Come on in! What's your name, anyway?"

Jake followed the man inside. "Jake Turner," he answered, deciding to stick to his new name.

"Well, Jake, you wear those guns like you know how to use them." The man walked behind a counter and laughed nervously. "'Course, it makes no difference to me why you wear them. Men come through here from all walks of life, I don't ask questions. I just sell them what they need and mind my own business."

"Sounds like a good idea," Jake answered. He looked around inside the stuffy building, seeing no wanted posters there either. He picked up a can of tobacco and set it on the counter, telling himself to stay alert. There were two more men inside the post, probably friends of Nemus. *That makes six,* he told himself. "Actually, I'm looking for some travelers," he said aloud, "friends of mine that I'm trying to catch up with. They're a preacher-family, name of Jennings." Again he spotted the quick look of guilt and worry in Nemus's eyes, a look he quickly covered with one of curious thought. "They're traveling with a trader named Hap Dearing. Did they pass through here?"

Nemus rubbed his chin. "Well, let me think. I don't always pay attention to names, you know. But some preacher-family did pass through here, four, five days ago. I couldn't tell you their name was Jennings, but I do remember the trader they traveled with, and it seems his name was Dearing. He had three big wagons loaded down with supplies for Virginia City."

Jake picked out a box of thin cigars. "That's the one. Four or five days, you say?"

"Yes. You just might be able to catch up with them, since you're traveling with just horses. That bunch has wagons, and those supply wagons especially won't be moving too fast. I pity them when they get to the mountains."

Jake turned to take inventory of where the other two men were standing. He looked back at Nemus, who was re-arranging some items under the counter that Jake figured didn't need rearranging. He had a feeling the man was nervously trying to keep busy, wanted to keep from having to look directly at Jake.

"How about flour, sugar?" Nemus was asking. "I know anyone traveling who stops by here around noon like you have are usually in a hurry to get in some more miles before sunset. I'll get your supplies together right fast. Just tell me what you need."

Jake moved to a wall of shelves where boxes of ammunition were kept, turning so that he could see all three men. "You seem in a big hurry to get me out of here, Nemus," he told the trader.

He watched the other two men straighten to an alert position. Nemus himself slowly lowered his hand from where he had reached up to take down a sack of flour. The man turned to face Jake. Again came the nervous smile. "Well, it's like I said. Most travelers this time of day are in a hurry. I'm just trying to get you what you need, Mr. Turner. Hell, if you want to stay and rest a while, that's fine too. The men outside are cooking up a hind quarter of beef. You're welcome to stay and eat with us."

Jake eyed all three of them, taking a cheroot from his shirt pocket and lighting it. He smoked quietly for a moment. "There's one lady in particular I'm looking for," he finally spoke up. "A widow woman, named Miranda Hayes." Again Nemus looked away. The other two men glanced at each other, and Jake knew something was terribly wrong. Was Randy here? Why? And why were these men hiding her? "Any of you remember if she was with the Jennings group?"

One of the other two men cleared his throat. "Don't rightly remember, mister."

Jake studied the man a moment, taking a drag on the cheroot. "Oh, I think you'd remember. Men out in a lonely place like this don't soon forget a single woman as pretty as this one."

"Lots of women come through here, single and married," Nemus put in, his friendly, nervous attitude now changing to one of hostility. "Hell, hundreds of people come through here, probably thousands. How are we supposed to remember one in particular?"

"You remembered the Jennings party. If you remembered them, you'd remember Mrs. Hayes." Jake kept the cheroot between his teeth, and a look of dark fury came into his eyes. "You were right, Nemus. I *do* know how to use these guns," he said, his voice low and threatening. "And believe me, you don't want to test me out. Why don't you just tell me the truth about what you know about Mrs. Hayes?" All three men eyed each other, none of them looking willing to talk. Jake threw down the cheroot, stepping it out. "One of you is going to get his goddamn kneecaps shot out if somebody doesn't tell me what the hell is going on here," he seethed. "That's Mrs. Hayes's trunk sitting out there by that sod hut, isn't it?"

"She's dead," Nemus spoke up quickly. "She got snakebit, and Jennings didn't know what to do with her. They left her off here and we tried to help her, but she died on us."

The first words brought a wrenching pain to Jake's chest, and it felt like knives were moving through his blood. Dead! Why did it bother him so to think that could be true? He had known Randy for such a little while.

The thought stabbed at him only for a moment. Something in Nemus's eyes and the quick way he had answered told him the man was lying. He *had* to be lying! For some reason he felt like he didn't even want to live himself if Randy was really dead. "Show me the grave," he told Nemus.

Before any of the three men could even blink, Jake had drawn one of his revolvers and was aiming it at Nemus. The movement had been sleek and instant, the click of the gun as he cocked it, the determined look in his eyes . . . it gave all three men the shivers. He moved his arm to point the gun at the other two men.

"Wait a minute," one of them spoke up, backing away. "I don't want no part of this, Nemus. I ain't dyin' for no woman just because you want to keep her for yourself!"

"Shut up, Stanton!"

"She's over in Nemus's shack next door," the one called Stanton told Jake. "She really did get snakebit, and she's awful sick. Nemus, he's been takin' care of her."

Jake held the gun steady, moving it back to Nemus. "I'll just bet you have. What have you done to her, Nemus?"

The man's eyes widened, and he swallowed. "Nothin'! All I've done is keep her cooled down. You know the fever a person gets when they're snakebit. She's lucky she's even alive. Hell, I offered to take care of her. Those people she was with just wanted to dump her off like a sick animal. I . . . I helped her. What's she to you, anyway?"

"She's my woman," Jake answered without even thinking. The words had come out so easily that he was hardly aware of what he had said.

"Then what's she doin' travelin' with somebody else?"

"That's my business. You take me next door."

Nemus looked helplessly at the other two men, who both put up their hands. "We don't want nothin' to do with this, Turner," they told Jake.

"You bastards," Nemus growled. "You wanted to keep her around as much as I did. You did your share of lookin'!"

Jake felt such rage he wondered if his head would explode. Looking? Had they all taken advantage of Randy's condition to ogle her naked body? What else had they done?

"We never touched her though," one of them protested to Jake. "Honest to God, mister."

Jake backed to the doorway. "Let's go, Nemus." When the man hesitated, Jake fired, the bullet skimming across Nemus's cheek.

Nemus cried out and jolted back against some shelves. Several sacks of flour fell, one landing on his head and spilling white powder through his hair and over his face. "Jesus Christ!" the man swore as he got to his feet. He coughed and brushed flour from himself, then grabbed a rag and pressed it to his bleeding face. "What the hell is wrong with you, Turner! You could have killed me!"

"That's right," Jake warned, still pointing the gun. "I *could* have. You give me any trouble and the next one goes right between your eyes! Now let's go next door, and I'll decide whether or not you live or die!"

"Shit," one of the others whispered. Both men backed farther away. Nemus came out from behind the counter, his hair still full of flour. "You're a goddamn crazy man," he grumbled, leading Jake outside. Others were heading toward the post, and Nemus shouted to them. "Stay back! This sonof-abitch will kill me if you make trouble!"

Jake turned his gun on them, watching them carefully as he followed Nemus next door. "All of you stay out of this and mind your own business and you'll live," he told them. "I've got no quarrel with you."

Only one of them was armed. Jake looked back at Nemus, but his side vision did not miss the armed man's movement as he went for his gun. Instantly Jake turned and fired before the man had a chance to pull his own weapon. The loud crack of his gun made Nemus jump with fright, thinking at first he must have been plugged in the back. Jake's victim made no sound as his body lurched backward. A hole in his chest spurted blood for a few seconds, before his body stopped twitching.

"I'm gettin' out of here," one of the others yelled. He turned and ran for his horse. The two men from inside the trading post hurried over to see to the one who had been shot, and Jake followed Nemus into the sod hut. He immediately curled his nose at the smell of smoke and filth and urine, and he felt as though someone were tearing his heart from his chest when he heard a whimpering sound come from a small cot in the corner.

He herded Nemus to a chair, making the man sit down and remove a rawhide string belt from his pants. Jake used the belt to tie the man's wrists tightly behind him and to one of the back rungs of the chair. The towel Nemus had held to his wounded cheek fell to the floor. "I'll bleed to death," the man protested.

"You break my heart," Jake answered, jerking the rawhide as tightly as possible. He holstered his revolver then and went to the cot, bending over Miranda, drawing in his breath in a gasp at the sight of her. If not for the honey-blond hair, he would hardly know it was her. Even the hair looked different, it was so stringy from sweat and filth.

"Randy?" She whispered something, but he couldn't understand her. A tear slipped out of one eye, and he wiped at it gently. "It's me, Jake. I'm right here, and I won't leave you."

"Jake?" she whimpered. She opened her eyes, but he had a feeling she couldn't really see him. Her tears came harder then. "It's . . . not true. Leave me . . . alone . . . don't . . . touch me."

Jake frowned, pulling the blanket away from her to see that the cot was soiled and she was naked. She had urinated, and Nemus had not cleaned her up. "No," she whimpered. "Please . . . don't . . ."

In all the horror he had seen his father inflict on others, Jake had never known such fury, except the incident between his father and Santana. There was no damn reason for her to be lying here naked other than to allow Nemus and the others to get a good look at her whenever they wanted, probably more than a look. He spotted dirty fingerprints around her breasts, and his anger was so intense that he thought he might black out. He covered her again and pulled the blanket away from her feet to see that her left foot was badly swollen and discolored. A cut in the form of an X was scabbed over, and he could still see fang marks near the cut. He touched the foot lightly, and Miranda groaned and shuddered.

Jake looked at Nemus and the fury in his eyes made the man begin to sweat. "Who lanced the bite?"

"One of them traders with Jennings. He sucked out the venom, enough that she lived, anyway."

"It's infected. Have you done anything to try to stop the infection?"

The man shrugged, blood still running down his jaw and neck from where Jake's bullet had grazed him. "What the hell can you do?"

Jake left her and walked over to Nemus, whipping out his revolver and setting it against the man's throat. "You sonofabitch! There's *plenty* you could do! But all you found time for was giving her a good *feel*! What the hell else did you do, Nemus!"

The man swallowed and trembled. "N . . . n . . . nothin'. I swear. I ain't that bad, mister. But, hell, she was burnin' up with fever. I had to get her clothes off, don't you know?"

Jake stood up. Unable to control his rage a moment longer, he brought the barrel of the gun down hard across the unwounded side of the Nemus's face, opening another deep gash. Nemus's body tumbled backward from the blow, chair and all, and the man cried out when the back of the chair smashed into his arms. The awkward position made the fall even more painful.

"Goddamn it, untie me, Turner! Let me up from here!"

Jake cocked his gun and placed the end of the barrel against the man's ear. "You're fucking lucky I don't blow your brains out, Nemus, but I can promise you I *will* if that woman dies! I'm taking her out of here and I'm going to try to save her. If she dies on me, I'll be coming *back*! You can *bet* on it! I've killed enough men that it won't bother me in the least to let you die slowly, the way you're letting that poor woman die!" He raised a booted foot and brought it down hard between Nemus's legs. The man screamed, but because he was tied to the chair he could do little to help his position or find any comfort.

Jake moved to a window to check on the other three men. They stood just outside the cabin with rifles in their hands. He broke out a window and cocked his revolver. "Put those guns down or they'll just go down with you when you fall from my bullets," he warned. "One of you has already died. Why add any more to the list?"

"What did you do to Jack?" one of them asked.

"He'll live. The rest of you get me that buckboard over there by the corral. Hitch it up to my two horses and put all the supplies from the horses into the wagon, along with Mrs. Hayes's trunk. Who owns the wagon and harness?"

They looked at each other. One started to raise his rifle, and Jake fired. The man grunted and fell, a hole in his head. Before he hit the ground and before the other two could react, Jake had fired again, deliberately grazing the arm of the second man, just enough to frighten him but not do much damage. The man yelled and dropped his rifle, grabbing his arm.

"Don't either of you move!" Jake commanded, "or you're dead! Now drop that other rifle," he ordered the third man. "I don't aim to kill either of you if you do what I say. Now, I asked you a minute ago who owns that wagon out there?"

"Nemus owns the wagon," the wounded one answered.

"Good. In that case I don't have to pay for it. If he gets out of this with nothing more than a good beating and sacrificing a wagon, he'll goddamn lucky! Now go hitch my horses to the wagon like I said in the first place!" He left the window and quickly went to the door, opening it and stepping out, still pointing the revolver. "Do what I ask and you'll live. Get going!"

The one called Stanton hesitated. "Who the hell are you, mister? Really?"

"None of your damn business. Just get that wagon ready!"

The two men turned and walked toward the wagon, and Jake closed the cabin door. He hurried back to Miranda. Nemus lay groaning, now on his side, the chair still braced to his back with his arms wrapped behind it. Jake paid him no attention as he leaned over Miranda again. "Randy? Don't be afraid. I'm taking you out of here. Everything is going to be all right."

"Hurts bad," she wept. "Please don't . . . touch me again. Let me . . . die."

He grasped her face, pressing his big hands to either side of it reassuringly. "Randy, it's Jake. Nobody is going to touch you like that again. Do you hear me? It's Jake." She was so hot that the palms of his hands were wet within seconds after touching her. He wondered if she was beyond saving, wondered how he was going to live with himself if she died, knowing none of this might have happened if he had come with her when she asked. One thing was certain: If she died, Jack Nemus and the two men outside would also have to die. Then he would find Jennings and make the reverend pay for abandoning her. Maybe then he would just let himself be caught and hanged. There wouldn't be anything left to live for anyway.

In her own delirium, Miranda struggled to think straight. She was so sick. She had never known such pain. She was aware that strange men had been taking care of her, if it could be called that. She had vague, foggy memories of being naked, of men leering at her, touching her in private places. Her foot and leg hurt so bad, but no one seemed to be doing anything about it. She was sure she was dying and wondered why God didn't let it happen quickly. The way she felt was certainly much worse than death. How she would welcome the blessed release if death claimed her.

Hot, so hot, so much pain. The slightest movement sent excruciating agony from her foot through her whole body. She could remember the sound of the rattlesnake, remember the feel of the bite. She had cloudy memories of the Jenningses leaving her somewhere, with some man who said he would take care of her. She groaned at the memory of the man taking off her clothes, rubbing his hands over her body. She had begged him to stop touching her, to help her somehow. She had even asked him once to kill her.

Now here was a man close to her saying he was Jake. Jake Harkner? That wasn't possible. Surely she was hallucinating, probably on the brink of death. She hated the thought of dying alone out here where no one knew her. Would the wolves dig up her grave and eat her flesh? Would Wesley ever know what had happened to her? And Jake. He would never know either. Oh, the pain, the awful pain.

Someone was wrapping the blanket tighter around her now, picking her up. Oh, it hurt so much to be moved! She screamed in protest, and again came the familiar voice. "It's going to be all right, Randy. I'm taking you out of here and I'm going to help you." She rested her head against a strong shoulder, opened her eyes to see traces of a scar on his neck, another small scar on his left jaw. Jake? It couldn't be. If only she could think more clearly. Right now all she could think about was the awful pain. She wanted to talk, but all she could do was cry with the pain, cry in desolation. She had promised herself she would not cry over being left alone, but the pain was too much, especially when strange men were touching her, looking at her. Where was her Winchester? If she could just find her rifle, or her pistol, she could shoot them and make them stop touching her.

Someone was laying her down again. Was that bright sunshine? Fresh air? It smelled good. She had smelled nothing but sweat and urine for days. "Hang on a little longer, Randy," someone was telling her. It was a familiar voice. Jake? No, she told herself again, it couldn't be. She heard a horse whinny, tried to determine where she was, whether or not she was in a bed. She felt movement then, was vaguely aware she must be in a wagon, going somewhere. But where? Was she being taken out for burial? Was this what it was like to be dead? Surely not. Surely with death the pain would go away, but it hurt worse than ever because she was being moved around.

Everything after that happened as though in a strange dream. She had no conception of time, how long she rode in the wagon, where she was when someone lifted her down and laid her on soft blankets in green grass. She felt a light breeze. Someone drew her hair back and tied it at her neck, away from her face. "We'll wash your hair later," a man's voice said.

She slipped into a restless sleep. For how long she wasn't sure, but when she awoke she was vaguely aware of a fire nearby. She felt herself being bathed then, gloried in the feel of the warm, wet rag, the smell of soap. It felt so good to be clean, and for some reason she didn't mind that whoever was washing her saw her nakedness. Why didn't it matter? He was so gentle. He slipped something over her head . . . a gown! Finally she had something to cover herself. She reveled in the feel of the soft flannel.

"I've got to reopen the wound, Randy," the man told her. "It's going to hurt worse than anything you've ever known, but I've got to drain the infection and get something on it to help it heal, or you're going to lose your foot. I'll try to find some of your pa's laudanum to help kill the pain." He was leaning close now. "I'm sorry, Randy. It's all I can do. I hate like hell to bring you even more pain."

She opened her eyes, finally able to focus them a little. Jake? It looked like his face, but it seemed too impossible. He had ridden off over a week before she had even left Kansas City. How could he be here? "Jake?" she whispered. "Is it really you?"

"It's me. You're going to be all right, Randy. I won't leave you for a minute now until I get you to Nevada."

She stared at him, trying to believe he was real.

"I'd like to find that sonofabitch Preacher Jennings and blow him away for what he did, leaving you alone with those bastards at that trading post!"

Jake! Such language! She almost felt like laughing. Who else would talk like that? And it was his face she saw hovering over her, his dark, handsome, familiar face. Fever and tears mixed with joy overwhelmed her. She said his name over and over, trying to convince herself she was not dreaming. He drew her into his arms and she sat up slightly and wrapped her own around his neck. Somehow he had found her, but how? And why? It didn't matter for now. It only mattered that he was here. Jake Harkner had found her and he said he'd take her to Nevada.

"Don't let them touch me again," she sobbed. "Those men . . ."

"Hush, Randy. They won't touch you again. You have my word."

His cheek was resting against her own, and it was comforting. "It hurts so bad, Jake. I've never known . . . such pain."

"I know. Once I drain it, it's going to feel a lot better."

She wished she could stop crying, but everything seemed to hit her at once, her desperate fear of being left alone with the strange, rude men; the false accusations; the abandonment; her horror of being snakebit and the unbearable pain that followed; the thought that she would surely die alone on the prairie with no one who cared to pray over her grave. Most of all, the thought that she would never see Jake Harkner again. "I love you, Jake," she sobbed, unable to control her emotions in her weakness. "Don't let go. Don't ever let go!"

He held her a moment longer, saying nothing at first. He pulled her arms away then and made her lie back down. "You don't know what you're saying," he told her. "You're just sick and all mixed up right now, but that's okay. In a few days you'll be back to your old self."

Jake rose, turning away and breathing deeply, removing

his hat and running a hand through his hair. "Jesus," he muttered. Would she misinterpret the reason he had come to find her? All he wanted to do was repay her kindness by helping her get to Nevada. There was nothing more to it than that . . . or was there?

She couldn't have meant what she just said. She was just delirious, that's all. She would probably forget all about it when she was better, probably be horribly embarrassed, if she did remember. Women like Randy didn't love men like himself. It was then he remembered what he had shouted to Jack Nemus. *She's my woman,* he had told the man. The words had come out so easily and felt so right.

He shook away the unfamiliar emotions this woman stirred in him. First things first. She could die on him and there would be no more need to think about these feelings. There would only be a strange, unbearable emptiness in his life. He climbed into the wagon and searched through her trunk to find her father's medical bag. Inside were three small bottles of laudanum. He also found a small surgical knife that he knew would cut better than his own pocketknife.

He closed his eyes, breathing deeply. "God, let me do this right," he said quietly. "And don't let her die." He climbed down, bag in hand, not even thinking about the fact that he had said a prayer for the first time since he was a little boy and used to pray with his mother.

CHAPTER NINE

 Jake sat back and watched Miranda sleep, hoping she really was finally experiencing a peaceful sleep and not passed out again. He would not soon forget her screams of agony when he recut her wound and forced out the infection, and he had no idea if he had done any of it right. That had been yesterday afternoon, and she had tossed in fever and delirium since. The laudanum had done little to help deaden her feeling, and he figured it was because the wound was just too badly infected. Early this afternoon her fever had finally broken, and she seemed to be resting at last.

He leaned over the fire and lit a small stick, holding it up to a cheroot held between his lips. He lit the smoke and rested back against his saddle again, smoking quietly. Dusk was settling into darkness, and it was cool tonight. He studied Miranda's pale skin in the firelight, the fine lines of her small face. He wondered if she would remember his holding her, bathing her; and he wondered how he was supposed to forget the look of her, the beautiful, firm breasts he had been so careful not to touch with anything but the washrag, the flat stomach and slender thighs, the golden hairs that hid that sweet part of woman he had not enjoyed in a long time. For now it was not so hard to see and touch her without having thoughts of passion and desire; but what about when she got well?

He sighed, knowing what was happening to him and wanting to kick himself for it. These feelings were exactly what he had been afraid of, yet he had let himself go looking for her, fool that he was. Now he would have to fight his emotions all the way to Nevada, for he did not intend to bring the pain and sorrow into her life that any good woman would suffer hooking up with a man like him. No. He would simply get her to Nevada. That was what he had felt obligated to do. After that, he could get rid of the guilt and get on with his life, and she with hers. Maybe her brother had a place to live up there and she could have a home again.

Her eyes fluttered open then, and he watched her a moment, trying to determine if she was really alert or still in a daze. "Randy?"

She just stared at him at first, letting the reality set in. "Jake," she whispered. "It really has . . . been you," she added in a somewhat stronger voice. "I thought maybe . . . these past hours . . . days . . . I don't even know how long it's been. I thought it was . . . all in my mind."

He picked up another blanket and came closer to put it over her, touching her cheek with the back of his hand. "I found you yesterday at that trading post. I took you out of there and I lanced your wound to get the infection out."

Her eyes teared. "Those men . . ."

"I don't want you to think about them. Two of them are dead, and a couple more are *wishing* they were dead."

"What did you do . . ."

"Doesn't matter." He took hold of her hand, the cheroot still between his lips. "What matters right now is how that foot feels. I'd like you to try to eat something."

How good his strong hand felt around her own small one. Jake was here! She could hardly believe her eyes. An outlaw, a wanted man, was looking after her. How odd that she felt safer with him than she had among the Jenningses or the men at the fort. The men at the fort. She shuddered at the vague memories, and Jake squeezed her hand.

"What did those men do to me?"

He rubbed a thumb over the back of her hand. "Nothing, at least not the worst. You've got nothing to be ashamed of, Randy. You were sick and they were filthy bastards who are wishing they would have taken better care of you. I think I'm more angry with the sons of bitches who left you behind in the first place. What the hell kind of so-called Christians were you traveling with, anyway?"

She sniffed back more tears at the hurt. "The reverend's nephew . . . Clarence. He was eighteen. He kept . . . bothering me . . . got mad when I told him to . . . leave me alone . . . thought because I was a widow . . ." She closed her eyes. "He did his best . . . to make me look bad. The reverend and . . . his wife thought . . . I was a bad influence. When I got . . . the snakebite, it just gave them an excuse . . . to leave me behind . . . said I'd slow them down."

Jake let out a sigh of disgust. "They'd better hope I never catch up with them. Hell, even *I* wouldn't do a thing like that!"

Miranda looked at him through tears, thinking how handsome he looked in the firelight, the cheroot between his lips. Some might think he looked dangerous, but she knew better. *No, you wouldn't do that, would you, Jake?* "I don't . . . understand . . . how you found me. Or why."

He sat down cross-legged beside her, wondering if she remembered what she had told him yesterday when he had held her. He hoped she did not, that it wasn't even true. She shouldn't love him. She was much too good for the likes of Jake Harkner. "I don't understand the why myself," he said aloud, "except that I felt like a bastard for not going with you like you asked. I kept thinking how guilty I'd feel if something happened to you. As it turns out, it's a damn good thing I did try to find you. As far as how, I just went to Independence and started asking around, rode poor Outlaw and my packhorse nearly into the ground trying to catch up. I just happened to stop at that trading post, spotted your trunk. I knew then something was wrong."

"My trunk! I . . . need it."

"I've got it. I kind of borrowed a wagon from the owner of that trading post. Figured he owed you that much. You couldn't very well ride. Between that foot and wanting to bring your trunk, I needed a wagon."

Miranda smiled weakly. "I never thought . . . I'd see you again. I prayed for you . . . every day . . . thought about you . . . so many times, especially when I got scared. I wondered . . . if you were thinking about me too . . . worried if you were all right." Her eyes teared anew. "I wanted so much . . . to see you again. It just . . . didn't seem right . . . the way you left. And now . . . here you are . . . helping me get to Nevada. You see? You *do* have some good in you."

He grinned and moved away, setting a fry-pan on the fire. "Don't be putting labels like that on me. I just figured I still owed you, that's all." He took some potatoes from his supplies.

You don't fool me, Jake Harkner, she thought. "You took a chance, going . . . to Independence like that."

He shrugged. "I did like you said, stayed cleaned up, kept my guns off. People thought I was just an ordinary citizen. I found that Reverend Bishop and told him I was an old friend of the family. He told me about you traveling with the Jennings party." He looked back at her. "You never answered me about how you feel. Can you eat a little? It would be the best thing for you. You need to get your strength back."

"I'll try." She moved slightly and realized her foot and lower leg were tightly wrapped. The pain was not nearly as bad as it had been for the last several, horrible days. "My foot feels much better." She laid back, feeling under the blankets. She remembered someone bathing her, putting on her flannel gown. Jake? She felt a cloth wrapped between her legs, and embarrassment took over. She was grateful that at least it was dry. She tried to get up then to relieve herself, but could hardly get to a sitting position without feeling faint. In an instant Jake was at her side.

"What the hell are you doing?"

"I have to go . . . relieve myself."

"You can't even walk." He picked her up in strong arms and carried her several feet away out of the firelight. "When I put you down, don't put any pressure on that left foot. I'll raise your gown and keep hold of you when you squat. You don't have to support yourself at all. Let me do it. Can you get that towel off you?"

He kept one powerful arm firmly supportive around her middle under her breasts and lifted her gown with his left hand. Miranda wanted to die of embarrassment. "I can't! I can't do this with you here." She started to cry.

"Bullshit! I can't see a damn thing just leaving the firelight like that. It's black as tar tonight. Hell, you're sick, Randy, and I've already seen everything there is to see, so just go. Hell, it's better than having to clean up after you."

She removed the towel, sniffing back tears, realizing he was right. She couldn't do this alone, and the need was too great to hold back. She forced herself to think about something else for the moment, wondering if there was any way she would be able to cure Jake Harkner of his constant cursing by the time they reached Nevada. Nevada. Jake was taking her. He had promised. She was sure she had heard him promise. She remembered an embrace, suddenly remembered she had told him she loved him. She couldn't remember hearing him reply, wondered if he just thought she had said it in delirium. She clung to the strong arm that held her. "Do you . . . have paper?" she asked, brushing away tears.

"Yeah, but I can't let go of you to get it. Use the towel. Hell, it's just water. I can wash the towel out in the river. Leave it right here and I'll pick it up in the morning."

Miranda cleaned herself and Jake let go of the gown and picked her up again, carrying her back to the fire. She clung to him, weeping against his chest. "I'm sorry," she told him. "When I asked you . . . to take me to Nevada . . . I didn't mean . . . to be such a burden."

"You didn't ask to get snakebit, either, and if I had come along in the first place, none of this would have happened. Don't worry about it." He started to set her down, but again she clung to his neck, almost like a child. He thought about all the times when he was a little boy when he would have welcomed someone's strong arms to hold him and tell him everything was all right, that he would be protected and safe.

He sat down himself then, keeping her in his arms. "Randy, I don't want you to be embarrassed or afraid or sorry, all right? It isn't like you to cry, and I know it's just because of what you've been through and because you're so sick." He stroked her hair. "In a few days you'll feel a lot better and doing everything on your own. Hell, I've seen it all and done it all. Don't be embarrassed to let me help you."

"I still can't believe you're here," she sobbed, clinging to his shirt. "You meant it, didn't you, about taking me to Nevada?"

"I meant it."

"I won't be afraid at all if I'm with you."

You're getting in way too deep, Jake Harkner, he told himself. Jake looked into her blue-gray eyes, his heart aching at the gaunt look of her too-thin face, the tears on her cheeks. He gently wiped at them with his fingers. "I told you I meant it about getting you to Nevada," he repeated. "Just don't cry, Randy. I can't stand to hear a woman crying."

She forced a weak smile through her tears. "I'm trying to stop," she told him. "I just hate to cry. Did you ever . . . feel like there was so much . . . to cry about that you might as well . . . not bother crying at all?"

He grinned. "Most of my life."

She saw the sadness behind the smile. Yes, he did know what she meant. Who would understand better than a man who had been through what he had? She wanted to tell him again that she loved him, but she suspected that if she did, now that she was fully awake, his mood just might change on her again, as had happened so often back at the cabin. The old defenses would rise, and the spell would be broken.

As though he read her thoughts, he suddenly scooted her back into her own bedroll. "I'd better get those potatoes cooking," he said, quickly turning away.

No, Jake, she thought. *You aren't ready to hear those three words. Not yet.* A woman had to be careful with a man like Jake, but then it was a long way to Nevada. For now she just had to be grateful he had found her at all. Again fate had brought them together, as though it was all meant to be. Maybe Jake didn't realize that yet, but she did. God was moving to change Jake Harkner's life, and she was all part of His plan.

The next month was spent following the regular route west, easy to identify from twenty-five years of emigration to California and Oregon, from discarded debris and old campsites. The horizon seemed endless, and never had Miranda felt so insignificant, a tiny moving dot on the vast, open plains. Her foot slowly healed to the point where she could wear a shoe again and could dress and ride up front in the wagon seat. Although she still limped a little, it felt good to be so close to normal again.

With Jake at her side she felt stronger and surer than ever, safe and protected. He had stopped at a fort and purchased two oxen, since Outlaw and his packhorse were really not meant to be wagon horses. The daily work had been hard on them, and Jake knew they would never make it all the way to Nevada. Miranda grinned at the memory of an experienced driver at the fort showing Jake how to guide oxen. With oxen, a man had to walk beside them, goading them along with a switch. She supposed Jake had never dreamed he would be doing such a thing, and it warmed her heart that he was grudgingly trudging along like some common settler just to get her to Nevada. On horseback, he could be much farther ahead by now, but he did not complain.

She wondered if he ever wished it was true that she was his wife. That was what he had told the men at the fort, and the group of prospectors who had passed them on horseback yesterday. He did it to protect her, knowing what most men would think about a single woman traveling alone with a man.

That man had been as respectful as he could be, other than his cussing. Miranda thought how, if they could never be anything else, they were certainly good friends by now. Jake was learning to trust her, learning not to be so defensive, learning to laugh. He was always looking out for her, had even had a wheelwright and blacksmith at the fort work together to make some curved iron bars that could be bolted to the wagon so that it could be covered with canvas to keep everything inside dry in case of rain. He had taken a great risk staying around the fort as long as they had, considering the fact that soldiers were there, men who would have arrested him in a moment if they knew who he really was. He wore just one of his revolvers at his side, kept his rifle and shotgun, as well as her own rifle and his spare revolver, under the wagon seat.

The days were spent covering as many miles as humans and animals could stand, and so far there had been no major mishaps. Jake preferred not to hitch up with a bigger wagon train. He felt they could make better time on their own and he didn't want to take the risk of being recognized. Once they reached Nevada, he figured there wasn't much chance anyone would know who he was. In the meantime, he was sticking to the name Jake Turner.

Miranda didn't mind the two of them traveling alone. She reasoned she should be missing the company of other women, should be afraid with just one man for protection; but she found she enjoyed just being with Jake, and she trusted in his skills and his unique survival experience to keep them safe. She had never been happier, and she knew she was in love, whether Jake Harkner realized it or not. Nothing had been said about it, and she knew Jake was doing everything he could to avoid the subject, pretending he was just taking her to Nevada because he "owed her"; but she had not missed the hint of pride and possessiveness in his voice when he had told other men she was his wife, and she was sure it was not all an act. Did he really think he could take her to her destination and then just leave her there and go on alone?

"Storm's coming," he called out then.

"I see it," she answered. She watched the dark clouds billowing toward them from the western horizon. So far they had been blessed with beautiful weather, but men at the fort had warned them how fast a storm could sweep over the plains, and now she realized they were right. She had never seen clouds move so fast.

"Get under the canvas!" Jake shouted. He headed the oxen into a gully just ahead, where the wagon and animals could drop down just enough to at least be more sheltered from the suddenly cold wind that began whipping at them. Rain joined the wind as Jake hurriedly climbed into the wagon from the front seat. "Close the back flap and I'll get this one," he told Miranda, uncurling the front flap and letting it down. He secured it with rawhide strips at the corners, and wind and rain began pelting the canvas from the outside. "Damn good thing we had this canvas put on back at that fort," he told her, taking a cheroot from his shirt pocket.

"Yes," Miranda answered, moving near him to take her shawl from where it lay on top of her trunk. She wrapped it around her shoulders and shivered, noticing then that his shirt was wet. "You should get out of that wet shirt and put something dry on."

He lit the cheroot and took a drag. "I'm fine." He removed his leather hat and set it on the trunk, then leaned back against a pile of blankets. "Actually, I don't mind an excuse to stop for a while. Hell, it will be dark in another hour anyway. Maybe we'll just camp right here."

He closed his eyes for a moment, and Miranda watched him, realizing this was the first time he had had cause to get into the wagon with her when it was closed. At night she had slept inside with the canvas down, while he slept outside under the wagon. She dressed and undressed inside, he outside. The wagon had been like her own little dwelling, the outdoors had been his. It disturbed her in ways that it shouldn't to have him in the small enclosure with her. His virility seemed to fill the wagon, making her suddenly feel almost uncomfortably aware that he was a man and she was a woman, more aware of how she had not minded being thought of as his wife. For three years now she had buried old needs and desires.

She found it hard to stop looking at him. Because he was

sitting there with his eyes closed, she could study him freely. She liked watching him, liked the square jaw and high cheekbones, the full lips and the shadow of a beard. She liked his thick, dark hair, the way it lay in gentle waves and softly graced the collar of his shirt.

Jake suddenly opened his eyes, and she quickly looked away, feeling her cheeks going hot at being caught staring. Thunder suddenly exploded, and the wagon jerked a little as the restless oxen balked at the storm. "Might be safer if I unhitched them," Jake told her. "If I leave them yoked together, they can't go so far that I couldn't find them again."

"Jake, it's pouring out there!"

"I don't like the thought that they could start dragging this wagon around." He put his cheroot into a tin cup and untied one corner of the canvas, quickly moving outside, glad himself for an excuse to get out of the wagon for a moment. Did she know what it did to him, being confined so close to her, catching her staring at him? She had never mentioned what she had told him that first day he rescued her. Had she forgotten, or was she just afraid to say it again?

Thank God she had let it go. He didn't want to have to tell her she was crazy to love him. He didn't even want to know if it was true. It would hurt too much, because he couldn't possibly return that love. That would mean bringing her into his life, and there was no future there, only danger.

He worked quickly to unhitch the team, then climbed back inside, where Miranda waited with a towel. "Get your shirt off," she told him. "I won't take no for an answer this time. It was blistering hot all day and now it's suddenly almost cold. You'll get sick."

He took the towel and rubbed his wet hair with it. "Damn, what a downpour," he said, trying to position himself so that his boots did not soil anything inside. "Sorry to get your things wet."

"Don't worry about it. Just don't go and get sick on me."

"Hell, I've been a lot wetter than this. I've kept right on traveling on Outlaw in worse weather. Speaking of Outlaw, take a look out back there and make sure the horses are still tied to the wagon."

Miranda looked to see the animals standing in the pouring rain. "They're still there, poor things."

"They'll be all right. A spring rain won't hurt them."

"Well, it's not exactly what could be called a *gentle* spring rain."

Jake grinned. "Agreed." He picked up the cheroot and tried to light it with a match from his shirt pocket, but the match had no spark. "Damn. My matches got wet."

"Here. I have some." Miranda moved near him to open the precious trunk that seemed to carry whatever they needed. Jake began unbuttoning his shirt while she searched for the matches. He wondered at how a woman could look so pretty after riding day after day in a wagon across the hot plains, unable to always bathe the way she would like, or do her hair or wear any color on her lips. He had seen plenty of painted women, shared the bed of many, but this small woman with no makeup and her hair brushed back into a plain tail at the neck, dressed in a light blue calico dress and worn high-button shoes, was the most beautiful he had ever set eyes on.

He got his shirt off and Miranda turned with the matches. She lit one and he leaned forward. She held it for him, and as he drew on the cheroot he met her eyes, eyes that told him things he did not want to hear aloud. God, he wanted her, and that was the hell of it. No, the real hell was knowing by her eyes that she wanted him too. If he were an ordinary man who led an ordinary life, he would pursue that want, and he would know how to love a woman like Miranda Hayes.

He decided he had to find a way to make her stop looking at him the way he had caught her looking at him earlier. There was one thing he could do. It just might make her find him revolting, but then that was probably best. It would be easier if she would look at him with horror or animosity than with that look of loneliness and longing.

"I need a dry shirt," he told her. "My gear is behind you."

Miranda closed the trunk and turned to his saddlebags, taking out a dark blue shirt. "It needs to be pressed," she told him, handing it out.

Jake laughed lightly. "I don't think anybody out here gives a damn."

Miranda watched him pull on the shirt and begin buttoning it. She had seen that broad chest and those muscled arms before, when she had nursed him. Now seeing him barechested gave her a different feeling, stirred in her a terrible lust that almost startled her. She didn't just love Jake Harkner, this outlaw to whom no woman of her morals and values should give a second thought; she also wanted him . . .

physically. She moved into her own corner and picked up another one of his shirts, one that needed mending that she had not been able to finish the night before. "I might as well get this shirt done," she said, jumping slightly again when thunder cracked overhead. "No sense just sitting here wasting time."

Jake put his head back again, closing his eyes and listening to the storm, remembering another storm, one that hit on a night he would never forget. Should he tell her? He knew she was wondering, and what better way to make her hate him than to tell her the truth? The storm only brought it all back more vividly anyway. Thunder clapped again, and he could hear the gun going off at the same time. He could see the look of astonishment on his father's face.

He waited a moment longer, another crash of thunder making him wince and put a hand to his forehead.

"Jake? What's wrong?"

He ran his hand through his hair. "Where's the whiskey I bought back at that fort?" He saw her hesitate, knew what she was thinking. Giving whiskey to an ailing man was one thing, but it was something completely different when given to a perfectly healthy man with a notorious reputation. "Don't worry. I don't react to whiskey like my pa used to," he told her, "although he didn't need alcohol to bring out the worst in him."

Miranda watched him a moment longer, then nodded toward the pile of blankets. "You're leaning against it—in the crate under those blankets."

Jake turned to search, grinning to himself at the realization she must have put it out of sight in hopes he would forget he had it. He removed a flask from the crate and uncorked it, turning back around and taking a swallow. He let it burn its way down his throat and into his stomach. He seldom drank much, hated the memories of what whiskey did to his father, how mean it made him. Still, right now it gave him the added courage he needed to shock Miranda Hayes out of any feelings she might have for him. He did not need or want to talk about this, but if it would take the light out of Miranda Hayes's eyes when she looked at him, it would be worth the telling.

He lowered the bottle, staring at it for a moment, taking another drag on the cheroot. "I killed him," he told her.

Miranda frowned, taking her gaze from her sewing and meeting his eyes. "Killed whom?"

Jake held her eyes, giving her his darkest, meanest look. "My *pa*! I shot him dead. What do you think of that?" To his frustration and amazement, he saw no shock, no animosity, no horror. He saw only a strange sorrow.

"I know," she answered. "I'm sorry, Jake."

He just stared at her a moment, astounded at her reply, suddenly angry with her. "What the hell do you mean, you *know*! And you're *sorry*? I didn't tell you in order to get your damn *pity*!" He let out a nervous laugh. "Jesus, woman, what the hell is the matter with you?"

Miranda put down the sewing. "You expected me to be surprised? After all, that always has been the rumor. After what you told me back at the cabin, I had no doubt it was true. What I'm sorry about is you must have had good cause, which means your father must have been doing something terrible to you or to someone you loved. What did he do, Jake? Does it have something to do with Santana?"

He rolled his eyes and took another swallow of whiskey. "You're incredible, you know that? What the hell kind of a man kills his own pa?"

"A desperate one, and I'm betting he wasn't a man at all. He was probably still a boy, and sometimes that same boy comes charging out of the man, fighting, angry, defending himself, refusing to have feelings because he might hurt again, and he doesn't want to hurt. He's afraid—"

"Shut up!" He wanted her to flinch, but she didn't. Damn her! Damn slip of a woman! "Maybe what I ought to do is show you just how much of a man I *really* am!" he deliberately snarled. He turned and crammed the whiskey back into the crate, then dropped the cheroot back into the tin cup. He began unbuckling his gunbelt.

Miranda truly wondered if she had gone too far this time. The man hated it when someone saw through the outer meanness to his vulnerability. It made him furious, and a furious Jake Harkner might not be as safe as she had supposed. Had she trusted too much?

He tossed the gunbelt aside, and before Miranda could react, he lunged at her and grasped her arms tightly, painfully. Her eyes widened, and she dropped her sewing when he lifted and moved her like a ragdoll, pushing her against the blankets against which he had himself been resting. "I *want* you, Randy Hayes," he snarled. "What do you think of *that*!"

Miranda drew in her breath and faced him boldly. "I think

that whatever you want to do to me, you will. After all, you're stronger than I am. Just don't take me like your father would take a woman, Jake. And don't do it just to try to scare me off, because you can't. I love you, Jake Harkner, and you damn well know it! You'd never hurt me!" Unwanted tears suddenly filled her eyes, and she felt his grip relax. He massaged her arms for a moment.

"Damn you, woman," he said softly then. "How do you know me that well?" He leaned closer, kissed her eyes, licked at her tears, found her mouth and licked at that too. Miranda found that her instinctive response to him was powerful, as though it was always supposed to be this way. She closed her eyes and met his tongue, letting him slake his own between her lips in a kiss more delicious than any kiss Mack had ever given her. Had she just been too young then to fully enjoy a man? Or perhaps she had just been too long without. She only knew this felt more wonderful than anything she had ever experienced.

Jake groaned, and his kiss grew hotter, deeper. He moved his hands behind her, and she felt him pull a few blankets down, let him lay her down on them. Never had she wanted a man like this, with such wantonness, such an agonizing need. She returned his kisses with a fiery passion she had not known she was capable of feeling.

His lips left her mouth for just a moment, moving to her throat while with one hand he pushed up her dress and felt along her thigh, up to the waist of her bloomers.

"Jake," she whispered, wondering if she had spoken his name with desire, or if it was just a feeble attempt at protesting. She felt the bloomers coming off, groaned when strong fingers moved into her intimately, drawing out the moistness that told him she needed and wanted him. He stroked and caressed her in magical, circular movements, his strong fingers much gentler than she thought they could be. It was so easy to let him touch her. She wanted and needed this so badly. There was no room for reasoning, only this burning desire to be a woman again. In seconds she was gasping his name in an intense climax, and somehow both of them knew that this first time was too urgent to even bother fully undressing. This was something they both had known was coming, something they both had been fighting uselessly.

She opened her legs willingly, inviting him to take his pleasure in her. She boldly met his gaze to see a blazing fire in his own dark eyes, a fire that spread through her whole body when he suddenly surged inside of her, filling her to ecstasy. She cried out with the thrill of it, wondering somewhere in the back of her mind how he had so quickly gotten himself undone and inside her. He moved in exotic rhythm, and she found herself moving with him, arching herself up to him, grasping his arms and feeling his hard muscles. She groaned his name over and over, giving herself to him in sweet abandon.

She felt as though she was floating in another world. His big hands covered her bottom, pulled her to him in perfect, exhilarating union. She had seen that most manly part of him, knew he was a man built to give a woman great pleasure. It was even more wonderful than she had dreamed it might be. He surged hard and deep, groaning with every thrust, meeting her mouth again and running his tongue deep as though claiming her mouth as he possessed her body.

He was wild and hard and determined, just the way she knew a man like Jake would be. She wondered why it had been so easy to open herself to him, was surprised at her own boldness. He came down close then, kept one hand under her bottom and gently molded her breast with the other, kissing it through the material of her dress, arousing an ache to be naked so that she could offer him the breast fully, enjoy the feel of him tasting her nipple. Never had she had such lustful, near-sinful thoughts, not even with Mack. Was it because of the kind of man Jake was, dangerous, forbidden?

"God, I love you, Randy," he whispered, kissing her so fiercely it almost hurt. She felt his life surge into her then, and he uttered her name in a kind of whimper, as though in an agony of his own. When he was finished, he lay quietly for several long seconds, his face resting against her breasts.

"My God," he finally muttered. "What the hell have I done?"

Miranda ran her fingers into his thick, dark hair. "Made love to me. That's all. It wasn't something terrible, Jake."

"Wasn't it?" He rolled away from her, pulling down her dress and covering himself with a blanket. "Jesus, I'm sorry, Randy." He put a hand to his eyes. "My God," he repeated. "I'm sorry I talked to you like that. For Christ's sake I half forced you."

She raised up on one elbow and leaned over to touch his face. She kissed his cheek. "You have got to stop cussing, Jake

Harkner." She put her head on his shoulder. "If I had felt forced, I would have fought back and you would have stopped. Don't tell me you wouldn't. You've just never done this before when love was involved. You don't understand what just happened to you, but I know what happened to me, Jake. I let the man that I love be a part of me. Just for tonight let's accept the fact that we want to be together. Let's not worry about how right or wrong it is, or what is going to happen tomorrow or next week or next month. I want you, Jake. It's already dark outside. Why not just stay in here with me tonight? I'm so tired of sleeping alone."

He turned, pressing her shoulders into the blankets and hovering over her, searching the eyes he thought were so pretty, eyes that had cast some kind of spell on him. "I hurt every person who comes into my life, Randy."

She touched his face lightly, tracing her slender fingers over his eyebrows, his nose, his lips, studying the longing in his dark, fiery eyes. "Only because they hurt you first. I'll never hurt you, Jake. We have a good six weeks of travel left, maybe longer, plenty of time to talk. Tonight let's just be together."

He closed his eyes and stretched out beside her, kissing her hair. "I'm no good, Randy. There's no future with a man like me."

She ran a hand inside his shirt and leaned closer to kiss his chest. "We don't know that, yet. And you *are* good, Jake."

He wrapped his fingers into her hair and rolled on top of her. "If I was really good, I would never have let things go this far with you. You mean too much to me, and if you stay with me you're going to suffer, Randy. You'll always be running, always wondering when someone might find out who I am and come gunning for me. Life is hell with me, believe me—"

She touched his lips again. "Tell me you can take me to Nevada now and just leave me there and ride off without me. Can you do that, Jake?" His only reply was to meet her mouth in a savage kiss.

CHAPTER
TEN

 Miranda opened her eyes and stared at the saddle stored in the wagon. Jake's saddle. She lay still, gathering her thoughts, realizing the strong arm that was secured around her from behind belonged to Jake; remembering then a night of heated, sometimes almost violent lovemaking.

Had she really let it all happen, even welcomed it? A dull, yet pleasant ache deep in her belly told her she had, and now she lay here naked, her back snuggled against this man she once thought any decent person should surely hate. She had let Jake Harkner make love to her, not just once, but several times and she had responded. He had tasted and explored and claimed and invaded her, and not once had she felt it was wrong or sinful. Maybe to others it would look that way, but not to her. She had fallen in love with a man who desperately needed to be loved, even if he didn't know it himself.

There was no going back now, no changing what she had let happen, no denying how she felt. She couldn't worry about the future or the past, or about the danger of being an outlaw's woman, for now it was impossible to think of not being at his side. She had never felt more beautiful, more daring, more alive. She moved slightly, grasping his muscled forearm and kissing it.

"So, you *are* awake," he told her, kissing her hair then. "I wasn't sure. I didn't want to move and disturb you."

She smiled with sweet satisfaction, glorying in once more experiencing the ultimate pleasures of being a woman. "Yes, I'm awake," she answered, keeping her back to him. Now that morning light made its way through the canvas, she felt suddenly shy about her nakedness. It had all been so easy in the dark of night. She pulled a blanket farther over herself. "Have you been awake long?"

He sighed, nuzzling her neck. "Maybe a half hour." He smoothed her hair back from her face and leaned forward to kiss her cheek. "Do you know how beautiful you are? I've never seen a woman who could hold a candle to you, except maybe my mother, but she was dark and you're fair." He kissed and licked at her satiny shoulder, gently massaging her breasts as he did so. "Thank you for last night, *mi querida.*"

She smiled. "What does that mean?"

He moved his hand to gently massage her belly then, thinking how small she was, how he had worried last night at times that he might bruise her, or break something if he held her too tightly. Surely he had hurt her when they had intercourse, yet she had taken him with a wild passion he never dreamed she had in her. In his whole life he had never wanted a woman like he had wanted Miranda Hayes, or ever gotten so much pleasure with one.

"Something I've never said to a woman," he answered. "Something I never thought I was capable of saying . . . too mushy for somebody like me." He kissed her shoulder again. "It means 'my darling' in Spanish. My mother used to say it to me and my little brother, but certainly not the way I mean it with you."

Miranda rubbed at his arm. "It's a pretty language. Do you remember much of it?"

"Sure. I just haven't used it in years because it makes me think of her, how good she was. It is a beautiful language, maybe too gentle for a man who raids and kills and has his face on wanted posters all over the state of Missouri."

He reached past her to get something out of one of his saddlebags, and Miranda studied the hard lines of his upper body, still having a little trouble coming to terms with what had happened last night. Why hadn't she stopped him? It had all seemed as natural as breathing. He moved back beside her, leaning down to kiss at her breasts. She closed her eyes and breathed deeply, relishing the ecstasy of letting him lick and taste at her nipples. She had never been this bold with Mack, but Jake had a commanding way of touching her that destroyed all her inhibitions.

"I got us some peppermint," he said then, showing her a pink stick of candy. "I want to kiss you," he told her, "but I don't feel like getting up just yet and looking for the baking soda, so the candy will have to do."

Miranda smiled, watching his dark eyes, thinking how handsome he looked even in the morning when he needed a shave and his hair was a mess. He put one end of the candy in her mouth, put his own mouth over the other end and moved his mouth to her lips. He bit off his end of the candy, and they both sucked on it while their lips brushed.

She felt his hardness, closed her eyes when he entered her again. This time he took her slowly, gently, quietly. She tried to remember how many times he had drawn from her the exhilarating climaxes that left her feeling weak this morning. Little was said between them. They simply enjoyed the quiet morning, the feel of warm bodies touching, the joy of their union. He swallowed the candy and leaned down to taste at her nipple again, enjoying seeing her in the light of morning, thinking how ripe and beautiful she looked. He wanted to see more in the light, wanted to explore other parts of her, taste her again. Maybe they would just stay here all day. He could teach her all the things he knew about pleasuring a woman, show her there was more than one way to enjoy a man.

But then maybe not. Maybe none of this was right. God, he loved her, but what could he really give a woman like Miranda? Only unhappiness. He shuddered when the life flowed out of him once more, tried to remember if he had ever taken another woman this many times in one night.

He relaxed beside her, and Miranda snuggled against him. "You should use your Spanish more often, Jake. I like to hear it. Maybe you can teach me some."

"Maybe." He rubbed her shoulder, thinking how good it had felt to be with someone who really seemed to care. Her response to him had fed a long-buried need, but had any of it been right, or fair to her?

"Randy," he said softly, turning on his side to meet her eyes. "This whole thing." He closed his eyes for a moment, and when he opened them, Miranda saw the pain there. "If last night is all we ever have, I'll have to be satisfied with that, and I'd never blame you one damn bit for deciding it was a mistake."

"Jake—"

He touched her lips with his fingers. "I'm not a man to think any the worse of a woman who has needs. One thing we sure as hell have become is good friends, but considering who I am—" he sighed deeply, "the way you look at me, I don't ever want that to change, and if we take this further, stay together, it will change. I'll see hatred in those eyes, remorse, despair. You know damn well what life with me would be like. If you want to just pretend last night didn't happen and feel like you ought to think twice about hooking up with somebody like me—"

She grasped his hand. "Do you really think I could go on now as though nothing has changed? Do you think I could forget you, Jake? Pretend that I don't love you?" She scooted slightly away from him. "I didn't lie with you just out of some lustful need, Jake. I *wanted* you, not just that way, but *all* of you. I wanted to belong to you, give you pleasure in return, make you happy. I wanted to love you, teach you how to love me in return."

He closed his eyes and turned onto his back, putting an arm over his eyes. "You'd better think real deep on this, Randy."

She lay on her back, staring up at the canvas and pulling the blanket back up to her neck. "I didn't come this far without thinking about it, much more than you know. I know what I want, Jake. I know that I love you."

He let out a kind of hiss. "You've had enough tragedy in your life."

"And so have you!"

"The difference is, there are always going to be men looking for me. I've brought on a lot of my own tragedy."

"No one will know you in Nevada. We could even go all the way to California. You can start over, Jake. I know you want to. You talked about it once. The tragedy in your life— your father brought it on, not you. You've got to let go of the past, Jake."

He sat up, keeping a blanket around his waist. He rummaged through his things to find a cheroot. He lit it, moving then to sit up against the sideboard of the wagon. He smoked in silence for a moment, watching her eyes. "I don't know if I can let go. It eats at me, Randy, like rust slowly eats up metal.

It haunts my dreams at night, brings out the worst in me when I feel threatened, warns me never to allow myself to have feelings."

Miranda turned to her side to face him, supporting her head with one arm. "Maybe if you talked about it, it would help. I have a right to know, Jake. You started to tell me last night."

He glanced at her exposed arm, noticing the bruises on it. "Good God, I left marks on you," he said, disgust in his voice. He stuck the cheroot in his mouth and angrily threw off his blanket. He grabbed his long johns and began pulling them on.

Miranda felt a disturbing heat move through her at the sight of his naked splendor. She wanted him—and she wanted to cry. Again his anger and defense had taken over at the mention of talking about things that hurt.

"I'm sorry about that part of last night," he was saying. He jerked on the underwear and began buttoning it. "I had no right talking to you like that, grabbing and threatening you that way."

"Jake, we have a lot of things to talk about, some decisions to make. We can't do that until you get that anger out of you and open up to me. Please tell me about your father. Talk to me, Jake."

He grabbed his pants and began pulling them on. "The horses have to be tended to. The poor things have been tied to this wagon all night in that rain." He pulled up the back canvas flap and looked out. "At least the sky is blue. I'll get a fire going and heat some water so you can wash and dress." He climbed out of the wagon.

"Jake, wait!" Miranda held a blanket around herself and scooted to the back of the wagon, where he was untying the horses. "You aren't going to shut me out again, Jake Harkner, not after last night! I suppose you think it's all right to get as close to me as you want physically, but that you don't have to share yourself *emotionally*! It doesn't work that way, Jake, not for a woman, anyway. Why don't you just tell me all of it and let me decide what's right for me, who I want to 'hook up' with, as you so eloquently put it! Is that how you think of it, just as 'hooking up'? I *love* you, and you said last night that you loved me. Was it a *lie*, Jake, just to have your way with me?"

"No!" he yelled. He let go of the horses' ropes and let

them wander to graze. "Damn it, woman, it's got nothing to do with whether or not I love you! It's got to do with who I *am,* the things I've done! For Christ's sake, Randy, I'm a wanted man! I have killed and I'll probably kill again! I've robbed trains, stolen guns, robbed banks; I've run with some of the worst, gambled with them, drank with them, slept with their whores, and shot down men just for cheating at cards! I killed my own damn *father*!"

"Why, Jake? *Why* did you kill him?"

"Because," he roared, "he was *raping* her! He was raping Santana! She was my friend, and she was only twelve years old and he was *raping* her!" His eyes suddenly teared, and he turned away. He put his hands on his hips and threw back his head, breathing deeply. "I've got to get a fire started."

Randy let him go, wishing there was some way she could erase the memory, but knowing there was not. She was glad to have gotten this much out of him, knew he would tell her more when he was ready.

For the next hour she said as little to him as possible. She straightened the inside of the wagon, folded the blankets. Jake brought her some hot water, and she washed and dressed. She climbed down from the wagon to see a pan of bacon and beans cooking over the fire, thought how self-sufficient he had learned to be, living on his own over the years. She longed to make a home for him, cook nice meals for him, create a whole new life for him, and with him.

She stirred the food, watching him in the distance rounding up the oxen and goading them back to the wagon, where he hitched them. He told her then he wanted to wash, too, and he climbed into the wagon, emerging several minutes later wearing clean denim pants and the blue shirt he had worn the night before. He carried his Winchester and laid it beside him when he squatted near the fire.

"I'll wait till tomorrow to shave," he told her. "We've lost a lot of time this morning. I was thinking of staying here all day, but that would be foolish. Every day is precious when you've still got mountains to cross." He picked up one of two plates Miranda had set near the fire and he spooned some beans and bacon onto it. "I didn't know what else to fix. We're getting low on food. We can stock up at Fort Laramie. From there maybe we'd better see about joining up with a wagon train or supply train for the rest of the trip. I doubt I'd be recognized way out here, and they say the trip over the Rockies is pretty rough. I don't think we should try it alone. We're lucky we've come this far without Indian trouble. I know a lot of Indians down in Indian Territory, lived with some Cherokee and Osage when I was hiding out sometimes. But these Plains Indians, that's a different matter."

Miranda thought how his talk rambled more than usual for a man normally of few words. He was avoiding the subject they really should be discussing. She scooped up a spoonful of beans for herself, not really very hungry. "There are probably plenty more travelers only a few days behind us." She sat down on an overturned bucket he had set out for a chair.

"Probably." Jake finished eating and set his plate down, pouring himself a cup of stiff coffee heated from the day before. He rose and walked a few feet away. "I told you about my father being a drunk and a wanderer," he said.

Miranda waited, knowing it was wiser to say nothing.

"He was born in Connecticut, did I tell you that? He ran away from home and wandered all the way down to Mexico, ended up with the troops at San Jacinto. It was during that time he bought my mother off a drunken Mexican. I guess I already told you that too. He liked them young. She was only fourteen, fifteen when she had me. As I grew older and began to understand things, I realized it broke her heart never to have been legally married. I know now that her first night with my father must have been nothing more than rape. After that she felt obligated to stay with him, or maybe she was just too damned ashamed and too damned scared of him to try to run away. She used to cry a lot, used to pray with those beads a lot. My pa's name was John Harkner, and he was big like me. My mother was small, like you."

He took another swallow of coffee, then turned, staring at the fire. "From what I told you back at your cabin, you can guess what life was like with my father. Sometimes I think he was just plain crazy, and it scares me to think I could turn out like him, scares me when I lose my temper. I was eight when he killed my mother and my little brother. He beat me for crying about it. By the time I was ten he had me stealing for him so he could buy whiskey and women. I did whatever he told me, because I knew what he would do to me if I didn't. I was scared he'd find me and kill me if I tried to run away, and I was too small to fight back. Fear can make you do a lot of things you wouldn't ordinarily do."

"Like when I shot you that day in the store," Miranda said quietly.

He finally looked at her, and a trace of a smile passed across his lips. "Yeah. Kind of like that." Miranda saw the pain in his eyes. and she knew the moment was delicate. She looked back at the fire, waiting for him to continue. He walked away for a few minutes, returning with a smoke. He poured himself another cup of coffee. "This stuff isn't much better than mud, but I hated to throw it out yesterday. Bad coffee is better than none at all.

He swallowed some and made a face, then puffed on his cheroot for a few quiet seconds. The wind began to pick up, and it blew his dark hair around his face. "Over the years after my mother died, there were lots of other women, mostly all young Mexican girls my pa bought off *bandidos* who stole them from nice families. Many nights I had to try to sleep while I heard young girls crying and begging my father not to rape them, heard the blows when he would beat them. Sometimes I even threw up, wishing I could stop him. When I was fifteen I befriended this homeless Mexican girl . . . Santana. She was only twelve, but she looked sixteen. There was nothing physical between us, but I knew that some day there would be. I never let Pa know about her. I used to take food to her, steal money and clothes for her. She lived in an abandoned shack in a worthless little town full of poor Mexicans just south of San Antonio, where Pa and I lived. He had moved up there after killing my mother and brother."

He drank a little more coffee, walking a little farther away again and watching the horizon. "Somehow Pa found out about Santana. I don't know how. I only know I came home one day and there she was, in our house, him standing there holding her wrist so tight I could tell it hurt. She was naked, her face all bruised and wet with tears. I could even see blood . . . on her thighs." His voice nearly broke with the words. "Pa just grinned at me, told me I was learning to pick them good, just like him. 'She's tight, boy,' he said, sneering. 'I couldn't hardly get into her, but I did.' "

Miranda felt sick, and she put her head in her hands.

"I loved her." Jake nearly groaned the words. "As much as a fifteen-year-old boy who's been kicked around all his life knows how to love anyway. He took her, took what belonged to me, what I was going to take someday in a nice way. I was going to make her my wife, show her it didn't have to be ugly and painful. I felt crazy knowing what he'd done to her. He dragged her back into that bedroom and started having at it with her again while I was standing right there in the house. I just . . . I don't know. It was like that was the last of it. I had taken all I could take. I went in there and started beating on him, screaming at him to stop. I was a lot bigger by then, but still not as big and strong as he was. He landed me a good one, sent me flying against the wall, and almost knocked me out. Then he got on top of her again."

He tossed his cup out in front of him in anger, and what coffee was left in it splattered against sand and rock. "I knew there was only one way to stop him. All reason left me. I told myself he was hurting Santana; but it wasn't just for her. It was for my mother, my little brother, all the young girls he had hurt; mostly maybe it was for me. I don't know. I only know I went and got his pistols. He had two of them, and I wanted to be sure I did the job right, because I knew what he'd do to me if I missed. I brought the guns back into that room and I shot him in the back with one of them. He fell away from Santana onto the floor. I walked around the bed to where he lay, and I put the second pistol to his forehead and I shot him again. I'll always remember standing there looking at him with that hole in his head and not feeling a damn thing."

His voice broke on the last words, and Miranda's heart ached for him. She wanted to go to him, but she waited, sensing he did not want her pity, did not want to be touched. Not yet. He turned to face her, and the agony in his eyes tore at her insides. "It wasn't until I turned to Santana that I realized the first shot had gone through his neck, not his back, right through him and into Santana's throat."

Miranda's eyes widened in horror. She saw the tears in Jake's eyes before he turned away again. "She just lay there staring at me, unable to speak. I went to her, held her. There was blood . . . everywhere. I told her how sorry I was, and I could tell by her eyes she understood it was an accident. Within a minute or two she was dead too."

He stopped and cleared his throat and wiped at his eyes. "At first I was too scared even to cry. Hell, I had killed my own father, killed Santana. I just grabbed a few things and ran, took Pa's guns and horse and rode north. It wasn't long before Texas Rangers were after me. I rode into a camp of *bandidos* my father had done business with, and they protected me.

They shot it out with the Rangers, and I helped, killed a couple of them myself."

He drew in his breath and let out a sigh of a man in pain. "I guess that's when it all began. I hated everybody because I had lost Santana, felt the pain of knowing I was the one who had killed her. I knew I was no good because I had killed my own father. The *bandidos* didn't care. He was nothing to them, and I was young blood and was learning how to shoot. I fell in with them easy enough, and from then on that's all I ever knew—raiding and killing and stealing. After a while I went off on my own, landed in Indian Territory and took up with whiskey traders and gunrunners." He shrugged. "You can figure out the rest. Word spread among others of my kind that I had killed my own father. Somehow that made me even more notorious. Some men taunted me about it and I shut them up with my guns. I got to be real good with guns of all kinds, and men began challenging me. Once you get a reputation like that, there is always someone who wants to prove he's better."

He came closer and stirred the fire. "Anyway, it all just kind of got away from me. My life was out of control, and I didn't know how to change it. When I was young I used to think about having a wife and being good to her, figured maybe some way I could make up for how my pa was, prove to myself I wasn't going to be like him. But then I've got that mean streak, got it beat into me, I guess. For most of the past few years I just made up my mind I was meant to be bad and to never have a normal life, so I just let go and raised hell and did all the things people expected Jake Harkner to do, took out my hate and anger on anybody who even looked like they were going to get in my way. The last couple of years, though, I don't know . . ."

He stuck the cheroot between his teeth. "Maybe age does something to a man. I'm getting tired of the way I live. I just don't know how to change it."

He faced her then, taking the cheroot from his mouth. "You've got no obligation to stay with me, Randy. I'll understand if you don't want to. I'm not even sure if I know how to love anymore. You're right in what you told me once. The thought of having feelings about anything scares me to death; but from what I can figure, the way I feel about you has to be love, or as close as a man can get. I just don't know which is worse, living with you and seeing you hurt because of me, or taking you to Nevada and going on from there without you. You'd forget about me soon enough."

Miranda rose, studying the ruggedly handsome face, seeing both the little boy and the man who needed her in his eyes. "Never," she answered. "I could never forget you, Jake. I'd rather die than live without you now."

His eyes moved over her, and she felt flushed and warm at the memory of the things she had let him do to her the night before.

To Jake she looked like an angel, standing there in that yellow dress he liked, her hair brushed out over her shoulders, her blue-gray eyes softly glowing with love. Was it possible something this good could come into his life? "You just might die sooner than you should if you stay with me."

"Then so be it."

He sighed, rubbing at his eyes. "Randy, you're a beautiful, respectable woman, intelligent, probably well-schooled. Hell, I can't even read good. You could marry a banker or a doctor, live a normal, peaceful life—"

"Is that a proposal, Jake?"

He met her eyes and he just watched her for several seconds before answering. "I guess maybe it is."

"Then I accept."

He frowned. "Randy, you'd better give it some thought."

"I don't need to. I want to be your wife, Jake, no matter what the danger. We'll go to Nevada, maybe to California, someplace where no one knows you. You can start over, Jake. You're capable of loving and worthy of being loved in return. We'll just take one day at a time and enjoy that day's freedom to love and be loved." She stepped closer. "Your pa was wrong to tell you you were a bastard and no good. It isn't your fault that he bought your mother and never married her. It isn't your fault that a man like that fathered you. You might have his build, but you're nothing like him, Jake, not in any other way, do you understand? You've got to quit believing the things he told you, because he was just being mean. I can see right through you, and you *are* good, or you wouldn't be talking to me like this now. You wouldn't have ridden Outlaw half to death trying to find me, and you wouldn't have helped me like you did. You know now that you can't stay away from me anymore than I can stay away from you." She wrapped her arms around his waist and rested her head against his chest. "I'm not afraid of it, Jake. I'm only afraid when I'm not with you. I want to be your wife and know that you'll never ride out of my life again."

He embraced her, pressing her close, wondering if he had completely lost his mind. What the hell was it this woman did to him? Ever since meeting her it seemed like he hardly knew himself anymore, or maybe he was just beginning to find the real Jake Harkner. Whatever it was she did to him, he didn't seem to be able to fight it. He bent his head and kissed her hair.

"Maybe we can find a preacher or somebody at Fort Laramie who can marry us," he told her.

"I'd like that." He hugged her even tighter, and she felt him trembling. "It's all right to let that young boy cry, Jake. He's been holding things inside for a lot of years." He grasped her hair, and she felt his body jerk in a sob.

"I love you, Randy Hayes," he wept.

"And I love you, Jake Harkner. It's going to be all right, you'll see. God means for us to be together."

Part

Two

Woman with the golden hair,
You are my sunlight.
You are my joy.
You are my comfort in the night.
Now we walk together as one;
So much love I have never known.
We have laughed and cried and learned together.
You have brought me up from the darkness
Of despair and loneliness.

Woman with the golden hair,
You are my peace.

CHAPTER ELEVEN

Bill Kennedy threw in his cards and finished his drink. He picked up another five-dollar bill and added it to the pot at the center of the table for the next game. "I don't like this paper money," he grumbled. "A man don't hardly see gold or silver coins ever since the war."

"Banks got 'em," Juan Hidalgo answered, a hinting smile added to the words.

Kennedy stuck a new wad of tobacco into his mouth, saying nothing, but giving Juan a knowing look. After the bank robbery in St. Louis a few months back, money was running low again. Fancy guns, prime horses, women and whiskey could cost a man a lot. Part of the money he played cards with now had come from a settler family in northern Kansas that he and his men had attacked and robbed a week ago. They all had had a good time with the struggling, begging wife of the farmer before Juan had silenced her with his knife.

Juan dealt another round of cards, and Kennedy thought how the Mexican was damn near "artistic" with that big Bowie he wore strapped to his belt. The ugly scar that ran from the man's left eye across his nose and lips and on down his chin was clear evidence he had lived by that knife for a long time. He was a dark, ugly, evil-looking man that Kennedy himself would be afraid of if he didn't know him better.

"Lotta banks out west," Juan spoke up, adding to the ante. "Lotta gold and silver."

Kennedy gave him a warning look. He and his gang of eight men had taken a chance coming back into civilization as wanted men. They were holed up in an abandoned shack outside of Omaha, had come into town to gamble and spend their winnings on whores and whiskey. For over two months they had searched for Jake Harkner down in Indian Territory, where many Creek and Cherokee knew him. None had seen him. Kennedy didn't believe Jake was dead. A bullet from a little derringer like the one he'd been told the woman back in Kansas City had used wasn't generally powerful enough to kill a man as big as Jake.

Besides, Jake was too mean to die from being shot by a woman. He chuckled to himself at the thought as he picked up his cards. Jake Harkner, shot by a woman! How he would have loved to have seen that, and to have been there to finish the man off. Now the fact remained that Jake was likely still alive somewhere, and he was not going to rest easy until he found him and let Juan use his knife on him for stealing that pretty young girl away from them before they were through with her.

One of the strangers he was playing cards with opened a bid with two dollars. Kennedy turned and spit toward a spittoon, the brown saliva missing and sliding down the side of the brass container. He shrugged and picked up his two new cards, thinking maybe it was time to move on. Juan and the other men had been itching to head west, where they would be less likely to be recognized, and where there was no law.

They had all agreed that west was the best place to be now that the war was over and the law would try harder to find them; but they had lingered too long in Indian Territory, and now it was too late in the summer to try to get all the way to California or even to Nevada. They would leave in the spring, but he didn't like the idea of going without finding Jake first. The sonofabitch was good with those guns of his. In the shootout over that girl, Jake had killed Kennedy's own stepbrother and Juan's best friend, along with four other gang members. He still suffered pain from a bullet Jake had left in his right thigh, and several of the other men with him had been wounded. Jake was good, all right, but if he could be found and surprised, things wouldn't turn out the same. Jake Harkner would be begging for his life.

God only knew where the bastard had gone, let alone what

had gotten into him in the first place, taking that girl out from under their noses and returning her to her family. Hell, Harkner was handsome enough that he could have fucked the girl without her even protesting; but what did he do? Drew those damn guns of his and blew away half his men to get her out of there. Damn sonofabitch! He thought he knew the man. Hell, Jake had ridden with them for quite a while, robbed banks and trains with them, drunk and whored it up with the best of them.

He was pissed at himself for not realizing a man as good with those guns as Jake was would eventually decide to be his own boss. That was probably it. He might be gathering up a gang of his own right now. Whether he was or not, he had to be found. A man like Jake didn't stay low for long. Those guns of his were bound to get him into trouble.

He won the hand with three aces and pulled in his money, leaving a five-dollar bill in the pot and waiting for the next man to deal, spitting again and missing again. Juan raked in his own money. "I'm goin' to find me a woman for the night," he said in his raspy voice, forever damaged by an old wound that left still another scar on the man, across his throat. So far, no one had gone up against Juan with a knife and won. "One of the men in here told me about a whore at a saloon up the street who likes ugly men."

Kennedy chuckled. "Go ahead."

"I think we should go on west, boss. We'll all get bored sittin' around here all winter."

Kennedy glanced at the other men at the table, strangers who looked uneasy at their presence, especially Juan's. "We've got somebody to find yet. If we don't find him by spring, we'll leave then."

"I want to find him as bad as you do, *patrón*, but you will not find him if he don't want to be found. You know that." Juan scowled and pulled on his jacket, walking out.

"You, uh, you in for another hand, mister?" one of the others at the table asked.

Kennedy scratched at the stubble on his face. He supposed he ought to find a bathhouse, hadn't had a good soak for weeks. "Yeah, deal me one more hand."

One of the others at the table began dealing, glad the one called Juan had left and wishing the Mexican's friend would do the same. He had a pretty good idea that this Bill Kennedy and the men who had barged into their little town outside of

Omaha a couple of days ago were a bad lot, maybe wanted men; but dangerous enough that nobody around here was willing to go to the law in Omaha and start any trouble. Kennedy was a hard-looking man, with blue eyes that cut into you like a knife, his sandy-colored hair looking greasy, a scar down his right cheek. He was a tall, well-built man, perhaps in his thirties, the dealer guessed, and he could be pretty good-looking if he were cleaned up. Kennedy and his men were heavily armed, and the man couldn't help wondering if the money they were gambling with was stolen. The one called Juan kept talking about how much money there was in the gold towns out west, how he wished they would head that way before spring.

"Damnedest thing I ever seen," a man at the next table was saying, his voice growing louder from whiskey.

One of Kennedy's men who sat at that table turned to look at his boss. "Hey, Bill, come over here and listen to this."

"I've just got dealt another hand," Kennedy grumped.

"Throw it in. This is important, unless you don't care this guy over here might know somethin' about Jake."

Kennedy straightened, looking over at them. He threw in his hand and grabbed up his money, leaving the table and causing the rest of them there to breathe a sigh of relief. He dragged his chair to the next table and turned it, straddling it and resting his arms on the back of it. He looked at his friend. "This better be good, Jeb. I had a good hand."

The one called Jeb grinned, showing a missing tooth in front. He laid down his cards and nodded toward a man sitting across the table from him and looking a little nervous now. "That's Les Stanton. This past spring he was workin' at a tradin' post about three weeks west of here." He leaned back. "Les, this here is Bill Kennedy, a friend of mine, you might say. Tell him what you just told me."

Stanton swallowed. He didn't like any of these men any more than the others in this little town did, but he was no more ready to give them trouble than the next man. They all looked mean enough to kill a man for smiling wrong, about as mean as the one who had called himself Jake Turner looked the day he shot things up at the trading post over that woman.

Stanton took a swallow of whiskey. "Well, Mr. Kennedy, I, uh, I was just tellin' your friend here about somethin' that happened at the tradin' post where I'd been workin'. Some travelers came along, a preacher fellow, dropped off a woman name of Miranda Hayes who'd been snakebit. They went on without her, figurin' she'd most likely die, I expect. The man who owns the tradin' post, Jack Nemus, he took her in and took care of her." He grinned. "More than took care of her, if you know what I mean."

Kennedy scowled. "So? What's the point?"

"It gets better, boss," Jeb told him. "Hell, don't you remember that name, Miranda Hayes? That's the name of that woman from Kansas City I heard about when I was sniffin' around there askin' about Jake. That's the name of the woman who shot him."

Kennedy straightened further. Of course! Was it the same woman? "Might just be someone with the same name," he said. "Even if she *was* the same one, what good does that do us now?"

"Somebody name of Jake came lookin' for the woman," Jeb answered.

Kennedy's steely blue eyes narrowed, and he targeted them at Les Stanton. "Jake Harkner?"

"Called himself Jake Turner," Stanton answered. "Big man, dark, like maybe he was part Mexican or part Indian, wore his guns on two belts crisscrossed low on his hips and carried a rifle and a shotgun on his horse. He damn well knew how to use those guns."

Kennedy rose and leaned closer over the table, all ears. "What did he do?"

"Like I say, he was lookin' for that woman. Nemus, he tried to say she wasn't there, but somehow he knew she was. Damned if he didn't draw his gun and shoot Nemus right across the side of the face and told him he'd better take him to the woman. They went outside, and another man there drew on this Jake fella' and Jake shot him down easy as you please. The whole thing scared the hell out of me. This Jake, he took Nemus into his cabin where the woman was. We wasn't sure what went on in there till later. We found Nemus pistol-whipped and tied to a chair, but layin' on the floor, hurt pretty bad. Turner shot down another one of us when we tried to come in after him, wounded another in the arm. Another man rode off, scared shitless. I'm the only one who didn't get hurt. Turner, he brought the woman out and put her in one of Nemus's wagons, had us hitch up his horse and packhorse to pull it. Stole the wagon and lit out of there."

Stanton squirmed a little under Bill Kennedy's piercing

stare. "None of us was about to go after him," he added. "Figured he'd shoot us down if we did. He claimed the woman belonged to him. Headed west with her, far as I know. She'd been on her way to Virginia City to find her brother. That's what the preacher told us. I don't know what the hell Turner had in mind for her—whether he was gonna' help her or hurt her; but from the way he acted, I figure he had a soft spot for her and meant to help her."

Jeb Donner chuckled. "Sounds like ol' Jake is still into helpin' women in distress."

Kennedy straightened, his eyes bright with the thought of revenge. "It had to be Jake Harkner! I *knew* he'd give himself away with those guns!" He looked at Jeb. "Why in hell do you think he went after that woman? Hell, she's the one who *shot* him. I don't get it. The way he behaved over that woman—" He caught himself, not wanting to say too much in front of Stanton and the other strangers in the saloon. "Jake wouldn't hurt her. Then again, maybe he was pissed over her shootin' him and figured to get paid back—take it out of her flesh, so to speak."

Jeb shook his head. "Not Jake. He's gone soft lately, over women, anyway. Don't sound like he's gone soft when it comes to them guns."

Kennedy looked at Stanton. "Where's this tradin' post again?"

"About three weeks west of here, on the Oregon Trail."

"How long ago did this happen?"

Stanton shrugged. "Must have been a couple months. If they went on west, they'd be clear to Wyoming by now, I expect, unless Indians or the weather or an injury got them. Hell, all kinds of things can kill a man on that trip. The woman, she might have died from that snakebite."

Kennedy sat down and faced Jeb. "He's headed west, just like we were gonna do. Goddamn it! We should have thought of that sooner. Whatever he's got in mind for the woman, if she's dead or alive, he'll keep goin' west to avoid the law. And that's where *we're* goin'! We might not make it all the way this winter, but we can get pretty far before winter sets into the mountains. On horseback we can travel faster, maybe cut the distance between him and us." He rose, looking excited. "Jeb, you round up the rest of the boys. I'll go find Juan. Tell the others to meet tomorrow mornin' at sunup behind this saloon. We'll head out then." He reached into his pocket, slapping a twenty-dollar bill onto the table in front of Les Stanton. "Mister, you earned this. Thanks for the information."

Stanton grinned, picking up the bill and feeling a little more at ease. Kennedy turned and left, looking for Juan. *He'll love to hear this,* he thought. *Juan would like nothin' better than to carve Jake Harkner into a hundred pieces and feed him to the wolves!* And what if Jake *was* sweet on that Hayes woman? How in hell could that have happened? If it was true, and Jake had the woman with him, she would just be the icing on the cake for them once they found them. He and Juan and the others would lick that icing, right in front of Jake Harkner's eyes!

The Mormon women fussed over Miranda, helping her bathe, pressing the yellow dress Jake liked best on her, pinning her hair up into curls.

"Ah, you vill make beautiful bride," Esther Carlson said in her musical Swedish accent. "This vill be first time I see vedding in America." She ended the sentence with an up-note, as though it were a question, always making Miranda feel as though she was supposed to answer.

"Do you miss Sweden?" Miranda asked, holding still while the older woman pinned another curl.

"There has not been time to miss my home. Since ve come here, ve get right off boat and start out in vagon. There vill be time for settling and for missing home once ve reach Salt Lake. Soon ve vill think of that as home. This is good place, this America."

"Yes." Miranda wondered what these Mormons would think if they knew the truth about Jake. To them he was a hero, a daring, adventurous American who had saved them from certain death. Jake and Miranda had come upon their wagon train while it was being attacked by a small band of Sioux Indians. None of the Mormon men were experienced at shooting at other human beings, no matter how savage; only a few even knew how to use a gun, and had used them only to hunt game. They had apparently not even done a very good job of that, since Jake and Miranda found them all near starvation.

Miranda could smile now at the memory. Jake really had been a hero that day, but she remembered the terror she felt, sure he would be killed himself. He had heard the shooting and had sneaked up onto a rise near the surrounded wagon train. He had picked off several of the Indians with his Winchester, startling them with shots coming from another direction. Those remaining were frightened and rode off, except for two, who came at Jake after his rifle was empty. Jake rose and whipped out one of his revolvers, and with one quick shot he had downed one of the Indians. A second shot hit its mark also, but that Indian did not go down easily. He kept coming, and Jake fired twice more as the painted warrior whacked at him with a tomahawk. Miranda remembered the sick feeling the sight had given her, but Jake had managed to dodge the weapon, and the Indian finally fell dead from his horse.

It had been a harrowing experience, and the Mormons had treated Jake and Miranda like a king and queen ever since. Although Jake had wanted to continue traveling alone, both knew it was impossible. Because of the likelihood of further Indian attacks, they could not take the risk of being caught alone. There was only so much one man could do if it happened again. They had joined the Mormons and would stay with them to Salt Lake, where they hoped to find traders or settlers traveling on to Virginia City.

All the way here to Fort Laramie Jake had taken time to show the Mormon men how to shoot, had hunted game for them, helped with two different wagons that broke down. Miranda had nursed a little boy who broke his arm in a fall from a wagon, and had won the friendship of the other women. Because she and Jake wanted to get married as soon as they found a priest or a minister, they had been forced to admit to the Mormons that they were not married but planned to be when they reached Laramie. Miranda had explained that Jake was a "friend of the family" who had found her dying from a snakebite and had agreed to see her safely to Nevada.

Here at Laramie they had found a Catholic priest who ministered to the Indians. Today he would marry them, and the weather was perfect, beautiful, as though God had designed the day just for this special moment. There would be no fancy church, but they would be surrounded by new friends who truly seemed to want the very best for them.

Finally, tonight, after being unable to make love for the last three weeks, they would be free to be together. The Mormons had prepared a place for them to spend the night with a little privacy. They had cleared out one of their own wagons, one which was much bigger than Jake and Miranda's own wagon, and it had been pulled several yards from the fort grounds and covered with mosquito netting. A feather mattress and blankets, water and a washpan, and other necessities were left inside, and Miranda thought how that wagon would seem just as wonderful to her tonight as a fancy hotel. She would be with Jake, would be his wife, and that was all that mattered. The wagon was the Mormons' thank-you to Jake for all he had done for them. The women had baked a cake over a campfire in a Dutch oven; the fort commander had offered a four-piece band consisting of two fiddles, a trumpet, and a guitar; and the Mormons had offered some of their own precious belongings as gifts—handmade quilts, a few dishes and blankets, even a hand-crocheted lace tablecloth.

Miranda was overwhelmed by their generosity, and she knew Jake was still trying to get used to such niceties. He could not quite believe people existed who could be so kind, and he took his role as their hero with a grain of salt, totally embarrassed by all the attention and, Miranda knew, feeling unworthy of any of it. Miranda had to keep encouraging him to stop living in the past and accept the good things of the present, and although she trusted in the fact that he truly loved her, she prayed daily that he would learn to love himself. To her that was more important even than his learning to love others, and it was something she was not sure he would ever accomplish. He would be forever haunted by his childhood.

Today was not a day to dwell on the past, or on the fact that her husband-to-be had his face on wanted posters back in Missouri. Today there would be a wedding, and in the morning they would leave Fort Laramie and head for Salt Lake. She knew Jake would be glad to get away from the soldiers, always worried about being recognized when he was in such places.

"There now," Esther said. "Don't ve look beautiful! You are a picture, Randy! I think I have never seen a young voman so pretty. Your Jake vill not be able to take his eyes off you."

Miranda felt her cheeks flushing, not so much at the compliment as at the thought of lying with Jake tonight as his wife. They had had only that one night of making love; had come upon the Mormons later that next day after their long talk about Jake's father. The journey had been difficult, draining them physically from battling the elements and stubborn animals, crossing the river several times, bearing up to intense prairie heat, and fighting off insects at night. They had lived with the constant fear that the Indians would return, maybe in a bigger force the next time, and it felt so good to be within the safety of the fort, to have this little reprieve. Tonight, in spite of their weary bones and muscles, they would most certainly find the energy to share their bodies as husband and wife.

The little orchestra began playing the wedding march, and Miranda came out from behind the wagon where the women had been fussing over her. She walked toward the musicians, where Jake stood waiting with the priest. She carried a few wildflowers the Mormon children had picked for her, and she wore the yellow dress Jake liked best. A couple of the wildflowers had been stuck into her hair, and she had applied just a touch of rouge to her cheeks. She knew she had grown thinner from the hardship of their journey and from being so sick after the snakebite. Her dress was a little big on her, and she hoped she looked all right to Jake.

When she came closer, her heart soared at the look of love there in the eyes of a man who three months ago hadn't known the first thing about loving and caring. She saw something else in those eyes, that hint of fear, that little-boy look that made her heart ache for him. He was so afraid to care, so afraid that he would ruin her life by being a part of it. How handsome he looked, wearing clean denim pants, a white ruffled shirt, and a silk suit jacket loaned to him by one of the bigger Mormon men. A black string tie decorated the neck of the shirt, and he wore no weapons. He had bathed and shaved in the fort bathhouse, and his leather boots had been polished by soldiers. He wore a new black felt hat purchased at the fort supply store, a hat he removed as she came closer. He handed it out to a soldier who stood nearby and he reached out to take her hand. He squeezed it tightly. "You sure about this?"

"Very sure." She felt him trembling, wondered at her own daring to marry a wanted man. Everything they were discovering together could be destroyed so quickly, by a bounty hunter, or the law, or even other outlaws. Surely things would be different when they got beyond the Rockies. She smiled for him, felt like crying at the thought of how much she loved him.

The priest moved through his rituals, and they spoke their vows, Jake reddening and grinning a little on the words "for better, for worse." He felt removed from himself, as though it was a different man marrying this slip of a woman who had totally messed up his thinking. In a sense, it *was* a different man, one who wanted nothing to do with the life he had led up to now, one who wanted to put the past behind him, if that was possible, and settle with a good woman, find some peace.

Peace. That was what Randy brought him. Away from her, life was vicious and dangerous for him; but in Randy's arms he was safe, loved, free. Free of the past, free of the memories, free of his anger. He slipped the plain gold band he had purchased at the fort's supply store onto Miranda's finger. It was a little too big, but it was the only one available. He would get her something nicer, he vowed, either at Salt Lake or Virginia City.

He watched those gray-blue eyes, as she accepted the ring; he saw the love there. He wondered if a woman any prettier existed, or a man any luckier than he was today. Did he really have any right calling someone as beautiful and kind and understanding his wife? Would he bring her only pain and sorrow? He had wanted so much just to ride out of her life and leave her to better things; but it had been impossible to see her again and not want her. She had made it all so easy, and he saw no fear or doubt in her eyes now as the priest pronounced them man and wife.

He leaned down and kissed her lips lightly, and the people around them clapped, a few of the Mormon women actually crying. *"Yo te quiero, mi esposa,"* he told her softly.

"I love you, Jake." She saw tears in his eyes, and her own quickly misted. "We'll be all right."

"I won't let anything happen to you."

"I know that."

They embraced, and the orchestra broke into a snappy tune that put everyone in a party spirit. Miranda thought how she could tell their children that their parents' wedding was even attended by a few Indians. Children. How would Jake feel about being a father? It would surely be a traumatic experience for him. She had not even thought about it until now. They had not discussed it. She set the thought aside as their Mormon friends surrounded them and congratulated them, hugging and kissing and laughing. The little band changed to a slower tune, and everyone urged the newlyweds to dance alone. "The first dance for Mr. and Mrs. Jake Turner," someone shouted.

Jake put a hand to Miranda's waist, and they began to move in a circle. "I'm not very good at this—not much experience," he told her.

"Well, this farmgirl who hasn't gone out with a man in over three years is a little rusty herself."

He whirled her around to the music, both of them becoming less and less aware of those around them. Miranda wondered at how surprising life could be. She had shot this man, learned to hate his kind. Then there he was, lying in her own bed. How had she fallen in love with him? How had she known somehow, that first day in the supply store, that the tall, dangerous-looking stranger with the guns and wearing the canvas slicker would end up playing an important role in her life? Now here she was, Jake Harkner's wife. The bride of an outlaw. No, not an outlaw. Not anymore. If only society would leave him alone now, they could be happy.

They moved through the formalities in a near daze, both of them a little overwhelmed that they had really done this, both of them eager to prove it to themselves by consummating their vows. They visited, thanked those who had given gifts, ate cake, and drank lemonade. Jake drank a little whiskey given to him by the soldiers, but he allowed himself only two shots. As soon as it was dark, he whisked Miranda up into his arms and carried her off toward the waiting wedding wagon amid laughter and teasing remarks from those around them.

The voices faded, and Miranda rested her head on Jake's shoulder. "It was a perfect wedding, Jake, even without a church and all the fancy trimmings."

He set her on the gate of the wagon, bracing his hands on either side of her and leaning close to kiss her lightly. "Once we get settled, wherever that might be, you'll have a place of your own, Randy. I'll do the best I can."

She touched his face. "I know that. I'm just happy being your wife. When we do have a place of our own, we can make love whenever we feel like it. It gives us something to look forward to."

He grinned, kissing her harder then. He moved his lips to her neck. "If that's the case, when will I get any work done? I'll be in bed with you all the time."

She laughed lightly, savoring the feel of his tongue flicking at her throat. He climbed up beside her and they moved under the canvas and mosquito netting where they could see each other better by a dimly lit lantern. Jake drew her down into the feather mattress, glad the night was cooler than it had been for several weeks. He studied the trusting, gray-blue eyes, began pulling pins from her honey-blond hair, wondered at the perfect features of her face. How small it was. He could probably crush it with one big hand, and sometimes he wondered that he didn't hurt her accidentally, her being so small-boned and delicate; but she wasn't delicate on the inside. This was one strong woman who knew what she wanted and took any risk to have it.

"I can't believe you're really my wife." He traced his fingers over her face, her lips. "I'm not saying I'll be perfect. It's not easy pulling out of a past like mine, and trouble hunts me down like a wolf after a rabbit; but I'll do what I can, short of robbing a bank, to make sure you're taken care of and have a place of your own."

She smiled and touched his hair, liking the feel of it, painful urges pressing at her insides. She did not doubt his love for one moment. Jake Harkner had been starved of loving and *being* loved nearly all his life. He had a lot to make up for. "I'll be a good wife, Jake. Wherever our home ends up, I'll make it nice for you."

In the distant foothills wolves began their nightly songs to each other. Tonight the wailing seemed strangely ominous. They both felt it, and Jake met her mouth in a savage kiss as though to make sure she really was there and really was his. Miranda felt the same sudden need. She told herself she must not think about all the problems a woman might have being married to a man with Jake's past. It was the future that mattered, only the future. She had told him that, and she must believe it herself, for Jake's sake. He wanted so much to do this right. He needed her love, and she in turn had a mad desire for this man of danger and loneliness. Sometimes she felt that through loving the man she could also bring some love to the little boy in him who wanted so much to be held and comforted.

For now, at last, they could recapture the ecstasy of that first night he had taken her. It had been so hard being together, looking at each other, and not being able to sleep in each other's arms these last few weeks. Now they had all night, but this first time they needed to dispel the odd fear the wolves' howling had awakened in them, needed to make sure this was real and nothing could change it, needed to revel in the glory they had found in being united.

Jake's kisses grew deep and hot, his tongue slaking into her mouth suggestively, something Mack had never done. It made her feel wild and wanton. She thought about the kind of women he had been with before her, realized now there were probably things he knew that she had never been shown. His lips left her mouth and trailed to her neck. He pulled her to a sitting position and began unbuttoning her dress at the back. She closed her eyes and rested her head against his strong shoulder as he opened the dress and ran his hand under her camisole over her bare skin.

"I want to know all of it, Jake, all the things I don't know yet. I want to be as good as the women who do this just to show a man a good time."

He grinned at the mere thought of her being anything like the kind of women he had known. She leaned back, and he pulled her dress off her shoulders, untied the camisole and pushed it open, reaching inside to gently close his hand around a soft, full breast. "Just looking at you excites me more than anything those women did." He laid her back again, kissing her deeply, running his thumb over her taut nipple. "I'll gladly teach you anything you want to know, *mi querida*," he whispered, his lips moving down to taste at the pink fruits of her breasts.

The words stirred a passion in her that made her draw in her breath with the ache of it. In moments her dress and camisole and slips were pulled away. Jake sat up and pulled off her shoes and stockings, removed his shirt, boots and pants. Miranda lay there naked, on fire at how his dark eyes raked over her while he stripped off his underwear. She drank in the sight of his firm body, and that part of him that left no doubt he was all man. She touched the scar at his left side where her own bullet had come close to killing him.

Her own bullet. He had come into her life a wanted outlaw who had gunned down a bounty hunter, and now he was her husband. She leaned up and kissed the scar, as well as the one at his shoulder, at his neck. There were other tiny ones; Jake was a man battered physically and emotionally most of his life. She could hardly bear to set eyes on the faint scars on his back, knowing they'd been put there when he was small and defenseless.

He leaned over her, grasping her knees and parting her legs. She closed her eyes and let him drink in the sight of what now belonged to him. He ran his hands along the inside of her thighs, over her privates and belly. Then he leaned closer, licked at her neck, her cheek. "There are many things I can show you," he said softly. "Right now all I want is to be inside you, to make sure this is real."

She gasped when he quickly entered her then, filling her to ecstasy. His shaft was hot and hard, searching her depths. She leaned her head back, arching up to him and groaning at the way his penis teased her as he moved erotically, in moments bringing her to a delicious climax. He rose up then, grasping her hips and drawing her to him, thrusting himself deep. For several glorious minutes there was nothing but to enjoy the man and let him claim her. His hands gently massaged her bottom while he continued to fill her body in a sweet rhythm that made her forget everything else. There was only Jake, invading her, touching her everywhere, bringing out passions and desires she was hardly aware existed in her soul.

He pulled her closer then, met her lips almost savagely, and groaned as his life finally surged into her. He stayed inside her and took her into his arms. "We'll do it again in a minute," he whispered. "I'll never get enough of you, Mrs. Harkner."

She liked the sound of that name. To others and on paper she was Mrs. Jake Turner, but in her heart she did not mind being Mrs. Jake Harkner. If not for the danger for him, she would shout it to the world.

"Once we get someplace where we have more privacy, I'll teach you anything you want," he was saying. Already he was beginning to move inside her again.

Miranda met his eyes and was suddenly embarrassed at what she had said earlier. "You make me feel totally wicked and daring."

He grinned, leaning down to lick at her lips. "I want to see you and touch you and taste you all over," he promised.

"Jake," she whispered. Neither of them was about to let their weariness from the long, hard journey, or worry about the danger that might lie ahead interfere with this special night. It was done now. They were man and wife, and nothing could change that.

In the distant hills the wolves continued their mournful wailing.

CHAPTER TWELVE

October 1866 . . .

Clarence looked up and down the street to be sure none of his relatives was anywhere near. It had been easy to sneak away from his Uncle Wilbur's tent camp. They had been in Virginia City only two weeks, and his uncles were all busy building a log church, deciding the church must come even before a cabin would be built for Aunt Opal and the children. Within the religious camp he slept alone in his father's wagon, having taken over his father's possessions since the man's death from cholera in the mountains of Utah.

His eight-year-old cousin David, his uncle John, only twenty-eight, and his grandfather had also died from the dreaded disease, all before reaching the Nevada desert. The trip through the desert had been hell, and now that they had arrived at their destination, Clarence could not help wondering what kind of a God would put them through such hell when they were on their way to bring God's teachings to others.

Not that he believed much in God anyway. He had never really considered himself a missionary, never quite understood why God was so important to some people. He had hated having to be a part of the trip, hated the boring life his uncles led, always praying and reading the Bible, never having any fun. He had come along because it was expected of him, but now that he was here and his father was dead, he was not so sure he had to remain with the family and join in all that holy stuff. He was a man now, had been for longer than any of his family knew, ever since he'd lain with that farmgirl back in Missouri before they'd left. He should be old enough to make his own decisions about life and how he wanted to live it.

It seemed ever since that farmgirl, his appetite for women and the inability to be with any because of his family had been near painful. He had been so sure that widow woman, Miranda Hayes, would be hurting bad enough for a man that she'd let him under her skirts; but she had surprised him. God, how he hated her for embarrassing him the way she had! He hoped she had *died* from that snakebite, slowly and painfully. It would serve her right for acting so uppity around him when he knew damn good and well she was hungry for a man between her legs.

He stepped up onto the boardwalk. He liked Virginia City at night. It was wild and noisy and dangerous, a place for a man to prove himself. He pushed his way past drunks, glanced into each saloon to see smoky rooms full of men gambling and drinking, painted women hanging over them. Raucous piano music and wild laughter filled the night air, along with an occasional gunshot.

He could not help wondering if these were the people his family had come to "save." They sure didn't seem to think they needed it. What was so bad about this life? People were dancing and laughing and drinking, having a good time. He had felt drawn to the wilder side of this town since they had first arrived, felt a keen hunger to learn about this side of life. He wanted to taste whiskey, sleep with a whore and learn about all the ways women like that had of making a man feel good. He wanted to learn how to play poker, shoot pool; wanted to taste tobacco, smoke a cheroot, roll his own cigarettes.

These were his decisions to make now, not his Uncle Wilbur's. Maybe he would find a job up at one of the mines, or working at one of these saloons. Until then, he would continue using the money he managed to steal bit by bit from his uncle, most of it from the collections the man took after giving a sermon, collections turned over to Clarence to count. And count it he did, after taking out a portion for himself. He grinned at the thought of how stupid and trusting his uncle was.

He walked into one of the saloons where he spotted a young, blond-haired girl moving around the tables. She was pretty, reminded him a little of that Mrs. Hayes. Her bright green satin dress sported a neckline so low he was sure her entire bosom would spill out of it. An edging of lace was all that hid her nipples, and he felt a rush of excitement at the thought of being with a woman who would let him do anything he wanted with her. That farmgirl, she had been a little resistant at first, but she had given in once he told her that he'd tell her father about her if she didn't cooperate. He had made her cry, but he supposed that was how it was for a girl's first time. She'd get over it.

He edged closer to the prostitute, excited by the shortness of her dress, the hemline just above her pretty knees. He had never seen so much leg exposed on a woman before. She wore black net stockings and silver shoes, and her hair hung long and loose, unlike the tight buns worn by his Aunt Opal and most of the other women his family had known. He wanted to touch that hair, to see that slightly hidden bosom. "Hello," he spoke up, touching her arm.

She turned, and a bright smile parted her full, red lips. "Hello, kid." Her eyes moved over him. "Something I can do for you?"

Clarence grinned, already feeling an urgent pressure at his privates. "Maybe. You, uh, you one of those ladies who take money for showing a man a good time?"

She laughed lightly, tossing her head to flick her hair behind her shoulders. "A man? Is that what you are?" She came closer, moving her hand to his privates. Her eyes widened. "Well, I guess maybe you are at that."

Clarence reddened, on fire for her, already sure that this was all he wanted out of life, women like this, the smell of smoke and cards. "I'm man enough for you," he told her. "I've had my share of women," he lied.

"Have you now?" She gave him a teasing look and took his hand, pulling him to the bar and ordering a shot of whiskey "on the house" for him. Clarence thought of protesting, but he figured if he was going to learn about this life, he had to taste all of it. The bartender set a shotglass on the counter and poured the whiskey, and Clarence picked it up and slugged it down quickly. He could not help making a face then at how it burned going down. He shuddered, and the woman laughed.

"Pour him another one, Toby," she told the man behind

the bar. "He'll get used to it quick enough." She touched Clarence's chest, pressed her fingers across his nipple through his shirt. "For five dollars, I'll take you upstairs and show you all you want to know about women, honey. You got the five dollars?"

Clarence swallowed, wondering if he would explode with desire. "I've got *ten* dollars you can have if you let me stay all night." He grinned, imagining how his uncle would react if he knew his collection money was being spent on a whore.

"Let's see your money, kid."

Clarence quickly dug into his pocket, pulling out eight single-dollar bills and a two-dollar gold piece. The woman pulled the bodice of her dress away from her breasts so that he could see them fully. "Drop it in, honey."

He stared at the taut nipples eagerly, then shoved the money into her dress, his hand lingering there a moment to enjoy touching one nipple. Men sitting close by who had seen the display hooted and whistled and began teasing Clarence, asking if he really thought he was man enough for what he was about to do.

"You don't know Mellie, boy," one of them said with a laugh. "She'll eat you alive!" The others laughed with him, and Clarence reddened deeply but maintained a manly stance.

He drew his hand away. "That your name? Mellie?"

"That's it." She licked her lips seductively. "What's yours?"

"Clarence. Clarence Gaylord."

She traced her fingers over his lips. "Well, Clarence Gaylord, follow me upstairs, but don't expect to get any sleep tonight." She pulled at his hand, guiding him to the stairway while men continued to call out lurid remarks. Mellie just laughed, not at all offended. Clarence eagerly followed the woman up the stairs, wondering how old she was. She was so painted and had such a hard look to her, it was difficult to tell. She could be twenty, or maybe ten years older than that. It didn't much matter. Tonight he was going to do what *he* wanted to do. This woman wouldn't turn him away, and there was no Uncle Wilbur here to preach to him about how this life was wrong. He didn't see a damn thing wrong with it. All these people liked it just fine. If laughter and half-naked women and scraping in money from card winnings was sin, then where was all the sorrow and pain and repentance his uncle preached about? He saw nothing here but a good time. He followed

Mellie into her room, and she closed the door, keeping her smile when she turned to him. She knelt in front of him and began unbuttoning his pants. "Let's see what you've got in here," she said softly.

Clarence closed his eyes and breathed deeply. Yes, this was the life for him! This was where he belonged. He wanted some excitement out of life, and Virginia City held all the excitement a man could hope to find! Maybe after tonight he would never even go back to his uncle's camp, except to get his clothes and leave for good.

It was already getting dark when Jake led the wagon down the muddy main street of Virginia City. An early snowstorm in the Sierras had stranded him and Miranda and the Mormon supply train with whom they had traveled from Salt Lake, and he and Miranda were both weary from their struggle against the cold and snow. The duration of the storm had left them buried against the side of a mountain and had nearly starved them out. The supply train carried only hardware, no extra food, and it had been a harrowing experience.

The same storm had frozen the dirt streets of town, and now a slight warming and the tremendous traffic of wagons and mules and horses, combined with the warmth of all the animal manure that was dropped onto the ground, had warmed the streets just enough to bring on a thaw that created a sucking, smelly mud. Both Jake and the oxen found it difficult to trudge through the muck.

The Nevada desert had been beastly, and Miranda had gotten sick. Her illness had brought terror to his soul, for he'd been sure it was cholera, but she was better now. He had gotten a taste of what it would be like to be without her, and he didn't like it at all. As far as he was concerned, she was the best thing that had ever happened to him.

They had left the men of the supply train at a warehouse north of town, and now had the task of finding a place to stay for the night. The air was filled with screams and gunfire and piano music, and here and there a man could be seen lying on the boardwalk, out cold from too much whiskey. Jake thought how at one time he would have fit right in here among the wild women and smoking gamblers, and it still tugged at him a little, only because they had been so long away from any kind of civilization, which left him glad to see people and hear laughter. There had been times when they had both felt half crazy with the tedious journey and the fear of dying either from the heat of the desert or the cold of the Sierras. Before that there had been the Rockies to cross, pathways along the sides of mountaintops that made a man dizzy.

He glanced up at Miranda, who was gawking at the drunks and at whores who draped themselves over balconies, displaying their generous offerings. She had come through this journey with hardly a complaint, even when she had been so sick. She had shown courage and strength, and he hoped her worthless brother appreciated what she had been through just to find him.

He shuddered at the thought of her actually trying to make this trip alone, and a feeling of intense relief spread through him at having made the decision to try to find her and help her get here. Knowing now what the trip was like, the heat, the mosquitoes, the snakes, the dangerous roadways through the mountains, the horrendous and unpredictable prairie storms, Indians, men like those who had taken her in back at that trading post . . . Being a woman alone, she might never have made it, although he knew she would have given it a hell of a try and would not have let on that she was the least bit afraid. He'd never known anyone so strong and determined.

They were barely halfway down the street when the doors to one saloon burst open and two men charged out, fists flying. They were followed by a swarm of men who were taking sides and rooting for one man or the other, and the wagon itself was quickly surrounded. The oxen balked and the horses tied at the rear of the wagon whinnied. Two men climbed onto the wagon and began pulling at Miranda, who began batting at them with her fists.

"Hey, honey, you're new!" one of the men bellowed, holding up a whiskey bottle with one hand.

In a second Jake was up in the wagon beside Miranda. On the way up he grabbed one of the men by the collar and threw him off in one powerful movement, then raised a booted foot and kicked the second man in the chest, knocking him into the mud with a splat. The man just lay there sprawled on his back and grinning. Another tried to climb into the wagon from the back, and Jake pulled a revolver and shot at him, deliberately splintering a piece of the wagon gate beside the man's hand to warn him. The man jumped down, and the fight nearby suddenly stopped at the startling crack of Jake's gun.

"Get behind the seat!" he ordered Miranda. She quickly obeyed, her ears hurting from the firing of the gun so close to her head. She thought of another time that gun had been fired, its roar pounding against her eardrums, the weapon used against a bounty hunter who had had no chance against Jake Harkner.

Jake holstered the revolver and reached under the wagon seat to retrieve his shotgun. He waved it at the crowd of men, which had quieted. They stood all around the wagon now, just staring. "The next man who climbs on this wagon and touches my wife gets his guts blown out!" Jake roared. "Don't test me!"

Miranda could hardly believe how silent it had become in the immediate area. She could still hear laughter and piano music, but no one around the wagon moved.

"Sorry, mister," one of them finally spoke up. "We thought you was bringin' us a new woman. Ain't a whore in town pretty as your woman there."

"You've got it right. *My* woman! Now somebody tell me where one of the better hotels is in this goddamn town!"

Miranda peeked from behind the seat to see a short, dirty-looking, bearded man step forward. "Up at the other end of town. The International. You'll be lucky to get a room, though. I know a woman runs a real nice boardinghouse only a couple of buildings south of the hotel, a Mrs. Anderson— yellow house with white trim and roses out front. Friend of mine just moved out. You might could find a room there. It's nicer than the hotel on account of you can eat your meals all together at one big table, just like home, good food too."

They all stood staring, and Jake leveled the shotgun. "Thanks for the information. Now get out of my way so I can get my wife a decent place to stay."

They all hesitated. "Can you have her come out?" another one of them asked. "Just so's we can have another look?"

"No disrespect, mister," the bearded one told Jake. "Around here we don't see many young, pretty women who ain't . . . you know . . . we don't see many proper ladies." He removed his hat. "We just want to have a look, give your lady our apologies, that's all."

"Forget it!"

"Jake, it's all right," Miranda told him. "Maybe one of them knows Wes." She climbed back into the seat, her cheeks turning crimson at the stares. Several more of them removed their hats.

"Sorry, ma'am," the bearded man told her. He looked down and kicked at the man who still lay sprawled on his back. "Get up, Hoot, and apologize to the lady."

The one called Hoot just groaned and rolled over. The other two men who had tried to climb onto the wagon stepped forward. "Sorry to upset you, ma'am," one of them spoke up.

Miranda glanced at Jake, who looked ready to fire the shotgun at the slightest wrong move. She looked back at the rest of the men. "Do any of you know a Wes Baker? He came here almost two years ago from Kansas City. He has light hair and blue eyes and would be twenty-two now. He's my brother. I came here to find him."

They all looked at each other, shaking their heads. "No, ma'am," the bearded man answered. "Fact is, men come and go so much around here that we don't hardly ever get to know their names. Nobody really cares, I guess. A man is here today and gone tomorrow. You might have your husband there check at the mines. Most mine owners keep a list of the names of their workers."

"Thank you." She looked at Jake again. "Let's go, Jake."

Jake scowled at the crowd, climbing down and keeping his shotgun in his left hand.

"Hey, mister, you a lawman or somethin'?" one of them asked. "You look like you're right good with them guns."

"Good enough to kill any bastard who touches my wife." It was obvious this town was packed with men from every walk of life, mostly the wrong side of life. Jake hoped he wouldn't run into anyone here who knew him. The crowd of men parted, and he moved through them and headed up the street.

"Jake, that last remark was rude. They were perfect gentlemen once they realized I was your wife."

Jake gave Miranda a dark look. "You think anybody in a place like this cares about somebody being rude? You can't be too nice to men like that, Randy. You give them an inch and the gentlemen, as you called them, would turn right back into the animals that they are. I ought to know. I was just as bad."

A prostitute called down to Jake then, making a lewd remark about his size and asking him to come up and show her if he was big all over. Jake glanced at her, but said nothing, and Miranda felt a burning jealousy over all the other women who had touched him. Again a lack of privacy traveling with the suppliers had kept them apart, as well as the agony of the desert and the bitter cold of the mountain storm. They were both weak and spent, Jake obviously irritable; yet the sight of the prostitute made Miranda yearn to have her husband beside her in a real bed so that she could make sure he knew she could please him as much as any of the women who hung around these streets. Most of those outside wore coats, but the one who had called out to Jake as well as a few others braved the cold just to display bare skin.

She thought how this place fit a man like Jake. If not for her, he would probably already be inside one of the saloons, raising hell along with the rest of them. She wished it was not so far into winter. A town like this could mean trouble for Jake, and it was obvious they would have to stay here now until spring. They could not risk the danger of going on to California when the worst of winter storms in the Sierras was yet to come. She wondered if there was a decent doctor in this town. She hadn't told Jake, yet, didn't want him to worry while they were traveling; but she was sure now that she was carrying his baby. She wasn't quite sure how Jake would react to the news that he might have a child of his own. Just being married and thinking about honest work to support them was still new to him. Knowing his own childhood horrors, how would he feel about being a father himself?

One thing was certain. He loved her with a great passion, would defend her with his life. She had felt sorry for the look of terror in his eyes when he thought she had cholera back in the desert. She realized she should have told him then that she was just sick because she was pregnant, but she knew that knowledge would be a great burden to him for the rest of the journey. She didn't want to be pampered, and she didn't want to tell him he would be a father until they had reached their destination and settled in, if settling in was possible in a place like this.

They made their way through more rowdy miners and gamblers and drunks, all of them taking a step back when Jake threatened them with his shotgun. When they came closer to the International, the street became quieter. The worst of the wild nightlife seemed to be behind them, and Miranda breathed a little easier. Now if they could only find a decent room, either at the hotel or the boardinghouse; warmth, a real bed, perhaps a hot bath and hot food.

They approached the boardinghouse first, neither of them

aware that they were being followed by Clarence Gaylord. The crowd of men who had first surrounded them had been so confusing, and it had been just dark enough that Miranda had not noticed Clarence standing among them.

Clarence himself grinned at the realization that Miranda had not recognized him. After all, he had longer hair now, and had grown a mustache, was trying to grow a beard, too, but it was a little too thin for his liking. He was shocked to see Miranda Hayes had survived, even more surprised to see her traveling with a man who called himself her husband! When in hell had she met him? And who the hell *was* he? He didn't remember a man who looked like that at the trading post where his uncle had left her.

He kept to the shadows to see where she would end up staying, waited several minutes while the wagon was tied in front of Mrs. Anderson's boardinghouse. Finally her husband came out and began unloading the wagon, telling Miranda he had gotten them a room. Clarence watched the man lift her down from the wagon. Just looking at her brought back all the hate he still felt for her, and he wished he could find a way to get back at her now that she was in town.

The bitch! Acting like she didn't need a man, and here she shows up married to some stranger she must have met along the trail. She had let *him* get into her easy enough! Who the hell was he, anyway, brandishing that shotgun like he did? He figured the uppity Mrs. Hayes would have married some farmer or a banker or the like. The man with her now was no ordinary man, that was sure.

He put a cigar between his lips and lit it, turning and walking away. He wore a gun himself now, knew how to gamble, had slept with lots of whores. Uncle Wilbur was near to having a heart attack over his behavior, had even come into a saloon one day to beg him to give up his sinful ways. But Uncle Wilbur didn't know how good this life was. He was damn proud of himself for what he'd learned in such a short time. Real men didn't go around preaching and abstaining. Real men knew how to take care of themselves in a place like Virginia City. They knew how to bluff at cards and hold their whiskey. They knew how to chew and spit and cuss; and they knew a woman had her place, which was underneath him in bed, begging for more.

He decided he had better get back to his work at the Silver Shoes Saloon, where he did odd jobs for the owner, unloading crates of whiskey, cleaning up the place whenever the crowd thinned out enough to allow it. He liked it there, had learned a lot from the whores and the gamblers. Mellie worked there, and he liked Mellie, although sometimes she seemed a little irritated with him. Hell, she was a whore, wasn't she? Why wouldn't she just let him sleep with her whenever he wanted? Sometimes she pissed him off a little, and once he'd had to punch her. He almost got fired for it, but Toby had let him stay on.

He made pretty good money, had even won some at poker; and late at night, there were always the drunks to steal from. Mellie had taught him about that. Men often passed completely out in her bed, and it was easy then to sift through their pockets, after which the bouncer in the Silver Shoes carried them out to the alley. Clarence often roamed the city at night looking for other drunks who lay in the streets or in the alleys, and in this town most men carried a good amount of money on them. It seemed like in Virginia City everybody was rich. He didn't have to steal from Uncle Wilbur's collection plate anymore, hardly ever saw the man now, and that was just fine with him.

CHAPTER THIRTEEN

Miranda stretched, then snuggled back into the clean blankets that covered the feather mattress. She moved against Jake's warm, naked body, luxuriating in the reality that they had found a room at this pleasant boardinghouse, a place where they could shut themselves away from the danger and the reckless life of Virginia City only a block or two away. Even with doors and windows closed, a person could hear the rowdy yells and gunfire coming from the saloons and gambling halls, as well as the rumbling explosions at the mines in the surrounding mountains; but the coziness of the boardinghouse made Miranda feel safe and protected.

The owner, Virginia Anderson, was an aging widow woman whose husband had been killed in a mining accident two years ago. In spite of the rough-and-tumble life that went on in the streets of town, the woman kept a tidy, pleasant home, renting rooms only to married couples or single men who appeared clean and respectable. Her cooking was wonderful, and everyone sat at a big table in the dining room and ate off lovely china set out on a lace tablecloth. It was as close to home as she and Jake had been, and she thought how nice it was going to be to truly have a place of their own, where she could do the cooking and the decorating.

At least for now she could get a taste of being settled

again. She needed something to do here for the winter and she wanted to make this place feel as much like home as possible. Yesterday morning she had offered to help Mrs. Anderson with the cooking and baking and kitchen cleanup, and to her relief the woman had agreed, explaining that she was getting a little too old to keep up with all of it. In return for her help, she and Jake would not have to pay for their meals, and they would get two dollars a week off the cost of their room. With what they had already learned about living expenses in this silver town, and with their own money reserves getting low, Mrs. Anderson's offer was a welcome relief. It would make the winter's stay here much easier.

She turned and put an arm across Jake's middle, moved a leg over his own legs. Last night had been their third night here, and the first time both of them felt settled and rested enough to make love. They were finally beginning to get their strength back and get their bearings after the arduous journey. Once they located Wes and Jake found a job, life could be almost normal for them, except that they wouldn't have a place of their own until they reached California. By then Jake would have a son or a daughter, and they would truly be a family. Maybe Wes would want to come to California with them and help Jake build a cabin, start a ranch or a farm. She so looked forward to seeing Wes again, even though she could not quite forgive him for leaving her and their father when they both needed him most.

"I'd better go out and start looking for your brother and for a job," Jake spoke up, as though to read her thoughts.

She raised her head and looked at him. "I wasn't sure you were awake."

"With you crawling all over me? How can a man sleep through that?"

She smiled, and both of them relaxed in the luxury of being safe and warm and living in something that didn't have wheels. He rolled on top of her, and Miranda closed her eyes as he entered her softly, gently. She thought how they just seemed to know each other's minds sometimes, how lovemaking with him could sometimes be a desperate, grasping, urgent need; or just a gentle "good morning," like this. They were both relaxed and warm, snuggled into the feather mattress with a down-filled blanket covering them, their body heat shielding them against the cold room, their coupling building that body heat. The potbellied stove in the corner needed stoking, but for the moment they would stoke the fires in their souls.

"I could stay right here all day," Jake told her, kissing her eyelids.

"I wouldn't mind," she answered. She ran her hands over his broad chest, toyed with his nipples.

Jake drew in his breath and pushed harder, wondering at how easily she could make him want her, loving her to the point of worship. What a sweet feeling it was to wake up with Miranda beside him, wanting him this way. Now that they had this place to stay and a little privacy, he could teach her all of the delicious ways of making love, show her the things she had said she wanted to learn.

He had always figured proper women like Miranda would be stiff and unsatisfying in bed, but she had surprised him with the bold offering of her body to him for his pleasure. He loved knowing she was his wife, loved possessing her, claiming her, proving to himself she really belonged to him.

She drew the life from his depths, and it seemed that each time he did this she took a little more of the old Jake Harkner away and filled him with more of the new man. He belonged to her now as much as she to him. She had made him open up to her, share his deepest horrors and ugliest memories. Somehow she had made them easier to bear. Nothing must ever be allowed to destroy what he had found with this woman, yet he feared sometimes that the destruction would come from himself and not from outside forces. Could he really do this? Could he really leave the past behind and be a proper husband for her? Hell, he had no experience with this, no background to teach him how to do it right. The only thing he had going for him was her sweet, loyal love, the passion they shared, and his own desperate need never to be without her.

He leaned down and kissed her forehead, then rolled away from her, stretching and lying on his back. "I've got to get going, find work."

"Maybe I should go with you. After all, I know what Wes looks like."

He tousled her hair. "No, ma'am. The best way to find him is to hit the saloons and the mines, and I won't have you seen either place. You remember what happened that first night we got here. If you want *me* to stay out of trouble, you stay right here with Mrs. Anderson and help her out like we agreed on. I've got Wes's picture. That's all I need."

"I hate for you to be out there at all." Miranda stroked his arm and kissed it. "Everything out there represents the old Jake. Maybe you'll go out there and never come back to me."

He grinned. "Hell, I hope you have more faith in me than that."

She smiled and caressed his chest. "It's the troublemakers and the prostitutes I don't trust."

He turned to her and moved down to kiss at her breasts, then her neck. "You're more exciting than any woman I've been with, and you make it beautiful because you love me." He kissed her lightly.

She touched his face. Was he ready for the additional responsibility he would face in a few months? "Jake, before you go, I have to tell you something. I put it off until now because I wanted to get that trip over with first. You had so much to worry about just getting us here."

He frowned. "You saying there's something new to worry about? You think your brother is in trouble or something?"

"No, it isn't that." She breathed deeply for strength, not quite sure what the news would mean to a man like Jake. "I'm going to have a baby, Jake. My guess is around next April you'll be a father."

She watched him closely, saw the familiar fear fill his eyes. He sat up and looked her over, touched her belly.

"You sure?"

"I haven't had my time for three months now, ever since our wedding night. You were too tired and busy keeping us alive to notice."

He closed his eyes and turned away, throwing back the covers and rising to pull on his long johns. "I've got to wash up." He walked into the small, curtained-off room where a washstand and a chamber pot were kept.

Miranda waited, wondering if the news would send him running back to that old life because he was too afraid to face being a father. He emerged from the washroom, turning to pick up his shirt. She studied the scars on his back, inflicted on a small boy by a vicious man who was his own father. He pulled on the shirt and buttoned it, then stepped into his trousers. "I'm no material for being a father, Randy." He tucked in his shirt. "I guess I knew in the back of my mind it would happen, but somehow I hoped it wouldn't."

"Hoped?" She sat up, keeping a blanket over her breasts. "Jake, when a man and woman get married and make love, babies usually follow. It's a fact of nature. I'm sure the women you've known have ways of avoiding such things, but I don't know how to do whatever it is they do to keep from getting pregnant; and I certainly don't believe in letting quack doctors do horrible things to women to abort their babies, so I'm having this one. You're going to be a father whether you want to or not."

He began pulling on socks and boots. "It isn't a matter of whether or not I *want* to be a father. I *can't* be one."

"And what is that supposed to mean?"

He rose and walked to a nightstand where Randy had left her brother's picture. He put it into his shirt pocket and took his gunbelts from a nearby chair and began strapping them on. "It means that because of my own childhood, I can't turn around and be a father to a kid of my own. What if the kid pisses me off and I hit him? What if I find out I'm just like my own pa?" he said bitterly.

She watched him tie the rawhide holster-straps around his thighs. "Jake, that's ridiculous. You would never be like that. Don't you understand? This is your chance to make up for all the terrible things your father did to you. I have no doubt in my mind that you'll make a better father than most men would, because you remember all the things you wished you had in your own father. Of course there will be times when he'll be naughty and need a spanking. That isn't the same, Jake."

He took his sheepskin jacket from a hook on the wall and put it on. "And what if a spanking turns into something more? I'd rather shoot myself." He put on his hat. "I figure I can handle settling and being a husband, Randy, but not a father." He turned to the door.

"And just what do you propose we do about it, Jake? This baby is going to be born, no matter what."

He kept his back to her. "I don't know. I need to think."

"I love you, Jake. I want this baby to know its real father, to experience the love I know you're capable of showing him, probably more than most men."

He hesitated at the door. "You, uh, you need a doctor or anything like that?" His voice was gruff with emotion.

She felt an anxious panic at his leaving without settling their discussion about the baby. "I don't think so, but I wouldn't mind you finding out if there *is* a real doctor in this place, so I'll have one when the baby comes."

"Fine. I'll check it out. Between that and looking for your brother and for work, I expect I'll be gone most of the day, maybe all night. Don't worry if I don't show up."

All night? He was running! He was scared to death and running! "Jake! Is that the only reason you might not be back? Do you think you can run from this baby by going out there and getting right back into the kind of life you used to lead, pretend this isn't happening? It *is* happening, Jake! You're going to be a father, and I know in my heart you'll be a *good* father. Don't give up trying to change at the first sign of too much responsibility. I can *help* you. We can do this together. We can make a home for our children, like the home you always wanted yourself!"

He sighed deeply and opened the door. "Get some rest." He walked out, and Miranda slumped back into the bed, refusing to let the tears come. Surely he wouldn't go out there and get into trouble. Did he think that would make her stop loving him, make her leave him and find some other man?

You're the only man I want, Jake Harkner, the only proper father for this baby.

She rose and pulled a blanket around herself, then walked to a window. Their room faced the street, and she parted a curtain to see Jake walking across the street. "You'll be back, Jake," she said softly. "You'll be back because I can give you more than that life out there. You've had a taste of love and you want so much more. I'm the only one who can give it to you, me and this baby you made inside of me."

Jake lit another cheroot, glancing up at the sign over the saloon that read SILVER SHOES. He had been in practically every saloon in town asking about Wes Baker and showing the picture. In most of the taverns, he had encountered the expected one or two men ready to challenge a newcomer, either with whiskey or cards or by bellowing about how strong they were or how good with a gun. After a second look, they had all backed down from him or decided to be friendly. Jake figured it must be the look in his eyes or the way he wore his guns, slung low, like a man who knew how to use them.

He decided it was mostly the look in his eyes. He was pissed off today, and he expected men could tell. His anger was not at Randy or over the baby, but at himself for just leaving the way he had, without settling what was really bothering him. Part of him wanted that baby as much as Randy did, but another part of him told him he wasn't worthy of being a father. Who was Jake Harkner to think he should deserve the honor of having a small child call him Pa? And what if that child found out the truth about its father, that he had been a killer, a man who whored and drank and gambled and raided innocent farmers; worst of all, a man who had killed his own father, the child's own grandfather!

Somewhere in the back of his mind he had considered the possibility of being a father, and every time it happened, he had not allowed himself to dwell on it, had refused to discuss it with Randy. How could he have been so stupid as to think he could put it off forever? For all his skill with his fists and guns, for all his wild daring and fearless exploits, he was a damn coward when it came to the thought of being a father. How did he know he wouldn't be just like his own father? And if the child found out about his past, just think of the shame he would see in his son or daughter's eyes. He couldn't bear that look, couldn't stand the thought of his child hating him and being ashamed of him the way he had hated and been ashamed of his own pa. And if he did turn out to be a crummy father, think what it would do to Randy. He would lose her. No woman chose a husband over a child. She would surely take the kid and leave him.

He walked up the steps and into the saloon. It was nearly dark now, and the place was packed with every sort of lowlife imaginable. *Including me,* he thought. Lowlife was right, for the way he had walked out on his wife, a good woman, devoted. She had taken a big risk marrying a man like him, and already he was proving she had made a mistake.

God, how he wished he could just stay away, stick to his first idea that maybe she should get rid of him right now and find some other man. But life without Randy would be the worst hell of all, worse than what he had suffered as a child, worse than taking a bullet or being cornered by Kennedy and his bunch. He couldn't live without her, and that was that. He'd have to face this father thing and own up to his responsibilities; but if he ever hit that kid, ever found himself even *wanting* to hit him, hell, he wouldn't want to live.

He walked up to the bar and asked for a whiskey, and a pretty blond prostitute sauntered his way, her breasts almost fully revealed by the low bodice of her purple satin dress. Her diamond earrings dangled nearly to her shoulders, and she was a little more pleasant to look at than most whores. He thought how at one time he would have grabbed this one up and enjoyed her for the night. Now she didn't interest him in the least. She wasn't Randy. There *was* nobody like Randy. He'd never gotten such pleasure from being with a woman as he got from his wife, and he supposed it was because he was really making love.

"Buy you a drink, mister?"

Jake allowed himself a look at the low neckline. "No, thanks," he answered. "I'm just looking for someone."

She smiled, rubbing up against him and moving her hand to his rear. "If you're looking for a good lay, you've just found her. My name is Mellie."

Jake picked up his shot of whiskey and downed it. Yes, it would be so easy to go back to this. He'd played a few hands of poker at one of the other saloons, as a way of getting to know the men better, finding out about the different mines and trying to determine where Wes might be. But all the while he had been unable to get his mind off of Randy.

"You're a big man, right handsome, too," Mellie purred. "I like those big guns you wear." She moved her hand to his privates. "You got another one in there?"

Jake took hold of her wrist and pulled her hand away. "That's for my wife to know." He gave her a wink and she looked disappointed.

"She must be some woman. Not many married men turn me away."

Jake let go of her wrist. "I don't expect they do. And if I *wasn't* married, I'd be whipping out my money right now." He swallowed the second shot of whiskey, then turned to scan the room, always wary of walking into a saloon in a town like this, where there wasn't much law. Some men who regularly frequented favorite taverns had a kind of possessive feeling about the place, didn't like newcomers.

A few glanced his way, looked him over. One in particular looked awfully interested. He was young, maybe eighteen or twenty. His blond hair hung nearly to his shoulders, and he sported a poor semblance of a beard and mustache. Jake pegged him as a boy who thought he was a man. He even wore a gun on his hip and he was giving Jake a challenging look. Jake hoped the kid wasn't stupid enough to try to start something.

He looked back at Mellie and pulled out Wes's picture for

what seemed the hundredth time that day. "There is one thing you can do for me," he told her, handing her the picture. "His name is Wes Baker, and he's about twenty-two. He's my wife's brother. We came here to find him. His last letter was from Virginia City. You know him?"

Mellie's mouth fell open as she studied the picture for several seconds. When she looked up at Jake, he was surprised to see tears in her eyes. "Yes. He used to come in here a lot." She looked back at the picture. "He was a nice kid. He used to say I was his favorite and we, I don't know, we got to be pretty good friends. He was sweet, liked to drink and gamble a little too much, never had any money because he gambled away his earnings every weekend." She looked back up at Jake. "I'm sorry to tell you this, but Wes Baker is dead. He was killed in a mining accident last year."

Jake felt like someone had hit him in the chest. Dead! How the hell was he supposed to go back to Randy with news like that? "Maybe you're mistaken. A lot of men hang out in these places. Maybe you've got him mixed up with somebody else."

She studied the picture again. "No. That's my Wes, all right. There's no mistaking it. I mean, that was his name, and this is his face. He even used to tell me about a sister he had back in Kansas City. I expect I knew more about him than anybody. In a place like this, men don't generally share too much about where they came from and all." She wiped at her eyes. "I'm the one who made sure he had a decent burial. The men where he worked told me his body had been brought down to town, so I went and saw it for myself. There were five or six mineworkers at the funeral, and me." She handed back the picture. "I guess I should have maybe tried to find his sister, maybe sent a letter to a Miss Baker in Kansas City or something. He never even told me her name. I wasn't sure she'd get the letter and I sure as hell knew she wouldn't want to know he'd been hanging around with the likes of me."

Jake took the picture. "Sorry I upset you. You want a drink yourself?"

"Yeah, I think so." She called out to the bartender and asked for a whiskey. "I'm awful sorry, mister, your wife coming all the way here from Kansas just to find him."

Jake sighed, shoving the picture back into his pocket. Poor Randy. Here he'd walked out on her this morning when she was trying to share something wonderful with him, wonderful to her at least. She probably thought he didn't want the kid, maybe even figured he wasn't coming back and she was stranded here alone. Now this. He'd have to go back and tell her Wes was dead. Wes was all the family she had left. It didn't seem right, when folks had decent family, that they should have to lose them. And now *he* was all she had left, him and the baby. She would need him now more than ever.

Mellie sniffed and swallowed the whiskey, wiping at her eyes again. Jake noticed the kid with the blond hair had moved closer. He approached Mellie. "This guy giving you trouble, honey?" he asked, a possessive ring to the words.

"No, Clarence, nothing like that. We're just talking about somebody who used to mean a lot to me."

Jake ordered one more whiskey, and the kid named Clarence came around Mellie and stood before him in a challenging stance. Jake tried to remember why the name Clarence rang a bell. Wasn't that the name of the kid who had tried to rape Randy? This couldn't be the same one. That kid had been traveling with a preacher. He couldn't be the tobacco-chewing, gunslinging man-child who stood before him now.

"Part of my job here, mister, is to keep an eye out to make sure nobody comes in here and hurts or upsets the girls," the boy told Jake. "You made Mellie here cry, so maybe you'd just better leave."

"Clarence, I told you it's got nothing to do with him. Leave him alone." Mellie moved in front of the young man, but Clarence shoved her out of the way.

Jake drank down another shot of whiskey and took his cheroot from an ashtray on the bar. He stuck it in his mouth and puffed on it a moment, studying the snot-nosed kid before him. Why in hell was he doing this? "I think you've had a little too much whiskey, boy. It's making you do something real stupid. Now I'm warning you, I'm in a damn bad mood right now, and you don't even want to see what I can do when I'm in a *good* mood, so if you have any brains in that skull at all, you'll back off right now while you're still healthy."

Clarence rested his hands on his hips in a haughty stance. He was standing up to this big man with the big guns, and he liked the feel of it, especially with Mellie and his boss and others watching. He felt confident. After all, he knew most of the men in here, figured they'd back him up. This man surely realized it wouldn't be wise to try anything when he was surrounded by men who would jump in against him.

"I saw you the other night when you came into town with Mrs. Hayes," he told Jake. "I've been wondering about that, who you really are, how the pretty widow woman ended up taking up with the likes of you. Are you really her husband, or just another traveler helping out the poor widow in distress?"

Jake straightened, slowly setting down his shotglass and studying the young man. Good God, was this Clarence Gaylord? The little sonofabitch! "Her name is Mrs. Turner now, and I'm *Jake* Turner. Maybe you can tell Mellie here and anybody else who's listening just how you know my wife, Clarence. It *is* Clarence Gaylord, isn't it?" Several men sitting closest had already stopped their drinking and cardplaying to watch the confrontation.

"First you tell me how in hell she ended up with you," Clarence challenged.

Mellie herself backed away then, confused by what was happening. She didn't like Clarence. Ever since that first night she had taken his money for sex, he had begun hanging around, being a nuisance. He seemed to think he ought to be her favorite, that he should be able to come and see her for free whenever he had the yen, just because he worked here now. He was a cocky, stupid kid eager to be a man and prove he could hold his whiskey with the rest of them. "You'd better be careful, Clarence. This man doesn't look like any ordinary Joe," she warned.

"Shut up, Mellie! I know he's pretty good with a gun once it's drawn. I just don't know how fast he is at drawing it."

Jake almost laughed. "Go dry yourself behind the ears, boy. You try drawing on me, and I'll blow you clear into the wall behind you! Fact is, I ought to do it anyway after what you did to my wife!"

"Yeah? Well, before you do that, maybe you'll tell me how it is Mrs. Hayes got to *be* your wife, if that's really true."

"I don't owe you any explanations, you little sonofabitch! Why don't *you* tell everybody how she trusted you and that preacher uncle of yours, how she was a widow woman trying to get here all the way from Kansas just to find her brother. Tell them how you attacked her and tried to rape her, and how your good Christian uncle left her to die after she got snakebit!"

Clarence began to redden a little. He didn't like being embarrassed this way in front of men who knew him, especially not in front of his boss and Mellie. He hadn't wanted any of them to know his uncle was a preacher. God, he'd like to kill this man! It would make him look big, really big. And it would leave Mrs. Hayes or Mrs. Turner or whatever she called herself a widow again, alone in a town where all kinds of things could happen to a woman like her.

He backed up a little, and men began moving out of the way. Was this man really fast with a gun, or just a big bluff? He'd gotten pretty good himself, had been practicing. "Your wife lied to you, mister. It wasn't that way at all. I never tried to rape her. She was a widow woman hungry for a man, and I accommodated her. When my uncle caught us, she cried rape, but my uncle knew what she *really* was. She was a trouble-maker! That's why my uncle left her at that trading post. She was too much a temptation for me and his brothers. He was afraid we'd all end up fighting over the slut."

The whole room quieted at the words, and Jake moved to face Clarence more squarely. "You're a cocky, lying little rap-ist, Gaylord! You're itching to draw on me, so go ahead. I'd like nothing better than to blow your privates clear down the mountain! I tried to warn you, but you're too fucking stupid to know when to quit! I'd advise you to take back your words and tell these people the truth."

"*I* believe your side, mister," Mellie put in. "You'd better apologize, Clarence. You've got yourself in too deep already."

"That's right," Jake seethed. "Only it's too late for an apology." He pushed his jacket behind his guns. "Go ahead, boy. Show Mellie here what a big man you are!"

Clarence swallowed, his whole body suddenly bathed in perspiration. What had he gotten himself into? He'd started this. Now he had to finish it. Maybe, just maybe, he was faster than this man. He went for his gun, but he had barely touched the handle to pull it out when Jake's was already out and aimed directly under his nose.

"You dumb sonofabitch," Jake snarled. He came closer, grabbed Clarence's gun from its holster and tossed it aside. Quickly his booted foot came up between Clarence's legs, making the boy cry out and bend over. Before he went all the way down, Jake brought his knee into his face, and the sound of his nose breaking could be heard all over the room. No one made a move to interfere, most astounded at the speed with which Jake had drawn the gun.

Clarence crumpled to the floor, gasping for breath and holding his privates. Jake was on him then, shoving him onto his back and forcing the barrel of his ivory-handled .45 into the boy's mouth. Blood poured from Clarence's nose across his cheeks and into his ears, and he stared wide-eyed at Jake, making little whimpering sounds as terror engulfed him. Jake shoved a knee against the boy's chest to pin him down, and he cocked the gun.

"You know what happens when you stick a gun in a man's mouth and pull the trigger, boy?" he growled. "It's not a pretty sight! Now you listen up good. If you were a grown man, I'd splatter your brains all over this room! You're getting a break because you're a stupid, goddamn kid! But if I ever see you anywhere near my wife, or if you give her or me any trouble at all, I won't be so accommodating next time! You picked the wrong man to prove yourself, you little bastard!"

Clarence began to choke at the feel of the end of the gun barrel against his throat, the taste of metal. He had never known such terror in his life, nor such humiliation. Jake finally yanked the gun out of his mouth, and he rolled over and threw up, grunting with fear when Jake yanked at his shirt to grab a piece of it to wipe off his gun.

"You've had your warning, kid." Jake shoved the gun back into its holster. "Pay attention to it and thank God you're still alive!" He stepped back to the bar and glanced around the room, seeing no one who looked willing to give him any trouble. He looked at Mellie then. "Will you come with me and tell my wife what you know about her brother? She might have questions only you could answer."

Mellie looked down at herself. "If she won't mind talking to a . . . to somebody like me. Let me change clothes first. I'll be right back."

She turned and hurried up the stairs, and Jake watched Clarence, who was apparently not so well-liked. No one made a move to help him as he bent over, crying and choking.

"Clean up that stinkin' mess, Clarence," the man behind the bar shouted. "If you're gonna' puke again, do it outside."

Clarence got up and ran out the back door, and the bartender offered Jake another whiskey. "Don't worry about anybody believin' that kid," he told him. "He's been hangin' around here puttin' on airs about bein' a big man. He talks big, but we all know he ain't nothin'."

Jake took the whiskey, figuring he needed one more to deal with the torrent of emotions churning inside him. He had to tell poor Randy that her brother was dead. They had come to this hellhole for nothing. Now she would have to have her baby here, and he wasn't sure he could be a decent father. Now this thing with Clarence Gaylord. The stupid kid was only eighteen, but he had hurt him bad. Was he wrong to do that? Visions of his own father landing into him brought knots to his stomach.

Mellie came back down the stairs wearing a woolen coat. She walked up to the man behind the bar. "I have to go talk to this man's wife, Toby about her brother. I knew him. I'll be back in an hour or so." She looked up at Jake. "Let's go."

Jake followed her out, and the rest of the men returned to their cardplaying. At nearly every table the conversation was about the man with the guns who called himself Jake Turner. None had ever seen anyone draw so fast. A few glanced at Clarence when he came back in holding a handkerchief to his nose, tears on his pale face. He carried a few rags and used them to clean up his vomit, still shaking from thinking Jake Turner would blow his head off.

The way he was raised, Clarence never knew a man could hate so much. He felt humiliated, felt like a fool, and it was all because of that sonofabitch Miranda Hayes had married. Indirectly, the bitch had brought him down again, embarrassed him again. If he could ever find a way to get back at her and that big bastard she married, he'd find it! He hated both of them so bad it made him feel sick again, and he ran back outside to throw up for the third time.

CHAPTER FOURTEEN

 Jake closed the doors to the tidy parlor of Mrs. Anderson's boardinghouse. He liked this place. It was the nicest home he'd ever lived in, and he hoped he could make as nice a place for Randy someday. Lace curtains and braided rugs and lovely plants decorated the room, a warm fire crackling in the fireplace. He was not used to living like this, but it was something he wouldn't mind *getting* used to. Then again, maybe he wasn't meant to live this way. Maybe it was too late for a man who had lived in shacks and above saloons all his life. It all depended on Randy and if she still wanted him. He'd hurt her badly this morning, and he saw how she watched him now, knew what she must think of him bringing someone like Mellie here. She probably thought he'd been with the woman. Mellie had changed into a simpler dress, but the paint on her face and the dangly earrings readily told what she really was.

"I asked Mrs. Anderson to let us be alone in here," he said, turning to Randy.

She looked from Jake to the woman he had introduced as Mellie. Was he trying to throw this in her face to make her hate him more so she would leave him? Jealousy raged in her soul. How dare another woman touch her Jake!

"This isn't what you think, Randy," Jake spoke up quickly. He came over to kneel in front of her. "I brought Mellie here because she knew your brother. I've been asking all over town all day long and I finally found somebody who can settle things for us." He took her hand but she pulled it away, glaring at Mellie.

"You know my brother? Why isn't *he* here? Did he make a habit of hanging out with women like you?"

Jake grasped her arms. "Randy, don't insult her. She was a good friend to Wes. I brought her here in case you had any questions I might not think to ask. Randy, look at me."

She met his eyes, her heart quickening at the sorrow there.

"I'm damn sorry about this morning. We have a lot to talk about, but right now—" He sighed deeply. "Wes is dead, Randy. He was killed in a mining accident almost a year ago."

Miranda just stared at him, the words roaring in her ears. That couldn't be! Wes was her last living kin. "Do you have proof?"

"I'm your proof," Mellie spoke up.

"Why should I believe you?"

Mellie stepped closer. "Honey, I've got no reason to lie about it. Wes and I were good friends. Some of the other men knew it. When he was killed in an explosion, they brought his body to town. I saw it with my own eyes. It was Wes. I made sure he got a nice burial. If you want, I can take you to the graveyard and show you where he's buried. I made the undertaker put up a headstone with his name and age on it. I'm real sorry you came all the way here for nothing."

Miranda felt the tears wanting to come. How could this be? Her father, her mother, her husband, now her brother. And Jake. Did she even still have Jake? She looked at him, felt his hand come over hers again. This time she did not pull away. "Do you believe her?" she asked. "You . . . you know women like her better than I do."

"I believe her. She even started crying when I showed her the picture. And don't be rude to her, Randy. She didn't have to come here." He squeezed her hand. "I'm damn sorry about Wes. If I could change things, I would. I'd even take his place, if that would make you happier."

A tear slipped down her cheek. "Don't say that."

He put a hand to her face and wiped at the tear with his thumb. "Is there anything you want to ask Mellie?"

She sniffed, pulling a handkerchief from the pocket of her dress and wiping at her eyes more. She looked up at Mellie.

"I'm sorry to act so rude. There are other reasons I was upset when you walked in with my husband."

Mellie felt a little embarrassed at witnessing a tender scene between a husband and wife. "It's all right. Women like me are pretty tough-skinned."

Just like Jake, Miranda thought. "Was Wes happy?" she asked aloud. "Did he ever talk about our father? About me?"

Mellie smiled. "Sure he did, but he mostly referred to both of you as just 'Pa' and 'my sister.' I wasn't even sure what your name was, or I might have tried to write and let you know what happened. Besides that, I didn't know if you'd appreciate hearing about him from somebody like me. He was happy, because he was doing something he really wanted to do. He told me he had gotten bored with farming, but he felt a little guilty about leaving you and your pa." She shrugged. "Hell, he was young and wanted some adventure, that's all. Lots of men that age get the yen to strike out on their own. He had big dreams about finding his own claim, but he ended up working at one of the mines instead. He made good money, but I'm afraid he gambled most of it away every week. He only had about twenty dollars on him when he died. I used that for his burial and grave marker. I hope that was all right."

Miranda rose and walked closer. "If you don't mind, I'd like you to take us tomorrow to show us his grave."

"Sure. I don't mind."

Miranda studied her, guessed her to be perhaps thirty. It was hard to tell. The woman had a hard look to her, had obviously had a rough time. What made women choose this life? She thought of Jake's remark back when she first met him, about how some women like this did what they did because they'd been abused as he had. Who was she to judge? "I hope you were good to him."

Mellie almost laughed at the innocent remark. She glanced at Jake and knew he was thinking the same thing, but she kept a sober look. The sadness of the occasion far outweighed the humor the remark would otherwise have evoked. "As good as I could be," she answered. "We didn't always . . . well, you know." She reddened a little. "Sometimes he just wanted to talk, so I listened. That happens a lot here. These men get lonely, miss their family, get their expectations dashed to the ground. It's not as easy to come to a place like this and get rich as one might think."

Miranda swallowed back a lump in her throat. "Did he . . . suffer?"

Mellie shook her head. "They told me he was killed instantly. They use lots of dynamite in those mines. Accidents like that are pretty frequent."

Miranda nodded. She reached out and surprised Mellie by hugging her. "Thank you for being his friend, and for coming here to tell me. Can you be here tomorrow morning around ten?"

Mellie glanced at Jake again. She had a feeling he knew that women like her seldom got up before one o'clock in the afternoon. There was something about the man that told her he was familiar with saloons and whores. How had he ended up with this lovely woman who was obviously a proper lady? He was so big and dark and dangerous-looking, and she was so small and refined.

"Why don't we make it around two, Randy?" Jake suggested, to Mellie's relief. "It will be warmer midday. I don't want you getting chilled in your condition."

"Fine. I'll see you at two then."

Mellie nodded.

"You want me to walk you back? It's dark out there," Jake spoke up.

Mellie laughed lightly. "You don't really think that matters, do you?"

"Sure it matters."

"I'm all right. Just about every man in this town knows me. I'm safe." She smiled rather sadly. "Besides, there isn't much a man can do to me that hasn't already been done now, is there? You stay here and comfort your wife, Mr. Turner. I'll be by tomorrow."

The woman left, and Miranda just stood staring at the doors. The ordeal of the journey to get here, the horror of being left to die at the trading post, and the terror of her pain and of the men who cared for her, all combined with the thought today that Jake might go back to his old life, crashed in on her on one wave of emotion. Now to learn that Wes was dead, that she had given up so much and risked so much to come here for nothing, brought her such terrible grief and disappointment, she grabbed the back of a chair to keep from falling.

In an instant Jake was there, lifting her up with strong arms and carrying her to their own room. He kicked the door shut and sat down on the bed, holding her tightly on his lap. "I'm sorry, Randy, not just about your brother but about all the rest. Just tell me what you need, *mi querida.*"

"I just need you to hold me," she sobbed. "I need you to want our baby."

He kissed her hair. "I told you I do want the child. It's just that my whole life I never gave one thought to being a father, figured I'd never be very good at it. I just don't know if I'm even worthy to have a kid call me Pa."

"You are, Jake. How many times do I have to tell you you're as worthy as the next man? I know you love me, Jake, and you'll love our baby. But you've got to learn to love yourself too."

He felt an ache in his chest at the remark. He realized how right she was. It was hard learning how to love and be loved, harder still to learn to love himself; but then he figured if a woman like Randy could love him, there must be a part of him that was worth something.

"It's more important to me now than ever for us to be family, Jake," she was saying. "You and the baby are all I've got, and we're all *you* have." He smelled of whiskey and smoke, and she clung to him. "I was afraid you wouldn't come back."

He stroked her hair. "I'll do and say a lot of things that don't make sense sometimes, Randy, but one thing I know is I can't be without you. There are times when I might leave because I've got to be alone to think things out; but I'll always come back. Always." He began unbuttoning her dress. "Let's get a nightgown on you so you can get some rest. Tonight I'll just hold you, and tomorrow we'll have a nice breakfast and go visit Wes's grave. When you feel stronger, we'll talk about the baby."

He undressed her and put on her gown, insisting she stay in bed while he went to the kitchen to see about bringing her something hot to drink. Miranda pulled the pillow to her, her emotions torn. The news about Wes was so disappointing. She had gone through so much to get here. The only thing that made the grief more bearable was the fact that Jake was here. She had trusted that he would come back, and he had. She put a hand to her belly, realizing her waist had gotten thicker. If Jake Harkner didn't fully understand about love, the baby would teach him the rest. "You'll be the best father who ever walked the earth, Jake. I know it in my heart."

Miranda laid some flowers on Wes's grave as Mellie left them. She put a hand to her aching chest, her grief more piercing at having never gotten to see her brother again. It felt strange to know that all that had been a part of her blood and her past was gone.

"There is nothing left now, Jake." She rose and faced him. "No past, for me or for you. This is a sign that we have to go on and look only to the future, our baby, a life together. All we have is each other."

They stood high on a hill that overlooked Virginia City. With the influx of thousands to the silver town, the graveyard had also quickly expanded, filled mostly with men killed in mining accidents or in fights in town. In the distance someone was conducting a funeral. A hawk flew overhead and screeched, and Miranda thought what a sad place this was, full of the graves of lonely, forgotten men come here in search of a dream and finding only death.

"I don't want you to be afraid of being a father, Jake," she told him. "You know exactly what you would have liked to have for a father, and I know in my heart you'll do everything you can to make life very different for your child than it was for you. You think you know what love is all about now, but you won't know until you hold this baby in your arms. I have a feeling our biggest problem will be you spoiling him or her to death."

Jake walked a few feet past her. "I'll tell you what bothers me most, Randy," he said, his voice strained with emotion. "It's the same thing that hurts the most about my own pa. It wasn't the beatings so much as the fact that I hated him so much, was so ashamed of him. A kid needs to be *proud* of his pa, Randy. If I ever saw that same hate and shame in my own kid's eyes . . ." He turned to face her. "That's why this baby and any others we have can't ever be told about my past. If they find out what I used to be, find out I killed my own pa, they'd look at me with those same eyes, and any love they had for me would be lost."

"I don't believe that, Jake." She drew her coat closer around her neck, a cold mountain wind blowing her hair away from her face. "We'll *make* them understand."

"No." He came closer, his dark eyes determined. "I don't

want you ever to tell them. We'll find a peaceful place in California to settle. They don't ever need to know."

She frowned. "Jake, my own father used to say that telling the truth right away was always better than letting it be found out some other way farther on in life. It saves a lot of hurt and misunderstanding."

"I mean it, Randy. If you ever say anything, I'll leave, because I'm not going to stay around and have my children look at me with that shame. I don't ever want them to know. You've got to promise me."

"Jake—"

"Promise me! I never want them to know about my past."

She folded her arms, seeing again that little-boy fear in his eyes. "All right. I think you're wrong, Jake. If they find out later, it will be worse, but if that's what you want, I'll agree to it." The wind suddenly blew a little harder, and she shivered, something deep inside telling her the promise she had just made was a decision they would both one day regret.

Jake breathed deeply in relief. "I found an honest-to-goodness doctor in town," he told her. "I think you should go and see him, get to know him. At least you'll have some help when the time comes. Soon as that baby is born and you're both strong enough, we'll get the hell out of this place." He leaned down and kissed her cheek. "I'm sorry about Wes."

Miranda looked back at the grave. "We used to be close when we were little. Now that I think about it, he seemed to start drawing away after Mother died. My father was so lost in his own grief, he didn't pay any attention. I don't think any of us realized how much her death affected him." She looked back at Jake, realizing how much more traumatic for him the death of his own mother had been. She reached out and took his hand. "Let's go back."

Those who had attended the funeral nearby had broken up and were also leaving. Miranda glanced their way, only then realizing that the preacher for the service had been Wilbur Jennings. She drew in her breath, and Jake frowned. "What is it?"

"It's Preacher Jennings!" She left him and briskly walked closer to the man. Jennings and his wife stopped still when they saw her, and Miranda noticed that one of the man's brothers was also with him. She saw no sign of Clarence.

"Mrs. Hayes!" Preacher Jennings looked startled and immediately began to redden.

"Well, if it isn't the fine preacher," Miranda said, loud enough for some of the other people leaving to hear. They stopped and turned. "Have you told the people here the truth about the kind of man you really are?" Her grief and the strain of the last two days made her want to lash out at someone. What better target than this man who had left her to die! She turned to the rest of them. "You can tell any others who listen to this man preach about God and faith and goodness that he's a hypocrite! I traveled part way here with the good preacher and his family from Kansas—"

"Please, Mrs. Hayes," Opal spoke up, her face pale.

Miranda glanced at her. "You're as guilty as your husband," she sneered. "And my name is Turner, Mrs. Jake Turner. It's only thanks to my new husband that I am *alive* today! He found me at that trading post, dying, being abused by those horrible men you knew good and well wouldn't take good care of me!" She looked at the others again, as Jake stepped up behind her. "The Reverend Jennings left me behind at a stinking, dirty trading post back in Nebraska after I had been bitten by a snake," she told them. "His own nephew tried to rape me before that, and the preacher chose to believe the boy when he said I had done the seducing! It was a lie! That is how forgiving the preacher is. Even if it had been true, a true Christian would have given me the benefit of the doubt, would have still seen to my safety until others came along with whom I could travel. Instead he chose to leave me behind like a dying mule!" She looked back at Jennings. "Never have I known such pain and humiliation. Mr. Turner came along and rescued me from that filthy place and lanced my wound to drain the infection! He saved my life, while you continued on as though I never existed!"

"Reverend, is that true?" one of those in the funeral party asked.

"I . . . it wasn't quite that way. I mean . . ." He looked at his wife. "Say something, Opal!" The man's stammering told the others all they needed to know.

"And we thought somebody had finally come to this godforsaken town who could be trusted," one of the others said. He and those with him just stared for a moment, shaking their heads. They turned and left, and Miranda enjoyed the withered look on Jennings's face.

"I'm glad I've seen you again." Miranda was seething. "Every chance I get I'll tell others about how poorly you practice what you preach! And where is your oh-so-perfect, innocent nephew, Reverend? Is *he* out preaching too?"

Opal blinked back tears, her hard, thin face showing her sorrow. "Clarence has been taken in by the sin of this town," she answered, looking embarrassed herself. "He has strayed from us and has fallen into the ways of the wicked."

"Well, today Clarence isn't feeling too much like sinning or doing anything else," Jake spoke up, surprising Miranda. "He and I had a little run-in last night in the Silver Shoes. I found out who he was and I can guarantee he's damn sorry about what he did to Miranda."

"What did you do to him?" the reverend demanded, his face livid.

"Nothing he didn't deserve," Jake answered.

The preacher literally shook, turning to Opal. "I must try to find him and make sure he's all right. James would want me to do that much." He grasped his wife's arm and stormed off with her, his brother glaring at Jake for a moment, looking him over, studying the guns he wore. The momentary challenge he had shown quickly changed to a look that said he thought better of it. He followed Jennings down the hill.

Miranda turned to Jake. "What happened with Clarence? Why didn't you tell me?"

He moved his hat back farther on his head. "You had enough to think about last night. He had seen us that first night, knew who I was when I went into the Silver Shoes. Apparently he works there, and apparently it pissed him off that the woman who had spurned him turned around and married me. I'm only guessing at how the stupid kid thinks." He took a cheroot from an inside pocket of his jacket. "The dumb kid decided to challenge me. He insulted you in front of everybody in that saloon, then went for his gun."

Her eyes widened. "You *shot* him?"

"Hell no. You don't want to know what I did, except that I gave him a damn good scare. I have to tell you, though, there was a time when I *would* have shot him." He cupped his hand against the wind and lit the square cigar. "On the one hand I feel good about letting him live, but I only did it because he's a smart-mouthed kid trying to be a man." He puffed on the cheroot. "The only thing that bothers me is the rage I felt when I lit into him. It reminded me of my pa. I've beat the hell out of plenty of men, but never somebody that age."

Miranda folded her arms stoically. "He deserved whatever

you did to him! If he thought he was man enough to try to rape me, then he was man enough to take what he had coming!"

He squinted, keeping the cigar in his mouth and studying her intently. "Well, Mrs. Turner, for such a slip of a woman, you can be pretty damn ornery."

"If I'm going to be married to you, I expect I have to be, just to keep you in line, if nothing else."

He grinned a little, stepping closer and putting his arm around her. "Come on. Let's get you out of the cold."

Miranda looked back once more at the lonely grave. It broke her heart to think of Wes dying without any family close by, but it had been his choice to leave. She only wished he could have been buried next to their father. She turned to Jake, resting her head against his chest. "It hurts, Jake, to think our once-close family is so scattered and broken now. Mother is buried back in Illinois, Father in Kansas, now Wes here in Nevada. I'll be moving on to California come spring. It feels strange, like I'm floating on the wind."

"You'll feel more secure when you have that baby and have a place to call your own. There won't be any more wandering after that. I promise. Come on now. It's getting colder. I think another snowstorm is coming."

He walked her to Outlaw and lifted her up onto the horse, then took the reins and began leading the animal back to town. An explosion in a nearby mine made Miranda jump, and she looked back at the grave once more, thinking of the awful way poor Wes had died. Her throat ached, and she turned away again. Snowflakes began to take shape, and before the day was out, the graveyard would be buried in three feet of snow. Winter was settling into the Sierras with a vengeance.

CHAPTER FIFTEEN

 January 1867 . . .

Miranda read the headlines of the *Territorial Enterprise* again. BANK ROBBERY FOILED BY LOCAL CITIZEN. "Oh, Jake," she whispered. What he had done would be laughingly ironic if it weren't for the unwanted attention it had drawn. She read on. *Local gunsmith Jake Turner yesterday interrupted a bank robbery in progress at the Nevada National, catching the thieves as they came out of the bank and shooting it out with them. Turner, an ex-lawman himself, is known to be an excellent gunman and has worked for Ike Jones, our local gunsmith, since arriving in Virginia City last October. Of the five thieves, two are dead, two wounded, and one is sitting in the local jailhouse. All the stolen money was recovered, and Sheriff Lane is grateful for Mr. Turner's quick thinking and prompt action.*

Quick thinking. The whole town thought Jake's reaction had been because he was an experienced lawman from back East. That was the only explanation Jake could think of. How else could he explain the wild shoot-out? He couldn't tell everyone that the reason he had recognized a robbery was in progress was by the look of the men who waited outside the bank; that he knew why they were there because he had robbed more than one bank himself and knew the setup. Miranda had tried to make him feel better by telling him that at least he had had the right idea for once, had stopped a robbery instead of being a part of one. On the one hand he had done a good thing, but he had paced and smoked half the night worrying about the attention he had drawn to himself.

If we weren't in such a dangerous place where I might run into somebody who knows me, I'd take these damn guns off, he had grumbled. *Once we get out of here and settle in California, I won't wear them anymore. I promise.*

Miranda was just as worried about the bold headlines as he was. He could hardly walk out the door without people surrounding him, slapping him on the back, asking about his skill with his guns, wanting to know where he had been a lawman. She knew it irritated him that he had to pile on lie after lie. At the breakfast table this morning, the other guests of the boardinghouse peppered him with more questions.

She set down the paper when she heard the outside door close. She walked from the parlor into the hallway to see Jake hanging up his coat and hat. "You're late," she told him. "You know I worry when you're late."

He stomped snow from his feet, then sat down on a bench Mrs. Anderson kept in the hall and removed his boots. "I was talking with the owner of the Yellow Jacket mine." He set his boots aside and rose, kissing her cheek before leading her into the parlor. "He offered me a job, and I think I'm going to take it." He moved to the fireplace to warm his hands.

"The Yellow Jacket! You won't be able to come home at night."

"I know." He turned to look at her, still warming his hands. "The pay is good, Randy, five times what I'm making here in town. We'll need the money if I'm going to set you up right when we reach California. I've already let these guns bring me more attention than I want, so I might as well go all the way. Management at the Yellow Jacket wants me to come up there and be a troubleshooter, keep men in line up at the mine, make sure shipments from the mine to town make it without any trouble and that payroll money gets back up there the same way."

"Jake, that sounds dangerous."

He laughed almost bitterly. "For me? Hell, I can take on an army, remember? The damage is done now as far as people knowing how I handle myself. If that's how it's going to be, I might as well make all the money I can with these things while I have the chance." He unbuckled the gunbelts and threw the weapons onto a chair and held his hands near the fire again.

"I'm taking the job, Randy. I want to get us started right when we reach California. We're going to need a lot of things, a house, furnishings, cattle and such. I don't have any choice. If I can use what I know for good, then why not do it, especially when it means making a better life for you and the kid."

He turned, glancing at her swollen belly, loving the sight of this beautiful woman carrying his child. He wanted more than anything to make life good for her, and he hated the disappointed look in her eyes. "It's just till spring, Randy. I can make a lot of money over the next four months, and I can come home for two days out of every eight. As soon as you're able, we'll get the hell out of here and life will be more peaceful, I promise." He turned back to the fire. "You'll be fine if you stay right here with Mrs. Anderson. After we get to California and settle into some little nameless town, things will be different. I'll hang up the guns and just be a common farmer, a man with a wife and a kid who's no different than the next man."

She hated the thought of his being gone so much, but he wanted so badly to earn all that he could so they could live well in California. "Will you come and stay when the baby is due? I don't want to have it alone, Jake."

"I'll be here. Nothing can keep me away." He turned and folded her into his arms. "I don't like it much more than you do, Randy, but I can't turn this down. If I'm going to work to earn money legitimately, I might as well be doing what I do best, and making as much as I can."

"If you feel right about the job, then take it." Her eyes rested on the guns that lay in the chair, and she thought about the promise she had made not to tell their children about his past. Could they really keep that past a secret like he wanted? The only possibility of doing that was if he hung those guns up forever. She felt like part of this was her fault for having brought him here. They should have headed north to Oregon.

April 1867 . . .

The smell of spring was pungent in the mountain air, and Bill Kennedy wondered how soon it would be safe to travel on to Nevada. The cold and snowstorms had lasted into April, and they were all anxious now to be on their way. He stepped off the porch of the small cabin he and his men had taken over since the owner, an old trapper, had died, and he thought how good the air smelled compared to the stink of eight men sleeping practically on top of each other inside. At least most of the time two or three of them were gone, sleeping with the few whores in the little town of Bear River, women who by now were beginning to look pretty ugly.

Word was a transcontinental railroad would be coming through here in a couple more years. That was hard to believe, but if it was true, the town was sure to grow. Trouble was, with a railroad, more people would come, meaning more lawyers and judges and civilization and lawmen and all the things that would give them trouble. They had come out here to be free to do whatever the hell they wanted and live off what they could take from others. In little towns like this, he and his men could rule like kings. All winter they had eaten and drunk and slept for nothing, holed up here while they waited for the vicious Rocky Mountain winter to end so they could go on to Nevada. There wasn't one person in this town brave enough or skilled enough to stop them from whatever they wanted to do, and he figured that before they left, they would clean out the town and take as much food and money as they could get off the "generous" citizens of Bear River.

He stretched, then scratched at his beard. There had been no reason to shave while they were here, and he supposed he could use one now, maybe a bath too. As soon as the danger of avalanches was past, they would be on their way. He'd been told there was also the danger of spring flooding, small streams turning into rushing torrents in minutes. It was a chance they would have to take. The longer they waited, the more risk they took that Jake Harkner would leave Virginia City. Once he did, he'd be harder to find.

He thought about the wide-eyed soldier back at Fort Laramie who had cried, begging Juan not to slit his throat when Juan and the others had got the young man alone and forced him to tell them what he knew about the destination of Jake and Miranda Turner. They had inquired when first arriving at the fort, but the commander had refused to give them the information. Kennedy had not bothered to tell the man who Jake really was, but later that night he and Juan and the others had caught a young private alone and forced the information out of him. He figured that soldier had never told his commander how he had been threatened. After all, Juan had described to the young private just exactly what he would do with his knife when he came back for him if they discovered soldiers were on their tail.

Now they at least had a definite destination. If the woman's brother was in Virginia City, it was likely she and Jake would settle there. Hell, there must be plenty for a man to do in a place like that if he knew how to use his weapons.

"Do we go soon, *patrón?*"

Kennedy turned to see Juan standing behind him, looking uglier than ever from having just awakened. He turned back around to study the foreboding mountains ahead. "Yeah. Soon. Six months in this dead little town is too much for any man."

"*Sí.* It is time for some action." Juan fingered the handle of his knife. He never slept without it. All winter he had only used it to clean animals, each time imagining it was Jake Harkner or the man's wife at his mercy.

"You'll get your action, soon as we find Jake," Kennedy told him. "Some old scout offered his services last night to ride out and check the trails, see if maybe we can get started. I expect he volunteered only because the people in this town are anxious for us to leave." He chuckled. "Chicken-shit bastards. We'll go, all right, but not before we clean them all out good. I just hope that scout says we can ride. I don't want ol' Jake to get away from me. If he slips through our fingers this time, we might never find him."

Jake charged up to the boardinghouse on Outlaw, jumping off the horse before it even came to a complete halt. He whirled the reins around a hitching post and rushed inside, not bothering to clean off his wet boots this time. He trooped down the hallway, a man who just didn't quite seem to fit in the tidy home with its lace and knickknacks and flowered wallpaper and plants. His canvas duster brushed against a fern as he hurried into his and Miranda's room to see the doctor bent over his wife, taking her pulse. Mrs. Anderson was gently washing perspiration from Miranda's forehead.

"Randy!" Jake threw off his duster and moved closer. Mrs. Anderson moved out of the way, and he looked down at Miranda's pale face. He put his hand to her cheek, and in spite of the perspiration that showed in her hair and on her neck, she felt cold. It startled him so that he drew his hand away. "What's happened?" He looked at the doctor.

The doctor straightened. "The baby came a little early. It's a boy. I think he'll be all right, and your wife should be, too, now that we've stopped the bleeding. She had a bad time of it. For a while, there, I was afraid she would bleed to death, but it's stopped now. She'll be pretty weak for a while."

"You sure? You'd better be a real doctor like you said! You'd better know what you're doing! If she dies . . ."

"Jake," Mrs. Anderson interrupted. "Don't talk to him that way. He did the best he could. These things happen."

Jake glared at the doctor, who had paled from the threat. The man stood there wide-eyed and practically shaking, and Jake realized the reputation he had developed after foiling the bank robbery and making a living with his guns since then. He realized he had behaved for a moment like the old Jake, his fear of losing Randy outweighing all reason. He removed his hat and hung it over the bedpost. "I'm sorry," he told the doctor.

"You should take those guns off, Jake," Mrs. Anderson told him. "You're in the presence of your new son, and you know I don't like them worn in the house anyway." Jake began unbuckling the guns, wondering how it was some women had a way of ordering around men who could probably kill them with one swipe of the hand. They had grown close to Mrs. Anderson, who sometimes seemed more like a mother to them—at least that was what Miranda had said. Jake felt it but wouldn't admit it. He slung the guns over a nearby chair and returned to bend close to Miranda. "Randy? Can you hear me?"

She opened her eyes and managed a weak smile. "You have . . . a son," she whispered.

No. He couldn't think about that. He couldn't really have a son of his own. It was all so unreal. Maybe if he didn't look at the kid, this would all just go away. "You hang on, Randy. Don't you dare leave me with a kid to raise on my own. You know I can't do it."

She smiled more. "Yes, you . . . can."

He put his hands to either side of her face and bent down to kiss her forehead. "You listen to me. I love you like I never thought I could love another human being." He felt a lump rising in his throat, a desperate fear at the thought that he could lose her. "I need you, Randy, and you know all the reasons why. Don't you go and die on me, you hear? If I lose you I'll go right back to that old life. You don't want me to do that, do you?"

"You talk . . . big," she whispered. "Don't . . . mean it . . . got to take care of . . . our little son."

He brushed her cheek with his own, tears forming in his eyes. "Damn it, Randy, don't you leave me," he said, his voice raspy. "Don't you dare leave me! I'm so sorry I wasn't here. I was going to come down tomorrow to stay. I should have been here, should have been with you through all of this."

"It's . . . okay. Get the baby, Jake. I want . . . to see you . . . holding your son. Please, Jake."

"Come and see your son, Jake." Mrs. Anderson touched his arm.

Jake straightened, looking over at the cradle he had asked a local carpenter to build for the baby. He had brought it home two weeks ago, finding it difficult to picture a child of his own lying in it. Why did he dread this? What if he really did love the child? What if he found out his son meant more to him than his own life, more even than Randy? That meant he couldn't bear for anything to ever hurt the child, especially not his past.

The sins of the father are visited upon the son. He remembered hearing a street preacher shout that to a crowd once back in Missouri, recalled how he had applied those words to his own father, figuring it must be true. Look how he had turned out, just as mean and unfeeling and murderous as his father. To think his own past could somehow scar his son . . .

Mrs. Anderson was lifting the child from its cradle. She handed him out to Jake, smiling. "He won't break. Just let him rest in the crook of your arm, Jake." The woman wondered if this man had ever held a baby in his life. Lawman or not, this Jake Turner had surely led a wild, violent life. It was written in his eyes, and in the scar on his neck. She and the others who lived at the boardinghouse had talked about Jake and Miranda a few times when the couple was not present, trying to figure how they had ended up together. The big, dark, dangerous-looking Jake Turner simply did not seem to fit with the tiny, pretty, quiet woman he had married, yet they seemed very much in love.

Jake took the baby into his arms. Mrs. Anderson signaled the doctor that they should leave the couple alone for a few minutes, and she and the doctor left. Jake just stood there staring down at the red-faced, dark-haired infant that looked back at him with big, nearly black eyes. *So,* he thought, *the kid even looks like me.* Was this real? God, what if he hurt him? His legs actually felt weak, and he walked back to the bed and sat down on the edge of it. Never had he had such a feeling. It was all he had dreaded. He had a perfect, beautiful son, and already he knew he would die for the kid. He didn't want to feel this way. It just wasn't a feeling he was used to. A father! This kid was going to call him Pa, was going to look up to him for guidance. Who the hell was he to give direction to another human being when his own life was such a mess? Who was he to teach a child about tolerance and living right?

"Jesus," he whispered. He stuck a big finger against the baby's tiny palm, and the child grasped it lightly. "I never saw anything this little in my life," he said a little louder.

"Let me . . . see," Miranda spoke up, her voice a little stronger.

Jake held the child up slightly so she could look at him. Miranda smiled. "Jake, he's . . . so beautiful!"

The boy made little gurgling sounds, and Jake quickly wiped at his eyes with his shirtsleeve. "I can't do this, Randy. He deserves better than me."

She managed to move her hand to touch his arm. "He's got . . . the best father any child . . . could want. You'll . . . try harder than most, Jake. It's going to be . . . so good for us now. We'll go . . . to California . . . as soon as the baby is a month old . . . and we can get through . . . the mountains. We'll have a good . . . life there, Jake. You'll see. Now . . . let me have . . . my baby."

Jake carefully laid the infant beside his mother, and the child started to squall. Jake felt a chill at the memory of how his father used to toss his little brother around when he was hardly any bigger than this, roaring at the child to stop crying.

"He's hungry. Help me . . . roll onto my . . . side, Jake."

"Are you strong enough?"

"I . . . don't know, but . . . he's hungry . . . no choice."

He leaned over and propped some pillows behind her. He opened her gown and positioned the baby so that the infant could reach a full breast. As soon as he found his mark, the child stopped crying and sucked away contentedly. Jake watched, never believing he'd see such a lovely, intimate mo-

ment, let alone know the mother and baby belonged to him.
That promise Randy had made not to reveal his past to this
child meant more to him than ever now.

"I want . . . to name him Lloyd," Miranda spoke up.
"Your name . . . is Jackson Lloyd. His will be . . . Lloyd
Jackson . . . Lloyd Jackson Harkner."

A rush of regrets over a past he could never erase whipped
through Jake with near pain. "Turner," he corrected her.
"Lloyd Jackson Turner." That was the only name his son
would ever hear. "Don't ever mention the name Harkner in
front of him."

Miranda looked at him in a way that told him she still
thought he was wrong. "If that's how you want it."

"That's how I want it."

She smiled a little. "You love him . . . already . . . don't
you?"

Jake touched her hair, leaning down and kissing the baby's
soft cheek, then kissing her breast. "I love you both. You've
got to help me on this, Randy. You've got to live and get
stronger."

"I'll be fine . . . now that I've seen . . . how you look
. . . at your son." She touched his hand. "Jake . . . my Jake.
You'll be a good father. You'll see."

She closed her eyes and seemed to drift off. The baby kept
nursing, and Jake watched, wondering if a man could experience anything more wonderful than this. But then he wasn't
just any man, and he didn't deserve to have this happening to
him. He rose and went to a chest of drawers, opening one and
taking out his mother's Rosary, which he kept under his shirts.
He had never felt much need for it until now. He grasped it
tightly and closed his eyes. "God help me," he muttered. He
didn't know what else to say, how else to put it. He just
squeezed the jeweled cross and hoped that by some miracle
there was a God who did listen to men like him.

Mellie sauntered up to the tall, sandy-haired man at the bar
who was throwing money around as though its source was
endless. She thought how he could be considered good looking, if not for the chilling meanness in his icy blue eyes, and
the fact that he needed a shave and a haircut; but, then, most
men in this town needed that. She had gotten used to the
smell of whiskey and perspiration, had a lot of money in the

bank from putting up with those very things. Some day she intended to start a business of her own, maybe a restaurant or something, anything to get away from this miserable life. In the meantime, she would do what she did best. There were plenty of other men she could approach tonight, but she had heard this one asking about Jake Turner, and that got her curiosity going. She rubbed a hand over his bottom, and he turned to look at her, grinning, a stub of a cigar between his teeth. "Well, hello there, honey."

Mellie smiled. "Can I do something for you tonight?"

He set down his glass of whiskey and his eyes fell to her exposed bosom. "I expect so. You cost much?"

She looked past him at a dangerous-looking, scarred Mexican who stared at her in a way that made her shiver. That one she would definitely *not* do business with. "Five dollars," she told the first man. "But first you have to tell me your name and why you're looking for Jake Turner."

He took the cigar from his mouth. "You know him?"

Mellie noticed the Mexican lean closer, a murderous glint in his eye. She had no doubt that their reason for finding Jake was not a friendly one. She never had been able to determine the truth about Jake, had always wondered about him. She knew men pretty good, and if Jake Turner was an ex-lawman, she was a nun. Had he once run with the likes of these two? If so, how had he ended up with a woman like Miranda Turner?

"I knew him. He's not around here anymore."

"Shit!" the Mexican cussed. "I knew it!" He pulled out a big knife and slammed it into the bar, making Mellie jump and a few people nearby turn and look. Some of them quieted, feeling uneasy even sitting close to the dark man with the crazy eyes.

"Relax, Juan," Kennedy told him, his gaze on Mellie. "Why don't you go find a card game or something? This lady and I have things to talk about."

Juan jerked the knife out and shoved it into its sheath, turning and stalking out.

"Don't mind him," Kennedy told Mellie. "He's a little short-tempered from that long journey through the Nevada desert. I never knew it could get so hot in June. Never been in country like that. At any rate, it was a journey through hell, and we're all exhausted. Had mountains to cross first. We've been looking for Jake for a long time. He's an old friend. The rest of my men are spread out in town, asking at other saloons about him."

"An old friend?" Mellie looked him over. "Why do I doubt that?"

Kennedy laughed. "You know people pretty good, don't you?" He ran a finger over one milky shoulder. "You, uh, knew Jake *real* good? I mean, I heard he got married, but then I'll bet that wouldn't stop the Jake I knew from goin' 'round with somebody like you now and again."

Mellie decided that the less this man knew, the better for Jake. "I just saw him around a few times. I don't know much about the wife. She never showed herself much." Why was she so sure it was best this man did not know that Jake Turner had a son? She glanced at Clarence, who was working behind the bar tonight. She knew he had heard, knew he hated Jake. She took Kennedy's arm and pulled him toward the stairs to get him away from Clarence. "You still haven't told me your name. Mine's Mellie."

"Bill Kennedy," he answered, following her up the stairs eagerly.

"Well, Bill Kennedy, Jake Turner has left Virginia City for parts unknown." She figured she had only half lied. She knew he had gone to California, but where in California she wasn't sure. For some reason Jake had not wanted anyone to know. Actually, she had only seen Jake one other time, other than when she went to meet his wife to tell her about Wes. Jake had surprised her by coming to tell her good-bye and to thank her for helping them find out about his wife's brother. She had asked around after they left, but no one in town knew where in California Jake and Miranda Turner and their new son had gone.

"You must know if he went to California, Oregon, Arizona?"

"No," she lied. "I had known his wife's brother and knew he was dead. That's how I met Jake. He was asking about the brother." She led Kennedy into her room. "Because I had helped him find out about Wes Baker, Jake came to tell me good-bye. He was a pretty private man, never said where he was going. I don't think anyone else in town knows, either. My guess is he'll take his wife back to Kansas. I expect she'd just as soon go back home since her brother is dead."

Kennedy chuckled. "Honey, he's not going back to Kansas, believe me." He suddenly kicked the door shut and grasped her around the throat in a choking hold, startling her. "Now, why don't you tell me everything you know about ol' Jake?" He slammed her against the bedrail, and she grunted from pain in her back. "I can get real mean, Miss Mellie! You don't want to know *how* mean!"

Mellie's eyes teared, and she grasped at the man's wrist, but he just squeezed harder so that she began losing her breath.

"It's real easy," he told her. "Just tell me everything you know, no lies. Then we'll have us a good time and I'll be on my way and you can go on about your business."

She watched the wild, blue eyes, knew instinctively he'd kill her in the blink of an eye if she fought him. How was it Jake Turner knew men like this? Could he have been this way once? Surely not with women. There had been something about him that told her he could never lay a hand on a woman. But she did remember how he had treated Clarence, the vicious blows, the gun stuck in the kid's mouth.

Kennedy released her and backhanded her, knocking her to the floor. Mellie lay there a moment gathering her thoughts, putting a hand to her throat and trying to get her breath. She felt Kennedy bend over her then, stroking her hair. "Now don't make me do anything worse. Where's Jake?"

"I only know . . . he went to California," she gasped, her voice husky from the injury to her throat. "Nobody knows . . . where in California . . . I swear it. You can . . . ask all over town . . . or up . . . at the Yellow Jacket. He worked there."

"How long ago did he leave?"

"Six weeks, maybe."

"By wagon?"

"Yes."

"His wife with him?"

"Yes." He didn't ask about a baby, so she was not going to volunteer the information.

"What did Jake do when he was here? He have a job?"

"I told you, he . . . worked at the Yellow Jacket." She sat up slightly, still rubbing at her throat. "He was . . . some kind of troubleshooter."

Kennedy grinned. "So, he made himself a reputation with those guns, did he? I figured as much. I'll bet there are other people in this town who know as much or more about him than you do. Men like Jake don't go unnoticed for long."

"Why don't you . . . leave him alone? He's . . . happily married . . . not doing you any harm."

He grasped her hair and jerked her head back. "The harm's already done! He stole a good piece from me, shot up a lot of my men doing it, including my stepbrother! He went against my orders. *I* was head of our gang. Nobody goes making decisions on his own!"

"Gang?"

"I guess out here folks don't know much about names like Bill Kennedy and Juan Hidalgo and Jeb Donner. But by the time we're finished out here, they'll know our names well enough! There used to be another name connected with us— Harkner, Jake Harkner! Your happily married man used to ride right at my side until he turned traitor!"

Mellie eyed him maliciously. "Maybe he rode at your side, but I don't believe . . . he was ever the stinking coward *you* are . . . beating up on a woman to get . . . information!"

He grabbed the front of her dress and ripped it away from her breasts. "Honey, I've done more than just beat up on a woman, and I don't generally pay a slut like you to get what I can get for free!" He punched her hard in the side of the face, and Mellie felt a blackness closing in on her, felt her clothes being ripped away. She knew that if she fought him he would only hurt her more, maybe send the scarred one up here. She lay still and let him get it out of his system, wondering how it was that even someone like herself could feel sick and humiliated when she was forced. Whoever these men were, she prayed to God they never found Jake and poor Miranda.

Clarence watched the stranger emerge from Mellie's room, wondered why Mellie herself didn't come back down. He had not gotten the man's name, but he was excited that he was asking about Jake. Anybody could tell that he was looking for vengeance, and the thought of bringing harm to that damn bitch Miranda Hayes Turner and the SOB she had married got his juices flowing. He moved out from behind the bar and walked over to the man, grabbing his arm.

"You looking for Jake Turner, mister?"

Kennedy's steely blue eyes bored into the youngster. He studied the young man's crooked nose and front teeth that were turning black. The kid might have been good looking at one time, but he wasn't anymore. "You heard me askin'."

"He went to California, him and his wife and their kid."

Kennedy's eyes widened. "Kid! Jake's got a kid?"

"Yes, sir, about two months old by now, a boy. Everybody in town knows, on account of Jake stopped a bank robbery not long after he got here and got a write-up in the *Enterprise.*"

Kennedy grinned. Jake had a kid! That would slow him up even more, and it would give them yet another way of torturing the man before they killed him. What the hell had gotten into him, marrying and having a kid! That sure didn't sound like the Jake he had known, but then, Jake had been changing a little those last few months, talked sometimes about getting out of the life they led and maybe settling. He had just never believed Jake would really do it.

He glanced up at Mellie's room, wanting to hit her again for not telling him about the baby. She'd pay for that one. He looked at the young man standing before him. "You know where in California he was headed?"

"No, sir. But if you don't mind, I'd like to go along with you to find him. Something tells me you've got a big grudge to settle, and so do I."

"You?" Kennedy looked him over. "You're just a kid."

"I hate his guts. He's the reason my nose is crooked and my teeth are rotting out of my head. Besides, I'm getting sick of this place. I want to do something new."

Kennedy leaned closer. "You ever rob a bank, boy? You ever raid a farm and take what you wanted, including the women?"

Clarence swallowed. From the looks of the Mexican who had been in here earlier, these men were obviously dangerous, probably killers. If he rode with them, he'd have plenty of protection when they did find Jake; and in the meantime he could learn a lot about how to handle a gun and all. It could be exciting taking up with a gang like this. "I've never done those things, but I'm willing to learn. And once you find Jake, I'd be one more gunhand against him. He's awful damn good with those guns, but a man can take on only so many men at a time."

Kennedy grinned. "Well, you're right there, boy." He put an arm around his shoulders. "We can always use new blood. Ol' Jake, he used to ride with us, but he got the crazy notion to try to turn good."

"I knew it!" Clarence told him, following the man back to the bar. "I knew he wasn't any lawman back East. Was he an outlaw?"

Kennedy frowned. "Don't say that so loud, boy."

"Damn!" Clarence ordered a whiskey, and the bartender scowled at him.

"You *work* here, remember? Get back behind the counter and help me out."

"I don't work here anymore, Mr. Steed. I work for this man now." Clarence pulled at his beard, which was getting a little fuller. "What's your name, anyway?"

"Kennedy, Bill Kennedy." Kennedy looked the boy over. He'd take him in. Why not? Might be fun teaching the kid a thing or two. He would either end up being a good man to have along, or a pest. If he was a pest, Juan would slit his throat and they'd leave him in the Sierras. No big problem. He glanced at the bartender. "By the way, Mellie said to tell you she won't be down anymore tonight," he told the man. "She's not feelin' too good."

Toby Steed glowered at Kennedy, and the look in Kennedy's eyes told him not to ask any questions. Kennedy ordered another drink, then held the glass up to Clarence. "Welcome to the group, boy. Here's to findin' Jake Harkner."

Clarence grinned and joined him in the drink.

Jake pushed on the brake, and he and Miranda scanned the valley below them. It stretched out for endless miles like a soft green and yellow painting. As soon as they had moved down out of the mountains and the huge fir trees on their slopes, the sun hit their skin with a radiating warmth. Birds flitted about, their songs soothing and pleasant to the ear. Wild roses bloomed seemingly everywhere, filling the air with their sweet perfume.

"Jake, it's beautiful! I've heard so much about California, how the weather is always lovely, how a man can grow just about anything in the valleys."

Jake took a good look around, feeling like he had driven straight into heaven. "Sure is pretty." He looked at her, glanced down at the baby in her arms. "So is what I'm looking at now."

She smiled, resting her head on his shoulder. "Oh, Jake, we can be happy here, I know it. We'll start a brand new life here, you and me and little Lloyd. Let's not make camp just yet. Let's go on closer to Sacramento. The sooner we get there, the sooner we can see about land for sale, decide where we'll settle and whether we'll farm or ranch—"

"Not Sacramento."

She raised her head and looked at him. "What? I thought we had decided."

Jake looked behind them, then out over the valley. "Don't ask me why, Randy. I just have a gut feeling we should head farther south. I expect most folks who come through here figure on settling in Sacramento or San Francisco. Others probably decide to go on down to Los Angeles. I don't want to do the expected. Nobody has even seen us yet to say where we might have gone. I'm turning south. We'll follow the foothills and look for some little out-of-the-way place most folks haven't heard of. California is a big state—easy to get lost in— and that's what we need to do—get lost."

"Jake, we left no enemies back in Virginia City. They all wished only the best for us."

He pushed his hat back, wrapping the reins around a peg and taking a cheroot from his pocket. "It's not the people of Virginia City I'm worried about." He lit the cigar and puffed on it quietly for a moment.

"Then who? The law wouldn't bother tracking you all the way from Missouri."

"Probably not. But I know somebody who would, and if he gets even the slightest taste of my trail, he won't quit."

"Bill Kennedy?"

Jake sighed. "I hope you never meet him, not just because of what he'd do if he found us, but because you'd see even clearer just what kind of man I used to be."

She quelled the hint of fear he had stirred in her soul. "Jake, Sheriff McCleave told me clear back in Kansas that Kennedy and his men had gone on to Indian Territory to try to find you. There is no way they would ever track you back to the Oregon Trail and clear out here."

"He's one of the best trackers I know, him and Juan Hidalgo." He picked up the reins to the mules that pulled the wagon. "I don't want to upset you. I wasn't worried in Virginia City, because I knew if they did track us, they'd have a late start and probably get stranded by winter; but part of the reason I wanted to get the hell out of Nevada as soon as you could travel was to stay as far ahead of him as I could, if he's even following us at all. I knew once we got here we'd be almost impossible to find, especially if I hang up my guns and lay low so I don't draw any attention to myself. Maybe I should change my name again."

"But the baby's last name is Turner."

He took the cigar from his mouth. "He'll never know the difference. How about Logan? John Logan?"

"Jake, I don't want to—"

"You don't know what they're like, Randy! Now more than ever I want a peaceful life, a nice place for you and Lloyd. I never thought too much about Kennedy and his bunch till Lloyd was born. Then I knew I want to make it as good for the both of you as I can, take no chances. Kennedy carries a mighty grudge. It never mattered to me when I was on my own. I still don't care just for myself, but if they ever got hold of you and Lloyd." He looked away. "We're heading south, and we're changing our name again. Our last name is Logan, understand?"

She put a hand on his knee, knowing the pain he suffered at thinking he might be the cause of harm coming to them. "All right. But we might as well keep the first name Jake. I'm so used to calling you that, I'd probably slip up and cause more attention than if we just keep your right name."

"Fine. It's Jake Logan then." He put the cigar back in his mouth and rubbed at his eyes. "I'm sorry, Randy. Maybe I'm just getting too anxious about the whole thing. Here in California, farther south in the valley somewhere, we can be lost to the rest of the world."

"We'll settle wherever you want, Jake. All that matters is that we're together."

Jake moved his arm to rub at her back. "I love you. I'll get you settled soon and there won't be any more of this living out of a wagon, I promise." He kicked off the brake, flicking the reins and shouting at the mules to get moving. He headed the wagon down the hill, Outlaw and the pack horse following. As soon as they reached the valley, he headed south.

CHAPTER
SIXTEEN

September 1869 . . .

Jake came inside for lunch, hanging his hat on a hook near the door. He had left his boots just outside, not wanting to dirty the bright braided rugs Miranda had so painstakingly made herself to decorate their three-room log home.

He smiled at the thought of how good life was here in California. The main room of their house, which he had built with his own hands, along with help from generous neighbors, was large and pleasant, with several windows to let in the California sunshine. Lace curtains graced the windows, and a huge stone fireplace took over one whole wall at the kitchen end of the room. It wasn't needed often for cooking, since he had bought Miranda an iron, coal-burning cookstove, which was her pride and joy.

The other two rooms were bedrooms, one for them, the other for two-year-old Lloyd, who was taking a nap. Miranda greeted him with a smile and told him lunch was nearly ready, and he watched her pop a loaf of fresh-baked bread from its pan. She was wearing that yellow dress he liked. She hadn't worn it for a long time. He remembered the first time he saw her in it, when she first started making him think maybe he wanted to change his life.

"That foal is doing great," he told her. "I'll have a good herd to show that buyer who comes to the fair every year. We ought to make some good money, besides the profit we made on the feed corn and the onions. By next year we'll have to hire help. The grapes will start to produce enough by next year to ship to market in San Diego."

Miranda set the bread on the table. "I have to admit, Jake, I never thought you'd take to farming and ranching quite this well."

He came around the table and pulled her into his arms. "You should have more faith in me, woman." He leaned down and met her mouth, giving her a long, deep kiss. He moved his lips to her eyes. "I'm hungrier for you than I am for that food," he told her.

"Jake, it's the middle of the day! Someone could come, or Lloyd could wake up."

"Nobody will come and you know it, and Lloyd wouldn't know what we were doing." He swept her up into his arms. "Hell, Randy, I've been so busy getting in the crops and worrying over that mare and her foal that all I've done is collapse into bed at night and hardly given you any attention at all."

"Jake Harkner, put me down!" She liked to use his real name in private, felt he should hear it and learn to be proud of it. She made a mild protest when he dumped her on the bed and moved on top of her, but her weak objections vanished when his lips covered her own again in a penetrating kiss. This was so like the man she loved, spontaneous, gently demanding, sometimes a little wild and unpredictable. "Jake, this is crazy."

He moved his lips to her neck and ran his hand under her dress. She wore the dress alone today, except for a camisole and drawers. It was warm, and she hadn't bothered with slips. "Just a quick little sign of affection, *mi querida*," he said softly. She felt the drawers coming off. "Maybe tonight we'll do this again, take our time."

Just the words brought on a surge of hot desire. When Jake Harkner "took his time" with a woman, he had the most exotic ways of taking her to a world of ecstasy. She never dreamed she could let a man do such things, or that there were so many ways to make love. With Jake it always seemed so right and natural.

For now there would be this quick but sweet sign of affection, clothes still on, pants unbuttoned. He moved into her, the penetration hot and hard, and she remembered how glad she was to know even after the baby that they could still get so much pleasure out of this. His thrusts were deep and stimulating, and he patiently held back until she arched up to him in her own climax. She wondered if it was like this for other women, or if she was simply lucky to have found a man who knew all the right ways to arouse her, to bring out this wanton desire. She could not quite understand why some women complained about this, acted as though allowing their husbands their pleasure was such a chore. Perhaps they would faint if she told them all the things she had let this man do to her. There was not an inch of her body that had been left unexplored. It was the nature of the man to have a woman completely at his command when she was in his bed, and she had never minded one bit. He carried a deep and amazing passion for a man who at one time thought he could never love, and never once had she felt used or dirty. Every touch, every taste, every joining was filled with sweet pleasure and grew out of a desire to express their love.

He moaned with his own throbbing climax as she finally drew the life from him. He let out a deep sigh, and stretched out beside her.

"This is not the way to get chores done, Jake."

He grinned, rolling to his side and tugging at her honey-blond hair. She'd brushed it out long and straight today. He liked it that way. "Maybe if you'd put your hair in a bun and wouldn't wear this yellow dress, I'd just come in to eat."

She touched his lips. He smelled of sweat and leather and out-of-doors, but it was a good smell, the smell of a man who worked hard to make a good life for his family. She supposed there was a time when he smelled only of liquor and smoke and cheap perfume . . . and maybe blood. "When you have a need, I doubt it would matter what I was wearing or if I was bald."

He laughed lightly, then noticed Lloyd standing in the doorway to the room staring at them. "Hey, you, what are you doing out of bed?" The boy grinned and ran on chubby legs to the bed, tugging at Jake. "Wait a minute!" Jake rose and quickly washed. He tucked in his shirt and buttoned his pants, then whisked the child up, holding him in the air so that he giggled. "Come on, let's walk around outside a minute while your mommy washes."

"Daddy pooay," Lloyd said, grasping Jake's nose.

"Yes, Daddy play, but we also have to eat."

Miranda watched them walk out of the bedroom, her heart

full of a sweet joy. It had been just as she had suspected between Jake and his son. The man doted on him every free moment he had. In fact, the child had been a source of a few arguments when it came to the subject of discipline. Jake would not lay a hand on the child, and around his father Lloyd got away with any naughty thing he wanted to do. Since he had started walking, he got into endless trouble. He was spirited and daring, everything his father was. The older he got, the more he looked like Jake—dark, wavy hair, snappy, black eyes, a winning smile.

She got up to wash, thinking about that smile. Since they had come here, Jake had become more relaxed about not being followed by anyone. She realized it had been months since she saw that old look of wild anger in Jake's own dark eyes. He seemed to be healing emotionally, and most of the time he wore that smile that had nearly startled her the first time she saw it on the old troubled and unhappy Jake Harkner. That smile just seemed to totally change his looks. He seemed to feel better about himself, had learned to read and to work with his hands, even discovered he was a good farmer. It was good to see him so happy.

She washed herself and straightened her dress, then brushed her hair and tied it at the back of her neck. She went back into the main room to finish preparing lunch, cutting a few pieces of ham and thinking how good life was here in California. The weather was nearly always perfect, except for occasional earthquake tremors, to which they had become more accustomed. Their neighbors had explained that it was those who lived in bigger cities who had to be afraid, and that it seemed the quakes were more often and more violent farther north. Last year just about the only topic of conversation had been the devastating earthquake in San Francisco. For weeks the newspapers out of San Diego ran bold headlines about the loss of lives and property. The destruction and fires had been terrible, and Miranda was glad Jake had decided to come south.

She set the ham on the table, thinking about some other headlines that for several weeks had changed her Jake back to the old, restless, scowling man she had first met. In the north, especially along the winding mountain roads to mining camps, there had been several stagecoach and payroll robberies by an outlaw gang whose leader, according to surviving victims, was called Bill. Another of the outlaws was described as a scarred

Mexican called Juan who had done horrible things with his knife and had raped several women.

Jake had stormed about, had hardly spoken to her, and would not play with Lloyd. He had even threatened to head north and "wipe out" Kennedy and his gang before they could come here and do the same to them. The words had struck fear in her heart that he would never come back, that he would be gunned down and she would never see him again.

Jake had no doubt it was Kennedy and his men who were the culprits. His worst fear, that Kennedy would come west, had been realized. Miranda had finally convinced him that it was most likely they had come to California only because things were too dangerous for them back in Missouri. They were wanted there, and now that the war had been over for four years, lawless men could no longer enjoy the freedom they once had. She had finally convinced him and herself that Kennedy's coming west had nothing to do with hunting Jake. How could the man possibly know Jake had come west? Even if he did, he would never find them in this peaceful little valley few people frequented. Jake's last name was Logan, now, and he was a farmer and a rancher. He never even wore his guns anymore, except to carry his rifle to go hunting for meat or to protect himself from wild animals when he rode into the foothills. That was certainly not the Jake Harkner Kennedy would be looking for. And how could he know? The regular trail to California did not go through Virginia City, and that was the only place Kennedy might have heard about Jake and put things together.

She sliced some bread and went to the door to call out to Jake to draw some water from the well and come in to eat. He was walking around with Lloyd on his shoulders, and she smiled at the sight. After several days of going out every afternoon with his guns strapped on, practicing his draw over and over, target practicing, Jake had finally hung up the weapons again and decided it was highly unlikely Kennedy would ever find him here or even know he was in California. The Kennedy gang finally faded from the headlines, and a growing law enforcement in the San Francisco area was having its effects on thieves and murderers. The last article they read about Kennedy had said it was believed things had gotten too hot for him and his men. A trap had been set for them in which four of Kennedy's men were killed.

"Brad Helmsley, Luke Stowers, Frank Smith, Bert Jackson,"

Miranda had read aloud to Jake. *I knew all of them*, he had answered. *Bert Jackson was called Buffalo by his friends, if men like that can be called friends*.

The article had said the rest of the gang had headed farther north, a couple more of them believed to be wounded. They were most likely headed for Canada.

There had been no more word of Bill Kennedy and his gang, and Jake had finally begun to return to the new Jake she loved even more than the old one, a hardworking man who had built this ranch on land purchased from their closest neighbor. Joe Grant lived two miles distant and wanted to sell off part of his land to reduce his workload now that he was getting old.

The people they had met in the little town three miles to the east called Desert, were some of the kindest, warmest people Miranda had known, even friendlier than the people she had known back in Kansas City. Some of them, as well as ranching neighbors, had helped build this lovely cabin she called home, as well as the barn and two sheds out back. Life was good, better than she had ever known it to be. She realized this was the happiest she had been since her mother died nine years ago. It seemed life had been a matter of turmoil and wandering and loss ever since then.

Her family was gone, but she had a new family now, a beautiful son. She hoped there would be more children. She suspected she might finally be pregnant again, but she didn't want to get her hopes up too much, so she had said nothing to Jake yet. Maybe she would tell him today. She had been trying for two years for a second child but had had trouble conceiving after Lloyd's difficult birth.

She walked over and opened the door for Jake, and a sweet fragrance from the rose bushes she had planted around her front porch penetrated the air. Lloyd toddled in ahead of his father, and Jake followed behind, setting the bucket of water on the counter he had built along one wall for her. "I took Lloyd to see the foal, set him on Outlaw for a few minutes. The kid isn't afraid of a damn thing. I swear he'd take off riding if I let him."

"Like father, like son," Miranda teased.

She picked Lloyd up and glanced at Jake whose eyes had quickly changed from joy to a look of deep hurt. "Don't ever put it that way, Randy," he said, scowling.

"Oh, Jake, I only meant that you aren't afraid of anything

either. If our son is daring and full of adventure, it's because you've put that spirit into him. It's a *good* thing, not bad. I *want* him to be like his father. I'm *proud* of his father."

Jake walked over and took Lloyd from her, setting him into a high chair he had made himself. "He'll be a thousand times *better* than me," he said quietly. He leaned down and kissed the top of the boy's head, and Miranda turned to retrieve a pot of coffee from the stove, realizing how delicate the subject of fatherhood still could be for him sometimes. "How many horses will you take to the auction at the fair next month?" she asked, deciding to change the subject. She poured the coffee and set a little plate of boiled and buttered potatoes in front of Lloyd, then served more potatoes to Jake.

"I don't know. About ten, I guess. Next week I'm going hunting for more mustangs, now that the crops are in. I'd like to catch that black stallion that keeps getting away from me. He'd make a hell of a stud horse if I could ever get a rope around his neck and get him back here." Jake stabbed three pieces of ham and laid them on his plate with the potatoes, cutting into the meat zealously. He was a big man who always had a big appetite, and Miranda enjoyed cooking for him. He always made her feel appreciated, made anything she did for him enjoyable because it was all so new and pleasurable to him. "Joe Grant wants to go after the mustangs with me. I want you and Lloyd to go stay with his wife while we're gone. Joe's brother will come over here to tend to our place."

"Jake, I can stay here alone. There has never been any trouble around here."

"Well, there's a first time for everything." Jake cut up some meat into smaller pieces and gave them to Lloyd. "This is still pretty lawless and remote country. We've offered food and water to enough migrant Arizona prospectors who wander this way that I wouldn't want you alone here when another one comes along. No arguments. You'll go stay at Joe's."

She sighed and shook her head. "Are you going to enter the shooting contest again this year?"

"I don't know. I suppose. I didn't really want to last year. It isn't very fair to the others."

"Maybe not, but the fifty-dollar prize will come in handy."

Jake glanced at her and scowled. "It's a hundred dollars this year, but it doesn't seem right, us knowing the rest of them don't have a chance against me. If they knew the truth—"

"Well, they don't. They just think guns are your hobby and you happen to be an excellent shot. You shouldn't worry so much, Jake."

"I can't help it. If Joe Grant hadn't seen my Peacemakers hanging in the barn last year, none of this would have started. He kept after me to show him if I was any good with them, put me in that contest at the fair last year against my will. I tried to miss a few, pretend I wasn't any better than anybody else, but then I started thinking about the money and how much we needed it. I hope I don't answer for not leaving well enough alone."

"Jake, it's just a simple shooting contest at a little fair in a little town. And these are good people around here. They don't think anything about it. Their biggest thrill is that fair and you just made it more exciting for them. Hetta Grant says Joe's been practicing ever since last year to try to beat you."

Jake finally smiled a little. "I know. He ribs me about it constantly, tells me I'd better be ready this year." The smile faded a little. "Only thing I don't like is he talked about advertising the fair this year in the San Diego paper to get outsiders to come. It would bring in more money. He wanted to put in some kind of challenge to come to the shooting contest and try to beat the best shot in Southern California—wanted to use my name. I told him I didn't care if he advertised the fair, but I made him promise not to mention my name. That's the last thing I need. I don't even like the thought of a lot of outsiders coming."

"No one in these parts knows you, and they certainly won't recognize the name."

"You never know. I don't like it, but maybe it will be all right."

"I enjoy the fair. Everyone looks forward to it after a long, hard summer of farming and all."

"You baking your famous pumpkin pies again?"

She smiled. "Yes, and I'm taking that quilt I've been working on."

Both of them enjoyed this, being at the table together in their own home, being a family. Jake thought how this was the kind of life he only used to dream about, and he was at last beginning to relax and believe it could always be this way.

They finished eating, Lloyd eating his potatoes and ham

with his fingers. Miranda rose and poured the boy a small glass of cow's milk and helped him hold the glass while he drank it. She cleaned his face and hands and took him from the chair, and he immediately ran on quick little legs to reach for the handle of the fry-pan in which she had cooked the ham. Miranda rushed after him, grabbing his hand back and slapping it. "No, Lloyd! It's hot and it's heavy. It will hurt you!"

The boy's lips puckered and he started to cry, and Jake scooted back his chair. Miranda gave him a warning look. "Don't you dare pick him up and cuddle him. He's got to learn to stay away from the stove!"

Jake frowned. "I wish you wouldn't smack him. I'd rather he learned the hard way and burned his hand. Then it's the stove he'll remember hurting him and not one of us."

She rolled her eyes, putting her hands on her hips. "And would you rather he pulled that skillet off the stove and have it fall on his head and break his skull, maybe kill him, let alone the fact that the hot grease could burn his face and scar him?"

Their eyes held in a challenge, and Jake turned away. Already Lloyd's tears were subsiding, and he toddled over to a tin pie-plate he liked to play with, the incident quickly forgotten, but not by Jake.

"You know I can't stand to see him cry because he's been spanked. We've been through this before, Randy."

She stepped closer. "Jake, you have to learn there is a difference between senseless beatings and minor spankings to discipline a child for his own good. There are some things he has to learn early so that nothing happens to him. The right kind of discipline is nothing more than a form of love. You have got to let me teach him right from wrong. You've got to *help* me teach him, or he'll end up getting badly hurt, or being so spoiled that no one will be able to stand having him around. What if he wanders to the creek out back? Should I let him just toddle in and risk drowning?"

He sighed, rubbing at his eyes. "I know what you're saying. It's just that when I hear that smack and see those tears . . ."

She touched his arm. "Jake, that child is loved more than most. Believe me, a little spanking now and then is not going to destroy his trust. I got a few spankings of my own when I was little, but I knew it was because my parents loved me and didn't want anything to happen to me. I never doubted that love for one minute, and I was never afraid to turn to them and let them hold me when I needed holding. You have to learn the difference between proper discipline and senseless hitting. That little boy knows his daddy loves him, and it isn't fair of you to make me be the only one who shows him discipline. I need your help on this, especially if we have more children."

He pulled her close. "It isn't just that. I'm afraid that if I hit him for something, I won't be able to stop. What if something takes over, something inside of me that I can't control? Besides, he's so little, and I'm so strong. I could hurt him without even wanting to."

She sighed deeply. "Jake, what should I do with you? You are *not* your father. There is no chance you would ever get carried away and hurt him." She leaned back and looked up at him. "Part of being a father is teaching your son the right way to go, that the wrong way can hurt him. If you never discipline him at all, he'll grow up to be a wild young man who no one likes and who goes out and gets himself in trouble. Is that what you want?"

Jake looked over at the boy, who sat playing with the plate, still sniffling. "I just want him to love me."

Miranda leaned up and kissed his cheek. "Jake, you're a kind, gentle, attentive father. He *does* love you. Nothing is going to change that."

Lloyd looked over at them and got to his feet, toddling over to grasp at his mother's skirt. Miranda smiled and stooped down to pick him up. He hugged her around the neck and she patted his back. "It's all right, baby," she said softly. "The stove is a no-no. You know that." She looked at Jake. "Does it look like he is afraid of me now or doesn't love me? He's only two and a half, Jake, but he knows what I did was out of love."

Jake pulled both of them into his arms, and Lloyd turned, putting his chubby arms around his father's neck. Jake took him into his arms, thinking how much he would have loved to have had the same affection and reassurance shown to him when he was small. "I'm taking him back out to the barn with me for a while."

"Fine. But if he goes toddling up behind a horse, you'd better make sure he understands it's dangerous. And do it in a way that makes him think twice about doing it again."

"Yes, ma'am." He walked toward the door.

"Jake."

He turned, keeping the boy in his arms and patting his bottom.

"I mean it. I need your help in this. Jake, I think I'm going to have another baby. I can't take care of a newborn and be running after a two-year-old who won't obey me."

He watched her lovingly, slowly setting Lloyd back down to the varnished hardwood floor Miranda kept dusted daily. "You're making me do this twice?" he teased. "Hell, I'm not sure I can do it right one time around."

"You're doing just fine. Just go tend to your chores."

He gave her a rather tentative smile, his emotions mixed. The responsibilities were growing. There would be a second child depending on him, another mouth to feed, another baby to love and to look up to him as a father. He walked closer to Miranda, bending down and kissing her cheek. "You all right?"

"I'm fine."

"What if it's like the last time, maybe worse? I can't lose you, Randy. I can't do any of this without you."

"Nothing is going to happen to me. I'm sure Mrs. Grant and some of the other neighbor women will help when the time comes, which won't be until at least next March. Now get going."

He kissed her once more, then left her, picking up Lloyd on the way out. Miranda walked to the door to watch them head for the barn, Lloyd riding on his father's shoulders again and laughing. She thought what a sweet and peaceful sight it was. Lloyd had been like a healing ointment to his father's tortured soul. Already they were so close. She prayed nothing would ever happen to destroy that.

Bill Kennedy put a fat cigar in his teeth and settled into the tub of hot water, making a growling sound of pleasure as he let the warm water come up to his neck. "You can scrub my back and anything else you want to rub after I soak a few minutes," he told the young Mexican woman whose job it was to keep adding buckets of hot water as the tub water cooled. The woman stared at Kennedy dully, a mixture of hatred and resignation in her dark eyes. It was obvious she hated her job, and that pleased Kennedy, made him feel powerful. She worked here, therefore she had to do what he asked. He gave her a wink and she turned away.

Three other Mexican women kept clean towels coming, provided soap and were required to scrub down any man who asked. Kennedy and his men had been told this was the most luxurious bathhouse in San Diego, and they had all converged on it after a hot, dusty trip back from Mexico. The others laughed and splashed and made lewd remarks to the Mexican women. Juan stood up and gestured with his penis, and the men laughed more, Clarence asking the women if any of them would please get in the tub with him and let him give them a soap massage of their own. He reached up and felt the breast of one older woman when she bent over to give him a towel, and she slapped his hand.

Clarence made kissing sounds at her and picked up his own cigar from a nearby ashtray. He thought how good it felt to be here after over a year of running. He watched Jeb Donner use his right arm to support himself as he knelt into his own tub. Jeb had lost almost all use of his left arm after the shoot-out with Wells Fargo detectives up near San Francisco over a year ago. Jeb had been slammed with two bullets that day, one in his left shoulder and another that smashed his left elbow. The trap the lawmen had laid had come close to killing all of them. Brad and Luke, Buffalo and Frank were dead. Juan still limped from a bullet to his right thigh that had broken a bone. Joe had taken a bullet in his side, but he'd lived.

The terror of that day still haunted Clarence. He'd never been that scared since the day Jake Harkner stuck a gun into his mouth and threatened to pull the trigger. He'd never seen so much shooting in his life, and he hoped he never would again. He felt lucky to have gotten away with his life, and he had even considered leaving Kennedy, going back to Virginia City and staying with his uncle a while until things cooled down.

They had eluded the law by heading north and making those who hunted them think they had gone to Canada. Instead, after finding a farm family who put them up and treated their wounds at gunpoint, they had circled around and headed back south, killing the entire family first so that they could not identify them. They had moved on through the Nevada desert and into Utah, where there was a whole network of hangouts for outlaws all along a north-south trail from Arizona clear into Wyoming called the Outlaw Trail. It was a haven of caverns and canyons and desolate country where no lawman

ventured, unless he wanted to commit suicide. It was along
that trail that Kennedy had picked up the two new men, Oran
Peters and Cliff Remington. With himself and Kennedy, and
long time gang members Juan, Joe Stowers, and Jeb Donner,
Kennedy's gang now numbered seven.

Still only twenty-one and the youngest of the group, Clarence felt proud to be a part of this formidable bunch of outlaws who took what they wanted wherever they went—money,
women, anything they needed. It was mostly women he
couldn't get enough of, and the innocent ones who protested
pleased him most. He drank down some whiskey. This was the
good life, a hell of a lot better than sitting around listening to
his uncle preach. The way he lived now was dangerous and
daring, but he liked the power that came with being one of Bill
Kennedy's men. He had gotten pretty good with his gun,
thanks to lessons from Bill and Jeb. After each robbery that
turned out especially lucrative, they lived high on the hog,
buying new clothes, buying the prettiest women.

That had been the case after their last robbery of a little
bank in some nameless town in Arizona, where they had
found a surprising amount of cash on hand. They had ridden
into Mexico to lay low for a while and now returned, coming
up into Southern California. Here in San Diego they had
bought new clothes and decided to get baths and shaves. His
new felt hat hung on a hat rack nearby, and he wore a diamond ring on his right hand. Nearby lay his brand new .45
Peacemaker with a cutaway trigger guard to make his draw
and shooting time even faster. The gun rested in a new gunbelt with his name etched into the holster.

The only trouble they had found since fleeing Northern
California was along the Outlaw Trail itself. At a place called
Robber's Roost they had run into two men who had known
Jake Harkner in his gunrunning days, men Jake had known
before he took up with Bill Kennedy. They seemed to have a
certain loyalty to Jake and didn't like the idea that Bill Kennedy had been hunting for him. One of them, who called
himself Jess York, claimed Jake had saved his life once, and he
didn't want anything to do with anybody who was out to kill
Jake. He and several other men had come after Kennedy,
warning all of them to forget about finding Jake. That was the
only time Clarence could remember Bill Kennedy and even
Juan running from anything, but it was obvious the men meant
business.

Clarence had realized then that being an outlaw didn't always mean just the law was after you, but sometimes men of your own kind. Word had spread, and they had suddenly become unwelcome practically everyplace they stopped along the Trail. They had been forced to the southern end, into Arizona, and after the bank robbery there, they had finally gone on into Mexico. After a few weeks in Mexico, Kennedy had decided to come back north, this time into Southern California, where they weren't so well known. There was plenty of wealth to be had here, too, and they could always make it back to Mexico, where the law couldn't touch them, in just a few days. And in Mexico there were no outlaws who wouldn't make them welcome there. In fact, Kennedy had made friends with some rough-looking *bandidos* and was planning to do business with them, raiding Southern California towns and ranches and trading horses, guns, and women to the *bandidos* for Mexican gold.

One of the bathhouse women gave Kennedy a copy of a San Diego newspaper, and the man handed it over to Clarence, the only one among them who could read well. "Take a look, boy. Let us know what's goin' on around here that's exciting."

Clarence took the newspaper and studied it, proud to be the best educated one of the bunch. They all seemed to look up to him a little for that, all except Juan, who had no respect for anything. Clarence stayed away from Juan, after an argument they'd had over which one got to rape a young Mexican girl first. Juan had come after him with a knife, and Kennedy had managed to talk the man out of using it on him. Clarence had seen Juan's "talent" with the big Bowie he carried, and he wanted no more run-ins with the man.

"Nothing much here," he said aloud. "They're having some kind of sailboat races off the coast."

Kennedy chuckled. "Big deal. This town's a little too big for my liking anyway. We'll hit a few saloons tonight with our new duds, find us some card games and some women and get out of here in a couple of days. I like these Mexican women. The ones who are easy are hot mamas who know how to please a man, and the ones who *aren't* easy fight you so hard they're even more excitin' than the whores." He laughed a throaty laugh, joined by the others.

"Says here they're planning to bring in a railroad to Southern California, partly following the old San Antonio–San

Diego stage route." Clarence looked over at his boss. "Hell, at the rate they're bringing railroads out here now, we might as well start robbing trains instead of banks and stagecoaches. Now that they've completed the transcontinental railroad, they'll be putting in more tracks all over the place."

"Yeah, and bringing in more civilization and more law," Kennedy complained. "And don't be tellin' me what kind of jobs I should pull."

Clarence reddened a little. "Sorry, Bill." He always felt his position among them was tentative, and did his best to prove he was worth having along, even though he had never quite gotten used to being the target of lawmen's bullets. He turned back to the paper, hoping to find something to interest Bill Kennedy and stay on the man's good side. He turned the page and saw a headline reading COME TO THE FAIR. He read on a ways and then spoke up.

"Some small town east of here name of Desert, they're having a fair—stitching contests, baked goods, a horse auction —hey, and a shooting contest! Hell, we could go there and win every prize they got. Nobody in a little town called Desert is going to be any good with a gun."

"Now that could be fun, boss," Jeb Donner spoke up, rubbing at his left arm. "If the town is small enough, while everybody is at that fair, we could check out the bank, break in and rob it before anybody knows what's happening. Maybe there isn't even any law there."

"Yeah, and maybe there's no *bank* either!" Joe Stowers said, joking.

They all laughed again, all but Clarence, who sat up straighter in his tub. "Hey, Bill listen to this!" They all looked his way. "It says here that the prize this year at the shooting contest will be a hundred dollars instead of fifty, and that they're offering a special challenge to outsiders. They have a citizen of their own that none of the locals can beat. They want to draw as many people as they can and will take side bets on top of the hundred-dollar prize."

Kennedy smiled smugly. "Well, the guy might be good, but he would never beat any of us."

"That's not what's important here, Bill. What's important is the man's name. It's Jake Logan."

Kennedy's eyebrows arched. *"Jake* Logan?"

"Jake Logan," Clarence repeated. "Doesn't that make you wonder? If this guy is so good that they're challenging men

from all over to try to beat him, then he must be *damn* good. How many men do you know named Jake who are that good with a gun?"

Kennedy just sat there a minute, then straightened, looking over at Juan, who was beginning to grin. He looked past the man at Jeb. "What do you think, Jeb?"

Jeb's eyes sparkled with pleasure at the thought of possible vengeance, finally, after three years of searching! Actually, they had given up looking for Jake, but just the slim hope of finding him brought new life to his veins. "I think we ought to check it out. We know Jake came to California. Maybe he picked that little-ass town so he'd be harder to find."

"If it is Jake, *patrón*, when I am through with my knife, I will personally drink his blood and spit it in his face!"

Kennedy looked back at Clarence. "Boy, I knew there was a good reason to keep you on. If you couldn't read, we'd never have known about this."

Clarence grinned with pride, his teeth already stained brown from chewing tobacco. The two teeth in front that Jake had blackened were getting even more rotten. He had finally done something that showed them he was valuable to the gang. If this Jake really was the one they were looking for, he'd be favored in Kennedy's eyes the rest of their days. He checked the article once more. "We don't have much time. This is an old paper. The fair starts in two days."

"Well then," Kennedy said with a sly grin, "looks like we've got some riding to do." He settled back into his bath water. "Boys, let's get done with these baths and get dressed. We're goin' to a fair!"

CHAPTER
SEVENTEEN

Miranda set her pies on the checkered tablecloth beside the tags designated for her entries. The judging would take place in one hour. She mingled with the other women, many whom had become close friends. They exclaimed over other entries, fancy meringues, cinnamon-topped apple, berry pies oozing their sweet juices over the edges of the pans.

"There are so many more entries this year," Miranda said to Hetta Grant.

"Oh, you'll still win a prize, I just know it. Nobody makes a pumpkin pie that ends up as light as yours. Why, I could eat a whole pie in one sitting."

Both women laughed, and they wandered to the table that held cakes. Hetta was older than she, a woman whose children were already grown. Miranda enjoyed their talks, enjoyed the woman's company when she had stayed with her while Jake was hunting mustangs. He had captured the black stallion, his pride and joy. He had brought it to the auction just to show, and advertise the animal for stud service.

Lloyd was with his father. The boy refused to leave the man when they were in a crowd. He was shy, but where most toddlers clung to their mothers in such times, Lloyd clung to his father. She knew she would have to get over to the horse-showing stands soon and take the boy whether he liked it or not, since Jake did not like him playing around the unpredictable stallion. She smiled at how excited Jake was this year about the auction. He had several quality horses to sell. They would make a good profit.

"This fair is much bigger than last year's," she told Hetta.

"Thanks to Joe's advertising in San Diego," the woman answered, putting an arm around her waist and walking with her to where handmade quilts hung on display. "I think the challenge involving your husband and the shooting contest is what brought a lot of these people. I notice there are a lot more men here this year. They probably want to know who Jake Logan is."

Miranda felt a hint of alarm. "Did Joe use Jake's name in the newspaper article?"

Hetta laughed lightly. "Yes. Jake didn't want him to, but Joe thought that giving a name for people to look for would make it even more interesting."

Miranda stopped walking and faced the woman, unaware that a bearded, blond-haired young man who had spotted her was running off toward a scarred Mexican who carried a big knife. "Hetta, Jake asked Joe not to use his name. He would have preferred the challenge against one man wasn't even mentioned."

"It's all right. It's all in fun, dear. Come now, let's see if any of these other women can make a quilt pretty as yours."

Three other women friends caught up to them. One, Betsy Price, was a year younger than Miranda and a newlywed. Betsy and Miranda worked together on church projects for the one-and-only church in town, a Catholic mission around which the little settlement had been built.

Desert had never been so busy or so populated. Baked goods, quilts, canned goods, and all sorts of homemade wares were on display in the town's only street. Jake had joked once about it being called "Main" Street. *Only Street is what it should be called,* he had said. There were booths set up for children's games and for adult games. In the distance some children played tug-of-war with a rope over a man-made mud puddle, their parents cheering them on. The weather was beautiful, and Miranda thought what an enjoyable day it was going to be. She had made a picnic lunch of fried chicken, which they would share with the Grants. She decided to ignore the uneasy feeling she had over Jake's name being used in the San Diego newspaper, and she decided it would be best not to mention it to Jake. The town was full of strangers, but they all seemed to be good-natured people come to enjoy the fair, many of them probably here for the one-hundred-dollar pot raised for the shooting contest. Since there was a charge to enter the contest, even with the hundred-dollar prize, Desert stood to raise a good deal more than that from the entries; and to top off the day, she was confident Jake would be the one to walk off with the prize.

Behind her the blond-haired young man was pointing her out to the Mexican with the ugly scar. A few people glanced at the Mexican, thinking to themselves how very ugly he was and not too sure he and the men some of them had seen him ride in with were the kind they wanted around Desert. The blond-haired man left, flagging down some more of his friends, and the Mexican and a light-haired, blue-eyed man walked casually toward where Miranda stood visiting with her women friends.

Somewhere in the distance a band struck up "Sweet Betsy from Pike," and it was the last lovely memory Miranda had of that day. A strong hand suddenly came around her middle, and something poked her sharply at her right side, making her gasp. "Miranda Logan?"

Her name had been spoken by someone with a raspy voice. She started to struggle away, but whatever was poking her cut deeper, and she cried out with the pain of it. She heard the women around her screaming, and some man was waving a gun at them.

"Just stay out of the way, ladies, and nobody will get hurt." Other men were joining him, and she saw a few people running. The band still played "Sweet Betsy," and in the distance people went about their business, unaware of what was happening near the quilt booth.

Miranda watched a man with a stubble of a beard and a scar on his right cheek step closer to her. His steely blue eyes gave her shivers. He grasped her jaw and yanked her head around so she had to look up at a dark, ugly man with a deep scar across one eye, his nose, and lips, another scar across his throat. "This is Juan," the blue-eyed man told her. "Ol' Jake ever tell you about Juan?" He squeezed her jaw painfully, and she could feel blood soaking her dress at the side.

Juan! Jake had mentioned the name several times. She remembered him saying something about how good the man was with a knife. Terror engulfed her, for that knife was stuck in her side now. A little deeper, and she would be dead. Jake! These men were after Jake! The one called Juan rode with Bill Kennedy.

This couldn't be! Bill Kennedy had found them after all! She tried to wrench free, but Juan just held her tighter, yanking the knife from her side and putting it against her throat, pricking the skin. "Take it easy, *mujer bonita,*" the Mexican growled in her ear. "We will not kill you yet. We will wait and do it in front of your husband. But first we will have a good time with you, no? Now, you take us to Jake, or maybe I will change my mind and kill you now. I can push my knife a little deeper next time and maybe go all the way into your kidney. It will take you a while to die, and it will be very painful, but I assure you, you *will* die!"

"Hey, what's going on here?" Miranda could not see the man who had spoken the words. She only felt Juan whirl, heard a chopping sound and a grunt. More people screamed and ran, and Juan held a bloody knife before her eyes. Had he just killed some innocent man who had tried to help her?

"We would have waited for the shooting contest, honey," the blue-eyed man told her, "but then there would be a lot of men around with guns. We prefer to do it this way." He patted her cheek, hard enough to make it more of a slap. "Now, just tell us where to find Jake. Maybe we can get to him before the rest of my men find him and the kid. Is that where the little boy-pup is, with his pa?"

"You're Bill Kennedy," she said, the words choked. She was already beginning to feel weak from loss of blood.

The man in front of her grinned. "I see Jake told you all about us. Now, where is he, sweetie?"

"He'll *kill* you. You know that."

"You let us worry about that. You just tell us where he is, and we won't hurt the kid. But it's got to be quick, honey. If my men find him first and I'm not there, they might act without my orders and shoot down the little pup like a bunny rabbit."

She knew by his eyes this man would think nothing of killing a little boy. She had to get to Lloyd, even if it meant telling these men where Jake was. Jake was the only person in this whole crowd of people who might be able to help this situation, but how many of them were there? Would she see her husband gunned down today?

"Randy," Hetta Grant cried. "What is going on? What can we do?"

"Nothing!" Miranda answered in a low voice, terrified Juan or Kennedy would hurt the woman. "Just please stay out of the way."

Kennedy squeezed her jaw again. "Smart woman. Now, where is Jake?"

Juan kept a strong left arm around her, moving a hand to close it over her breast and wiping the blood that was on his knife onto the front of her dress, pressing the flat of it against her stomach to warn her how easily he could sink it into her. Miranda felt sick with fear and dread. "You're fools to do this with so many people around," she answered, her voice shaking.

Juan gave her a jerk. "Do not waste time, woman!" he growled in a chilling voice. "Your son's *life* is at stake!"

Lloyd! "He's over at the stands . . . where they're holding the horse auction," she told them.

Kennedy grinned. "Let's go!"

They hurried off, forcing Miranda to go with them. Shock and pain and loss of blood left her weak, and Juan had to half drag her to keep up. She sensed there were a couple more men following. All around them people scattered and women screamed. Miranda could feel blood trickling down her right leg under her dress. She walked as fast as she could to keep her feet ahead of Juan's, but it was impossible, and his boots kept kicking into her ankles. When she would start to fall, he would hoist her up again, making sure to keep a hand over her breast.

"What's going on there? What the hell are you doing to that woman!" someone shouted.

Bill Kennedy turned and fired. A second innocent person dead. Her fear faded into a dread of what this would do to Jake if he did survive, to know innocent people had died. Would she lose everything today? Her husband? Her son? Was this to be her destiny then, always to have her loved ones taken from her? "Please don't hurt my son," she begged.

Juan laughed. "Now you know the kind of man your Jake used to be, no? You have spread your legs for a man just like one of us, *señora bonita,* so you will not mind doing it for us, too, no? We will all have a good time. Maybe I will not even kill you. Maybe I will keep you." He squeezed her breast painfully and laughed. "After being with Juan, you will not want Jake anymore anyway."

"Somebody get Jake!" a man shouted.

Kennedy shot again, hitting the man in the back. *Three* innocent people! Miranda could see the stands now, heard shouting, more screams, children beginning to cry. Plenty of the men sported guns because of the contest, but none seemed willing to get involved. A couple of men rode off on horses, deciding just to get out of there. The band stopped its playing. She could see Jake now, standing in the middle of a corral. To her horror, another man, obviously part of Kennedy's bunch, held a crying Lloyd, pointing a gun to the baby's head. The black stallion was trotting nervously in a circle around the inside of the corral fence.

So, the rest of Kennedy's men had already found Jake. She spotted two more men lying dead, and her stomach churned when she saw that one of them was Joe Grant. He must have been watching Lloyd while Jake showed the stallion, and had likely lost his life trying to keep the outlaw from grabbing the boy away.

She took faint hope in the fact that Jake was still alive and standing, and he wore one of his revolvers. He had put it on because of the shooting contest, but it was only one gun with six bullets. How many men did Kennedy have along? People scattered, no one willing to argue now with the defiant intruders who seemed to think nothing of shooting people down in cold blood. Most people had run off; others stood transfixed, probably afraid that if they moved, they would be shot.

Now you know the kind of man your Jake used to be, Juan had told her. She would not believe he had ever been this bad. He would not stick a knife into a woman's ribs. He would not threaten a little boy. Never. He would not rape, or come to something like this and shoot people down like rabbits. Still, he had ridden with these men at one time, and now it seemed he would pay a much higher price for it than if he had gone to prison. Her heart ached at the look in his eyes when Juan dragged her around the corral fence to stand next to the man who held Lloyd. The baby reached for her, screaming "Mama."

"Let him go, you bastards!" Jake shouted. "Let him go to his mother and release both of them! You can have me if you want! Just let them go!"

People stared, no one making a move. Jake had never felt

such desperate rage. This was his son! And the woman he loved more than his own life! Was that blood on her dress? What had Juan already done to her! The very thing he had feared most was happening. By some cruel twist of fate, Bill Kennedy had found him, and he knew that if he survived this, the sweet, gentle life he had found here was over. He had everything to lose, and he was not going to lose it without a fight!

"Oh, we'll take you, Jake," Kennedy shouted. "But you've got to suffer a little first. You and your kid and your woman are comin' with us." He turned to one of the other three men who had come around to stand in front of Jake. "Shut that kid up. Gag him or something."

"Leave him alone!" Miranda screamed.

One of the men untied a sash she was wearing around her waist and yanked it off, going up to Lloyd and tying it tightly around the baby's mouth.

"Jake, what the hell is this about?" the small town's mayor shouted.

"It's about this man here being Jake Harkner, not Jake Logan," Kennedy shouted. "It's about him bein' just like us once, rode with us back in Missouri, robbed a few banks, killed a few men, raped a few women—"

"You *liar!*" Miranda shouted.

Kennedy lashed out and backhanded her, and blood appeared at the corner of her mouth.

"Don't you move, Jake," Jeb called out when he saw Jake stiffen. "You just drop that gun."

Jake stood still, weighing his chances, telling himself to hang on and make every shot count.

"Jake's a wanted man back in Missouri," Jeb shouted to the others. "Don't any of you be feelin' sorry for him. There's five thousand dollars on his head alive, three thousand dead."

People mumbled. More women had scurried away, herding their children with them, taking a chance on being shot rather than letting their little ones witness what might happen.

"Joe! Joe!" Hetta Grant was running toward her dead husband, but several men grabbed her and held her back.

"Don't go over there, Hetta!" one of them pleaded.

The woman began sobbing and crumpled to the ground. Lloyd kept up his screaming, the sobs muffled now by the hideous gag on the child's mouth. He arched wildly to get away, and the man who held him had trouble keeping hold with one arm while he held a gun in the other. Suddenly the baby wiggled loose and started crawling under the railing.

"Let him go," Kennedy ordered, grinning. "Let him go to his daddy." The words were sneered sarcastically. "If Jake doesn't want to give up his gun and come with us, the boy can be shot down just as easily there in the corral."

"You're making a mistake thinking I'll go anywhere with you, Kennedy," Jake answered, forcing himself to concentrate in spite of Lloyd running up and grasping his leg. He wanted desperately to get the gag off the boy, get him out of the way. He saw the terror in Miranda's eyes, worried about the stallion hurting Lloyd, but he noticed by an alert side-vision that someone had grabbed the horse and tied it to the fence rail. The animal was whinnying and jerking his head, trying to get loose. "If you want me dead, do it right here."

"Why, hell, Jake, then we wouldn't get the pleasure of having a little fun with you and the woman first."

"Exactly. You're going to kill her and my kid anyway, so why not get it over with? I'd rather they died right here on the spot than suffer what you'd do to them if you took us away with you."

Kennedy's smile faded. This was not working out quite like he had expected. In his desperate desire to show Jake up in front of these people for what he really was, and to corner him and make sure he didn't get away again, he realized he had not taken enough time to plan this. He knew how fast Jake could be, had watched this man shoot it out with more men than this and live to tell about it. Still, every man he had was a good shot, except Clarence still needed some practice. And where in hell *was* Clarence? He couldn't see him, but then he couldn't take his eyes off Jake right now either.

"What's it going to be, Kennedy?" Jake asked.

Miranda watched him, saw in his face the old Jake. He was on even ground now with men he used to ride with. This called for the old ways, and the look in his dark eyes would have frightened her if she didn't know him better. The meanness was back, the aura of danger.

"I'll tell you what, Kennedy," Jake was saying. "You go ahead and shoot me and my son. But I guarantee something. I guarantee that today *you're* going to die too! No matter what else happens, before I go down, you'll be *dead,* and I'll shoot my wife myself if I have to, to keep your men from getting her. Make your choice, Kennedy! Back off and get the hell out of here right now, or *die,* because I'm not going anyplace with you, and neither is my wife!"

The few people left backed farther away, and Miranda's heart beat so hard her chest ached. Lloyd! There he stood, hanging onto his father's leg and sobbing, his little lips stretched tight from the cruel gag.

"What do we do, *patrón?*" Juan asked.

"Shut up!" Kennedy barked.

"I say I slit the woman's throat right now!"

"I said shut up!"

"Don't listen to him, Bill," Jeb spoke up. "He knows he's a dead man."

Jake noticed the man's left arm hung limply at his side. He took note of it, realizing Jeb could shoot only with one hand. He recognized Joe Stowers and Jeb Donner, but not the other two men who stood to his left and his right. He kept them in his side vision, counting. Six. Kennedy, Juan, Jeb, his front tooth still missing, Joe Stowers, and the two new men. Was that all?

Clarence watched from a barn behind Kennedy. He had never forgotten Jake's gun in his mouth. He wanted to be in on this, but only if and when Jake went down or was taken away by Kennedy. Then he could strut in front of Jake and get back at him for the way he had humiliated him back in Virginia City; he could help torture the man and he could finally have a turn at the woman who had spurned him. He had never gotten used to these shootouts, was still nervous about such things after their narrow escape from the Wells Fargo men. He would stay near the barn until most of the shooting was over.

The young man's eyes widened then when the black stallion suddenly broke loose and reared, running between Jake and where Kennedy and Juan stood with Miranda. After that everything happened so fast he could hardly believe what he was seeing. With the speed of lightning, Jake ducked down, his gun drawn and fire spitting from its barrel. More people screamed and ran, and in spite of his wife being used as a shield by Juan, Jake's first bullet hit the man square in the forehead, knocking him backward.

Jake was screaming for Miranda to hit the ground as his next bullet hit Kennedy. It all happened in perhaps three seconds, and Clarence realized how good Jake had to be to risk shooting at Juan when he could easily have missed and shot his own wife. The rest of the men were firing back at Jake, who scrambled on the ground clinging to his son with one arm and keeping the boy under him for protection. He moved around, bent over, trying to use the frightened, pacing stallion as a shield. Several of the bullets from the other men's guns hit the horse, and it crashed to the ground, whinnying and kicking wildly. Jake kept firing, even though it looked as though he'd been hit. Joe and Jeb cried out and fell, and Oran and Cliff started running. His shirt stained with blood, Jake rose, and Clarence noticed more blood near his hip. Jake raised his revolver and fired, hitting Oran in the back. He whirled, getting a shot off at Cliff, also in the back.

Six shots, six men. Clarence realized that meant Jake's gun was empty. If he moved fast enough, this was his chance for fame—to be the man who killed Jake Harkner. He could collect three thousand dollars! He would never go up against him if Jake had a loaded gun, but now . . .

Miranda was screaming Jake's name. "Stay there!" he ordered, not sure he'd gotten all of Kennedy's men. He let go of Lloyd and scrambled to reload, got only one bullet in the gun's chamber when he saw someone running toward the corral. He ducked over a violently sobbing Lloyd when a seventh man started firing at him. The first two bullets missed, the third grazed across his shoulder but did little damage. The man hesitated then, and Jake took advantage of the moment. He rose and fired. The man grunted, his body jumping slightly into the air before crashing backward into a watering trough with a splash.

Jake quickly reloaded again, waited, saw no one else who looked eager to challenge him. He looked down at Lloyd, while a dazed crowd gawked at the bloody sight around them. Two innocent bystanders were groaning with bullet wounds they had suffered from stray bullets. Jake reached for Lloyd to get the baby to his feet and take off his gag, but the boy screamed and fought him, afraid of the blood on his father, and of the smoking gun in Jake's hand that had roared in his ears. He sensed his father's fury, and he looked at him with terror in his eyes.

Devastated, Jake watched his son scramble over to his mother . . . his mother, her dress soaked in blood. Kennedy had destroyed all that was dear to him, and in spite of his bleeding wounds and the fiery pain in his right hip, he managed to stay on his feet and walk over to where Kennedy lay.

He stared down at the man, heard him moan. So, he was still alive. He finished reloading his revolver.

Onlookers remained stunned, hardly able to believe what had just happened. Jake Logan, or Jake Harkner as the outlaws said he was called, had taken down six men without a miss, even though one of them held his wife as a shield, and even though Jake himself was wounded. He'd hardly had time to reload more than one bullet when he shot down the seventh man. Now that the gun battle was apparently over, they all remained rigid and staring, still trying to grasp all that had happened. They watched Jake point his gun at Kennedy's head, and no one made a move to stop him.

"You'll never do this to me and my family again," he said gruffly. People gasped when Jake deliberately fired the gun.

Miranda jumped at the roar of yet another gunshot. "Jake, you can't—" she protested.

Jake turned to her, panting and bleeding. "Never again," he repeated. He limped to every man he had shot, and wherever he walked people backed away. He looked down at the man who had fallen into the watering trough. He was wounded and struggling to get out. Jake recognized him as Clarence Gaylord.

"You little sonofabitch!" he snarled.

"Please! Let me go!" the young man begged.

"You did this, didn't you? You knew Miranda. You pointed her out to Juan! You little bastard!"

"Please, wait—"

Jake jammed his revolver into the man's mouth. "I *told* you what I'd do if you ever messed with me or my family again!" He fired, and blood poured into the trough water as Clarence's body slumped.

"Oh, my God," someone said softly.

Jake dipped the barrel of the gun into the water to swish off the blood, and the hot metal hissed. He turned and staggered back to Miranda and Lloyd, looking horribly tired and beaten, blood oozing from several wounds. He slipped the revolver back into its holster, and as he came closer to his wife and son, the dreadful look in his dark eyes turned to one of great sorrow. "Look at you," he groaned, his eyes tearing. "Hurt and bleeding, my own son afraid of me. *I* did this."

"No, Jake," Miranda sobbed. "Kennedy did this. Not you. All you did was defend yourself." She sat there in her bloody dress, holding Lloyd close. She had taken the gag from the

boy's mouth, and he clung to her, screaming. Jake went to his
knees, reaching out to touch the baby's dark hair, and Miranda supposed she would never forget the look in Jake's eyes
when Lloyd curled up tighter against her, still seeming terrified of his own father.

Jake closed his eyes and put his head down against the
earth. Miranda wept his name, moving to touch his hair. "It's
not your fault, Jake," she repeated. She looked up at the
crowd of people that had gathered. "Please find a doctor."

"I'm right here," the town doctor spoke up, pushing his
way through the crowd. He knelt over Jake, who rolled to his
side, grimacing with pain.

"Help my wife first," he groaned. "Juan . . . stabbed her
. . . I think."

"Somebody help me get them over to my office," the doctor barked. "And bring those other two wounded men."

A few people began moving to help them, everyone acting
slowly as they came out of the shock of what they had just
witnessed. Four men picked Jake up, and two others helped
Miranda get to her feet. Betsy came running up to her, trying
to take Lloyd from her, but the still-crying child would not let
go of his mother. They walked past Hetta Anderson, who
stood looking helplessly at Miranda, her eyes full of questions
and disappointment and not a little animosity.

"I'm so sorry, Hetta," Miranda said, her throat aching with
grief.

"That won't bring back my Joe. You lied to us! And now
my husband is dead because of your lies!" the woman sobbed.

The words cut deep. Hot pain pierced Miranda's right
side, and nausea grabbed at her stomach. She felt the whole
world closing in on her. The day had started out so happy and
peaceful. Now it was all destroyed, the friendships she had
valued, the love they had felt in this little town. Maybe she
would even lose the precious baby in her womb, the baby none
of these people even knew about yet.

And Jake. What would this do to him? It had taken so long
to teach him that he could be as good as the next man, that he
could have a happy life, a family, love. These people would
turn against them now. She knew it in her heart. His prize
stallion lay dead in the corral, and his son had recoiled from
him, terrified of the look on his own father's face. More than
the fair had been ruined. Lives had been ruined. Perhaps
some of these people would even hold Jake prisoner after his

wounds were tended to, take him back to Missouri and collect the reward on him.

Jake had been right. Bill Kennedy was a damn good tracker. The only good thing that had come out of this day was that the man and those who rode with him were dead and could never hurt them or anyone else again. But the way Jake had cold-bloodedly killed the two wounded ones had surprised even her. In that moment she had seen the worst of the old Jake. Could she ever get back the man she had loved these last three years? Could life ever be as sweet and peaceful for them again? Maybe he wouldn't even live. Maybe he had hung on just long enough to kill Kennedy and his men and make sure they could never hurt her or little Lloyd.

People surrounded her, talked among themselves. She kept hearing Jake's name, heard someone else crying in the distance. She felt consciousness slowly leaving her as the loss of blood drained her of strength. Finally her world went black and Lloyd slipped away from her. Someone took him and someone else lifted her. She slipped into a kind of dreamworld, where she saw Jake coming toward her, holding Lloyd. Both were smiling. Jake reached out to her and enfolded her into his arms with their son. She was safe there, wasn't she?

Yes, everything was fine. She would wake up and find out none of this had happened. They would have their picnic and sell their horses and Jake would win the shooting contest. They would take the hundred dollars and go home to the ranch they had built together, where they had always been so happy.

CHAPTER
EIGHTEEN

 Miranda could hear the doctor talking in a loud voice somewhere outside. "Let them rest for now!" he was shouting. "You can all settle this later."

"We'll settle it all right! And we're waiting right here until they can talk to us!"

She recognized Jack Stewart's voice. Jack owned the livery in town, had been a good friend to Jake. She did not doubt now that that friendship was over, not because Jake would want it to be, but because Jack and probably everyone else in town hated Jake for the bloodshed that had taken place this morning.

She opened her eyes, trying to gather her thoughts. What time was it? It felt like late afternoon. She had drunk a lot of laudanum before the doctor began stitching up the stab wound in her side, and she felt groggy. She raised her head to see little Lloyd sleeping soundly on the cot next to hers. Her heart ached for the child, who had been so confused and terrified by this morning's events. His little face was still stained from a mixture of dirt and tears, and there were red spots near the corners of his mouth from the cruel gag.

She closed her eyes again and took a moment to thank God that her son was still alive. It seemed a miracle that he had not been hurt in all the flying bullets, but then he had had his daddy protecting him. The whole event whirled in her mind. She could still hear the roaring guns, see the blood, hear people cry out, women scream. She could see that beautiful black stallion Jake had been so proud of, lying kicking and dying in the middle of the corral, could see Jake rolling and dodging, trying to keep his body over Lloyd's.

"Hang him right here, that's what we should do!" she heard someone shout.

Hang him! These were people who hours earlier had called themselves friends! Didn't they care about the kind of man Jake had become? Were they so quick to judge?

Jake! He had been shot! How many times? Was he even still alive? She vaguely remembered his own cries of pain, had been too sedated to get up and go to him. My God! Had he died without her at his side? She had to find Jake! She sat up, gasping at the awful pain in her lower right side. It was an area that could not be favored. Every movement, every breath, brought the stinging agony.

She realized she wore only her drawers and a camisole. Her dress and slips had been removed so the doctor could stitch her side, and her entire middle was wrapped with gauze. Grunting with pain, she rose and pulled a blanket around her, but before she could leave the little room where she had been resting, she heard the door to the outer office close. In the next moment the doctor came into the room.

"What are you doing up?" Dr. Henderson rushed to her side.

"I have to see Jake. Is he all right?"

"He'll be fine. He's down the hall," the man told Miranda. "You really shouldn't be walking around, Mrs. Logan. After what happened, it's a miracle you didn't lose that baby you're carrying."

"Harkner. It's Mrs. Harkner. Everyone knows that now, Doctor, so you might as well call me that. Please, I have to see my husband. Do you have some kind of robe I can put on?"

The man sighed in resignation. "You're both pretty stubborn, aren't you?" He brought over a cotton smock for her to wear. "I took three bullets out of him, and it's a good thing you were out so you couldn't hear his yelling. He refused anything for the pain, said he *deserved* to feel it. He *wanted* to feel it. I think he wants desperately to see you and the boy and make sure you're all right, but he thinks *you* won't want to see *him.* He kept talking about how his son is afraid of him now, and he couldn't bear to see him look at him like that again."

"I know all the things he's thinking, Doctor, heard some of his shouting when you were working on him. I should have gone to him right then—"

"I wouldn't have let you, even if you *could* have gotten off that bed. I shouldn't let you up even yet. You're liable to pass right out on me, and if you fall, you'll ruin my artwork."

She gave him a weak smile, but her eyes filled with tears. "I'm glad you decided to come here last month. Our little town needed a doctor."

They talked softly so as not to wake up the baby. "Well, as far as calling this 'your' little town, I'm afraid a lot of the citizens out there don't like that idea anymore."

"I heard." She wiped at her eyes. "They were once our friends."

The doctor sighed. "Well, these people aren't used to seeing what they saw today. It's true Jake had to defend himself, but all they know is that he shot down seven men, and in the process five more people died who were perfectly innocent, and two were wounded, but not badly. Joe Grant's wife is so worked up I had to send some laudanum out for her neighbors to give her to calm her down."

Miranda put a hand to her stomach. "Joe and Jake were close friends. I know this is hurting Jake as badly as if he had taken a bullet in the heart." She sniffed. "Who else was killed?"

"Well, Brad Shaker, that young farmer out south of town, the one who was engaged to Tilly Boone. Herbert Hughes, a man from San Diego. We found papers on him to see who he was and we've wired San Diego to tell his relatives. Then Joe Grant, of course, and Bob Liberty, the owner of the hardware store; Larry Bates, another neighbor of yours. Luke Bradshaw and Billy Kuntz each took a bullet, but they were only flesh wounds."

The names rang in her ears—all men they knew except for the one from San Diego. "Does Jake know all the names?"

"He knows. He must have asked me a dozen times, wanted to know if I was sure that was all. He's pretty devastated, but I don't think those people outside care."

Miranda touched at the superficial wounds on her neck, wondering if any of them would leave a scar. They had scabbed over and stopped bleeding. "Don't they understand

that none of the innocent ones were shot by Jake? It was
bullets those outlaws fired that killed them. Three of them
were killed deliberately when they tried to help me. That isn't
Jake's fault."

"Try to tell that to those people out there. Those men
came to get Jake. They blame him for the whole thing. They
don't think a man with his past should have come to Desert."

"I wonder if they realize that Jake will blame himself much
more fiercely than they ever could." She closed her eyes
against the pain of the thought. "How about Jake's wounds?
Are any of them dangerous?" She spoke in a near whisper
because Lloyd had stirred.

"No. The one in his hip was the deepest. He'll be walking
with a cane for a while, but eventually I think he'll get back to
normal. It's the kind of wound you can't really predict how it
will affect him later. Things like that have a tendency to turn
into arthritis and such in a man's later years. He might be
limping again when he's older."

Miranda looked over at Lloyd again. "My poor baby. I just
thank God . . ." She choked in a sob, which only brought
pain to her wound. The doctor patted her arm.

"That was the one thing Jake asked about more than anything else, that boy and you. He told me if I was lying to him
that you were all right, he'd have my head." The man turned
and took a clean handkerchief from a dresser drawer. He
handed it to her. "The crowd outside is talking ugly. I'm afraid
the two of you won't be able to stay in Desert, Mrs. Harkner,
not without a lot of trouble."

She blew her nose lightly, unable to take deep breaths. "I
know. I want to talk to Jake. Please take me to him."

"I don't think he wants to see you, or rather face you, I
should say."

"I don't care what he wants. I know how to handle Jake."

"Right now he's like a volcano ready to erupt, blames himself for all of this."

"You don't have to tell me that. Please, help me to his
room."

The doctor sighed in resignation and took her arm. "He's
just down the hall." He led her out of the room and into the
hallway of the small frame house he rented from a grocer in
town who had built himself a bigger house. The doctor used
the three bedrooms of the house as rooms for patients. Miranda felt disappointment, knowing this man would not be

around to help her when her second baby came. She and Jake would have to leave Desert. She had liked Dr. Henderson. He was a middle-aged widower with a sincere desire to help others. He reminded her in many ways of her own physician father.

The portly man with graying hair and eyes just as gray helped her to another doorway and patted her arm. "He's in there."

She breathed deeply for courage. She had a feeling it would take some clever talking to keep Jake from letting this destroy all the confidence and pride he had managed to build over the past three years. Somehow she had to find a way to keep him from blaming himself for all of it. "Leave us alone, please" she told the doctor.

The man just shook his head, as though he felt sorry for her. "You must be one hell of a strong woman to be married to a man like that."

"He's easy to love, once you know him and understand all the reasons behind what he's done. He's a good man, Dr. Henderson."

The man squeezed her arm. "I'll keep an eye on your son and see what I can do about making the people waiting outside go home for now."

Miranda blinked back more tears. "Thank you." She opened the door to the room and looked inside to see Jake resting on his left side, his right shoulder and left forearm bandaged. He wore only his long johns, and a lump near his right hip bone told her there was a heavy bandage there too. More scars on a man who already carried too many. His eyes were dark, glowering with anger, and again she saw for a moment the old, fierce, hardened Jake. She knew that this time the anger was directed at himself.

As soon as she appeared in the doorway he lay down on his back and covered his eyes. "Thank God you really are all right," he said quietly. "Is Lloyd really unhurt?"

"Thanks to your quick thinking. He's fine. He's sleeping."

"My quick thinking?" He lay there quietly for a moment. "Don't gloss it over, Randy," he spoke up then, his voice gruff with passion and grief. "Because of me, my son could be dead, and so could you." He let out an odd groan, as though he needed to sob but couldn't. "I wanted to be with you through your stitches and all, but the doc told me you'd be all right, and I decided you were better off not having to look at me. I heard you crying and I wanted to puke at the thought that I was the cause of all of it. I'm sorry, Randy, so goddamn sorry that I wish *I* had been killed out there."

"Jake—"

"Just leave, Randy," he told her. "Take the baby and just go home."

She closed the door. "And just what do *you* intend to do?"

He opened his eyes and glared at her. "I intend to get the hell out of your lives, out of the lives of everybody in this town, in this state, for that matter. Joe Grant is *dead* because of me. I've made Hetta a widow, terrified my son, nearly got you killed. There really isn't much to talk about, is there?"

"There is plenty to talk about. We still have each other and Lloyd. I haven't lost the baby I'm carrying. We still have the farm—"

He interrupted her with a grunt of disgust. "Haven't you heard that crowd outside? They want more blood, Randy, *my* blood! We don't have any farm anymore because they'll never let us stay there. They'll run us out of town on a rail, if they don't come after me with their shotguns first and turn me in for the reward, or maybe just hang me on the spot."

"I don't think any of them is brave enough to try to do that."

"They wouldn't need to be brave. I'd never shoot any of these people I know."

"I don't think they're too sure of that after what they saw this morning. *I* understand why you went back and shot the two who were still alive, Jake, but they don't."

He grimaced as he turned back on his side to rest on his left arm again. His eyes were so dark and angry, she shivered at the pain he was feeling. "The one in the watering trough was Clarence Gaylord."

Her blood chilled. "Clarence! He had joined up with Bill Kennedy?"

"Apparently. Kennedy probably came to Virginia City looking for me, and Clarence must have figured it might be exciting to join him—and that he'd get his revenge against us both if Kennedy ever found us." He sank back into the cot and turned his face toward the wall. "Damn, stupid kid," he groaned. Miranda noticed the hand he rubbed over his eyes was shaking. "I went right back to my old self today, Randy. I couldn't control that rage. I saw you lying there bleeding, heard Lloyd screaming, and I had to finish them off. If any of them had lived, they might have come back to do it again, and God only knows how many others they'd rape and kill in the meantime. The worst part is, I used to ride with them, and those people out there know it. Most people figure a man can't change, Randy, and I expect they're right. I was a goddamn fool to think life could be different for me, but it can still be different for you. It isn't too late for you to get out of this mess."

She felt a growing alarm. "Get out of it? How?"

"You *know* how," he almost growled. "As soon as I'm able, I'm getting the hell out of here and leaving you and Lloyd and the new baby to a life of peace."

"Is that so?" She walked closer, hanging onto a chair to support herself. "And just where are *we* supposed to go? We can't stay here. And how am I supposed to support the children?"

His pain was obvious as he slowly sat up then. "There are a hundred men who would marry you in an instant." He sat there a minute, breathing deeply against the pain, while Miranda tried to grasp what he was telling her. He reached over to the foot of the bed to get his shirt, sweat breaking out on his face from the effort. He took a thin cigar and a match from the shirt pocket.

"And I am supposed to just go out there and announce that I'm available?" Miranda asked, hardly able to believe his words. " 'Oh, sir, will you marry me and support my two children? My husband ran off on me.' "

"Stop it, Randy!" He closed his eyes, and a tear slipped down his cheek. "Do you know how I felt, how scared I was you and Lloyd would be killed? And my best friend, my first real male friend, is dead. It's going to keep happening, Randy. My past is going to keep coming back to try to destroy us—"

"*Try.* Yes, *try* is the word!" She breathed deeply against pain and dizziness, realizing she could barely raise her voice without hurting, but not wanting the pain to stop her from being here with Jake and convincing him he must not let this ruin the love they had found together. "People don't love each other only in the good times, Jake," she said in a softer voice. "They love each other no matter what, for better or for worse, remember?"

"And *I* get all the better being married to you, while *you* get all the *worse*! It isn't fair to you, Randy. I never, never should have let this happen! I never should have let my feelings overcome the cold, hard facts!"

"I had a big part in the decision we made, Jake. I knew exactly what I was doing when I married you. I went in with my eyes wide open. And what about Lloyd? How am I supposed to explain that the father he practically worships has suddenly disappeared from his life?"

Jake lowered the cigar, still not lighting it. "You saw the way he looked at me out there, the way he ran from me. I can't live with him looking at me like that! I told you before that if I ever saw that look—" He squeezed his eyes shut. "That's why I never wanted him to find out about my past when he's older. He'd look at me the same way, only he'd be old enough to also be ashamed. He might even be ashamed of himself because of who fathered him, just like *I've* always been ashamed. I don't *ever* want him to feel like that! It's best I get out of his life now while he's still young enough to forget me."

Miranda felt the panic rising, sensed that there would be no reasoning with him this time, not even a way to reach his emotions. As soon as he saw her hurt, saw his son recoil from him, he had quickly buried all feelings like the old Jake would have done after a beating from his father. Oh, he was so good at it. Seeing Kennedy and his men had brought back all the meanness and all the hardness he'd once possessed, and everything she had accomplished with him emotionally had been wiped out.

"I'll leave you every dime I have," he was saying resignedly. He stared at the floor. "I'll take just enough to survive on for a while. Hell, I've lived off the land plenty of times."

"And what you need, you'll steal?"

He looked at her darkly. "Maybe. You can have the farm. Sell it and keep the money. Maybe you should go to San Diego. You can file for a divorce there, live pretty nice there. Maybe you'll meet a banker or a lawyer or some other decent, educated man who can make a nice life for you."

"*We* had a nice life, Jake!"

"*Had* is the word."

"And you're a damn coward!" Her voice broke on the words, her eyes filling with tears. He looked at her in surprise. "For all your bravery with those guns, all you pulled through as a little boy, you've grown up to be a coward, Jake Harkner!" Miranda struggled to keep from breaking down. "You could face Kennedy and his men, but you can't face your own past and stand up to it! You won't hold up your head and look your past straight in the eye and say, 'Look, this is the Jake Harkner I am *now,* and I'm strong and I'm sure of what I want. I love my wife and my son and I am going to protect them and provide for them and be *happy;* and nothing that has happened in my past can change what is real for me right now!' "

She felt suddenly faint and moved to sit down in the chair. In spite of his own fierce pain, Jake rose and grabbed her, and she sank against his chest. "Don't leave me, Jake," she said softly. "You promised, remember?"

He threw the still-unlit cigar onto the bed and moved his arms around her carefully. "You should *want* me to leave you, for Lloyd's sake if not your own."

"You're his daddy and he loves you. What happened out there was just frightening to him, that's all. When he's settled, he'll come to you like he always has, because he thinks you're the greatest thing that ever walked."

He stroked her hair. "And when he gets older, he'll find out differently."

"Maybe not, now that Kennedy and his men are dead. We'll just move on from here, Jake. We did it once, we can do it again. All that matters is that we have each other. I don't want to be without you."

"How can you talk that way?" he said gruffly. "After today . . . you saw what I did."

"You defended yourself and me and Lloyd. That's all I saw. The world is better off without Kennedy and Clarence and Juan and *all* men like that!"

She felt his grip tighten. "*I* used to be like that, Randy. That's the hell of it."

"No! You were never *like* them." She leaned back and looked up at him. "You rode with them, but left because you couldn't keep associating with the things they did."

"I left them, but I also didn't do anything to *stop* them."

"You stopped them from hurting that girl!"

He moved away from her and helped her sit down in the chair. "I can't keep doing this to you, Randy. Look at you, in so much pain."

"Juan did this, not you."

He eased himself back onto the bed, just watching her a moment, feeling sick at the thought of what would have happened to her if Juan had gotten her alone. Kennedy had not planned his capture very wisely. He must have been so excited over finding him almost by accident that he lost all sense of reason. All they would have had to do was take Miranda off with them. He would have gone with them quietly if he knew Juan already had Miranda.

Thank God she hadn't suffered being alone with Juan and the rest of them. He was glad they were all dead. At least that much had been accomplished today, but at what horrible cost? "Randy, some of those people out there want to hang me for being responsible for the loss of innocent lives, and I can't say as I blame them. Now they're afraid I'll bring more trouble to Desert. This is going to be in the newspapers of major towns all around here, which means men are going to smell reward money and come after me. Even if we decided we *should* stay together like you want, it's too dangerous for you and Lloyd right now. I'm going to have to leave, Randy, and leave alone —get the hell out of Southern California if it isn't already too late. Once I'm sure no one is coming for me, and I find a place where I can settle safely, I could send for you."

Her throat ached so fiercely she could hardly talk. He was going away! He could be hunted and killed and she would never know it! Or without her he could start thinking she was better off this way and never send for her, maybe even return to his old ways. "Jake, I can't let you go off alone. I *belong* with you." Her voice trembled, and she broke into tears.

Jake reached out and touched her hair. "Randy, you know I'm right. You know that right now you've got to let me go. Alone I can dodge anybody who tries to come after me. We have to do this, for Lloyd's sake. We can't go dragging him all over the country, risking being bushwhacked by bounty hunters and the like. The best thing for him right now is to go right back to the house, to familiar things. You can tell him I went hunting for more mustangs, that I'll be coming back, or that I'm looking for a new place to live and he'll be back with his daddy soon enough."

"Will he? Will he ever hear from his daddy again?" She begged him with tear-filled eyes. "You need us, Jake, and we need you. Don't let this destroy everything we have together. Don't go back to the way you used to live, thinking we're better off without you. I love you. Lloyd loves you. Don't just disappear from his life and never let him see you again. He's little, Jake, but he'll remember. He'll know his father deserted him, and you said you'd never hurt him. Deserting him is just as bad as beating him."

Silent tears traced their way down his own face, and he took hold of her hands. "I don't want to be separated from my son, Randy, but for now it's better than either one of you being hurt or killed because of me. Thinking it's best for both of you if I go on without you is as painful as somebody ripping my heart right out of my chest. I'd love right now just to go home to that peaceful ranch and be with you and Lloyd and have everything the way it was, but it's all changed now, Randy. In fact, you can't even stay out there alone. You've got to get someone to stay with you, or sell the place and stay here in town somewhere, after Lloyd has been home a few days and settles down." He squeezed her hands. "If you're brave enough to still want to be with me, then somehow we'll make that happen. I promise."

"You promised you'd never leave."

"And I won't, not forever. But for now I don't have any choice, and you know it. You *know* we have to do this to protect Lloyd. You *know* I'm right!"

She put her head down, drawing his hands to her face to kiss them. She choked in a sob. "I'm so afraid for you. What if you're hurt and I'm not there?"

"I'll just rest easier knowing that at least you and Lloyd weren't in danger, knowing you're right here, safe. Not everybody out there hates us, Randy, and those who do don't hate *us*. They hate *me*. Once I'm gone, some of them will be willing to help you. Even so, it's going to be hard, Randy. Some of them are going to say cruel things. I'm so damn sorry about that."

"I don't care what they say. All I care about is you being all right and not giving up on us." She rubbed her cheek against his hand. "Please write me, Jake, or send me a wire once in a while telling me you're all right. Please don't take too long to send for us. Wherever you are, I'll come. I don't care where we live, as long as we're together, as long as Lloyd can be with his daddy again."

He pulled his hands away to reach over to where his pants lay. He took a handkerchief from the pocket and wiped at his eyes. "I don't understand you," he told her. "I knew you were a strong woman, but most women would end it right here and now. Maybe you should think about this, Randy. Being apart will give you time—"

"I don't need to think about anything! I love you, Jake Harkner, and Lloyd loves you. You fathered the baby I'm carrying, and he or she will love you too. I meant every vow I took when I married you, and I don't care how you feel about it, you *do* deserve to be happy and to have us with you. *You* have to be strong, too, Jake, and running from this, going back to that old life is *not* being strong, even if you think you're doing the best thing for us. The best thing for us is to be with you, and the only way you're going to overcome the past, Jake, is to stand up and refuse to let it destroy your future."

She paused, then went on. "Not giving up on us is the best way for you to show your father and men like Kennedy that you're *better* than that, *stronger,* that you're strong enough to overcome all the things they did to try to destroy your spirit, to show them you've found a love strong enough to bear up to anything your past throws at you. You've proven you're capable of loving and letting yourself be loved, Jake. You've proven you can provide for a family, that you can give us a home and be a good husband and father. We'll just do it again, someplace else."

He ran a hand through his hair. "It was so beautiful here."

"Anyplace we can be together is beautiful."

He shook his head. "I don't deserve—"

"I don't want to hear that. You know how strangely our lives kept getting entwined together, and you know that means God intends for us to be together. You're stuck with me, Jake, whether you like it or not."

He took hold of her hands again, studying her reddened eyes, her hair hanging in loose strands from the once-neat bun it had been pinned into. The horror of this day had taken its toll on her. "If you or Lloyd had been killed, I would have pointed my gun right at my own temple and pulled the trigger. You're the only good thing I've ever known in my whole life, and that's why for now I've got to leave you both behind, Randy, until I know things are safe again. Fact is, for your own safety, you ought to tell people around here that you plan to divorce me. They have to think that you didn't really know the whole truth about me. They have to think that what you found out today about me is as new to you as it was to them, and that because of that you can't bring yourself to stay with me. If they think I'm out of your life for good, they'll be more willing to help you."

"Jake, I won't do that. I'm not ashamed to be married to you. I knew exactly—"

"Damn it, Randy! For once will you do what I ask, for Lloyd's sake if nothing more? You've got to pretend to disown me and just get on with your life as though you mean to live it without me. If you sell the farm and all the horses, you'll have money to live on for a while, plus the money we've got in the bank. Somehow I'll get more money to you, and somehow I'll find a way to send for you without anyone realizing it. When the time comes for you to leave and come to me, you've got to make up some story about going back to Kansas or something. They can't ever think you might be coming back to me, or you might be followed. Do you understand?"

She reached out and touched his face, shivering in another sob. "I understand," she wept. "But I don't want to do it that way, Jake."

He took hold of her wrist and kissed her palm. "It's the only way. And I want you to stay here till that baby is born. Doc Henderson is good, and he's an understanding man. I need to know you'll be with someone who knows what he's doing when the baby comes."

"But that's at least six months away!" Their eyes held, and she shook her head. "Jake—"

"It's the only way. It could be longer than six months. We have to allow enough time for people to believe we've really parted ways."

The voices outside grew louder again, and it sounded as though someone had come inside. "Get out of our way, Doc!" someone shouted. Jake managed to get to his feet just as the door burst open, and Jack Stewart barged inside with four other men and two women. At the sight of Jake standing there bare-chested and looking too big for the small room, they all hesitated, the women looking away when they realized he was wearing only his long johns. Jake glared at all of them, angry that the men were seeing Randy wearing the light smock the doctor had given her.

"You people might have a little respect for other people's privacy," Jake glowered.

Jack puffed up his chest, stepping forward. "Respect? For the likes of you?"

"Yesterday I was your friend."

"Yesterday I didn't know you were a murdering, thieving rapist who's wanted back in Missouri!"

Miranda wanted to stand up and defend her husband, but sick as it made her to keep quiet, she knew Jake was right that these people had to believe she was innocent of his background.

"I was never a rapist," Jake said in a low voice. "Believe the rest if you want, but not that! That label got pinned on me by mistake!"

"So what?" Milt Owens spoke up. "That still leaves murder and robbery!"

Jake glared at him, thinking how just yesterday he had bought oats from this man who owned a feed store in town. Owens had been pleasant, had even given him a special price, joked with him about the shooting contest that was to have been held today. There had been a shooting contest, all right, of the worst kind. "You folks believe what you want. I'm in too much pain to stand here and try to explain any of my actions to you. Now you all listen to me! I'm damn sorry about what happened today! *Damn* sorry! I came to Desert to try to start a new life with my wife and son. Now I know that's impossible, and I know why you're here. You want me to get the hell out of Desert. You're afraid more trouble will come."

"You bet we are!" Jack answered, feeling braver by the minute. "If you don't leave Desert we'll—"

"You'll what?" Jake stepped closer, towering over the man. Stewart swallowed and looked at the others. Jake just shook his head. "You're all a bunch of hypocrites! What kind of friends condemn a fellow friend without sitting down and listening to all the facts! I didn't ask those men to come after me today, and I wasn't about to let them hurt my wife and son! But as it turns out, that's just what they've done, because they've destroyed my marriage!"

Miranda closed her eyes at the words. She wanted to stand up and shout to them that they were all wrong about Jake, and that she would never stop loving him.

"I'll leave your perfect little town," Jake snarled. "But I want all of you to know that Miranda didn't know everything about my past until today. She had no idea I was a wanted man! I lied to her about a lot of things, and I don't want her abused because of me! Every damn one of you knows what a good woman she is, and she's going through hell right now! She needs your support after I'm gone."

"We have nothing against Miranda, if she truly did not know about your past," one of the women spoke up. It was

Leona Stewart, Jack's wife. "It's too bad you had to destroy her life the way you have, and your son's life—"

Shut up, Leona! Miranda thought. Words like that could make Jake think the woman was right, that he *had* destroyed their lives. He could decide never to come back to her or send for her.

"—But what's done is done," the woman continued. "We will help her, Mr. Logan, or Mr. Harkner, whatever you call yourself."

"We're not the hypocrites you think, Jake." The words came from Lester Thomas, a neighboring rancher. "If we were, we'd string you up right now, or herd you back to Missouri for the reward money."

Jake laughed bitterly. "The only thing keeping you from that is you're too damn scared to try it!" He deliberately reached for his gunbelt, disgusted at the way their eyes widened with fear. They actually thought he'd shoot them! One of them ran right out of the room. He threw the gunbelt onto the bed. "I'm leaving Desert as soon as I can get some supplies together. I'll be out of here by sundown."

Miranda's heart quickened. No! Not that soon! They had to talk more, hold each other again!

"You ought to know my wife is going to have another baby," he added. "I want her taken care of, and protected if some bounty hunter comes through here and tries to give her trouble. That's all I ask."

"She'll be all right with us," Mrs. Stewart promised, literally shaking at being so close to a killer. "She is as much a victim as those others who were killed and wounded."

Jake stepped closer. "You just remember, they weren't killed by any of *my* bullets! All *my* bullets hit their targets, and every one of the men I killed *deserved* to die! If I could have kept them from hurting the others, I would have! But what's done is done, and by nightfall you won't have to worry about Jake Harkner making trouble for this town because he'll be gone! Now all of you get out of here! I have a son to say goodbye to!"

They all seemed to shrivel slightly at his tirade, and they quickly filed out of the room. Jake hit the wall with his fist. "Damn hypocrites!"

"They know and understand nothing about you, Jake, or about the side of life you saw growing up." Miranda managed to get to her feet. She walked over to him, touching his back.

"Jake, I want to shout to them how much I love you. I want them to know the truth."

"You can't. Promise me."

She put her head against his arm. "Can't you wait one more day to leave? You're hurting, Jake. How can you even ride?"

"I'll find a way if it means your safety. Word about things like this spreads fast. The sooner I get out of here the better for all of us."

"Jake—"

"Take me to Lloyd. I want to see my son." He refused to look at her, and she knew what this was doing to him. He was hardening himself once again, using his old ability to pretend he could bear the emotional pain and would be just fine. He moved an arm around her, and she put hers around his waist so that they supported each other down the hall to Lloyd's room. Jake drew in his breath at the sight of him lying there, his little face still dirty and stained with tears.

"If you ever doubt why we're doing this, just remember that sight," he groaned. He moved away from her and managed to kneel beside the bed, reaching out and touching the child's hair. He put his head down beside him then, his shoulders shaking with tears of grief and heartache.

Miranda felt as though someone was slowly carving her heart from her chest. Lloyd stirred and opened his eyes, and to her great relief he smiled and reached out for his father. "Daddy hold," he said, his little voice raspy from so much screaming earlier.

Jake took the boy into his arms, hesitantly at first, fearing he would start screaming again. Lloyd hugged him tightly, and Jake hugged him tighter then, ignoring the pain in his hip as he remained kneeling there with his son in his arms. What man could ask for more than this, he thought. He had been so blessed, and he could not let some other man raise this boy, some other man who would never love him the way he did. He thought what he would give to have had one moment like this with his own father. Thank God his son was alive and unharmed, and thank God he had not seen that look of terror in his eyes. He would do whatever he had to do to keep this precious child safe and happy, even if it meant leaving him for a while.

Miranda came closer and stroked Jake's hair, wondering if this was the last time she would see father and son together this way. "Now you know I was right about how much this little boy loves you, Jake. You can't ride out of his life forever and think he will forget you. You have to send for us. You have to come back into his life."

He could not find his voice to reply, and he could not for the moment stop his open weeping. How strange that there was a time when he thought all he ever needed was himself and his guns. Now his whole reason for existing was right here in his arms, and he knew it could never again be just Jake Harkner alone. "I'll find a way," he promised.

Part

Three

We have walked together many years.
Your spirit is my spirit.
Your breath is my breath.
Our hearts beat with one rhythm.
I know your soul, and you know mine.
Even when we cannot be together,
We are one.

CHAPTER NINETEEN

March 1870 . . .

Miranda slowly opened her eyes, moving them just enough to see familiar flowered wallpaper. She realized then that she was in one of the rooms at Dr. Henderson's house. She tried to move, but realized she was too weak to even wiggle her fingers.

Gradually it all came back to her. She had delivered her baby. She remembered she had been helping bandage a man's arm when she went into labor. Thank God it had happened here at the doctor's office and not while she was alone with Lloyd in the tiny apartment she rented above the hardware store. A man named Jerry Eastman had bought the store after the former owner, Bob Liberty, had been killed in the now-infamous shoot-out the day of the fair. Eastman was new in town, so he was at least friendlier to her than most of the others, but, oh, how she hated those two tiny rooms above his store. She had had no choice but to find the cheapest place possible. She had to be careful with money now, and being pregnant and having Lloyd to watch and unable to afford help, she couldn't have kept running the ranch.

She thought about the lovely home she and Jake had shared, the home Jake had built with so much love. Each time she remembered the happiness they had known at the ranch, the peace Jake had found, it felt as though someone was squeezing her heart in a vise.

Now there was a new baby. If they were still living as a family at the farm, this event would be such a joy, but the only remnant of that life was the small profit she had made selling the property and livestock, most of the furnishings, the coal cookstove Jake had so proudly bought for her. She had carefully packed her lace curtains and her braided rugs into her trunk, the one pitiful constant in her life, and she continued to promise herself she would use those things again in the new home she trusted Jake would make for her and the children . . . somewhere.

For six months now she had managed to live off the money Jake had left her in a savings account, as well as the money from the ranch. To keep from using it up too quickly, she helped Dr. Henderson with his practice. Betsy Price, one of the few women in town who had remained her friend since the shoot-out, graciously watched Lloyd for her when she worked for the doctor; and she spent her evenings doing ironing and mending for others. She was determined to survive this awful time away from Jake, determined to find ways to support herself and stay in Desert until Jake could send for her.

She heard hushed voices outside the door, heard Lloyd, nearly three now, running about and playing, heard the tiny squall of a baby. She remembered the doctor saying it was a girl. Why was the memory of the birth so vague, and why was she so weak? Pain. She remembered horrible pain, something worse than just birthing a baby. Something else had happened; someone had made her breathe chloroform. *Stop the bleeding,* she remembered Dr. Henderson saying. How long ago was that? What time was it now?

Dr. Henderson came into the room then, deep concern in his brown eyes. "You awake, Miranda?" He bent close. "How are you feeling?"

Miranda studied the man's plump face and kind smile. He was a widower, had a son in college back East, also studying to be a doctor. Henderson was a hefty man of perhaps forty, with receding hair, and she thought how at the moment he looked somewhat distorted, his eyes seeming bigger, his voice far away. Why did she feel this way, as though she was removed from her own body?

"My . . . baby," she whispered.

"You had a little girl. She's doing just fine. Betsy is feeding her goat's milk right now. You just rest. You won't be getting out of that bed for some time yet." The man felt her pulse. "Much stronger," he said after a moment. "That's good." He patted her hand. "I'll be right back."

He left her, and Miranda heard the door close. She managed to move her arm to put her hand to her eyes. *Where are you, Jake? Are you alive? You have a little girl. Don't let her and Lloyd grow up without their daddy.* The day Jake rode out of her life again, they had agreed she should stay in Desert so that he could get word to her more easily when he found a new place to settle and was sure it was safe. For the first several weeks she had been pestered by reporters and lawmen alike, the reporters wanting to know everything about her and Jake: how they had ended up together, if he was a good husband. She had refused every one of them, other than to inform them in no uncertain terms that she intended to divorce Jake Harkner as soon as her baby was born. Letting them think Jake had left her and that she was ending the marriage seemed to be the only way to quell the excitement about her being his wife.

It had to be this way, so that when she finally left Desert, no one would think she was going to Jake. Otherwise, she might be followed, by lawmen or outlaws or bounty hunters. Even Betsy thought the marriage was over. Miranda hated lying to the one woman in town who still was a friend to her, but it was the only way to protect Jake. Friends and enemies alike had to think she had no idea where Jake was; and for the present, it was true. That made the hell of waiting all that much worse.

How long should she wait thinking he would send for her? He could be dead. He might decide that she and the children would be better off if he never sent for them. That was her biggest fear. She knew how the man thought, knew he still blamed himself for the tragedy the day of the fair.

The door opened again, and Henderson returned to her bedside. He felt her forehead. "Your fever seems to be gone," he said, looking relieved. "You haven't told me how you feel, Miranda. Are you in a great deal of pain?"

"Yes," she whispered. "And . . . I'm so . . . weak."

The man took her hand. "It will take some time to get your strength back. You nearly died. I've never seen so much bleeding after a birth. I am afraid I was forced to make a decision you may not like to hear." He squeezed her hand, and Miranda felt a deep ache in her heart, suspecting in that moment what he was going to tell her. "I performed an operation on you, Miranda. I removed your uterus but not your ovaries. The bleeding was from the wall of the uterus and simply would not stop. I am sorry, but you won't be able to have any more children."

She watched his eyes, saw true sorrow there. He was not telling her just as a doctor, but as a friend, and she knew he would not have done this if it had not been absolutely necessary to save her life. She closed her eyes against a feeling of deep loss, needing to mourn for all the babies she would never have now. She was only twenty-four years old.

The tears came then, and the doctor wiped them away with a clean handkerchief. "I'm sorry, Miranda. You just aren't made to have a lot of children. I don't think you would have survived another birth." The man pulled a chair to her bedside and sat down. "You have two beautiful and healthy children now. Be glad that they're strong and normal, and that you're still alive." He took her hand. "I'm going to give you a little more laudanum now for pain—"

"No. I want . . . to see my daughter first."

Henderson sighed, feeling sorry for this beautiful young woman, deserted by her outlaw husband, left with two children to support alone. "All right," he told her. "I'll have Betsy bring your daughter in for a minute or so. Then she's going to take the baby and Lloyd home. She brought Lloyd over here because he kept asking about his mommy, and Betsy wanted him to see you so he'd know you were here and all right."

The man left, and Miranda wanted to cry for Lloyd. Of course he wanted to see his mommy. He was probably afraid she had gone away like his daddy. How much longer could she bear this emotional pain? She had not heard from Jake, had no idea when she would.

Henderson came back into the room, carrying the tiny bundle that was her daughter. Betsy followed, holding Lloyd's hand and telling him to be very quiet. The doctor held the baby close to Miranda and opened the blankets so she could see her. Miranda was overwhelmed with a mixture of sweet joy and deep sorrow. The baby was beautiful, dark like Lloyd and Jake.

"Do you have a name for her?" Henderson asked.

"Yes," she answered. She had thought for a long time what she might call her baby if it was a girl. She wanted a name that would be important to Jake. "Evita," she answered. "E-V-I-T-A. Evita Louise. Louise was . . . my mother's name."

"Evita. What a pretty and unusual name," Betsy spoke up.

"Yes," she answered. "I heard it somewhere once and always liked it." Evita had been Jake's mother's name. Miranda couldn't tell them the truth, but she knew that naming the baby after her would mean so much to Jake.

"Mommy hurt?" Lloyd asked, pouting as he moved beside the bed.

"Mommy . . . is fine," she answered. "Mommy . . . has to sleep. You be . . . a good boy . . . for Betsy."

The boy reached out and touched her arm. "Mommy come home."

"I will, Lloyd, after I sleep for a few days."

"Daddy come home too?"

"No, darling, not just now."

"Mommy don't go away?" Lloyd asked.

Miranda fought against more tears, not wanting to cry in front of the boy and frighten him. She knew Lloyd was thinking about his father. Not a day went by that he didn't ask when his daddy was coming home. "No," she answered her son. "Mommy isn't going away, Lloyd. Mommy will always be with you. She'll never go away."

Daddy is with you, too, Lloyd, in spirit. You'll be with him again soon. Daddy loves you. He would never desert you. How she wished she could say it aloud, but as far as the doctor and Betsy were concerned, Jake was gone from her life forever . . . and maybe he was . . . maybe he was.

Jake tipped back his chair and let it rest against the wall. He took another swallow of whiskey and drew deeply on the cigarette he had rolled for himself, watching the only whore in this hole of a saloon lift her skirt to show a bare bottom to a prospective customer. She was a wild, dark thing, looked half Indian. The two men at the table made kissing sounds and got up to follow her to a back room.

Jake watched quietly until the door closed. Then his dark eyes took note of every man in the little log tavern run by a man called only "Bates" by the outlaws who frequented the smoke-filled, dirt-floored establishment. Bates supposedly sold guns and whiskey to Indians in return for valuable skins and even gold, and it was rumored he had robbed many a wagon train and stagecoach out West. He had built this little "business," such as it was, as a way to make money when in hiding, and he liked to brag about selling the best whiskey on the Outlaw Trail—whiskey Jake figured was either stolen or bought with stolen money. The man had even stolen the woman in the back room from a trader who owed him money. He had shot the man and taken all his belongings, including the woman, who didn't really seem to mind, just as Bates didn't seem to mind sharing her with every man who wanted a piece of her.

Bates's full background was a mystery, like every other man who hung out along the Trail. In these surroundings, a man didn't ask too many questions and he couldn't be too careful. There was hardly a man anywhere in these parts who wasn't wanted by the law and wasn't capable of killing another man at the drop of a hat. Jake had himself been challenged three times by men wanting to prove they were the most notorious and most feared of those who traveled this trail, which stretched from southern Arizona all the way into Montana. It was dotted with several small "hideout towns" with names like Hole-in-the-Wall and Robber's Roost.

The only law here was the gun, and survival was often a simple matter of how fast a man could draw. That was how arguments were settled. All three of the men who had challenged him had died, and he was so full of anger and loneliness that he had felt nothing when he killed them. After all, this was where he belonged, wasn't it? This was the Jake he was meant to be. Word traveled fast in this network of outlaws, and now it seemed that whenever he reached a new hangout along the Trail, men stepped back when he told them his name. Harkner. Jake Harkner. People might as well know it.

Here, at least, he was free to say who he was. No man wearing a badge dared venture into this country. The vast and desolate canyonlands and valleys and mesas of this mostly uninhabited and forbidding land were a haven for men like himself, men with an ugly past, men with their faces on wanted posters. Here such men made no bones about who they were and what they had done when bragging to fellow robbers and murderers. In spite of their lawless natures, most of them shared an unspoken code of honor. Here they were safe.

He had heard about this network of outlaw hideaways

through rumors when he worked at the mine in Virginia City. A few miners were familiar with the Trail, and it was the only place he could think to go for the time being, until lawmen and bounty hunters might stop looking for him. He was supposed to find a way to start over, to send for Miranda and Lloyd and the new baby eventually, but now he wasn't so sure he should. Maybe this was where he belonged, out of their lives.

He had made a few friends along the way, if men like this could be called friends. He had even met one old friend from his gunrunning days. Charlie Tate was fat and bearded now. The man had seen one of Jake's gunfights down in Arizona not long after Jake left California, and Charlie had ridden with him for a while. He had talked incessantly, liked to brag to others who Jake was and that he had known him during the war. Jake liked Charlie well enough, but he was glad when the man had ridden off with some cattle rustlers. Right now he didn't want to be around someone who blabbed so much. He needed to be alone . . . alone. That was how he was meant to be, wasn't it?

In his rage and personal agony, he had made more enemies than friends along the Trail, almost looking for an excuse to kill. He had made his way up and down the Trail aimlessly, worked for a rancher for a while just for extra money. Ranchers in these parts cooperated with outlaws, even let them graze stolen cattle and horses on their land. It was better to get along with such men than to risk having their own herds stolen, or chance being murdered. It was simply an understood way of life, and most ranchers didn't even ask a man's name.

He heard the whore scream with delight in the back room and he thought how ugly and used she looked compared to Miranda. He had never ached so badly for a woman in his life, but there were none here or anywhere else that he wanted. There was a time when women like the one in the back room would have been enough for him, but not anymore. Memories of Miranda's firm but supple naked body pressed against his own haunted him at night when he bedded down alone, usually on the cold ground.

God, how he missed her! He felt tortured with the need to touch her, hold her, feel her arms around him in return. He needed to know that she was all right, yet for her own safety he could not go back to her or even make contact with her.

Being away from her was only made worse by being separated from his little boy. He felt real pain at the thought that Lloyd would probably forget him in time, that he would never know his second child. It had been ten months now since he'd left California. The baby should have been born at least four months ago. He could only hope Miranda had gotten through the birth with no problems.

He finished his cigarette, lit another one, drank another shot of whiskey. It was early summer now. A harsh winter had pretty much kept him holed up here at Robber's Roost, but soon it would be time to make up his mind what the hell he was going to do. Miranda would run out of money eventually, and if he decided not to send for her, he at least had to find a way to send her money and to tell her he was not coming for her. She had to know. He couldn't leave her dangling forever, never knowing what had happened to him.

Whether he returned to his family or not, he sure as hell wasn't going to let them starve. He knew he could get money easily enough if he wanted to use his guns to get it. Just to the east were the gold towns of Colorado, more up north in Montana, or south in Arizona. Gold towns meant payroll runs, banks, people riding stagecoaches with money in their pockets. To the north was the Union Pacific Railroad. Only wealthier people could afford to ride the train, people who carried money and gold watches and wore diamonds.

Yes, it would be easy, but something kept him from that life now. That something was a woman whose face he could see as vividly as if she were sitting right in front of him. She looked at him with those scolding gray-blue eyes and told him that if he returned to a life of crime, her faith in him and her love for him would be destroyed. He could see the disappointment in her eyes, and even if he never went back to her, he knew that look would haunt him forever. Damn woman! That was the hell of it. He couldn't get her out of his mind or his heart or his blood. He felt torn between two worlds now, belonging to neither.

He glanced at the swinging doors then when someone new entered the tavern. The man looked familiar to him, and when the newcomer took his own inventory of those inside, his eyes lingered on Jake for a moment, as though he, too, realized maybe he should know him. The man nodded to him, but Jake made no sign of recognition. He took a deep drag on the cigarette, watched the man step up to the bar, which Bates had built out of wooden planks laid over barrels. The man ordered a beer, paid for his drink, and turned to face Jake again.

Jake stayed put, squinting his eyes to study the man, searching his memory. The man looked friendly enough, but Jake was always wary. If this man did know him and remembered how good he was with his guns, he might turn out to be another fool stupid enough to challenge him. To his surprise the man smiled, then headed toward his table. Jake guessed him to be about the same age as he was, and cleaner in clothes and appearance than most men in these parts, about ninety-five percent of whom were in bad need of a bath and a shave, himself included. This man was downright good-looking, his blue eyes friendly as he approached the table.

"By God, it *is* you, Jake!" the man exclaimed, a strong southern accent to the words. He set down his beer. "I heard you were makin' your way through these parts. I've been trackin' you all the way from northern Arizona. Saw Charlie Tate down there. He's the one who told me you were hangin' around here somewhere." He put out his hand. "It's been a long time!"

Jake's eyes narrowed in puzzlement. He glanced down at the extended hand and noticed there was a thumb missing. It was then he remembered. "Jess! Jess York," he said, grasping the hand and shaking it. "You rebel bastard, what are you doing out here?"

"I could ask the same of you. First I hear you're wanted back in Missouri. Next thing I know, some asshole by the name of Bill Kennedy and a rough bunch of no-goods is hangin' around places like this askin' about you and lookin' ready to cut you up and feed you to the wolves."

"They came here first?"

"Traveled all up and down the Trail askin' if anybody had seen a Jake Harkner or Jake Turner. You know how men in these parts feel about rats who go after their own kind. We chased them out but good." The man pulled up a chair and turned it, straddling it backward. He looked Jake over. "You can be sure they never found you because of anything any of *us* told them. Hell, we didn't know where the hell you were anyway. I read in the newspapers down in El Paso that you shot the hell out of all of them out in California." He grinned. "Man, I sure would have liked to have seen that."

"El Paso! The news made it all the way there?"

York shrugged. "Hell, it ain't every day a man shoots it out one against seven and lives to tell about it." He looked Jake over, thinking the man hadn't changed much since the war, still big and handsome as ever, but he needed a shave and a haircut. He didn't look like any family man, and York couldn't imagine he ever had been. "The article said you had a wife and a kid. That true?" He watched the pain darken Jake's eyes, and he knew he'd hit a sore spot.

"It's true." Jake took another swallow of whiskey, and York said nothing for a moment. Jake knew it was out of respect. Men like himself and York shared personal triumphs and tragedies only when they felt like it, not because someone asked.

Jake had met Jess York during his gunrunning days. Jess had lost his wife and a little daughter to a group of brutal Yankee raiders who had burned his home and farm and raped his wife before killing her. The incident had turned him into a ruthless raider himself for several months, and after the war he had continued an outlaw life, caring about nothing but revenge and trying to deal with the bitter pain he suffered.

The two men had become good friends for a while, finding it easy to talk to each other. Both had suffered from brutal pasts, and they understood each other's motives for living the way they had. After the war, though, they had gone their separate ways, and Jake had taken up with Kennedy's gang.

Jake took another deep drag on the cigarette. "I know what you're wondering. Where's the wife and kid? By now there's two kids. My wife was carrying when I left California after the shoot-out."

York took a swallow of his beer and licked at foam on his upper lip. "Left her for her own safety, I expect, if you don't mind my askin'."

Jake sighed deeply, aching to taste Randy's mouth, to be inside her, to love and protect her, provide for her the way a husband should. "You've got it," he answered. "I knew the shootout would draw every lawman and bounty hunter for miles. I couldn't expose my wife and son to that kind of danger. Fact is, she's got everybody in the little California town where we lived thinking I've left for good and she's divorcing me. That's the only way to keep reporters and bounty hunters off her back. She doesn't even know where I am, and that's the best way to protect her."

"I expect. She *really* divorcin' you?"

Jake stared down at the cigarette in his hand. "If she had any sense, she would. But when it comes to me, she *doesn't* have much sense. Seems to think she still loves me and wants to be with me, no matter what."

"Sounds like a hell of a woman. She know about your past before she married you?" York laughed lightly. "Come to think of it, how in hell did you find a woman like that in the first place? I sure never imagined you'd marry, let alone have a kid."

Jake met his eyes. He used to trust this man, but now that he had a wife and children, he had to be careful. Still, he knew York was basically honest. He'd been a simple family man himself once, until the war destroyed everything that meant anything to him. "It's a long story," he answered. "What about you? What have you been up to?"

"No good, mostly. I'm on my way to Colorado to see about a job. Lots of jobs in those mining towns, in Denver, too, I'm told."

"An *honest* job?"

York chuckled, showing clean teeth. "Hell, yes! I do still find ways to make money the easy way, but mostly I find honest work when I can. Now if I could find me another woman as good as the one I lost . . ." His smile faded.

Jake knew the man still suffered on the inside, still felt lost, a man with no direction in life, just as he had been before Miranda came along. "Maybe I'll go with you to Colorado," he said aloud. "I'm getting tired of these hellholes, and I need to make some money. You want somebody to travel with?"

The man's eyes lit up, both men understanding the unspoken loneliness the other lived with. "Sure." He grinned. "Hell, I'm glad I found you. When I heard you were roamin' these parts, I started checkin' out every settlement and hideout along this trail. It's good to see you again, Jake. It's been a lot of years."

Jake nodded. "I've just been laying low here myself, biding my time till things die down. I've got to figure out what I'm going to do next, whether or not to send for my wife and kids." He took one last drag on the cigarette and threw it down, stepping it out. "I just don't know what the hell to do, whether to get back into their lives or just end it."

"End it?" York shook his head. "I'll tell you somethin', Jake." He made a gesture toward Jake's bottle of whiskey. "One thing I remembered about you was out of all the hell-raisin' and shootups and robberies and anything else you did, you never was much of a drinker. Maybe you don't remember I'm probably one of the few people you used to talk to about your pa, how much you hated him. You told me once heavy drinkin' reminded you of him, that you always hated it because of him and was scared whiskey would take control of you like it did him."

Jake scowled, pouring himself another shot. "So what? How much I drink is nobody's business."

"Hell, I know that. I'm just sayin' somethin' must be eatin' at you good to make you sit there with a whole bottle of whiskey in front of you. My guess is it's the woman and the kids. If your wife is willin' to forgive and wants to stay in your life, hell, grab what you can." The man finished his beer in two gulps and leaned closer. "Shit, Jake, do you know what I'd give to have my wife and kid back? You could chop off both feet if it meant I could be with them again. I don't know the whole story, but it sounds to me like you've got a good thing waitin' for you back there in California. I wouldn't even *think* about not goin' back to it. Were you close to your kid?"

Jake looked at his whiskey glass. "I'd die for him. He means more to me than my own blood. Yeah, we were close." He took a deep breath, twirling the glass against the table. "You sonofabitch. You always could cut right to it."

He met Jess's eyes, and Jess was stunned by the tears brimming in the eyes of this man he remembered being mean as a snake at times. The pain in Jake's eyes almost startled him.

"I never thought I could learn to give a damn about anything," Jake told him. "And I sure as hell never thought I'd like being a father, or that I could be any good at it, after the kind of childhood I had. Trouble is, I love the woman and the kid enough that I'm not sure it isn't better for them if I stay out of their lives for good.

York took a cigar from his pocket and lit it.

"When are you leaving for Colorado?" Jake asked.

York took the hint. Jake was through talking about personal things. He shrugged. "Now that I've found my old friend, I'll go whenever you feel like going."

Two men at a nearby gambling table began arguing over a hand, one accusing the other of cheating. The argument quickly became more heated, one of the men kicking the table over. Cards and drinks went flying. The other man pulled a gun on the first and shot him before he could draw. His body flew backward, landing near Jake. The man holding the gun glared at Jake, the sudden shooting making him feel brave.

The whole room hung silent for a moment. "Don't even think about it," York told the man holding the gun, noticing the way he was looking at Jake. He rose slowly and moved his chair out of Jake's way. "I've seen this man in action, mister. You'd be best to put that gun back in its holster."

Jake still sat with his chair tipped back, a cigarette in his mouth. "Mister, if you want to die today and join your friend on the floor here, that's your business," he told the man.

The man watched him, breathing hard. "I know who you are. All I have to do is cock this thing and fire it, and I've shot Jake Harkner. You have to draw. You ain't got a chance."

"I can draw faster than you can cock that gun. I guarantee it. Now I don't really feel like killing anybody today, so why don't you put that thing away?"

The man looked at him for a long time, and Jake did not take his eyes off him for one split second. The secret to these confrontations was watching the man's eyes, not his gun or his hand. Hesitation, that was his edge over these men. They always hesitated. That was their downfall. The man began to shake a little, then lowered his gun, slowly putting it back into its holster. He turned and left, and Jake just shook his head, looking up at York. "How about tomorrow morning?"

Jess was grinning. "I see you ain't lost the old fire or confidence." He nodded. "Tomorrow mornin' is fine with me."

"Just remember I'm going to have to go by some other name to keep bounty hunters off my back."

"Whatever you want. One thing is sure, I don't have to worry about my safety with you along."

Jake just smiled with a hint of bitterness. "Yeah. I guess I'm good for *some*thing." He picked up his whiskey bottle and handed it out to the man. "You can have this if you want."

Jess grinned. "Thanks, friend." He sat back down and took Jake's glass, pouring himself a shot.

Jake knew Jess was right. A good woman and a loving family was not something a man gave up easily. Every bone in his body ached for Miranda, ached to hold Lloyd close and touch his baby-soft cheek, ached to see the new baby.

Jess began talking about Colorado, and Jake thought how strange and ironic it was to see the man again after six or seven years. He recalled Miranda's belief that all things happened for a reason. He had always laughed at her for her silly

ideas, but now she had him thinking like her. *Was* there some
reason Jess York had walked through the door and asked him
to go to Colorado with him, right at a time when he was
feeling his lowest? Was this the answer to some prayer of
Miranda's?

There was one way to find out. He'd go to Colorado with
Jess. Maybe he could get a job similar to the one he had had in
Virginia City, working at a mine. There sure weren't any op-
portunities around here to get honest work, and he couldn't
go back to California yet. As long as he had an old friend to
travel with, he might as well go.

"I'm going to check my gear and turn in," he told Jess.
"I'm camped out behind the livery. Meet me there at sunrise
and we'll head out."

"Fine with me," Jess answered.

Jake left, shaking his head and realizing that even after
months apart, Miranda was as much with him as if she were
walking right beside him. The woman was keeping him from
returning to his old ways, scolding him, holding him tight,
even though they were separated by hundreds of miles.

Damn slip of a woman. He supposed he would never again
be the same man he was before he'd met her.

December 1870 . . .

Miranda came from the tiny bedroom where she had put
Lloyd and Evie down for their naps. At three-and-a-half and
nine months they were a handful, and she welcomed the afternoon quiet. She walked to a rocker and picked up some mending that she had to finish for Mr. Eastman. She needed the
money. She was working as many hours as she could, many of
them at night while the children slept, had taken Evie off
breast milk early so that she could spend more time away from
the baby working odd jobs to make money.

She sat down wearily in a rocker, her neck already aching
from hours of mending. She was not sure how much longer
she could survive this way, not knowing about Jake, loving him
and wanting to believe in his promises, wanting to uphold her
marriage vows. She missed him so, needed to feel him holding
her, but if she was to survive, she couldn't stay in Desert forever. She had to get to a bigger city where she might be able to

find a steadier job, but if she did that, how would Jake find her? Would he even try? How much more was her love and faith in him to be tested?

She glanced at the sad little Christmas tree in the corner, decorated with popcorn strung by her and Lloyd. There was no extra money for presents. Lloyd had asked about his father again today. He never stopped asking, and she never stopped promising he would see his daddy again, never stopped praying that her promise would come true.

She had continued her charade of divorcing Jake. She had even made a trip to San Diego with Dr. Henderson, on the pretense of seeing a lawyer. While the doctor ran some errands and stocked up on medical supplies, she had gone into the lawyer's offices, but she had never really talked to anyone. Now all she told people was that it was taking time, but that she should have her papers by the end of the year. In order to make people believe that and keep protecting herself and the children, she would soon have to tell them the divorce was final; and to continue providing for her family, she would have to get out of Desert.

Tired. She was so tired, more from the strain of not knowing what to do than from the long hours she put into a hundred odd jobs to keep food in the house. There was still some money left in their savings, but she knew she might need that to find a place to live when she left Desert. She leaned back in the chair, suddenly unable to find the energy even to pick up the shirt in her lap and sew on the buttons.

She heard footsteps then on the outside stairway that led to the apartment, and she sat up and put the mending aside. She had been on the verge of tears over her emotional quandary, and she quickly wiped them away when someone knocked at the door. "Mrs. Harkner? It's Jerry Eastman. Got some mail for you."

Miranda quickly walked to the door and opened it before the man could knock again and wake up the babies. He handed her an envelope. "Kind of fat," he commented with a grin. "You got a long-lost relative in Denver or something? Somebody owed you a long letter."

He handed her the envelope and she glanced at the return address. "Lawrence Baker, Denver, Colorado," she read quietly. Lawrence Baker! That was her *father's* name. Who would use . . . Jake! It had to be from Jake! Who else would put that name on a letter to her! He knew she would realize who it was from, and he certainly couldn't use his own name! "Yes," she answered aloud. "Lawrence Baker is my uncle. I didn't know he was in Denver!"

"Well, then, when you leave Desert, maybe that's where you should go. You've been worryin' about where you should settle. Maybe the man would take you in."

Miranda was still staring at the envelope. Jake! It had to be from Jake! "What?" She looked up at Eastman. "Oh! Yes, maybe he would. Thank you, Mr. Eastman."

The man nodded and left, and Miranda closed the door, hurrying over to the rocker and sitting back down. With shaking hands she carefully opened the envelope, taking out a letter and gasping when a wad of money fell into her lap. "My God!" she whispered. She gathered it up and began counting . . . one hundred, one-fifty, two-fifty, three, four hundred dollars! She hugged the money to her breast. "Jake!" She sighed. "Oh, God, please don't let this be from him going back to his old ways. Don't do it, Jake. I can forgive anything but that."

She barely held back tears of joy as she picked up the letter, almost afraid to read it, afraid it would say he was never coming back, that the money was just to keep her going until she really could get a divorce.

Dear Randy, Here's four hundred dollars. I'm okay. Found work. Will find a way to send for you soon as possible. Work! He had a job. It must be a very good one to be able to send her so much. Had he sent her every dime he had earned? *Took a chance sending money this way, but couldn't wire it or somebody would know it was from me. Sorry it's taking so long. When the time is right to send for you, I'll understand if you don't want to come. I love you, Randy. Sorry to put you through this hell. Give Lloyd and the new baby a hug for me. Hope all went well and you and the baby are all right. If you do still love me, don't give up the faith. If you're crazy enough to still want me, just come when I send for you. I can't say exactly where I am in case someone sees this. Am with an old friend. He might be the one to come and get you, so don't be afraid of him. His name is Jess York. You can trust him.*

I love you, Randy, and I hope nothing bad has happened to you while I've been gone. You have already put up with more than any woman should. I respect that and will honor whatever decision you make. All my love, Jake

Some of the words were misspelled, and the handwriting

was shaky, but what a letter from a man who didn't even know how to read or write when she'd first met him, a man she had taught herself, and who had learned eagerly the things he had never been taught as a child.

She smiled, broke into tears, hugged the letter close. "Oh, Jake, how can you think I wouldn't come?" He couldn't have timed the letter better. She had plenty to live on now until he sent for her, and he *would* send for her! She wasn't sure if her tears of joy were more for the fact that he was alive and working and was sending for her, or for the fact that he had conquered his old feelings of defeat and had not returned to his old ways. He had gone out there alone and he had kept his pride and determination and had not let old feelings of worthlessness make him give up all that he had struggled to gain for himself! It was a personal victory for him, an emotional victory for her. He had needed her love, her belief in him, and he had survived one of the darkest moments in his life. They had *both* survived!

She jumped up and carried the letter and the money into the bedroom, leaning over to kiss little Evie and Lloyd, both of them looking so sweet and innocent lying there asleep. "We'll be with daddy soon, my babies," she whispered. "Merry Christmas."

CHAPTER
TWENTY

July 1871 . . .

Miranda set her iron aside when through the window that faced the outside stairway she saw the figure of someone coming up the stairs. She quickly wiped at the sweat on her brow with a handkerchief she took from her apron pocket, and she imagined she must look terribly wilted. It was miserable ironing in the sizzling heat all of Southern California was experiencing this month, but things like ironing never went away and it had to be done. Besides that, she had to keep up a pretense of needing to work for money, since others might begin wondering where she was getting enough to live on while she decided whether or not to leave Desert. She didn't want anyone to know about the money Jake had sent her.

She smoothed her apron as someone tapped on the door and she pushed a strand of hair behind her ear. Her hair frustrated her in this weather. It was so fine that it was difficult to keep it pulled up on top of her head without pieces of it constantly refusing to stay put. She opened the door to greet a clerk who worked downstairs at the hardware store. "Hello, Luke."

The young man nodded to her. "Mr. Eastman told me to come up here and tell you there's a man downstairs who says he's a relative of yours, name of Lawrence Baker. You want I should send him up? Mr. Eastman don't like sending strangers up here unless you say it's all right. He asked the man if he was the uncle you said you got the letter from in Denver, and he said he was."

The uncle she had gotten the letter from? Miranda's heart beat faster with anticipation. Could it finally be happening? Had Jake sent Jess York for her? She put a hand to her pale cheek, realizing that besides looking wilted and tired, she wore no cheek color today, no lip color. Her hair was a mess and she was wearing one of her oldest dresses.

For God's sake, what does it matter! she scolded herself. "Stay here with the children for just a moment while I go and see," she told the clerk. She rushed past him, hurried down the stairs and through the front door of the hardware store. Eastman turned to look at her, and standing beside him was a man she guessed to be about Jake's age. He was quite handsome, with a quick, bright smile, pleasant features, thick, sandy hair. He held a black felt hat in his hand, and he wore clean denim pants and a white shirt with a black string tie. He was not as tall or broad as Jake, but he was well-built. She had wondered after getting Jake's letter if this man had also been an outlaw. Jake had said he was an old friend, and what other kind of "old friends" did Jake have?

The man stared back at her with near awe in his hazel eyes, and both of them felt hesitant at first. Miranda realized then that it was important for Eastman to believe this was her uncle. She would take the chance of making a fool of herself. "Uncle Larry!" She rushed closer and threw her arms around him.

A stunned Jess York embraced her, realizing he had better go along with the ploy. Actually, he did not mind it a bit. Jake had described this woman to him, but he had not really believed she was as small and beautiful as he'd said she was. How in hell did an ornery cuss like Jake Harkner end up with someone like this? "Hello, Randy," he spoke up, struggling to act casual.

"I'm so glad you came." Miranda pulled away, her cheeks flushed at having to embrace a complete stranger; but Jake apparently trusted this man, and that was good enough for her.

"I, uh, I brought a wagon, sweetheart," he said, a teasing grin now showing. "I was hoping you'd come back to Denver with me. You divorce that murdering liar you married yet?"

Miranda watched his eyes, knew the man was deliberately

goading her now. He gave her a wink, and Miranda found it
difficult to remain serious. "Yes," she answered, her smile
fading. "Come upstairs and I'll tell you all about it." She
glanced at Eastman. "It's all right. I expect I'll be moving out
tomorrow or the day after, Mr. Eastman. Thank you for letting me rent the rooms upstairs."

"No problem. I'm just glad you've got someplace to go
now, with somebody who can take care of you."

Miranda glanced at York again, wanting to jump with joy,
and full of questions about Jake. "Follow me." She led him
out and up the stairs, and young Luke left them alone. Immediately Miranda grasped Jess's arm and led him to a table.
"You *are* Jess York, aren't you?"

"Yes, ma'am." He looked her over as he took a chair.
"And I've got to say, Jake didn't do you justice when he described you to me."

Miranda blushed again, putting a hand to her hair self-
consciously. "Well, I'm afraid I have to apologize for the way I
look. I've been ironing all day, and in this heat—"

Four-year-old Lloyd came bounding out of the bedroom
then, followed by his little sister, who toddled after him on
chubby legs. At sixteen months, Evie was walking well. She
looked like the prettiest of little Mexican girls, her black hair
hanging past her shoulders, her big, dark eyes staring at the
stranger. She hurried to her mother's lap and crawled into it.
Lloyd walked right up to Jess and boldly asked who he was.

"I'm Jess—"

"This is my uncle Larry," Miranda interrupted. She looked
at Jess. "He's four years old and very bright. He might say
something to someone, so let's just let you be my uncle until
we get out of Desert."

The man nodded, studying the dark, handsome boy, who
seemed too big for just a four-year-old. "I wasn't sure what
your explanation would be for my presence. The man downstairs asked if I was your uncle Lawrence from Denver, so I
just went along with it and said that I was."

Miranda smiled. "I'm sorry to put you on the spot like
that. When Jake sent that first letter and the money and used
my father's name, telling people here I had an uncle in Denver
was all I could think of, so I'd have an excuse when Jake sent
for me." She sobered, her eyes showing her anxiety. "Is Jake
all right?"

"Yes, ma'am, and itchin' for me to get you to Colorado."

The man stood up and reached into his pants pocket, pulling out the Rosary. He sat back down, handing it to her. "Jake said you might be a little suspicious about me, so he told me to give you this—said you'd know it was okay to go with me if I gave you somethin' that was special to him."

Miranda hardly heard the man. She took the precious beads, clutched them in her trembling hand. She could not hold back the tears then. "I'm sorry," she wept. "I've waited so long. When Jake sent that money, I knew he really would send for me. I just didn't know when . . . or how." She breathed deeply, still clutching the beads. She set Evie on the floor, and the girl ran off to play with Lloyd. "What has he been doing? How is he? Will we be going to Colorado?"

Jess still could not get over how beautiful she was, even all frazzled from the heat and wearing no color on her face. It was difficult to believe the Jake he had known back during the war had a wife and a beautiful family like this. No wonder he had worked so hard preparing a home for them.

"Well, ma'am, the man talks about you constantly, so's sometimes I wish he'd shut up." Miranda smiled through tears. "I've got to tell you, he's gone all out to make a lot of money so he could send for you, risked his life for it, in fact. He's been workin' as a guard for gold and silver shipments from the Gooseneck Mine, west of Denver. Fact is, he got wounded in a shoot-out with robbers a few months back, but he foiled the robbery and saved the shipment."

Miranda's eyes widened with concern. "Wounded! Is he all right? Dear God, I should have been with him!"

"Well, he's feelin' a lot worse for not bein' able to be with *you* for almost two years now, believe me. Jake's fine. Took a bullet in his left shoulder that landed him in a Denver hospital. He said to tell you it didn't hurt as bad as when you shot him, but I think he was pullin' my leg. He's been a long time gettin' back the use of his arm."

Miranda covered her mouth with her handkerchief in surprise. "He *told* you about me shooting him?"

Jess laughed lightly and shook his head. "I gotta say, you two had one strange way of gettin' together." His smile faded. "He loves you an awful lot, ma'am, you and the boy. When I found him, he was drinkin' himself stupid, pinin' over you, thinkin' maybe it was best to leave you be and stay out of your life. Him and me, we've done a lot of talkin'. I knew Jake back during the war. Some people just get along and can talk with each other easy. There's no explainin' it. That's how it was with me and Jake."

They talked quietly while Lloyd played with Evie, apparently lost in a set of blocks enough that he did not grasp the conversation. "Me, I lost my wife and kid to Yankee raiders back during the war," Jess went on. "The Yankee bastards murdered them both, burned our place down. I wanted revenge, so I turned to raidin' Yankee trains and stealin' their rifles and ammunition, and money when it could be had. I helped smuggle the guns to the Confederates. That's when I met Jake. He was doin' the same thing. At any rate, after the war we kind of lost track of each other, both of us continuin' to live on the wrong side of the law, except I never got into as much trouble as ol' Jake managed to get himself into. Then a few months back I run into him at a place called Robber's Roost. It's on the Outlaw Trail and it's a place where men wantin' to avoid the law go to hide out. When I found Jake, it was pretty obvious he was thinkin' about goin' back to that old life. He'd already had a few run-ins with some men who figured they'd try to take down Jake Harkner. They're pushin' up flowers now. But Jake, he never really got back into the rest of it, rustlin', robbin', things like that. I was on my way to see about gettin' some respectable work in Colorado, and Jake decided to go with me."

Miranda's mind whirled with a thousand questions. Surely she could trust this man. He had an honesty about him in spite of having lived on the wrong side of the law part of his life. "I'm sorry about your wife and child," she told him. "It must have been terrible for you. I lost my own husband in the war, and then my father was killed by rebel raiders. Now it doesn't seem to matter who fought for which side. So many lives were destroyed."

A sadness came into York's eyes as he pulled an envelope from his shirt pocket. "Yes, ma'am. I was just a law-abidin' farmer before it all started." He handed her the envelope. "That there is a letter from Jake. By the way, he calls himself Jake Hayes now, decided to use the name you had before he married you so's it wouldn't feel so foreign to you."

Miranda laid the Rosary carefully on the table and took the letter, quickly opening it. She wiped at tears first so that she could see the writing better. *Dear Randy, I'm sorry this all took longer than I thought it would. I have a place for us now in Colorado. It's real pretty here, not as warm all year as California, but prettier. Jess will explain how I ended up here. I'm a ranch foreman, and it's steady work that means we can settle here. I hope this letter finds you okay. I don't even know about the new baby, if it's a boy or a girl, how the birth went. How can I tell you how sorry I am about that? I miss you and Lloyd so much that I can hardly stand it sometimes.*

You can trust Jess. He's an old friend and he knows all about us. He's probably the only person besides you who knows the whole truth about my past, about my pa. You know I wouldn't tell those things to anybody I didn't trust.

I'll be going crazy waiting and wondering if you're going to come back with Jess. I sent him off when there was still snow in the mountains so he could reach you in time to get back here through the mountains during the summer months. I can only pray he'll reach you and get you back safely.

I love you, Randy. It's safe now and I need you, but you do what you feel is right in your heart, what is best for you and for the babies. I won't give you any trouble over it, but I'll never know another day of happiness or ever love again like I love you.

I'd tell you in Spanish, but I can only speak it. I can't write it. If you want to hear it in Spanish, you'll just have to come to Colorado. Love, Jake

Miranda refolded the letter, smiling at the last words. She bent her head and wept quietly, the letter crushed in one hand, her handkerchief in the other. "Thank God," she whispered.

York watched her, understanding now why Jake had been so hell-bent on making a home for this woman. How many women were strong enough to put up with such a long separation, to live not knowing whether or not they would ever hear from their husband again? She and Jake had both gone on blind faith, and it was obvious this woman's love was uniquely strong. How he would like to find a woman like this for himself. He just hoped he could get her back to Colorado with no trouble. He wouldn't want to answer to Jake if anything happened to the woman or the children. He wondered if he should comfort her somehow, but then she was Jake's woman, and he didn't think he ought to touch her. The embrace for the sake of Mr. Eastman downstairs was a necessity, but this woman was not for just any man to hold without a damn good excuse.

He cleared his throat, not quite knowing what to say to her. "Jake, he's workin' for the man who owned the mine. His name is Zane Parker, and he was along when Jake had the big shootout with the robbers. Parker figures Jake saved his life as well as the gold shipment. The man owns a huge spread south of Colorado Springs, about twenty thousand acres. He wanted to repay Jake for riskin' his life to save that gold shipment, and for savin' *his* life. Jake told him the best way to pay him was to let him work at the ranch for him, where he could settle some and send for his family. He told Parker he had a wife and two kids in California waitin' for him to find steady work, so Parker, he give Jake a piece of land in the northwest corner of the ranch—loaned it, so to speak. He had his men help Jake build a real nice home there, and put Jake in charge of the whole damn ranch. It's a hell of a good job, Randy, pays good, prettiest place you'd ever want to live. A job like that, stayin' on that ranch near the mountains, it ain't likely anybody will ever know who Jake really is. He's sure now it's safe for you to come there."

Miranda shook her head. "I can hardly believe it's all real. I *won't* believe it until I feel Jake's arms around me again."

"Well, we can leave as soon as you're ready. We'll head up into Northern California and hitch a ride on the Union Pacific, wagons, mules, and all. Jake gave me money for the train. We'll take it to Cheyenne and then take the railroad connection south from there to Denver. Then we'll head out to where Jake is. You'll like it there, I guarantee. It's workin' out real good for Jake. Parker really likes the man, thinks he's pretty valuable. So far Jake's doin' a damn good job. The men respect him. I'm working at the ranch myself. You ought to know Jake will be gone at least two weeks out of every month. Him and me, we travel the line, the borders of the ranch, lookin' out for squatters, watchin' for strays, rustlers, that kind of thing. Sometimes Jake has to do it alone, but then we both know he's damn good at takin' care of himself."

Miranda smiled through tears. "Yes, he certainly is that." Evie came toddling back to her, and Miranda hugged the baby close. Lloyd walked back to Jess and handed him a piece of paper, asking if he'd help him write something. "Well, boy, somethin' tells me you can already write and spell better than I can," Jess teased. He looked at Miranda. "The boy ain't shy, is he?"

"No. He's always getting into mischief. Does that remind you of anybody you know?"

Jess laughed. "I expect it does."

Miranda rose, keeping Evie in her arms. "I'll start packing right away. I'll need a day or so to pay some debts and get everything ready. You should be able to get a room at the boardinghouse south of town. Be here the day after tomorrow. We'll need a wagon and mules."

"I figured as much. I bought both in San Diego. That's my rig out in front of the store, my horse tied at the back. Jake gave me plenty of money for the whole trip. He wants it to be as comfortable for you and the kids as possible. That's why he's payin' for me to bring you back by train. It might be closer to go by wagon along the Old Spanish Trail and through Arizona and New Mexico up into Colorado. But that's one hell of a trip, pretty desolate country and full of Indians. I wouldn't think of taking a woman and kids back through there. I traveled with a pack train through that country to get here, and I ain't goin' back."

The man rose, and Lloyd, who didn't fear a person on earth, reached up for him. Jess picked him up, grunting a little at his size. "He not only looks like his pa, but he's gonna' be big like him."

"Yes. Evie looks like Jake, too, but she's much tinier than Lloyd ever was."

Jess looked her over again. Good God, she was small. "Like her ma. Jake's gonna be right surprised and a little taken aback when he finds out he's got a daughter. I just feel sorry for any young man who wants to date her when she's older. Ol' Jake will probably nail every one of them to the wall, tellin' them if they lay a hand on her, they'll have to answer to him. I don't think they'll want to do that."

Miranda laughed at the remark and kissed Evie's cheek. "Her name is Evita. I named her after Jake's mother."

York sobered, touched. "Jake will like that." He shook his head. "This has been real hard on him, ma'am. I know it was hard on you, too, but he had the extra worry of you bein' a woman alone with two babies, and him not bein' able to fill his responsibilities of takin' care of you. It ate at him real bad, and it just about drove him crazy not bein' able to come back here and see to you himself, but he had to make sure everybody thought he was out of your life so's you won't be followed when you leave with me."

Miranda closed her eyes, saying a quick prayer of thankfulness. "I understand. I always understood. I never stopped believing I would hear from him." She wanted to ask if Jake had been true to her. They had been apart nearly two years. She knew that in his heart Jake had never strayed, and she decided that if he had turned to someone a time or two out of physical need, she didn't want to know about it. All that mattered was that he was waiting for her and they could be together again, and once that happened, she would make sure he had no needs left unsatisfied.

Jess put Lloyd down and turned to the door. "I'll be by day after tomorrow then, bright and early," he told her.

She looked at him with tear-filled eyes. "Thank you. I'll be ready."

The man gave her a wink and left, and Miranda sat down again. She held Evie close with one arm and reached for the letter, opening it with her other hand and reading it over again. *I love you, Randy. It's safe now, and I need you . . .*

"Jake," she whispered, kissing Evie's hair. They would be together again, and this time it would be forever.

Miranda studied the barren Nevada desert as the train rumbled through hard-packed sand and here and there pools of green, poison water. She remembered that first journey west, coming to look for Wes, the torture of traveling through the desert while she was pregnant with Lloyd. She remembered how frightened Jake had been for her when she got sick.

It had been five years since she and Jake first came out here; five years since she first set eyes on the outlaw Jake Harkner and heard his gun explode in her ears. Somehow she had known since that first time he rode out of her life back in Kansas City that she could never be fully happy without him.

How sad that they didn't have this railroad completed when she and Jake first came west. They could have avoided so much hardship. She thought how Jake had come out here to get away from civilization, but civilization had followed the railroad, and she had seen new little towns all along the way that had not even existed when they first came west. A mere five years had brought amazing changes. Jess said Denver was quite a big city, with hotels and horse-drawn trolley cars. It was expected that soon the whole city would be lit with gaslights rather than oil lamps.

She turned to Jess, who sat beside her. He had been every bit the gentleman on their journey. Again it seemed fate had stepped in and sent someone into Jake's life to bring him up from the pits of despair and show him there was always hope. Life in California had been so good, so sweet and happy. Maybe it could be that way for them again now in Colorado.

"Jess, do you think with all the growth out West and the way the country is coming back from the war . . . do you think there is any chance the wanted posters will come down in Missouri and men like Jake will be forgotten and allowed to be free?"

Jess sighed, puffing thoughtfully on a cheroot he had lit minutes earlier. "I don't know. The country might be pickin' up again, but hard feelin's from the war, they ain't gonna die easy. I still carry a lot of hate myself, and those times right after the war, people carried a lot of revenge in their hearts, just like I did. It's too bad about the mixup—Jake bein' accused like that. If he could ever find that girl he rescued from Kennedy's bunch, get her to testify that he helped her, maybe he could wipe his slate clean. But she might not even remember enough to be any help. A thing like that happens to a woman, she gets kind of crazy."

His voice trailed off and he smoked quietly for a moment. Miranda knew he was remembering what had happened to his own wife at the hands of the Yankee raiders.

"I don't reckon it's worth him takin' the risk of goin' back. He might not be wanted anymore, or then again he might get hauled in and pushed through a trial and hanged in two days. It's hard to say. All I know is with Kennedy and his bunch wiped out, none of the rest who know who he is is gonna say anything because they either respect him too much or are too afraid to come after him. Fact is, none of the others even know where he is now. Just me. And livin' out there on the Colorado plains under a new name and all, hell, ain't nobody that works on that ranch gonna know. After enough years, maybe then it won't matter anymore. It's already been well over six years since it all happened."

Miranda stroked little Evie's long, dark hair as the child shifted in her lap. Lloyd was turned in his seat, resting on his knees and watching the scenery out the window. He pointed to a herd of wild mustangs. "Horses, Mommy," he said excitedly.

"Yes, I see them," she answered, leaning forward slightly to look past Jess.

"Is Daddy there?" the boy asked, his dark eyes wide with hope.

Miranda felt a stab at her heart, realizing he must be re-membering when Jake would bring in a herd of wild horses to their ranch back in California. The child had a surprisingly keen memory of things from when he was only two, and he had never forgotten his father, nor would she have let him forget. "No, Daddy isn't with those horses, Lloyd, but we'll see him soon—just a few more days now."

She couldn't wait for Jake to see how much Lloyd had grown, how bright he was. He could already write his name. Although he was sometimes reckless and daring, he was an obedient child with a sweet nature, a child with a lot of love to give, love Jake needed right now. Most of all she was anxious for Jake to see that his son had not forgotten him. He would see that this product of his seed was good and loving, just as she imagined Jake must have been when he was small. Now when she watched Lloyd and imagined a father treating him the way Jake had been treated, she could understand all the better the horrors of Jake's childhood, the terrible pain he must have suffered when he had so much love to give and no one who wanted it. If Jake's father were still alive, she thought, she would shoot him herself.

"We'll be in Cheyenne in a couple of days," Jess told her. "Another day or so to Denver and another to the ranch. Won't be long now."

Miranda kissed Evie's hair and smiled, trying to imagine what it would be like seeing Jake again. "I'm scared, Jess."

He looked at her with a frown. "Scared? Of Jake?"

"No. Scared of how he'll feel, scared it won't be the same."

He chuckled. "Oh, it will be the same, all right. Better, I expect, because you've both been through so much and you both know now how much you need to be together. If you want to know the truth, I don't think you're anywhere near as scared as Jake is. When I left, he was as nervous as a bobcat up a tree with sixteen huntin' dogs barkin' at it. I have a feelin' he'd rather shoot it out with ten men than go through this first meetin' with a woman he worships and who he's afraid maybe won't love him the same anymore. He's even scared you won't show up at all. You ain't got nothin' to be afraid of, Randy. You've got that man hog-tied but good. Whatever it takes to keep you and make a good home for you, he'll do it."

Miranda met his eyes. "Thank you for being his friend, Jess. I hope you can find love again someday for yourself."

He blushed a little and turned away, grabbing Lloyd and

making the boy giggle when he tickled him. He moved into Lloyd's seat and held the boy on his lap, needing to be a little farther away from Miranda for a moment. Did she have any idea what she did to a man? Traveling with her night and day, he'd gotten to know her pretty good, and it was easy to understand why Jake loved her. She was a good woman, beautiful, devoted . . . hell, he could love Miranda Harkner easy as breathing. Watching her and her children reminded him of what he had lost eight years ago. She was the first woman he'd met since then that he thought could help him forget and start over, but any man could see there was only one man for her, and that was Jake. She loved the man so much she was practically blind to the way other men looked at her.

"Jess play cards?" Lloyd spoke up, straddling the man's lap then. He pulled open Jess's jacket and took a deck of cards from an inside pocket where he knew Jess kept them. Jess glanced at Miranda, who he knew wasn't too fond of her son learning how to gamble. She smiled and shook her head.

"I guess you don't have much choice. He's restless and bored and stuck on this train for two or three more days. It's all right."

Jess grinned and took the cards from their carton. "We'll let you guess what each one is. It's up to your pa whether or not you learn what to do with them," he told Lloyd. "Lord knows he's won his share of money and got into his share of brawls over these fifty-two little troublemakers." He held up a queen of hearts. "What's this?"

Lloyd grinned. "Lady," he answered, pointing his finger against the picture.

Jess laughed. "You got that one right. That's just what your pa would call this card if he had two or three of them—'Pair of ladies,' he'd say." He laughed again and held up a king.

Miranda moved to a window seat, keeping Evie on her lap. The scenery outside began to change to beautiful red rock formations. In the distance she could see the outline of dark mountains on the horizon. The Rockies. One more chain of mountains to cross, through Utah, into Wyoming, then Colorado . . . and Jake. There it came again, that quick stab of excitement that made her chest feel tight, made her heart beat a little faster.

CHAPTER
TWENTY-ONE

 A hawk flew overhead as Jake urged Outlaw down the steep embankment and into the open valley ahead. He herded three young calves ahead of him that had strayed too far into the rocky crags at the base of the mountains that made up the western border of Zane Parker's land.

He breathed deeply of the scent of mountain wildflowers mixed with the rich scent of pine. He liked it here. It was the prettiest country he'd ever seen, and he hoped Miranda would like it, too, if she came back with Jess. Maybe since the new baby was born she had found some other man, someone who could give her peace and a normal life that held no physical or emotional dangers. The worst hell was not even knowing if she was alive and well. He had not dared try to get in touch with her, other than to send her the letter and money he could only hope had reached her safely. He couldn't even send Jess until now, when he was sure the man could bring her right back.

What the hell was he going to do if Miranda didn't show up with Jess? He rubbed at his left shoulder, which still ached fiercely at times, especially when it was damp. The shootout over the gold shipment had put him through a lot of pain, but Zane Parker's payoff had made it all worth it. At last he had a real home for his family, a place where they could all live in peace. Parker's men had helped him build a sprawling, five-room log home that was a palace compared to anyplace else Miranda had lived. He wanted a big house, big enough for more children they might have. The home was set against a backdrop of mountains that displayed brilliant colors of purple rock, white snow, deep green fir trees, yellow-green aspen with stark white trunks. This was the kind of country a man, and, he hoped, a woman, would never want to leave.

Parker's vast spread ran from this place, which was just south of Colorado Springs, east to Fountain Creek, south nearly to Pueblo and back west to the mountains. It was a huge ranch that took in mountains, foothills, valleys, and streams. A man could ride for miles out here and still be on Parker land, and he had been put in charge of it all. It wasn't always easy to make his rounds. Physical pains from old wounds were beginning to set in. With all he had been through, at thirty-five he supposed there were times when his body thought maybe it was much older. Sometimes he felt pain deep in his side where Miranda's bullet had landed, and his hip still hurt him often from the gunshot wound he'd suffered at Desert. Now there was this damned ache in his shoulder. He suspected he'd be practically a cripple when he was an old man, if he even lived to *be* an old man.

Today, other than the shoulder, which he figured would get better as he healed over time, he felt good, strong, stronger than he had felt in a long time. Maybe it was the air here in Colorado, or maybe just the realization that he might be united again soon with his family. Whatever it was, he was not going to let his aches and pains interfere with his daily life, certainly not with his love life if Miranda came back to him. He'd been a long time without a woman, and he reminded himself that the first time wouldn't be easy for her after being apart for so long. They would have to get to know each other all over again.

He headed back toward the house. With Parker's permission, he had stayed close these past two weeks, sure that if Jess made it to California and was on his way back, he would show up any time. He had wanted to go to Denver and meet them at the railroad station, but with no knowledge of exactly when they might arrive, all he could do was wait here and watch for a wagon. He whistled to the strayed calves and rode after them, forcing them to head back into the valley by riding behind them in zigzag motions, not allowing them to turn back.

Outlaw had turned out to be a good, dependable mount
for this work. He'd had the animal for seven years now, and
over these past two years the horse had been about the only
steady thing in his life. He remembered how Lloyd had liked
to sit on him. It wouldn't be long now before he could teach
the boy to ride on his own. He longed to make up for the last
two years, hoped the boy had never felt abandoned. His biggest fear was losing the closeness they had once shared. He
would never forgive himself if this separation had affected the
boy emotionally. Over the past two years he'd had nightmares
about the day of the shoot-out, how easily Lloyd or Miranda
could have been killed.

It took nearly a half hour to come in sight of the house,
and he drew Outlaw to a halt when he saw a wagon far in the
distance, coming down the roadway that led south out of Colorado Springs past his own spread. He told himself it could be
anyone, but every time he saw a wagon coming he could not
help hoping that maybe this time it would be the one carrying
Jess and Miranda. He goaded Outlaw into a gentle lope, heading for the house.

Miranda could not quite get over the splendid beauty of Colorado. If she and Jake were going to know anything close to
paradise, this was it. She drank in the blue sky, the purple
mountains in the distance, the lush green valley spotted with
groves of aspen. To the east they had followed for part of the
way a sparkling run of water Jess had called Fountain Creek.
It was hard to believe that for as far as she could see to the
south and east, the land belonged to Zane Parker, the man for
whom Jake now worked.

The day was pleasant, and Lloyd rode in the back of the
wagon amid a pile of blankets. Miranda held Evie in her lap as
the wagon bounced over the dirt road toward a beautiful log
home surrounded by a split-rail fence. Wildflowers bloomed
here and there in the thick green grass that surrounded the
house, and a few horses grazed in a corral nearby. "What a
pretty house," she commented to Jess. "Is that where Mr.
Parker lives?"

Jess laughed. "No, ma'am. He has himself a mansion in
Denver and a house a lot bigger than that one, farther south
on his land. You're lookin' at your own home. This is Harkner
land, or should I say Hayes land?"

Miranda put a hand to her chest, gasping with disbelief. "That's *our* home? Are you sure?"

"Oh, yes, ma'am," Jess answered, still grinning. "I figured you'd like it. So did Jake. Parker's men helped him build it. You ain't never seen men work so fast over the winter. Jake needed the help because of his shoulder bein' wounded and all. It's still a little bare inside. Jake wanted to wait and let you furnish it however you like."

"Oh, Jess, it's beautiful! It's so big!"

"Well, Jake, he figured maybe there'd be more babies eventually, so he wanted plenty of room."

Pain gripped her heart at the words. There would be no more babies. Would Jake be terribly disappointed when he heard? How much difference would it make in how he felt about her? She thought she had learned to accept the fact there would be no more children, but now the ache was re-awakened deep in her soul. She told herself she must not think about it now. She was here . . . home. That was all that should matter to either of them—just being together.

She saw a rider then, approaching from the south, and she wondered if her heart might stop beating. She recognized Outlaw. "Jess, look! Is that Jake?"

Jess pulled the wagon to a halt. "I believe it is."

"Oh, dear God," she whispered. "I'm shaking."

Jess just grinned and shook his head. He took the baby from her. "Go on and get down and go out there to him. You two ought to be alone at first. I'll drive on up to the house with the children."

Miranda turned to Lloyd. "You be good for Jess. Mommy will be right with you." She climbed down, wondering if her shaking legs would continue to support her. Was this really happening, or was it all a dream? Jess drove on with the wagon, and she began walking toward where Jake had halted Outlaw and was watching them. She saw him urge the horse into a slow walk then, heading toward her.

She hardly knew where she was, was unaware then that she had started running. Jake in turn had urged Outlaw into a faster trot, then a full run. He was farther away than she had first thought, and she realized that's how it was in this land. Nothing was as close as one first thought. It was big country, and it fit men like Jake. The next two or three minutes it took for them to reach other seemed like forever.

"Jake!" she called out as he came closer. In the next mo-

ment he was off his horse before the animal even came to a
complete halt and she was swept into his strong arms. "Jake!
Jake! Thank God!" She breathed in the scent of man and
leather and fresh air as he lifted her off her feet and whirled
her around.

Jake ignored the pain in his shoulder. It hardly seemed
real that he could be holding her again. Here she was, this slip
of a woman he thought might not even want to come back to
him, embracing him, weeping against his shoulder, obviously
happy to be here in his arms. At first he just held her, unable
to find his own voice.

Now she was kissing his neck, his cheek, weeping his name.
Their lips brushed, then met again in a deep, hungry kiss that
told both of them nothing had changed, that each had waited
for the other, that there had been no one else and never could
be. He could taste the salt of her tears, his own mixed with
them.

He left her mouth and kissed her eyes, her hair. He slowly
lowered her to her feet but she would not let go of him. She
rested her head against his chest, and so far neither of them
had even taken a good look at each other. They wanted only
to hold, to touch.

"I didn't quite expect this," he finally managed to say. "I
wasn't sure you'd even come."

"How could you think that?" Miranda finally allowed herself to move away from him. She took a handkerchief that was
tucked into the sash of her dress and wiped at her eyes, and
Jake wiped at his own with his shirtsleeve. He looked her over,
thinking how she hadn't changed at all. In spite of another
baby, she was as slender as ever, and as far as he was concerned, she had never been more beautiful.

"Tell me about the baby." He sniffed and wiped at his eyes
again. "I'm so damn sorry you went through another birth
alone, Randy."

"You have a daughter, Jake. Her name is Evita. I call her
Evie."

She watched his dark eyes, saw the love there, the surprise
at what she had done. "You named her after my mother?" He
reached out and touched her face. *"Gracias, mi querida.* We'll
have more, as many as you want. Did you see the house? It
has five rooms, Randy, three bedrooms. I can add more if—"

"No." She turned away, and a mountain breeze blew her

honey-blond hair across her shoulders. "There won't be any more babies, Jake."

"What?" What was she saying? Had she decided not to come back to him after all?

"I wasn't going to tell you until later, but . . . talking about the house." She hugged herself tightly. "I had the same problem with Evie that I had with Lloyd, only this time it was worse. Jim Henderson said the only way to save me was to . . . remove my uterus. That's what holds a baby." She pressed a hand to her stomach. "I have a scar. There won't be any more children."

For a moment there was only the sound of a soft mountain breeze. Then she felt a hand on her shoulder. "My God, you could have died! That's all that matters, Randy, that you're alive."

She hung her head. "I wasn't sure—"

He turned her and folded her into his arms again. "Thank God the man knew what to do. I'm so damn sorry, Randy. But if you think it makes any difference to me—hell, all that matters is you're here and alive and the baby is fine." He pulled away but kept hold of her arms. "She is all right, isn't she?"

"Yes. She was a year old in March, Jake. She's beautiful, dark like Lloyd."

He looked her over. "You went through all that alone." He touched her hair lovingly. "I wish I could change it all. I should have been there. I'll do everything I can to make it up to you, Randy."

"You already have, by just being here, sending for us, building this home for us. Jake, it's so beautiful. We can be happy here." She stepped back from him, studying him a moment. He looked more handsome than ever. There was a peaceful look about him she had not seen before. "You're happy, aren't you? You look good, Jake. Jess told me about your shoulder. Are you all right now?"

God, how he loved the sight of her. How had he lived all that first part of his life without her? Why had he been so blessed when he was so undeserving? "It's still healing, but hell, I'm used to the aches and pains. Considering what I went through the first thirty years of my life, I guess I'm lucky to be walking on my own two feet." Their eyes met, and they both smiled. "God, you look good, Randy, prettier than ever."

A little older. Yes, he looked a little older, but the new lines around his eyes only made him more handsome. "I was so afraid you would decide we were better off apart. I never want us to be apart again, Jake. We belong together, no matter what happens."

He looked past her then at a small boy running toward them. "Daddy!" Lloyd shouted.

Miranda smiled through tears at the look of utter worship that came into Jake's eyes. "He remembers me?"

"I never let him forget, Jake. We talked about you every day, prayed for you every night at bedtime. All the way here he asked if this was the day he would get to see you again."

Jake walked toward the boy, grabbing him up into his arms, laughing, crying. Lloyd squealed and hugged his father tightly. Jake turned to Miranda. "He got so big!"

"Well, he's over four years old! And he knows his numbers up to ten and all his A-B-Cs and can print his first name. And thanks to Jess he knows all the suits in a deck of cards!"

Jake grinned, turning to kiss his son. Lloyd kissed him back and pointed to Outlaw. "Sit on your horse," he demanded.

Jake laughed and carried him over to the animal, plunking him in the saddle and telling him to hang onto the pommel. He turned to Miranda. "How about his last name?"

Her own smile faded. "I never taught him that. I was waiting to find out what it would be."

"I'm sorry, Randy. It's got to be Hayes now. I've told my boss it's Jackson Hayes but that some call me Jake instead of Jack. Mr. Parker is a pretty fair man, a little demanding, wields his power pretty good when things call for it, but he's been fair to me."

"I wanna' ride the horse, Daddy." Lloyd wiggled in the saddle, and Jake turned and put a hand behind him to make sure he didn't fall. He looked back at Miranda.

"We have a lot to talk about. Let's go to the house. I want you to see it, and I want to meet my daughter." He reached out to her. "Here. You get up on Outlaw and hang on to Lloyd. I'll walk the horse back to the house."

She stepped closer, shivering at the reality that Jake was standing right in front of her. She took his hand and he drew her closer again, bending down and kissing her lightly. She rested her head against his chest for a moment. "I love you, Jake. I never stopped loving you." She felt him tremble.

"I almost went back, Randy. I almost said the hell with it, figured that it would be best. I hung out with men like the kind I used to be, gunned down three men who wanted to prove they were better than I was. I thought I could go back and be the old Jake, but I couldn't do it. I couldn't find him. I think you killed him that day you shot me. He just slipped away and died, but I didn't even realize it until I tried to find him again."

He let go of Lloyd and put his hands to her tiny waist to lift her up onto Outlaw. Miranda noticed him wince slightly when he did so, and she knew he was still in pain. She glanced at the familiar guns he wore. He was still using them to make his living, but at least it was an honest living, although she didn't like the idea that he'd had to risk his life to earn the position of Zane Parker's right-hand man.

She sat sideways on the saddle and held on to Lloyd. She smiled as Jake stood back to study them.

"That's the prettiest sight I've ever set eyes on, my wife and my son."

"Go, Daddy, go!" Lloyd began bouncing in the saddle, and Miranda laughed, hanging on to him.

Jake grinned, walking to take up Outlaw's reins to lead the animal back to the house. Lloyd giggled as the horse began walking, and the sound was music to Jake's ears. Life was going to be good now, better than it had ever been yet. He would make sure it stayed that way.

They talked well after midnight. Jake wanted to know all the "firsts" about his son and daughter, wanted to hear again how Lloyd asked about him every day. He told Miranda about his work, warning her that for two weeks every month he would be gone. Yes, it was dangerous at times, what with the weather and wild animals and sometimes cattle rustlers, but he argued that the pay was good and they got to live on this beautiful land and be together again.

They went into the bedroom where they had put the children down together in a log bed Jake had made himself, with a rope spring and feather mattress. It would have to do for now until he could take her to see a Mexican carpenter in Pueblo who made beautiful furniture. Miranda was to order anything she wanted, buy whatever she liked in the way of carpets, material for curtains, and anything else she needed. Jake said he would even take her to Denver if she couldn't find anything good enough in Pueblo.

"We'll have a good life here, Randy," he told her quietly as they watched the children sleeping. He leaned over the bed, kissing each child, still overwhelmed that they were finally here, that Lloyd still adored him and that Evie had taken to him so easily. "They're beautiful. I never thought something so sweet and innocent and good could come from me, but then I expect their goodness comes from you."

He straightened, and Miranda moved her arm around his waist. "It comes from you, too, Jake. How many times have I told you I don't want to hear any more of that kind of talk?"

He turned and pulled her close. "We'd better turn in ourselves."

Miranda saw the question in his eyes. "I want to sleep with you, Jake. I feel like the last two years never even happened, and I have ached for you every night since you left. I don't need to wait, if that's what you're thinking."

He leaned down and captured her mouth. Now that the talking was done and the children were asleep, they could let the hot coals that had slept in their souls for all these months flare into the searing flames of passion they had forced themselves to ignore until now. His kiss felt like fire on her lips, and all her buried needs were awakened when his tongue slaked into her mouth suggestively. The kiss lingered as he picked her up in his arms and carried her into their own bedroom.

He pressed his lips gently against her cheek as he laid her on the bed. He sat down beside her and took a deep breath. "It's been so long," he told her, touching her face, moving his hand down over her breast, still hidden by her dress. "I don't want to hurt you."

She took hold of his hand and kissed it. "You won't hurt me, Jake. But I'm afraid for you to see my scar. And after two babies, my breasts—" She sat up beside him, looking at her lap. "I'm not quite so firm and unblemished as I was before."

He grinned, leaning over and kissing her deeply again, laying her back on the bed and stretching out beside her. "You don't really think any of that matters, do you?" He touched her breasts again, kissing her neck. "You're as beautiful as ever, but it wouldn't matter if you'd come back fat and wrinkled." He grinned again, biting lightly at her lips. "I need you for much more than that. You loved me when no one else did, *mi querida*. You saw through the beard and the long hair and the meanness and touched the man beneath all that. You are my life."

She closed her eyes and let him undress her, sighed deeply,

first with apprehension, then with pleasure, as he caressed her breasts, her stomach, kissed at her full nipples, trailed his tongue down over her belly and kissed at the scar that reminded them there could be no more children.

As far as Jake was concerned, that scar was beautiful, because it meant she was alive. He had noticed how Jess had looked at her before he left them earlier in the day. Jess had spent a lot of time with Miranda. Had he fallen in love with her too? God knew the woman was easy to love, a woman a lot of men would like to call their own; but she belonged to him, and he was going to make sure she never regretted that. He adored her for her faithfulness, her trust, for the children she had given him, for the chance he had at love, at being a father and making up for his own sorry childhood.

He moved to kiss at the lovenest he had so longed to invade, and she groaned his name, reaching down to weave her hands through his hair. From then on there was no stopping either of them. He savored the taste of her, made her wild with desire.

Miranda wondered how she had gone so long without this, and she realized it was only because there was just one man who could do these things to her, one man who could make her so bold and free. If she could not be with this man, she had no need of any other. When she was with Jake, all her womanly needs and passions came alive.

Jake left her a moment then to remove his clothes, and she curled up to watch him, drinking in the still-hard body, the flat stomach, the magnificence that was Jake Harkner. There was another scar on his abused body, at his left shoulder, and she noticed it seemed to hurt him a little to move his arm to get his shirt off. He turned to throw his clothes on the floor, and she saw the scar left on his hip from the wound in the shootout at Desert. His right forearm also bore a scar from that same fateful day.

He was right when he said he was lucky to be walking on his own two feet. So many times he could have been killed, and so many times he had defied death. Now he had overcome something even worse, his past. He was a happy husband and father, and life was going to be good for them here.

He stretched out beside her and drew her into his arms. *"Siento el fuego bajo tu piel,"* he said softly. He kissed her deeply, and she tasted her own sweetness on his lips. He had spoken those words before, and tonight they were never more true. *I feel the fire under your skin,* he had told her, and never had she felt that fire burn so hot.

He moved on top of her, his kiss desperate and almost violent. In the next moment he was surging inside of her, and she knew in that instant that nothing had changed, that in spite of two babies none of the pleasure of this act had been lost. If anything had changed physically, their love and their desire made up for it. With every breath he groaned her name, and in moments she felt his pulsating release, but he kept up the rhythmic movements.

"I'm going to stay right inside you all night," he whispered, kissing, nibbling at her ear. "As long as I'm inside you, I know this is real." In only seconds he was filling her again, raising up slightly then to brace himself so he could drink in her nakedness.

Miranda caressed the scar at his shoulder, the one at his neck that his father had so cruelly given him. She leaned up and kissed his chest, his neck, met his mouth and drew him back down to her in hot, desperate kisses that left them breathless. "Tell me again," she whispered, her skin feeling branded as it rubbed against his own hot, damp body. "Tell me what you're going to do to me all night."

He groaned the words. "I'm going to make love to you all night," he said softly, kissing at her eyes. "I'm going to stay inside my woman until neither of us can move. Tomorrow I'm going to spend all day with my kids, but tomorrow night, it's just you and me again in this bed."

He kissed her wildly again. He raised to his knees and grasped her under the hips, moving in the way only Jake could to make her feel wild with desire. This time he held back longer, wanting her to enjoy it for as long as possible, realizing she had needs of her own that had been long neglected. He thought about that first time he had taken her almost violently in the wagon on their way west. She had surprised him with her response, releasing a wild passion he never thought this slip of a woman possessed.

Again came his release, and he still remained inside of her. He lay down close to her, pulling a blanket over them. "Just stay right there," he told her.

"I'm not going anywhere," she whispered, opening her eyes to study his handsome face. "I need to know this is real just as much as you do."

"It *is* real, isn't it?" He kissed her softly. *"Gracias, mi esposa,* for never losing faith in me, for being so strong, for loving me."

"You had to be stronger, Jake. You had to rise above your past. You had to believe in yourself and in our love, and in your responsibility to those children in there."

"They're my whole world, Randy."

"I know."

Their eyes held, and he knew what she was thinking. "No, Randy," he said softly. "You made me a promise. They can't ever know about my past. I want them to always be proud of their father."

She still felt it was wrong not to tell the children someday about their father's past, but she wanted no arguments tonight. Tonight was just for them. She reached up and stroked his thick, dark hair. "Those children will always love you and be proud of you, Jake, just because you're their father and they know how much they're loved. And *I'm* proud of you for what you've done here, for the beautiful home you've given us, for not giving up on us or on yourself."

She felt his life returning, and she closed her eyes and breathed deeply as he began moving again, more gently this time. "It feels so good, Jake, to be with you like this again," she whispered.

"El gusto es mio, mi querida. Yo te quiero mucho."

In the distant foothills wolves began their nightly wailing. Jake and Randy clung tightly to each other, ignoring the menacing, wild cries that in the past had always given them a feeling of impending disaster. That was not going to happen again. They were together, a family, in a beautiful land where they would find the peace they so longed for. This time was forever.

CHAPTER
TWENTY-TWO

April 1881 . . .

Lloyd blew out the fourteen candles on his birth-day cake, and eleven-year-old Evie laughed as he used his last breath to get them all. Beth Parker joined in the laughter, and Lloyd glanced at her, wondering why he was suddenly so self-conscious around her. He'd never thought of girls as particularly pretty, but Beth sure was. He found himself thinking about Zane Parker's daughter a lot, since she had started coming over often to play with Evie. She was always accompanied by her nanny and one of Mr. Parker's men, but her wealthy father didn't seem to mind that his pampered daughter played with the children of the men who worked for him. He studied her white-blond hair and sky-blue eyes, and he thought she looked like one of Evie's china dolls, so perfect and smooth. Sometimes he felt foolish thinking about a twelve-year-old girl that way. He had kept his feelings a secret, even from his father. If anyone were to ask, he'd say he thought of Beth Parker as nothing but his sister's silly friend.

"What did you wish for, Lloyd?" the girl was asking.

Lloyd noticed she blushed when he met her eyes, and he reddened in return, realizing she thought he was handsome and that in her eyes he was a man. Evie had teased him about it, told him things Beth had said about him.

"That's supposed to be a secret," he answered.

"Oh, come on, Lloyd, you can tell," Evie begged.

Miranda began cutting the cake, and Lloyd glanced at his father, who was watching and smiling. He wondered if he should bring up the subject again. "I wished that my father would figure I was old enough now to learn to use a rifle and learn to hunt," he answered.

Jake's smile faded. He glanced at Miranda, who had stopped cutting the cake and was watching him. She gave him a look he knew well, telling him with her eyes what he knew she would say aloud if they were alone. *You can't take your past out on Lloyd, Jake. Teaching him to use a rifle isn't going to turn him into an outlaw. It's something every father has to teach his son, and in country like this, it's dangerous for him not to know how to shoot. Out here a man needs to know how to defend himself against wild animals when he's riding alone, needs to know how to hunt for game. What if something happened to you? It's Lloyd who would have to bring home the meat.*

He knew she was right. They had been having the same argument for two years now. Like he'd been, Lloyd was big for his age. At fourteen he looked more like sixteen, and he was a damn handsome kid. Jake suspected Beth Parker felt the same way. She was too young now to understand it all, but give her a few years and those girlish feelings would become womanly ones. He wondered if Zane Parker would mind if his daughter fell in love with the foreman's son.

He got up from his chair and walked over into one of the spare bedrooms that they used for an office, opening a desk drawer and taking out a can of tobacco and a cigarette paper. He began rolling a cigarette, and before he could light it he heard Miranda's voice. "You can't put it off any longer, Jake. It isn't fair to Lloyd. The more you fight it, the more he'll wonder why. You're the one who doesn't want him to know about your past, so quit acting like you have something to hide every time he asks about learning to shoot."

In the outer room the girls laughed when Lloyd showed them a card trick Jess had taught him. "Hurry up, Mother," Evie called out. "We want our cake."

"Yeah. Come on, Pa."

Jake turned to look at Miranda. "He's fourteen. Do you know what I see when I look at him? I see *me*! I see what I *could* have been. I see what a kid he is, and then I realize that at fourteen I killed my father. Fourteen! I was a damn *child*,

Miranda, and putting a gun in his hand makes me remember all of it!"

Miranda stepped closer. "And now at fourteen, your own son worships the ground you walk on. He thinks the sun rises and sets with you, Jake, and as his father, it's your duty to teach him how to be a man. If you keep refusing to teach him how to use a firearm, he's going to start resenting it. Is that what you want? To refuse to teach him is to insult his attempts at being a man, Jake. That's very important to him right now. If he learns from you, then he'll learn from the best. He'll learn to respect his firearms and use them wisely. You know darn well that teaching him to shoot doesn't mean he's going to run out and turn bad. You ended up using your guns for the wrong things because you were forced into that life by a brutal father. It's all different between you and Lloyd. He's a good boy who's loved and who honors and respects his father. Learning to use a gun and to be a man isn't going to change that."

Jake smoked quietly for a moment, his eyes moving over her. She was nearly always right, and he wondered just when and how he had come to be unable to say no to anything she wanted. At thirty-five, his wife was still slender, but round in the right places now, a full, ripe woman who knew how to please her man and who was still beautiful. The tiny lines about her eyes spoke of a woman of strength and courage and experience; and so far there was not a hint of gray in her honey-colored hair. In the nearly fifteen years since they'd gotten married, he had found a peace he had once never thought possible.

They both loved it here in Colorado, or was it that they both loved each other so much that it didn't matter where they lived? They had both survived the grasshopper plague of seventy-four, a run-in with Cheyenne Indians that same year; in seventy-six they had survived an epidemic of measles that had brought them even closer when both the children took sick and it seemed possible that Lloyd might die. Last year they had survived the worst winter in the nation's history. That time it was he who nearly died, lost in a snowstorm trying to find stray cattle that Parker was afraid would freeze or starve to death. It had been a rough year for Parker and other big ranchers, and a year ago this time he and other Parker men had worked for two months just dragging stinking cattle carcasses into piles to be burned, burying others.

"Hey, Pa, come have some cake," Lloyd yelled.

"Do you want to go riding tomorrow?" Beth was asking Lloyd.

Jake looked at Miranda, and she smiled. "She has a terrible crush on him, you know," Miranda said in a near whisper.

Jake stepped closer. "I know, and I'm not sure I like it."

"They're just children, Jake."

He scowled. "Maybe she is, but *he* isn't. I thought *I* was in love at fourteen, remember?" He took another drag on the cigarette. "That isn't what bothers me. What bothers me is that she's Zane Parker's daughter. If the interest should last when they get older, Parker's going to think twice about it, maybe decide to check me out a little more, make sure just who his precious daughter is falling in love with."

"She couldn't find anyone better than Lloyd, and Mr. Parker knows it. He's good, he's honest, he's smart. We're even going to send him to college with that money we've been saving. If Zane Parker ever dares to say my son isn't good enough for his daughter—"

"Mama, come on!" Evie came into the room, grabbing Jake's hand. "You, too, Father. I want Lloyd to open his presents."

Jake grinned, releasing her hand and putting an arm around her shoulders. His daughter was already exotically beautiful, even though she wasn't even developed yet. She had big dark eyes and dark lashes. Her nearly black hair hung in thick waves down her back, and her olive skin was like satin. She looked so much like his own mother. He wondered how he was ever going to let young men come calling on her. She was sweet and innocent and full of love, and he couldn't bear the thought of any man taking advantage of that. If anything could make him turn back to his murdering days, it would be if someone hurt either one of his children.

He stuck the cigarette in his mouth and put his other arm around Miranda, finding it almost humorous how neither of their children bore any resemblance to their mother, except for their goodness. He could see Miranda in Evie's smile and her small-boned frame, but the physical resemblance stopped there.

Miranda returned to cutting the cake, and Lloyd opened a small present that Beth handed to him. His eyes widened when he took out a pocketknife with a handle made of real silver.

"Wow! Look at that," Evie exclaimed.

"My father bought it last time he was in Denver," Beth told her proudly. "I told him I wanted to give Lloyd something for his birthday."

"Look at this, Pa." Lloyd handed the knife to Jake, who glanced up at Miranda, who in turn raised her eyebrows in their shared knowledge that Elizabeth Parker was enamored with Lloyd Hayes.

"This had to be pretty expensive," Jake said, looking over at Beth.

"Not for my father," she answered. She blushed deeply then. "I didn't mean that like it sounded." She looked down at the cake on her plate. "I just meant . . . I mean, I wanted to give Lloyd something nice, and if Father had thought it was too much, he wouldn't have bought it." She looked back at Jake, and he could see she was about ready to cry. He gave her a smile.

"Well, it's the nicest gift Lloyd has ever gotten."

"Yeah. Thanks, Beth," Lloyd said, taking back the knife. "I'll be real careful with it."

"I'll be right back," Jake told them, turning and walking outside.

Miranda finished serving the cake, then went to a window to watch her husband returning from the barn. At forty-five, he had the virility of a man much younger, but he limped a little now, just like Jim Henderson said he would probably do as he got older. It was that bullet wound to his hip. She knew he had aches and pains he never talked about, but the handsome build and the strength was still there, and at night in his arms he still made her feel like the twenty-year-old he had married, still knew how to bring out her deepest passion. He had been an even better husband and father than she had first believed he could be, and the past seemed so far away now. Surely it couldn't hurt them anymore.

She smiled then when she saw what was in his hand. She turned away and took some lemonade from the icebox to pour for the children, her heart beating with excitement for Lloyd because she had seen what Jake was bringing him. So, he had decided on his own after all. He had kept his gift hidden until he could make up his mind for certain.

The door opened, and they all looked up to see Jake standing there with a brand new rifle in his hand. The room got quiet, and Lloyd slowly rose. "I told Beth that the knife was the best present you had ever gotten," Jake told his son. "Until now." He handed out the rifle, its barrel oiled to a blue sheen. The wood stock was polished to a beautiful finish, with the initials L.J.H. carved into it and finished off with a gold butt-plate; the metal casing was gold with beautifully etched designs, including a picture of an antlered moose.

Lloyd's eyes widened, then teared as he came closer and took the rifle from his father. Jake glanced at Miranda, and she knew how hard it was for him to put a gun in his son's hands.

He looked back at Lloyd. "That's the latest model Winchester .44-.40 repeater," he told the boy. "It even has an extra rear sight for more accuracy. I had it all polished up and wrapped in a blanket out in the barn."

"Pa," Lloyd said softly, studying the rifle. "When in heck did you get this? They don't sell anything like this in Pueblo. The last time you went to Colorado Springs was last fall, when you bought those new Colt Peacemakers for yourself." He looked up at Jake and realized that was when Jake must have bought the rifle. "Why'd you wait so long to give it to me?"

Jake watched him almost sadly, wondering if his son could ever understand about his past. Was Miranda right in saying he and Evie should be told? Maybe she was, but the pain was too deep, the fear of losing his son's love and respect too great. He struggled to control his own sudden urge to weep. "I just figured fourteen was a better age than thirteen, that's all. Besides, I didn't know if I'd get back to Colorado Springs again before your birthday, so I went ahead and bought it. Your mother didn't even know."

"Jake, it's a beautiful rifle," Miranda said, coming closer to look it over.

Lloyd quickly wiped at his eyes with his shirtsleeve. "Thanks, Pa. When can we go practice shooting it?"

Jake shrugged. "This afternoon, if you want. Fact is, I thought maybe you'd like to go with me this time when I ride the line and check things out. It would be a good time for you to do a little hunting, but it means sleeping on the cold ground at night for a good two weeks. Think you can handle that?"

Lloyd smiled through tears. "Heck, yes! You know how bad I've been wanting to ride out there with you." He looked at his mother. "It's all right, isn't it? I can catch up on my lessons when we get back."

Miranda wondered when she had ever been happier for

her son and his father. She knew what Jake was suffering deep inside, remembering how different things had been for him at fourteen. Another barrier from the past had been hurdled. "Of course, it's all right. Now let's all eat our cake. Jess will be coming soon with Beth's guardian to take her back home."

Beth and Evie began whispering and giggling while Miranda poured more lemonade. Lloyd set the rifle against the wall and looked at his father, then grinned and walked closer to embrace him. "Thanks, Pa," he said again. "It's the best gift I've ever had."

Jake closed his eyes and hugged the boy. How ironic, he thought. At fourteen he'd murdered his father. Now he hugged his own fourteen-year-old son. If only he could have enjoyed such an embrace at this age.

Lloyd sat back and watched the rabbit sizzle over the open fire, proud that he was responsible for the meat they were eating tonight. Jake had told him that rabbits were hard enough to hit even with a shotgun, but Lloyd had shot it with his Winchester. He figured it was mostly luck, but then it was a damn good rifle, a "straight-shooter," Jake had called it. *Some guns hit above or below the sight mark,* he had explained. *Some are straight-shooters. You just have to get used to the gun.*

Lloyd had practiced every day and was proud of his progress, proud to be the owner of such a beautiful rifle, most of all proud to be Jackson Hayes's son. He watched his father light a cheroot, wondering when he'd be old enough to smoke. "How'd you get so good with guns, Pa? Mom told me your own pa died when you were about my age and that your mother was already dead. You didn't have anybody to teach you."

Jake smoked quietly for a moment, staring at the campfire. *Tell him the truth,* a little voice nagged him. *There couldn't be a better time.* "I just taught myself," he answered. "I was orphaned at your age, had no other family. That was down in Texas in the thirties. Things were pretty lawless then. A kid my age had to know how to defend himself, how to provide for himself. You just do what you have to do. I never had a home or anybody to take care of me like you and Evie have, like your mother had. She lost her mother at a young age, too, but she had her father and brother until she was about twenty."

Lloyd leaned closer over the fire and turned the spit. Fat

dripped from the rabbit onto hot coals and made little hissing sounds. "You ever have to kill a man back then?" he asked.

Jake met his eyes. *Yeah, my own father. And a hell of a lot of others.* How in hell could he tell him that? The kid looked at him sometimes like he was a god. If he knew the truth . . . "A few, in self-defense. That's just how it was back then."

Lloyd shook his head. "I don't think I could ever kill a man."

Jake watched him lovingly. "I hope to hell you never have to. It can come back to haunt you sometimes, but if you have to do it to save your own life, then you don't have much choice."

Lloyd remembered something, but he couldn't remember enough to ask his father about it. He recalled guns exploding in his ears, could hear his mother screaming, but it seemed it was only something he had dreamed. He met his father's dark eyes and wondered sometimes about the terrible sadness he saw there. Sometimes he felt like the man wasn't telling him everything, almost like he was afraid of something, but then it was hard to imagine his father being afraid of anything. He'd seen Jake throw out a drifter once who had wandered into the house and threatened his mother. The drifter was a big man, but Jake had picked him up, shoved him right out of the house, then landed a punch that sent the man flying right over the porch railing and into a rosebush. The man had run off cussing a blue streak.

There were other things his father had done that he was proud of, although Jake never seemed to want to talk about them. It was Beth who had told him the story her own father had told her about how Jake had become his foreman—that he'd shot it out with a whole gang of robbers when he worked at her father's gold mine west of Denver. Being foreman of the Parker ranch was a big responsibility, and riding the line presented a lot of dangers for a man alone, but his father always made it back home. He remembered the winter before last, when his mother had wept thinking Jake had been lost in a snowstorm. He remembered how scared he'd been when his father finally made it home and fell ill with pneumonia and frostbite. For a while they were afraid he'd lose some of his toes and fingers, but he had survived.

Jake Hayes always survived. Lloyd had never seen anybody better with guns. Three years ago they had gone to a Buffalo Bill Wild West Show in Denver. It had been an exciting trip for the family, one of the best times Lloyd could remember. Buffalo Bill had asked for challengers to a man who was a part of the show and was his best shot. The challenger would win two hundred dollars in silver if he could beat or even match the showman. His mother had urged his father to take the challenge, but at first Jake didn't want to do it. That was another thing he liked about his father. The man was probably the best shot in Colorado, but he never made a big thing out of it. In fact, it seemed like he didn't even want people to know.

Jake Hayes had won that two hundred dollars that day, hitting his target every time with both his hand gun and a rifle, even while riding a horse. He'd been so good that Buffalo Bill had offered him a job in his Wild West Show, but Jake didn't want anything to do with the publicity. It seemed like after that he'd been anxious to just get out of Denver and go home. He hadn't even told his good friend Jess about what had happened when they got back, and sometimes it seemed like even Jess was keeping secrets about his father. He liked Jess York a lot, but the man was always evasive whenever Lloyd asked him questions about Jake.

"I don't want to go to college, Pa," Lloyd said aloud then. "I want to stay right here and work on the ranch with you."

Jake leaned back and drew deeply on the cheroot, glad for the change of subject. "Your mother wants better things for you, and so do I. Besides, you want to make a good impression on Beth Parker, don't you?"

Lloyd grinned bashfully. "Beth Parker? Why would I care about making an impression on her? She's only twelve years old."

"Twelve going on sixteen. She's a damn pretty girl, and she watches every move you make. A man like Zane Parker isn't going to let his daughter get too interested in a cowhand's son, not that you aren't worth more than any young man raised with a silver spoon in his mouth. I just want you to be careful, son. People like Parker can get a little rankled when it comes to who's interested in their children. If you're college-educated, you can get a high-class job, maybe work in Denver—"

"Pa, I don't give a care about Beth Parker, and even if I did when I got older, hell, I wouldn't want her if she looked down on me for some reason. I'm proud of what you do, and if that's what I end up doing, I'll be proud for myself. Hell, you've got a damned important job with a lot of responsibility.

How good this ranch does is because of you, not because of Zane Parker. Sometimes you act like you think you're not good enough or something. You're one of the smartest, bravest, most skilled men I know. Every man on this ranch looks up to you."

There it was again. Jake's eyes held that strange sadness that made Lloyd wonder.

"And you're a good son. Don't put me on such a pedestal, Lloyd." Jake threw the cheroot into the flames. "I'm just a man, and all men have faults and shortcomings. Nobody is perfect, that's for damn sure." He looked over at Lloyd and smiled for the boy. "Except maybe you."

Lloyd laughed lightly then, leaning back against his saddle again. Night was upon them, and he wondered how many millions of stars there were in the sky. He liked looking at that sky, liked the night sounds, even the sounds of the wolves in the deeper mountains. A man might find sleeping out in this wild country at night a little frightening, especially in the spring, when the grizzlies awoke from their long winter's naps and began roaming about looking for food. This was the time of year when bears were their orneriest, according to Jake. He'd had more run-ins with angry bears than he cared to talk about. He'd even lost his beloved Outlaw to one of those bears, but he had managed to shoot the grizzly before it got to him. Outlaw had been tied while Jake went after a buck, and Jake had not been able to get back to the horse in time to save him. Lloyd remembered his father had actually wept over the loss of that horse. Even his mother had felt bad. She said Outlaw was the horse Jake had been riding when she first met him.

That was another subject that was not quite clear to him. His parents always seemed a little evasive about how they met. He only knew it was in Kansas City. They had fallen in love, and Jake had brought Miranda west originally to find her brother, who they discovered had been killed in a mining accident. Then they went onto California, but Jake thought he could do better someplace else and had left for two years to build a better life for them.

Lloyd couldn't quite understand why. He seemed to remember a nice house in California, but it wasn't real clear in his mind. He thought they had been happy there. Still, that dream he had about all the shooting—it seemed like in the dream they were living in California at the time. In the dream his father was kissing him good-bye, and he was crying, as though something terrible had happened. He had wanted to tell Jake about the dream, but it seemed kind of silly.

A coyote yipped not far away, and he watched his father's dark eyes check the shadows beyond the campfire. The darkness and the sound of prowling wolves and coyotes didn't frighten Lloyd, because he was with Jake Hayes. What was there to be afraid of when his father was along? Besides that, he had his own rifle now.

He breathed in the smell of pine and mountain breezes. It was still pretty cold at night around here, and there was still a lot of snow up higher in the mountains. The stream near which they had camped was swollen with sparkling, icy water from spring melt-off, and here in the foothills the lush, spring grass was dotted with brilliant wildflowers.

Jake took a knife from his boot and leaned forward to cut a piece of rabbit off the spit. "This ought to be done. Sure doesn't compare to your mother's home cooking, does it?" He put the meat into a tin plate and handed it over to Lloyd.

"Sure doesn't," Lloyd answered. "You miss her when you're out here, don't you?"

Jake cut off another piece. "What man wouldn't miss a woman like that?"

Lloyd grinned and bit into the rabbit. It made him happy to think how much his parents seemed to love each other. He remembered once when he was little running into their bedroom when he heard strange sounds coming from there, and he thought maybe his father was hurting his mother. He knew better now, and much as they tried to be quiet and wait until he and Evie were asleep, he still sometimes heard those sounds. Somehow it was comforting to know his parents still made love and seemed to enjoy each other's company so much. He hoped to find someone as good as his mother someday. He didn't very often think about girls, certainly not about marriage and making love. But his father had been more right about Beth than he cared to admit. She sure was pretty, and if the truth were known, he didn't mind the thought of how beautiful Beth was going to be when she was older, or of maybe thinking of her as his girl in a couple more years. In spite of her wealth, Beth was sweet and generous. There was nothing snooty about her, and she treated him and Evie like equals. She was nice, and sometimes she was fun to be with, for a girl anyway.

He chewed on a piece of rabbit and discovered it was a little tough. "You're right, Pa. I think I like Mom's home cooking better."

Jake chuckled, feeling an ache in his heart to be lying next to Miranda tonight. God, she was nice to come home to after two weeks of sleeping on the hard ground. He'd seen how Jess York looked at her sometimes, suspected how the man felt. Jess didn't come around very often, and Jake figured he knew why. Jess was a good man, had been a good friend, and Jake wished he could have found love again after the brutal way he had lost his wife and daughter during the war. There had not been another woman for Jess, but Jake supposed that if he were out of the picture, it was Miranda Jess would like to be holding. That didn't upset him. In fact, it made him feel a little better. If anything ever happened to him, between Jess and Lloyd, Miranda and Evie would be taken care of, protected, loved.

He heard the snap of a branch then, and he tensed, slowly putting his rabbit meat back onto his plate. "Say, Lloyd, I've got something to show you," he said, trying to sound casual. Was it a bear sneaking around in the shadows, or wolves? Or was it a man, maybe more than one man? Were they after the horses? Money? He had warned a gang of hunters earlier to get off of Parker land and do their hunting elsewhere. He had been worried then about trouble, feared Lloyd would get hurt, but the men had reluctantly ridden off. Jake had not liked the look of them. He knew that look, men who would shoot another in the back if they could get away with it. He'd ridden with men like that long enough to know one when he saw one.

"What is it, Pa?" Lloyd was asking.

"Come over by the horses." He picked up his rifle and walked around the fire to a puzzled Lloyd, picking up the boy's rifle also. In the next instant Lloyd heard a shot ring out, and his father tackled him to the ground and rolled with him into the darkness away from the fire. "Stay right here!" he growled.

"Pa! Are you hurt?"

"Just do like I said and stay out of the firelight." Jake shoved the boy's rifle into his hands and left him, moving off into the trees beyond. Lloyd clung to his rifle, rolling onto his belly, his heart pounding with fear for his father.

"Where'd the sons of bitches go!" someone growled.

"They run off like scared rabbits," someone else returned,

laughing. "Hell, let's finish that fine meal they was eatin' and get their horses and leave."

Two men stepped into the firelight. "Be careful. That boy's nothin' to worry about, but the pa looked like somebody you don't take lightly."

"There's two of them and six of us," came a third voice. Another man stepped into the firelight. "They know it, and that's why they lit out. Probably figured it was us come back and knew they didn't have a chance."

"Maybe," the first man answered, looking around. "But they won't go far without their gear. Better keep your eyes open. I'd feel better if you wouldn't have stepped on that branch and given us away, Lenny. We could have shot them both down and made off with their food and gear and horses, and nobody would ever have known the difference."

A fourth man came into view, and Lloyd forced himself to breathe quietly as he gripped his rifle. Could he really shoot one or more of these men if he had to? Where was his father? Was he all right?

Suddenly he heard two more shots, recognized the loud bang of his father's Winchester. The four men in the light of the fire whirled, and Jake stepped into view then, leveling his Winchester at them and retracting the lever to cock the gun. "All of you shed your guns," he ordered. "You can answer to Zane Parker for trespassing on his land again and attacking one of his men. This is Parker land, and out here Zane Parker also sets the law! Murderers and thieves can find themselves in a whole lot of trouble!"

Lloyd noticed blood trickling down the side of his father's face. That first bullet must have grazed his head! A fraction of an inch, and his father would be dead!

"Now, look, mister, we just wanted—"

"I heard what you wanted, to kill me and my son and make off with everything that's ours! Now drop your guns! Your two friends out there are already dead. You want to join them?"

Lloyd rose and leveled his own rifle. The unexpected noise made one of the men go for his gun, and the next thing Lloyd knew, his father's rifle was blazing. He only had two bullets left in it, as he had not yet cleaned and reloaded the rifle that night. Two men went down, and Jake dropped and rolled, whipping out one of his Peacemakers and shooting down the other two men. It had all happened so fast that Lloyd had not even had time to raise his own rifle and fire at any of the men.

Jake got to his knees, and it was then that Lloyd saw another man step from the shadows and point a gun at Jake from behind. Lloyd raised his rifle and fired, and the man cried out and fell. Jake whirled, cocking and leveling his six-gun, only to see the man was already dead. It was one of the two he had shot at in the dark, and he realized he must not have quite hit his mark. He walked over and checked the body to see a hole in the man's head, put there, he knew, by a bullet from Lloyd's Winchester.

He slowly turned to face Lloyd, who walked out of the shadows to come over and stare at the dead man. "My God," Lloyd uttered, looking down at his rifle then.

In that moment Jake saw himself standing over his father. This was what he had feared the most, that his son would use a gun against another man. In his mind it was the worst thing that could have happened. For an instant he felt only rage, at himself, at society, at his own son. He grabbed the rifle from his hands. "What the hell do you think you're doing!" he roared. "I told you to stay put, not shoot somebody!"

Lloyd turned to face him with startled, tear-filled eyes. "What was I supposed to do, let him kill my own *pa*?"

Jake just glared at him a moment, burning, painful memories stabbing at him. *I killed my own pa!* How could this son of his ever possibly understand something like that? He would surely think it was the most despicable crime a man could commit, and he guessed it probably was.

Lloyd could not stop his tears or his own rage. "You told me just a little while ago, Pa, that if I have to shoot a man to save my own life, I wouldn't have any choice. Doesn't that go for saving my *pa's* life?"

Jake studied his son, weeping because he had killed his first man. He could only hope to God there would be no more, or that the boy would never find out just how many men his father had killed in his lifetime. He told himself Lloyd had not shot the man out of a pure mean streak like he had done so many times. The boy had shot the man because he was afraid he would kill his father. He had done it out of love. He closed his eyes and sighed, laying the rifles against a fallen log. He faced Lloyd, saw the boy struggling against tears. He folded him into his arms.

"I don't like it, Pa," Lloyd wept. "I didn't mean to kill him. I just wanted to stop him from hurting you."

"I know, son. It's all right. You did the right thing, and if it makes you feel any better, I don't doubt the man would have died from my own bullet anyway. I got him before you did, and close to the heart. He was already dying."

He warned himself not to be angry with the boy, not to take out his own pain on him. It was the first time he could ever remember raising his voice to his son, and he reminded himself that at least the boy was bothered by having killed a man. He himself had lost that feeling of regret long ago, except to regret how all the killings might come back and destroy all that was dear to him. He remembered how scared and sorry he had been that first time, when he looked down at his father's dead body. He'd had no one to hold him and tell him it was all right, no one to talk to about what was right and what was wrong.

"I'm sorry I yelled at you, Lloyd. I just didn't want you to have to use your rifle that way so soon. I understand why you did it, but you have to remember to do what I say in situations like this. I can take care of myself. I heard that man behind me. I would have got him."

Lloyd pulled away and wiped at his eyes with his hands. "I never saw anybody act so quick." He looked his father over. "You're so fast, Pa. I never—" He hesitated. The dream! His father was shooting fast and furious, his handgun booming in Lloyd's ears just like tonight. Jake was holding him, hovering over him to protect him, shooting at several men who were firing back. He remembered it all now! It wasn't a dream at all! His mother was bleeding and screaming. His father was rolling on the ground with him. He'd been hurt that time, too, and he'd gone away after that.

"California," he muttered, watching a strange alarm come into his father's eyes. "Something like this happened in California when I was little, didn't it? What happened, Pa? We were at a fair or something like that. Why were men shooting at you? I remember you trying to protect me. I thought it was just a dream, so I never told you about it. But tonight, with all the shooting, I remember."

Jake turned away and walked around to check the bodies. "We'll have to get their identifications, if they have any on them, and bury them, then tell Mr. Parker about this."

"Pa, what happened in California?"

"Just some outlaws who tried to spoil the fair, that's all," Jake lied, feeling the desperate fear again of being found out. "I was the only one there that day who was good enough with a gun to stop them. They had already hurt your mother and a few other people, were threatening to hurt more and rob the bank, so I put an end to it, that's all."

Lloyd ran a shaking hand through his hair, looking at the rabbit that still hung over the fire. It was beginning to turn black. "But you left after that," he said, meeting his father's eyes again.

Jake just stared at him, looking as though he wanted to tell him something very important. "I had already been planning on that," he answered. "It was just strange timing, that's all. I'd heard there was good money to be made in the gold and silver mines near Denver, and I wasn't doing so well out in California, so I decided to come to Colorado and see if I could do better. I left your mother in California, figured the mining towns weren't a good place for her and you to be. I didn't know she was already expecting another baby when I left. It turned out I did the right thing. As soon as I landed this job and had a home ready for you and your mother, I sent Jess to get you, and that's how we all ended up in Colorado."

Lloyd had more questions, but something told him his father wouldn't want to answer them. Why would he leave so quickly? That still didn't make sense, especially since he remembered Jake had been wounded. And why hadn't he come himself to get his family, instead of sending Jess? He turned and looked at the man he had shot, feeling a little sick. Maybe the questions didn't matter. He trusted his father, figured if there was something the man didn't want him to know, there must be a good reason.

"Do you think Mom will be angry that I shot a man?"

Jake walked closer to him again, relieved the boy had asked no more questions about California. "She'll understand." He put a hand on Lloyd's shoulder. "You did what you had to do, Lloyd. But you can see how dangerous this job is. You're meant for better things than this. Someday you'll make your living with a pen in your hand instead of a gun. The land is changing, son. Things like this won't happen so much in a few more years, and men won't set their own law. There will be more courts and judges for things like that. Maybe you'll be a lawyer, one of the men who makes sure men like this"—*the kind of man I used to be*—"don't bring harm to people anymore."

Lloyd nodded. "Maybe." He looked up at his father. "I don't feel too good."

Oh, the memories. Jake remembered vomiting after shooting his father. "I know, son. I know. You just remember there was nothing else you could have done." He pulled the boy close again, cursing himself for teaching him to use the rifle, yet knowing he'd really had no choice. Lloyd was becoming a man, and there was no stopping it, just like Randy had said. Trouble was, the older he got, the more questions he asked, and the harder it was to lie to him, but in moments like this, when his son saw the ugliness of the kind of man his own father used to be, it only seemed all the more important to keep the truth hidden.

"You go sit back down by the fire, Lloyd. I'll pull these bodies out of the way and we'll bury them as soon as it's light."

Lloyd nodded and walked on shaking legs back to the fire. Suddenly, he wasn't hungry anymore. He lay down in his bedroll and pulled a blanket over himself, watching his father strain to pull the bodies out of sight. He knew he should probably help, but it was a strange feeling killing a man. He couldn't bring himself to touch the dead bodies, and somehow his father understood that. He couldn't help wondering how his father could kill so many men and not seem terribly upset by it. Maybe it just came with age, or maybe when a man was older it was easier to hide his emotions. After all, these weren't the first men his father had killed.

He figured Jake had had a pretty rough life when he was young, being orphaned at fourteen and all. He wished his father would talk more about it, but he never seemed to want to. He pulled the blanket closer around his neck, remembering the look in his father's dark eyes when those men had attacked them. It was a mean, frightening look he'd never seen there before, and it was still there when Jake had ripped his rifle from his hands and hollered at him. He'd never done that before, either, yelled like that. The meanness had quickly turned to something akin to fear . . . no, more like horror, and somehow he sensed it had nothing to do with the fact that his son had killed his first man. It was something else—something deep inside his own father—something to do with that terrible secret Lloyd was sure the man was keeping from him.

He'd seen that look before, remembered now. It was the day of that shootout back in California. Something was being left out, but he loved and trusted his father enough to believe that whatever it was, it must be best that he didn't know.

CHAPTER TWENTY-THREE

June 1885 . . .

Jake swallowed a drink of cold beer from a glass handed to him by one of Zane Parker's servants. He watched Lloyd dance in a slow waltz twirl with Beth, both of them laughing as Beth taught him the right steps.

"He really loves her," Miranda spoke up, coming to stand beside him.

"I know," Jake answered. "It's pretty obvious." Lloyd was eighteen now, and Jake had to agree with others that the boy was damn handsome. Other young girls at Zane Parker's annual hoedown were watching him, and Jake could see the envy in their eyes for Beth, who was the only girl there Lloyd cared about. Both of them would be going off to college in the fall, Lloyd to the University of Colorado at Boulder, Beth to a finishing school in the East.

Already Lloyd was talking about writing Beth every day, and Beth was talking about not wanting to go. They didn't want to be apart, and it had taken several long conversations to convince both of them they were doing the right thing.

Jake wanted more than anything for Lloyd to have the education he'd never had; he also did not want Lloyd to risk losing Beth to an irate father who was determined that sixteen was far too young to be thinking about spending her life with someone. She had barely been out in the world away from the ranch, except to school in Denver in the winters. Zane Parker had big plans for his daughter, including sending her to Europe. Jake knew Parker liked and respected Lloyd, but this was not the time for getting too serious. He had to agree with the man, but from the look on Lloyd's face, things had already gotten beyond the mark of casual friendship. He set his beer aside and put an arm around Miranda's shoulders. "How about a dance?"

She smiled and put her own arm around his waist, and they walked onto the wooden platform Parker had erected for his guests to dance on without getting dusty. It was in front of a huge barn where tables of food and drinks were set up for the one-hundred-fifty-plus people who had turned out for the annual spring celebration held at the ranch after roundup and branding. Not only all the men who worked on the ranch and their families came, but people were invited from as far away as Pueblo and Colorado Springs. There were even two couples there from Denver.

Jake put a hand to Miranda's waist and slowly began turning with her, thinking how beautiful and petite she looked in the new dress she had made, white cotton with pink and yellow flowers. He remembered that first dance at Fort Laramie on their wedding day. How was it, he wondered, that after nineteen years she had hardly changed; or did he just see her through the eyes of love? Maybe it was only in his mind and heart that she had not changed. She felt the same in his arms, looked the same to his eyes, except that just this year, a tiny hint of white had begun to appear in little streaks through her honey-colored hair, which sported so many shades of blond and ash that the white hairs were difficult to detect. He usually hardly noticed them at all. It was Miranda who fussed over them.

She couldn't really be thirty-nine years old, could she? That meant he was forty-nine. Some days he felt much younger, like today; but there were also days when he felt a hell of a lot older, especially when his hip acted up on him.

Miranda glanced at Evie, who was dancing with a young cowhand Jake had recently hired. Lonnie Mix was only seventeen, and had been on his own for two years. Jake felt sorry for him because he was orphaned and alone, but now he scowled when he glanced at the young man and saw his hand at Evie's waist.

"Evie is growing up, too, Jake. Don't go getting all upset. It's just a dance."

"And she's just a little girl," he grumped. "If any man ever hurts her, I'll land into him so bad he'll never walk again."

"Jake Hayes, you'd better face the fact that your little girl is going to fall in love and get married. She's fifteen years old. I was married myself at sixteen and I was perfectly happy."

He looked down at her, still frowning. "Well, I'm sorry about what happened to your first husband, but I'm a little jealous of him too." He pulled her a little closer. "I don't like the thought of any other man being with you." He leaned down and kissed her cheek.

"Jake, people are watching!" she chided, blushing.

"Let them watch." He studied her lovingly. "You know, there could have been any number of other men in your life. I've always wondered why you picked me, why you hung in there through all the bad times."

She thought how age only seemed to make him more handsome. The shoulder on which her hand rested was still solid and strong. "We don't always pick the person we're going to love, Jake. It just happens. I stuck with you because no matter how bad things got, I knew nothing could be as bad as having to be without you." She smiled. "Besides, the good times have far outweighed the bad. And look at your children, how happy and secure they are. Remember how worried you were when Lloyd was born, how scared you were of being a father? I don't think you could have done a better job of loving them, Jake."

They watched Lloyd and Beth walk off together. "Yeah, well, as far as Lloyd is concerned, he's got a new love, but I worry about Parker suddenly deciding Lloyd isn't good enough for his daughter. I'm not sure I could keep working for the man if he hurt Lloyd that way. I've raised him to be honest and responsible, and he's as good as any of Zane Parker's fancy friends."

"Jake, stop worrying. Mr. Parker seems to be very much in favor of their seeing each other, or he would have already put a stop to it. He told us himself he doesn't mind, as long as nothing interferes with Beth going to finishing school. It's very possible that once they're both off to college, they'll find other interests." She shook her head. "Do you realize that you spend most of your waking hours worrying about those children? There comes a time when you have to let go and let them do their own growing up."

The dance ended, and Jake walked her back to the table where he had left his beer. "It's hard to stop. And don't tell me *you* don't worry." His smile faded when he noticed a small troop of soldiers riding in to join the party. He had been aware that Parker intended to invite the new commander from Fort Lyon to the event, and it made him uneasy. Parker was working on striking a deal with the government to sell beef to the fort and also for shipment to Indian reservations to the south. As Parker's foreman, Jake would have to deal with soldiers.

He watched Parker greet the soldiers and shake hands with their commander after the man dismounted. He immediately began introducing the soldier to several of his business cohorts. Jake had always liked Zane Parker, in spite of the rather pompous airs the man sometimes showed. He was always dressed in a dapper suit, gold chain-watch dangling from the pocket of his vest. The balding, blue-eyed man was not very tall, but he was stout, and he was seldom seen without a cigar in his mouth. He was probably one of the richest men in Colorado, owned several mines now, as well as this ranch, which was one of the biggest in the state; but most of the time he didn't brag or flaunt his wealth.

Parker had been fair to Jake over the years, paid him well, treated his family like his own. Several times the Hayes family had been invited to the sprawling Parker ranch-home for meals, and so far Parker did not seem to be upset by Beth always wanting to see Lloyd when she was home summers. When she was away winters, she and Lloyd wrote each other often. Jake had to admire the man for the good job he had done raising his daughter alone these past few years. Beth could sometimes act spoiled and snooty, but usually she was a sweet girl who seemed unaffected by her wealth.

Parker began walking toward Jake and Miranda, the ever-present cigar in his mouth, his arm on the fort commander's shoulder. "Jake!" the man called out. "I want you to meet the man you'll probably be dealing with often over the next couple of years." They came closer. "This is Lieutenant Phil Gentry from Fort Lyon. Lieutenant, this is my top man, Jake Hayes."

Jake put out his hand, and the lieutenant took it, squeezing lightly. Jake thought the lieutenant studied him a little too closely, and there seemed to be a hint of surprise in the man's eyes when he first looked at him and heard his name. Did this man know him from somewhere? Jake tried to place him, but he did not look at all familiar to him.

"Good to meet you, Mr. Hayes," the man was saying. *"Jake* Hayes, right?"

"That's right," Jake answered. "I've worked for Mr. Parker now for almost fifteen years."

"Yes. He's told me how you saved his life once, says you're faster and more accurate with a gun than any man in Colorado," Gentry said, studying Jake closely.

"And Jake knows me and the cattle business so well, I let him make all the decisions for me in that department," Parker put in. "Once I strike a deal with the government to sell my beef, it's Jake you'll be dealing with from then on. Whatever he tells you, you can figure it's me talking. You won't need to verify anything through me first." The man turned to Miranda. "Oh, and this is Jake's beautiful wife Miranda."

Miranda blushed a little as the lieutenant nodded and tipped his hat to her. Jake kept watching the soldier, figured him to be about the same age as himself. He was tall and skinny, his eyes pale blue. From what he could see of the man's hair beneath his hat, it was sandy colored; at the left side of his neck was a dark brown discoloration of his otherwise light skin, a birthmark, Jake figured. That was what bothered him. He had seen that birthmark before, but when? Where? If he had ever met this man, did the lieutenant remember? He had an uneasy feeling that the lieutenant was having the same thoughts.

"Oh, and over there is my daughter, Lieutenant, with Jake's son," Parker was saying. "Now, have you ever seen a more beautiful couple?" The man grinned and looked at Jake. "Jake, I always thought you were a handsome man, but that son of yours is a heartbreaker if I ever saw one." He laughed. "He wouldn't break my Beth's heart now, would he?"

Jake grinned. "He's too good-hearted himself to break someone else's heart. And speaking of heartbreakers, your daughter has every man's head turning."

Zane guffawed, a proud look on his face. "She's the image of her mother. My wife was a beautiful woman." His smile faded a little. "I miss her terribly, but having Beth around makes me feel like she's still with me. Just wait till she gets back from finishing school. I'll wager there won't be a more beautiful, more elegant young lady in all of Colorado."

"And by then Lloyd will be practicing law in Denver, if we can get him to leave the ranch," Miranda spoke up. "He loves it here."

Parker nodded. "I kind of hate to lose him. He'd be a good replacement for Jake some day." He gave Jake a teasing look. "When Jake's too old and decrepit to keep up with this kind of work."

Beth and Lloyd joined others in a square dance, and the conversation turned to sheepherders and barbed-wire fences. Miranda left to help some of the other wives serve up pieces of pies they had all brought to donate to the hoedown. The dessert tables were set up just outside the barn where all the food was being served, and not far away a whole young steer was being roasted over an open pit of hot coals.

Miranda watched people visiting and catching up on a winter's news, and she supposed this must be the biggest crowd she could remember. The dancers were shouting and laughing, as were the onlookers, as a man called out a confusing square dance that kept the dancers turning in circles and bumping into each other. A ten-piece ensemble of banjos, fiddles, a trumpet, a drummer, and a guitar played a variety of songs, from slow waltzes to sing-alongs to wild square dances.

She liked these get-togethers as a chance for Jake to relax after the long, hard hours he and Lloyd both put into helping with spring roundup and branding. It was a wonderful opportunity to see neighbors who lived miles away, a chance for Evie to meet new young people, and it felt good to see so many people after a long, lonely winter spent buried against the mountains, sometimes unable to get out for days on end.

She watched Lloyd and Beth leave the crowd then and walk off alone together. They seemed so happy, had been good friends for so many years now, a good foundation for love.

She was glad there had been no more incidents like the one four years ago when Lloyd had killed that squatter who had attacked him and Jake. She did not doubt that the incident had affected Jake more deeply than Lloyd. It had shattered him to see his son shoot a man, but he had since come to realize it did not mean Lloyd was going to take the wrong path in life.

Lately the problem had come up again. Over the past year Zane Parker had set his men to ridding his land of sheepherders who had begun letting their animals graze on land Parker claimed was meant only for cattle. Jake had been left with the responsibility of leading raids against the sheepherders and he didn't like the assignment. He had talked about quitting as Parker's right-hand man if the raids had to continue. They brought back too many memories of his own days as an outlaw, and he no longer cared to go gunning after innocent people.

Legally, a lot of Parker's land was really public land, and the sheepherders had every right to be there. The situation left Jake caught in the middle and had been a source of contention between Jake and Lloyd, which upset him even more. Lloyd wanted to go with his father and the other men on the raids, but Jake would not let him go. Lloyd had thought he was old enough and skilled enough now to be allowed to participate in all phases of ranch work, but Jake knew there could be trouble, maybe shooting, and he worried that Lloyd would be forced into a situation again where he had to use his gun against another man.

"Why is it all right for you, and not for me?" Lloyd had asked.

"Because you're a hundred times *better* than me," Jake had answered. "You belong to a new generation, Lloyd, of men who do their fighting in the courts and not with guns. That's where this whole mess with the sheepherders is going to end up, in the courts. I'm doing what Parker pays me to do, and only because he pays me well, and that money is sending you to college so you can learn to live by the law and not by *these.*" He had held up his Peacemakers, and it was one of those rare times when he was genuinely angry with Lloyd.

The whole situation was eating at Jake, and he was hoping the sheepherders were gone for good. He wasn't sure he could keep obeying Parker's orders, and he was worried about the attention he could draw if someone were killed and the sheepherders tried to have him and the other men arrested. Jake and other Parker hands had spent the winter putting up barbed-wire fencing around land Parker considered his, even though under new edicts from Congress most of it was declared public government land on which anyone could settle to farm, to raise sheep or do whatever else they wanted to do with it. The matter was causing tremendous problems all over the West, as longtime settlers like Parker, who considered the land they had used for years their own, butted heads with newcomers who felt they had a right to it.

"Do you want some help, Mother?" Evie walked up beside Miranda and began cutting another pie. "Why don't you go back and find Father? You should dance some more and be together. Father was gone so much this spring during roundup."

Miranda brushed her daughter's hair with her hand and smoothed it back from her shoulders. "That's very nice of you, Evie." She looked around. "Where is Lonny?"

Evie blushed a little. "Oh, he decided to wait a while before asking me to dance again. I think he's a little bit afraid of Father. I wish you'd tell Father to stop giving him those dark looks of his. He scares boys away from me."

Miranda laughed lightly. "I've already mentioned it to him, but I'll remind him again."

"Well, I'm a big girl now, Mother, big enough to dance with a boy without Father acting like I'm going to run away with him."

Miranda grinned more, but inside she felt a sudden urge to cry. She had so wanted to have more children. Now the only two she was blessed with were growing up and within two or three years would probably leave them. How lovely Evie was, with her dark beauty.

"You just enjoy yourself," she told the girl. "I'll take care of your father." She left the girl then to find Jake, wondering where Beth and Lloyd had gone. She couldn't see them anywhere as she moved through the crowd. She did spot Jess York, whom she had not seen for weeks.

"Well, you finally made it, Jess! Be sure to try some of my pumpkin pie."

The man tipped his hat to her. "I wouldn't think of leavin' without a taste of it," he answered. "Where's Jake?"

"He's over there," she pointed, "talking with Zane Parker and those soldiers, probably feeling very uncomfortable at the moment. You know how he feels about soldiers."

Jess squinted to see better in the bright sunlight. "Yeah. I kind of wish Mr. Parker hadn't got that government deal, but maybe it will work out okay. After all these years and bein' clear out here in Colorado, I don't think Jake ought to get all worried about it."

Miranda touched his arm. "Jake worries about *every*thing. You know that."

Jess smiled, a sadness to his eyes as his gaze moved over her. "Well, he just loves all of you so much, he's scared of losin' it all." *I love you, too, Miranda. I've loved you for years now. Jake knows it. I'll bet you do, too, down deep inside, but it will always only be Jake, won't it?* "Listen, I, uh, I see the widow Adams over there servin' up some of her famous honey biscuits. She's still a right handsome woman, don't you think? Maybe she'd like to dance."

Miranda smiled. "I expect she would, especially with you. She had her eyes on you last year, and her husband had only been gone for eight months. Maybe it's time you did something about the woman's loneliness." She squeezed his arm. "And your own."

Their eyes held for a moment, their smiles fading. "I expect so," Jess answered. He readjusted his hat and gave her a wink. "You'd better go rescue Jake from them soldiers."

"I'll do that," Miranda said with a laugh.

Jess left her, and Miranda turned toward Jake, her heart a little heavier. She knew Jess loved her. It was just one of those silent matters that was understood and never talked about. It could never affect her love for Jake, or go beyond the friendship Jake and Jess shared.

The orchestra started up another foot-stomping, handclapping tune, and while everyone was involved in partying, no one noticed Beth and Lloyd darting into a barn several hundred yards away.

"Alone at last!" Lloyd said, pulling at Beth until they were well inside where no one could see them. In the next second she was fully in his arms, and their lips met in a hot kiss. Their youthful urges had exploded two weeks ago into a new awakening of desire for both of them. Now they could hardly wait to find ways to be alone so they could share this newfound ecstasy, this wondrous world of kissing and touching and holding and petting.

Beth finally pulled away, her face deeply flushed. She smiled and ran teasingly from him, going to pet one of her father's prized Palominos. "This is our last summer together for a while, Lloyd," she told him, her smile fading as she softly stroked the horse. "After a winter of schooling, Father wants to send me to Europe next summer. Then I'm to go right back to school for another year."

She looked up at him with tear-filled eyes. She had loved Lloyd Hayes since she was just a little girl. As far as she was concerned he was the most handsome young man who ever walked the face of the earth; but that wasn't why she loved him. They were the best of friends, had played together when they were very little, had talked often when she would go to visit Evie, had watched each other slowly grow and change. They knew each other so well, respected each other's dreams. This summer, when she saw him again after coming home from Denver, he had told her that he loved her, that he would wait however long it took to be able to marry her, would fight anyone who tried to stop him from making her his wife.

"Europe! Beth, we'd be apart almost two years if you don't come home next summer."

"I know." Her eyes began to tear. "I can't go that long without seeing you," she told him. "I love you so, Lloyd."

He studied her exquisite face, her skin so clear it looked like porcelain, her white-blond hair reminding him of an angel. He wondered if this was how his father had first felt about his mother, wanting her so badly he thought he might die if he couldn't touch her. He wanted to do more than taste her mouth, more than just feel her breasts. He'd never even been with a woman in the fullest sense, hated it when Parker men teased him about sex and talked about the female anatomy.

He knew from being around animals all his life how the physical part of it was done, had dreamed about being with Beth that way many a night; and he knew from the deep love his parents shared that there was something beautiful about it, knew by the way his father talked about his mother when they were camped alone that there was something wonderful about having one special woman at his side. He knew it was something that transcended age and beauty, something that stayed the same no matter how long a man and woman were together. His parents still made love often. They tried to hide it, but it was impossible to shut out all sound in the cabin.

He touched Beth's face. "I love you, too, Beth. You know that. I don't want to be apart either, but it's best you do what your pa wants. What if we stayed right here and got married? You'd always wonder if maybe you should have gone on to finishing school, seen Europe and all. I want you to know for sure about us." He pulled her close. "Besides, the way things are now, your pa so wealthy and all, hell, I've got a ways to go to be able to take proper care of you. I don't want to leave you or my folks or this ranch, but I know I need the schooling. Your pa would never settle for you marrying a cowhand. The only reason he lets us see each other is because he knows I intend to go on to college and be a lawyer. He's a powerful, determined man, Beth. He'd never let us be together any other way."

Beth swallowed back tears. "You know I love you just like you are, Lloyd. I'd stay right here and live on your pa's land with you if that was what you wanted. I just want to be together."

He pressed her tighter, enjoying the feel of her against him. He allowed his hand to wrap itself into her long tresses that felt like silk. "I'd like that just fine myself, but if we ran off and got married now, your pa would always hate me, and I don't want it to be that way. Besides that, you're only sixteen. Someday you might wish you never would have settled so soon and for so much less than you're meant for. We'll just have to find a way to make the next couple of years go as fast as possible."

She leaned her head back to look up at him, tears on her cheeks. "What if you go off to school and find somebody else?"

He wiped at the tears with his fingers. "You know me better than that. You're my best friend, besides my own folks. In some ways we're closer, because we share things we can't even talk to our folks about. It's going to be worse for me, you know, you being rich and beautiful and traveling the world. Hell, rich young men will be after you like . . ." God, how he hated the thought of any other man touching her. "I couldn't stand it if you up and married somebody else, Beth. I feel like you already belong to me."

"I *do* belong to you, Lloyd. My *heart* belongs to you, and if we have to be apart, I want this summer to be wonderful for us. I want to belong to you in every way, Lloyd." Her cheeks reddened, and she rested her head against his chest, hugging him tightly. "I want you to remember me in a special way, to make me yours so I know I belong to you and you belong to me and that no matter what happens, you were my first man and I was your first and only girl. You've never been with anybody else, have you, Lloyd?"

He took a moment to weigh what she was telling him. Was it right? How could it be wrong, when they loved each other so much and this was their last summer together for two years, maybe longer? He kissed her hair, feeling a fire move through his body that culminated in an ache deep inside that made him feel like he might die with the want of her. "It's always been you, Beth."

She looked up at him again and whispered his name, and he bent closer, brushing her lips lightly at first, feeling the heat there. He kissed her then, a fierce passion ripping through him in that one moment that made him want to taste her with his tongue. She whimpered when he pushed his tongue between her lips and ran it deep, and he gripped her tighter when he felt her fingers dig into his shoulders.

The kiss was long and delicious, the most wonderful kiss they had shared yet. Both of them fantasized about what it might be like to be together, like a real man and woman. He moved a hand from her slender waist along her ribs to a breast, and she left his lips and kissed at his neck, whimpering his name. Their lips met again in a groaning kiss, and he lowered her to a pile of hay on the floor, leaning her back into it and kissing her wildly then, enjoying the feel of her breast, the way her aroused nipple was raised so that he could feel it through the material of her dress.

He had never wanted her so badly. Maybe it was because of the news that they would be apart for so long. He wanted to touch her everywhere, to see and explore every part of her. He moved his hand down to catch the hem of her dress and push it up so he could run his hand along her leg. It was slender and silken, and he thought how beautiful she must look naked. He felt himself growing hard with an ache for her, the same thing that happened when he dreamed about this in the privacy of his bed at night and he had to rub himself to relieve the terrible need. He moved his hand to pull at her bloomers, but she pulled away from him slightly then.

"Not here," she whispered, her face flushed. "There are too many people here today. Father might bring someone in her to see the Palominos."

Lloyd ran a hand over her breast again, kissed at her neck. "Where then? When?"

Beth shared his excitement. It was understood what they needed to do. She wanted him as badly as he wanted her. She couldn't imagine how it could be wrong, when they knew each other so well, loved each other so much. It seemed the only right thing to do. She smiled and snuggled against him. "Father lets me ride alone down to the pond behind the house. He knows I like to sit there and read, and write my poems. I could go there tomorrow, only I could ride a little farther south, meet you at Fisher's Creek. It's secluded there." She sat up and faced him. "You'd have to come up through Devil's

Canyon to get there without being seen. Can you get away tomorrow?"

He studied her beautiful face, tried to argue it was wrong, but the temptation was too great, her willingness too impossible to deny, his love for her too strong. "Pa says I can have a few days off, now that the roundup is over. I'll tell him I want to go hunting alone." He frowned, pulling her close. "You sure, Beth? What if I hurt you?"

"You know how happy your parents are, and I know my mother and father were happy. It must be wonderful, Lloyd. I'm not afraid of it. I just want to be as close to you as I can get. I want to love you completely, to know you belong to me and will never forget me when we're apart. If it was anyone else, I'd be afraid of it, but not with you. And I know you understand why I want to do this and won't think less of me for it."

"I could never think less of you for anything." He kissed her hair, thinking how he ought to talk to his father about this, but sure the man would tell him it was wrong. He loved his father as much as he could love anyone, but it seemed like sometimes the man worried too much about things. He'd find some reason why he shouldn't make love with Beth, and he didn't want to hear the reasons. He was old enough to make his own decisions now, and this was as right as it could be.

"We'd better go back before we're missed," Beth told him.

He met her mouth again in a long, hungry kiss that made him wonder how he was going to wait another whole day to be one with her. "I love you, Beth," he said softly when he left her mouth. "I'll meet you tomorrow, one o'clock down by Fisher's Creek then." He quickly rose and helped her up, sure if he stayed here one more minute with her, he wouldn't be able to wait until tomorrow. "You go out first, mix with the others for a few minutes. We'd better not be hanging on each other too much the rest of today or your pa or mine might get suspicious."

She shook straw from her dress and turned to let him pick more out of her hair. "I'll dream about you tonight, Lloyd. Will you dream about me?"

He wondered how he was going to get rid of the fire under his skin. "You know I will."

She turned and stepped back to study him, wondering if a more handsome young man existed in Colorado. She didn't care that he wore denim pants and a plain cotton shirt and

leather vest. That was part of what she loved about him, his
brawn, his ruggedness, the smell of leather. She took a deep
breath and smiled. "Tomorrow then."

She hurried off, and Lloyd watched after her, studying her
tiny waist, wondering how her bottom looked bare, how her
long, blond hair would look hanging over her shoulders and
caressing her bare breasts. Tomorrow he would know. He
would be a man, and she would be a woman, and they would
be one. After that, nothing could change the fact that she
belonged to him. Nothing could take her away from him, and
no other man could say he had been the first to claim Beth
Parker. *He* would be her first man, her only man.

Miranda breathed deeply as Jake took her slowly, both of
them trying to be quiet about their lovemaking. She arched up
to her husband, the feel of him inside her as glorious and
fulfilling as ever. Age had not changed this for either of them.
There were more nights now when they were simply too tired
or ached too much to make love, but the desire had not
changed, nor their ability to please each other.

Jake licked at her breasts, savoring the taut nipples that
had been offered only to him for the past nineteen years. He
was still feeling good about the successful roundup, about the
way the Parker herd had bounced back from the last few lean
years since the terrible winter of 1880. It was good to be home
again, good to have a few days off to just be with his family, to
relax and make love to his wife, the woman who had been so
faithful to him.

He pressed close to her, ignoring the pain in his hip as he
moved in circular motions that he knew excited her. She felt
the muscles deep inside her pulling at him in her climax, and
he met her mouth, licking and tasting in response to her
groans of pleasure. Her own sweetness was on his lips, for he
had tasted her intimately, slowly, quietly pleasing that part of
her that only he could satisfy, the passionate woman deep
inside who was so bold and free in his arms. He figured if he
died tomorrow, he would die the richest, happiest man on
earth.

His life spilled into her, and for a moment he felt the
sudden ache he often felt when he thought how she could not
take that life and have it blossom into another child. He knew
she suffered silently the pain of never having been able to

have more babies. He didn't care so much for himself, but she was such a good woman and good mother, it didn't seem fair that she should have been denied the chance to have as many children as she wanted.

He kissed her several times over before pulling away from her. He pulled her against him then, her back to him, and he caressed her breasts as they lay there quietly for a moment. "That lieutenant we met today worries me a little," he told her quietly.

"Why do you say that? Did he say something?"

"No. He didn't do or say a damn thing I can pinpoint. It's just the way he looked at me, like he was trying to remember me. I could swear I've never met him before, except for one thing—that brown mark on his neck, like a birthmark. I've seen that before, and it's driving me crazy."

"Maybe you saw a similar mark on someone else."

"No. It's too distinctive." He sighed deeply and rolled onto his back. "I don't like it, Randy."

She turned and raised up on one elbow, studying him in a ray of moonlight that came through the window. "Jake, it's been nineteen years since you left Missouri. I doubt there are any wanted posters left anywhere around, if that's what you're worried about—or any lawman left back there who remembers you. Maybe after a certain number of years you can't even be arrested anymore. Is that where you think you know him from?"

"I'm not sure I know him at all. If I do, it isn't from Missouri. It must have been before that." He sat up, lighting the oil lamp beside the bed so he could roll himself a cigarette. He took a deep drag on the smoke and turned the lamp down again, lying back in the bed and smoking quietly. "Damn," he muttered. "I just don't know what to make of it."

Miranda moved an arm around his middle. "You've got to stop worrying about things that haven't happened, Jake. It might be nothing at all."

He sighed deeply. "A man with my past always has to be alert. If it was just me, it wouldn't be so bad. But there's you and the kids . . . if they ever found out about me . . ."

"Jake, they love you. They will always love you."

He finished his cigarette and put it out, settling in beside her and pulling her into his arms. "What would I do without you, *mi esposa*? You've been my strength all these years, you know. If you hadn't come along when you did, I'd probably be dead by now from some man's bullet, maybe hanged. If I wasn't dead, I'd be some drunken, worthless bastard wasting my life away at Robber's Roost or Brown's Park or some other hole along the Outlaw Trail."

She raised up and kissed his mouth lightly. "I don't believe that. You were wanting to change your life, and I think you would have done it even without me."

He grasped her hair and pulled her to him, returning the kiss she had just given him. "You're a damn good woman, Miranda Hayes."

She rested her head on his shoulder. "It's Miranda Harkner, and I never would have been ashamed to use your real name, Jake."

He sighed deeply, never getting over the fear that someone *would* remember that name and connect him to it. If only he could remember where he had seen Lieutenant Gentry before.

CHAPTER
TWENTY-FOUR

Lieutenant Phil Gentry poured himself another shot of whiskey, then leaned back in his chair to think. It was late, and the grounds outside were quiet. There wasn't much activity at Fort Lyon anymore, what with most Indians living on reservations now and troubles over sheepherders having calmed somewhat. Law had come to the West, and a lot of army posts like this one would close over the next few years.

He didn't mind. He was about ready to retire from the army anyway. For the first few years after the war he had had to suffer the abuse of being considered a "Galvanized Yankee," a former Confederate who had come into the regular Union army after the war. He had originally belonged to the Union troops, until the war broke out. Because he was from Tennessee, his conscience had not allowed him to fight on the Union side, and he had joined the Confederates, a cause that had ended up being useless.

It was the war period that he needed to think about, because it was during that time he was sure he had met the man who called himself Jake Hayes. He had spent a couple of days at the Parker ranch, then ridden on to Denver on army business and had just got back to the fort yesterday. There had not been a lot of time to think about Parker's right-hand man, but now he could study on it. The name Jake sounded familiar when associated with the size of the man, his dark good looks, and those guns he wore. He'd seen the man and those guns before, and when he first shook hands with him, he could have sworn Jake seemed to recognize him too. He had even looked a little worried.

Why would he be worried? Men who seemed uneasy around an army officer were usually men who had a past to hide. A lot of men hiding from the law came West, changed their names, their lives. Was that what Jake Hayes was doing? He leaned forward again and opened a drawer, taking out a thin cigar and lighting it. His eyes squinted as he forced himself to remember. If Jake Hayes was wanted, then if he knew him, maybe it went back to the war. A lot of men who dealt in illegal gunrunning and that sort of thing ended up outlaws after the war was over. Jake Hayes had that look to him, an air about him that told a man he could be ruthless if necessary. Maybe if he could see the man under different circumstances, maybe if he hadn't been smiling and happy the day of Parker's shindig, maybe then it would be easier to remember him.

He thought back to when he acted as an agent for the Confederate army and bought stolen guns for the South— guns taken from Union supply trains robbed by outlaws who sold them to whoever needed them, men who didn't much care who won the war. Sometimes the guns came from small regiments of Union soldiers who were attacked and shot. Either way, the gunrunners managed to procure rifles and ammunition for the Confederates, who paid for them in gold, sometimes taken from the wedding rings of generous, courageous Southern women who wanted to donate to the cause.

He remembered that one man in particular was mentioned often among the Confederate spies and agents he had worked with. He could swear that man's name had been Jake too. He was known as one of the best with his guns, had taken on six Yankees once who were supposed to be protecting a wagonload of rifles. When he was through, the Yankees were dead, and the rifles were delivered into Confederate hands.

Zane Parker had bragged about how good Jake Hayes was with guns. "Fastest I've ever seen," the man had told him.

Jake, he thought. *Jake . . . Harper? Harker?* The last name of the Jake he had known was something like that. He knew just the man who would remember—Otis Benson. Otis had worked with him during the war as a Confederate spy, had dealt often with the gunrunners, and he had kept in touch with the man after the war. Otis was a sheriff now in Carothersville, Missouri, had told him that if he ever quit the army, he ought to come there and see about a job in law enforcement. Maybe Otis would remember a gunrunner named Jake who had a reputation himself with guns—a big man who looked part Mexican or part Indian.

He puffed on the cigar absently as he took a piece of paper from his desk and penned a wire to Otis. He would give it to his dispatcher in the morning.

Beth stood waiting with an eager heart as Lloyd rode toward her on the familiar roan gelding. It was a big horse, necessary to carry a big man. Lloyd Hayes was no boy in her eyes, and whenever they got to see each other again, it brought a rush to her heart. He looked so grand on the horse. Already he was one of her father's best hands. He was a skilled marksman, the one who did most of the hunting, providing the meat when the men were out on roundup or mending fences. He could outdo any of the other men when it came to busting mustangs, and thanks to his mother, he was so well educated he was able to go off to college in the fall. Their house was filled with books Miranda had made him read and study, books she had ordered from the East so she could educate him. Lloyd had passed an exam to enter college, and she was so proud. What a handsome lawyer or doctor he would make!

Once that happened, there would be no reason why they couldn't marry. He would be just as worthy as any of the sons of her father's fancy friends. Her father liked Lloyd a lot, but sometimes he urged her to consider seeing boys who came from prominent families in Denver. But that's just what they were—boys, and pampered ones at that. They couldn't hold a candle to Lloyd, in looks or skill or brawn.

He came closer, smiled when he saw her. Oh, how was she going to stand being without him? It was already July. One more month, and they would have to go their separate ways. She was so glad she had decided to give herself to him. He had been so gentle that first time. They had both discovered something wonderful, had shared bodies in a deep love she knew she could never feel for any other man; but then Lloyd had to leave the next day when her father asked him to accompany some of the other men to Colorado Springs to buy horses.

Their separation had lasted three weeks when she was

compelled to go to Denver shortly thereafter, three precious weeks lost out of the short summer they would have together. Every summer her maternal aunt in Denver insisted she visit. The woman had stayed with her and been like a mother to her for several weeks following her mother's death, and had continued to insist she visit every summer so that she would continue to have a "woman's influence," as her aunt called it, in her life.

Beth had never minded the visits before, but this summer she had hated every minute of it, in spite of how good her Aunt Trudy was to her. She supposed other girls would think it was wonderful attending balls and operas and plays, being measured and outfitted with a whole new wardrobe for the coming trip east to her finishing school. But she would much rather have been here on the ranch where she loved it best, wearing her riding skirt and spending her time with Lloyd. She had longed to talk to her aunt about her new sexual awakening, but she knew she dared not. Aunt Trudy would never understand. No one could know. It was her and Lloyd's secret.

He rode closer, smiling that handsome smile that made her shiver. He dismounted, and in the next moment he was sweeping her into his arms. "Beth! God, I missed you!"

This was the first chance they had had to be alone again after that one glorious day of passion when he had made a woman of her. He had come to the house first thing this morning to call on her, where they had made whispered plans to meet again here at Fisher's Creek. It had been so hard not to touch him or let him hold her when he was at the house, but her father and servants had been around. Now they were alone again at last!

"I missed you, too, Lloyd. I hated every minute I was in Denver. I couldn't wait to get back."

She offered her mouth to his, whimpered when his full lips parted her own, his tongue exploring, teasing. The very moment he wrapped his arms around her she felt fire in her blood, passion exploding inside of her at the feel of his arousal pressed against her belly. It seemed she had wanted him this way since she was very small; she had simply been too young to realize how love could be expressed in body as well as word. She had loved Lloyd Hayes since her first memories, and there would never be another for her, no matter how long they had to be apart, no matter what her father thought.

He picked her up in his arms and carried her to the blanket she had already spread out on soft sand along the creek. She rested her head on his shoulder and kissed at his neck. "I hope we can meet like this every day while you're home again."

"I'll try to get away." He knelt to the blanket and laid her back. "I have to be gone a few more days after today. Your father asked me to take that prize stud Palomino of his to Pueblo to service some guy's mare. I can't turn him down or ignore my work, or he'll get suspicious. We have to be careful." He kissed her eyes. "It's not that I think what we're doing is wrong, but I'd never want your father to get angry and try to keep us apart."

"Maybe we should just get married before we go away to school."

He removed his hat and vest, sat down and removed his boots. "When I marry you, I want to be a man graduated from college making good money. I want it all to be done right, Beth—a big, grand wedding for you, a home that's just ours." He turned and moved on top of her. "It's all going to happen, Beth, you'll see. We'll show all of them we can do it." He moved a hand over her breast. "And they'll never know you already belonged to me, and me to you, for a long time before that."

He met her mouth again in a wild, hot kiss that told her there would be time later for talking. For now they were both eager to enjoy the exquisite pleasures they had discovered could be had from making love. It seemed like he got her clothes off as if by magic, and moments later he lay naked on top of her. It was all so natural and right, and she wanted desperately to please him.

The first time he took her, it had hurt so much that she had cried. Lloyd had been deeply worried, and she could see that worry in his eyes now as he hesitated.

"I don't want to hurt you again, Beth."

"It must get better," she answered. She reached down and gently grasped him. "I'm not afraid." She touched him out of purely innocent wonder, moved her hand over his hard muscles, felt his nipples. Her beautiful eyes were glazed with desire.

Lloyd looked down at her slender body, her full, firm breasts, her satiny white skin. Could there be any more pleasure for a man than drinking in the nakedness of a beautiful woman whom he loved with great passion? God, how he had hated hurting her that first time, but he could not keep from doing this, any more than he could keep from breathing. Her slender thighs were parted, the silky blond hairs of her lovenest inviting. He touched it first, toyed with her until she gasped and he felt her sweet juices on his fingers. He leaned down to taste at her nipples, then pushed himself inside her, muffling her cries with a hot kiss. The way she returned that kiss told him there was no pain this time, only ecstasy. To his surprise and pleasure she arched up to him in a natural rhythm, driving him wild with a new boldness she had not shown the first time. He thrust himself deep inside her, excited that he was pleasing her so. His release was quick, for he had done nothing but dream about doing this again ever since that first time.

He released his kiss, panting with emotion. "Just stay there," he whispered. "I'm sorry it was so quick. Just give me a minute." He studied her blue eyes, seemingly glazed with desire. "Was it better this time?"

"It was wonderful," she answered, her lips looking a deeper pink, her breathing coming hard. "I want to stay here and do this all day. I love you so much, Lloyd. When we're together I like to pretend time has stopped, and the day will never come when we have to be apart." She leaned up and kissed hungrily at his lips.

He had wanted so badly to tell his father about that first experience, but there was something so beautiful and sacred about it that he hadn't even been able to tell the one person in whom he had always confided, and who he trusted beyond measure. Besides, he wasn't sure his father would understand. Jake had not fallen in love and married until he was thirty years old. Lloyd had always been too bashful to ask, but he could not help wondering if his father had learned about this in his early years through prostitutes, or if there had been some other love for him before his mother came along. If so, who was she, and what had happened? There were still things about his father's past that seemed a kind of blur, but he had given up asking.

For the moment it was all just a quick, passing thought. For the moment there was only Beth, sweet, trusting, beautiful Beth, who had been his friend for as long as he could remember, who was now his lover and would one day be his wife. Maybe they should have waited for this, but their passion was too intense, their desire to know they belonged only to each other too strong.

They made love a second time, more slowly this time. He discovered he enjoyed moving in teasing ways that seemed to heighten her passion, and together they learned the glorious wonders of being man and woman.

Again his life surged into her, and he came closer, folding her into his arms and pulling a blanket over them both. "We'd better be careful, or you'll be sunburned in places you shouldn't be," he teased.

She snuggled against his shoulder. "This place will always be so special to me, Lloyd. For the rest of my life, no matter what happens, I will remember how it was here that I became a woman and first lay with the man I love. It almost makes me want to cry."

"I'll always remember it too. We'll have good memories to take with us when we have to be apart. We'll write every day. It will be like my mother says about my pa when he's gone. She says they're together in thought and dreams and in the heart. She says they're never really apart."

"That's how I feel about you. We were friends for so long before we were lovers. We understand each other, Lloyd. It's like we're one person."

"We *are* one person."

He rolled on top of her again, and she studied the handsome face, traced her fingers over his lips. "I'll wait forever for you, Lloyd. Promise me you'll wait for me too."

"You know I will. I don't know why you even ask." He smoothed some of her hair back from her face and kissed her tenderly. "One more time," he whispered. "We can't stay much longer. You'd better get back before they come looking for you."

"I wish you could come tomorrow again."

He sighed. "I have to take that horse to Pueblo. It will just take a few days. I'll come see you soon as I get back and we'll meet here again."

"Then come back just as fast as you can."

"You know I will." He met her mouth once more, and she eagerly gave him his pleasure. Lloyd Hayes was her friend, her lover, her man. He would always come first in her life.

.　.　.

Zane Parker shaded his eyes as he stepped away from the veranda of his sprawling ranch house. Jess York had ridden in to tell him Lieutenant Gentry and twelve of his men were riding onto Parker land and wanted to talk to him about "one of his men."

Jess waited now beside his horse, wondering himself what was going on. The lieutenant had brought along a prison wagon, and the sight of it gave him a sick, uneasy feeling. He remembered a conversation with Jake only two weeks ago about meeting the lieutenant at Parker's hoedown last month. Jake had been worried Gentry might know him from somewhere, but Jake couldn't quite place him. Jess stood prepared now to ride out and warn Jake if this visit involved him.

Parker took a cigar from his mouth and walked a little farther away from the house, his balding head shining in the sun. "Hello, there!" he called out in greeting as the lieutenant rode up close to him. "You're lucky I was here. I'll be heading for Denver tomorrow on business."

Gentry nodded to him, looking serious. He dismounted, shaking Parker's hand. "Good to see you again, Mr. Parker, although my reason for coming isn't sociable." He glanced at Jess, remembered seeing Jess and Jake Hayes talking and laughing the day of Parker's party. Men who worked together on a ranch often stuck together in other ways, and he had a feeling taking Jake Hayes might be a difficult enough task in itself. He didn't need or want to go up against half the men on the Parker ranch. "Can we go inside? I need to talk to you in private."

Parker shrugged. "Certainly." He turned and led the man inside, and Jess mounted his horse, riding over to where Gentry's men waited.

"Any of you know what this is about?"

They looked at each other before one of them answered. "We ain't supposed to say. The lieutenant would have our hide. Besides, he hasn't even told us the name of the man involved."

Jess glanced back at the house. He had a feeling he already knew the name. "You boys just might have your hands full," he told the soldiers. He turned his horse then and rode off, deciding maybe he'd better try to find Jake.

Inside the house, Parker started to close the doors to his parlor when Beth appeared at the doorway. "Father, what are those army men doing here?" She spotted the lieutenant and smiled. "Hello, Lieutenant Gentry."

The man nodded, but did not smile.

"Beth, I want you to go to your room for the moment. The lieutenant wants to talk to me in private," Parker told her. "Go on with you now."

Beth wished her father would stop treating her like a child. She was old enough to be at his side, helping him make decisions like her mother used to do. She was a woman now, in every sense, and she felt like telling him so, but she was afraid it would turn him against Lloyd. "Yes, Father," she answered, turning and heading toward the stairs.

Parker closed the doors and faced Gentry. "Would you like a drink, Lieutenant?"

"No, sir," the man answered. "I don't want to waste time, Mr. Parker. Every minute I'm on this ranch the word will spread through your men that we're here. One of them, the one I'm after, is going to find out and I could lose him. I just came to explain to you first so you can order your men to stay out of this. I don't want innocent people to get hurt. This is army business, and I'd like to keep it that way, but in a sense it does involve your daughter too. What I'm doing is for her good as well."

Parker set his cigar in an ashtray, frowning. "What the hell are you talking about?"

Outside the doors, Beth snuck back to listen. She could see just a little through the crack between the doors.

Gentry took a yellowed piece of paper from inside his shirt. He unfolded it and held out an old wanted poster to show Parker. "It's about this man, Jake Harkner. You know him as Jake Hayes. The reward on him is still good, and I aim to collect it."

Parker's eyes showed shock and disbelief as he took the poster and studied it. He shook his head. "I . . . I don't believe this. How do you know this is even Jake, with that long hair and that beard?"

"I know because during the war I was a Confederate agent. I bought guns from him. He didn't have all that hair on him then, but it was Jake. He was bad, Mr. Parker, as bad as they come. He killed men at the drop of a hat. It was wartime, so we didn't particularly care how the man got us the guns, and I suppose the war can be used as an excuse for some of the things he did, but not the things he did *before* and *after* the war. He was a murderer and an outlaw from the time he was just a kid, when he murdered his own father."

Beth stifled a gasp, a sick feeling engulfing her. Beyond the doors Parker took his eyes from the poster and looked at Gentry, stunned. "What!"

"Most men who ran with him back then knew. I don't know the circumstances, but I know he killed the man and continued killing after that. He rode with some of the worst outlaws, including Bill Kennedy and his gang, who were wanted in Missouri for robbery and murder and rape, just like what Jake's wanted for on this poster. I did some thorough investigating for this, Mr. Parker. This isn't just a hunch, it's a fact. Before coming here, there was a big shootout between Jake and Kennedy's bunch out in California. I don't know what the beef was, but Kennedy went after Jake, and Jake killed Kennedy and every last one of his men. He's good with those guns of his, as good as they get. That's why taking him isn't going to be easy. I hope twelve men is enough."

Parker let out a gasp of shock and sat down in a silk brocade chair. "This is incredible! Jake is the best man on this ranch! He's been my right-hand for fourteen years now. I've known him even longer. He worked as a payroll guard for me up at the mines before he came here. Why, he even risked his life *saving* the payroll, and my life! That doesn't sound like this man."

"And how many men did he shoot it out with to save the money?"

"Why there were at least . . ." Parker hesitated, realizing what Gentry was telling him. One fact was indisputable, Jake was damn good with those guns.

"I don't know or care what the man has been doing the last twenty years, Mr. Parker," Gentry told him. "I only know what he did before that, and bad is bad. Maybe he's married and got kids, but that doesn't erase what he did. You ask his wife about it. I'll bet she knows."

Parker kept staring at the poster. Robbery, murder, rape! Jake? "Miranda Hayes is a wonderful woman. She wouldn't marry a man who did these things."

Gentry sniffed. "Who knows what attracts some women? Maybe she had some big idea she could change him, or maybe she didn't find out the truth about him until after they were married. All I know is she was already married to him when he got in that shootout back in California. That was back in sixty-nine, and that son of his is older than that. Think about it. Why did he come here after that? Was his family with him when he worked for you at the mines?"

Parker ran a hand through his thinning hair. "No. He sent for them later."

"Because he was trying to find a place where he could start over, hide his identity. He got found out in California. He left his family out there so they'd be safe till he knew it was all right to be together again. Don't you see? Working here on this ranch, hardly ever leaving this land, changing his name, it was his way of hiding out. He didn't count on running into somebody who would remember him."

Parker just kept shaking his head, an anger beginning to build toward Jake. It wasn't so much that he cared what the man did twenty years ago, but his own daughter was in love with Jake's son! Didn't Jake realize what it would do to the Parker name if society found out his daughter was married to the son of a wanted man, a man who had robbed and raped . . . raped! Good God, he had let Beth go over there to visit so many times over the years! And what about Lloyd? Was he as trustworthy as he had first thought? Bad seed usually begat bad seed. Jake had killed his own father! What worse crime could a man commit? He couldn't have Beth getting involved in this sordid mess.

Gentry came over and took the poster from the man, refolding it. "You're thinking of your daughter, aren't you? I remember from your party that she was sweet on Harkner's son. I don't know what the boy knows about any of this, Mr. Parker, but once I arrest Jake, who knows what he'll do? Maybe he's a good kid. I don't know him. But I do know it would be best for your daughter's reputation if she quit seeing him."

Parker rose. "Yes, I agree."

Beth walked a few feet away, grasping a stair rail and bending over to try to find her breath. Lloyd! Did he know about this? Surely not! He thought the world of his father. If only he were here on the ranch so she could ride out and find him, warn him, but he had taken that horse to Pueblo.

Her father had actually agreed with the lieutenant that she should no longer see Lloyd! She could not let that happen! She just couldn't! Tears of horror and disappointment welled up in her soul, and she ran up the stairway, ignoring one of the maids who tried to stop her as she ran to her room.

In the parlor Parker slowly rose. "Yes. I agree Beth should not be seen with the son, once this gets in the news. If the boy doesn't know about this, it will be hard on him too. Maybe it's a good thing that for the moment he's in Pueblo." The man's pale complexion showed he was still bewildered.

"It's a good thing for more reasons than one. He'll be out of the way when we go after his father. He might try to defend the man, and someone could get hurt."

Parker rubbed at the back of his neck, feeling numb. "You going after him right away?"

"Right away. I just need to know where you think he is."

Parker shook his head, walking to look out a front window at the waiting soldiers outside. "I'm not sure. This is a big ranch, Lieutenant. You could ride for days and not find him. He could be anywhere. I sent him out to check again for sheepherders and squatters. I suppose the only thing you can do is go to his house up at the northwest section. He's been such a good man I let him build a home up there and use a piece of land like it was his own." He turned to face Gentry. "Whatever he's done, he does seem to care deeply for his wife and children. If he thinks they're threatened, perhaps he'll turn himself in to you to keep them safe."

Gentry sighed. "I'd rather not do it that way, but so be it. You just be sure to send a messenger out to tell your men to stay out of this."

"Yes. Yes, I will." The lieutenant started to leave, and Parker touched his arm. "Be careful, Lieutenant. Whatever Jake has done, he has a lovely family. I don't want to see them get hurt."

"They won't, if they stay out of my way; but if his wife knows about his past, then she knows the risk she takes being married to him. If she chooses to expose herself and her children to that danger, then that's her problem."

The man walked out, and Parker followed, watching him mount up. "Where's the man who brought us here?" he asked the others.

"He was askin' questions, Lieutenant," a sergeant answered. "We didn't tell him anything, but he rode off like he was in a hurry."

"Damn! The sonofabitch probably knows who I'm after!"

He looked at Parker. "The man who rode in here with us—who is he?"

"Jess York."

"He good friends with Jake?"

"Best friends."

"Jesus Christ," Gentry mumbled. "What's the quickest way to Harkner's place?"

Parker stepped away from the house again, pointing to a road in the distance to the west. "Ride back out of here and head up to that right fork you see up there. That takes you right to his place. It will take you a couple of hours."

Gentry turned his horse. "Follow me, men!"

The soldiers rode off, and Parker watched them for several minutes, until they headed out on the right fork and disappeared over a rise, carting the prison wagon behind them. He turned and walked slowly back into the house, wondering how he was going to break this to Beth, how he was going to convince her to stay away from Lloyd Hayes, or Lloyd Harkner, as the lieutenant claimed he should be called.

With the lieutenant on his way to arrest the man, he supposed he should tell the girl right away. The charge of rape was difficult to believe. In fact, none of the things he had heard seemed to fit the Jake he knew, but then the man's past had always been a bit of a blur, and when Jake did use his guns, he could be ruthless. He had proved that up at the mines, and again when he'd had that shootout with the squatters.

Lloyd had killed that night too. Was it in his blood to become like his father? He seemed like such a good kid, but this could set him off in a whole different direction. He was going to be an angry, shocked, confused young man, maybe turn to Beth for something more than friendship. There were things Lloyd was going to have to learn to live with, and he simply could not have Beth involved in the drastic changes that would take place in the boy's life.

Thank goodness Lloyd was in Pueblo right now. If he had been home, it would be just like Beth to try to ride out to him once she heard about his father. She would have gotten involved in the whole dirty mess and the dangerous arrest. He decided he had better get her out of here as fast as possible, and he had to convince her to stay away from Lloyd. Neither task was going to be easy, but it was for her own good.

Thank God the relationship to this point had not seemed to grow too serious. Both still had plans to go off to school in the fall. Once Beth met some of the refined young men in the eastern schools, she would forget about Lloyd Hayes soon enough.

CHAPTER
TWENTY-FIVE

Jake listened to the birds of summer, watched them flit about. He loved these mountains in summer, loved the smell of the pine, the beauty of gray and purple rock still glazed with snow at the peaks. This particular spot was his favorite, a rocky foothill that overlooked a wide, green valley and a small, blue lake. Behind him the bigger mountains loomed like fortresses.

He missed Lloyd. He had let his son head home a couple of days early, knowing he was anxious to see Beth before he took that horse to Pueblo. He still worried about Lloyd's intense feelings for Zane Parker's daughter, hoped the boy was being smart enough not to let himself get carried away physically.

He drank down the rest of his coffee and began breaking camp when he heard a gunshot echo through the valley below. Alarmed, he walked to a rocky ledge to see who had fired the shot. "Jake!" someone shouted, the voice barely discernable. "You up there? Got to talk to you!"

Jake recognized Jess York's horse, pulled out one of his handguns and fired a shot in the air. "Here!" He watched Jess turn his horse and head toward him. He slid his gun back in its holster, wondering what was so urgent that Jess had come looking for him. He would have been home by tonight, wouldn't even have stopped to make himself any lunch if his horse hadn't bruised his leg.

He stayed in sight while Jess made his way up the steep pathway, which took several minutes. From the urgent, almost careless way Jess headed up the slope, he suddenly worried something had happened to Randy, or to Lloyd or Evie. "What the hell is wrong?" he shouted anxiously.

Jess kicked his horse into a loping gait until he reached Jake. By the time he came close, his horse was lathered and breathing heavily. "Soldiers!" Jess told him. "I think they're comin' for you." In spite of Jake's dark complexion, Jess watched the man visibly pale. "I just come from Parker's place. That Lieutenant Gentry was there with twelve men, said he'd come for one of Parker's men, went into the house with Parker to talk private. You said Gentry seemed familiar to you, so I figured you're the one he's after. I tried to get it out of his men, but they wouldn't tell me. I figured you'd be somewhere in this section. Just wanted to come and warn you. He's got a prison wagon with him, Jake."

Jake turned away, a feeling of numbness moving through his entire body. Suddenly there were no birds singing. Suddenly the beauty around him existed no more. He didn't want it to exist, for then he would have to face the fact that soon this freedom, the enjoyment of these simple things, all the love he had found these past years with his work and his family, all of it was going to be taken from him. "Lloyd already left for Pueblo, didn't he?"

"He left early yesterday."

Jake closed his eyes. "Good." Lloyd! His son was going to discover the awful truth now! In the blink of an eye all their lives would be changed. What was it Randy had said all those years ago? Something about the truth catching up with you and hurting more than if it was told in the first place. As usual, his wise, patient, devoted wife had been right, and oh, how it would hurt Lloyd and Evie!

"You've got time to light out of here, Jake," Jess told him. "You know I'll look after the family till you can send for them again."

A quick gust of wind swept down from the mountains and blew Jake's hat off. He breathed deeply of the sweet smell of pine and mountain wildflowers. "No," he answered, running a hand through his still-thick hair. Its near-black color now showed streaks of gray at the temples. "No more running. It wouldn't do any good this time." He turned and faced Jess, and Jess was almost startled at the change in his face, suddenly older, a look of defeat in his eyes. "Before it wasn't just to keep my own freedom. It was to be able to raise my family, to keep the truth from the children. I won't be able to do that now, so what reason is there to run? If I did, and I sent for them later, the only one who might come is Randy. The children won't want anything to do with me after this. That's what it was all for, Jess, for Lloyd and Evie."

Jess felt a deep ache in his chest. "I'm sorry, Jake. Whatever happens, I'll look after the family for you. They're like family to me too."

Their eyes held, and Jake nodded. He knew without their ever talking about it how Jess felt about Miranda. "I'd appreciate that." He stooped down to pick up his hat and put it back on his head.

"I think you're wrong about the kids, Jake. You underestimate how much they love you."

Jake shook his head. "Evie has her mother's forgiving heart." He turned and dumped his coffee over the fire to put it out. "Lloyd and I have been closer because of working together these last few years, being alone together. He trusted me, and I've destroyed that trust. So many times he asked questions about my past, and so many times I almost told him but couldn't. I know him. He has a fierce pride. This will crush him." He sighed deeply and faced Jess. "I'll need your horse. Mine has a bruised leg, and I don't want to waste time getting back to the house. Maybe I can get there before Gentry and his men do. I don't want them to make trouble for Randy and Evie."

"They could already be there, Jake."

The two men just looked at each other for several long, silent seconds, realizing this could be the last time they saw each other. There was no more running this time. Jake could be facing a firing squad or a noose before it was all over. Jess could see the man fighting tears as he put out his hand. "You've been a good friend, Jess. I'm trusting you to keep my family safe, help them however they need it."

Jess grasped his hand and nodded, clearing his throat to find his voice. "This ain't your fault, Jake, when you think about it. It's your pa's fault. If not for him, none of the other would have happened."

Jake released his grip and walked to Jess's horse, feeling as though someone had set a boulder on his chest. "Trouble is, Jess, Lloyd's going to say the same thing. This is going to change his life, and he's going to say it's all my fault." He mounted up. "He'll be right."

He turned the horse, and Jess noticed his jaw flexing, knew the man was struggling not to break down. "It's been close to twenty years, Jake, and you've been a good husband and father and a law-abiding man all that time. Maybe the judge who hears your case will take that into consideration."

Jake smiled bitterly. "It won't matter. Even if they let me go, I'll have already lost something a lot more important to me than my life." He turned the horse and headed down the steep embankment.

Jess turned away and viciously kicked dirt over the fire. This wasn't fair. After twenty years, Gentry should have left it alone. Goddamn bastard! He must have found out the reward was still good on Jake.

He picked up Jake's gear, his thoughts filled more with Randy than with Jake. Not many women loved with the kind of devotion and forgiveness that woman showed. She'd risked so much to be with Jake. He wished there would be more he could do to comfort her, but if Jake was hanged or put in prison for life, there would be nothing he could do but watch over her, provide for her as best he could. Nothing would take away the pain, and he knew he could never take Jake's place in her heart.

Miranda heard the creaking of leather saddles, the clinking of stirrup irons and bit and spur chains, the soft thud made by many horses as they trotted on the dry, dusty trail that led to the house. Many riders were coming! She had lived in this remote area long enough to know one had to always be wary, and she quickly took down her Winchester from where it was cradled over the door. "Stay inside, Evie," she ordered her daughter. She opened the door and stepped out onto the porch to see soldiers coming.

Immediately her heart leaped to alarm. They were led by that tall, skinny Lieutenant Gentry. Had Jake's suspicions about the man after meeting him at the picnic been valid after all? She couldn't be sure that was why the man was here, didn't want to give Jake away by being too defensive. Maybe there was some other reason the man was here, but a sick feeling began to churn in her belly when she saw Gentry was hauling along what looked like a prison wagon.

She lowered the rifle, nodding to Gentry as he rode closer. "Good afternoon, Lieutenant." She set the gun aside. If not for Evie, she supposed she would gladly shoot the man right out of his saddle and suffer the consequences, but she wanted no bullets flying with Evie around. "What brings you way out here?"

Gentry looked around warily. "Your husband about?"

The sick feeling became a sharp pain in her stomach. "No." Jake! He was here for Jake! Why? After all these years, why had God let this happen!

"How about the boy? He still in Pueblo?"

Miranda folded her arms, dread turning to anger. It seemed a silly thing to come to mind all of a sudden, but she thought how ironic it was that today she was wearing the yellow dress Jake had always liked. She had kept herself trim enough all these years that she could still wear it, kept the dress cleaned and pressed for special occasions. She always wore it when she knew Jake could be home any day. "Yes. I'm here alone with my daughter."

Gentry turned and motioned to one of his men. "Get the rifle. Check the house and get rid of any weapons that might be inside."

Miranda quickly hoisted the Winchester. "I want an explanation first!" she demanded, aiming the rifle at the private. The man stopped in his tracks, and Miranda moved her gaze and her line of fire to the lieutenant. "You can't just come riding onto people's personal property and invade their home without a damn good reason, Lieutenant!" Miranda said firmly.

The lieutenant dismounted, facing her then with a look of authority. "Lady, I think you know the reason I'm here. Your husband is a wanted man, and I have every right to come here and arrest him." He stepped a little closer, a victorious look in his steely blue eyes. "You'd better think this through. My information tells me that Jake Harkner is no easy man to take down, but he'll come in quick enough if he thinks his family is in danger. Now, do you really want to use that thing against twelve men? I'll have you shot down, woman, you and the daughter both, if you interfere, and I'd be within the law to do it. You've knowingly harbored a fugitive for years, and pointing that rifle against me and my men creates a picture of self-defense. You want your daughter to get hurt over this, or be left without a father *and* a mother? It's your choice, lady."

Miranda slowly lowered the rifle. "You bastard!" she nearly growled. "Why are you doing this? Jake has led a decent life for nearly twenty years now! You have no good reason to do this!"

The man reached out and yanked the rifle from her hands. "Go on inside and check it out," he told the private. The young man hurried past him, and Gentry kept his eyes on Miranda, thinking what a pretty woman she was for her age. "I have a lot of reasons, lady. Five thousand of them, to be exact, unless your husband gives us trouble. Then I've only got three thousand reasons."

Miranda struggled to keep her composure. The last thing she wanted to do was crumble and weep in front of this haughty man. "How did you know Jake? How did you find out?"

"He looked familiar to me that day I saw him at Parker's shindig. I started scratching my memory, remembered a man named Jake who was damned good with those guns he wore. I bought stolen rifles from him during the war. A friend of mine remembered him too. He's a sheriff now, down in Southern Missouri. He knew more about Jake than I did—sent me this." The man reached into his jacket and pulled out the wanted poster. "Doesn't look a whole lot like him anymore, except for those eyes. It's Jake, all right. I checked with the Missouri authorities, and the money is still good. I aim to collect."

Miranda unfolded the poster. There was the Jake she had found that day lying on her bed, the old, hard, bearded, mean Jake Harkner, the man he had left behind so many years ago when he discovered he was worth something to someone, discovered he could actually love and be loved in return. She handed the poster back to Gentry. "The man you will be arresting is not the man in this poster. Turning him in now would be like turning in an innocent man."

Gentry just grinned. "A man is never innocent of his past, lady. What's done is done, and can't be *un*done. I'm hauling him back to Missouri for the reward money."

Oh, how she hated him! "And I wonder who is truly the decent man here. If someone offered Jake ten million dollars to do what you're doing, he wouldn't take it! *You're* the sinner, Lieutenant, and you'll burn in hell for this!"

"Will I?" His eyes moved over her insultingly. "Well, then, I expect you'll be there with me, after spreading yourself all these years for a no-good outlaw." He watched the crimson come to her cheeks. "Tell me, Mrs. Harkner, just what was it that attracted you to the man? Was it the danger? Did it excite you to know he'd raped women?"

Miranda could not control the urge to slap him. She hit him hard across his cheek, with such force that the man stumbled slightly sideways. In an instant he backhanded her with a shocking blow to her left cheek, knocking her to the ground.

"Mother!" Evie screamed. The girl had just come to the door to ask why the soldiers were there, why one of them was tearing through the house looking for weapons. She ran to Miranda and knelt over her, cradling Miranda in her arms and looking up at the lieutenant with tears in her eyes. "What are you doing!" she screamed. "How can you hit a woman like that!"

"Don't tell me your *pa's* never hit her," Gentry sneered. "I expect that's why she married him. He probably forced her into his bed and then she felt obligated. You've got a lot to learn about your father, little girl. You take your mother in the house and let *her* explain." He pulled a pistol from its holster on his hip and pointed it at Evie. "Do like I say. I don't want any trouble and I don't want anybody to get hurt. Soon as we have your father in our custody, we'll leave you be. Now, you tell me when your father is expected home, and don't lie to me, girl!"

Evie stared at the gun in shock. What was happening? What did her father have to do with all of this? "I . . . he . . ."

"Leave her alone," Miranda demanded weakly, putting a hand to the side of her face as she managed to get to her knees. Pain shot through her left cheek and eye like thousands of needles. "He was due home . . . yesterday, so he should show up . . . anytime."

"Mother," Evie whimpered, helping Miranda get to her feet. A dark bruise was beginning to swell on Miranda's left cheekbone, just under her eye.

"It's all right," Miranda tried to assure her. "Come inside." She glared at Gentry. "We'll let this angel of Satan do his dirty work." She forced back tears, standing proudly in front of Gentry. "Jake didn't do the things he is wanted for, Lieutenant, but you want that five thousand dollars, so you don't want to hear that he's innocent." She forced her voice to be strong, ignored the pain in her face. "I just hope when you're off spending that money, that you'll think about all the lives that have been destroyed by what you're doing today! Of all the things Jake did in his past, he's still ten times the man you are. He's never hit a woman or threatened a child! You're a *coward*, Lieutenant Gentry, a stinking *coward*!" She smiled defiantly. "How interesting that you had to bring twelve men along to help you arrest just *one* man in return! What you don't even realize is that if he didn't have to worry about his family's safety, even *twelve* men wouldn't be enough, Lieutenant! Not enough to take down Jake Harkner!" She turned and put her arm around Evie, leading her into the house just as the private came out with her derringer.

"This is all I could find besides the rifle, Lieutenant," the man told his officer. "Harkner and the boy must have any other weapons they own with them."

Evie helped Miranda to a chair, and Miranda looked around to see every cupboard opened and emptied, every drawer. Her trunk was open, everything tossed out of it. She looked into Evie's frightened eyes. "I'm sorry, Evie. Your father had a very tragic past that he never wanted you or Lloyd to know about. Now I suppose there is no choice but to tell you. You mustn't hold it against him. He loves you so much. People can change, Evie. They can be very sorry for some of the things they have done, but sometimes the law doesn't forgive, and they have to answer for things in spite of how much they might have changed. That is what is happening to your father. He's going to need our love and support more than ever now."

"Mother, what are you talking about? I don't understand!"

Miranda took hold of her hand. "I know, Evie." She closed her eyes, struggling to stay strong. Jake! Lieutenant Gentry was going to take him away! He would surely be hanged, or imprisoned for the rest of his life. He would not come today and sweep her into his arms like always. She would not sleep beside him tonight. He might even react defensively when he came home and saw soldiers there, might shoot it out with them, be killed today. And what about the children? How was she going to explain all this in the midst of such tragedy? For years she had warned Jake to tell them, and for years he had put it off, had been so afraid of losing them.

If only she could get out of here, ride out to him, hold him once more before he was arrested. There was no way around it, and she knew Jake would not run again. Not this time. The running was over. The pain in her chest was so fierce she was afraid she might pass out. "Sit down, Evie," she told her daughter.

Evie pulled a chair around the table and sat down near Miranda, who again took hold of her hands. "While we're waiting for your father to come home, I have something to tell you."

"Surround the house!" Gentry was shouting outside. "Make sure the woman and the girl stay inside! Private Bale!"

"Yes, sir!"

"Take two other men and keep a lookout—all directions! Harkner is due back anytime. He's a man who's always well armed, dangerous when he's cornered. Watch out for the boy too. He could come back unexpectedly."

Lloyd! Thank God he was still in Pueblo. He could get hurt if he rode in here now and didn't understand what was happening. Miranda squeezed Evie's hands reassuringly. "Evie, your father was once an . . . an outlaw; but certain things happened to him as a boy that forced him into that life at a time when he had no guidance, no love, no family. I want to tell you about it so you'll understand what is happening; and I want you to try to find it in your heart to forgive him for keeping the truth from you. He did it only because he loves you so very much. He never wanted you to hate him or be ashamed of him. For twenty years he has worked hard at changing his life and trying to make up for his past. Now it has caught up with him, and I'm afraid we can't do anything to help him except to be there for him and let him know he's loved and has our support."

"He's my father. I could never stop loving him."

Miranda could only hope she would hear the same words from Lloyd, but there was something else involved there. If Lloyd lost Beth Parker because of this, there would be no forgiving; and if their son looked at his father with the hatred and shame Jake had always dreaded he would see in the boy's eyes, it would destroy Jake. He would go to the gallows willingly. The love of his wife and daughter would not be enough to make him want to live, to fight for his rights. Nothing worse could happen to him than to lose his son's love.

. . . .

"Look sharp, men! That could be him coming now!"

Almost two hours had passed. Miranda heard the shout and rushed to the door. "Stay inside!" she ordered Evie. "No matter what happens, stay in this house."

Evie ran to a window to watch, her heart pounding with fear for her father. The lieutenant had told them Jess York had ridden out when they arrived at Mr. Parker's house. She and her mother both hoped Jess had warned Jake about what was happening. Evie had prayed her father would not come at all, that he would get away while he had the chance. She could not imagine him being hanged, or spending the rest of his life in prison. Not her father! Her heart ached over the things her mother had told her, and she was struggling to understand, to forgive. She prayed Lloyd would be able to do the same. She watched her mother move away from the house and past some of the soldiers. Gentry grabbed her arm. "That's far enough."

"Please, let me go to him!" Miranda begged. "Let me have a few minutes alone with him."

"No, ma'am. As long as you're here and he's there, he'll keep coming."

"I know him. He'll come anyway. Evie is still here." She jerked her arm away. "Please! He'd never try to ride off when I'm with him. He'd be too afraid I'd get hurt. And he wouldn't leave Evie behind. For God's sake I haven't seen him for over two weeks! Let me have two *minutes* alone with him!"

The lieutenant watched Jake move a little closer. "All right, long as you go out to him on foot. A man can't get far carrying two people on his horse." He turned to one of his men. "Holt, you and Webster and Bates get inside with the girl. I want him to know that if he tries to shoot the rest of us down, his daughter is still inside with more men."

Miranda glared at him. "You're such a fool, Lieutenant. Nothing you're doing could stop Jake if he decided he'd rather shoot it out with you. He's faced nearly as many men before, also with a wife and child at stake." She smiled, wincing a little at the pain it caused. "He doesn't miss, Lieutenant. There are other reasons he won't try anything this time, and none of them have anything to do with your efforts." Her defiant smile faded, and her eyes teared. "He knows he has already lost something more precious to him than his life or our physical presence. He's lost the pride and self-respect he's worked so hard over the years to learn to have in himself. He's lost his children's honor, maybe even his son's love, but then you wouldn't understand how important those things can be."

She whirled and walked off toward Jake, and Gentry glared after her, frustrated at the woman's refusal to crumble and beg or to show fear. There was no look of defeat about her as she walked out to meet her husband. She stood erect, walked in bold steps. It seemed to him the woman ought to be regretting a lot of things by now, but she actually still seemed to be proud to be married to Harkner. "Stay alert, boys," he ordered.

Miranda's steps became more rapid as she drew closer. Jake had stayed a good three hundred yards back. She watched him dismount, noticed he was riding Jess's horse instead of his own. So, Jess *had* warned him. Something must have happened to his own horse, so he used Jess's to get back here faster. He walked toward her, and her heart ached fiercely at the look of him, suddenly older, a look of defeat about him. "Jake," she whispered. She hurried to him then, wrapping her arms around him.

His own arms encircled her, and she thought how this might be the last time her husband would hold her. She clung tightly to him, visions of him hanging or imprisoned stabbing at her like a knife. Not Jake! Not her Jake! Why had God let this happen? Why had He let them come this far, only to let it all be destroyed?

Jake took hold of her arms and pushed her away, studying her face, a look of fierce anger coming into his dark eyes. "What the hell happened! Who did that to you!"

"It's all right, Jake. I'll be fine!"

"It was Gentry, wasn't it! The sonofabitch is after *me*! He had no right hitting you!" He started walking away from her.

"No, Jake! Evie's in the house. They'll hurt her for sure! This is the *army*, Jake, not just one gang of men you can eliminate! If you shoot them down, they'll just send more men after you!"

"Bastards!"

"Jake, please! I know you came here to turn yourself in to protect us. Don't let what happened to me make you do something that could get Evie hurt!"

He turned away, breathing deeply for control. "The sonofabitch knows he's holding all the cards this time. He's probably laughing right now over getting away with hitting you. If I could ever get him alone—"

"Jake, we have so little time." She choked in a sob, and he turned to face her. He realized what she meant. They couldn't spend these last few minutes fretting over Phil Gentry. He came closer again, reaching out to lightly touch the bruise. "You're still so beautiful," he nearly groaned. "My precious, faithful *esposa*. You took all the risks, turned down so many chances at peace and happiness. I thought we had finally found it here. I'm so sorry, Randy."

She grasped his hand and kissed his palm. "Don't ever be sorry. I don't regret one minute of it." She moved her arms around his waist again. "This doesn't change anything, Jake. The man they are arresting doesn't really exist anymore. You have to believe that. Evie knows, and she still loves you. She's trying to understand." She looked up at him. "Lloyd will too."

He pressed her head against his chest, unable to speak at all for a moment. She could feel him trembling. "He won't," he finally managed to say. "He'll lose Beth over this. He'll never forgive me for that. I'll see it, Randy. I'll see the one thing in his eyes that I never wanted to see. I'm just glad he's not here today."

"I'll explain to him, Jake."

"It won't matter. I know him. Everything he ever believed about me will be thrown in his face, all the pride, the trust. It will be worse for him. He'll be the son of an outlaw. I know what it does to a boy to know terrible things about his father."

She could not stop her own tears. He would never hold her again this way. He had lost the only love and happiness he had known in life. For the moment he was not Jake Harkner the man, but was back to being Jake Harkner the boy, who wanted so much to be loved but felt unworthy. "I'll stay with you . . . every step of the way, Jake. Evie and I both will. Lloyd will, too, once he finds out what has happened."

"I don't want you there, not any of you. Everything I've ever done is going to come out, as well as things I *haven't* done but people want to believe I did."

"The children will know the truth, Jake. They know *you*. They won't believe the lies." She looked up at him, hardly able to see him for her own tears. "That's what family is for, Jake, for love and support in time of need. Love is as strong and important in the bad times as the good. I've stayed with you through a lot of things. I'm not going to desert you now."

He stroked her hair, kissed her eyes. *"Yo te quiero, mi querida."* He kissed her lightly, thinking how just this morning he had looked forward to coming home to a home-cooked meal, seeing his wife and daughter, sleeping with Randy beside him tonight. Lloyd would likely be back in two or three days, and they would have talked about his trip to Pueblo. There would be no more camping alone with his son, no more hunting with him, no more talk about sending him off to college. There would be no more sweet nights with this woman he loved with more passion than he ever dreamed possible, no more sitting by the fire and listening to Evie read to him.

He leaned down to gently kiss her bruise. "Thank you, Randy, for all the good times. We tried, but it's over." He closed his eyes and breathed deeply, but he could not control the tears that slipped down his cheeks then. "You know . . . how much I love you . . . but the worst part is still . . . losing Lloyd's love and trust. I figure . . . I can stand anything but that." He squeezed her shoulders. "Love him for me. Help him through this. There can't be any more running, Randy. The worst damage has already been done, and it won't do any good . . . to put this off any longer. *Vaya con Dios.*"

He walked past her, unbuckling his gunbelts one at a time as he walked toward the soldiers and the waiting prison wagon.

"Jake," she whimpered. How was she going to go on without him? She left the horse behind and followed him, picking up first one gunbelt, then the other. He took a knife from his boot and dropped that too. She picked it up and pressed the guns to her breast.

"Father!" As Jake drew closer, Evie started to run from the house to hug him. Two soldiers held her back. Jake glared at Gentry. "Let her go, you bounty-hungry sonofabitch! I've dropped all my weapons!"

Gentry smiled victoriously. "I give the orders from here on. You're too dangerous, Harkner. I remember just *how* dangerous, when I used to buy stolen rifles from you back during the war."

Jake looked him over and nodded. "So, that's why you looked familiar to me."

"I just didn't stand out enough for you to remember good enough. You, on the other hand, are a man not easily forgotten. Now, get in the wagon."

"Just one thing first." Before Gentry realized what was happening a big fist slammed into his jaw and sent him sprawling to the ground in a cloud of dust. "That was for my *wife,*"

Jake growled. He grunted and crumbled then when another soldier smashed a rifle butt into his lower back. The rest of the soldiers joined in then, kicking and punching. Miranda dropped the guns and ran toward them, Evie's screams of terror and horror ringing in her ears.

"Stop! Stop it!" Evie shrieked.

Jake fought back viciously, but ten men against one were odds no unarmed man could handle. Miranda tried to push some of them away, but a fist landed in her stomach and landed her on her rear so hard it knocked the breath out of her. Evie also tried to help, but the two soldiers holding her kept their grip, laughing at the sight of her father being beaten bloody. "He deserves it," one of them told her. "A man's got to pay for his sins sooner or later."

Miranda struggled to her feet and stumbled over to her daughter, tearing her away from the two men and holding her tight, pressing her head against her breast in an effort to keep her from having to see.

"Get him in the wagon!" Gentry ordered, now on his feet again himself. The words were slurred through a bleeding, already-swelling mouth.

It took four men to lift a nearly unconscious Jake into the wagon, which looked hot and uncomfortable to Miranda. She could not control her sobs then as she watched them handcuff both of Jake's wrists behind his back to wagon bars. He sat on a hard bench, his head hanging, blood dripping from several face and head wounds. He managed to lift his head just slightly to look back at her as two soldiers climbed into the wagon seat and whipped the mules that pulled it into motion.

"Where will you take him?" Miranda screamed at Gentry.

One of the men who had been holding Evie answered for the man. "To Fort Lyon. Authorities from Missouri will pick him up there and take him to St. Louis."

"Then *I'm* going to Fort Lyon, *and* to St. Louis! And I'll damn well find out who Lieutenant Gentry's commanding officer is! He'll know what happened here today! Arresting a man is one thing! Beating him and his wife is another!"

The soldier frowned, walking to help Gentry mount up, then mounting his own horse. The rest of the men climbed onto their horses, and they all rode to catch up with the wagon.

Miranda watched after them, feeling crazy with a need to

go and help Jake. How badly was he hurt? Would they help him at all? Would he get food and water?

How could life turn so quickly? This morning she had been happily baking, planning for Jake's return. She clung to a weeping Evie, and from inside the house she could smell her bread burning. She had been baking it for Jake. How he loved her homemade bread, loved it when the house smelled of it. She remembered the first time he'd mentioned how he liked that smell, back at her little cabin in Kansas City close to twenty years ago.

In the distance Jake watched his wife and daughter grow smaller as the wagon bounced and clattered away. He thought how Randy was still a slip of a woman, how strangely sad it was that she had been wearing that yellow dress today.

CHAPTER TWENTY-SIX

Lloyd led the Palomino stallion into the corral, glancing at the Parker ranch house in the distance, anxious to see Beth again. He would have to wait until tomorrow to meet her at Fisher's Creek, since he was dusty and sweating and needed a bath. It was already late afternoon, but in spite of his condition, he decided to at least go to the house before he left.

"It's about time you got back, boy," one of Parker's men yelled out to him.

Lloyd grinned. "I know. I would have been back two days ago if the damn mare hadn't been so stubborn. She wouldn't let Pacer near her for three days." He thought the man would laugh, but he only nodded, a strange look in his eyes that made Lloyd feel like he was in some kind of trouble. He had done everything as he had been requested, and he had the money Parker's friend had paid for the stud service. He glanced toward the house again, wondering why Beth didn't run out to greet him like she usually did. She always watched for him when he'd been gone a while.

He dismounted and took the bridle from the stallion's head, pulled the bit from its mouth. "There you go, boy. You ought to feel damn good after making love with that pretty mare." He patted the horse's neck, and the animal reared and whinnied, then pranced around the corral. Lloyd led his own horse back out of the gate and locked it. He tied his horse and started toward the house when the same man called out to him.

"She ain't there, kid! Her pa took her off someplace four days ago." The man started toward him, taking a piece of paper from the pocket of his vest. "I'm supposed to give this to you. It's from your ma. She's gone, too, her and your sister and Jess York—gone to Fort Lyon to be with your pa."

Lloyd frowned, totally confused. "Fort Lyon? Why would Pa take my mother and Evie there just to sell a few cattle to the government?"

Will Brewer leaned against the corral gate, hating to be the bearer of bad news. He liked Lloyd, had liked Jake, too, for that matter. He and the other men were still shaking their heads over the events of the last few days, still found it all hard to believe. "I guess you don't know anything at all yet, do you? I thought maybe the news had got to Pueblo before you left."

Lloyd took the folded paper from the man. "What news?"

Will rubbed at his mouth nervously. His shirt showed sweat stains, and he sported a three-day-old beard. He had never been one to shave or bathe regularly, and his eyes were always puffy from too much whiskey. Right now those pale gray eyes showed a true concern for Lloyd. "Soldiers come here about four days ago, son. They took your pa away, arrested him."

"*Arrested* him! What the hell for?"

Will watched his dark eyes. "For a lot of things. They had an old wanted poster with them showin' your pa was an outlaw back in Missouri during and after the war. On the poster he was wanted for bank robbery and murder, and rape."

The man watched the blood drain from Lloyd's face. He suddenly grasped Will's shirt and shoved him against the gate. "You're lying!"

Will grasped his wrist. "Don't be pushin' me around, boy! I'm tellin' you the truth! I liked your pa. Why would I lie about it?"

Lloyd glared at him, then released him and stepped back. "My pa would *never* murder and rob and rape!" he growled.

"Maybe not, but there's a lot of people back in Missouri who seem to feel otherwise, so much so that the wanted poster was still good on him after pretty near twenty years. It was that Lieutenant Gentry who arrested him. He knew your pa from the war, bought stolen rifles from him, found out he was still wanted."

Lloyd stared at the man, dumbfounded. His father, a wanted man? An outlaw?

"Word is he rode with a real bad bunch led by a man called Bill Kennedy," Will continued. "Kennedy raided settlers during and after the war, robbed trains, banks, you name it, took women hostages. Apparently Kennedy and your pa had some kind of fallin' out, had a big shoot-out out in California a few years back. It was after that your pa went to work for Mr. Parker, then sent for you and your ma and your sister. He's been hidin' here on the ranch under a different name."

A sick feeling engulfed Lloyd. Beth! Did she know? Did she hate him now because of this? He struggled against a growing panic. "A different name?"

"His real name is Jake—Jackson Lloyd Harkner."

"My . . . mother knew?"

"I reckon so. She decided to stay by your father's side through his trial and all—wrote that letter for you and left it with me. She knew you'd likely stop here first thing when you got back from Pueblo. Your pa is probably on his way to St. Louis by now. I ain't sure if they hang men anymore in Missouri, but—" The man halted midsentence when he saw the look of horror in the boy's eyes. "Sorry about that. You just ought to know things don't look good for your pa. I'm sorry you have to come back to all of this, but I figured I might as well get it out right away, seein' as how you were headed for the house. Parker done took Beth away somewhere. Most likely it was to keep her away from you and all the scandal. He wouldn't want a daughter of his seen with the son of an outlaw. Mind you, now, I don't think any the less of you for it, but some people will."

Lloyd looked toward the house, then back at Will, tears of anger and frustration forming in his eyes. "Where did he take her?" He stepped closer and shouted. *"Where!"*

Will shook his head. "He wouldn't say. I reckon that was his way of keepin' you from findin' out so you couldn't go after her."

Beth! He had to find her! They had sworn that nothing would keep them apart. He headed toward the house again.

"I wouldn't bother, boy. Ain't none of the servants inside know where they've gone. You'd best read your ma's letter. It's your own family who'll be needin' you right now."

Lloyd looked down at the folded letter in his hand. Was this some kind of joke? Some kind of nightmare? What the hell was going on? How could his father do this to him, hide such a lawless, sinful past? All his life Jake had taught him about honesty and truthfulness. He had preached to him about doing the right thing, wouldn't even let him touch a gun until he was fourteen, and even then only because he had practically begged for it.

The sick truth began to sink in, bringing literal pain to every nerve in his body. He felt betrayed, humiliated. Suddenly it was difficult to remember what time of day it was, *where* he was. Nothing around him seemed real. He was supposed to come home and see Beth, then go home to a cozy house and a happy family, talk to his father about his trip to Pueblo, eat one of his mother's good meals, joke with Evie. He was supposed to clean up, put on the new clothes he had bought in Pueblo and visit Beth tomorrow down by Fisher's Creek, hold her again, make love to her.

"I'm sorry to be the one to tell you," Will was saying. His voice sounded far away. "Me and some of the boys, we was told to stay out of it, but we rode out to catch up with Gentry and his men to see if it was true they was arrestin' your pa. By then they already had Jake in a prison wagon. That's when Gentry told us what all he done, showed us the poster. Your pa was in a pretty bad way. Looked like them soldiers had beat up on him pretty good. I reckon' your ma got in on it, too, on account of when we rode out to your place, she had a pretty nasty bruise by her eye. Jess was there by then. Bein' your pa's best friend and all, he's lookin' out for your ma and your sister, stayin' with them through the trial."

Lloyd slowly opened the letter, nausea gripping his stomach.

"There's, uh, there's one more thing maybe you should know, before you hear it some other way," Will told him.

Lloyd turned dark, angry eyes to the man. "What is it?"

Will scratched at his beard. "I hate tellin' you these things, son, but you've got to know. That Gentry fella', the lieutenant, he said your pa killed his own father some years back."

Lloyd stared at him in wide-eyed horror. "That *has* to be a lie!"

Will shook his head. "One of the men asked your ma if it was true. Your sister started cryin', and your ma just looked him straight in the eyes and said as how he didn't understand all of it; but she didn't deny it.' "

Lloyd let out a gasp, turning away again, finding all of this incomprehensible. "Go away, Will," he said quietly.

The man reached out and patted his shoulder, then left him. Lloyd blinked back tears so he could see to read his mother's letter. His hands trembled as he opened it. *My dearest son,* it read. *By the time you read this letter, you will have heard the awful news that your father has been arrested. I would give anything to be there when you come home, to explain all that has happened myself, but your father needs me. I have no idea how much longer I will be able to see him, talk to him, whether he will be imprisoned or executed. There is so much you need to know, and I hope that when you do know, you will find it in your heart to forgive.*

I wanted Jake to tell you everything long ago, but he was so afraid of losing your love, something he treasures beyond life. Through you, he has been able to heal terrible wounds from his own battered youth, to make up for all the love he never knew as a child. Please don't blame your father or turn away from him in this, his hour of need. All your life he has been there for you, has loved you as much as is humanly possible.

Please come to St. Louis. Check at Fort Lyon first to make sure we are not still there. Come as quickly as possible. There may not be much time left to see Jake once more, and he very much needs to talk to you. I need to see you, too, to know that you're going to be all right through all of this. I am so sorry you have to bear this news alone. We love you, Lloyd. Poor Evie needs her brother. Life is going to change for us, and we need to stick together. Please don't judge your father until we have had a chance to talk.

God be with you. We will be waiting for you in St. Louis. Love, Mother.

He choked in a sob, wadding the letter into his fist and throwing it on the ground. He threw back his head and groaned deeply, loving his father, hating him. How could he do this? Why had he bothered to marry and have children, knowing the legacy he could one day burden them with? Why had he lied to him all these years?

So many things made sense now—the way his father always avoided details about his past, the reason he was so good with guns, the shoot-out back in California that he had first thought was just a dream. Now he understood why his father reacted so emotionally when he shot that squatter four years ago, why he had ripped the gun from his hands. He was afraid his son would turn out just like him, would grow to enjoy killing. Was that how it had been for Jake? Did he enjoy it? His own father! How could anyone shoot his own father? How was he going to live with that kind of shame, the son of a murderer, a thief, a rapist? That was the hardest to understand. His father had never been anything but gentle and respectful of his mother and Evie, a pure gentleman to any women he met.

Still, there was that mean streak he had seen just a couple of times. He remembered the night the man had shot up those squatters, downing them with a cold gleam in his eyes that was rare, but there, nonetheless. How many innocent people had he killed in raids and robberies? He'd been a gunrunner in the war. Maybe it was true that he was innocent of the charges he was wanted for; but that didn't negate the fact that he had done a lot of other terrible things. That much had been admitted.

What must Zane Parker think? That he had the potential to be just like Jake Harkner? Did he consider him a "bad seed" now? Maybe he was at that. It was already obvious Parker was going to make sure he didn't get anywhere near Beth. He wouldn't want her mixed up in this dirty business, and maybe the man was right. Beth was too innocent for this, too refined and well-bred. Why would she want to be married to the son of an outlaw?

God, the ache of it! He loved her so much. She was everything to him. He'd never find another woman like Beth, never feel that way about anybody else. He suspected that if not for her father, sweet Beth would be right by his side in spite of this ugliness; but her father was going to keep her away, and right now, for her sake, maybe that was best.

He felt as though everything his father had done had been laid on his shoulders. He never dreamed he could feel this way about the man. He had lost Beth, and it was Jake's fault. He would probably even lose his job here at the ranch. They would lose their home. Parker wouldn't want them there now. His mother had talked about forgiveness, but how could he feel anything but hatred? In a few short minutes his life had been shattered by a past he'd never known existed. He had trusted his father, looked up to him, held him up as a kind of hero, only to find out he was nothing more than a common, murdering outlaw who had even killed his own father!

He stumbled to his horse. Yes, he would go to St. Louis, but not for the reasons his mother wanted. *She* had betrayed him too. All these years she had known! Why had she even married the man? He would go to St. Louis and get some answers. He would confront his father with all of this. Maybe, just maybe, this would all get cleared up, and he would still have a chance with Beth, if he could find her. It all depended on what happened at the trial, what was done with his father, what other ugly things would come out about the man.

He headed his horse toward home. He would need to clean up and change, repack. It made him sick to think of going to an empty house, all the laughter and happiness and togetherness gone. There would be no more nights alone in the mountains with his father, no more hunting together, working together, sharing their feelings.

So, now he knew why so many questions had been left unanswered. After all the years of togetherness, all the talks alone over night campfires, he realized now that his father had never really shared himself at all. It had all been a lie, an unforgivable lie.

Beth lay curled up in bed, shivering at the news the doctor had given her. It couldn't be possible! She had been so sure she was only sick over her separation from Lloyd. If only she could find a way to talk to him, to explain! How could she go on living without Lloyd? How could she face never seeing him again? It wasn't fair of her father to whisk her away so quickly, not even to allow her to talk to Lloyd just once more. It wasn't fair that Lloyd wouldn't know she was going to have his child.

She had been in Denver eight days, eight days that had changed her life. Aunt Trudy was being good to her, but she could feel the woman's consternation. *Why didn't you talk to me?* the woman had asked her a thousand times. *I could have told you, child, that it takes only one moment of passion to become pregnant. How could you have done such a thing? You're so terribly young and impressionable. Your father never should have allowed you to see so much of that boy. It's obvious now that he's from bad seed. That evil young man took advantage of your love and your trust.*

Nothing she said in Lloyd's defense seemed to matter. She

had cried and begged her father not to make her go away, but the very day the soldiers had come and said those awful things about Lloyd's father, her own father had packed her into the carriage and whisked her off to the train at Colorado Springs and on to Aunt Trudy's. On the train she had become violently ill, and had suffered the same sickness every day since. Her father had become so alarmed that he called in a doctor, who, after a thorough examination, asked the embarrassing question of when she had had her last period. It had been at least six weeks ago, before that first time she and Lloyd had loved each other by Fisher's Creek. Then came the even more embarrassing question. Had she been "indiscreet" with some young man? Her tears and her crimson face had given her away.

She had never known such fury from her father when he found out about her and Lloyd. *Even if none of this had happened with his father,* the man had roared, *in spite of how much I liked the boy, I would have had his hide for this! I have a feeling Jake would have too! What makes it worse is all this mess with Jake! You're carrying the grandson of a murderer and a rapist!*

She had screamed that she did not believe that of Lloyd's father. She had never known him to be anything but a good man, a loving father and husband. *You know I'm right, Father,* she had pleaded. *You trusted him to run the ranch almost single-handedly for years! How can you believe all those things so easily now! What kind of friend are you to turn your back on him this way? And you know what a good person Lloyd is!*

I only know what the man is wanted for. Things like that don't happen by accident. I'd like to stick up for the man, and I might testify in his behalf because he saved my life once. But that doesn't mean I can let my daughter be involved in the whole sordid affair or be married to the man's son!

There was no arguing with her father, and now there was no denying she was pregnant with Lloyd's child. Lloyd should know, but her father was watching every move she made. She knew Lloyd would marry her in an instant if he knew. She had never been so miserable, and she wondered how it was possible to cry so many tears.

The door to her room opened, and she smelled the familiar cigar smoke. "Please, Father, the smoke makes me feel sicker," she told the man as he came into the room. He stepped out into the hall and put out the cigar, then came back inside, coming to sit by her side. She waited for another tirade, but the man seemed calmer now.

"I have decided what to do," he said, sounding heart-broken.

Her heart pounded with dread. "I'm sorry I disappointed you, Father, but I'm not sorry for loving Lloyd." She remained lying very still, afraid that if she moved the nausea would return.

Zane Parker sighed deeply. "The boy took advantage of you. I don't blame you now for any of it. I should have kept a closer eye on what was going on. I was gone too much, gave you too much freedom. It's been hard, Beth, trying to raise you without a mother. I took it for granted that a couple of weeks every summer with your Aunt Trudy and winters at the girls' school here in Denver would make up for it." He leaned forward, resting his elbows on his knees. "Something has to be done. I'll not have this child bearing the Harkner name. I don't even want other people to know who the real father is. I've already sworn the doctor and your aunt to secrecy."

More tears started to come. "But I have to marry Lloyd. I can't have a baby out of wedlock."

"That's right. You can't, and I won't even consider an abortion. Women die from such things, especially young ones. You'll have this baby, and you'll be a married woman when it is born. He or she will carry a reputable name and will never know he was conceived out of wedlock or carries the blood of an outlaw."

"I don't understand," she sniffled.

The man cleared his throat. "I have a friend in Chicago, a widowed druggist. He's thirty years old and very wealthy in his own right but also comes from a wealthy family. He owns several drugstores in Chicago. He never had any children by his first wife, but they always wanted them. You met him at the spring party. He was visiting in Denver and came to the ranch. You played the piano for him the night before the party. Do you remember? His name is David Vogel."

A terrible dread began to creep through her blood. "Yes," she answered quietly. She remembered an attractive young man whose hands seemed too white and clean when he sat down beside her and joined her in a tune. He had smelled like scented perfume instead of leather and the out-of-doors. He had seemed pleasant enough, a man of moderate build who wore very expensive suits. He'd had a bright smile, a pleasant personality.

"He's still here in Denver, on an extended stay because of an older brother of his who is dying of some kind of cancer. I remembered he was quite infatuated with you at the party. I had a lengthy talk with him last night, and he is willing to marry you and take you back to Chicago. He will allow everyone to believe the baby is his, and he has promised not to touch you until after the baby is born, and then only when you are ready."

Beth slowly sat up. "You want me to marry a perfect *stranger*?"

"He's not a total stranger. He's a very nice young man, wealthy and responsible, and, I might add, very generous to do this. Not many men will marry what they consider soiled goods." Pain showed in his eyes. "I don't like to put it that way, Beth, but you should know how most men look at something like this. It's a cold fact of life, and David is being very noble. You'll marry him, and that's that. It sickens me that you won't be able to attend that finishing school or travel to Europe, that you won't be able to do any of the things I had planned for you. Maybe David can see that you take a trip to Europe after the baby is born, and he has plenty of servants, so you'll have help with the child."

Beth just stared at him, feeling cold and damp and abandoned. "It's *Lloyd* I should be marrying! I love *Lloyd*! I can't be some other man's wife!"

"You have no choice. You've got to think about the baby now, not yourself. You've heard the charges against Jake. I've wired home, and Lloyd has left for St. Louis. God knows how long this thing will take, and if you're going to fool people about this pregnancy, you can't wait around. It's important to marry as quickly as possible so people will believe the baby is David's."

He leaned closer, his eyes drilling into her. "No matter what happens at Jake's trial, Beth, the charges against him are not going to go away. They will follow him and Lloyd both wherever they go. You can't do that to your child, nor can you take the risk of people calling him or her a bastard. The child is all that matters now. If you love the baby in your belly, you'll do what's best for him and forget about what *you* want! David is a good man. After a time you'll appreciate what he's done, especially when he loves that baby like his own. You'll learn to love him and be a wife to him. That's the way some marriages are, Beth. Not everyone marries out of childish passion, and that's all you had with Lloyd. When you're young, it isn't always easy to control your emotions. Lloyd should have known what he was doing was as wrong as it could be, that you were much too young for him to be taking advantage like that." He let out a sigh of disgust and leaned back in the chair again. "Sixteen! My God!"

"He just loved me, Father," she wept, lying back down. "And I love him. I *can't* marry David Vogel."

"You have no choice. You have to do what's right for that baby. Lloyd is going to be a very confused young man for a long time. He's better off never knowing about the baby. Once you're married to David, you've got to never say a word to anyone about the real father, never see Lloyd again."

"What will he think," she sobbed, "finding out I married someone else so quickly?"

"He'll probably think I pushed the marriage to keep you away from him. Let him think whatever he wants. You'll be in Chicago, away from it all."

Away from it all? "Don't send me away alone married to a man I hardly know," she begged.

Parker moved to sit on the edge of her bed and took hold of her hands. "I trusted you, Beth. You're my beautiful, precious, only child, and I know you think this is cruel, but I'm doing it because I love you and am trying to salvage what we can from this. I want to save your reputation and my grandchild's name. If it will make you feel better, Aunt Trudy will go to Chicago and stay with you for a while. Would you like that?"

Lloyd! He would be shattered. He would hate her. He would *never* understand this. So much of his trust in life and those he loved was surely already destroyed. The worst part was, she knew her father was right. She had to think about the baby, give Lloyd's son or daughter a good home, never let him suffer the ugly names people called babies sired out of wedlock.

"Yes, I'd like Aunt Trudy to come along," she answered in resignation. She turned away from her father. "I need to sleep. I wish I could just sleep forever, or wake up and find out none of this is true."

Her father touched her shoulder. "I wish it, too, darling. And I'm not deserting you. As soon as possible, I'll come to

Chicago and spend some time with you, and I'll come and stay a while when the baby is born."

Her throat ached with a need to cry again. "Will you love it, Father?"

He sighed, rising and leaning over to kiss her cheek. "Of course I will. I may not approve of the father, but my daughter is the mother, and that's all that matters. That baby has my blood too."

The man turned and left, furious with himself for not seeing what was going on with his daughter and Lloyd Hayes. If the boy were here now, he'd kill him! He'd do everything in his power to keep him away from Beth from now on, which meant forcing Miranda Harkner off Parker land. She would have to find a new home. He hated to do that to the woman. He actually thought her quite remarkable, but she knew the risks she was taking when she married Jake Harkner. She would just have to suffer the consequences, as would Lloyd. Beth came first.

CHAPTER TWENTY-SEVEN

Jake looked up as two deputies led Lloyd to his cell.

"That the young one?" a prisoner across the way spoke up. "Sure looks like his pa. Hey, boy, you've got a pretty famous pa there, famous here in Missouri, anyway. 'Course it ain't the nicest things in the world he's famous for. What's that other word? *In*famous?"

The man laughed, as Jake slowly rose, keeping his eyes on Lloyd. He supposed that if God wanted to punish him for his sins, He had found the perfect torture. He had let him get close to this son of his, love him, nurture him, feel his love in return, only to have it all be destroyed. What he had feared more than death was in Lloyd's eyes: shame, humiliation, hatred . . . yes, the hatred was there too. How well he knew what the boy was feeling, and he wished he had done something to cause Gentry to shoot him dead so he wouldn't have to see that look in Lloyd's eyes.

One of the deputies unlocked the cell door while another held a shotgun on both men. "No funny business," the first man said, letting Lloyd inside the cell. He closed and locked the door, and the prisoner across the way began his teasing remarks again.

"Shut up, Collier, or you'll get no damn supper tonight!" one of the deputies warned him. "You know I mean it!"

Collier just chuckled and went back to his cot, curling up with his back to Jake's cell.

"Have you seen your mother? Jake asked. "She's worried sick about you."

Lloyd swallowed. Could this be the same man he had loved and trusted all these years, had shared his dreams with over campfires? They should be back in Colorado, riding the line, laughing together. Jake Hayes didn't belong in a prison cell, possibly to be executed. But then this wasn't Jake Hayes. He was Jake Harkner, the outlaw.

"I haven't seen her or Evie. I didn't know where to look," he said, trying to keep his anger in check. "I went straight to the courthouse and found out where they were keeping you."

"Your mother's at the Carriage Hotel, but she's looking for a rooming house, something less expensive until the trial is over. Jess is with her, but she needs you."

The boy smiled bitterly. "Needs *me*? *You're* the one she needs. We *all* need you. Why in hell did she marry you, anyway? Did she know from the beginning?"

Jake could see already that the boy had put up a wall too high for him to climb over. It was going to take a long time for him to get over this, if he ever did. His chest felt tight, and it pained him to breathe. Lloyd! He couldn't have had a son to be more proud of. He didn't see him as a man, but as the little boy he'd loved so; the child who had ridden on his shoulders, laughed and screamed the first time he'd put him on a horse; the young boy who had struggled not to cry the day he gave him that first rifle.

"She knew," he answered. "She also knew I needed and wanted to change my life. She knew things had happened to me that led me into a life I never really wanted—"

"Like killing your own *pa*?" Lloyd sneered. He watched his father literally wilt. The man closed his eyes and sat down on the cot, putting his head in his hands. "As much as I hate you right now," Lloyd went on, "I couldn't *kill* you, because you're my flesh and blood! Only right now I have trouble calling you pa because I'm not sure I want to face the fact that a man wanted for murder and rape and robbery, a man who killed his own father, is *my* father! What does that make *me*? Do *I* have bad blood? Zane Parker apparently thinks so! He's taken Beth away, and I don't even know where! I *love* her! I need her! But she's gone, and it's all *your* fault! You've *lied* to me, all these years, lied about your past, about what happened back in California, *everything*! How could you do it? How could you kill your own *father*?"

Jake looked up at him, struggling against the old feelings of guilt and worthlessness Miranda had been telling him for years he shouldn't feel. He rose, facing Lloyd squarely. "You tell me what you would've done when you were fourteen years old, feeling like you did then about Beth, if you found me *raping* her!" His heart ached at the horror on his son's face. "What would you have done if you weren't strong enough to stop me, and you could hear Beth crying and begging you to let her go! What would *you* have done, Lloyd? I was fourteen years old, and my father was big like me! The girl's name was Santana, and we were friends, just like you and Beth! Sometimes you just do what you have to do! For a long time after that I figured I must be just as mean and rotten as *he* was, so I lived a mean and rotten life! I didn't give a damn about myself or anybody else! But you wouldn't understand that, because you grew up in a home filled with love! I've never raised a hand to you in your entire life! My father beat me practically every day of my life. He *murdered* my mother and my little brother! It wasn't until I met your mother that I began to learn the meaning of love, to learn how it felt to *be* loved! I made the mistake of wanting that to last forever, so I ran from my past. I wanted to protect you and Evie from the ugliness of it all, so I never told you; but the biggest reason was that I never wanted you to feel about me the way I felt about *my* father! I never wanted to see that shame and hatred in your eyes. I know how it feels, Lloyd. I know too goddamn well how it feels!"

Lloyd closed his eyes and turned away, grasping the bars of the cell. Jake's eyes teared and he reached out to touch the boy's shoulder, but Lloyd jerked it away. "Don't, Pa."

Jake took a little hope in the words. It was the first time the boy had called him Pa since arriving. He swallowed to keep from breaking down. "Son, if there was any way I could change all this, make us all just be back home, a happy family again; if I could erase all of this for you, I'd do it in an instant, even if it meant putting a gun to my head."

"Did you rape women?"

"No," Jake answered quickly. "No, I never did that. I'm accused of it only because of certain men I rode with. I've never raped a woman or hurt a woman any other way, never shot a woman or a child. You've got to believe that much. You must know that from the way I've treated Evie and your mother all these years."

"*Others* will believe it. They'll believe all the charges. Beth's father believes them, and he's taken Beth away somewhere." He faced his father. "I *love* her! We had even *made* love, more than once, made promies to always be together, and now he's taken her away!" Tears of anger and despair formed in his eyes. "How am I ever supposed to hold a decent job or marry a decent woman, being the son of an accused murderer and rapist? People will say like father, like son."

Jake quickly wiped at tears, hating to have his son see him this way, needing a bath and a shave, locked up in this hellhole. Would he also have to watch him hang, or be executed some other way? He didn't mind dying, probably deserved it. He just wished that by dying he could erase all of his past and ensure a happy life for his wife and children.

"They might," he answered. "But you have to learn to be your own man, Lloyd, to be proud of who *you* are. You have to be strong, to show them they're wrong."

Lloyd closed his eyes, a tear slipping down his cheek. "That night I shot that squatter, you told me you'd killed a few men, mostly in self-defense. How many is a few, Pa? Ten? Twenty? Thirty?"

Jake sighed deeply. "I honestly don't know."

Lloyd snickered bitterly and shook his head. "You don't even know. And they *weren't* all in self-defense, were they?"

"Some weren't, but most were. Men knew I was good with guns. The kind of men I ran with, I was constantly being challenged. Somehow it all got out of hand. I was young, full of hate."

For the first time Jake saw that dark meanness in the boy's eyes that made him look almost like the wanted poster of himself. "Well, that's how *I* feel right now! I hate your father, I hate *you* for lying to me, I hate Lieutenant Gentry for turning you in, I hate Beth's father for taking her away! I even hate *God* for letting all of this happen! Why did you even have us, Pa? Why did you let the evil seed of your father be spread any further?"

Jake felt as though the boy had rammed a knife into him. "Because I loved your mother, and she wanted babies. If she could have had more, I'd have let her have *ten*! She's a good woman, full of love and forgiveness. Evie is just like her. With you, I can see that forgiveness is not something that's going to come easy, but in a way I don't need it, Lloyd. I've paid my dues. The things I did were the result of years of beatings from my own father, of being called a bastard and told I was worthless, to the point where I *believed* it. The man standing before you right now is not the man who committed all those crimes. He died the day I met your mother!"

"Did he? Maybe he lives on in *me*, Pa! Maybe there's a side to me I don't know anything about. Maybe I should put on those guns of yours and go out there and find out who the *real* Lloyd Harkner is! That's my real name, isn't it? Harkner! Lloyd *Harkner*, son of Jake Harkner, the *outlaw*!"

Jake's reaction was instant. It was a quick reflex from a sudden need to stop his son from his foolish ideas. Lloyd was nothing like him! He must never go searching for that dark side! Not Lloyd! With the old force that controlled his reflexes before he could think, he slammed a fist into the boy, knocking him across the cell and against a cement wall. Lloyd slid to the floor, dazed, and Jake looked down at his fist as though it were a weapon that was not a part of his body.

"My God," he groaned. He looked at Lloyd, saw himself at his father's hands. "Lloyd." His breath would not come. He gasped to find it, shook as he knelt to help Lloyd up. The boy shoved at him; turned away. A deep gash on his lip bled profusely as he stumbled to the cell door and yelled for a guard to let him out.

"Lloyd, wait!" Jake growled. "Anything I've done was to keep you from suffering, to love you the way I was never loved."

Lloyd turned as the two deputies came back inside. He wiped at his bleeding lip, his face a livid red. "I've got a lot of thinking to do," he answered, his voice shaking. He gasped in an effort not to cry. "For the first . . . time in my life . . . I'm afraid of my own father. I don't know you, Pa. I guess I never did, did I? Well, maybe . . . you don't know me either."

One of the deputies opened the door. "What the hell is going on here? For Christ sake, Harkner, what kind of man are you, hitting your own son when he comes to visit you?"

"Just shows you the kind of man he really is," the other deputy put in.

"Better keep an eye on the boy there," Collier shouted from the other cell. "He's a lot like his pa, mean and stubborn."

Lloyd looked back at his father, tears on his face. Part of him wanted to go to the man and embrace him, tell him he loved him in spite of his past. He wanted to hug the father he had always known, but he couldn't bear to touch the man Jake Harkner once was. He needed him, but he wanted to hurt him like he'd been hurt. The look in Jake's eyes right now tore at his guts, but he couldn't bring himself to utter any words of affection. He turned and left.

Jake drew in his breath in a shuddering sob, all the old frustration and shame and hatred for his own father welling up in him and exploding in a rage pent up for thirty-five years. He looked at his fist again in disbelief, then slammed it into the concrete wall, over and over, so full of fury that he did not feel the pain. With every blow he growled like a wild man. He kept up the self-abuse until he literally ran out of strength and wilted to the floor, his hand bloody and broken.

Miranda braced herself, ignoring the dark dampness of the lower prison cells, ignoring the smell of sweat and urine. Jake hated for her to come here, but when the deputy sheriff told her Jake had badly injured his hand and had been seen by a doctor, she insisted on seeing him right away.

She struggled to stay in control when she was let inside his cell. He slowly rose, looking terribly thin, his face haggard. It was obvious he had not been allowed to clean up. He needed a shave, and his right hand was heavily bandaged clear up to the elbow. "Jake," she whispered, stepping closer.

"I told you I don't want you in this stinking place." He moved past her, leaned against a side wall. "That lawyer you hired came to see me this morning. You keep doing things I ask you not to do! You're going to need every dime we have left. Don't be spending money on a lawyer. There's nothing to defend."

She saw him now, the old, hard Jake. There was the meanness in his eyes, the old crust that refused to let anything else hurt him. This was the Jake she had first come to know.

"What happened, Jake? What happened to your hand? You're in terrible pain. I can see it in your face. You're pale, and you've been sick. What caused all of this?"

He smiled bitterly. "Lloyd was here. Didn't he tell you?"

Her eyes widened. "Lloyd! When? I haven't even seen him!"

He closed his eyes. "Damn," he moaned. "He's left then. God only knows where he's gone or what he'll do." He opened his bloodshot eyes, breathed deeply as he looked down at his hand. "I hit him."

She closed her eyes and sucked in her breath, knowing what must have gone through his mind. "Oh, Jake," she whispered.

"He said maybe he was . . . just like me." The words came in broken stutters as he refused to let himself break down. "He said maybe he should put on my guns . . . and go find out who the real Lloyd Harkner is. He's lost Beth because of me, and that's what's eating at him the worst. When he said those things, I lost control. I wanted to stop him . . . just stop him; but it came out of me the same way it used to come out of my pa, through my fist."

"Jake." She started toward him but he waved her off and turned away from her.

"The way he looked at me—" He breathed deeply. "I saw myself, saw all the hatred, the hurt, even the fear. I never thought I could hit my own son. After he left, all the old hatred for my own father and for myself just . . . welled up inside of me. I started hitting the wall . . . over and over until I passed out."

"I can bring you something for the pain—"

"I don't *want* anything for it! Don't you understand, Randy? I *want* to hurt! I *deserve* to hurt!"

"No! You're wrong, Jake! How many years did it take me to convince you of that? All that happened was your father's fault, not yours! And when you hit Lloyd, it wasn't out of cussed meanness like your father, it was out of love, out of a desperate need to keep him from suffering and making the same mistakes you did when you were young. When he has time to think all this over, he'll realize that. You've loved him too much over the years for him to turn away from that love forever. Jake, please let me hold you."

"No. It only makes it harder for me." He winced with pain and supported his right arm with his left hand as he walked over to sit down on the cot. "You've got to find him, Randy. You're the only one who might be able to talk some sense into him, make him understand. He won't listen to me right now." He met her eyes. "You have a way of making ornery men listen. You bring out the best in people. Jess can help you find him."

She stood in front of him. "He's my son too. As a mother, I see him as a helpless boy running around out there in a cruel world. You know I'll try to find him. I'll have the police search the city. Surely he'll come and see me and Evie, he'll come to the trial."

"Trial? There's no sense in even having one. I'm already a condemned man."

"The crime is twenty years old. We're bringing in people to testify as to the good man you've been over those twenty years. I'll tell the judge what a good father and husband you've been. We've even subpoenaed Zane Parker to testify to the fact that for years you've been his right-hand man, carried important responsibilities, risked your life to save a miners' payroll. The man might not want Lloyd near his daughter now, or want us on his land, but he can't deny the truth about the kind of man you've been these past years. I'm getting an affidavit from Betsy Price as to the kind of man you were when she knew you in California, and from Mrs. Anderson in Virginia City. The judge can't ignore the way you've changed your life, Jake. He has to take all that into consideration."

He shook his head. "Damn it, Randy, it doesn't matter. I've lost Lloyd. I did some terrible things and I'm getting my just punishment."

"Jake Harkner, don't you dare give up on me! All these years I've held on, stayed by your side through the worst of it. Be strong for me, Jake!" Her voice broke, and she turned away, her shoulders shaking in sobs.

She felt him touch her then. She turned and wept against his chest, took comfort in the feel of his left arm embracing her. "My poor Randy," he groaned. "You've always been far too good for me."

"No. Not nearly good enough. You're . . . the one who had the strength to rebuild your life . . . after all the obstacles . . . all the horror. I've always admired your courage, Jake. Don't lose it now."

"I don't think I can go on with my son hating me," he told her. She felt him tremble. "I can't stand it, Randy. You didn't see how he looked at me."

She rubbed at his back. "If you won't fight for yourself, Jake, then fight for that, for Lloyd. You never had the chance to confront your own father, to truly know him. You can't tell me you wouldn't have liked to be able to just see him once more and tell him that deep inside a part of you loved him.

You never got over his life ending through such hatred and hard feelings. Don't let it be that way for you and Lloyd. Some day he's going to see he was wrong, and you're going to want to be here for him when he does."

Jake pulled away and rubbed at his eyes. "The only thing he understands is that he's lost Beth. He admitted that things between them had gone a lot further than we thought. I'd be angry, too, if somebody caused me to lose you."

She touched the bandages on his arm. "Jake, your hand. It must be so painful."

"I'd cut it off if it would bring back Lloyd and keep him from trouble," he said resignedly. He walked to the cell door, feeling restless. "When is the trial?"

"Just a few more days, Attorney Mattson says. He'll be coming to talk to you again soon. Tell him the truth, Jake. Don't leave anything out." She rose and walked over to put a hand to his back. "Don't lose hope, Jake."

He smiled sadly. "How can I, with my ever-hopeful wife around?" He faced her, putting a hand to her face. "See if that attorney can arrange it for me to clean up and shave before I have to face the judge. Get me some clean clothes."

"I will."

"Jess with you?"

"He's out in the main area with Evie."

"Good. I don't want you walking around without him, understand? Some men get strange ideas about women married to criminals."

"Oh, Jake, you're no criminal. Not now."

"I mean it. Keep Jess with you. He'll watch after you, gladly." He met her eyes. "The man loves you, you know."

She felt herself blushing. "Jake Harkner, what makes you think that?"

"I don't think it. I know it. If something happens to me . . ."

"Jake, stop it! There could never be anyone else for me."

"You aren't that old and you're a beautiful woman. I need to know someone will love you, take care of you. I wouldn't mind if it was Jess."

Her throat ached with a need to cry. "I can take care of myself, Jake Harkner! I did it before you came along and I can do it again. Don't go pushing me into some other man's arms just yet. You might be coming home with me."

He shook his head. "You know I won't, Randy."

Their eyes held. They both felt the agony of needing to be together just once more. They would not make love again, never again enjoy the freedom and happiness they had shared for the last nineteen years. There had been bad times, but they had gotten through them. This was the worst, and, she thought, perhaps he was right. Perhaps he wouldn't be coming home, ever.

A guard came to the cell door then. "Time to go, Mrs. Harkner."

Miranda blinked back tears. "Keep faith, Jake." Her voice began to break. "Remember what I said, about how we were meant to be? I still believe it. God will bring us through this. Lloyd, too. You'll see."

He gave her a weak smile. "I'll see you at the trial."

The guard unlocked the door, and she stepped out. She looked back at Jake. They had not even kissed, and she knew he wanted it that way. "Good-bye, Jake," she said softly, re-membering the day she had said it years ago when he rode off and left her back in Kansas City.

The courthouse was packed, as it had been for the three days of Jake's trial. The general public, many for whom the days of lawlessness during and after the war were a vague memory, or younger ones who did not remember those days at all, were there out of curiosity, to see a "real outlaw." Others who had stronger, more painful memories of those days, were there to see that the "goddamn, murdering rapist" paid his just dues.

A few testified against Jake about the robbery and the abduction in question, and Attorney Steven Mattson, a young lawyer who had taken the case for Miranda at a reduced fee because she'd convinced him Jake was innocent of the charges, did an excellent job of discrediting some of them. He pointed out the fact that after twenty years, memories can become vague. After so long a time, how could they possibly remember seeing Jake at the scene? Several of the others in Kennedy's gang dressed like Jake did then, carried several guns, were just as big, some bearded.

Miranda was furious at the prosecutor for bringing up things totally unrelated to the specific charges for which Jake was being tried. The man kept mentioning other raids and robberies that "men like Jake Harkner" had committed be-fore and after the war. He put Lieutenant Gentry on the stand. The man testified that as a Confederate agent during the war he had bought stolen guns from Jake, guns Jake had killed to get.

Mattson protested vehemently. "But you had no reservations about *buying* those illegal guns, did you, Lieutenant?" he shot back. "Even though you knew men had died in their taking. I will remind you, Lieutenant, that there was a *war* going on at the time! Men do strange things in time of war. A lot of innocent people usually die, but it's forgiven because it was war. How many innocent people did *you* kill in the war, Lieutenant?"

The courtroom had broken into pandemonium for several minutes. Once the judge managed to calm things down, Mattson argued that nothing else Jake did or was rumored to have done should be considered. Affidavits from old acquaintances supporting Jake were read to the court. Zane Parker showed up to testify that he had indeed been a dependable ranch foreman for years, but Miranda did not miss the man's cool attitude toward her and Jake. There had been a brief recess after his testimony, and the man had stopped to talk to Jake.

"I'm sorry about all of this, Jake. I've done all I can do." He looked at Miranda. "I just hope you understand why I can't let your son see my Beth any longer. In fact, Beth has married and moved to Chicago."

"Married!" Miranda's heart fell.

"Who?" Jake asked. "And why? Why didn't you just send her to school?"

"I can only tell you the man is reputable and is quite fond of her. Marriage was the only way to make sure she didn't try to see Lloyd. She understands it was the best thing to do."

Miranda had watched after him in disbelief. The man had forced his daughter to marry a man she didn't love!

"This will kill Lloyd," Jake had told her. "Maybe he already knows." He had looked around the courtroom, as he was doing now, searching for his son, but still he had not come. There was only Evie, faithful Evie, who had wept so many tears and stayed by her mother's side through it all. She sat behind her father, with her mother and Jess.

Finally Miranda herself was able to take the stand. Jake watched her with an aching love. So brave and strong and devoted. She looked especially beautiful, in a russet-colored, beautifully pressed cotton dress with white lace trim around the moderately cut bodice. Her hair was done up in curls, topped with a fashionable hat that matched her dress and sported tiny flowers. She was every bit the lady, looking refined, sitting straight and proud, showing absolutely no shame or embarrassment for being Jake Harkner's wife.

Miranda's testimony as to the kind of man he was left the courtroom silent, until the prosecutor asked her to explain how she had met Jake. When she told about shooting him, a courtroom mumble grew to a near roar of gossip and laughter that caused the judge to pound his gavel in order to bring order. The prosecutor began badgering her, asking her about other violent incidents, Jake's work in Virginia City, the shootout in California. "Why in God's name did you marry such a violent man, Mrs. Harkner?"

Miranda watched Jake quietly for a moment. "I married Jake because I fell in love with the real man beneath all the bravado," she answered, facing the jury. "I learned about his battered childhood. His father beat him severely and often, killed his mother and little brother. You have heard the awful story that he killed his father. He did it because he was only fourteen years old, and his father was raping a girl even younger. He didn't know how to stop the man, so he shot him. After that, he was an orphaned young man with no direction in life, a young man who knew nothing about love, either how to give it or receive it. He led a life of wandering and getting into trouble. I taught him it was all right to be proud of himself, all right to let people love him. With me and through the children he found a whole new world like nothing he had known before."

"That's enough, Mrs. Harkner," the prosecutor interrupted.

"Let her finish," the judge told the man.

Miranda kept her eyes on Jake. "I have loved Jake Harkner for almost twenty years," she continued. "I have never for one moment regretted marrying him, and at his side I have known nothing but happiness. He has been a gentle man who never once raised a hand to either of his children. He never told them about his past because he loved them so much and was afraid of losing their love."

She looked up at the judge. "The man on trial here today, sir, is far different from the man whose picture is on those twenty-year-old wanted posters. The old Jake Harkner is a stranger." She looked at Jake proud of how nice he looked today, in spite the weight he had lost, the way he had aged. He was still her handsome Jake. She had picked out a pair of black cotton trousers and new leather boots for him. He wore a white silk shirt that made him look even darker. The collar of the shirt was dressed with a black string tie, and he wore a black suitcoat.

She turned to look at the jurors then. "Jake is a man with many scars, both physical and emotional, all put there by a violent, brutal father. He survived and brought himself out of that hell. He is a changed man, and the new Jake Harkner does not deserve to be hanged or put in prison. He has already suffered much worse punishment through his own struggles and nightmares. As far as the things he is charged for here, he was not with Kennedy's men that day. If the girl he helped that day were here, she would tell you he risked his life to rescue her from them. That's why Bill Kennedy searched for Jake afterward, for revenge. That is what led to the shoot-out in California."

She looked defiantly at the prosecutor, as though to dare him to come up with something else to try to make Jake look bad. The man glowered at her. "You're a clever woman, Mrs. Harkner, but then a woman who lives with a wanted man has to learn to *be* clever, doesn't she? She has to constantly be changing her name, lying to her children and her friends. She has to pretend life has been all honey and roses to try to convince others her husband is a changed man, because if she doesn't, she might suffer at his hands."

"I have never suffered at my husband's hands. I have suffered more these last few minutes under your questioning than I ever did in nearly twenty years of living with Jake Harkner."

The man's face reddened as several in the courtroom chuckled. The judge pounded his gavel and things quieted again. Jake's attorney rose, smiling. "Your Honor, I was going to ask Mrs. Harkner a few more questions, but she has already answered them. I daresay her testimony just now has done more than anything else I could say at this moment. I would like her to step down and I will call Mr. Harkner himself."

Miranda rose as deputies unlocked Jake's handcuff but left ankle cuffs on him, making it difficult to walk to the stand. As they passed each other, Miranda touched his arm. *Yo te quiero, mi esposo,* she said softly, giving him a supportive smile. If only the girl he had rescued were here to testify. Louella Grif-

fith, the court had said her name was, but there was no longer
any trace of her in St. Louis.

For close to an hour Jake was grilled. He refused to react
with anger or violence when the prosecutor kept bringing up
other facets of his past, including what had happened with his
father. Miranda was proud of his composure. He fully denied
having any part of the robbery in question, told his own story
of how he had found Miss Griffith with Kennedy's men and
had stolen her away from them and taken her home.

"Miss Griffith never said anything about anyone 'rescuing'
her," the prosecutor put in. "It was assumed she was dumped
on her parents' doorstep after you and Kennedy and the others were through with her. She suffered so much shame and
horror that she was delirious. Her family moved away without
a trace, probably to go somewhere where others wouldn't
know what had happened to their daughter."

"I can only tell you the truth about what I know happened," Jake answered. "There is nothing I can do about the
fact that the woman isn't here to back up my testimony."

The questioning finally ended, and Jake returned to his
seat, looking weary and beaten. The finishing arguments were
given, and the jury was sent to deliberate. Miranda watched
the guards take Jake out of the room and back to his prison
cell, and she sat down in her seat, putting her head in her
hands to pray. It was done now. His life was in the hands of
twelve people who didn't know him, didn't know the kind of
man he really was. Jess put an arm around her, and she allowed herself a good cry on his shoulder. She had told him
that it was not necessary for him to be there, but secretly she
was glad for his quiet presence and gentle understanding . . .
glad for his silent love.

It was only two hours later that the jurors returned and the
judge had Jake brought back into the courtroom. Jake turned
to look at Miranda when he reached his chair. She rose and
leaned forward, touching his shoulder and kissing his cheek,
not caring that others watched and whispered.

"I love you, Father," Evie told him from where she sat, her
eyes puffy from crying.

Jake nodded to her. "I love you too." He glanced around
the room again, and Evie knew he was still watching for Lloyd.

"He'll come back, Father. He loves you."

Miranda's heart ached at the words. Lloyd! Where was
their son?

The judge brought the court to order. People waited anxiously, some excitedly, as the foreman of the jury rose and read each charge. "Guilty" of robbery. "Guilty" of murder. On the charge of rape, "guilty."

Miranda gasped. People mumbled, a few sounded disappointed, others nearly cheered. It took several minutes for the judge to quiet them down. Jake turned to look at Miranda, deep pain in his eyes. If only he could hold her. Whatever the judge handed out to him in punishment, it couldn't be as bad as losing his son's love, having his marriage destroyed, knowing his daughter would go out into the world without her father's protection.

The judge ordered Jake to rise. Jake obeyed, facing the judge squarely. "Do you have anything to say, Mr. Harkner?"

Jake drew in a long, deep breath, suddenly seeing his father. *Well? What do you have to say for yourself, you little bastard!* Any little thing that went wrong was always his fault. *I didn't do it, Pa. Honest!* "I did not commit the crimes for which I was tried here," he said aloud, "but I rode with the men who did do them, so I suppose I should expect to be judged for that. I can only say that for the last twenty years I tried to make up for it."

"Mr. Harkner, I have no doubt that part of your guilty verdict was based on the known fact that you did ride with the Kennedy gang. We will probably never know the truth about the day of the robbery in which innocent people died and a young woman was ruined for life; but I must tell you that since twelve people feel you were involved, it is my duty to see you get the proper sentencing. However, I also must tell you that there is as much *lack* of proof in this case as there is proof; twenty years is a long time to remember details amidst such quick violence and shock as those involved suffered that day." The man glanced at Miranda, who sat wiping at her eyes. "You can thank your lovely, gracious wife for impressing me deeply with her testimony. I might add that your own testimony, the sincerity and love that show I have seen you feel for your wife and daughter, shows me that you are indeed a changed man. But, being changed does not erase your past."

The man cleared his throat and looked at some papers, then back at Jake. "I have given this a lot of consideration. I don't believe you are any longer a danger to society; however, that same society expects men to pay for their crimes. If they were not made to do so, this land would remain lawless, and we all know that is no longer so. Men like the Youngers, the Daltons, the James gang, are all either dead or in prison. It is true that the terrible war this country suffered had a great deal to do with giving birth to such outlaws, but a man chooses his own way, and he must answer for it. In weighing your punishment, because of your behavior the past twenty years, I am going to be more lenient than I would normally be. The punishment for your crimes would ordinarily be death or life imprisonment. However, in your case I sentence you to fifteen years in prison, with a chance for parole in eight years."

Jake closed his eyes. He heard Miranda gasp and break into tears. He knew what she was thinking, what he already knew. At his age, living in a prison, the sentence was the same as life. He was used to the out of doors, to the sweet mountains and wide valleys of the West, used to riding free on the back of a horse. The arthritis that had set into old wounds would only get worse staying in a small, damp cell where he couldn't get any exercise. He would not last fifteen years, probably not even eight. He'd been in local jails more than once in his younger days, had known men who'd been to the bigger prisons, knew what hellholes they were. A lot of men died there from tuberculosis.

"I feel this is a lenient sentence," the judge was saying, "given the severity of the charges. Your final destination will be determined at a later date, but I will request that you be sent to Joliet in Illinois, where I usually send those with long-term sentences. They have better facilities for such prisoners." The man pounded his gavel. "This ends the matter of the State of Missouri versus Jackson Lloyd Harkner."

The courtroom broke into loud talking, and Jake turned to Miranda. Evie was already around the railing and running to her father. She embraced him, as Miranda approached him more slowly, their eyes meeting in mutual understanding and horror. She knew that if her husband had to stay in a penitentiary for very long, she would never see him alive again.

The disappointment in her eyes tore at Jake's gut. She had tried so hard, had been so sure she could get him off with a lighter sentence. She came closer, and he drew her into his arms, hugging her and Evie both. "Let it go, Randy. End the marriage and get on with your life."

"No! Never!" she groaned. "Something will happen. It won't end this way."

"It's already ended." He kissed her hair, held her tightly when he felt her body tremble in sobs.

"Let's go," one of the deputies told him.

"No, wait," Miranda begged.

Another man pulled her and Evie away. Jake glanced at Jess. "Take care of her." His eyes showed their terrible grief as the deputies forced him to leave.

Jess put an arm around both women. "You two had better get on back to the hotel and get some rest. Randy, I'll bring you back tomorrow and you can see Jake. We'll find out where they're sending him. Maybe we can get the judge to send him out to the territorial prison at Laramie. There's lots of federal prisoners there. That wouldn't be such a terrible move for you, and we could maybe both find work in Cheyenne. That way you'd get to go see Jake once in a while."

Miranda pulled away from him, meeting his eyes. What a good man he was. There were more lines on Jess's face, too, now, put there by long years under the western sun. His sandy hair was streaked with gray, but he still had a rugged handsomeness to him. He had done his best to keep her spirits up, and he was doing it again.

"You knew I'd move to wherever they send him, didn't you?"

"I knew." Jess gave her a reassuring smile, but he ached inside, knowing he would never take Jake's place in her life. As long as Jake was alive and she was able to find a way to be near him, there would be no one else. He had accepted that a long time ago. "Let's get Evie back to the hotel."

She nodded, wiping at her eyes again and putting an arm around her daughter. "What about Lloyd, Jess? I'm so worried about him, and angry with him too. He should have been here."

"It's different for the boy. As far as him findin' us after we move from the Parker ranch, the men there will know where we are. If he shows up there, they can tell him. And he *will* show up, Randy. You'll see. Besides, don't think he hasn't been keepin' an eye on what's goin' on here. He might be pretendin' he don't care, but he damn well does. He'll know where they sent his pa, and he knows that where Jake goes, you go."

How she hated the thought of leaving the lovely home Jake had built for them in Colorado. More tears wanted to come. Jake had loved it there so much, loved his work there.

Life would never be like that again. Leaving that house would be the hardest thing she had ever done, but she would do whatever it took to be near Jake. She would not let him rot away in prison alone. She had to be stronger than ever now, for the children, for Jake. If she could find a way to be near him, she could take him decent food once in a while, nurse him if he needed it, do all she could to keep his spirits up.

"I've got to find Lloyd, Jess. I promised Jake I would."

"Then we will. I'll help you. But first we've got to see about talkin' to that judge and gettin' Jake sent to Laramie. After that we've got to get you resettled."

So, she thought, time to move again, from Illinois to Kansas, to Nevada and California, Colorado, and now either Illinois or Wyoming. This would be the last journey for her and Jake both. A few people stayed to gawk, and one reporter pushed his way through to Miranda. "What do you think of the sentence, Mrs. Harkner?"

It struck her then that she could finally use her real name. It seemed so ironic. For years she had wanted to be able to use it, but not this way.

She turned away, keeping one arm around Evie, and clinging to Jess's arm with her other hand. She had to be strong for Evie, but she didn't feel like being strong right now. It took every ounce of effort she could muster to keep from screaming. Jake! He was as much gone from her life as if he was dead.

CHAPTER
TWENTY-EIGHT

 Lloyd waited across the street from the mansion owned by David Vogel. He'd never seen a city as big as Chicago, had gotten lost several times, finally found the neat row of homes on the street where Beth was supposed to be living. Under a gaslight he looked again at the newspaper article he had spotted while in St. Louis.

Elizabeth Ann Parker, daughter of mine-owner and rancher, Zane Parker, of Colorado Springs and Denver, was wed to Mr. David Vogel, a prominent druggist from Chicago, Illinois, on Saturday, August 1. There was much more, about Parker's wealth, about how the newlyweds planned to take a trip to Europe soon.

Why had she done this? Had she been so quick then to judge him because of his father? Was she that vulnerable to her own father's wishes? This wasn't Beth. She had made him promises. She would have talked to him before doing something like this, explained it to him.

He was determined to confront her. He had intended to stay around St. Louis until the trial was over, had bought himself some whiskey and camped out in the wooded hills beyond the city to wait for the big day. Pangs of guilt stabbed at him for not going to his mother and Evie, not being with them through the trial, but anger and bitterness still burned in his gut like hot coals.

Because of his father, Beth was lying in some other man's arms. He had seen the article and had left St. Louis right away, feeling betrayed, even angrier. He hadn't even been given the opportunity to see Beth once more, to talk about any of it. It was as though someone had ripped out his heart and he was standing back staring at it. Knowing she was with someone else was worse than if she had died.

He had loaded up his horse and taken the train to Chicago, where he had spent three days trying to find the right David Vogel, the right address. Now he was here. All he had to do was find the courage to go over to that house and get the truth out of Beth, husband or no husband. He took a fifth of whiskey from his saddlebag and took another swallow. He'd gotten to like this stuff, liked the way it soothed the pain in his heart, made the ugliness of life a little less ugly. He tried to ignore the little voice inside that told him if he really loved Beth, he'd not bother her, the voice that told him she was better off. He took a deep breath, put the whiskey back and adjusted his hat, then stomped across the street and up to the double front doors of the elegant home. Lace curtains graced the frosted door-windows. He rang the bell, and moments later a servant answered. "Yes?"

"I'm here to see Miss, I mean Mrs. David Vogel."

"Mrs. Vogel and her husband are at the opera. Are you a friend? May I leave a message?"

"When will they be back?"

"Oh, quite late, I suppose. They're attending a small party afterward." The old woman smiled. "Mr. Vogel is enjoying showing off his new wife to all his friends, you know. Who shall I say called?"

Showing off his new wife? She belonged to Lloyd Hayes! No, Lloyd Harkner . . . Harkner . . . son of Jake Harkner. "Is she happy?"

"Well, as happy as a new young bride can be, I suppose. She is very young, but we're all helping her, and Mr. Vogel is terribly kind to her."

Lloyd nodded and stepped back. "Thank you." He turned.

"Sir!" the old woman called out. "May I give Mrs. Vogel a message?"

Lloyd looked back at her. "Just tell her I think I understand. Tell her good-bye."

"But . . . what is your name?"

"She'll know." Lloyd hurried down the steps and disappeared beyond the house lights. The old woman stared after him curiously, then closed and locked the door.

Lloyd walked back across the street and mounted his horse. Its hooves clattered against the brick street as he headed away from the rows of elegant homes and toward distant lights that told him there were plenty of taverns and wild women waiting in the night in a city like this.

So, she was happy, was she? Well, he wasn't. Did she care? Maybe he should listen to that little voice. His own life was miserable enough now. Why should he make hers miserable too? This wasn't Beth's fault.

He rode on for several blocks, passing buggies and trolley cars, finally coming into an area where he could hear laughter and piano music. More whiskey, that was what he needed, whiskey and women, cards and a good smoke. His father had always told him to stay away from those things, especially the whiskey. *Whiskey can make a man do foolish things,* he had warned. *Sometimes it makes him do cruel things.* Had the man been talking about his father? What did it matter? If his father didn't want him to drink, then he *would* drink! He would do every damn thing his father had told him *not* to do. After all, the man had lied to him all his life. Maybe whiskey and whores and gambling weren't so bad after all. Hell, Jess had taught him how to play cards when he was just a kid. If there weren't a law in this town against carrying weapons, he'd strap on Jake's Peacemakers. Might as well go all the way. He'd been practicing drawing those guns, was getting pretty fast at it, he thought. That was something else his father had never let him do—wear a handgun. Well, once he got out of this city, he was going to wear *two* pearl-handled, perfectly balanced Colt .44-.40's, the guns that belonged to the infamous Jake Harkner.

He rode past a telegraph office and noticed someone was inside working. He thought what a big city this was to have some businesses that were open all night. He drew his horse to a halt and tied it, walking inside. Might as well find out what had happened at the trial. "Say, mister, can you find things out from other cities, before they might hit the papers, I mean?"

"Like what?"

"There's an outlaw being tried down in St. Louis, name of

Jake Harkner. Can you find out if the trial is over, if he's been sentenced? It should be any day now."

"I can try, but it's probably already been in the paper, if the man is famous enough. The name sounds familiar to me."

"Yeah. He was a bad one."

The man looked at his pocket watch. "Only one telegraph office is open this time of night in St. Louis. I'll try them." The man began tapping out a message, and Lloyd watched the night life through the window. Beth was out there somewhere, being shown off by her new husband to his rich friends like she was some kind of trophy. God how it hurt to think of her going home to his bed tonight. "Now we wait," the telegrapher told him. "It should only take a minute or two."

Lloyd nodded, walking outside and lighting a cigar. His father had loved to smoke, but he had never cared for it, until now. Now he wanted to do it all, enjoy every aspect of life he had not experienced.

"Here it is," the man called to him.

His heartbeat quickened. Pa! He didn't want to care, told himself he *didn't* care. He walked back inside, trying to act casual. "Well?"

"Just a minute." The man finished scribbling. "Jake Harkner sentenced yesterday on charges of robbery, murder, and rape," he read. "Fifteen years in prison, possible parole in eight." The man looked up at him, alarmed at the sudden pale look on the boy's face. "You all right, kid?"

"Yeah. Sure. Where did they send him?"

"Says here he's gonna be sent to Joliet. Hell, that's a state prison just a few miles southwest of here."

Lloyd reached into his pocket and laid a dollar bill on the counter. "Thanks."

"This is too much, boy."

"Forget it." He walked out and untied his horse. Yes, maybe he'd leave Beth alone after all. Who was he compared to a wealthy Chicago druggist who could give her everything? He was just the son of a murdering outlaw. He'd drink away the pain, maybe get the hell out of Chicago tomorrow and go someplace where he could wear those guns. He sure as hell wasn't going to stay around until his father arrived. What use was it to see him now? It would only be torture for them both. Jake probably didn't want him to see him rotting in a place like that, and he didn't want to see his father anyway.

He'd go back West. Maybe he could find the real Lloyd out

there in the country where he'd grown up, maybe on some of the trails he used to ride with his father; or maybe on a different trail Jake Harkner had known, the trail of the outlaw. He needed to see that world, to know if there was a part of him that belonged to it as his father had.

His mother would probably move to Illinois now. Miranda Harkner would want to live near wherever her husband was incarcerated. How bitterly ironic that they would be living so near to Beth again, but the old friendships would be over. Nothing was the same now. Nothing.

Beth awoke and stretched against satin sheets, then pulled a pillow to her, wishing it was Lloyd. At least for the last few days she had not been so terribly ill, but she was still plagued with waves of nausea, and she could not eat. She told herself she must eat, that she had to start taking care of herself for the sake of the baby. This child was all she would have of Lloyd, a little piece of the love she had shared with the only man who could ever be in her heart.

What must he be thinking by now? She had no news yet of what had happened with his father. Did Lloyd know she was married? Did he hate her? Thank God David had kept his word not to touch her. He slept in an adjoining room, but he had made no attempts to come to her bed. She shivered at the thought of his ever demanding his husbandly rights. She could not let another man touch her. So far Aunt Trudy was still here, and that made her feel safer. Her father had only stayed the first few days, then had to leave. He had said nothing about Lloyd or his father, if he had heard from Lloyd. She knew that he wouldn't tell her if he had. He was determined to try to make her forget him, but she never would. He would always be with her every time she held her baby.

The door to her room opened. "Good morning, ma'am," her personal maid said, coming into the room with a tray of food. The old woman came closer, an ever-present smile on her face.

"Good morning, Louise." Beth liked the old woman, who mothered her as if she were her own child. "I still don't think I can eat."

"Well, you must try." Beth sat up a little, and Louise placed a tray over her lap. "Did you have a good rest?"

"Pretty good, I guess." *I would have slept better in Lloyd's arms.*

"Well, you got home so late, I didn't have a chance to tell you about your visitor."

Beth felt a quick rush of hope. "Visitor?"

"Yes, it was the strangest thing. He came knocking on the door late last night, and I do believe he'd had some little bit to drink. I could smell the whiskey. He asked specifically for you. When he found out you were not here, he asked the strangest question. He wanted to know if you were happy."

Beth looked away to hide the mixture of excitement and sorrow she knew showed in her eyes. "If I was happy?" Lloyd! "What did he look like? Did he give his name?"

"No, ma'am. He was tall, quite handsome, dark eyes and dark hair, as much as I could tell in the dim light. I would guess he was twenty or so. He said to tell you, well, he said, 'I think I understand.' And then he said to tell you good-bye."

Beth closed her eyes and put a hand to her stomach. "Take the food away, Louise."

"Oh, but you really must eat—"

"Just take it away."

"Oh, my, did I say something to upset you? Is he someone you're afraid of? Shall I tell Master David?"

"No!" Beth lay back against her pillow, struggling against tears. "No, you must not tell him. I'll be all right. Just leave me alone for a little while."

The old woman sighed, taking the tray. "If you don't eat by lunchtime, your Aunt Trudy says she will send for the doctor again. I know being newly married can be difficult sometimes, especially for one so young; but Master David is ever so kind a man. You'll get used to being a wife and learn to run this big house for him."

The old woman left, and Beth curled up against the pillow again. "Oh, Lloyd," she whispered. She had no doubt it had been him. He must have wanted to talk to her and then changed his mind. He had said to tell her good-bye. What an awful thing to discover on top of the shocking news about his father, to find out the girl he loved had married someone else. What did he mean by saying he understood? Did he think she had married because she thought he was a terrible person now and wanted to be sure he left her alone? If only he knew the truth, but that was out of the question. For the sake of the baby, she had to keep up this charade of a happy marriage, had to let the baby think David was its father.

Poor, sweet, trusting Lloyd. He had no one now. Everything familiar had been taken from him. Everything. She at least had the baby to remember him by. And what would happen to his father? How his mother and poor Evie must also be suffering. Evie had been such a dear friend.

She thought how she would trade all the luxury of living here in this mansion in Chicago, as well as all the land and riches she would inherit from her father one day, all for a crude little cabin in the mountains where she could live with Lloyd, if only it could be so.

Tell her I said good-bye, he had said.

"Good-bye, my love," she whispered. He would not be back. She knew it in her heart. Everything he had loved and trusted had been destroyed, and she in turn had not only lost the love of her life; she had lost her best friend. She wept into her satin pillow.

June 1888 . . .

Miranda waited impatiently for Jake to be brought out of the dark entrance to Wyoming's territorial penitentiary. With each monthly visit, all that she was allowed, he looked a little older, limped a little more. Sometimes she felt she was in a prison of her own, having to watch her husband slowly die, a big man cramped into a six-foot by eight-foot brick cell for most of the twenty-four hours of every day for three years now. He would never make it another five. Of that she was certain, and every day she prayed for a miracle that would see him freed.

She had suffered her own torture through all of this, and Jake knew it. That was killing him too. She had waited nearly a year for him to be sent to Laramie. During that year she had had to pack and leave the beloved home they had shared in Colorado.

She lived in Laramie City now, worked as an assistant to young Doctor Brian Stewart, who had come to Laramie a year ago from New York with a sincere desire to come to a place where he was most needed. She had delivered babies, helped remove bullets, and knew how to stitch wounds. Laramie was one of those cities that was still rough and sometimes wild, and there was plenty of work for the doctor, who was sweet on Evie. She did not doubt that before long he would ask for her hand in marriage.

Brian was not the least bit bothered by the fact that Evie's father was in prison. He was a good-hearted young man who in turn saw the goodness in Evie, but Miranda knew the man also was surely taken by the girl's exotic beauty. Evie was tall and dark, a woman now at eighteen, gracious and beautiful. How she wished Jake could see her, but he had literally begged her never to bring the girl to the prison. He didn't even want his wife to come, had asked her several times to divorce him and get on with her life.

She looked toward the doorway again. No, she would not leave Jake Harkner. For the first thirty years of his life he had known only loneliness and desertion. She would not allow him to know those things again, and she could not bring herself to turn to Jess, as Jake had hinted she should do. Jess had remained in Laramie, worked at the stockyards in order to stay close to her and Evie. They were good friends, and she knew Jess would like their relationship to be much more than that. There were times when she had turned to Jess, only because she needed so badly to let out her grief and let someone else be the strong one. In those times he had only held her, and sometimes she felt torn between two different loves; the deep, passionate, determined love she felt for her Jake; and the gentle, abiding friendship she had with Jess, something that in another time and situation could have been much more. Jake Harkner still owned her heart. It would always be Jake, whether they could be together or not.

She rose from the bench and paced, worried about getting back in time to help Mrs. Rose at the boardinghouse with supper. Besides working for Brian Stewart, she had taken part-time jobs cleaning and cooking for the woman, in return for rooms for her and Evie, which helped keep down expenses. She also helped teach at Laramie's little schoolhouse. She did everything she could to stay busy, so busy that she didn't have time to think about the past and everything she had lost, no time to think about how much she needed her husband beside her, no time to think about poor Jake rotting away in that tiny cell, dying not just from malnutrition and lack of exercise, but from a broken heart over what this had done to Lloyd.

She wished that for once she had news for Jake about their son, but for three years she had heard not one word. She had promised to look for him, but she didn't know where to begin. She had placed ads in newspapers all over the country, asking Lloyd to please get in touch with her. She had spent money on a private detective, who had come up with nothing. Jess had searched the Outlaw Trail a year ago, thinking the boy might decide to turn to men like those his father used to run with, but he had turned up nothing.

If only Lloyd would return, come and see his father, tell him he forgave him, loved him, Jake might survive this horror. It was not knowing what had happened to Lloyd that was killing him more surely than anything else, and worry over the boy was taking its toll on her own emotional health.

Finally Jake emerged from the prison entrance, four armed guards accompanying him. He limped toward her, the pain in his hip made worse by long hours in a damp cell with no exercise. She forced a smile as he came closer, and she rose from the bench to embrace him, but he just looked at her with that hopelessness in his eyes and sat down wearily on the bench.

"Why do you keep doing this, Randy?"

She sat down beside him, touching his arm. "Because you're my husband and I love you, and I need to keep seeing that you're all right." It pained her to see how much he looked like the old posters now. He had a full beard, didn't bother to shave anymore. His hair hung to his shoulders again, and the only difference between the way he looked now and when she'd first met him were the lines about his eyes, the hint of gray in his hair. "I don't want us to be complete strangers when you get out of here," she added.

He rubbed at his eyes. "What difference does it make? I'm not going to be around five years from now and you know it." He moved his hand to run it through his hair self-consciously. "I hate you seeing me like this. I wish to hell you'd give up. The next time you come, I'm not coming out, so don't even bother. This is all too damn hard on you."

"I'll decide what I can handle, Jake. Love doesn't go away just because things go wrong. This would all be much worse for me if I *couldn't* see you. Don't begrudge me the only bit of pleasure I have left."

He looked at her with the dark eyes of the old Jake, angry, full of hate for himself. *"Pleasure!* You call this pleasure?"

She watched his eyes, knew he was trying to discourage her. "Don't look at me that way, Jake. I know what's going on inside you, so don't pretend with me." The words were spoken almost as a command. "You say you don't want me here, but if I didn't show up for next month's visit, you'd die just a little more inside." She turned to a basket that sat on the ground. "I brought you some decent food. I'm afraid it's been fingered over by those damn guards. They always think I'm going to sneak a weapon in to you."

She opened the basket and took out a plate, then opened the lid of a pan inside the basket and took out two pieces of fried chicken. "Eat this," she said, turning and handing him the plate. "I have pie, too—apple, your favorite. And my homemade bread that you love so much."

He took the plate of chicken and stared at it a moment, wishing he had an appetite. "Have you heard from him?"

Her smile faded. "No," she answered softly. "I've tried everything, Jake. It's like he vanished off the face of the earth."

He set the plate aside, putting his head in his hands. "He could be dead. Maybe he got himself into trouble, got himself shot someplace where nobody knew who he was. Maybe he died all alone."

She put a hand on his shoulder. "Stop torturing yourself, Jake. I am not going to lose faith that Lloyd will come back to us someday soon. He's alive and well. I know it in my heart."

She felt him shiver. "I can't stand it, Randy, not knowing. He's been haunting my dreams lately. What have I done to my son?"

She rubbed his back, resting her head on his shoulder. "Jake, the Bible says that if you raise your son right in his early years, even if he strays from you, he will always come back. He will remember the good things he was taught, the love he knew, and that will sustain him when he becomes a man. It will guide him through the bad times, and he will eventually follow the teachings of his youth." She kissed his cheek. "You taught him well, Jake. You loved him as much as is possible for a father to love his son. He's going to remember that. He's going to realize that no matter what your past was, and no matter what is happening now, he had the best father a boy could have." She began stroking his hair. "I'll keep trying to find him, Jake; but you have to help me through this by giving me a little less to worry about. You can do that by having more faith in the love you and Lloyd shared, more faith in the goodness deep in Lloyd's heart; and by taking better care of yourself. Please eat something. It frightens me to see you this way."

He threw his head back and breathed deeply, wiping at tears on his cheeks. "How is Evie?"

"She's fine, and in love. I expect Brian Stewart to ask for her hand in marriage any time."

He picked up the plate of chicken and set it on one knee, but still he did not eat any. "You sure he can be trusted to be good to her? You sure he respects her, being the daughter of an outlaw and all?"

Miranda could not help a smile. "Jake, young women like Evie command respect no matter what their situation. A man can't help but see the goodness in her. She's sweet and intelligent, loving and beautiful." She reached into the basket to take out a loaf of bread. "She prays for you every day, Jake. You have to try to get through this, because Lloyd is going to come home, and both of them will want to see you free again. We can and will be a family again, Jake. All you have to do is hang on and take as good care of yourself as possible in this place."

He set the plate aside again, the chicken still untouched, and turned to face her. His eyes were bloodshot and watery, and they showed a look of near shock and disbelief when he met her own eyes. "You really believe that, don't you?"

She set the bread in her lap. "Of course I believe it. I've told you so every month since they sent you here. What do you think keeps *me* going?"

He shook his head as though he was looking at something startling and wonderful. "I don't know. I honest-to-God don't know how you do it, or why."

She touched his hand. "Wouldn't you do the same if the tables were turned? When will you ever understand how much I love you, or that *any*one could love you enough never to leave you no matter how bad things get?"

"But I know you're out there alone, working to support you and Evie, crying at night alone over Lloyd, no one to hold you, comfort you . . ." He turned away. "What about Jess? Is he still watching after you?"

How could she tell him Jess had not been well? It would only make him worry more. "He's still working at the stockyards. He visits once or twice a week to see how Evie and I are doing, and he asks every new stranger in town if they've ever heard of or seen Lloyd. He's a wonderful comfort and support."

He looked at her again, taking her hand. "You know how I feel about him, Randy. Sometimes a woman just needs the strength she can get from a man holding her in the night. I'd understand, if . . . ." He took his hand away. "Hell, I'm not getting out of this place alive, so don't waste yourself. You're still beautiful and—"

"You *are* getting out of here! I don't need any man but you, Jake Harkner! I love Jess, as a friend. He's been wonderful to me and Evie both. I couldn't have gotten through those first months of moving up here from Colorado and waiting for you to be sent out here without him; but there can't be anything more between us, no matter how much he might want it, or how sincere you are in saying you would understand. I don't want to hear any more about it, Jake."

Did he sense she had weakened once since last she was here? It had been for just a moment, late one evening after Jess had visited and Evie had left with Dr. Stewart to go for a moonlight walk. She had been so tired that night, had let her faith and hope weaken, was depressed over Lloyd. Sometimes it was just impossible to hold it all in and put on a show of courage. She had broken down and wept bitterly, and Jess had held her for the longest time. He had begun kissing her hair, her eyes, finally her mouth. It was just like Jake had said . . . it had felt so good to give it all over to someone else, to pull strength from his still-virile demeanor, to let his strong arms enfold her and shore her up.

Jess had wanted more, knew she didn't love him, but was willing to accept that, willing to just take Jake's place for a while if that's all there could be to it. He was willing to make love to her and risk the hurt of saying good-bye again once Jake was free, but she could not do that to Jess, or to herself or Jake. They had come so close, but she had made him leave. Truth was, he had not been back to see her since. That was almost two weeks ago. She understood and she ached for Jess, wished she could return his love, wished he had long ago found some other woman so she wouldn't feel this guilt for not being able to love him the way he deserved to be loved. Now he was sick with a bad cough. Brian had told her Jess had been to see him, that he suspected the man had lung cancer.

Jess! Poor, sweet Jess! And how could she tell Jake that awful news? She could only pray for now that Brian was wrong.

She looked down at the bread and broke off a piece. "Please eat something, Jake."

She handed out the bread, and he caught her wrist. "Something happened, didn't it?"

She kept staring at the bread. "No."

"Randy, it's been over three years, and five to go. It's all right."

She shook her head. "It's not all right, not in my heart." She met his eyes, her own misty. "You're the only man I love or want, Jake. If you really love me as much as you say, you'll stop talking like you're not getting out of here, and you'll stop trying to push me into some other man's arms. My place is beside you." She put a hand to his face. "Jake, you're letting your father win this fight. You're going back to being the man who thought he was no good, that he wasn't worth being loved. You're giving up, Jake, behaving like the little boy who would curl up in a corner after his father beat him and think maybe he deserved it. You didn't deserve it then, and you don't deserve it now. The strength I need isn't going to come from some other man. It comes from these visits, but then only when I see hope and determination in your eyes; only when I know you're going to fight to survive this and come *back* to me! You're giving up, and that's what shatters me. You fought so long and so hard to bring yourself up from the horrors of your past. You became a strong, determined man, a loving father and husband, and you released the goodness in your soul. And you smiled! You have the most wonderful smile, Jake, and someday you will smile again."

He studied her lovingly, wanting her so. "My God," he said in a near whisper. "I never should have ridden back into your life."

She smiled through tears. "Oh, but just think if you hadn't. For one thing, I probably would have died. For another, we never would have had all those years of happiness. You never would have found out what it was like to love and be loved, and you never would have had the chance to be a father and make up for all the things you missed as a child. Evie has already forgiven your past, and she understands, Jake. It will be the same for Lloyd. He just needs more time. You and Lloyd were so much closer, and a father and son share a different kind of relationship and trust. He'll come to realize

you kept your past from him because you loved him so much."
She squeezed his hand. "We *are* going to be a family again,
Jake. You'll see. Haven't I been right about everything else?
Didn't I say we were meant to be, and that you could lead a
normal life, and you'd love being a father? Wasn't I right
about those things?"

"Time's up, Mrs. Harkner," one of the guards told her.

She saw the tiny glimmer of hope in Jake's eyes quickly
vanish at the words. "You think about what I've said, Jake. My
strength comes from your own hope and faith."

She kissed his cheek, and he breathed in the sweet scent of
her, ached for her. Five more years was such a long time. Hell,
even if he lived, he'd hardly be able to walk by then. What
kind of man would she have coming home to her? A near
cripple. His hip was getting worse, and his right hand had
healed so poorly he doubted he had the strength in his fingers
to pull a trigger. What kind of work could he do? How could
she keep hoping like she did, keep talking like five years was
just two weeks away?

"Take care of yourself," he told her, kissing her forehead
in return. How he wanted to kiss her mouth, but that would be
torture.

"Take the basket, Jake." She put the bread back into the
basket and put the chicken back into the pan and covered it
again. "I can get it when I come next month. Please take this
back with you and promise me you'll eat it. Please, Jake."

He sighed deeply, picking it up and nodding. "I promise."

"Let's go," one of the four guards told him, nudging him
lightly with a the barrel of his shotgun.

Jake watched Miranda a moment longer. She stood there
straight and sure, showing pride and strength and trying to
encourage him with a weak smile. God, how he hated the sight
of her standing there alone. He gave her the best smile that he
could, knowing she needed to see some sign that he was not
giving up after all, and even though he knew a part of him was
already dead.

He turned away and followed the guards inside without
looking back again. The guards led him to his tiny cell, which
for the moment he was not sharing with another prisoner.
He'd had to pair up a few times, and it only made things even
more miserable in the small enclosure.

"Either of you want some chicken?" he asked the guards.
"I don't think I can eat more than one piece."

One of the men opened the basket and lifted the lid to the pan. "Smells damn good. You ought to eat it, Jake. Your woman brought it for you."

Jake took out the loaf of bread. "Just leave me this." He turned away and sat down on his cot while one of the guards locked the cell door. The men took the basket and walked off with it, one of them already chewing on a chicken leg. Jake looked down at the loaf of bread, broke it in half and put it against his nose and mouth so he could smell it. What memories that smell brought to mind, good memories of coming home to the smell of baking bread, being greeted by a slip of a woman with blue-gray eyes and honey-colored hair. What he would give to hold her again in the night.

CHAPTER TWENTY-NINE

Lloyd trotted his horse along the Milk River. Being back in the United States again brought back old aches and memories, but he had vowed not to give in to them. For three years he had lived in Canada under another name, working odd jobs, learning to enjoy whiskey to the point that it had gotten him into numerous fights and landed him in jail more times than he could remember. He had thought that by going away and shedding his infamous name he could somehow find himself, discover if he had it in him to be the no-good his father had once been. He expected he had proved that he could. He'd done enough drinking and fighting to earn him some kind of bad marks; and in trying to forget Beth he'd lain with plenty of whores, taking his need for Beth out on women who meant nothing to him, some pretty, some damn ugly, most forgotten by the next morning.

He was tired of Canada. It was too damn cold there for most of the year. Montana wasn't much better. He'd head south, maybe find a way to hook up with the kind of men his father used to ride with. He'd heard from plenty of men about the Outlaw Trail. A lot of men he'd run into in Canada were bandits and outlaws who had fled the States. They knew a lot about places like Brown's Park and Robber's Roost. Most of them had also heard about Jake Harkner, but he'd never told any of them he was Jake's son.

Maybe now it was time to find out what being a Harkner really meant, how people would treat him. One thing he had learned while in Canada was how to use his father's guns. They were damn good six-shooters, perfectly balanced, with beautiful ivory handles, and he figured he was as fast with them now as his father had once been.

He still wanted to hurt the man. Making a reputation for himself with these guns, making sure his father heard about it, would surely cause him some pain and feelings of guilt. His grandfather had been bad, his father had been bad, so there must be a bad streak in him too. It must be so, because he'd sure taken a liking to whiskey easily enough, and he didn't mind at all when he got into fights and landed in jail. He needed to fight. It felt good to hit and hit and hit, even felt good to get hit back and feel pain; but no man's fist had hurt him so deeply and fiercely as when his own father had hit him that day in his jail cell back in St. Louis.

Why did the look on his father's face that day still make him feel like crying? He didn't want to feel sorry for him. He didn't want to care. It seemed he was constantly fighting that side of himself that told him to go back, that tried to remind him of how things used to be between him and his father.

He headed south. What better place to prove his reputation as the son of Jake Harkner than along the Outlaw Trail? He liked whiskey too much to hold a decent job, and he wasn't about to give up the liquor. Maybe the only way to earn a living now was by the gun, the way his father had once made his money. There were still some pretty lawless places in the West. He'd find them, and the men who ran them. They'd soon learn that the son of Jake Harkner was to be every bit as feared as the father.

He had no idea if Jake was still at Joliet, or where his mother and sister might be. He didn't want to know. His mother and Evie wouldn't like seeing him like this. He didn't like hurting them, too, but if that was the only way to hurt his father, then so be it.

He drew his horse to a halt as a wave of nostalgia hit him again. He remembered his fourteenth birthday, the way Beth watched him, giggling and whispering with Evie. He remembered the pretty cake his mother had baked for him that day.

Most of all he remembered his father bringing him that rifle. He looked down at his gear. He still carried that gun.

Pa! a voice cried from within.

No, this wasn't good. He wasn't supposed to get these feelings. He reached into his saddlebag and pulled out a flask of whiskey, uncorking it and taking a long swallow. He liked the way it burned from his throat all the way to his aching gut. Most of all he liked the way it helped him get through the painful memories, made him reckless, made him feel like he didn't give a damn.

He took one more swallow and put the flask away, then lit a cigarette and urged his horse into motion again. From what he'd been told, the Outlaw Trail ended somewhere up here in Montana near the old Bozeman Trail. He'd find it and head down into Wyoming, check out a place called Hole-in-the-Wall in the Wind River Mountains. It was time to start telling men who he really was and see how many wanted to try him out, see if he was as good as his father with the infamous Peacemakers he wore. If he got real lucky, somebody would come along who *was* faster, and that would be the end of him; he wouldn't need whiskey anymore to end his pain. There wouldn't *be* any pain; just the blissful peace of death.

April 1889 . . .

A biting mountain wind made Miranda shiver, and she had never felt more alone, never realized just how much she had depended on Jess's friendship and quiet support. Now a preacher prayed over his fresh grave, and she could not control the tears. So much had been lost to her. She had still heard nothing from Lloyd, and the last time she visited Jake, he had tried to put on a good front for her, but he had a bad cough, and she was terrified of losing him the same way Jess had died.

It had been a long, slow, agonizing death. The man had wasted away, his last days spent in terrible pain, every breath a gasp for air. She had stayed right by his side, held his hand, and he had admitted how much he loved her. She had assured him she loved him, too, that if not for Jake, she would have gladly embraced him fully into her life. He had seemed com-

forted by that, and had clung to her hand in those last agonizing hours.

It didn't seem fair for a man to die like Jess had. And what
if Jake died that way? He would suffer alone in that awful cell
without her at his side. Evie wrapped her arms around her
mother. Thank God for Evie and her husband. They were so
good to her. They were after her to come and live with them,
but she refused. Newlyweds should be alone. Besides, she was
no shriveled old woman yet. She was only forty-three years
old, still slender and strong, still plenty able to take care of
herself. She had her work, enjoyed nursing others and birthing
babies. She had remained living at the boardinghouse, and
Evie had moved into the fine new frame home Brian had built
for her.

Miranda did not doubt that before too many months she
would be helping deliver her own grandchild. It was obvious
Evie was ecstatically happy. She remembered the glow of that
first time of becoming a woman. She had felt it with Mack, but
that was such a vague memory now. She had experienced it
again with Jake, remembered the wild abandon he brought
out in her, the almost painful passion and aching need. If he
could ever be free again . . .

Still, even if Jake were freed now, there would be so much
healing to do, and there'd always be the pain of Lloyd's ab-
sence that would keep them from being truly happy. Jake
simply had to live long enough to be released. His deteriorat-
ing condition haunted her nights, and combined with the last
two agonizing weeks sitting day and night with Jess, nursing
him, bathing him, trying to make him eat, wishing she could
help him breathe, she was exhausted.

"Ashes to ashes, and dust to dust," the preacher was saying.

"Oh, Jess," she whispered, wiping at her eyes again. "I'm
so sorry." She leaned down and put some wild geraniums on
the grave. She had found them sprouting up through lingering
snow on a hillside behind the boardinghouse, their bright red
beauty reminding her there was life after death, and hope in
times of darkness. "I did love you, my dear friend."

How was she going to tell Jake he was really dead? They
all knew it was coming, but the actuality of it still hurt. The
preacher said a final prayer, and she turned to Evie and wept
in her daughter's arms.

"He's better off now, Mother. He can finally be with the wife and daughter he lost in the war."

Several men who had known and liked Jess moved past the grave, stopped and spoke with Miranda.

"Some of the ladies at the church have prepared a meal," the preacher told the men. "All of you be sure to stop by Evie's house and have a bite to eat. Jess would have liked you to enjoy a good meal in his honor."

The men nodded and thanked him. "We'll stop over," one of them told him. "We'll give Mrs. Harkner and her family a few minutes here at the grave."

Everyone left but Miranda and Evie and Brian. The minister stayed behind to see what he could do to comfort them. Miranda was in tears again, embracing her daughter.

"You mustn't worry about Father," Evie was telling her. "He's strong and he loves you. He'll make it until he can be free again." Evie patted Miranda's shoulder. "And I don't care how much he is against it. I'm going with you to see him next time. I don't care what shape he's in or how terrible that place is. He's my father, and I love him. I want to tell him so. I want to see him again, touch him again."

"It will break his heart for you to see him that way," Miranda wept.

"He just thinks it will. I think he'll secretly be happy about it, and I want him to meet Brian." She pulled away. "Besides, I don't trust those doctors who work at the prisons. I want Brian to look at him. I want Father to meet my new husband, and I want him to see a doctor who knows what he's talking about."

"I think she's right," Brian spoke up. "I'd like to take a look at him myself, Randy, considering that bad cough you described. Besides, I'd like to meet this infamous father-in-law of mine."

Miranda managed a meager smile. Brian was a good man, a dedicated doctor. He was fair-skinned, with sandy hair and blue eyes, a sharp contrast to his dark-skinned, dark-haired wife. He was a handsome young man, not really very tall but built solid. He had a crisp smile and a wonderful sense of humor that helped put patients at ease. She was grateful that he was obviously good to Evie, for the girl simply glowed with happiness, except for today. Today they both felt the sorrow of the loss of a good friend. Evie had long ago taken to calling

Jess "Uncle Jess," and Miranda knew her daughter felt a painful loss at his death.

She wiped at her eyes. "We'll go next week. Jake will be furious at first that I brought the both of you, but he'll get over it. I long ago stopped getting upset at his temper. He's all bluff most of the time." She looked back at the grave. "Jess knew that too."

The preacher came up and put a hand on Miranda's shoulder. "Some of the ladies from the church have prepared a meal and are ready to bring it over to Evie's house as soon as you go back," he told her. He looked at Brian. "You make sure this woman eats right and takes care of herself, Doctor."

"Oh, no problem there," Brian answered. "She's my most important patient." He took his mother-in-law's arm and led her away from the grave and back toward town, noticing someone walking hastily toward them then. A man called out to her.

"Mrs. Harkner! There you are!"

Brian frowned, wondering who this was. Miranda and Evie both continued to be approached at times by curious onlookers or newspaper reporters, asking questions about Jake and about Lloyd. It irritated Brian to no end to have Miranda and Evie both harassed by rude people who kept bringing up painful memories for them. When they had first arrived in Laramie City, they had been followed around almost constantly, but for the past year things had finally died down and they had been pretty much left alone.

"I'm Tom Chadwick, from Cheyenne," the stranger told them. "I've just moved here to start my own newspaper. I, uh, I heard all about you, saw you coming up here today for a burial. I wondered if you could tell me a little bit about the man who died. Did he know Jake Harkner? Did he ride with him once?"

"For Pete's sake, mister, can't you see these women are in mourning?" Brian fumed. "What a damned rude thing to do!"

The man reddened. "Well, I just . . . I thought—"

"Jess York was his name," Miranda put in. "He was my husband's best friend. They knew each other back during the war. Jess had lost his wife and daughter to raiding Union soldiers, so he took to gunrunning for the Confederates. Is that enough for your story, Mr. Chadwick?"

The man whipped out a pad of paper and a pencil. "Yes, yes." He met her eyes. "Mr. York stayed here in Laramie with you and your daughter then, to kind of watch over you while you wait for your husband to be released?"

"He was a loyal friend," Miranda answered, suspicious of what the man was thinking. "Yes, he had promised Jake to watch out for us."

"That's enough," Brian said, leading Miranda away from the man.

"Oh, wait! Mrs. Harkner, I heard something in Cheyenne you might want to know."

Miranda stopped and turned, hoping for news about Lloyd. "Yes?"

Chadwick shoved the pad of paper back into a pocket on the inside of his winter coat. "Someone called me from the newspaper office in Cheyenne. Great inventions, those telephones, aren't they? Who would ever have thought a while back that there would be railroads connecting East and West, or contraptions we could talk into and speak to somebody miles away?"

Miranda thought how wild this West was when she and Jake first came out here. So much had changed. "Yes, they truly are a miraculous invention. What did you hear from Cheyenne, Mr. Chadwick?"

"Well, they say it was a Lieutenant Gentry who turned in your husband four years ago. Is that right?"

The remark brought a sharp pain to Miranda's heart. "Yes."

Chadwick grinned. "Well, ma'am, maybe it will give your husband a little satisfaction to know Gentry is dead. He was transferred from Colorado to Arizona. He'd gotten promoted to general, so he decided to stay in the army. At any rate, he was out on patrol, and he and his men were attacked by renegade Apaches. Killed every last one of them. Tortured and scalped them. I just thought maybe you'd like to know."

Miranda felt a glimmer of the satisfaction of revenge, but it was dimmed by the fact that Gentry's death had come too late to help her husband. "Yes," she answered. "It's just too bad that didn't happen a few years earlier. If it had, my husband wouldn't be rotting away in prison right now, and we would still have our son with us." She faced the man squarely. "Don't bother me again, Mr. Chadwick, unless you have news about my son." She turned away and headed toward town with the preacher and Brian and Evie.

So, she thought, Lieutenant Gentry was dead. What good

did that do anyone now, except the satisfaction of knowing perhaps he had never even got to spend all his bounty money. She hoped he was tortured longer than any of the others, that he was now burning in hell!

Jake stayed on his cot when the new prisoner was brought in along with a second cot. Two guards positioned the legs of the upper cot into the holes in the legs of Jake's cot to create a bunk bed for the new man who would share the tiny cell with Jake. Jake made no move to get up, stared at the springs overhead, hated the closed-in feeling that engulfed him when he had to look up at another bed.

"You get to stay with somebody famous," a third guard told the new man. "Your bunkmate is Jake Harkner. Used to be the fastest gun anywhere around till he busted up his own hand in a temper fit." The guard chuckled and the other two left the cell. The third man closed and locked the door. "Next meal is at six, Peterson. Try to get along with Harkner. He gets a little ornery sometimes. Maybe the two of you can practice drawing on each other to keep busy." He laughed again and turned away.

"Fuck you," the one called Peterson muttered. He turned to Jake. "You *really* Jake Harkner?"

Jake felt the cough coming again and he sat up to clear his lungs. This cough was getting worse, and he wondered if he had tuberculosis, or maybe he was dying from the same lung disease that had killed Jess. Poor Jess. Jake had gotten the news in a letter from Miranda. His best friend was dead, and he had wanted to die himself at the news. Another ray of hope was gone, and now Miranda was even more alone. He coughed for several seconds before he could answer his new cellmate. "Yeah, I'm Jake Harkner," he finally answered, "and I'm not feeling too great, so don't try to strike up a conversation." He felt like he was burning up with fever, yet he felt cold at the same time. He pulled a blanket around his shoulders.

"I'll be damned," the one called Peterson answered. "Ain't that a coincidence? I get put in with Jake Harkner. Hell, man, you *are* famous! I read about your trial and all." The man rubbed at the scratchy prison suit he'd been given to wear. "These things ever get any softer?"

"Never," Jake answered, lying back down, shivering in spite of the sweat on his brow. "You'll get used to it."

Peterson looked around the small cell. "I don't think so."

Jake watched him a moment, always hating having to get used to some new man. Peterson was perhaps a little younger than he, not quite six feet tall, he guessed. He was freshly shaved, a requirement of every new prisoner, although once inside, the opportunity to bathe and shave came up only once a week. He looked like a man who had led a hard life. His face showed several scars from cuts, probably from fights, and two teeth were missing on the bottom. His dark hair was thinning, and he had the paunchy look of a man who drank too much and didn't take very good care of himself.

"This is what I get for stealin' a few horses," he grumbled, standing at the bars and trying to see down the narrow hallway of cells. "I couldn't help killin' that damned rancher. The guy was shootin' at me. What was I supposed to do?" He turned and faced Jake. "Hell, there was a time when a man could get away with murder out here. Not anymore. The West is gettin' too damned civilized, you know it? Too damned civilized. I expect you feel that way too." He rubbed at his chin. "I've heard a lot about you. Men on the old Outlaw Trail talk about you a lot."

"I said I didn't want to carry on a conversation right now." Damn the pain in his chest. God, it hurt just to breathe.

Peterson shrugged. "Fine with me." He sat down on the one stool in the cell. "I guess that means you don't want to hear about your son."

The mention of Lloyd made Jake sit up so suddenly that he hit his head on the frame of the top bunk. He winced and put a hand to his head, glaring then at Peterson, forgetting about his cough, his fever and chills, the pain in his chest. "My son? You've heard of him? Seen him?"

Peterson grinned. "I figured as much. The kid ain't been to see you, has he? How long you been in here?"

"Four years." Jake rose, walking over to stand at the cell door, grasping one of the bars. The cough overcame him again, and it took him several seconds to find his breath again. "What about Lloyd? What do you know?"

Peterson frowned at the sudden desperate look in Jake's eyes. He shook his head. "The kid ought to come see his pa. He's carryin' a big grudge, aint' he? That's too bad. You don't

look too good, Harkner. You got TB or somethin'? The boy
ought to know you've got that cough."

Jake ran a hand through his damp hair. "I'll be all right.
Just tell me what you know about my son. Where is he? I'll
give you a month's ration of cigarettes if you'll tell me what
you know."

Peterson chuckled. "Hell, you don't have to pay me to tell.
Men like us, we have to stick together. Hell, I feel honored
just bein' in the same cell with you. How long you in for?"

"Four more years. You?"

"Ten. Ten fucking years." The man let out a sigh and rose.
"You want a smoke?" He walked over to his little sack of
supplies and took out a cigarette.

"I'll smoke my own. Right now my chest hurts too much."
Jake coughed again, wondering if he could get himself well
enough to break out of this place and get to Lloyd. "What
about my son?"

Peterson lit his cigarette and sucked on it for a moment. "I
seen your boy at Brown's Park, on the Outlaw Trail. The kid
has taken to drinkin' rotgut whiskey, pretty heavy." He saw
the pain in Jake's eyes. "Maybe you don't want to know it all,
seein' as how you're cooped up in here and can't do nothin'
about it."

Jake turned away. "You can tell me."

Peterson sighed. "Well, he's carryin' a big chip on his
shoulder. Goes around spoutin' to everybody about how his
father is the notorious Jake Harkner, how he killed a lot of
men, killed his own pa, robbed trains and banks. He wears
your guns, shows them off to people, brags about how he's just
as good with them as you were."

Jake felt the nausea growing in his stomach. Lloyd was
doing the very thing he had dreaded most, doing it just to hurt
him, he was sure. "*Is* he as good?"

"Well, I ain't never seen you in action, so I can't compare.
I will say, the boy's good. He killed two men who tried to
prove otherwise. He's ridin' with cattle rustlers now."

Jake literally bent over in pain. He moved back to his cot
and sat down, putting his head in his hands.

"Hey, I'm sorry, Harkner. You asked."

"It's all right." Jake coughed again. "I've got to find him,"
he said then. "I've got to get out of here somehow and find
him, stop him from throwing his life away."

"You ain't gonna get out of this place except by some

miracle, mister. Do you know how fast they'd shoot you down
if you tried to escape? Besides, you don't look in any shape to
be tryin' to break out of here and run. Fact is, you don't look
too good at all."

Lloyd! Jake hardly heard what the man was saying. Lloyd
was out there somewhere, asking to get himself shot or
hanged or thrown in prison just like himself. What was he
going to do with Jess dead? Who was there to go and find
Lloyd? He didn't dare tell Miranda what he knew. The
damned, stubborn woman would be crazy enough to try to find
Lloyd by herself. It would be just like her to take that Winchester and that stupid little pistol and ride into outlaw country to find her son. She was brave enough and he knew she'd
do anything to find the boy.

Boy. He wasn't a boy anymore. He was twenty-two years
old and asking to die young. Things were different now than
when he was Lloyd's age. There was more law now. Men
didn't get away with things like they used to. If some gun-
slinger didn't get Lloyd, some lawman would, if he wasn't
stopped.

What the hell was he going to do? God, how he missed
Jess! Jess would have gone after the kid if he could have.
There was no other man he knew who could have gone into
outlaw country and knew how to handle himself. Jess had
lived in those places before, knew how to handle those kind of
men. He sure couldn't expect that Eastern doctor husband of
Evie's to go after Lloyd. Brian wouldn't last two days in country like that, around men like that.

He lay back on the cot, wishing his chest didn't hurt so
much, wishing he didn't feel so dizzy all the time. He needed
to be stronger, needed to get out of this place and find Lloyd.
It had been hard enough keeping insanity away, penned up in
this place, but now, knowing where Lloyd was, what he was
doing, he really *would* go crazy being stuck here and unable to
do anything about it. The hell of it was, he couldn't even tell
Randy.

"Damn!" he groaned. He sat up again, and Peterson
backed into a corner at the dark look in Jake's eyes. Jake
walked over and picked up the short stool Peterson had sat on
earlier. He slammed it against the cell door, busting it into
several pieces. "Guard!" he screamed. He turned and ripped
the mattress off the top bunk, threw it down. He lifted the

frame, springs and all, and threw it at the bars. "Get me out of here!" he roared.

Two men came in to see what the commotion was about. "What the hell—"

"Get me the hell out of here!" Jake yelled. "I've got to go find my son!" He grasped the bars, his eyes wild and menacing.

"Hey, do somethin' with this maniac before he turns on *me*," Peterson hollered.

"Calm down, Harkner! You've got four years to go before you get out of here! Pick up that bunk and put it back where it belongs!"

Jake reached out and grabbed the man's shirt, slamming him up to the bars. "You get me out of here—*now*!"

One of the other guards slammed a nightstick down over Jake's wrist, bringing new pain to the already partly crippled hand. He cried out and let go of the first guard's shirt. He turned then, picking up the slop bucket and throwing it at the guards, showering them with urine and excrement.

"Goddamn sonofabitch!" one of them cursed. He unlocked the cell door, and the second guard called for help, then joined the first man in trying to wrestle Jake to the floor to get handcuffs on him. Other men in the prison began rooting for Jake as he fought the men wildly. Peterson moved out of the cell and backed away as more guards rushed in. Jake held his own for the first few seconds, getting in some solid blows with a fierce strength few thought he had for being so sick; but there were too many guards and he was too weak to hold up for long.

Jake was quickly showered with fists, feet and nightsticks until he lay groaning in a pool of his own blood. The prison warden hurried into the wing where he'd heard there was trouble, and he winced at the sight and smell. "What the hell happened here?" he demanded.

"I don't know," one of the original guards answered, his mouth bleeding badly. He wiped at the blood and turned to Peterson. "What the hell did you say to him when we put you in here?"

Peterson shrugged. "I just told him I'd seen his son at Brown's Park, told him he was good with guns now, shot two men in a gunfight. He went crazy."

"What a damn mess," the warden growled. "Hell, everybody knows he asks about that son of his all the time." He ran a hand through his hair. "Damn. His wife is due to visit him tomorrow. What's she going to think when she sees him like this? That woman can be a real she-cat when it comes to how we treat her husband."

"We'd better get him to the hospital ward. He's been burning up with fever as it is," one of the guards told him.

"Why wasn't I told?"

The man shrugged. "Men get sick all the time. You know that, Warden."

The warden stepped closer, glowering at the guard. "Yeah? Well, they aren't all Jake Harkner either. They don't have the public asking about them all the time, or a watchdog of a wife coming to see them." He sighed, looking down at Jake's battered face. "Get him to the hospital ward and see what you can do with him. Find that doctor we use, and I'll try to find some excuse to keep his wife from seeing him tomorrow."

Four men moved to pick up Jake and they carried him out.

"Clean up this mess!" the warden barked to those remaining. He turned to follow the others. "I'll have one hell of a time keeping this from his wife."

CHAPTER THIRTY

 Miranda ignored the cold mountain wind that chilled her to the bone. It seemed that winter just did not want to let go this year, and the weather over the last couple of warm spring days had turned again to a damp cold, with a mixture of sleet and snow spitting through the air. For the moment she was too angry and worried to care that she was standing in the ugly weather while Brian and Evie waited in Brian's enclosed buggy at the prison gate.

"I want the truth," she demanded of the guard at the gate. "Why can't I see my husband? I've never been refused before!"

"Ma'am, it's the warden's orders, that's all."

Miranda saw the look of nervousness and guilt in the guard's eyes. She stepped closer, her eyes on fire. "Well, you go back and tell the warden that I am going to stand right here until I'm allowed inside! I don't care if it takes all night or if I die from the exposure! And you tell him that if I'm not allowed in by morning, I will phone or wire or write every damn newspaper in every major city in this country, as well as the judge for Jake's case and Congress and anybody else who will listen! I'll tell them all kinds of stories about this place, some true and some *not* true; but by God, your warden will get more attention than he'll ever want! Something has happened to my husband that he doesn't want me to know about, so you just tell him that if he'll let me see him, I'll keep quiet! If he doesn't, he'll be out of a job! I'll make sure of it! I have already been writing letters to Washington about prison reform, mister, and Wyoming is going to become a state soon. When it does, I'll be among the first to see about better treatment for prisoners at *this* facility! You tell your warden he can save himself a lot of headaches if he lets me see my husband right now!"

The man scowled at her, then turned and left.

"Mother, what's wrong?" Evie shouted.

Miranda walked back to the carriage. "I don't know yet. Something has happened to Jake. They won't let me see him, but I'm not leaving until they do! You two wait here. I'm staying right at that gate!"

Miranda stormed back to the gate and Brian shook his head. "She's something, isn't she? It's not good for her to be out in that cold, you know."

Evie smiled. "She'd walk through fire to see my father. I guess it's her love for him that helped me forgive his past. If she could love him that much, marry him in spite of his past, I guess as his blood child, I certainly had no reason not to love and forgive him. He was always good to me and Lloyd, Brian. I just don't understand how Lloyd could stay away. It's killing Father."

"Feelings are different sometimes between men than women. I think a boy expects more of his father than a girl. There's a special bond between a father and a son. From what you tell me, your father and Lloyd were pretty close. Lloyd must have felt betrayed when he heard the truth, maybe thinks he's no good now because his father and grandfather were no good."

"But father *is* good. He was *always* good to Lloyd. I think Lloyd is angrier over losing Beth because of all this than anything else." Evie watched the guard return and begin unlocking the gate. She smiled. "I don't know what Mother told him, but they're letting her in." A few more words were exchanged between Miranda and the guard, and then Miranda turned and walked back to the buggy, a kind of terror showing in her eyes.

"You can both come. Bring your bag, Brian. Jake's been hurt and he's even sicker than the last time I was here! The guard says you can look at him. I don't trust the prison doctor."

Brian and Evie climbed down, and Brian tied the buggy horse. They followed the guard inside, and Evie shivered at the cold dampness of the place, wondering if all the cells were this cold. They were led through a narrow hallway to a door where a man in a suit waited for them.

"Mrs. Harkner." The man nodded.

Miranda folded her arms. She had met the warden a few times before, and there were no good feelings between them. She saw the look of anger mixed with worry in his dark eyes. He was a short, balding man, with a hard mouth and a round, fat face. It irritated her that he obviously ate well, while most of the prisoners looked malnourished after several months in his prison. "Warden Pruett," she acknowledged. "What has happened to my husband?"

The man glanced at Evie and Brian, then back at Miranda. "I trust you will keep your word, about not spreading lies and rumors about this place?"

"I will. But I'm not so sure I can keep quiet about the truth," Miranda answered boldly. "What *is* the truth, Mr. Pruett?"

The man sighed, putting his hands on his hips. "The truth is your husband brought this on himself. I was about to put him here in the medical ward anyway because of his cough and fever, but he went into a rage yesterday, tore bunks apart, broke a stool to pieces, threw a chamber pot at the guards and showered them with the filth in it. He had to be stopped before he hurt the other man in his cell or hurt himself."

"Stopped? What did your guards do to him? He's fifty-three years old, for God's sake!"

Pruett scowled. "Look, Mrs. Harkner, when your husband loses his temper, he fights like a *twenty*-three-year-old! I have a few guards with split lips and cracked ribs to prove it! It took six men to get him under control, and the only way they could do it was to beat him into unconsciousness. I'm sorry, but they had no choice. He's come around a little, but he's in pretty bad shape. If you'll keep quiet about this, I'll let your son-in-law here take a look at him, and I'll allow you to stay with him through the night, if you like."

Miranda put a hand to her chest, feeling literal pain. Jake, sick and beaten. She struggled against tears. "I would like that very much. What brought this on, Mr. Pruett?"

The man ran a hand over his balding head. "I'm not sure. We brought in a new prisoner to his cell yesterday. The man apparently had some news about your son Lloyd."

"Lloyd!" Evie stepped closer. "What about him? Can we talk to this other prisoner?"

"We'll see. All I know is what he told me—that he'd told Jake he'd seen Lloyd along the Outlaw Trail, at Brown's Park, I think. Said Lloyd was drinking heavily, wearing his father's guns. He shot two men in two separate gunfights and he might be riding with rustlers. Your father just went kind of crazy then, yelling for the guards, demanding he be let out so he could go to his son."

"My God," Miranda whispered, turning to Evie. "It's all the things he dreaded most, that Lloyd would turn to the kind of life he once led." She closed her eyes. "With Jess gone, he must feel he's the only one who could find and help Lloyd now. He'll want to stop him before it's too late for him. He must feel so helpless, so desperate."

"He's going to have to live with it or be chained in solitary," Pruett told her. He opened the door to a long, narrow room with ten cots in it. Only three of the cots were occupied. A guard stood at the other end of the room. "He's in the third bed over there."

Miranda hurried inside, her whole body aching with dread, for both her son and Jake. Lloyd! Her little boy, that was how she still thought of him, her precious son. She could still remember vividly the look on Jake's face when he first held him, the desperation in his eyes when he made her promise never to tell his son about his past. What a terrible mistake that had been! Now Lloyd was out there risking being shot, drinking heavily. It wasn't the Lloyd she had always known, her sweet, trusting, loving son. If only he hadn't lost Beth on top of everything else. He might have been all right if not for that.

She drew in her breath and made a little choking sound at the sight of Jake, his face bruised and swollen. "Oh, God, Brian, look at him! God only knows where else he's hurt."

Brian quickly moved to Jake's bedside and opened his medical bag. He pulled the covers away to see the man was shirtless. His arms and chest were covered with bruises, but Brian noticed with a bit of surprise that Jake's body still had a hard, lean look to it, the chest and arms of a much younger man. He'd never met his notorious father-in-law. He was a big man, dark. There were several scars on his body. He'd heard about some of them, how Jake's own father had put that scar on his neck, that there were more on his back from belt-whippings. He had laughed and shaken his head when Miranda told him and Evie how the first time she'd met the man she'd shot him. There was the scar from that wound, on his lower left side.

He moved his hands over the man's arms, ribs. "I don't feel any broken bones," he told Miranda, "but I don't doubt he's got more than one cracked rib. His ribs should have been wrapped." He took out a stethoscope and listened to Jake's breathing.

"He's so hot, Brian, and his breathing sounds so labored." Miranda smoothed Jake's still-thick, dark hair back from his face. She leaned close. "Jake? You'll be all right, *mi querido*. I'm here with you and I'm not leaving."

Brian examined Jake for several minutes, pressing the stethoscope to his chest again. He looked across the bed at Miranda. "Sounds like pneumonia, Randy. We've got to get him into more of a sitting position or his lungs will fill and he'll suffocate."

Evie hurriedly gathered pillows from some of the empty beds and the three of them worked to prop Jake up higher. Randy and Brian wrapped his ribs, and Randy shivered with fear when he began coughing, a deep, prolonged cough that was obviously painful, from both the pneumonia and the cracked ribs. The pain was written on his face, and he groaned with every breath for several minutes after the coughing stopped.

"Dear God, don't let him die," Randy whispered, kneeling beside the bed. She took hold of his hand, which was closed into a tight fist, tighter than she had ever seen him close the crippled hand. He was clinging to the Rosary beads.

"Lloyd," Jake muttered. "Got to . . . help . . . my son."

Jake breathed deeply for Brian, who held a stethoscope to his back. "He sounds a little less congested," Brian told Miranda, who sat on the other side of the cot. He still could not get over feeling a chill at the sight of the scars on Jake's back, always recalling the horrid vision of a grown man beating a little boy with the buckle end of a leather belt.

"This is one hell of a way to meet your father-in-law," Jake said, lying back against the pillows. He glanced at Evie, overwhelmed by her utter beauty and by the realization she was a grown, married woman. "Have you really all been here for three days?"

"Slept right on the empty cots over there," Brian answered. "Can't you tell by our wrinkled clothes? They at least gave me shaving equipment. Randy and I used it to shave that grizzly beard of yours." He grinned. "Randy told me what a handsome man you were. I knew you had to be because of how beautiful Evie is, but under that beard and all those bruises, it was hard to tell."

Jake put a hand to his hair. "I'm a beat-up, half-crippled *old* man is what I am." This morning was the first he'd awakened knowing who and where he was, and who had been talking to him in his dreams, that the woman he had thought was his mother was Evie.

A fit of coughing hit him, and he grasped Randy's hand tightly until he could get his breath again. He held his ribs and lay back, groaning with pain, and Miranda brought his hand up to her lips and kissed it. Brian pulled up a chair and sat down beside the bed. "You should know you've got pneumonia, Jake, so you've got to stay in a sitting position. Don't lie all the way flat or you could suffocate. If you take it real easy and they let you stay in this bed with plenty of blankets for warmth, you'll be all right in time. What you really need is fresh air."

Jake looked at his son-in-law, a handsome, clean-cut young man who he supposed had never seen any of the ugly side of life he had seen. He glanced at Evie, saw the glow on her face. "This man being good to you?" he asked.

"Can't you tell?" She smiled. "We're very happy, Father. That's partly why I wanted you to meet Brian, see us together. It gives you that much more to come home to. By the time you're free, you'll have grandchildren to meet."

Jake frowned. "You sure you want them to know me?"

Evie rolled her eyes. "Of course I'll want them to know you. You're my father, and you've been a very good father. That's all that's important. I'm proud of the man who raised me. I don't care what he did before that."

Jake smiled sadly, looking at Randy, squeezing her hand. "Lloyd *does* care. He's throwing his life away because of my past."

Miranda reached out and stroked his hair. "The warden

told us what that prisoner told you about Lloyd." She felt him tensing.

"I've got to find a way to get to him, Randy. I can't stay in this place three more years while he's out there either drinking himself to death or risking being caught by the law and put in a place like this. If I didn't have this need to find him and help him, I'd let myself die right now, or find a way to end my life for what's happened to him." He closed his eyes. "It's my fault. It's all my fault."

"Jake, if you did anything wrong, it was to love him too much, shelter him too much from reality. You taught him the right way to go in life. If he's chosen another way, it's *his* doing. He's being a foolish, stubborn young man who is going to come around someday to face the truth, and the truth is he can't deny how much you loved him or how much he loved you. This won't last. He's too good a man deep inside."

Jake tried to breathe deeply against unwanted tears, but his lungs would not allow it. The result was another coughing spell that led to deep, jerking sobs. Randy tried to comfort him, but he wouldn't let her touch him, embarrassed to be so weak and sick and in such an emotional state. He took a handkerchief Brian handed him and managed to control his despair, wiping at his eyes with a shaking hand.

Brian watched in dismay. The things he had heard from others about this man's past did not fit the man he saw now, a devoted father weeping over his son's wayward life. In spite of his condition, Jake Harkner still emanated an aura of power and danger. Somewhere behind those tired, dark eyes he could detect the man who could be ruthless, who could kill, the battered boy turned murderous outlaw. Miranda Harkner had tamed that part of him, and his children had taught him the true meaning of love, so much so that the man was shattered by the loss of his son's affections.

"It's the whiskey," Jake said, once he was able to speak again. "He just needs to get off the whiskey. It's just like my pa. He could never control his drinking. That's why I never drank a whole lot and never wanted Lloyd even to try it. He's got it in him, Randy. He's got that damned weakness for whiskey my father had, and it's making him do crazy things."

"There is one difference, Jake," Miranda answered firmly. "Lloyd is *not* your father! He doesn't have that meanness in him. He's soft-hearted and a good person deep inside; and the one biggest difference is how he was raised. Look what a good person Evie is. Lloyd is the same. He just needs to learn a few things the hard way, but he *will* learn, and he'll remember. He'll come home. If I have to go into outlaw country myself and fetch him, he'll come home!"

"Don't you dare!" Jake sat up a little straighter, and Brian saw the flash of meanness. "Don't you dare go into that country alone, you hear me? I wasn't even going to tell you about Lloyd because I was afraid you'd do exactly what you're talking about doing! Those places are filled with bastards as ruthless and worthless as the men I used to run with. It's no place for someone like you!"

"Then I'll find someone who can take me."

"Who? Who besides Jess could you trust? With Jess gone there's *no*body! There's only *me*! I'm the only one who can do it! I just have to get well and find a way to get the hell out of here!"

Miranda glanced at the doorway. A guard stood just outside. Jake was the only one left in the medical ward today, so there was no one to hear. "Please don't talk that way, Jake. If you try to escape, I'll never see you again! They'll either catch you and shoot you down, or put you back in here for the rest of your life! If that doesn't happen, you'll have to run forever. Either way, you'll be gone from my life." Her eyes teared with terror. "Please don't try it, Jake."

"What the hell else am I going to do? Lloyd's the only one who matters here. It's for our *son*!"

"Jake, I could go with Randy, or help her find someone trustworthy," Brian put in.

Jake glanced at him, leaning back against the pillows with a scowl. "Don't get me wrong, Brian. I'm sure you're a brave man who can hold his own, but you don't know the kind of men you'd be up against. The only way to know who to trust among such men is someone who was once just like them, someone who can read them inside and out. They're ruthless. Most of them don't give a damn about another human life. They'd just as soon shoot you in the back for the rings on your fingers as to look at you. I sure as hell ought to know."

"Father, we'll find a way to help Lloyd," Evie put in. "We'll do whatever it takes."

The door to the ward opened then, and all four looked up to see Warden Pruett coming toward them, a piece of paper in his hand. The man had a look of chagrin on his face, and he scowled at Miranda as he came to stand at the foot of the bed.

"Well," he said with a hint of sarcasm. "I don't know what you've been telling that judge back in St. Louis, but something is up."

Miranda's heart quickened, and she rose. "What do you mean?"

Pruett held up the paper. "This is a letter from Judge Mitchell. Soon as Jake is able to travel he's to go back to St. Louis for a possible resentencing. All it says is that some new evidence has been discovered. I've got no idea which way he means, good news or bad."

Miranda took the letter from him and read it to the others. *To the attention of Warden Howard Pruett, Wyoming Territorial Penitentiary, Laramie, Wyoming Territory: You are ordered to transfer prisoner Jackson Lloyd Harkner to St. Louis, Missouri, St. Louis County Jail, where he will be temporarily under my jurisdiction until decision has been made regarding new evidence and resentencing. Transfer is to be made as soon as possible.* Miranda looked at Jake, her eyes alight with hope. "This is something good, Jake! I feel it. I've prayed too hard for too long to have it mean anything but your freedom!"

Jake put a hand to his head. "What the hell kind of new evidence can they possibly have after twenty-four years? It's probably just somebody else who wants to testify to some raid or some other murder."

"It can't be. The judge said at your trial that evidence pertaining only to the charges you were wanted for could be used against you."

"They can always come up with new charges, open a new trial for different reasons. I don't think you've ever understood the kind of reputation I had back there." He took the letter from her and studied it. "Maybe Texas has decided to try me for my father's and Santana's murders. They figured I killed *both* of them deliberately."

"Jake, read the letter. It says new evidence—resentencing. You're being transferred to Judge Mitchell's jurisdiction, not to Texas. That can only mean it pertains to the charges you were already tried for, nothing new." She handed the letter back to Pruett. "Thank you for letting us stay here this long."

Pruett took the letter. "Frankly, I'll be glad to see all of you leave, including Jake. I hope *none* of you will be coming back." He folded the letter. "I'll wire the judge and tell him Jake is sick and that we'll send him back as soon as he's well enough. In the meantime, all three of you will have to get out of here. I've gone against the rules letting you stay this long." He saw the worry in Miranda's eyes. "Look, Mrs. Harkner, I want to get rid of him as bad as you want him out of here. We'll take good care of him."

The man left, and Miranda pulled the blankets up closer around Jake's neck. "You've got to get well just as fast as you can so we can go back to St. Louis. After that, we'll decide what to do about Lloyd. This could be something that might change everything for us."

Jake watched her, grinning slightly. "Damn slip of a woman," he muttered. He looked at Brian. "She's like a damn mother hen. I don't know what to do with her. I've tried to make her give up on me a hundred times over the years, but she just keeps hovering around. I can't get through to the woman."

Brian smiled. "She loves you."

"Yeah? Well, I should have left her back there at Fort Laramie all those years ago and just ridden out of her life. She would have been a hell of a lot better off."

Miranda took his hand. "I would have been very unhappy for the rest of my life."

Jake studied her gray-blue eyes. "I want to take hope in the letter from that judge, Randy, but after four and a half years in this place, it's pretty hard for a man to take hope in anything."

"In a few days, when you're well enough, we're going to leave this place, Jake Harkner, and we're never coming back." She kept a tight hold of his hand. Their eyes held, and Brian saw in Jake's eyes an amazing love and adoration he would not have thought possible for a man with his past. He had always thought that all of Evie's love and passion and sweet devotion came from her mother. God knew Miranda Harkner had shown a great capacity to love beyond all obstacles and disappointments, a patience few people possessed. But it was obvious now that a great deal of Evie's loyalty and compassion came from her father, the notorious outlaw Jake Harkner. He realized now more clearly than ever that Jake had never been a killer at heart. In his worst days the man had really been an angry, frightened boy, lashing out at the world. Randy had understood that.

He closed his eyes and said a quick, silent prayer that the news in St. Louis would be good. He didn't want to see the looks on either Randy's or Jake's face if they were told Jake would be coming back to this place to spend the rest of his life here.

Jake waited in the St. Louis County Jail, grateful that at least these cells were bigger than those at Laramie. He was waiting to see the judge, still in the dark over what this was all about. Attorney Mattson was still in town, and Miranda had gone to see him, but the man had told her he couldn't say what it was about. He didn't want to give her too much hope when it might all come to nothing.

Right now he was not in his cell. Guards had brought him to a windowless room where there was just a table and chair. He sat in the chair, nervously rubbing his hands together. He'd been guarded by six men on the train ride back to St. Louis, kept in a separate car from Miranda, Evie, and Brian, who had all come along. In spite of both his hands and ankles being cuffed all the way there, just being outside of the Laramie penitentiary, being on that train and able to look out a window at a world he hadn't seen in over four years, gave him a taste of freedom that persuaded him he'd do anything not to have to go back.

All that mattered now was Lloyd. Somehow he had to help the boy. If he was sent back to prison, he'd break out. He felt better now, stronger. He wasn't fully recovered, but he'd gotten plenty of rest on the trip, which had taken nearly a week, and for two weeks before that at the prison before he left. He'd forced himself to keep still, to eat right, to keep warm and drink plenty of water like Brian had instructed. He hadn't touched a cigar or cigarette for over three weeks because Brian said it would only irritate his lungs, but he figured he sure as hell could use a smoke right now. Whatever was going to happen, it would happen today, and the waiting was torture. Finally he heard voices outside. "You sure, lady?"

"Yes, I'm sure," he heard a woman answer one of the guards. "I want to see him alone."

Jake couldn't see outside the door. He heard the key turn in the lock, and the door opened. A woman stepped inside. She was beautiful, dressed in an elegant, deep green velvet dress that spoke of a person of wealth. Her feathered hat was perched perfectly atop dark red hair that was drawn up and pinned into a cascade of curls. She held her head erect and proud, her eyes as green as the dress, her skin lovely but slightly lined, telling him she was probably older than she actually looked. He took a rough guess that she was about Miranda's age, maybe a little younger. Something about her looked familiar.

He rose from the chair to greet her, surprised when the guard closed the door and left them alone. After all, he was supposed to be a notorious outlaw, a rapist, and he hadn't been alone with a woman in years. Why wasn't this woman afraid of him? He stood there before her in confusion, glad he'd been given the opportunity to shower and shave, had been given a haircut and a new shirt and denim pants to wear before having to go before the judge. He wouldn't want this elegant woman to see him looking his worst and wearing prison clothes. But why was she here? He studied her intently just as she was studying him in return. Her eyes moved over him, rested again on his face, met his eyes.

"It *is* you," she said softly. "You don't know who I am, do you, Jake?"

Jake frowned, trying to remember. "You look a little familiar. Am I *supposed* to know you?"

She smiled with a hint of sadness. "You should. You risked your life to save mine about twenty-four years ago. I was only sixteen then. I was devastated and terrified and suicidal at the time. It took me a while to remember what really happened, who helped me, but after a year or two of healing, I remembered."

Hope welled in Jake's heart. That red hair, those green eyes! "Louella Griffith?"

She stepped a little closer. "Louella Adams now. My parents moved with me to New York. We never told anyone what had happened to me. I eventually married a very wealthy man who owned a shipping empire. I've been living in Europe for several years now. By the time I remembered all the details of what had happened to me, I was a married woman, and I didn't want my husband to know about—" She looked away. "Those men, what they did to me. You were long gone. No one had ever been arrested, so I let it go. I wanted to forget about it, all of it, if that was possible." She shivered, turned back to face him. "My husband died this past winter. I came home to spend some time with my parents while I'm in mourning. They told me then that you had been arrested and sentenced a few years ago. They had kept the newspaper article about it." She smiled. "Did you know you made the New York newspapers?"

Jake just stared at her in disbelief. Here was the woman he had rescued! Here was his proof of innocence. He couldn't find his voice.

Louella studied him closely again. "I remembered you. You told me your name was Jake Harkner. You wrapped a blanket around me and held me, and you told me not to be afraid of you. I remember the awful gunfire, the hard ride on that horse. You're older now, but the face isn't so different, especially not the eyes. I always remembered your eyes, how they could be so ruthless one minute and so kind the next. When I heard you were sitting in prison, that you had a wife and a son and a daughter, I knew I had to do something." She reached out and touched his arm. "You saved me, Jake. Those men would have killed me. You gave me a chance at life again. Now I can do the same for you. I have already talked to the judge. That's why he ordered you back here, so I could identify you. I couldn't be sure until I actually set eyes on you again. We're going over to the courthouse in a few minutes. I'll testify for the record that you had nothing to do with that robbery or the killings that took place or with what happened to me. I don't know what the judge will do then. I can only tell my side of the story. I'm just sorry I wasn't here when you were tried, but then my husband was still alive and I probably couldn't have spoken up anyway. I never wanted him to know." Her cheeks flushed. "I'm sure you can understand why."

He looked down at the slender hand on his arm, touched it hesitantly with his own hand. "I don't know what to say, except thank you. My wife and daughter are here with me. They have prayed and prayed for something to happen that might get me out of this. Seeing you walk in here is like a miracle. You're a godsend, Louella."

She met his eyes. "And you were a godsend all those years ago. Sometimes God uses the most unlikely people to answer prayer, Jake. He used you that day to answer my prayers that I be freed from those awful men."

He grinned. "I can't quite see myself in that light, but you can look at it however you want. I'm just glad as hell you're here."

She moved away from him and went to the door, turning again for a moment. "I went to the courthouse and saw your wife and daughter. They're both quite beautiful. I heard a reporter interviewing them, and I could tell by the way your wife spoke that she loves you very much. Your daughter talked about what a good father you were all of her life, wept with the hope that maybe you were going to be released. I knew then I was doing the right thing." She glanced at his hips. "You don't look fully dressed without those guns you wore. I'll always remember how fast you were." She turned and called for the guard. The door opened, and she left.

Jake stared after her, wondering if it was real. Louella Griffith had finally emerged from the past to tell the truth.

Judge Mitchell pounded his gavel and commanded the courtroom to quiet. Word had spread that Jake was back and that there was new evidence regarding his case, and by the time he was brought to court, the room was filled with curious onlookers. Louella Griffith Adams had just finished her testimony. "Jake Harkner is not guilty of any of the charges for which he has been imprisoned for the last four years," she concluded. "He had nothing to do with the bank robbery that day, or with my abduction and abuse. The man saved my life and risked his own in doing so."

The filled courtroom had come alive, and reporters wrote rapidly on their tablets. A photographer who had been allowed to set up his camera near Jake took a quick picture, the flash powder exploding in a *poof*. Jake turned and scowled at the man, and he backed away, grinning nervously. The judge kept pounding the gavel for quiet, and Miranda clung to Evie's hand, unable to control her tears. Louella Adams was like an angel from heaven as far as she was concerned.

Attorney Mattson rose. "Your Honor, I move that all charges against Jake Harkner be dropped and that he be set free," the man spoke up.

The courtroom quieted again, waiting for the judge's decision. Judge Mitchell told Louella to step down. The woman left the stand, glancing at Miranda with a gentle smile before taking her seat. The judge ordered Jake to rise, and all whispering stopped as everyone waited to hear Jake's fate.

"Jake Harkner, I have heard Mrs. Adams's testimony, and I am fully convinced the woman is telling the truth. She has no reason to make up such a story, and after the unspeakable acts committed against her, she most certainly would not now testify in your favor if you had anything to do with those acts. Her story coincides in every detail with the story you told me in this courtroom four years ago. All charges in this particular case will be removed from your record. However—"

Miranda's heart fell. However! What was the man doing? Jake should be set free now!

"You admitted of your own accord, and it is a well-known fact, that you did commit other crimes in your days as an outlaw. I am not so sure that four years is long-enough punishment for all the other crimes you committed, but then if I paid attention to the almost-weekly letters I have received from your wife ever since I sentenced you, I would have been convinced that four *days* was long enough." A few whispers and light laughter moved through the courtroom. "A woman that devoted doesn't love a man that much for no good reason. She has lauded your attributes to me for years, and I am convinced that no further time in prison, especially at your age, is going to do anyone any good."

Miranda breathed another sigh of relief until the judge continued. "I do believe, though, that some kind of further retribution is in order," the man said. "Do you still think you can handle yourself with guns?"

Jake was surprised at the question. "I don't know. It's been a while. And my right hand is partly crippled."

"You can shoot a rifle or a shotgun with it, can't you?"

"I suppose."

"And you were as good with a handgun with your left hand as with your right. Am I correct?"

"Yes, sir."

Miranda's heartbeat quickened. What was the man getting at?

The judge sighed, looking at some papers. "Well, I expect knowing how to handle guns is like riding a horse well or being good at blacksmithing or carving or any other thing a man does well. You never quite forget it. There is trouble in Oklahoma Territory right now, what with the recent land rush there. Towns like Guthrie that have sprung up overnight are in a state of lawless disarray, and there is trouble throughout the Territory between the Indians and ranchers as well as between ranchers and sheepherders; all kinds of problems that bring up a need for lawmen there, including the fact that outlaws still hide out in Indian Territory. Who would be better at hunting down such men than someone like yourself, someone who understands them, knows the best places to look for them and can outshoot the best of them? I am appointing you a Deputy U.S. Marshal to serve in Indian Territory. I am aware that you have been ill. I'll give you three months to rest and get your life in order before you have to report for duty in Kansas City to that state's attorney general. He will instruct you as to what area and to whom you will report in Oklahoma. You will then be given time to settle your family wherever that might be."

The man pounded his gavel, and Jake just stared at the judge, dumbfounded. A Deputy Marshal! Jake Harkner? He wanted to laugh at the irony of the sentence. Miranda was at his side in an instant. She threw her arms around him, and he embraced her, still feeling almost dazed by his new freedom. "Oh, Jake, it's real! You're free! You're free!" she wept.

There were more flashes from more photographers. Evie was hugging him, too, now. Jake glanced over at Louella Adams. She was watching him, smiling. She turned away then and left the courtroom, and in that one little moment Jake knew the true meaning of prayer and faith.

"Three months," he told Miranda, kissing her hair. "I've got time to go and find Lloyd." He looked over at Brian, who was shaking Attorney Mattson's hand. "Go find Mrs. Adams and bring her back here. Hell, the least we can do is treat the woman to a steak dinner tonight at the best restaurant in town."

"Oh, yes, Jake, we owe her so much," Miranda said, weeping.

Brian quickly left to catch the woman, and Judge Mitchell stepped down from the bench and approached Jake. He put out his hand, a stern look on his face. Jake let go of Miranda and Evie, reaching out to shake the man's hand.

"Don't make me out to be a fool, Jake," the judge told him. "Prove to me you're the dependable man I think you'll be."

Jake nodded. "I will be."

"Well, you can thank your wife for my generosity. She's a one-woman locomotive, let me tell you. She even has *me* talking prison reform to those who will listen, and her letters about you were beginning to give me quite a case of guilt. It made it very difficult for me to discern the law from personal emotion. You've got quite a woman there, Mr. Harkner. Her faith in you never waned."

"I'm well aware of how lucky I am to have her," Jake

answered, moving an arm back around Miranda. "If I can just find my son now and help him, I'll have my family back."

"I wish you luck in that, Jake. Heaven knows you can attest to the boy how wrong and pointless it is to get into a life of crime." The judge nodded to the others and left them, and the courtroom began to clear.

Jake closed his eyes and prayed he would be able to find Lloyd before he had to report to Kansas City. The thought of seeing his son again brought a quick ache to his chest, a mixture of fear, anticipation, joy, sorrow. All he could see was the little boy who used to ride on his shoulders, who looked to him with such love and trust, who cried the day he gave him his first rifle. How much of that little boy was left in the man? How much had hatred replaced the sweet love Lloyd used to have for his father?

He looked down at Miranda, and they embraced again. He could enjoy that embrace now. God, it felt good to hold her, smell her, feel her against him! For the first time since he was fourteen years old and had fled Texas, he was truly a free man.

CHAPTER
THIRTY-ONE

Miranda removed her hat and set it on a chair, glancing at the four-poster bed in the elegant room Brian had taken for them at the finest hotel in St. Louis. Miranda and Jake had both objected, but Brian and Evie had insisted that this first night alone together and Jake's first night as a free man should be spent in the most comfortable place possible.

Jake closed and locked the door. He turned to face her, watching her lovingly. She met his eyes, knew by the look there that he was just as unsure and hesitant as she. "It's been a long time for both of us, Jake. All I really care about is sleeping with you beside me tonight, lying in your arms, feeling your breath on my neck." Her eyes grew misty as she walked up and embraced him. "I can hardly believe this has happened. Life is going to be so good for us now, Jake. We'll find Lloyd and we'll all be together again, just like I said would happen." She looked up at him. "I told you to never stop believing, didn't I?"

He kept one arm around her and with his other hand he began pulling pins from her hair. "We haven't found Lloyd yet."

"We will. Tonight let's just enjoy being together, enjoy the news Brian and Evie gave us." She smiled. "Our first grand-child, Jake! Life is going to be so good for us now. Let's wallow in this wonderful freedom. For the first time in years you'll sleep in a real bed with me beside you."

He closed his eyes and leaned down to kiss her hair as he ran his hand through it to fluff it out from all the pins. He relished the silken feel of it, breathed in the smell of soap and lilac perfume. "Randy," he whispered, "I don't even know if I can be a real husband to you anymore. It's been so long, it's like, like that part of me died."

She pulled back and began unbuttoning his shirt. "I told you that all I want is to sleep beside you. Getting back to a normal life is going to take time. I know that." She looked up at him, leaned up and kissed his lips, lightly at first.

Memories and needs began flooding in then for both of them. Jake returned the kiss with a deeper one, the lingering, groaning kiss of a man long deprived of a woman's softness, a woman's love, a woman's pleasures. In all the years since he'd first met her, he'd never wanted her this badly, but to his horror nothing was happening physically to make that possible. He released the kiss, closing his eyes and turning away. He angrily removed his shirt.

Miranda went to her bag and took out a flannel gown, deciding it was best to say nothing. After four years in prison, being so sick the last two months, worrying over Lloyd, he was expecting too much of himself. This was a personal matter that she decided only Jake could work out with himself. The more she tried to soothe him, the worse he would feel.

She went into a changing room and undressed, coming out to find Jake already in bed, the lamp turned low. She moved into bed beside him. "Just hold me and never let go," she whispered. His arms came around her, and she snuggled into his shoulder. "Of all the times we've made love, this moment is the most pleasurable of my life, Jake Harkner, just having you beside me like this."

He stroked her hair, kissed it. She moved her hands over him lovingly, realizing then he had worn nothing to bed. She decided to just lie quietly, let him sleep if that was what he wanted. It had been a long day for them both. "I love you, Jake."

"*Yo te quiero, mi esposa,*" he answered softly.

It was the most blessedly wonderful experience of her life, as far as she was concerned. He was free! Free! They had shared a wonderful dinner with Evie and Brian and Louella Adams, Jake ignoring the stares of the other patrons. After dinner she and Jake had rented a carriage and sat in each other's arms while they were driven around and shown the city, which was lovely at night. Miranda remembered the last time she had been here, how she had hated it.

Now she loved it, loved the judge, loved Louella Adams, loved life, and oh, how she loved Jake! She was not sure how long she lay in his solid arms before she finally fell asleep, or how much time passed before she was awakened by his soft caress. By the pale lamplight he had untied the front of her gown and pushed it away from one breast. He touched the breast gently, his thumb stirring the nipple to life.

Miranda knew this was a delicate moment for him. She wanted to react with wild abandon. It had been so long, and she had dreamed of this moment every night for four years; but she knew she must let Jake move at his own pace. She closed her eyes and breathed deeply, allowing him his pleasure. His mouth came over her breast, and he groaned lightly, sucking at her hungrily as though to take nourishment.

He moved a hand under her gown, along her thigh, and she was glad she had deliberately left off her underwear. When his hand found her bare bottom, his need and passion seemed to intensify. His lips left her breast, and he whispered her name as he licked at her neck, met her mouth in a penetrating kiss, his tongue pushing deep while at the same time his fingers stroked between her bottom, moved to her lovenest.

"God, Randy," he groaned, leaving her mouth, trailing down to her breast again as he pushed up on her gown. "I need to touch you, taste you," he whispered, moving his lips down to kiss at her belly. She gasped and shivered in ecstasy when he moved to taste and explore that most intimate part of her that she had given only to this man. Mack had never done this to her. He had never brought out such wanton boldness in her or made her want to give every inch of herself to him this way.

She cried out his name when he worked his magic, fed her neglected needs until her breath came in deep gasps, her climax almost painful from the sheer euphoria of the moment.

Quickly he was on top of her. She tasted her own sweetness on his lips as he explored her mouth again while he surged inside of her almost violently from his pent-up needs. His release was quick, coming in hard, surging pulses, but his kisses did not let up and his body did not relax. "Stay there, just stay there," he groaned, kissing at her neck. "I'm sorry, Randy." He kissed her eyes. "I wasn't very gentle. I want to be."

"It's all right." She returned his kisses with equal passion. "I don't want you to be gentle tonight," she said softly. "The harder you take me, the better I know this is real, Jake."

Already the life was returning. He began moving inside her again, pushing hard and deep. He rose up to his knees, grasping her hips and pulling her to him, moving in circular motions that made her feel alive and brazen and all woman again. She grasped his strong forearms, so thankful he had survived prison, the pneumonia, the awful beating. Now he had overcome the ugly accusations and was free. Free! Jake was free! There would be no more running and worrying. Her man was here in her bed, making love to her. Yes, he was older now. The strain of the past four years showed in his face, but he was still her handsome Jake, still strong and getting stronger. She knew that once he found Lloyd, if he could win back his son's love, he would be like a new man. For now there was no doubt he was still virile, still her Jake.

He came closer again, resting on his elbows, licking teasingly at her lips as again she felt his life surging into her. He kissed her eyes, and she reached up to stroke his hair, wet with perspiration now. She worried a little that he would overtire himself after the pneumonia, but she did not want to interrupt this very important moment. He could sleep tomorrow.

He lay down beside her, took her hand and kissed the palm. "I don't think I'll sleep much tonight," he said softly. "I just want to keep touching you, be inside you."

"I need that just as much as you do, Jake."

He moved on top of her again, studying her eyes intently. "Tell me true," he whispered. "Tell me you never did this with Jess."

She was surprised at the remark. Did he think she had lied to him while he was in prison just to save him the torture of visualizing her with Jess? Her eyes teared, and she touched his face. "Oh, Jake, you must know I couldn't have. No, my darling, I never did this with Jess. That's the God's truth. If I can't have you, I don't want anyone."

She saw the tears in his eyes. "You don't know what it was like, lying in that cell day after day, week after week, knowing you had needs, thinking maybe . . ." He kissed her eyes. "I told you it was all right, and I meant it, but the torture of thinking it could really happen—"

"It *didn't* happen, Jake. You know I'm no liar. You'd know by my eyes if I wasn't telling the truth. There was one moment when Jess held me while I had a good cry. I let him kiss me, and for just a moment I thought how nice it would be to let a man hold me through the night." She ran her fingers through his hair. "But I couldn't go through with it. He wasn't you."

She watched the tears slip out of his eyes, realized more fully the agony he had suffered in that prison cell. "You know there is no man for me but you, Jake Harkner. Why do you think I've stuck by you through all of this when there were so many times it would have been easy just to walk away from it all? You are my life, my strength, my reason for being."

He put a big hand to the side of her face. "It's the same for me. I just can't believe you're really here in my arms, *mi querida.*" He met her mouth again, and there was no more to be said. By the time he was finished loving her, a hint of dawn light could be seen through a crack in the window curtains.

Jake rested beside Miranda, pulling her back against him. "I'll have to buy some new firearms before leaving St. Louis," he told her in a sleepy voice. "I want the best before I go into outlaw country. I'd better practice some too. It's been a long time since I held a gun in my hands."

"You'd better buy me a new rifle too," she answered lazily. "I'm going with you, you know."

"No, ma'am. I'll not take you into country like that, around men like that."

"With you along, what could happen to me? And what if you get hurt, or what if Lloyd gets hurt? You wouldn't find a doctor for two hundred miles in any direction. I'd be the closest thing to a doctor you'd have. He's my son, too, Jake Harkner, and I'm going to help you find him."

"I said no."

Miranda just smiled. "I'm going," she said, settling closer against him. "I just got you back, and I am never, *ever* letting you out of my sight again. There will be no more arguing about it."

She felt him sigh deeply. "Damn stubborn slip of a woman," he muttered.

.　.　.

Miranda guided her roan mare along a canyon wall above the
Green River. She led a shaggy, golden mare that carried their
supplies, and Jake rode ahead of her on a buckskin gelding
that closely resembled the now long-dead Outlaw. He had
named the broad-chested, powerful three-year-old Bandit,
and it had a black mane and black stockings just like Outlaw.

Miranda had traveled through the West and lived in it long
enough not to be totally surprised by the scenery, yet this
country was, to her memory, the most remote and desolate
she had ever seen, except perhaps for the Nevada desert. It
also carried a chilling beauty, a maze of buttes and mesas, of
wide valleys dotted with green sage and bunchgrass. A rancher
had headed them in this direction, where they would search
through Brown's Park for any news of Lloyd.

This was big country, and sometimes Miranda worried
they might get lost and never find their way out. It was no
wonder outlaws liked it here. There were thousands of places
to hide or take cover, caves, box canyons. Brown's Park was a
forty-square-mile area that took in both northeast Utah and
northwest Colorado. The Green River flowed through the
middle of it, and the area was flanked by Diamond Mountain
and Douglas Mountain, and a plateau called Owi-ya-kuts. According to the rancher, trappers used to gather here, men like
Jim Bridger and Kit Carson. Infamous outlaws such as Butch
Cassidy still roamed these areas.

Only the lawless who used these places knew them well.
Jake had traveled these parts himself after he'd left Miranda
in California, and the only reason he had asked directions
from the rancher was because they were approaching Brown's
Park from the east, a direction he had not used before.

It seemed with every day of travel Jake got healthier and
stronger. The sun was already tanning him even darker, but he
insisted Miranda wear gloves and long sleeves and a hat to
protect her skin. She thought how good he looked on that big
horse, how wonderful it had been to lie next to him under the
stars, to make love by moonlight, to feel this newfound freedom.

To Miranda it seemed they were lost in a maze of canyons
and gorges and high plateaus, but she trusted Jake to find the
way, and she was not afraid of trouble anyone might try to give
them. Jake had bought the best in weapons, a Colt Frontier
pistol for her protection, which she wore in a holster on her
own hip. For himself he carried a new .45-caliber Frontier

revolver that had a seven-and-a-half-inch barrel; a Colt Lightning magazine rifle that fired automatically without lever action; and a new sawed-off 12-gauge shotgun.

The firearms had been purchased in St. Louis with a special purchase order given to Jake by Judge Mitchell to buy necessary firearms to suit his taste, to be used on his job as Deputy Marshal. The cost would be paid by the U.S. Government, which suited Jake just fine. He had bought the best, figured he could use Miranda's snub-nosed pistol himself later. It was small enough to be hidden inside a jacket pocket or even a boot, but it packed a powerful punch.

It had been three weeks since they'd left St. Louis. During that time, both at Laramie and during their journey to reach the Outlaw Trail, Miranda had learned a lot about firearms. Jake had insisted she learn to shoot well before he brought her here, and she felt comfortable now using the snub-nosed pistol she wore. She had even practiced with the shotgun, but it still set her on her rump when she fired it.

You can blow a man in half with that, he had told her when helping her learn to load and shoot the shotgun. When it came to using guns, and to being the kind of man it took to face up to other men in these parts, part of him had reverted to the old, hard Jake. *You never hesitate,* he had warned. *You never feel sorry for the man you're shooting at, because he won't be feeling sorry for you. One second's hesitation, and he'll shoot first. You remember that. How in hell do you think I've stayed alive all these years?*

He had practiced himself, discovering that just as the judge had suggested, the old speed and accuracy were still there once he got rid of the "rust" of several years without holding a gun. He had amazed Brian and Evie with his target practice, drawing and shooting his handgun left-handed with speed and perfection, grabbing up the magazine rifle and getting off another round of bullets with astounding speed, hitting every single target Brian had set up for him. He was able to fire the rifle and the shotgun with his right hand, although it made his hand ache fiercely. Brian had fashioned a brace for the hand that helped the pain considerably.

They were well armed now, and with Jake along, Miranda did not worry about the kind of people they would face here. Jake knew them well, and he could handle them; but as long as they were in such dangerous territory, she knew he would not be the same man. He was Jake Harkner the outlaw now.

He would think like these men, act and react as they would. Part of the old Jake had reared up and come into action, and she would have to live with that side of him until this was over.

He motioned for her to ride up beside him, and she rode Lady to the edge of a canyon, seeing below what looked like some kind of settlement. "Brown's Park," Jake told her. "They even have a school. A few of the outlaws are married, mostly to ex-prostitutes. There is just about everything down there that any town has, except a jail. There is only one law in places like that: whoever has the fastest gun sets the rules. You ready?"

"Yes. This is the last place that prisoner saw Lloyd. It's all we have to go on."

Jake led her down a steep, winding path that trailed down the side of the canyon wall in a precipitous grade that made Miranda worry about the horses losing their footing. Tiny rocks scattered and tumbled before them as the horses made their way precariously on loose gravel, and she breathed a sigh of relief when an hour later they reached bottom. They moved through a cluster of juniper and wound through some brushy overgrowth and toward two huge red-rock formations.

"Hold it!" someone called out. They both looked up to see a man appear at the top of one of the rocks. "Who the hell is it?"

Jake rested his hand on his revolver. "Jake Harkner! I've come to find my son. Last word was he was here at Brown's Park."

The man lowered his rifle. "Harkner? I thought you were in prison."

"Not anymore. I'm coming through. Don't give me any trouble."

The man waved him on, and Jake and Miranda rode into an excuse of a town that was nothing more than a collection of rough cabins and stores. "At least we can get a few supplies," Jake told her, "although most of them were probably stolen from someone else." He rode up to a little building that read SALOON. "Best place to get information," he told her. "You keep that pistol handy." He dismounted and walked back to her horse, taking its reins and tying it. He grinned inwardly at the sight of the small holster Miranda wore at her right side. It carried the deadly pistol he had taught her to shoot. On her horse she carried his old lever-action Winchester, still a damn good gun.

Miranda dismounted. She wore a brown suede riding skirt and a yellow blouse, and Jake took pleasure in how good she still looked; but it also made him extra watchful. Not many decent women who looked like Miranda came to places like this. Her honey-blond hair was pulled back into a tail at the back of her neck, and she wore a wide-brimmed, brown leather hat.

"Don't pay too much attention to anything you see or hear," he told her. "Some of these men don't care what they say or how they behave in front of anyone. I wouldn't even take you inside, but I don't want to leave you *out*side alone, either."

Miranda followed him into the smoky log structure. It was late afternoon, and there were roughly twelve men there, eight of them sitting at card tables, three more at the bar, a bartender pouring one of them a whiskey. None of them was Lloyd. Twelve pairs of eyes moved to Miranda.

"Well, well, what we got here?" one of those at the table said with a grin. "My God, she packs a pistol even!"

Several of them laughed. "She knows how to use it too," Jake spoke up, moving to the bar. Miranda sat down on a stool.

"Yeah? Who taught her?" a man at the bar asked.

"Jake Harkner," Jake replied.

Most of them lost their smiles. "Harkner?" The man at the bar looked Jake over. "You Jake Harkner?"

Jake took a thin cigar from his vest pocket. "I am." He lit the cigar, watching them all carefully. "The woman is my wife, so quit ogling her."

Several quickly turned away and returned to their card playing. "We heard you was in prison," the man at the bar told Jake.

"I've been set free, and I'm looking for my son Lloyd. I heard he'd been here, shot a couple of men. Any of you know about it, know where he might be?"

A man at one of the tables looked up at him. "He *might* be dead by now," he told him.

Miranda gasped, and Jake slowly took the cigar from his mouth. He looked at the bartender. "Pour me a whiskey." His voice was gruff, and Miranda knew the statement had hit him hard. The bartender poured him a shot, and Jake quickly gulped it, then turned. "You want to explain that remark?" he asked the man at the table. "What's your name?"

The man had a hard, mean look to him, his beard full-growth, his dark hair oily and unkempt. He was not tall, but his brawny, heavyset build gave off an aura of strength. "Name's Mark Whitney," he answered, his steely blue eyes meeting Jake's boldly.

Jake moved closer to the man. "What do you know about my son?"

"I know the kid drank a lot. When he drank he did and said stupid things." The man spit toward a brass pot and missed. "I know he shot four men, two a while back, two more just recently. Them two was part of Jube Latimer's bunch. Latimer is a pretty big man in these parts, has a gang of at least ten men, sometimes more. He came ridin' in here a few days later, didn't much like hearin' about your son killin' two of his men, or the fact that the boy took their horses after he shot them." He bit off another chunk of chewing tobacco and stuck it between his cheek and gum. "I ain't seen the kid or Jubal and his bunch since." He looked Jake over. "The kid is good with them guns, I'll say that, but I expect you're better. Trouble is, ol' Jube wouldn't be impressed by that. Ain't many who'd dare go after the son of Jake Harkner, but Jubal would. He's got a lot of firepower. He wouldn't be afraid of just one man."

"Well, maybe the right one just hasn't come along yet," Jake fumed. "You must have some idea where Lloyd went, where this Jube Latimer and his men went."

Whitney shrugged. "Who knows out here?" He drank down some whiskey and spit again. "'Course, money talks and bullshit walks."

Jake kept the cigar between his teeth. "There are more things than money that can make a man talk."

Whitney's eyes dropped to Jake's revolver. "I expect so, but I'm one man who knows where Jubal and his bunch generally spend most of their time when they're not out on a job. I'll tell you for free it's up by Hole-in-the-Wall in the Wind River range, but it'll cost you a hundred dollars if you want me to lead you right to it. Just don't expect me to go in with you, not against that bunch. First off, you'd have to go up to Hole-in-the-Wall and see if your son's been seen up there."

"You crazy, Mark?" one of the others spoke up. "You shouldn't oughta be showin' nobody how to find Latimer, especially not Jake Harkner. Latimer will kill you if he finds out."

Whitney glanced at Miranda. "Maybe."

Jake startled everyone then when he grabbed Whitney by the lapels and jerked him out of his chair, throwing him against the bar with remarkable force, considering Whitney's bulk. Men scrambled for cover when in an instant Jake's revolver was pressed under Whitney's chin. Miranda jumped down from her stool and moved back.

"How fucking stupid do you think I am, Whitney?" Jake growled. "If you know where to find Latimer, then you used to *ride* with him! And if you used to ride with him, you're not about to turn on him! You'll lead me to him, all right, so Latimer can have the pleasure of being the one to say he killed Jake Harkner and took his *woman*!"

The revolver slammed across the side of Whitney's face, cutting into the man's cheek and sending him sprawling with a howl. He hit the floor hard and lay still. Jake holstered his revolver and turned to Miranda. "Come on. We're heading north to the Wind River range. Maybe somebody up there has seen Lloyd." He started to lead her out when he heard a click. In an instant Jake whirled, his gun out and fired before Whitney, who had already drawn his, could even pull the trigger. Jake opened a hole in the man's head, and Whitney just stared at him a moment, then slumped into death.

Miranda let out a little groan and turned from the sight. Jake held his revolver on the others. "Anybody else?"

"No, sir," they answered almost in unison, all of them stepping back. A prostitute came out from a back room, stark naked, and screamed at the sight of Whitney's body lying on the floor and Jake standing there with a gun in his hand. She ran back inside and slammed the door.

"Go mount up, Randy!" Jake ordered.

She quickly ran out of the smoky, smelly little establishment, glad for the fresh air. Jake soon followed, untying his horse and swiftly climbing into the saddle. "Let's go. We can make a few miles yet before nightfall."

Miranda did not question his judgment. She followed, wondering for the first several yards if she would feel a bullet in her back, but when she looked behind her, no one had even dared exit the saloon for fear of being shot. She shivered. From Whitney's brief description, Jubal Latimer sounded like one of the worst, and he rode with a lot of men. Not only had Lloyd killed two of them, but now Jake had killed another. Her ears still hurt from the explosion of his powerful revolver.

Was it true that Jubal Latimer was after Lloyd? Whitney was probably right. Lloyd could already be dead. She knew Jake was thinking the same thing, knew that was why he had so quickly lost his temper with Whitney. If they had come this far and found Lloyd dead, Jake's new freedom would mean nothing.

The night sky was filled with millions of stars, and wolves howled from seemingly every direction in the surrounding mountains. Miranda thought how frightening it would be in these mountains, if not for Jake. Not only did wild animals lurk beyond the light of their campfire, but wild men. She buttoned the top button of her wolfskin jacket. The nights were cold in the mountains, even in early summer.

She glanced across the flickering flames at Jake, who had said barely a word since leaving Brown's Park. He was quietly smoking, watching the fire, holding a cup of stiff, black coffee in his hands. As though aware she was watching him, he glanced at her.

"I'm sorry about the things you saw and heard today." He looked back at the flames. "I didn't really figure on having to shoot anyone. I guess I went a little crazy when that sonofabitch said Lloyd could be dead, blurting it out like that as though he was talking about some stranger."

"You had to shoot him, Jake. He was going to kill you."

He took the cigarette from his mouth and drank some of the coffee. "He wouldn't have tried if I hadn't hit him." He put the cigarette back between his lips. "I just wonder if it's true that Jube Latimer could be after Lloyd. I know what it's like to be hunted by outlaws. It's a lot worse than having lawmen after you. Lawmen have to treat you civilly once they catch you. Outlaws live by a different code. If it's true this Latimer might take his time killing him . . ." His voice trailed off and he rose, tossing down the coffee cup. "Damn it! It will take us a week or more to reach Hole-in-the-Wall. What if he really is in trouble?"

"Jake, you've got to get help if Latimer rides with that many men."

"Three of them are dead now."

"And he's probably already replaced the two Lloyd shot. You told me once yourself that men like Bill Kennedy pick up followers here and there, that their numbers are always about the same. Latimer probably isn't much different."

He took the cigarette from his mouth, squinting at her with dark, brooding eyes. "And here you are caught in the middle of all of it. I don't like any of this. I shouldn't have let you come."

Wolves began their wailing again, this time sounding closer. Miranda sighed. "Well, I'm here, and there certainly isn't anyplace out here you can leave me. You didn't teach me to shoot for nothing, and if it's possible Lloyd could be hurt, I wouldn't stay behind even if you *could* find a place for me to stay. I'll help all I can, Jake. I won't get in the way."

"I'm not worried about that. I'm worried about what could happen to you if I go down this time."

A sick feeling moved through her. She had never heard him talk about "going down." It hit her then how serious this could be. He knew the kind of men he might be going up against much better than she. The vision of seeing him shot to pieces sent a chill down her spine. She could lose her husband and her son both.

"Maybe you can find some help at Hole-in-the-Wall. You're Jake Harkner, remember? These men respect you."

"Maybe so, but that doesn't make them brave. Respecting me and helping me go up against this Latimer are two different things. Men like these don't make friends easily and don't go around risking their lives for each other. I wish to hell Jess was still alive. I could use him right now."

Miranda rose. "I do believe I saw you shoot down seven men back in California."

"That was seven, not ten, and they were all pretty much in one area. Out here men can spread out, hide in a thousand places. Wherever this Latimer hangs out, you can bet his men are scattered around keeping watch." He walked back to sit by the fire. "Get some sleep. We've got some hard riding to do tomorrow."

"What about you?"

"I can't sleep. I've got some thinking to do."

She lay back against her saddle, watching him, thinking how different he was in these situations. He had to draw on the old Jake for this, revert to the cunning, ruthless nature he'd shown when she first met him. There was that fire in his eyes, that mean look that would frighten her if she didn't know him so well. She had seen it when he slammed his re-

volver across Mark Whitney's face, felt actual chills at the look
in his eyes right after he shot the man.

She closed her eyes, telling herself she must try to rest, but
it would be nearly impossible, worrying about Lloyd and Jake
both. Jake sat down and leaned against his own saddle, his
revolver still worn on his hip, the magazine rifle and shotgun
both close by. "Keep that pistol handy," he advised. "You
never know out here when you might need it."

"It's right beside me."

Jake rubbed at his eyes. "I've got to find him alive, Randy.
If we don't reach him in time—" His voice broke.

"He's in God's hands for now, Jake. You've got to trust in
that. God didn't bring us this far for nothing."

He threw his cigarette into the fire. "I'll never learn to
have your kind of faith, but then I expect you've got enough
for both of us."

"You trust in me, Jake, and you're learning to trust in
yourself. Now trust in God. He's done pretty good by you so
far, considering your past, don't you think?"

He nodded. "Yeah, I guess He has at that."

The wolves continued their howling, and Jake rose, walking out of the light of the fire. Miranda knew there would be
no sleep for him tonight.

CHAPTER
THIRTY-TWO

They crossed the Middle Fork River, and although its waters were flowing gently, there was still a roaring sound because of the high cliffs on either side that caused everything to echo. They had been traveling for over a week now, moving through wild, gloriously beautiful country; but it was difficult to appreciate its beauty because of their worry over Lloyd. Jake pointed to a spot in the rocky cliffs that loomed over the river. Scrubby pine trees seemed to grow right out of the rock. "See that cave up there?" he called to her. "They call it Outlaw Cave. Civil War deserters used to hide up there. A prisoner once told me Frank and Jesse James used that cave to hide out after robbing a Union Pacific train in the late seventies. They killed two deputies. I knew where the cave was. Came across it when I was through this way back in sixty-nine."

How well Miranda remembered those two years of separation when she wasn't sure where Jake was or if he would really send for her. He had run into Jess in this wild country. Poor Jess. How he would love to be with them now, helping Jake find Lloyd. She would feel so much better if Jake had someone besides her to back him up. She dreaded the thought of Jake trying to go after Jubal Latimer alone, wondered if Lloyd would appreciate the risk the man was taking.

After a few hours they moved out into a wide, windy val-

ley, where a few horses and cattle grazed. Miranda had to tie
her hat under her chin to hang onto it. Jake pulled his horse to
a halt and she rode up beside him. He nodded toward the
stock. "Stolen, no doubt," he said matter-of-factly. "They
bring them here to fatten them up and change the brands,
then resell them." He looked above them at a steep, red-rock
cliff that was flat on top. "This is Hole-in-the-Wall, such as it
is. There are a few cabins up top there where someone might
be hanging out who knows something about Lloyd. Trouble is,
Latimer himself could be around here, so let me do the talking. Go easy on the way up. It's a damn steep, narrow climb
with steep cliffs on both sides and the path is full of loose rock.
You might have to get off and lead your horse on foot." He
turned his horse and headed toward a narrow opening in the
looming cliff. "This is a favorite spot because it's so hard to
get in and out," he called to her. "One man could hold off a
whole army up there."

Miranda followed him across the wide valley of yellow
grass, bending against the wind until they came closer to the
cliffs. Huge red rocks lay sprawled and scattered across the
edge of the valley, pieces that had broken away from the brit-
tle cliffs above and tumbled into the valley.

They approached the opening, and Jake took out his rifle
and raised it, waving it at someone above. With one hand he
fired into the air once as a signal, then put the rifle back in its
boot. It was only then that Miranda realized they were being
watched. She looked up to see three men, one not far away
behind a rock, two more at the top of the cliff, all of them
brandishing rifles. She shivered, wondering if they could be
Latimer's men. She told herself not to be afraid. After all, this
was for Lloyd, and she was with Jake.

Once she started up the steep pathway toward the mesa
above, she was sheltered from the wind. Jake had been right.
The climb was treacherous and at times terrifying. There was
nothing to do but depend on the surefootedness of their
horses. Miranda paid no attention to the fact that here and
there a man lurked in rocky crags on the way up, silent eyes,
watching. One could only concentrate on getting to the top
without a devastating fall. She understood now what Jake had
meant about one man being able to hold off an army here.
There was room only for one man at a time to come through.
No wonder lawmen seldom tried to penetrate this place. It
would be suicide.

They finally reached the top, and Jake stopped for a moment to turn to her. "You all right?"

She breathed a deep sigh of relief. "I am now, but I don't relish the trip back down." She huddled into her jacket. The view up here was magnificent, but it was high and windy and cold. She noticed Jake buttoning the top button of his sheepskin jacket, and he coughed as he took his rifle from its boot again. She worried about the pneumonia returning if he breathed too much of this cold air.

Jake took a careful look around. "Doesn't look like there are many up here today."

"I saw some men watching us on the way up."

"They always keep a lookout for lawmen. Hell, the Wild Bunch uses these places to hide out. Probably ninety-five percent of the men you've seen since we got to Brown's Park are wanted for *something*. Lawmen have tried getting into these places before and died in their efforts."

She thought about the fact that Jake was going to be one of those lawmen someday soon. She told herself she couldn't let herself worry about it. After all, he at least knew how such men think and behave, and he was better than any of them with a gun.

Jake was watching a man in the distance mount his horse. "Sit tight," he told her. "They'll want to check us out." The man began riding toward them, and as he drew closer, Miranda shivered at the look in his eyes. He wore a long, woolen duster, with gunbelts crisscrossed over his chest, a shotgun in his hand. He chewed on a thin cigar that looked like it wasn't burning anymore.

"Ain't seen you around before, mister," he snarled at Jake. "You wouldn't be wearin' a badge under that jacket, would you?"

"If I was, would I have my wife with me?"

The man's cold, dark eyes moved to Miranda. "I expect not."

"Is there a man around here by the name of Jube Latimer?"

The man looked him over. "What's it to you?"

"In these parts a man minds his own business."

The man watched Jake's eyes. "Jube ain't here. Him and his men are at his ranch north of here."

"How about Lloyd Harkner? Anybody seen him around here lately?"

To Miranda's surprise, a look of respect suddenly came into the man's eyes. He lowered his shotgun. "I'll bet you're *Jake* Harkner, ain't you?"

"I am."

"Ol' Charlie said he'd heard you was let out of prison. He also said you'd probably be comin' through here lookin' for your son."

Miranda took hope in the words, and Jake lowered his own rifle. "You've seen him?"

The man nodded. "You're a couple of days late. Latimer fetched the boy out of here day before yesterday, and it wasn't purty. You'll be damn lucky to still find him alive, if you can even get into Latimer's place without gettin' your guts blown out. Charlie might be able to help you there."

Miranda took hope in the word "help." Lloyd! Latimer did have him. What had he done to her son?

"Who's Charlie?"

"Charlie Tate. Said he knew you way back when you were gunrunnin' in the war, hung around some with you and Jess York when you was out this way some years back. He likes to brag that he knows you. You remember him?"

Jake nodded. "I remember. It was a long time ago."

"Charlie heard you was released. He'd seen your son at Brown's Park. Everybody knows the kid can't handle his whiskey and is lookin' to get himself killed. He might have already succeeded. Anyway, Charlie said if you was out of prison, you'd be comin' here lookin' for the boy to fetch him home. Said he remembered your woman and the boy was all you could talk about when you was in these parts them years back." The man glanced at Miranda, looked her over. "I can understand why you'd be anxious to get back to the woman," he added, looking back at Jake. "She's fine lookin'. Your boy is too. The whores love him."

Miranda closed her eyes and looked away, remembering a sweet, loving young man who was so much in love with Beth Parker.

"Watch your mouth around my wife," Jake told the man. "Where's Charlie? How can he help me?"

The man turned and pointed. "He's rollin' with the whores over there at Ella's place." He looked back at Jake. "He used to ride with Latimer, but it didn't last long. He ain't made of the same cut, ain't mean enough. I hate to tell you, but Latimer's as bad as they come. I seen him chop off a man's fingers once for cheatin' at cards. I've seen a lot of ruthless men, but Latimer's got them all beat."

Until now, Jake thought, his fury building.

"At any rate, Charlie knows how to get into Latimer's stronghold because he's been there himself." The man leaned forward, resting an arm on his saddle horn. "I'll tell you somethin' else. That boy of yours ain't got the ugliness he needs to go up against a man like Latimer. He thinks he does, but he don't. When Latimer is through with him, he'll wonder why he ever decided to go around wearin' them guns of yours. I can see by your eyes that you've got that mean spirit a man needs for this life. The boy ain't got it. If you can find him alive, you'd better get him the hell out of here. He's good with them guns, I'll grant you that. He's strong and all that, brave, too, in a lot of ways. He'd make a good lawman, maybe, but he don't belong on the other side of the fence, if you know what I mean."

Jake nodded. "I know exactly what you mean. Thanks for the information." He looked over at Miranda. "Let's find Charlie."

She blinked back tears and rode beside him toward the sprawling shack called Ella's Place. Jake had never mentioned this Charlie Tate, but then she knew he didn't like to talk about the time he spent here when he'd left California. He apparently had not been as close to Tate as he had been to Jess.

The man in the duster rode on the other side of Jake. "Name's Hank Downing. Me and Latimer had a run-in a few months back. Not many men around here would care if you shot the hell out of the man. If Charlie's gonna help you, I'll throw in my gun, if you need it. I'm pretty good myself, and it don't bother me one bit to blow a man's head off, especially if it's Latimer's."

Jake shoved his rifle back into its boot. "I'll need all the help I can get, which probably won't be much. I'll take you up on your offer. I can pay you, and I guarantee I'll get the job done because it's my son that's involved. Just make sure you leave Latimer for me."

Downing nodded. "I can understand that." The man put away his shotgun, each man beginning to trust the other a little more. "A lot of men around here know about you, Jake. We might be a bunch of bastards, but we got an idea how it must feel to be worryin' about a son. We've all kind of gone

easy around him on account of he was Jake Harkner's boy.
Otherwise, he'd probably have been dead or at least got his
ass kicked a long time ago. Like I say, he's a strong young man
and good with them guns, but he ain't got the spirit to be a
mean sonofabitch. He thinks he does on account of his pa was
that way."

They pulled up in front of the cabin, and Miranda could
hear laughter coming from inside.

"I'll go in and get Charlie," Downing offered. He dismounted and tied his horse. "You stay out here with the
woman."

The man walked up on a sagging porch and went inside.
Miranda could hear piano music and a woman singing. She
looked at Jake, still struggling against tears. "What has happened to our son?"

Jake looked away. "*I* happened to him." He took a cheroot
from his jacket pocket and cupped his hand around a match as
he lit it. He puffed on it quietly for a moment. "I can't get
sentimental about it right now, Randy, or upset over what he's
been doing. Until I get him out of there, I can't let myself have
any kind of feelings at all, so hold your tears for later." He
dismounted. "That's what I have to do." He glanced up at her,
his eyes showing bitter pain. "I'd better warn you about Charlie Tate. His mouth runs faster than a racehorse, and the
words he uses aren't made for delicate ears, so don't be surprised by anything he says."

He walked a few feet away, and her heart ached for him. If
Lloyd was already dead, she would lose Jake too. He would
never be the same man again. For now she understood what
he was saying. Emotions could get in the way when a man was
going up against someone like Latimer. For the next day or
two she would hardly know her husband. To take on someone
as ruthless as Jube Latimer, one had to be even more ruthless.
She did not doubt the old Jake could be just that, and that was
who he was now—the Jake Harkner who had shot down that
bounty hunter in Kansas City—the Jake Harkner who had
taken on Bill Kennedy's bunch.

The door to the cabin was flung open then, and a plump,
burly man who needed a shave and whose hair was thinning
on top walked quickly toward Jake. He wore pants but no
socks and no shirt, yet he seemed oblivious to the cold.

"Harkner! Lord Jesus, Jake, I ain't seen you in eighteen,
nineteen years!"

Jake turned, putting out his hand. "Hello, Charlie."

"By God, if it ain't the sonofabitch who cleaned my ass out at cards the last time you was in these parts. You always was one to outdo me, you bastard!" The man guffawed, and Miranda climbed down from her horse, trying to ignore his language. He was from another world, from another life Jake had led. Tate looked at Hank Downing, who had followed him out. "Hank, Jake here used to be the meanest sonofabitch you'd ever want to cross, and that ain't no exaggeration. Back in the war he tallied up more of them Union bastards than he could count. That's when me and him and Jess was runnin' guns to the Rebels. Wasn't *no*body much willin' to cross him. *No*body! He was good with his guns, good with his fists, and damn good with the women! Hell, the whores used to fight over him."

Jake grinned a little. "Watch your mouth, Tate. I've got my wife with me."

"Your wife! Jesus Christ, are you crazy or somethin'?"

"No. *She* is!" Jake answered.

"She must be, to have married you!" Tate glanced at Miranda, who nodded to him. He tipped his hat slightly. "Lord God, if she ain't a looker! Hello, ma'am. Name's Charlie Tate. I know Jake from way back when he was too damn mean and ornery for the likes of you. How in God's name did you manage to find any good in this ol' outlaw?"

The man turned back to Jake before Miranda could say a word. "You must have done some fast talkin' to get a woman like that, Jake. She's about the prettiest thing I ever laid eyes on, and God knows I've laid eyes on a lot of women." The man laughed again, finally letting go of Jake's hand. "This the woman you was pinin' over last time you was hangin' around these parts? Wasn't that right after you shot the hell out of Bill Kennedy and his bunch back in California?"

"It was." Jake looked at Randy, a hint of apology in his eyes for the way Charlie talked. "Jess and I both knew Charlie back during the war," he explained. "I saw him a time or two when I came here after California."

Miranda nodded to him. "How do you do, Mr. Tate."

The man laughed again, showing tobacco-stained teeth. He was a big man, but Miranda guessed it was more fat than muscle. He was obviously older than Jake, but looked sturdy in spite of his big belly. "Damned if I don't do just fine," he answered.

"What the hell are you doing still hanging around these

parts?" Jake asked the man. "I figured you'd have moved on by now, or else got yourself shot."

"Hell, I ain't fit for noplace else. I help out the Wild Bunch sometimes—you know, Butch Cassidy and them—worked for the James boys back in the seventies. I rebrand their cattle for them, sell stolen goods, that kind of thing. I make good whiskey money, that's about all, but hell, what else does a man need but good whiskey and a hungry woman in his bed at night? There's plenty of both all along this trail. I expect you sure as hell know that."

Miranda reddened, turning away and walking back to her horse, again fighting old jealousies. She never had asked Jake if he had turned to any prostitutes in their two-year separation, and she decided it didn't matter anymore. Nothing mattered now but finding Lloyd and all of them being a family again.

"I don't have time for reminiscing, Charlie. Downing says you expected I'd show up. You must know why I'm here. I'm looking for my son. Downing says Latimer's got him. I intend to get him back. Can you help me?"

"I can help," Charlie was saying. "Hell, I rode with Latimer myself for a while, but I got out of that bunch. They're bad, Jake. I've done a lot of wrong things in my life, but I ain't that bad."

Jake puffed on the cheroot, and Miranda could feel his fury. She walked back to his side. "Do you think Lloyd is still alive?" Jake asked Charlie.

Charlie was sober now. He glanced at Miranda, back at Jake. "Could be. Latimer don't like to kill somebody quick, if you know what I mean."

Jake took a deep breath for control. "You've got to show me where Latimer's place is, Charlie. I'll pay you. You don't have to go in yourself if you don't want. Just guide me there. I'll do the rest."

"Hell, Jake, I'll take you there. You don't have to pay me. I don't think you can do it alone, though. There must be fifteen men out there."

"I'm gonna help," Downing told Charlie. "I hate the son-ofabitch, but I could never go after him on my own. I figure the best chance I'll ever have is if it's Jake Harkner who's after the man, if Jake here is as good as everybody says he is."

Charlie watched Jake, feeling a little sorry for him. "He is. Ain't nobody faster. Anybody who can take on Bill Kennedy's bunch twice and live to tell about it has to be good." He walked closer to Jake. "I'll do what I can, too, Jake, for old times' sake. I'll get you in there. I know a way we can take that we won't be seen. What we need is ol' Jess helpin' too. Where is he?"

Jake held his eyes. "Jess died a few months back—lung cancer."

Miranda was surprised at the genuine sorrow in Charlie's eyes. How strange that these men could be so vulgar and lawless, yet be capable of affection and loyalty to each other. "I'm damn sorry to hear that. I know you was good friends."

"You know Lloyd, then?" Jake asked, his eyes bloodshot from fury and terror for his son.

Charlie nodded. "I seen him quite a few months ago down at Brown's Park. He was drunk as a skunk, hangin' with some rustlers, goin' around wantin' to know if anybody had heard of his father, the notorious Jake Harkner, sayin' it real sarcastic like. I tried talkin' to him, had a feelin' you wouldn't like him hangin' around these parts. He just shoved me away and told me to mind my own business, but I could see right through him. That boy loves you, Jake. He just ain't about to admit it."

Jake glanced at Miranda, and she saw the deep pain in his eyes. He turned to his horse then and mounted up. "There's no time to waste. Go get dressed, Charlie. There's plenty of daylight left."

The man nodded. "Just before we get there, I'll draw you a layout of the place."

The man turned, and Jake called after him. "You don't have to do this." He looked at Downing. "Neither one of you. You're risking your lives."

Downing just grinned. "I figure havin' you along is worth five, maybe six men. Besides, some men will do anything for money."

Jake adjusted his hat against the wind. "Money or not, I'm obliged."

"Hell, we've both been gettin' a little bored anyway," Charlie spoke up, but Miranda did not miss the worry in his eyes. She was grateful to the man, a little surprised that he and Hank Downing had offered to help. Apparently a lot of these men were like Jake, rough on the outside, but some of them had heart.

She mounted up, and Jake looked at her. "Where do you think you're going?"

"I'm going with you," she answered, surprised by his question.

Jake looked at Charlie. "Can those women in there be trusted to watch after her while we're gone?"

Charlie nodded. "Sure they can."

"No!" Miranda protested vehemently. "Lloyd could be hurt bad by now! I have to be there, Jake! I'll go crazy waiting here!"

"It's too dangerous!"

"I've come this far, Jake Harkner! I'll not wait here like some fainting flower! Why did you bother teaching me to shoot this pistol and that shotgun? I might be able to help you, and besides that, you or Hank or Charlie could get hurt. You *need* me, and that's my *son* out there! If I have to kill someone to get to him, then I'll do it! I've forgiven you for a lot of things, Jake Harkner, but I won't forgive you for leaving me behind now after the hell I've been through coming this far!"

Jake felt torn at the look of terror and helplessness in her eyes. She was right. She'd been through more hell than any woman should know in the years she had been with him, especially these last four years that Lloyd had been missing. "All right," he agreed. "You can go part way, but not all the way in. We'll find a place to hide you until I can come for you. That way you'll be close but safe." He wanted to hold her, but he was too full of fury and dread, too tense and full of thoughts of murder to have any gentle feelings for the moment.

Hank Downing mounted his horse, and Charlie stood at the door to the whorehouse, chuckling. "Now I know why you married her," he told Jake with a wink. "You finally come across somebody you couldn't whip. Takes a strong woman to handle the likes of you. I reckon you found one." He laughed again, going inside.

Jake turned to Miranda, edging his horse closer. "I reckon I did," he mimicked Charlie. He reached into his jacket pocket and took out his mother's cross and Rosary beads. He put them into Miranda's hand. "Keep these for me. Your prayers seem to have a lot of power, woman. Let's hope they're more powerful than Jube Latimer and my guns put together."

They stopped near the waterfall under which Charlie claimed Miranda could hide. The Bighorn River rushed past them as everyone dismounted and Charlie knelt to the sand along the bank of the river and began drawing a layout of Latimer's ranch.

"We're here, to the southwest," he explained. "The ranch is just on the other side of them bluffs we come past. The bluffs is what hid us. Now we're close to a couple of isolated buttes that form the south entrance to the ranch. They ain't very high, but big enough to shelter the entrance. There's always a man up top of each one keepin' watch. We're still safe along the river here where there's so much overgrowth." He pointed to a flat-topped butte just to the north of them. "That's the last barrier that's keepin' them from seein' us. I'm gonna move across the river, get your wife and her horse hid under that there waterfall. There's plenty of room underneath. She'll be safe there."

He looked at Miranda. "If nobody comes for you by nightfall, you head back come mornin'. The river will take you right back to Hole-in-the-Wall. You go to Ella's place. They ain't your kind of women, but Ella will see that you find somebody you can trust to take you back to Laramie. Nobody around Hole-in-the-Wall will give you trouble on account of you're Jake's woman."

Miranda tried to control the sick feeling the man's words had brought to her stomach. *If nobody comes for you by nightfall* . . .

"Do exactly what he says," Jake told her. "And don't you move from under that waterfall."

Their eyes held for a moment before he looked back at Charlie's drawing, and Miranda knew there would not even be a chance for a last good-bye, one more embrace.

"I'll head up the west butte the back way," Charlie was saying. "I think I can get to the guard there from behind. I'll knife him if I can, keep things quiet a little longer to give you time to position yourself to shoot down the man at the top of the east butte. Once you've killed your man, Hank can ride around the east side of the butte where you'll be and come in on the east side of the ranch. There's trees and fencing there to hide behind, and there's bound to be a couple of men out in this area where they keep stolen horses. Hank will take care of them, if he can keep himself from gettin' shot. From then on it's every man for himself. Jake, you can ride straight in. Hank will be to your right, I'll be to your left comin' in on the west side here. I'll head for the bunkhouse. It's right here."

The man drew a square at the northwest corner of the ranch. "To the right of that is a barn, and then a shed. There's liable to be men in every building and in the main house, which is right here in the center. We'll just have to take down whatever comes at us. Our only advantage is surprise, and your accuracy with them guns, Jake. Ordinarily I'd say we should just ride in there and demand Latimer hand over your son, but he don't behave like other men. We'd just end up with ourselves surrounded, and he'd have the pleasure of sayin' he killed both the Harkners. He thinks he's a big man. Fact is, I have a feelin' he didn't go after Lloyd just because the boy shot a couple of his men. He's probably figurin' like some of the rest of us, that you'd come after the kid once you was freed. He'd like to have your head mounted on his wall so's he can say he was the one to shoot Jake Harkner, even though he don't even know you. It's the name that counts." The man rose, looking from Jake to Hank. "You two ready?"

"You bet," Jake answered. He drew his shotgun and rifle from his horse and handed the shotgun to Miranda. "You use that if you have to, and remember what I said about not hesitating. These men will kill anything, including women and kids, so don't feel sorry for them. Just remember they've hurt our son."

She took the shotgun. "I'll do whatever I have to do."

Jake handed her a leather bagful of extra shells. "Just in case you need more."

Their eyes held as Miranda took the bag. "I'll be all right, Jake," she assured him.

"You and Hank take your horses," Charlie told Jake. "You can go in at a dead ride then. I'll leave mine here with your wife and go up the back side of that butte on foot. You and Hank go on this way, headin' east. Hide in the brush till you see my man go down, then draw a bead on the other guard. Once he's down, start ridin', Jake right up the center, Hank around here to the right like I said. Let's go."

The man took hold of the reins to his horse and to Miranda's and headed across a shallow section of the river toward the waterfall. Miranda looked at Jake, struggling against tears of terror. "I'll be watching for you," she told him.

He nodded. *"Vaya con Dios, mi querida,"* he told her softly. He turned and mounted up then, and Hank followed, both men heading east along the riverbank.

Miranda watched Jake a moment longer, then hurried to

catch up with Charlie, not wanting to slow anyone down. Charlie already had his and Miranda's horses tied to a fallen branch not far from the other side of the waterfall, where they would be difficult for an intruder to see. He motioned for her to come and stand under the raging water. She waded through the shallow river and stepped along slippery, flat rocks to come and stand beside the man.

"Remember what Jake said. You stay right here. You're close enough here to help your son real quicklike, once Jake's got him." He gave her a wink. "Don't you fret. They don't come any better than Jake."

"Thank you for helping, Charlie. You be careful too."

The man looked her over appreciatively. "Ol' Jake sure outdid himself when he put a ring on your finger. I got a feelin' that man would walk through fire for you." He chuckled again and shook his head, turning and disappearing into the underbrush.

Miranda breathed deeply in an effort to relax, but it was almost impossible. The waterfall roared in her ears, and she wondered if she would even be able to hear gunshots while standing under it. She set the shotgun aside and took the shells from the bag they were in and began stuffing them into the pockets of her jacket so she would have nothing to carry but the shotgun itself. Her pistol rested in its holster. She picked up the shotgun again and sat down on a rock that rested against the much larger boulder over which the water cascaded into the river. There was nothing to do now but wait.

CHAPTER THIRTY-THREE

 Hank hung back while Jake dismounted and ran farther along the riverbank to take a position where he could see the guard at the top of the east butte. He watched the west butte, where a man was sitting rather than standing. If either Hank or Charlie were as good a shot as he from a distance, they would have taken both men by gunshot. Jake had considered taking them both himself, but from their position, the minute a shot was fired, the other man could easily spread himself flat and be out of sight. It was important to get both guards to be sure Jake and Hank could ride through and around the buttes without being shot at from above.

He caught a glimpse of Charlie then. He crouched and took aim, waiting. Quietly and quickly, Charlie, who'd learned his stealthy approaches from living with the Indians for a time, had an arm around his man's throat and a knife rammed into his back. At the same moment, Jake fired at the second man. He watched the man's arms fly up, his rifle tumble from his hand. Slowly, almost gracefully, his body dived forward for the long drop to the bottom of the butte. Jake heard the thud as it hit a large rock, watched it bounce against a couple more boulders before sprawling in gravel near the riverbank only a few yards away. His side vision caught the body of Charlie's victim also plunging to his death from the west butte.

"Let's go!" Jake called to Hank. "They're both down!"

He mounted his horse, and Hank, already mounted, headed east, disappearing around the butte while Jake kicked Bandit's sides and headed the horse at a hard gallop directly between the buttes and toward the ranch. Charlie scrambled down from his killing point and headed up along the west side of the grounds.

Under the falls, Miranda caught the faint sound of a gunshot. She knew it would be Jake's. She took up the shotgun and rose from her resting place, feeling insane with wonder over what might be happening to her husband and son. She did not know a rider, who had been heading along the river to the ranch, one of Latimer's men, had spotted her. The man had glanced at the waterfall and saw her sitting under it. Quickly he had turned his horse and ridden out of sight, then dismounted and headed for the river. He moved alongside the boulder near where Miranda sat. Water splashed his hat and face, but he paid no attention. Something was up. What the hell was a woman doing lurking under that waterfall?

He peeked around the boulder, saw two horses tied beyond the waterfall on the other side. It was then he also heard the gunshot. He darted back again, unable to determine just where it had come from. When he looked around the boulder again, the woman was heading toward the other side of the fall. He quickly made his move, knowing the roaring water would keep her from hearing him.

Miranda gasped when an arm suddenly came around her chest and arms from behind. She felt a gun in her ribs. "Well, now, what do we have here?" came a man's voice.

Never hesitate, Jake had told her so many times. *It's either you or them.* She still held the shotgun, and her forearms were free. Quickly she turned the firearm in her hands and swung it backward, ramming it hard in the direction of the man's face and hoping to hit her abductor with the barrel end. Her quick thinking worked. She felt the jolt, heard the man grunt as the end of the shotgun barrel landed into his eye.

He let go of Miranda, and she swung around, firing the shotgun without a moment's hesitation. The jolt knocked her backward. She dropped the shotgun and landed on her back, then lay there a moment, struggling to get her breath. When she was able to get to her feet again, she saw her abductor lay sprawled on a rock under the waterfall, his middle a mass of blood.

Miranda gasped, vomit coming to her throat. In terror, she picked up the shotgun and ran, grabbing her doctor bag from her horse and heading out from under the waterfall. She followed the riverbank, searching for the two buttes Charlie had mentioned. "Help me, Jake," she whimpered. "I've killed a man!" She stopped to get her breath, telling herself to calm down. She would be no help to her husband and son in a panicked condition. "Jake, Jake," she whimpered, clinging to the shotgun. With shaking hands she hurriedly opened it and put another shell in the chamber she had emptied. They were both filled again. She closed the gun, then gasped when she heard more gunfire. She ran in the direction of the sound.

Jake was already heading straight into the ranch grounds. To his right he saw Hank running along the east fence. Two men were running toward Jake from a corral where horses were prancing about. A shot rang out, and one went down, shot in the back by Hank. Jake crouched in the saddle and shot the second man, trying to keep count. That was at least four down. On his way in he thought he'd heard the sound of his shotgun going off. The sound was so distant and muffled he couldn't be sure, but it had startled him for a moment. He had to fight to stay alert to what was happening right in front of him. Had Miranda fired the shotgun? What the hell was she shooting at? Had there been someone back there they hadn't seen?

He jumped off Bandit before the horse could even come to a halt. The horse kept running, and Jake ducked behind a large stump. He saw Hank moving closer to the shed across the wide ranch grounds to his right. To his left Charlie moved along the western fence line. Suddenly a man charged out of the shed and rode around the back side of the buildings. Hank fired at him and missed. At the same time three men came clamoring out of the bunkhouse several yards ahead of Jake and beyond the house. Everything was happening at once.

Jake raised up and shot at the three men, who were cursing and shouting and trying to get to the house. Two went down right away. The third cried out and rolled to hide behind a pumphouse. Jake got up and ran hard toward a wagon. The third man and the one riding around the west end fired at him, and he felt a sting across the top of his left shoulder. He jumped into the wagon and lay flat.

Charlie rose up then and shot at the man on horseback, hitting him in the leg. The man shot back, and Charlie felt a jolt to his left arm. He fell flat and the wounded man kept riding. The third man, who Jake had wounded and who had hid behind the pumphouse, got up and ran toward the wagon then, thinking Jake might be lying dead inside. When he peeked over the side, Jake's revolver was drawn. He fired, opening a hole in the man's face. The man made no sound as his head jerked fiercely. He slumped to his death.

Jake looked out of the wagon to see Charlie down. The man he had wounded was still riding. To Jake's horror he saw Miranda running along the fence then. He started to fire at the rider, but more gunshots erupted, this time from the house. They splintered into the wagon, and Jake dove flat again into its bottom. He heard the shotgun explode again, looked through a crack in the wagon to see the fleeing rider's horse go down, sending the man sprawling. Miranda was on her rump. She pulled her pistol from its holster and shot at the rider before he could get up again.

"Good shot, *mi esposa*," Jake muttered.

Miranda looked toward the wagon then, and Jake could see she was in a kind of daze. "Jake!" she screamed. "Jake, where are you?"

"Get the hell down!" he shouted. "Get down and stay there!"

More shots slammed into the wagon. Jake jumped out then, running and rolling to the pumphouse. Two men came charging out of the main house, and Jake caught sight then of Hank running at the house from the back. Someone fired from the barn, hitting Hank in the back. The man cried out and sprawled onto his face.

"Damn!" Jake fumed. There was only him and Charlie now, and Charlie was wounded. He whipped out his revolver and fired at the two men coming toward him from the house, swiftly ending their lives. Revolver in his left hand and rifle in his right, he made a mad dash for the bunkhouse, charging inside, revolver ready. The bunkhouse was empty. He scrambled to think, as he shoved two more bullets into his revolver to replace those he had used. He had downed at least seven himself. Charlie and Hank had each got one, and even Miranda had killed one. That made ten, maybe eleven, if Miranda had shot someone back at the waterfall. He was apparently the only one left to end this, and his own left shoulder was bleeding and hurting. As far as he could determine, there was someone left in the house and in the barn. He couldn't be sure how many, and now there was Miranda to worry about.

"What the hell is going on?" a voice shouted from the house. "Who the hell is out there?"

Jake scurried to a window. "That you, Latimer?" he shouted.

"It's me."

"It's Jake Harkner! You've got my son, you sonofabitch! You're gonna *die* for it!"

"Give it up, Harkner! The boy is already dead! Leave now, or you'll be dead too!"

Jake closed his eyes. The man had to be lying! He had to be! Lloyd!

Lying flat in the tall grass along the west fence, Miranda felt the tears coming. No! It couldn't be true that her son was dead! God wouldn't do this. She wanted to go and try to help Jake, but she knew the rest was up to him now. If she went running into the line of fire, she could be the cause of him getting himself killed.

Neither of them knew that their son was hanging by his wrists inside the shed, his body battered by a whipping and a beating, as well as two bullet wounds. The nearly unconscious young man thought he heard a lot of shooting outside. He decided he must surely be dying, for he thought he'd heard his father's voice. *It's Jake Harkner . . . you've got my son.*

"Pa," Lloyd muttered, tears forming in his eyes. How he wished it could be true his father was coming for him, but that was impossible. He hated him all the more for being in prison where he couldn't come to his aid, hated him for being the reason he was suffering this ungodly pain at the hands of Jube Latimer. His own father had been just as bad once, and it sickened him. That little voice that had plagued him since he had first deserted his family tried to tell him his father couldn't have done the things Jube Latimer was capable of doing, that he still loved his father and it was his own fault he hung here now near death. But he didn't like to listen to that little voice. If he could just have some whiskey, he could make the voice go away. Blood kept dripping from a bullet wound to his thigh, and wishing for the blessed relief of death, he slipped back into unconsciousness.

"You've got one chance, Latimer," Jake shouted from the bunkhouse. "Show yourself, and I'll give you a chance in a fair gunfight. That's the only way you can hope to live!"

"Fair? Against Jake Harkner after I've killed his son? No way, Harkner. You're gonna have to come in and get me. I'll blow your guts out before you reach the back door!"

"And you're a goddamned coward, Latimer! You're brave enough when you're surrounded by your men, brave enough to torture and kill one helpless kid, but you can't face a man one on one, can you?"

"Jake! It's Charlie! I'm comin' in!" Jake whirled to see Charlie plunge into the bunkhouse by a back door. His left arm was bleeding badly. "I managed to work my way around here. You go on and rout them out in the barn! I'll keep the ones in the house busy. I can do that much."

Jake nodded, heading for the back door. He ducked outside, and Charlie began firing toward the house, shattering windows. Jake ran for the barn, flattening himself against an outside wall. He was out of sight of the house now. He inched toward a door, then heard a click behind him. Like lightning he whirled and fired, hitting a man who had sneaked around the back side of the barn. At the same time someone shoved open the barn door where he stood, slamming the door into him and knocking him flat. Rifle and revolver both flew out of his hands, and he rolled onto his back just in time to see his attacker coming at him with a pitchfork.

Jake quickly rolled away, but one fork gouged across his upper back, leaving a deep gash. Jake forced himself to ignore the pain, rolled to his knees to see the pitchfork coming at him again. He managed to grasp it at the base of the tines and push up. He could hear gunfire, knew Charlie was doing his best to keep whoever was left inside the house right where they were. He had no idea if anyone else was in the barn and could only concentrate on the huge, determined man who had attacked him. The man kicked at him, caught him in the chest, but Jake hung on, managed to get to his feet.

The two men wrestled for the fork then. The bear-sized man managed to whirl the pitchfork around so that he held the handle crosswise in both hands. He forced Jake to his back, tried to shove the handle of the pitchfork against his throat. Jake grabbed on and pushed back, using his fury over the fact that these men might have killed Lloyd to draw on an inner strength he himself didn't even know he still possessed. In spite of the decreased strength in his crippled right hand, he managed to shove back and roll his attacker off him and onto his back.

Now it was Jake who pushed, just enough to make the
bigger man think he was going to try to choke him the same
way. Instead, Jake suddenly yanked upward, jerking the pitchfork right out of the man's hands. In an instant he whirled the
weapon forward and plunged it into the man's belly.

His attacker, so big that he had been too slow to roll out of
the way, grunted, staring wide-eyed at Jake then. He began to
tremble violently. Jake jerked out the pitchfork, his dark eyes
on fire with the ruthlessness of the old Jake. "This one is for
my *son,*" he growled. He plunged the pitchfork again, deep
into the man's throat, and blood spurted onto Jake's shirt.
"You fat, murdering bastard!" Jake shouted, enjoying the
gruesome sight. He left the weapon where it was and went to
pick up his revolver and rifle.

It was then he saw her. Miranda was crouched behind a
watering trough, gaping wide-eyed at the pitchfork sticking
out of the man's throat. Jake ran to the trough, crouching
down beside her. "What the *hell* are you doing back here!" he
demanded.

She just stared at him a moment, as though she didn't
know him. "I . . . I followed Charlie. I thought if I stayed
back here, out of the way, maybe I could still help somehow."
She looked again at the pitchfork. "I was going to try to shoot
him, but I was afraid I would hit you instead." She began to
tremble. "I never saw anything like that. When he came at you
with that pitchfork . . ." She looked at him again, her eyes
dropping to the blood on the front of his shirt.

"I *told* you before we left there would be no room for
mercy in this! God only knows what they've done to Lloyd. All
I can hope for is Latimer's lying about him being dead. I'm
going for Latimer! You stay *put* this time!"

The look in his dark eyes almost frightened her. "You're
hurt."

"Not bad enough to keep me from killing Latimer!"

A sob caught in her throat. "I killed two men, Jake. One
found me back at the waterfall."

His eyes moved over her. "Did he hurt you?"

She shook her head. He put a hand to the side of her face,
reminding himself what killing meant to someone like her.
"I've killed *nine* men so far," he said firmly. "You can't think
about it, Randy. You do what you have to do. Now stay here!
Promise me!"

She nodded her head. Jake left her then and moved inside

the barn, quickly searching through stalls, looking up then to check the loft area. The building was empty. "Just the house now," he mumbled, teeth gritted. "And Latimer." He leveled his rifle through a barn window, aiming it toward the house. "You're the only one left now, Latimer!" he yelled. "You and whoever is in there with you! Come on out!"

"You're a liar!"

"I got nine of them myself. Go ahead and call out! Nobody will answer! The big one is lying at the back of the barn with a pitchfork in his throat! You screwed up when you decided to hurt my son!" He began firing, rapid shots that tore through windows and ripped into the back door so fast that those inside didn't have a chance to shoot back. He charged out of the barn and headed toward the house. Charlie fired into two side windows from the bunkhouse, giving Jake more cover.

Miranda closed her eyes and covered her ears, hoping the bullets were coming only from Jake's and Charlie's guns and not from men shooting back. The barn was between her and the house, and she couldn't see what was happening.

Jake reached the back door, setting the rifle aside then and pulling out his revolver. He burst into the house then, firing instantly at a man who lurched into a doorway between the kitchen and another part of the house. The man went down, and Jake heard someone running, heard a door open. He charged through the house to the front door, aiming his revolver. "Latimer!" he roared.

The fleeing man stopped, turned, revolver drawn. Jake fired, opening a hole in his chest. The man went down, and Jake walked out to the body, his .45 smoking. The man lay panting, staring up at him. He was not a big man, actually looked thin. His dark eyes were full of terror, and his black hair was wet with perspiration. Jake stood over him. "You're Jube Latimer."

"How did you . . . do it?" the man groaned.

"You underestimate what a man can do when he's out to save his son. Where's Lloyd?" Jake sneered.

"In the . . . shed. I hope . . . he's dead. The sonofa-bitch killed two of my men. . . . stole their horses."

Jake knelt closer. "That isn't why you went after him, Latimer. You went after him to lure *me* up here, after you heard I got out of prison. You just didn't count on things happening the way they did. Maybe you thought I was too old and getting too soft to take on you and your bunch." He placed the still-hot barrel of his revolver against the man's forehead. "You hurt my son just to get to me, Latimer. That was a big mistake!"

He pulled the trigger, and Jube Latimer was instantly dead, his eyes still wide open. Jake just stared at him a moment, then wiped blood from the barrel of the revolver onto Latimer's shirt before rising and holstering the gun. He called to Charlie and Miranda, and both came running. Miranda still carried the shotgun. She stopped short at the sight of Jube Latimer lying on the ground with a gaping hole in both his chest and his head. Jake turned to her, suddenly looking weary and spent. "He told me Lloyd's in the shed. I don't know if I can get my legs to move. I'm afraid of what we'll find."

A look of ruthless revenge still lurked in his eyes. Charlie took the shotgun from Miranda's hand. "Where's your rifle, Jake?"

Jake tore his eyes from Miranda's and looked at the man, confusion in his eyes. "I don't know. I think I left it at the other side of the house." He put a hand to his head. "Do me a favor. There's a dead man in there. Get him out of there. If Lloyd's alive, I'll bring him into the house so Miranda can tend to him. Then go check on Hank. I think he's dead too. We'll bury him later. To hell with the rest of them."

"Sure, Jake."

Jake noticed the man's bloody sleeve. "You hurt bad?"

"You tend to Lloyd. Once you get him inside, your wife can tie somethin' around the arm to stop the bleedin'. I think the bullet went clean through. I'll be all right. What about you? What happened to your back?"

It was only then Jake began to feel the pain. "Pitchfork," he answered. "Doesn't really matter right now." He took hold of Miranda's arm. "Let's go find Lloyd."

Miranda put an arm around him, feeling him tremble. The gun battle and his pent-up fury had drained him. She knew he was terrified of what they would find, and so was she. She felt his weight, realized he was half leaning on her, suddenly weak. "He's alive, Jake. I know he's alive."

He smiled bitterly. "My ever-faithful, ever-hopeful wife."

They reached the shed, and Miranda gasped at the sight of Lloyd hanging from a beam, his wrists tied together. He wore only the bottom half of long johns, and his body and face were covered with bruises and cuts, his leg bleeding from what looked like a bullet wound, another similar wound at his upper left chest. "Lloyd!" she cried.

A new strength quickly returned to Jake's body. He hastily dragged a stool over to Lloyd's body and stood on it, taking a knife from his boot and cutting the boy down. He let the body slump over his shoulder.

"Oh, Jake, his back!" Miranda exclaimed. "They've whipped him!"

"I've got him. Let's get him to the house!"

Miranda hurried beside him, struggling to stay in control. Her beautiful son, so battered and wounded! What kind of men strung another man up like that and just beat on him? She knew that killing two men would always haunt her, but she did not regret it now. She would never regret it.

Jake kept the boy hoisted over his shoulder and ignored his own pain as he hurriedly carried Lloyd from the shed into the house. Charlie was dragging the dead man out the back door. Jake headed for the one bedroom, and Miranda pulled the bedcovers back. "We can't worry about his back right now," Jake told her. "The bullet wounds come first." He gently laid Lloyd onto the feather mattress, which was covered with a light cotton blanket.

Lloyd opened his eyes, focused them on the man hovering over him, expecting it to be one of Latimer's men come to bring him more pain. He saw his father's face.

"Pa?" He couldn't believe his eyes. Had he died after all?

"I'm here, Lloyd. Your mother is here too. We'll get you through this."

"Pa?" the boy repeated. "How did . . . you . . . find me?"

"That doesn't matter right now. The point is we're here."

Lloyd noticed his father was bleeding. He knew Latimer had a lot of men. How had Jake gotten through them? "Latimer . . ." he muttered.

"Latimer's dead. So are the rest of them."

Lloyd's eyes teared. As much as he must have hurt the man, thought he hated him, here he was. He must have risked his life to get here, his mother too! "I'm . . . sorry, Pa," he whispered, too weak to find his full voice.

"Don't be sorry, son. There's no sense in anybody being sorry anymore."

Lloyd's body jerked in a sob. "Hurts . . . everything . . . hurts."

"I know. I've felt the pain." Jake sat down carefully on the edge of the bed, facing the boy. He leaned over and drew him up so that Lloyd's head rested against his chest. Lloyd grabbed at one of his father's arms, breaking into deep sobbing.

"Pa," he repeated. "Don't let go."

"I'll never let go, son. You're not alone, Lloyd. You've never been alone, even when we were apart."

CHAPTER
THIRTY-FOUR

Miranda was not sure from where she drew the strength to bear the emotional drain the next several days presented to her. She had to remove two bullets from her own screaming son while Jake held him down. She was soon out of laudanum, and Jake had refused to let Lloyd drink any whiskey for the pain.

"He's got to get off the stuff," Jake had insisted. "I don't care what he has to suffer to do it."

She knew it was tearing Jake apart. Lloyd begged for a drink, suffered terrible fits of tremors and periods of hallucination, screaming that snakes were crawling on him. He shouted obscenities at his father, calling him every horrible name he could think of, including murderer and rapist and bastard. Jake refused to buckle, but Miranda knew the words gouged deep into his soul, in spite of the fact that he knew they were spoken only because of Lloyd's desperate need for whiskey. Along with a cleansing of Lloyd's body of the need for whiskey, there also seemed to be a cleansing of the soul for both Lloyd and Jake.

It was four days before all three of them enjoyed a solid night's sleep. Charlie had buried Hank Downing the day of the shooting, and over the last few days more men from Hole-in-the-Wall had shown up out of curiosity, having heard that Jake Harkner had gone after Jube Latimer. They helped

Charlie bury Latimer and his men, and Miranda did not doubt that word of what had happened here would be on the lips of men in these parts for a long time to come.

On their fifth morning at the ranch, Miranda awoke and stretched to realize it must be later than she usually awakened. She was surprised she had slept so well. Jake and Charlie had brought in cots from the bunkhouse for her and Jake to sleep on in the main room of the house so that they could be close to Lloyd. Jake had not really slept much since finding his son, had spent most of the last three days and nights watching over Lloyd. Often Miranda would wake up in the night to catch him smoking in the dark. She knew the worry over Lloyd that kept him awake was only enhanced by the painful back wound from the pitchfork that had left a deep cut across his shoulders, so that every arm movement was agony.

At last, this morning, Jake still slept. She looked over at him, hoping it would not be long before they could all just go home. Jake was only now beginning to return to the gentle, loving Jake who did not have that awful look in his eyes. It had taken the man time to control the rage he had felt over what had happened to his son, to calm the fierce temper that had given him the edge he needed to take on Latimer and his men. Right now he looked more peaceful than she had seen him look in years. She wanted to touch him, hold him, but she did not want to wake him. God knew he needed the sleep.

She rose quietly and went to check on Lloyd, surprised to find him wide awake and looking out the window. He turned to meet her eyes, and she saw in that moment her real son, the one she had known before Jake was arrested. He looked better today, and she realized he had actually slept all night for the first time since they'd found him, without waking up and yelling for a drink. He smiled with a hint of sadness. "Hi, Ma."

Miranda moved closer, sitting down on the edge of the bed. "How do you feel?"

He sighed. "Weak. But the pain isn't so bad anymore." He looked her over. "I can't believe you and Pa came here looking for me. You especially. You could have been killed, or something worse."

"I was not about to let Jake come alone. I just got him back after four years of prison. Besides, I knew you could be hurt and I might be the only one who could help."

He reached out and took her hand. "How did you get Pa to let you come?"

She smiled. "I have my ways."

Lloyd grinned. "Yeah, he is pretty soft when it comes to you." His smile faded. "You must both hate me. I deserted you, walked out on Pa, left you and Evie to fend for yourselves."

She squeezed his hand. "Lloyd, there is absolutely nothing a child can do to make his parents hate him. Nothing." She leaned down and kissed his cheek. "You had a right to be angry with your father, disappointed in him. But you also have a special gift now that your father never had, Lloyd. It's something I know your father would give anything for." She stroked his hair back from his forehead, thinking how utterly handsome this son of hers was, how wonderful it felt to have him looking at her with the gentle eyes of the old, trusting Lloyd. "You have a chance to make amends with your father. That's something Jake never had. If you think it hasn't bothered Jake that he killed his father, you're very, very wrong, Lloyd. That is what led to his confusion, to the desperate kind of life he led for so long. He was only fourteen, Lloyd. He didn't know what to do, where to turn. There was no one he could go to but the outlaw friends of his father, and he got caught in a vicious circle, thinking he was no good because his father told him so every single day of his life."

She reached over to a stand beside the bed and picked up the cross and Rosary Jake had left there. She held it up. "Jake never showed you this. It belonged to his mother. She was a good and gentle woman, sold to a brutal man. Jake's father killed her, and killed Jake's little brother. He beat your father viciously from the earliest Jake can remember. Your father saw some terrible things when he was growing up, Lloyd, but he knew that there must be some kind of goodness in this world. It just took him a long time to find it; and he always kept this to remind him of it."

She pressed the cross into Lloyd's hand. "Your father is *not* the bad man his own father was. He has his mother's goodness in him, and so do you. I hope to God you never believed those rape charges. The woman he risked his life to save the day of that robbery finally came forward to testify that your father had nothing to do with that robbery or her abduction that day. He actually rescued her and brought her back home. She had been living in Europe these last few years and didn't know your father had been put in prison. It was not an easy thing for her to come forward like that, but because of it your father is free now, and we can be a family again, Lloyd. Please, please come home with us. Evie is married to a doctor now, and she's expecting a baby. She wants so much for her brother to come home."

Lloyd lifted his hand and studied the cross. "I don't know if I'd fit in anymore. There's too much to forgive."

"There's *nothing* to forgive anymore. Don't throw away the gift of family, Lloyd. Your father knows how important family is. He never had the love and support you have always had. To him it's a wonderful blessing, something to be treasured. I'm not saying Jake didn't do other bad things. It's a fact that he did. He was an outlaw, but he was also a lost little boy just lashing out at the world that had hurt him so much. The man I married, the man who was such a good father to you, is nothing like the outlaw. You have to admit, Lloyd, that you could not have asked for a more loving, attentive father."

Lloyd's eyes misted, and he squeezed the cross. "That's the hell of it. He had a right to hate his father. I didn't. Not really. I was just so angry, I guess, that he never told me. I thought we were so close. Even at that, maybe we could have worked it out if not for Beth." A tear slipped down his cheek and he wiped at it, embarrassed. "I loved her, Ma. I still do." He breathed deeply and swallowed. "I don't understand why her father made her get married so quick, why she let him talk her into it. Every time I picture her with some other man, it makes me feel crazy, and then I need a drink, and that leads to blaming Pa all over again, makes me hate him." He sniffed and wiped at his eyes with his fingers. "Not anymore, though. What's done is done, I guess, and you're right about family. I want to come home. As soon as I felt Pa's arms around me when he cut me down out there, I knew I loved him and wanted to come home."

He looked past her then to see Jake standing in the doorway. "I'm sorry about Beth, son," the man told him, his own eyes looking misty. "Damn sorry." Jake came farther into the room, running a hand through his hair, still looking tired.

For the first time since Jake had rescued him, Lloyd took a good, clear-minded look at his father, realizing how much he had aged. His hair was peppered with gray, and the lines of hard prison life showed around his eyes; but he was still a good-looking man with an air of strength and power about him. He noticed the man limped a little as he walked around to the other side of the bed. He had a vague memory of the shoot-out in California, had a feeling the hip wound was from that and not from taking a fall from a horse, as his father had once told him when he was younger. There were so many things he wanted to know the truth about.

"I thought I heard voices in here. You look a lot better today," Jake was saying.

"I feel better."

Miranda rose, deciding to leave the room and let them talk. "You two need some time alone. I'm going to make both of you a nice, big breakfast," she told them. She leaned down and kissed Lloyd once more, then left, closing the door behind her.

Jake sat down in a chair beside the bed. "You still hate me for not letting you have the whiskey?"

Lloyd closed his eyes for a moment. "No. I'm sorry for the things I said, Pa. I'm sorry for a lot of things. I never hated you. I just *wanted* to hate you. The whiskey made it all easier."

"You've got to stay away from it, Lloyd. I lived with that hell for the first fourteen years of my life, with a man who went crazy when he drank. That's just the way it is for some men, and you're one of them. The difference is, my pa was mean clear through, and *all* the time. Whiskey just made him even meaner. I've got scars on my back you've never seen because I never let you. I didn't want to have to explain about a father who beat me with the buckle end of a belt from when I wasn't more than two; who murdered my mother and my little brother. You think it's terrible that I shot him, but he was a brutal, brutal man. He was raping a young girl I cared about very much, and I didn't know how else to stop him. After that I didn't know how to stop *myself* from falling into a life of crime. It just seemed like that was all I was fit for, and I had nobody to guide me."

He stopped to light a cigarette he had brought into the room with him, leaned forward, resting his elbows on his knees. "It's not like that for you. You had *me* to guide you, and I can tell you from first-hand experience that the path you're taking will only lead to a life of pure hell, full of regrets that eat at you on the inside like a cancer. If you hate things about my past so much, then why create one just like it for yourself?"

"I don't know." Lloyd stared at the ceiling. "I just wanted to hurt you like you had hurt me. Why didn't you tell me a long time ago, Pa?"

Jake took a deep drag on the cigarette, blowing out the smoke with a deep sigh. "I was afraid. From the day you were born I knew that through you I could somehow recapture my own youth and relive it in a whole different light. I could be the father *I* never had. I was ashamed of the man. I never wanted you to know the kind of man your grandfather was, and I sure as hell never wanted to see the same shame in your eyes for me that I had for him. I saw it the day you visited me in jail back in St. Louis."

Lloyd turned to look at him, for the first time noticing the crippled look to his right hand when the man put the cigarette to his lips again. "What happened to your hand, Pa?"

Jake took the cigarette in his other hand, flexed the crippled one as best he could. "I, uh, I made a vow when you were born, Lloyd, that because of my own pa, I would never, never lay a hand on you. That day you visited me, after I hit you, I felt a rage at myself. I guess I started hitting the wall, so they tell me. I didn't stop until I broke pretty near every bone in my hand, wasn't even aware of what I was doing until I wore myself out and couldn't keep it up."

"My God, Pa . . . I didn't know."

Jake smiled sadly and shrugged. "I can still shoot a rifle with it, but I have to rely on my left hand now to draw and shoot a revolver." He took another drag on the cigarette, staring at the floor then. "You want to talk about pain? I know pain, Lloyd, from this hand to bullet wounds to brutal beatings to losing someone you love. There isn't one loss or form of pain you can suffer that I can't understand." He raised his eyes then to meet Lloyd's gaze. "But I'll tell you one thing. I'd take on every bit of your pain, too, if I could do it. I'd take away the physical pain, the whiskey jitters, the pain in your heart over Beth, I'd gladly suffer all of it if there was any possible way I could take it all off you." He blinked back tears. "But I can't, and that's the hell of it."

Lloyd put a hand to his eyes. "I'm sorry, Pa, about your hand, about deserting you like I did."

Jake rose and put the cigarette into an ashtray. He leaned over the boy, grasping the headrail of the bed with one hand. "I'm not telling you these things to make you feel sorry for me or to try to force you to love me, Lloyd. I'm telling you so you understand what you mean to me. You could torture me, verbally abuse me the rest of your life, whatever. It wouldn't change how I feel about my son. It wouldn't keep me from turning right around and helping you the minute you asked for it. I'll always be here for you, Lloyd, any time you need me. I understand all the hurt, all the pain. You have advantages I never had, and you have a family's love. Don't turn away from all of that, Lloyd. Don't let my sorry life destroy your own good one. That was always my biggest fear."

Lloyd opened his fist to look at the cross. He handed it to his father then. "Ma told me this belonged to your mother."

Jake sat down on the edge of the bed, taking the cross from him and studying it a moment. "For a long time this was my only link to goodness in life, till I met your mother. The woman is nothing short of a saint for the things she's had to put up with being married to me." He sighed deeply. "I just hope to hell I'm the one who dies first, because I couldn't go on without her."

Lloyd touched his arm. "Yes, you could, Pa. You'd have me and Evie and your grandchildren."

Jake looked at the hand on his arm, met the boy's eyes. "Does that mean you're coming home with us?"

"Yes, sir, I'd like to. I'd also like you to sit down there and tell me the truth about everything—your past, how you met Ma, what happened in California, all of it."

Jake sighed, keeping the cross in his hand and moving to sit in the chair again. "Some of it isn't easy to talk about."

"I know. Hell, I've got all day, more than that. It's going to be a while yet before I can get out of this bed. We've got lots of time to talk."

Jake smiled, rubbing at the cross with his thumb. "Yeah, I guess we do, don't we?"

"I love you, Pa. I'm not ashamed, all right? I'm not ashamed."

Jake closed his eyes and nodded, suddenly unable to speak. He rose and walked to a window, clearing his throat and taking a moment to find his voice again without breaking down. *I'm not ashamed.* The boy really had no conception of what that meant to him. He quickly wiped at his eyes with the back of his wrist.

"Are you, uh, you really good with those guns?" he asked, needing to change the subject for the moment. Lloyd glanced at his father's old guns. They hung over the back of a chair. Jake turned to him, followed his gaze. "We found them hanging in the shed," he explained.

Lloyd met his eyes and grinned almost bashfully. "I'm

pretty good, but not as good as Jake Harkner, I'd bet on that."
He could see his father was struggling with emotion, sensed
that for the moment he couldn't go on talking about the past.

Jake smiled sadly. "Good enough to use your guns on the
side of the law?"

Lloyd frowned. "What do you mean?"

Jake sat back down in the chair. "I mean that if you come
home with us, you'll have to move to Oklahoma. Part of my
resentencing was to assign me to duty as a Deputy U.S. Marshal there."

Lloyd brightened. "I'll be damned! You'll be a *marshal*?
Hell, that's great, Pa!"

Jake shrugged. "I guess with opening up the land to new
settlers, plus some trouble between Indians and ranchers,
there's a need. Besides, a lot of that country is inhabited by
wanted men. Who better than somebody like me to search
them out? Lord knows I hid out there plenty of times myself."

"You think they'd deputize me too? We could ride together again, like when we worked on the ranch."

Jake nodded. "I'd like that." He walked over to the guns,
picked them up. "You couldn't use these old single-action revolvers, though. Double-action forty-fives, that's what you
want, and no more lever-action rifles. I've got a Colt Lightning
magazine rifle—a lot faster action." He stared at the guns,
turned to Lloyd. "I figured after prison I'd just give up my
guns and say to hell with it. But the fact remains I'm damn
good with the things, and Randy says that if I have a chance
now to use them for good, why not do it?" He grinned then.
"'Course that judge back in St. Louis isn't giving me a hell of a
lot of choice in the matter."

"I'm glad for you, Pa." Lloyd pushed with his arms, trying
to sit up straighter. He winced with pain.

"Let me help you," Jake told him, coming closer to the
bed. He reached around the boy to support him, helping him
scoot up; but before he could let go, Lloyd's arms were around
him. "I'm glad you didn't get yourself killed trying to help me,
Pa."

Jake crumbled, embracing the boy tighter. "Thank God I
found you alive," he said in a near whisper.

Lloyd felt the man tremble, and he hugged him tighter.
Miranda opened the door just then, and she drew in her
breath at the sight. Lloyd looked up at her. "I don't know

which one needs holding the worst," he told her, his voice shaky with emotion. "Me or Pa."

Miranda came closer, touching Jake's back. "I think it's your father, Lloyd. He was thirty years old before anyone held him in a loving embrace."

Jake kept a tight hold on the rosary beads, and a tighter hold on his son.

December 1890 . . .

Jake balanced his eleven-month-old grandson on his knee, making the boy laugh when he jiggled him extra fast. "Ba-ba," the infant said with a grin, using his word for grandpa. He reached out with fat little arms, and Jake took hold of him and let the child rest against his chest. He looked around the room of the rambling, frame house he and Miranda had rented in Guthrie, Oklahoma. His job compelled him to be gone for long periods at a time, but he was home for Christmas, and it was a good feeling.

He breathed deeply of the smell of Miranda's baking, watched her lovingly as she took some cookies from a baking pan and laid them out on a tray. She glanced at him, and he knew she felt the same stirring desire he did at the memory of their lovemaking last night, his first night home in six weeks. He chuckled at the way she actually blushed a little before turning to go back into the kitchen, and already he was anxious for night to come again. Age had certainly not affected their passion or their energy for making love.

In spite of the violence he sometimes experienced when out chasing men through the wilds of Oklahoma's back country, this was the happiest, most peaceful time of his life that he could remember. Living on the ranch in Colorado had been good, and they all missed it; but the cloud of being a wanted man had always been hanging over him. That was gone now. Brian was doing well in his practice, and he and Evie lived only a few houses away, close enough to be company for Miranda when he and Lloyd were out on an assignment.

Brian was out on call right now, and Evie was helping Miranda with the cookies. A Christmas tree stood in the corner, decorated with popcorn and ribbons and cookies . . .

and topped with his mother's beautiful cross and Rosary beads.

He patted little Jake's back, still a bit overwhelmed that Evie had named her son after his grandfather. He still fought the feeling that he did not deserve all of this happiness, this loving family, this peace; but he had long ago given up trying to convince Miranda she should never have married him, and deep inside he knew life would not have been worth living at all without her.

Lloyd came inside then from picking up the mail, and Jake grew a little alarmed at the look of surprise and near pain in Lloyd's eyes. He kept the baby in his arms as he sat up a little straighter. "What's wrong?" he asked.

Lloyd held up an opened letter. "It's to me," he said, "from Beth."

"Beth!" Evie was coming into the room then, followed by Miranda. "What does it say, Lloyd?"

The young man looked dumbfounded, keeping his eyes on his father. "She wants to see me . . . wants me to come to Chicago. Her husband was killed in a ferry accident two years ago, and she says she needs to talk to me about something very important."

"Then you'd better see about getting some time off to go," Jake told him.

Lloyd turned away, removing his gunbelt and hanging his weapons high on a hook where the baby could not get to them. "I don't know," he said quietly. "I just got over her. I don't know if I *want* to see her again." He looked back at his father. "Does she think she can just pick up where we left off? Do you think that's what she's thinking to do? I don't think *I* could do that, Pa, after the way she let her pa just whisk her out of my life like that when I never really did anything wrong. She said she loved me once, said she'd never let anything come between us."

"Lloyd, you don't know that's what she wants," Miranda spoke up. "Everything that happened was a terrible shock for her too. Maybe she just wants to explain. After all, she was only sixteen years old at the time, and she was under the thumb of a very powerful man. She must know how she hurt you. Maybe she just needs to get it off her mind."

Lloyd looked down at the letter again. "I wonder how she even knew where to write me." He looked back at his father. "Do *you* think I should go?"

Jake rose, keeping little Jake in his arms. "I think that when a chance for love and happiness presents itself to a man, he ought to grab onto it. And if it's nothing more than having a good talk to straighten things out, that's important too. You say you've gotten over Beth, but you won't really be able to get over her until you *do* have a good talk. It might do both of you a lot of good. There's something unfinished there, Lloyd. You and I both know it isn't good to leave things unfinished."

Lloyd shoved the letter into his pocket. "I guess you're right, but it scares the hell out of me."

Jake glanced at Miranda. "Yeah. A woman can do that to you sometimes. She can make you do things that are contrary to your whole nature and your better judgment." He grinned. "But it's usually worth it."

Lloyd shrugged, turning back to the door. "I'll go see if I can get some time off." He looked back at Jake. "What about you? You might have to go out alone on your next assignment. You'll be hunting that guy that killed that Cherokee up north of here. I should be with you."

Jake watched him lovingly. "Lloyd, I've been up against a hell of a lot worse things than that. Don't worry. This old man can still take on the best of them."

The boy had seen his father in action since riding with him, and he knew it was foolish to worry, especially after the way he had handled Jube Latimer and his bunch. His reputation as a lawman was already spreading, and some men had actually given themselves up rather than having Jake on their trail. "Yeah, I guess you can at that." Lloyd left, and Jake turned to Miranda and Evie. "I hope to hell she doesn't hurt him all over again."

Miranda walked up to him and put her hands on his shoulders, leaning up to kiss him lightly on the lips. "He'll be all right. He has his family now."

"I'd better go check the next batch of cookies," Evie said, leaving them alone.

Jake kept his grandson in one arm and moved the other around Miranda, pulling her closer and planting a deep, lingering kiss on her mouth. "Have I told you yet today that I love you?" he asked, kissing at her eyes then.

"No, but you told me enough times last night. Now quit teasing me, Jake. Evie is here, and I have cookies to bake."

"See you later," he told her. "I'm going to take Jake for a walk."

"Good! Go!" She hurried away from him before Jake could grab her back, and he watched the movement of her hips beneath the dress. Still just a slip of a thing, she was. And she was wearing yellow today. He sure liked that color on her. She always wore it when she knew he was coming home.

He turned and plopped little Jake into his chair so he could put on his own jacket and hat. He put a little woolen jacket and a hat on baby Jake then, and he picked the boy up again, carrying him outside, where the weather was cool today, but not cold. He decided he'd walk to the courthouse and see what kind of luck Lloyd was having getting some time off. He hoisted little Jake to his shoulders and walked across the street.

Miranda had come back into the room, and she went to the window to watch Jake. Her heart swelled with love at the sight. She remembered another little boy he used to carry that way, and she knew that in an abstract way he would always carry the weight of his son on his shoulders.

Beth waited in the study, smoothing her deep-blue taffeta dress, glancing in a mirror over the fireplace once more to be sure every hair was in place. Would Lloyd think she had changed much? She was twenty-one years old now. Lloyd would be twenty-three. How different would *he* look, and more important, how would he *feel*? She supposed he must hate her, but then if he did, he surely would not have agreed to come all the way to Chicago to see her.

She had no idea if she was doing the right thing, if any of this was fair to Lloyd. For all she knew he was in love with someone else by now, maybe even married, but that didn't matter. He had to know about his son. It had not been easy finding him. She had made a call to authorities in St. Louis after reading about Jake's release from prison and his assignment as a deputy marshal. She was happy for him, and for Miranda and Evie. She had found out through St. Louis where she could write the family, but she had not been sure Lloyd would even be with them anymore. She had completely lost track of him.

She had received the wire two days ago that he would be arriving today, and already she had been sitting here in the study for an hour, a thousand thoughts going through her mind. She had practiced a hundred ways of greeting him, had put on six different dresses before deciding on this one.

Finally she heard the door ringer. She glanced at the mantle clock. It was eleven A.M. She watched the maid walk past the study doorway to go to the front door, heard her greet someone. A man's voice replied, said he was here to see Mrs. Vogel. Her heartbeat rushed at the sound of the voice. It had not changed a whole lot, a little deeper, maybe. She backed away from the doors, went to stand near the fireplace, and a moment later the maid escorted Lloyd to the study door, taking his hat and jacket.

"Mr. Lloyd Harkner here to see you, ma'am," she said. The woman quickly left, and Lloyd and Beth just stared at each other for several long, silent seconds.

"Hello, Lloyd," she finally managed to speak.

He nodded. "Hi, Beth."

Beth wondered how he could possibly be so much more handsome than he was five years ago. There was a look of deep wisdom in his eyes, an air of grace and power about him as he walked farther into the room, looking hesitant. He was filled out in a more manly way, looking as tall and strong as she remembered his father looking, but even more handsome. He wore black, snug-fitting pants, a simple white shirt that made his skin look even darker. His dark eyes watched her carefully from a finely etched face that was perfect in every line, and his nearly black hair was slicked back from his face and just long enough to fall about the collar of his shirt.

She had not expected these sudden feelings of passion and desire. She planned to just have a talk with him, tell him about little Stephen. She had thought perhaps after all this time she would feel nothing more than a cool friendship toward Lloyd.

Lloyd looked around the room, a little overwhelmed by the mansion of a home she lived in. He noted lovely paintings on the walls, brocade rugs on the hardwood floors, several plants placed here and there, resting in expensive-looking pots. Two deep-green velvet settees sat near the marble fireplace, in which flames flickered softly. He met Beth's eyes again, astounded by how beautiful she had become. She was a full woman now, her figure showing delicious curves, her lips full and ripe, her eyes seeming a deeper blue. Maybe they seemed that way because of the elegant, lace-trimmed dress she wore, a deep-blue taffeta, perfectly fitted to her lovely form. He thought about her lying with another man, and he had to look away. "This is quite a place you have here."

She swallowed. "I'd rather be living in a plain little cabin in Colorado," she answered, surprised herself at the words. She had not meant to say that.

Lloyd looked at her in surprise. God, how those words hurt. "Yeah, well, we can't always have what we want, can we?"

She saw the hurt then, wished she had not said it. "No, Lloyd, we can't. That's why I asked you to come here."

He frowned. "I don't understand."

"I wanted to explain. It probably doesn't help much, and I suppose there is someone else in your life by now. That is as it should be. God knows you have every right to hate me. But there was a reason for what I did, Lloyd, and now that David is dead, I think you should know that I didn't just desert you because I stopped . . . stopped loving you or thought you were bad because of your father." She walked past him to pull a cord, ringing for the maid. "Sit down, Lloyd."

He walked over to the fireplace. "I think I'd rather stand." He met her eyes again, trying to keep a look of anger and defensiveness in his eyes, even though all he wanted was to pull her close and tell her he still loved her. He had not expected to feel this way. He thought he was finally over her. "My pa is out of prison, you know. He didn't do any of the things they arrested him for. Some woman came forward and said he actually saved her that day. He's a Deputy U.S. Marshal now. So am I. I expect Pa will be a full-fledged Marshal pretty soon. He's real good."

"I expect he is," she answered. "Considering how good he is with guns, and knowing what he knows about outlaws and such, he should be."

"There are reasons for the things he did, Beth. I want you to know that. I don't hate him anymore. We're closer than ever."

She nodded. "I'm glad." The maid came in then, and Beth ordered some tea. She looked at Lloyd. "Would you like some kind of a drink? Bourbon, perhaps?"

"No. I don't drink. I'll just take some coffee."

"Fine." The maid left, and Beth stepped a little closer. "I know all about your pa being a lawman now, but I wasn't sure about you. I found you by calling the authorities in St. Louis.

All I could get was where your father and mother lived. I was hoping you would be there too. I couldn't be sure."

He turned away, a little upset by the emotions she stirred in him. This was not supposed to happen. "I ran off after Pa's arrest, hung out in Canada for a while. You ought to know I developed a bad drinking problem, ended up holing up along the Outlaw Trail. I took up with rustlers, killed a couple of men." He turned back to face her. "I was pretty much going to hell, till Pa came for me after he was released. I had got myself in pretty deep trouble with a band of outlaws who were set to kill me. Pa risked his life to come for me. He helped me get off the whiskey. That's why I turned down the drink."

She nodded. "I understand. I'm glad you came through it, Lloyd, glad you're back with your family again. That's good. That's the way it should be. You and your father were always close."

He felt the anger welling up inside him then. "It wasn't just what happened with my pa that made me do those things, Beth. It was *you*! Why did you just run off and let your pa force you to marry somebody else? You *were* forced, weren't you? You couldn't have loved the man, not after the way you felt about me, or at least how I *thought* you felt about me. You told me nothing would ever come between us, remember?"

She closed her eyes and turned away. "I remember, but life can take some strange twists sometimes, Lloyd. Something *did* come between us, but it was something good, not bad."

The maid brought in a tray with two pots and two cups. She set it down on a table between the settees, and Beth moved to sit down. "Come and sit, Lloyd. Have some coffee."

The maid went out and closed the doors so they could be alone. Beth poured Lloyd some coffee, and he grudgingly came to sit down across from her. She poured herself some tea, took a sip, as well as a deep breath. "You're right," she told him. "I didn't love David. I grew to respect him, and in public we looked like a loving couple; but he never touched me, Lloyd. That's the God's truth. It was a masquerade of a marriage."

Lloyd frowned, setting his cup down. "I don't understand."

"I had to marry quickly, Lloyd, because I was pregnant." There, she had said it. She stared at her teacup, afraid to look at him. "David was a friend of my father's. He was a widower. They had an understanding that he wouldn't touch me until after the baby was born, but that he would say he was the father so my baby wouldn't be branded with those awful names people have for the babies of unwed mothers. I never did find the courage or the desire to be a true wife to David, and he was not the type ever to force me, so our marriage was never really consummated." She finally met his eyes, saw the tears in them. "I did what I did for our son, Lloyd. His name is Stephen, and he's four-and-a-half years old. He's a beautiful little boy, sweet and obedient. After David died, I knew I had to tell you, you had a son. No matter how you might feel about me, or if you're in love with someone else, he's still your son, and he should know you. I thought about how lies had nearly destroyed your life. I don't want the same lies for Stephen. I want him to know the truth right from the beginning, to know you're his real father."

Lloyd rose, walking to a window. "My God," he muttered. He shook his head. "You should have told me, Beth. You know I wouldn't have run off. I would have married you."

"I know. But Father had me whisked off to Denver and saying my vows before I had a chance to think straight. You had already run away, and I had no idea how to find you. I was already a good six weeks along when I married. Time was of the essence. Besides that, I was young and afraid, and I was so sick I could hardly hold my head up, sick from the baby, and sick with grief over you. I never wanted any of it, Lloyd. I just wanted you. I know it's probably too late for that now, but it isn't too late to get to know your son."

He closed his eyes for a moment. *When a chance for love and happiness presents itself to a man, he ought to grab onto it,* his father had told him. "There is no one else," he told her quietly, his back still to her. "There never has been. I thought I was over you, till I saw you just now. You want the truth?" He turned to face her, his eyes misty with tears. "You said you don't want anything hidden. Damn it, I still love you, Beth! You don't know what it was like, thinking about you being with some other man. I blamed my father for my losing you, hated him for a long time. But it's like he told me once, we're the only ones responsible for what we do with our lives. We can blame others all we want, but it's really up to us."

She rose, walking closer to him. "I never stopped loving you either, Lloyd, and Father can't stop me now from doing anything I want to do. All I've ever dreamed about since Stephen was born was us as a family. I hate it here in Chicago. I hate it anyplace where I can't be with you."

"We can't just pick up where we left off, Beth. Too much has happened."

She nodded. "I know. I'm so sorry for hurting you, Lloyd, but I did it for our son. Can you understand that?"

He searched her eyes, saw the same, sweet Beth he had loved so very much. "I said we couldn't just pick up where we left off. That doesn't mean we can't kind of start new."

She reached out and took hold of his hand. "I'd like to try, Lloyd. Can you stay a day or two? We have so much to talk about, and I'd like you to get to know Stephen."

He nodded. "Yeah, I'd like that. Can I see him now?"

She smiled and squeezed his hand. "I'll get him."

She turned and left the room then, and Lloyd inhaled deeply with a mixture of passion and joy. He still wanted her, and he could tell by the look in her eyes she felt the same way. He had a feeling he would not be going back home without a wife on his arm. Better than that, he had a son! He was sorry for what Beth had suffered because they'd made love before marriage, but sometimes the result of sin could be something good and wonderful, and where was the sin when they knew how much they loved each other? The child was the result of that love, not of their wrongdoing.

Moments later, Beth came into the room leading a little boy by the hand. Lloyd was struck with the most stirring feelings of love and protectiveness he had ever felt in his life. There stood a beautiful little child with dark skin and dark hair and big, brown eyes. The boy watched him carefully as he came closer. Lloyd knelt in front of him. "Hello, Stephen," he said.

"This is the man I told you about, Stephen," Beth told him softly. "This is your real daddy."

The boy pursed his lips and frowned, reaching out and touching Lloyd's cheek with his finger. "My daddy," he said matter-of-factly.

Lloyd understood now all the things Jake had told him about how it felt to be a father. He understood why Jake had been afraid to tell him about his past, afraid of losing his love.

He pulled the child into his arms. "My son," he whispered. Oh, how well he understood!

"My son, keep your father's commands
And do not foresake your mother's teaching.
Bind them upon your heart forever;
Fasten them around your neck.
When you walk, they will guide you;
When you sleep, they will watch over you;
When you awake, they will speak to you.
For these commands are a lamp,
This teaching is a light."

Proverbs 6:20–23

I hope you have enjoyed my story. To learn about me and other novels I have written about the American West, just write to me and I will send you a newsletter and book-mark listing all my other books. Send a #10, self-addressed, stamped envelope to:

Rosanne Bittner,
6013 North Coloma Road,
Coloma, MI 49038-9309.

Thanks so much for your support!

Rosanne Bittner

About the Author

An award-winning romance writer, ROSANNE BITTNER has been acclaimed for both her thrilling love stories and the true-to-the-past authenticity of her novels. Specializing in the history of the American Indians and the early settlers, her books span the West from Canada to Mexico, Missouri to California, and are based on Rosanne's visits to almost every setting chosen for her novels, extensive university research, and membership in the Western Outlaw–Lawman History Association, the Oregon–California Trails Association, and the Council on America's Military Past.

She has won awards for Best Indian novel and Best Western Series from *Romantic Times* and is a Silver Pen, Golden Certificate, and Golden Pen Award winner from *Affaire de Coeur*. She has also won several Reader's Choice awards and is a member of Romance Writers of America.

Rosanne and her husband have two grown sons and live on twenty-nine wooded acres in a small town in southwest Michigan. She welcomes comments from her readers, who may write to her at 6013 North Coloma Road, Coloma, MI 49038-9309. If you send her a stamped, self-addressed envelope, she will send you her latest newsletter and tell you of her other novels and her forthcoming books.